Mary Ellis
914 11th St
Eldora IA 50627-1338

# THE WINDHAVEN SAGA

\*      \*      \*

"A soaring, magnificent series of books . . .
I was caught up in every volume."

—Leigh Franklin James
*Saga of the Southwest* Series

---

# ROMANCE

"History comes to life in this engaging series
about a family with noble aspirations . . . the
Bouchards are an inspiration!"

—William Stuart Long
*The Australians* Series

---

# ADVENTURE

"Early America means a lot to me, and I was
captivated by this imaginative account of one
family's close association over several generations with the rich and beautiful country
along the Alabama River and in South Texas.
The Bouchards are a memorable clan, larger
than life."

—Donald Clayton Porter
*White Indian* Series

---

# HISTORY

**The Windhaven Saga:**

### ATTENTION: SCHOOLS AND CORPORATIONS

PINNACLE Books are available at quantity discounts with bulk purchases for educational, business or special promotional use. For further details, please write to: SPECIAL SALES MANAGER, Pinnacle Books, Inc., 1430 Broadway, New York, NY 10018.

### WRITE FOR OUR FREE CATALOG

If there is a Pinnacle Book you want—and you cannot find it locally—it is available from us simply by sending the title and price plus 75¢ to cover mailing and handling costs to:

Pinnacle Books, Inc.
Reader Service Department
1430 Broadway
New York, NY 10018

Please allow 6 weeks for delivery.
_____Check here if you want to receive our catalog regularly.

# WINDHAVEN'S BOUNTY

_Marie de Jourlet_

**Executive Producer: Lyle Kenyon Engel**

PINNACLE BOOKS      NEW YORK

This is a work of fiction. All the characters and events portrayed in this book are fictional, and any resemblance to real people or incidents is purely coincidental.

WINDHAVEN'S BOUNTY

Copyright © 1981 by Book Creations, Inc.

All rights reserved, including the right to reproduce this book or portions thereof in any form.

An original Pinnacle Books edition, published for the first time anywhere.

Produced by Book Creations, Inc.; Lyle Kenyon Engel, Executive Producer.

First printing, December 1981

ISBN: 0-523-41110-3

Cover illustration by Bruce Minney

Printed in the United States of America

PINNACLE BOOKS, INC.
1430 Broadway
New York, New York 10018

Dedicated to the memory of
I. I. Litwinsky

# Acknowledgments

The author expresses her grateful appreciation to the staff of Book Creations, Inc., for their help in completing this project.

Thanks are also due to Joseph Milton Nance, Professor of History, Texas A & M University, College Station, Texas, for his verification of obscure historical data; also to Fay J. Bergstrom, an enlightened transcriber who often catches the author's errors before they reach her editor.

Marie de Jourlet

# Prologue

It was the evening of January 2, 1877. For nearly two months, the American people had been awaiting, in growing wonder and fear, the results of the presidential election. On election evening, November 7, 1876, the popular vote had showed a majority of a quarter of a million for Democrat Samuel Tilden over Republican Rutherford B. Hayes, but the returns from four states were in dispute. The Electoral College, meeting in December, had been unable to resolve the dispute or choose a President, and there were ominous rumors now that Tilden, the upright bachelor governor of New York, was doomed to defeat despite his popular victory.

Hayes's party represented the punitive Reconstruction program that the victorious North had imposed upon the conquered South. Tilden, on the other hand, believed that the continuation of such tyranny could only weaken a nation that had just celebrated its glowing centennial. Almost to a man, the nation had been distressed by the corruption revealed last year within the Republican administration of Ulysses S. Grant. Although Republicanism went back to the idealistic days of Abraham Lincoln, the Republicans of this postwar era were not of Lincoln's caliber; their record was tainted by their open support of the carpetbagger regime that had emasculated and plundered the South.

And yet rumors persisted that by the time of the inauguration two months hence, it would be Hayes who was sworn in as President. Amidst the growing confusion and uncertainty—for never in America's history had so much doubt surrounded a presidential election—there were calls

1

for a special electoral commission, to be appointed by the Congress, to resolve the continuing conflict and at last select a chief executive.

The nation waited, its hopes and dreams held in abeyance, for the panic of 1873 had cast long-range shadows of pessimism and despair over the people. Unemployment was rife: there was restlessness among the workers, who were beginning to form unions for protection against exploitation by the bosses. The young nation prayed that idealism, honesty, and truth would finally rule the land, that the golden age hinted at in the Declaration of Independence a century before would at long last become a reality.

The land lay fallow; much of it was neglected due to deteriorating farm prices and the general unemployment. Generations ago, the rich land of the South had been depleted by the ceaseless planting of cotton and tobacco. Now that the guns of Appomattox had been stilled for more than a dozen years, the land was again fertile, as if enriched by the blood of thousands of soldiers. But if the land was ready for sowing, ready for the future, the people were not. . . . Fear, dissension, and prejudice were widespread; the heroes and preachers and politicos of the centennial year had proven to be tainted, and their vain and empty rhetoric had plunged many naively hopeful citizens into a black limbo of cynicism.

All day it had rained, and only toward sunset did the skies clear and the wind slacken. The farmers rejoiced in the abundant rain, so unusual for January, yet prayed that it would not be repeated in the summer, when it was time to harvest the cotton and the produce destined for market. Some of the more philosophical plantation owners reasoned that if the nation's politics were so awry in this new year after the centennial, the weather might be pardoned for a similar unpredictability. In the saloons as in the elegant houses throughout the South, wrangling about the as-yet-undecided presidential election grew with a kind of morbid intensity. There was a nostalgic yearning for things past, for an America that had existed long before the embittered years of the Civil War had created a seemingly impenetrable barrier between North and South. There were those who fervently wished that this rain, which

2

brought an end to drought, could also somehow wash away old hatreds and heal the festering wounds of civil strife and sectionalism.

West of the little bridge that crossed the Alabama River, near the outskirts of Montgomery, there was a strip of land that had always been a prairie. It was framed now by a curious mixture of trees—tall, gnarled oak, cypress, cedar, and stately birch. The tall grass rose to the height of a man's chest, and here and there it was dotted with errant clumps of elderberry, sumac, and thorny ivy.

In the days of old Lucien Bouchard, this site had been hallowed as the ancient gaming field of the Creeks. Here Lucien had won the right to ask the *mico* Tunkamara for the hand of his beautiful daughter, Dimarte. But then the Creeks had been forced to leave their hunting grounds— the land that had been their birthright—for the desolate country of the West and prisonlike reservations.

Now this prairielike stretch of land remained desolate and forsaken. Toward evening the people of Montgomery took pains to be nowhere near it, fearing that the spirits of the dispossessed Creeks returned there, once the sun had set, to hold their ghostly revels in memory of those days when they ruled the South.

Now, on this second day of January, as twilight fell, three elegantly dressed horsemen rode toward a huge clump of poison oak at the far western boundary of the clearing, each rider approaching from a different direction.

One of the riders was a man approaching his fiftieth birthday; he was short and dapper, with an ornate, elegantly waxed mustache. His name was Milo Brutus Henson, and he was known as a reputable surveyor who had recently retired and purchased a venerable white-columned house on the eastern edge of Montgomery.

The second man, who had come upriver from the south, was thirty-eight, tall and wiry, with blond hair and a neat spade beard. He wore riding breeches, gleaming black boots, and a red riding jacket. His brown eyes and sensuous mouth, together with the almost too-perfect casting of his features, gave him an effetely handsome appearance. There were shadows beneath the eyes, wrinkles along the smooth, high forehead, and the lips twitched nervously beneath the prissy mustache.

The third rider, also around fifty, had come from Tus-

3

caloosa to the southeast, after having attended the funeral of a friend of his, Judge Albert Siloway. He was a native of New Orleans, a suave, black-haired man with a distinguished touch of gray at his temples, a Vandyke beard, and imposing sideburns. He was elegantly dressed in waistcoat, cravat, and a new pair of breeches, which he had imported from London via an exclusive shop in the Queen City.

The three horsemen neared one another and lifted their hands in greeting. The man who had come from Tuscaloosa reined in his roan gelding, with an angry oath at the horse's restiveness, and exclaimed, "Milo, it's good to see you again, especially after the sorrowful journey I had to make."

"I know, William. Poor Albert, cut off in his prime."

"Well, I can't say as I'd agree with that—he was all of sixty-three, and he'd been twenty pounds overweight for the last ten years. Too much food and liquor killed him— harlots, too, if the truth be known. But he was a good man in his own way." He winked bawdily. "I don't much like funerals, and the only good thing about this one was that when it was all over, I had the pleasure of consoling Albert's last and youngest mistress, a pretty Creole bitch not quite twenty. That made up for all the solemnity."

"I never had the pleasure of making this Judge Siloway's acquaintance," the wiry, blond man from the south now spoke up. "My name is David Fales, by the by. Milo here sent me a telegram asking me to meet the two of you."

"I've heard your name," the dapper man from the Tuscaloosa funeral drawled. "Weren't you the one who arranged for a certain long-legged blond slut to vilify the name of our new, illustrious state senator, Andy Haskins?"

"Guilty as charged, Mister—Mister—?"

"William Brickley, at your service, Mr. Fales. Yes, I remember that scheme. Pity it didn't work out."

"It's been four years," Milo Brutus Henson interposed, in a strained, angry tone, his lips tightening, "since poor Homer Jenkinson and the judge and I teamed up together to get that naive country boy to help us in a little scheme that would have lined our pockets. The trouble was, he was so damnably honest it made you puke. And then with the help of Fales here, we set Judy up to blackmail him.

4

But that didn't work either, thanks to a certain lawyer all of us know about. Yes, it was that son of a bitch, Lopasuta Bouchard." Henson clenched his teeth, then hawked and spat.

"Whatever happened to Judy—do you happen to know?" David Fales turned to Henson and asked in a casual tone.

Henson shrugged. "Last I heard, after Haskins and his bosom buddy, Luke Bouchard, found out about our, ah, plan, they packed the bitch off. Curiously, a friend of mine mentioned that he thought he saw her recently in New Orleans. By now, she's probably married with a couple of kids. Besides, she wasn't really important."

"At one time," Fales hesitantly confessed, "I was hot for her. Even thought I might marry her, till I realized that she was bedding down with four niggers on the farm she took over when her folks died. Of course, no decent Southerner could abide to touch a creature like that."

"Of course not. And such a sentiment does you credit, Mr. Fales," Henson obsequiously observed. Then he chuckled humorlessly. "There's a lot of unfinished business to be settled in this town, William. That's one reason I asked you to come by after you'd paid your last respects to poor old Albert. This damned lawyer, Lopasuta Bouchard, is getting to be far more important than he deserves. He's not a nigger, but he's a dirty low half-breed—from what I've heard, the byblow of a Mexican whore and an Injun father. And Mr. Luke Bouchard, mind you, that fine upstanding gentleman who carries so much weight whenever he belches in Montgomery or Lowndesboro, went and adopted him as his son—that makes me puke, too."

"The South has fallen on hard times," William Brickley glibly commiserated with them. "But as yet I don't understand why you wanted to have me here at this touching reunion, Milo."

"I'm getting to that. This Lopasuta drove a few of my friends out of Montgomery with his so-called justice for the niggers against fine white men. It's a scandal, I tell you. And the judges ought to be retired or sent to the penitentiary for the way they let this low half-breed prance around in their courtrooms and come off with a favorable verdict just about every time. I knew a fellow, a pretty good attorney by the name of Vernor Markwell—well, thanks to Lopasuta Bouchard, poor old Vernor was driven out of town and died forgotten. And in my book, Vernor was by far the better lawyer."

"I still don't see what you've got in mind, Milo," Brickley interrupted.

"I'm coming to it. Lopasuta Bouchard rode out this way last month; I followed him, and I'm sorry to say that I missed the shot I had at him. I guess maybe my hand trembled because I felt such hatred for him. But ever since then, I've been thinking that a bullet's too good for a dirty half-breed like that. Especially since he actually went ahead and married a fine upstanding girl, a Geraldine Murcur, from one of the oldest families in Montgomery. A regular Southern belle she is—can you imagine anything more disgusting? The son of a bitch!" Milo Brutus Henson's mouth twisted with rancor, as he again hawked and spat.

"Get to the point. I'm eager to get back to my business in New Orleans, Milo," Brickley reminded him.

"All right. One of these days, if you get a telegram from me, just hang on to it. It will be in the code you and I always had. I've got a plan to get rid of this Lopasuta Bouchard once and for all. You can turn a pretty penny's profit for helping me out. And you, Fales, you'll make some money, too—all to the good, because from what I hear, you're not doing too well."

"What the hell business is that of yours, Henson?" Fales petulantly snarled.

"Look, I know all about you, Fales," Henson sneeringly interpolated. "You had yourself a little affair with this Judith Branshaw on the side while you were landing Henrietta Aylmers, who brought you a nice dowry and saved your own bankrupt plantation."

"That's none of your affair!"

"Oh, come, come now, Fales, it's no secret. I know that you've squandered your dowry, and that Henrietta is fair sick of you. Too bad. That property of hers was something special. You know that it was in one of those townships where Judge Siloway, Jenkinson, and I wanted to get the taxes lowered—through that bill that we wanted Haskins to sponsor in the House. You'd have been a rich man if Haskins had seen the light of day and put the tax bill

6

through. But he was too pure-minded for that. To think that I wasted money on you, Fales, lending you a thousand so you could put on airs and make Henrietta think you were a real catch. You know damn well I speculated on you because if Haskins had managed to vote through that tax reduction, Henrietta's property would have more than tripled in value. But the scheme fell through; besides which, you didn't have enough brains to keep your marriage from going on the rocks. The word is that if Henrietta should ever call it quits with you, she'd will her property over to an Eastern cousin and leave you penniless. So here you are, Fales boy, on your uppers again, in hock to me, and likely to go from bad to worse—"

"Goddamn it, keep your mouth shut, Henson!" Fales snarled, with an uneasy glance at the smugly smiling Brickley.

"Take it easy, Fales boy," Henson suavely interposed. "You can still pay off your indebtedness to me and be in on this new little scheme I've got in mind. Yes, and maybe recoup your losses, too. Just show some sense and listen to someone who knows more about what's going on than you do. You're not a good businessman, but you have a certain charm. Maybe it can come in handy. Now you go on back down to Tensaw and try to keep a good face on your marriage. You'll hear from William and me in due time. It's not only Haskins and Lopasuta Bouchard I'm after; I don't have much use for that high and mighty Luke Bouchard, either. He's getting on in years, and a little scandal, and maybe a financial setback or two, or the loss of his fine red-brick chateau should give him his comeuppance. And in memory of poor Homer, it would pay them all back for what they've done to my good friends."

"Whatever did happen to Homer Jenkinson?" William Brickley wanted to know.

Henson shrugged. "The poor bastard got blinded. His insipid little wife, Prudence, stumbled and spilled some lye in his eyes. She took real good care of him after it happened, but he died two years ago from pneumonia, and then that bitch of a wife of his sold his property. The last I heard, she was heading for Massachusetts to marry some pious Boston minister. Well, that's ancient history now."

"What a sorry tale," David Fales interjected.

"You just remember what I told you, Fales. And you,

7

William, if you're of a mind to turn a neat profit and to do me that favor you owe me, we'll all have a good time. This time we'll succeed, and we'll be able to laugh out the other side of our mouths when Lopasuta Bouchard gets what he's had coming to him."

"I'm with you, Milo. Well now, Fales, good to have met you. Maybe I'll be seeing you again soon. Now I think maybe we'd better skedaddle and not be seen together."

The three riders lifted their hands in token of parting, and then each rode off in a different direction.

Darkness had fallen upon the ancient gaming field of the Creeks. From afar came the twittering of night birds; then there was silence, and only the rustling of the wind suggested the presence of the murmuring ghosts of the Creeks, once rulers of this countryside but now banished and neglected, crushed to a life of meager subsistence in a land far away.

# One

On the morning of the third Friday in January 1877, Luke and Laure Bouchard took breakfast together as usual, surrounded by their children. It was a bright, beautiful day, and Laure talked in animated fashion both about the baby she was expecting—she was in her fifth month of pregnancy—and about her special plans for that evening: a festive dinner to celebrate the election of their friend and neighbor, Andy Haskins, to the state senate. She reviewed for her husband the menu she had selected with Annabel Leary—the assistant housekeeper, who was substituting as cook for the elderly, ailing Hannah Mendicott—and Luke smilingly approved all her selections, asserting that surely this dinner would see Andy off to the Senate in fine style.

After breakfast, Luke excused himself and retired to his study to write a long, informative letter to his eldest son, Lucien Edmond, now owner and manager of the family ranch at Windhaven Range. Closing the study door behind him, Luke walked to the window and stood for a long moment looking out at a landscape that was as familiar to him as every line and wrinkle on his face. It seemed to him it had not changed since his boyhood and the charmed hours spent there with his revered grandfather; it was a physical manifestation of the timelessness of the Bouchards and of the evergreen heritage that old Lucien Bouchard had bequeathed to those who followed him upon this fertile land.

Seating himself at the highly polished mahogany escritoire, so similar to the one used by old Lucien himself, Luke breathed a sigh and began his letter. "Dear Lucien

Edmond," he wrote, using an old-fashioned quill pen, "here we are at the outset of a new year, with the promise of a new President and Congress—though, to be sure, the identity of this new President has not yet been determined. I wish for you and Maxine and your children, for Mara and Ramón and their children, for Joe Duvray and Eddie Gentry and their families, and for all the vaqueros, a year of prosperity, health, and happiness. I also send special good wishes to Lucas and to his Felicidad and their children. . . .

"I am writing this letter at the escritoire that always reminds me of—"

Suddenly Luke felt an agonizing spasm, as if a hand had squeezed his heart. The quill pen dropped from his nerveless fingers and clattered on the desk, but for that instant he did not hear the sound. A black cloud obscured his vision, and for an incalculable moment he was not conscious of where he was or what he was doing.

And then, as swiftly as it had seized him, the spasm passed; his vision cleared, and he slowly turned his head to look out the window. The beloved, familiar landscape, gilded by the bright rays of the morning sun, appeared as normal as when he had first entered the study. The pain had vanished and his heart beat regularly, as if the entire episode had been imagined, like the echo of some vanished nightmare.

Luke frowned, drew a tentative breath, exhaled, and once again felt in full possession of his faculties. Reaching for the quill pen, he remembered the instant of blinding pain, too ominous to be ignored. He shook his head firmly. With the party tonight, no one—least of all Laure—must know of it.

Slowly he raised his eyes and said softly, "Almighty God, I am your servant, to do with as You will. I ask only to be granted a little time to provide for my family's welfare after I leave them. I ask this humbly, and I thank You who have given me such bountiful joy and love in my life."

That evening, as the warmth of the day was dissipated in the evening breezes, Luke Bouchard and Laure, looking radiantly beautiful, presided over the eleborately set dining-room table to celebrate the beginning of Andy

Haskins's senatorial career. Andy and his wife, Jessica—who was about to have their third child—were of course the guests of honor, and with them were his good friend Dalbert Sattersfield, a successful storekeeper, and his wife, Mitzi. Lopasuta Bouchard, Luke's stalwart adopted son, was also there with his lovely wife, Geraldine. Geraldine and Mitzi, having been formally introduced just before all of them went in to dinner, found that they shared a common good fortune: Geraldine was looking forward to bearing Lopasuta their first child, while Mitzi would present her one-armed husband with their fifth.

Marius Thornton and his Clemmie were also honored guests, for Marius's work as foreman of Windhaven Plantation had in Luke's often-professed opinion, earned for this thriving and idealistic commune ever-increasing profits at a time when not only the nation, but also most of Alabama, was blighted by the economic depression that had begun in 1873. Also present at this festive dinner were Andy's foreman, Burt Coleman, and his wife, Marietta, and two of Luke's own loyal tenant farmers and workers—Buford Phelps and Dan Munroe, who were accompanied by their wives, Dulcie and Katie.

What delighted Luke Bouchard most of all was the presence of the four children whom golden-haired Laure had given him. Lucien, named after Luke's grandfather, was now almost eleven, while his younger brother, Paul, at eight, was nearly as tall and in some ways sturdier. Young Lucien's kidnapping eight years earlier, arranged by the vengeful Henri Cournier, had left no traumatic blemish: the boy was frank and winning by nature, and outspoken almost to a fault. The latter trait Luke—with secret amusement—counted as a virtue: it was one of his own hallmarks, and its presence in his son only confirmed that the boy was following in his footsteps.

Then there were his two delightful daughters, Celestine, now five and a half, and Clarissa, now four. The two little girls were inseparable and in some ways reminded Luke of his half sisters, Arabella and Fleurette, when they were small. Yet while Arabella had always been the more dominant of the two in the older generation, sometimes overpowering Fleurette, Celestine in no way sought to take advantage of her little sister; when they played together, she looked after her and made certain that she did not hurt herself. Celestine in fact reminded Luke of Fleurette, who had married Dr. Ben Wilson after she had nursed him to health when he had been taken prisoner as a member of the Union medical corps. Perhaps—Luke had said to Laure only last night—Celestine might also become a nurse: at her tender age she already showed a remarkable concern and love for people. The workers in this commune adored her and were forever making her little toys, which she unselfishly shared with Clarissa.

After the children had had their dessert, Lucien, very solemn and adult, asked permission of his father and mother to bid the guests good evening and to take his brother and two sisters back to their rooms. Laure smilingly rose and went to embrace her older son, while the others chorused a warm good night to the four Bouchard offspring.

Luke watched Lucien leave the dining room and sighed. How he wished that his grandfather might be here tonight—how proud the latter would be to see his great-grandson, his namesake. Luke said a silent prayer that the destiny of this son might be as bright and purposeful as that of the pioneer Bouchard who had made all of this possible, and whose love for family and friends had transcended two generations so that the Bouchards today were still nourished by its lifegiving bounty. Then, rousing himself from his thoughtful mood, Luke rose and offered a toast to the assembled company, making a kind and thoughtful remark about each person present and speaking in particularly fervent tones about Andy, his record for honesty and good government in the past, and his bright future in the Alabama Senate.

Following dinner, Laure saw that her husband wished to talk privately with the men who had shared the lavish banquet. She proposed to the other ladies that they amuse themselves with a game of whist and led them into one of the larger rooms on the first floor of the chateau, where a card table was set up in front of a sideboard laden with decanters of cordials and plates of biscuits, cakes, and cheeses. At the other end of the room were a circle of comfortable chairs and a sofa.

Clemmie Thornton, Katie Munroe, Marietta Coleman, and Dulcie Phelps—declining to play cards—selected after-dinner refreshments and then seated themselves in the

12

circle of chairs to engage in some earnest conversation; Laure, Geraldine, Jessica, and Mitzi meanwhile took seats at the card table.

"Now, ladies," Laure began brightly, picking up a deck of cards from the table, "we can be much more at our ease. I'm sure all of us have things we'd like to talk about that we wouldn't exactly want our menfolk to hear."

"I don't know," Geraldine Bouchard smilingly countered. "Sometimes secrets can lead to deception, don't you think?"

"Well, perhaps just a few tiny little secrets, then," Laure amended. She had taken at once to the vivacious young brunette and bade Geraldine sit at her right, as she began to shuffle the cards and then presented the deck for the others to cut for the deal. She drew an ace of hearts and won the deal, and Geraldine marveled, "You handle the cards like a professional, Mrs. Bouchard!"

"I came from New Orleans, you see, Geraldine dear," Laure explained, "and my first husband, John Brunton, ran a kind of casino where Union officers amused themselves. I was the hostess, and I often found myself with time on my hands, so I got in the habit of playing on occasion."

"Why, I think you're good enough to be a dealer, Mrs. Bouchard," Geraldine rejoined with a laugh, then brightened as she looked at her hand.

"Now you see, Geraldine dear—and you really must call me Laure—you've already given away one of your secrets." And when Lopasuta's young wife looked puzzled, Laure explained, "From your smile, I can guess that I dealt you a very good hand. If you ever want to do any professional gambling, Geraldine, you'll have to adopt what is called in the parlance a poker face."

"I see what you mean. I'm sorry, Mrs. Bouchard—I mean Laure. I hope I haven't spoiled the game by my expression."

"Heavens, no!" Laure laughingly held up a protesting hand, "not in the slightest. And now it's your bid, my dear."

After the first hand, which Laure won, she passed the deck to Geraldine and murmured, "You know, Geraldine, dear, I couldn't be happier for Lopasuta, married to a girl like you—I wish you both every happiness. And Mitzi just

13

told me the wonderful news. There's nothing like having the very first baby; it will strengthen the bond between the two of you."

"I know!" Geraldine's eyes were radiant as she shuffled the cards, then let Mitzi cut them.

"And your parents—have they become reconciled?" Laure anxiously asked, keeping her voice purposefully low.

"I'm afraid not." Geraldine forced a brave little smile, as she began to deal the cards. "I do hope that when the baby's born, they'll come around."

"I'm sure they will. Well now, let's see what sort of hand you've given me, Geraldine." Laure sent Lopasuta's young wife a gracious smile, then picked up her hand and studied the cards.

"Andy, what I said in my toast tonight is just part of the way I feel about your being our new state senator," Luke Bouchard genially declared as he put his arm around the affable young man's shoulders. "But quite apart from any words I said at the table, or that I might say now, Andy, the real proof of your popularity was in that November election. All you have to do is look at the figures and you'll see that you were one of the few Republicans to win. That means the people didn't vote for partisan politics, but rather for an honest man; they remembered what you'd done in the House of Representatives."

"That's nice of you to say, Luke." Andy Haskins still didn't feel completely comfortable calling Luke by his first name, not only because of the difference in their ages, but also because of the gratitude he felt toward the older man. Andy could never forget that if Luke had not engaged Joe Duvray and him at the wharf in New Orleans when the Bouchard family was on its way to Texas to begin a new life, he and Joe might well have become hopeless drifters, along with thousands upon thousands of other Confederates who found themselves dispossessed and without any future at the end of the war.

Andy made an awkward gesture with his left arm, sheepishly grinned, and then finished, "I'd say that you had a lot to do with my success, Luke. You pointed out the way to me many times, especially in that business over the Alabama and Chattanooga Railroad."

"No, Andy, the credit is all yours. You had the foresight to do some studying on your own and, once convinced, to pursue the issues without flinching, even when you were bribed and blackmailed. But now, since we're here at the beginning of a new year, it's a good time to ask ourselves what's likely to happen to our country in the future. As of today, we don't officially have a new President to replace old Ulysses S. Grant."

"What do you think is really behind that, Luke?" Lopasuta wanted to know.

"Power politics, Lopasuta. I think the country was ready for a complete change, and Tilden—a clean, honest, and very personable candidate—was just about everybody's choice. But there have been some deals made, and, from what I've just heard, there's to be a special commission voted in by the Congress to determine who will win the election. And since there will be an odd number of commissioners, the outcome's going to depend on how many Republicans or Democrats are in the majority. That's inevitable."

"I don't like to think of a thing like that happening," Dan Munroe put in. "I'd hoped that we'd go back to electing people on merit, just the way the people of Montgomery County did with Andy here."

"I'd like to agree with you, Dan, because, like you, I'm something of an idealist, as all of you know." Luke looked around and chuckled to see nods of approbation from his listeners. "Here we had two terms of a Republican President, Grant, the hero of the war, only to discover that while he himself was basically an honest man, he was surrounded by corruption on every side. The natural and logical thing to suppose would be that the country would go Democratic, and with Tilden as their candidate, if you were a betting man, you'd be inclined to put your money on the Democrats. But I've a nagging feeling that it won't turn out that way, and all I can do is pray that if we do get Hayes, he'll ease up on the South, try to heal the wounds, and also try to forget partisanship."

"Isn't it strange, Luke," Andy spoke up again, his forehead furrowed with thought, "with the Republican party here in Alabama just about on its deathbed, we may be in

15

for another Republican President. It kind of makes one wonder."

"I've thought a good deal about that, too, Andy," Luke soberly replied. "Our governor, George Smith Houston, won his reelection last November over Republican Noadiah Woodruff by over forty thousand votes. The only lasting Republican influence in Alabama, apart from your own personal victory, Andy, is in the judiciary, where we still have some judges who were elected in 1874 and whose terms will extend through 1880. I've tried to analyze the Republican Party's decreasing strength, and I think one of the reasons for it is that even though the pro-Democratic Ku Klux Klan didn't openly demonstrate, a great many election officials refused to open polls in many Republican precincts. That destroyed Republican footholds without involving any bloodshed. The black vote was minimized, and those blacks who did go to the polls divided their votes rather evenly between the two parties last November. The white vote, conversely, was almost five times as much for the Democrats as it was for the Republicans—and that's what did it. I've a feeling that a great many loyal Republicans are going to switch to the Democratic side, out of sheer frustration—if, that is, they don't ally themselves with the Greenback movement under the label of Independent."

"What is that going to mean to us here, Mr. Bouchard?" Buford Phelps scratched his head and edged forward, his face anxious.

"Well, although Governor Houston didn't promise the blacks a total enfranchisement—not by any means—what he did do was imply that there wouldn't be the obvious and cruel oppression of blacks by whites. And apparently, that turned the trick. Economically, this state is still suffering from the follies of the past. The Alabama and Chattanooga Railroad is just about going to have to start all over again."

Luke paused to relight his cigar. "On the positive side," he continued, "Governor Houston is interested in bringing legitimate rail lines throughout the state of Alabama in order to facilitate the movement of crops and goods. That's a good sign. And actually, from what I've been able to learn, the small farmer, particularly in northern Alabama, has been able to make a decent living. It's the large plan-

16

tations that are in trouble. They still depend upon contractual labor from the blacks, they haven't pared their expenses, and haven't yet learned the lesson of rotating crops and trying for new markets. That's why I'm so hopeful about Windhaven Plantation."

"Because we have variety and versatility, isn't that what you once said to me, Mr. Luke?" Marius Thornton put in.

"Yes, Marius. Though by acreage Windhaven Plantation is about as large as it was in my grandfather's day, there's much more variety than even he could have contemplated back then. We've only a minimum amount of cotton because the price continues to be low, but we're well diversified, with cattle, hogs, and vegetables—and of course the poultry and dairy products we regularly send to the Montgomery or Lowndesboro stores to sell."

"I can vouch for that myself," Dalbert Sattersfield chuckled, as he accepted a cigar that Andy Haskins proffered him and nodded his thanks as Andy lit it for him. "One of the main reasons I've been able to draw new customers and to hold my old ones against some of the new stores that have been cropping up in the area is that Luke and Marius have been consistently furnishing me with the very finest foodstuffs at very reasonable prices, so I can make a decent profit without gouging my customers."

"We'll always continue to do that, Dalbert. You see, we're not greedy at Windhaven Plantation, and that's what sets us apart from the easy-money, get-rich-quick carpetbaggers who came upon us like a plague of locusts after Appomattox. There's enough food for everyone and their families, and still enough to be able to sell to give us our expenses and to put away a reserve, so when we need new machinery or tools or even if we have to buy a good boar or sow, a heifer or a bull, we don't have to dip into our savings. That's the premise on which Grandfather built his Windhaven Plantation, and even if everybody else considers it old-fashioned, I never intend to change it." Luke self-consciously lowered his eyes, aware that he had occupied the center of attention for some little time. To change the solemn tone that had fallen over the assemblage, he airily remarked to Dalbert Sattersfield, "You know, Dalbert, besides increasing the number of stores you have, you ought to think very seriously about replacing Mayor Daniel Fornage. I'm told he's in his seventies and isn't at all well, so he can't go on as mayor of Lowndesboro much longer."

"Me run for office, Luke?" Dalbert gasped. "I don't know a thing about politics!"

"You wouldn't have to in a little town like Lowndesboro. Everybody knows you. You just file an application if anything ever happens to Mayor Fornage. They'd have to hold a special election, and you'd walk right into the office with hardly a dissenting voice," Luke chuckled. "Don't forget, most of your customers come from Lowndesboro, and they've known you now for years as an honest, fair-dealing merchant. They'd rather have you than any carpet-bagger, not that a carpetbagger would particularly want that office—what does it pay, anyway?"

"Perhaps five or six hundred dollars a year at most. But really, Luke, you flatter me. I've enough to tackle just with thinking of opening a third store, I hope maybe by the end of the year."

"You're also thinking about your handicap." Luke came right out with it. "Take Andy here. He's in the state senate, and having only one arm doesn't hold him back at all. His brain, his personality, and the fact that he's a likable, decent man are what count. And that goes for you too, Dalbert. So think about it."

"All right, Luke. But when it comes down to cases, I'm not really sure that I'd have the gumption to go after anything like that," Dalbert Sattersfield almost apologetically concluded.

"I have to agree with Luke, Dalbert," Andy spoke up. "You ought to give it some thought. But right now—" he stretched and yawned, "I think I'll be taking my Jessica home. I've got to go back to Montgomery on Monday, and I'll be lucky if I see Jessica and little Horatio very often for the next month or so while we're in session."

"I understand," Luke Bouchard gently replied. "I'd be grateful to you, Andy, if you'd keep me abreast of the mood of the Senate after your first week back there."

With this, Luke rose to his feet. "Well now, gentlemen, a last toast. Lopasuta, be a good fellow and bring that decanter of good port you see over there at the end of the sideboard—that's the one. Fill all the glasses to the brim, and we'll drink to 1877 and a good year for all of you and your families."

"I'll second that, Luke, and wish you back a wonderful year for you and your wife and your kids," Andy at once retorted.

The ladies rejoined their menfolk in the dining room, they, too, having reached by mutual accord the decision to draw the evening's festivities to a close. As Luke stood with his arm encircling Laure's waist, bidding their guests good-bye, he suddenly closed his eyes and felt a cold shiver pass through his body. He remembered, for an instant, with a kind of stricken terror, this morning's seizure, and also the one at old Lucien Bouchard's grave the previous month. Even Laure had mentioned that she'd be happy if he'd go visit Dr. Kennery and have a thorough examination. And once again Luke Bouchard prayed inwardly that the kind Providence that had enabled him to build Windhaven Plantation according to his grandfather's dream would grant him time at least through this new year. For it was, in his considered and private opinion, likely to be even more critical than the year of the centennial.

# Two

The next morning—a Saturday—Luke Bouchard, on the pretext that he wished to ride to Montgomery to confer with Lopasuta on legal business relating to Windhaven Plantation, bade a tender farewell to Laure and his children, then saddled a black gelding and rode upriver.

He did not, however, go first to the house that Lopasuta shared with his spirited young wife, Geraldine. Instead, once he had passed by the state capital, he turned the gelding's head toward the northwest and tethered his mount to a hitching post outside a two-story building on Murchison Avenue. He climbed the stairs to the second-floor landing, knocked at the door of an office on whose opaque glass window was painted the name of "Abel Kennery, M.D.," and hearing an affable "Come in!" turned the knob and entered.

Dr. Abel Kennery was in his mid-thirties, slim, wiry, with friendly features and an outgoing attitude that Luke himself had greatly admired since he first met the eastern doctor who had bought out old Dr. Medbury's practice. The doctor came forward at once, extending his hand. "An unexpected pleasure, Mr. Bouchard! I trust you didn't come to consult me medically, because you certainly look fit. Matter of fact, I've been meaning to pay a social call on you and your lovely wife, and also, if I may have the privilege, of meeting your wonderful children."

"That I'd like you to do very much, Dr. Kennery. Perhaps next week, any evening you're free. Just tell me, and I'll arrange a very special dinner in your honor. I'm grateful to you for taking such good care of Laure."

"Thank you, Mr. Bouchard. Now then, what can I do for you?"

"Well, Dr. Kennery, to be perfectly honest, I did come here for medical reasons. I'd like you to give me an examination. You see"—Luke's face sobered—"I've had several small attacks, syncopes I think you would call them. The last occurred as recently as yesterday morning. And since I'm in my sixty-first year, it's only sensible to have you look me over and tell me what you think might have caused them, and what precautions I can take for the future—because now, more than ever, I've a great desire to go on living."

"I understand." The young doctor rose and, in a crisp, professional tone, directed, "If you'll remove your upper garments, Mr. Bouchard, I'll give you as thorough an examination as I can."

Luke swiftly divested himself of his waistcoat, then his cravat and shirt. Dr. Kennery tested his pulse and heartbeat, made him open his mouth and say "Ah," and proceeded through the steps of a general, routine physical examination.

"Well, Dr. Kennery, what's the verdict?" Luke smilingly asked, as he dressed himself.

"All your vital signs are excellent, Mr. Bouchard. Your blood pressure appears to be normal, your pulse is firm without any irregularity that I can detect. As to your heart, can you tell me in some detail what happened during the syncopes?"

Luke went on to explain his sensations during each episode. Dr. Kennery pursed his lips, frowned, then declared, "We're learning a good deal about the human heart, Mr. Bouchard. It's an extraordinarily complex and yet remarkably sturdy organ. Often emotional stress or physical excitement or overexertion cause brief spells in which the blood seems to be shut off in its circulation to the heart, which could cause these syncopes. Of course, I haven't given you a very intensive examination, but here under normal circumstances, at your ease, from what I've been able to detect, your heartbeat appears to be quite good for a man of your age. You're careful of your diet, I presume?"

"I've always been; Laure sees to that. Besides, I've never indulged excessively in strong spirits, nor do I smoke more

21

than an occasional cigar, perhaps two or three a week, at most. I go horseback riding, I walk a good deal, and of course my mind is active."

"That appears to be quite in moderation." Dr. Kennery smiled and seated himself, facing his patient. "You're being very sensible, as I've already said, in coming here to me now, but from what you've told me and from what I can observe at first hand, there is no reason to assume that you don't have at least another ten good years."

"But these fainting spells—"

"There may, of course, be a hidden abnormality of the heart, which I have no means of discovering, Mr. Bouchard," Dr. Kennery forthrightly averred. "Medical science in this country is just as young as the country itself. We can't yet examine the inside of the human body and detect what irregularities may be present. And yet, I shouldn't worry too much. I personally think that stress and brooding and introspection can do no good, and they certainly tend to aggravate symptoms."

"You don't think, then," Luke joked, "that I'm suffering from hypochondria?"

"Decidedly not," Dr. Kennery chuckled. "I'd just keep on with that sensible diet and regimen of physical exercise and activity. I still say you have at least ten good years and probably more, since you're concerned about yourself and, therefore, more than likely to take pains to preserve your health."

"That's a great relief, Dr. Kennery." Luke drew out his wallet and laid a greenback down on the doctor's desk. "That's for the consultation. And if you'll let me know what evening you might be free next week, I'll make advance preparations so that you can be our guest—Laure looks upon you, just as I do, as a friend and neighbor, not just a doctor."

"That's most kind. I really feel quite at home now in Montgomery, though as you know I'm an easterner. Would next Wednesday suit you?"

"Fine! I look forward to welcoming you to Windhaven Plantation. And I know that Laure and the children will be delighted to see you." Again, Luke Bouchard shook hands, and then left Dr. Kennery's office.

Lopasuta Bouchard opened the front door of his little

house and uttered with some surprise, "What joy it gives me to see you again—but I had not expected, after last night—"

"I didn't think you'd be at your office on a Saturday, Lopasuta," his adoptive father smilingly interposed, "so I came directly here. Now, apart from my pleasure in seeing you in your own house, I have formal business with you. May I come in?"

"But of course—I'm sorry Geraldine isn't here to greet you, but she's at the library looking up some references for me. Do come in. That sofa's very comfortable. May I get you some refreshment?"

"Thank you, no. Well now," Luke Bouchard looked slowly around the neatly furnished living room as he seated himself on the sofa. "It's evident to me that there's been a woman's touch here. The room is very attractive. Be sure to compliment Geraldine for me."

"I will. Yes, she is a constant delight to me in so many ways. And she has shown great courage in the face of the hostility which we both knew our marriage would generate. Well then, my father, how may I serve you?"

"Last night, Lopasuta, was a festive celebration. You and I had very little chance to talk in private, and that was why I decided, and not entirely on impulse, to visit you today. For one thing, I don't want to worry Laure. I've just come from Dr. Kennery's office."

"Oh? You're feeling ill?" Lopasuta solicitously inquired, as he half rose from his chair.

Luke Bouchard shook his head and made a gesture for him to resume his seat. "Actually, I've never felt better. But at my time of life, I thought it wise to be examined, to see if there were any unfavorable signs."

"I'm sure there weren't. Believe me, you look as strong and vigorous as ever," replied the young Comanche lawyer.

"You flatter me," Luke chuckled half to himself. "And so does Laure. And what you said about Geraldine's making you happy reminds me how lucky I've been with my Laure. I've never told you exactly how we met and what the circumstances were. Not that I'm in a mood for confession now—I told you that Dr. Kennery in no way read me a death sentence—but there's something I think you

23

should know about me, since you've honored me by allowing me to adopt you, and calling me your father."

"You owe me no explanations; you've done so much for me that I can never repay you."

"On the contrary, you've already repaid me and you'll do still more before I die, God willing. I think my grandfather, if he could look over all the acts of my life, would regard my having adopted you as one of the best and most unselfish. And that's enough talk of that subject, or I might become maudlin."

Rising from his seat, Luke went to the window, looked out, then turned back to the Comanche lawyer. "I want you to know the truth about me. While it is true that there is little I regret when I review my past, I have not been perfect by any means."

Luke took a deep breath, straightened, and then earnestly continued, "Right after the war, when I was still married to Lucy Williamson, I took my family to New Orleans, with the intention of emigrating to Texas, Windhaven having been burned and plundered by Yankee soldiers. While we were in the city, I naturally went to visit my banker, John Brunton. As you know, the major part of my cash is kept to this very day in what is now called the Brunton & Barntry Bank. And perhaps you know too that during the war Brunton saved his bank from being taken over by Union forces—General Butler was occupying New Orleans at the time—by a very clever ruse. With great audacity, he opened a house of pleasure to serve as a front for the bank."

"That took great daring, indeed," Lopasuta exclaimed.

"Quite so. If it hadn't been for his skill and loyalty, the Bouchard family would have been in terrible financial straits at the end of the war." Luke smiled ruefully. "But to get back to my story. In the course of one of my visits to John Brunton's bank, I met Laure, then Laure Prindeville. Her own father had owned a bank that Butler's men took over. She had been compelled to surrender herself to the corporal of a Union platoon, or else suffer violation by all of them. After her father committed suicide in his anguish over that atrocity, John Brunton took her in and made her a hostess at the house—but she never was one of those girls who entertained the Union officers who were constant patrons there."

24

"I understand. Mr. Brunton must have been a very good and compassionate man."

"One of the finest I've ever know, Lopasuta. Yet Laure summed me up—to use her expression—as an old sobersides, and one afternoon her teasing drove me to such distraction that I turned her across my knee and spanked her. It led to the only act of infidelity I've ever committed— you must understand, of course, that she was even more beautiful and maddeningly desirable then than now—*if* that is possible, for her beauty has in no way diminished. Then she married John Brunton, and Lucy and I went on to Texas, and my oldest son, Lucien Edmond, took charge of Windhaven Range."

Again, Luke took a deep breath, looked down at the floor, and then resumed: "When I was in Texas, after my poor Lucy was shot and killed by Mexican bandits, I learned that Laure had borne a son and John Brunton had died of yellow fever. I called my family together and I told them what I had done, and that I was convinced that Laure's child—Lucien—was really mine. I went back to New Orleans, and thank God I persuaded her at last to marry me and to share my life. I have been blessed in two marriages by devoted, loving women. But you must know that your adoptive father was guilty of that one lapse."

"You did not need to tell me this, not at all. But since you have, I have all the more respect and honor for you. You have done such good for my people and for all those with whom you come into contact that the Great Spirit Himself could never, would never, condemn you for what you call a lapse."

"It is kind of you to say that, Lopasuta." Luke's eyes were wet with tears, and he had to take a handkerchief and blow his nose. "Now, if you will forgive my intrusion into your house on a day of rest, may I ask you to do a piece of business for me?"

"I am always at your service, at any hour, at any time. You gave me a new life, you brought me to this happiness which I now enjoy with my Geraldine, and soon we shall be blessed with our first child. You have only to command me—"

"Never that," Luke shook his head and held up a reproving hand, "for such a term hearkens back to the days of ignoble slavery. My grandfather did not hold with

25

that, and that was why, when the *mico* of Econchate gave him black slaves, he promptly freed them. No, but I ask this favor of you: I want you to draw up my will."

"I will get paper and a pen at once and write it down. And then, in due course, it will be drawn up formally for you to sign."

"Very good. But mind you, not a word to Laure."

"I will send word to you by a discreet messenger when it is ready." Lopasuta reached for a pen and a sheaf of foolscap. "There now, I am ready to take down your words. But before I do, let me just say that we of the People have a saying that whenever even the strongest and wisest of men goes forth, the snake may deal him the death bite without warning. None of us has a covenant with the Great Spirit to guarantee long life. For myself, I pray to Him that He will grant Geraldine and our little child and myself, as you and your Laure and all of your family, untroubled, peaceful and happy years."

"To that I'll say a very humble amen, Lopasuta. But now, to business. You know the usual preamble, 'I, Luke Bouchard, being of sound mind and in full possession of my faculties, do hereby devise and bequeath—' and so forth."

"Yes. And now the will itself. I must say that I am not the best of secretaries, so please speak slowly, so that I may write down every word and phrase exactly as you utter it."

"You'll do fine, Lopasuta. Very well then, let me see. First, I devise and bequeath to my beloved wife, Laure Prindeville Brunton Bouchard, title to one half of the acreage that constitutes the present Windhaven Plantation, and one half of all monies, stocks, and bonds now presently held in the Brunton & Barntry Bank of New Orleans."

"I have it." Lopasuta looked up from the paper poised on his knee and attentively eyed Luke Bouchard.

"Secondly, I devise and bequeath to Lucien Edmond Bouchard, my oldest son, all my interests, financial and real, in the property known as Windhaven Range, near Carrizo Springs, Texas. This, together with any mementos from my personal belongings that he may wish to keep as a remembrance. Further, to Lucien Bouchard, my oldest son by Laure Prindeville Brunton Bouchard, the other half of the original acreage of Windhaven Plantation."

"I have that also," Lopasuta assured him.

Luke Bouchard leaned back on the sofa, clasping the back of his head with both hands, and closed his eyes, as he pondered a moment. Then, in a strong, clear voice, he resumed: "I have already provided for one half of all monies, stocks, and bonds to be left to Laure. Accordingly, I now stipulate that the remaining half of those monies, stocks, and bonds should be divided equally among my sons: Lucien Edmond, Lucien, Paul, my unborn child—if it is a son—and finally, my adopted son, Lopasuta—"

"No, my father!"

"This is my will, Lopasuta, and you are my lawyer. Write it down as I have spoken it." Luke stared sternly at the young Comanche, and then broadly smiled. "You bear my name and you have brought great distinction to it; besides, now that you have a family on the way, you'll be able to use that money. I can't think of anyone better to whom to leave it. Of course, my daughters, Mara Hernandez, Celestine, and Clarissa, are to receive bequests of fifteen thousand dollars each, as should my unborn child, in the event it is a daughter. The money for these bequests is to be taken from a special fund presently on deposit at the New Orleans bank. By the way, Lopasuta, Jason Barntry—who should receive a copy of the will, once it has been signed—will indicate to you that there are also special trust funds for my wife and each of the children, including the child about to be born, as well as a fund specifically designated for the maintenance of Windhaven Plantation. The income from these funds, which the bank administers as trustee, will be available without interruption, in the event of my death, even during the period that the will is being probated."

"That was very foresighted of you," Lopasuta remarked.

"I have tried to provide for every contingency, and I hope I have succeeded," Luke replied. "Now then, coming back to the will, I should add that since my four youngest children—and of course the unborn child—are minors, you will have to appoint an administrator for them—have you any objection to assuming that role?"

"None, my father, except that I can imagine a hypothetical case in which, if anyone should attempt to contest the will, they might find that I was guilty of conflict of interest. If I were a dishonest man, I might, as administrator, attempt to cheat your heirs out of their inheritance."

"There isn't likely to be any contesting of this will, Lopasuta, not the way you will draw it up. Besides which, you're the very opposite of dishonest, so, if you've no objection, I hereby appoint you as administrator. There's another reason for that, one of practicality. I might think of Jason Barntry, except that he's aging and he hasn't been too well the last few years, not after his wife's death, which shook him very greatly. You yourself know that you had to persuade him, when you and Geraldine were on your honeymoon, to continue working for us—"

"That's true. Very well then, but you do me too much honor."

"I give you only your due, Lopasuta. You've been as dear to me as my own flesh and blood; you've brought honor to the name of Bouchard."

"I can never thank you enough, but I swear to you that I will repay your trust in me all of my days, my father."

"I know you will. Now let me see, there's some other unfinished business. You are aware, of course, that part of the land on which Andy Haskins and Jessica now live used to belong to my first wife's father, old Mr. Williamson. He owned a total of four hundred acres. The land was left to me at his death; then of course it was confiscated at the end of the war. A few years ago, Jedidiah Danforth managed to buy back the acreage, and I turned it over to Andy. The title was supposed to be put in his name. Now, Lopasuta, I would appreciate it if you would investigate this matter for me, to make certain that Andy has full and incontestable legal ownership of the land. He has earned it."

"Certainly—I'll make sure that all the documents are in order. Now is there anything else you wish me to add to this will?"

"If you've gone through Jedidiah's papers, Lopasuta, you've seen the agreements that he drew up with me and the tenants—Dan Munroe, Hughie Mendicott, and the others."

"Yes, I remember them very well."

"By now, you will find that the recorder of deeds has the documents that transfer back their acreage to myself, thus restoring the original Windhaven Plantation. People like Dan Munroe and Hughie Mendicott are the very salt of the earth, and they have contributed greatly to rebuilding Windhaven Plantation, helping to make it as it was before it was set aflame. I wish to include an additional clause to the effect that, in the event of my death before the coming of age of either Lucien or Paul—and the baby, if it's a son—the tenants should be allowed to continue to live and work on the acreage that will be bequeathed to my young sons, and that they be allowed to keep half of the profits that come from the result of their labors on their own individual acreages. You may also express the wish to Laure, should I predecease her—which is very likely—that it is my dearest wish that she permit this also on that land that falls within her own inheritance of half the six hundred acres. Yes, I think that will do very nicely."

He frowned, then added: "Oh, yes, since Marius Thornton is still my foreman, I wish a clause granting him the sum of seventy-five hundred dollars in solid currency, whatever the accepted standard is at the time of my death, whether it be gold or silver or greenbacks. It is also my wish that he be allowed to retain his post of foreman of the acreage after my death, unless there be some reason or cause that he should wish to take employment elsewhere."

"I think you have covered everything very generously. You understand, of course, that when I draft the will, the specific smaller bequests—to your daughters, Marius, and so forth—will come first; then will come the larger bequests to your sons and to Laure."

"Oh, that's fine, Lopasuta. Please write it up however it should be done—you know the proper legal form. Yes, I should say that I have covered things pretty well, in the main. None of my children shall ever want for anything, providing that an economic catastrophe does not wipe out all of our holdings. In the Brunton & Barntry Bank, which has become one of the most solvent and reputable, not only in New Orleans, but in the entire South, wise investments and lack of greedy speculation continue to add growing interest to our capital. And if the crops are good this year—and there is every reason to believe they will be—more monies will be added to all of these funds. I believe when I appointed you as my lawyer, Lopasuta, I asked Jason Barntry to forward to you periodic statements of all the Bouchard holdings. These, of course, included the profits from Windhaven Range, but Lucien Edmond Bouchard controls those and he is not accountable to me."

"I understand that thoroughly. Well now, I think I have everything noted exactly as you dictated it. And, as I said, I'll send a messenger to you when the will is ready for your signature. But first, since you mention Jason Barntry, let me say that before the will is drawn up in final form, I would like to consult with him once more as to the current status of your holdings, in case there are any special provisions that should be in your will. That may take a little time—"

"That is fine, Lopasuta," Luke replied. "Please do whatever you feel necessary."

"Very well." Lopasuta rose, put the sheet of foolscap down on a little table, and then stood before Luke and held out his hand. "I thank you for the confidence you have shown in me. I pray to the Great Spirit that he hears me swear before you now that I will never violate either the trust you have shown me in telling me of your personal life, or the slightest term of any part of this, your final will and testament. I impose upon myself here before Him who is the Giver of Breath, the sacred oath of our people, that I should gladly die under torture before I would betray my vow."

"Lopasuta—" Again, Luke Bouchard's eyes were filled with tears, as he clasped the tall Comanche lawyer to him. When he stepped back, recovering himself, he reached into the portfolio case that he had brought with him and placed at his feet, as he had sat dictating his will. Opening it, he took out a wampum belt, ornate with shells and black, yellow, and red beads. Unfastening it, he clasped it round Lopasuta's waist and explained to the wondering Comanche, "This was the wampum belt of friendship that a Kiowa chief, Setangya, gave to me when I left Texas to go back to New Orleans to ask Laure to become my wife. He said that with this talisman, my life would be protected always. You, who only begin your life among us, and have already achieved such honor, you deserve this belt. And it is my wish that it will guard you, as well as your lovely Geraldine and the children she is sure to give you, through a long, rich, and happy life."

Lopasuta's eyes misted. "My father, I have no words by

which to thank you. And yet, I do not like the sound of your words, for they suggest a farewell—"

"No one is immortal, Lopasuta, as you yourself said. But no, I do not have a premonition of death—except that yesterday in my study I felt a little faint and was concerned, and that's really why I came to see Dr. Kennery. No, quite the contrary, with my beautiful Laure beside me, seeing the land fertile with crops that feed the hungry and give sustenance to all of our workers, knowing how well Lucien Edmond is doing at Windhaven Range, I rejoice in the gift of life that God has been good enough to vouchsafe me. Yes, this wampum belt brought me great fortune, great good luck, and I now wish you to have it. Perhaps the spirit of friendship that it symbolizes will be achieved in the hearts of all men before the end of your own life—on a day of wisdom and enlightenment when white men no longer look with suspicion or hatred at those whose skins are red or black or yellow."

He walked toward the window again, stood looking out for a moment, then at last said gravely, "That was what Grandfather yearned for, a world in which there would be understanding to take the place of ignorance and superstition, fear and hatred, the ugly handmaidens of war. Well, you can accuse me of being as idealistic and perhaps impractical a man as ever my grandfather was, but I'm not ashamed of it. And now, forgive me for imposing upon you at your leisure here at home. And give my warmest good wishes to your lovely Geraldine."

"She will surely be sorry to have missed you. But she told me what a wonderful time she had last night and how kind your wife was to her. Please tell my adoptive mother how grateful I am, in Geraldine's name as well as my own."

"Of course." Luke paused at the door and looked back a moment, then gravely added, "Laure said to me this morning before I left for Montgomery that she hoped that Geraldine's parents would be reconciled to you both, once your child is born. I would like to add my voice to her prayer."

"I can make no more overtures in their direction, my father. And Geraldine is too proud. She says that we have each other, and soon we shall have our child. She, too, prays, I know, that her mother and father will forget their

31

anger at her for having married me. I was afraid that would happen, and that is why I cherish her all the more because she braved their hatred to become my wife."

"Perhaps," Luke said smilingly, "that wampum belt will have magic enough to bring the reconciliation about. Thank you again, Lopasuta, and God bless you."

# Three

A week after the inauguration of Rutherford B. Hayes as President of the United States—though Tilden had received the larger popular vote, the electoral commission had chosen Hayes by a vote of eight to seven—Lopasuta Bouchard left his office to lunch at the little restaurant where he had courted his courageous young wife, Geraldine. As he walked by the capitol building, he was hailed by Andy Haskins: "Hold up a bit, Lopasuta!"

Lopasuta smilingly turned to see the one-armed former Tennesseean hurry toward him, broadly grinning. "We just recessed, Lopasuta," the newly elected state senator exclaimed, "and it's a stroke of luck your coming by this way—why don't we have lunch together?"

"Nothing could please me more, Andy. Come along. But I hope you've got a long lunch hour, because the place I've got in mind is on the outskirts of Montgomery."

"I don't think afternoon session will begin before three o'clock, and then there's going to be a motion to adjourn till Wednesday, to tell you the truth," Andy chuckled, as he clapped Lopasuta on the shoulder and matched the Comanche lawyer's strides with ease. "What's so special about this place? I thought I knew every good eating place in town."

"Well, I'll admit it's got sentimental value in its favor, too, Andy. You see, it's where I took Geraldine; I chose an out-of-the-way place for our meetings to try to avoid ugly talk and rumors."

"It didn't work, did it?" Andy sympathetically inquired.

"No, of course not." Lopasuta shook his head and

frowned. "You know how small-minded people are. And the worst of it is, her parents still reject her. She's a brave, wonderful girl. It's hard on her, now that she's going to have a baby in the summer."

"Good for you, Lopasuta! My Jessica can't wait to have her baby—it'll be any week now," Andy exuberantly broke in. "But tell me more about this place we're going to."

"Well, it's called Reuben's Dinery, and it's owned by a black couple in their early fifties, I'd say, and they not only make you feel quite at home, they also dish up the best fried ham or beef stew or pork chops with sweet yams you'll ever eat."

"That's good enough for me, Lopasuta!" Andy eyed his friend. "I might have figured you'd pick a place like that, just to show how little you are affected by the prejudice we've still got with us. And I suppose that's a good part of why your wife's parents are upset."

"Yes, it is. I've tried to get them to understand that we're very much in love, and it's my hope that when Geraldine has her child, they'll come around to our way of thinking. It's not as if I were a disreputable half-breed, or whatever—"

"I can lick my weight in wildcats even with my one arm," Andy vehemently declared, scowling and balling his fist, "so nobody'd better let me catch him saying that you're anything but a damned good lawyer and a fine man and husband, Lopasuta."

"Thanks, Andy. Coming from you, that means a lot to me. Well now, what do you think of this election?"

"I don't like it at all, Lopasuta, I can tell you that. If it hadn't been for Congress shoving through that special commission to decide who should get South Carolina's disputed electoral votes—and it just happened that there were eight Republicans against seven Democrats—Tilden would have won. Matter of fact, I voted for him. Hayes won officially by just one vote, 185 to 184, you know."

"Yes, I know. You might call it the stolen election—a lot of people are saying that, and so is the Montgomery *Advertiser*. Now that you're in the state senate, Andy, how do you think the election will affect us—not only the country, but us here in Alabama?"

"That's a powerful hard question to answer, Lopasuta.

34

Mind if I pass up answering till I've had some of the vittles you just mentioned to me? I left home early this morning and I had just a cup of coffee and a piece of cornpone, so I'm starving," Andy ruefully confessed.

As they entered the restaurant, the middle-aged black owner greeted Lopasuta with a beaming smile and ushered him and his companion to the most spacious table, located at the rear of the dining room and therefore protected from gaping viewers on the street outside. "Mighty good to see you again, Mr. Bouchard, suh," he effusively declared, "and my pleasure to serve you, Senator Haskins. Been readin' 'bout your good work in the Senate, suh. Jist like Mr. Bouchard here, you're on the side of dem what hasn't got much money. My wife Eunice 'n I, we sho 'preciates what you're tryin' to do for folks like us."

"I'm just one man, Mr. Henry," Andy Haskins deprecatingly replied, "but you're right about my wanting to give everybody a fair shake. Right now, though, I'd like to give my stomach a fair shake. My friend Lopasuta here has been telling me about your fine cooking, and I must confess I hadn't known about this place before."

"Den you let me fix you a real good lunch, me 'n Eunice, suh." Reuben Henry beamed from ear to ear and vigorously nodded his head by way of emphasis. "You sho won't be disappointed, I promise you dat!"

"I'll leave it to you, Mr. Henry." Andy chuckled, nodded, then turned back to his friend: "Judging from the delicious aroma coming from the kitchen, I'd say I was mighty lucky seeing you across the street when we adjourned."

"You'll have the best lunch in Montgomery," Lopasuta promised. Then, leaning forward, his face sobering, he went on, "I'm really glad to see you because I've been wanting to ask you what the feeling is in the Senate about our new President."

"Well, Lopasuta, there are lots of reactions, and they're all different. Mostly, the men are hoping that Hayes will keep his promise to take troops out of the South. Of course, you know that the Southerners in the House of Representatives blocked passage of the military appropriations bill just to make sure old Eight-to-Seven would do just that."

"Eight-to-Seven," Lopasuta repeated. "I'll lay odds he'll

be known throughout the rest of his political career by that phrase."

"Probably," Andy grinned. "And I've heard a few other things said about him, like 'Granny Hayes' and 'Goody Two-Shoes' and even 'Queen Victoria in Britches.' There's no doubt that most Americans figured that Tilden won the election. He certainly was the popular choice and would have made a fine President. But to answer your earlier question, the one good thing Hayes has already started to do is to sweep out of office any top government officials who had anything to do with the Grant administration, and he's putting in some good men. His choice of Carl Schurz as secretary of the interior is practically a stroke of genius. Schurz is a reformer, and he thinks the way you and I do, about giving equal opportunity to people who deserve it, not based on what fine houses they own, or how much money they've got in the bank."

"Do you think that Hayes will try to reconcile the North with the South?"

"In a way, yes." Andy Haskins pursed his lips and thought for a moment. "If he's really going to take all military forces out of the remaining occupied Southern states. Unfortunately, so far as getting along with the blacks is concerned, he and his administration seem to think that the Thirteenth, Fourteenth, and Fifteenth Amendments, along with the Civil Rights Act, ought to be enough to guarantee the freed blacks equal rights to labor, education and citizenship. That, however, I'm taking under advisement, as you lawyers might say."

"Why is that, Andy?"

"For the simple reason that we really don't have a truly effective federal civil rights law—you know that yourself from the cases where you've stood up for freed blacks who were being cheated by carpetbaggers. You've been very lucky, because the facts have all been on your side. But there are plenty of cities here in the South as well as even in the North, where a black whose rights have been violated isn't going to win a decision in a court case."

"Yes, you're right about that," Lopasuta slowly agreed. "In San Francisco, Cleveland, and Memphis, blacks have brought suit against theater managers for not admitting them. I've followed those cases in the papers. The courts upheld the defense in all cases. No, there's lots of work to be done before all men accept one another as brothers, I'm afraid."

"That's right. Now one more thing that we're talking about in the Senate," Andy put in, "is that Hayes got the critical electoral votes because he worked out a compromise with Southern Democrats. He promised that he and Congress would give strong backing to subsidies for a Southern railroad. It's going to take a while to get that accomplished, but everybody's thinking again about the Alabama and Chattanooga Railroad. We're going to have to wait and see if Hayes is able to get his bargain translated into hard, cold enterprise. I'm not so sure it's ever going to happen."

"Nor am I. But in general, Andy, what do you think the tone of this administration is going to be?"

"That's easy." Andy Haskins drew a long breath and shook his head. "For one thing, the whole atmosphere up in Washington is going to be changed. The cigars and the whiskey and all the important people going in and out of the White House to see General Grant and to get their pet schemes put through—that's all going to change. We'll just have to wait and see how things develop. When the *Advertiser* printed Hayes's inauguration speech, I declare, there was peace and sweetness but very little substance to it. I think what he's aiming at—and I can't say that I blame him—is to go back to the happy days when there wasn't any corruption or scandal in the White House; to get back to the prosperity that existed before the Civil War. And I'm sure he hopes he won't offend too many powerful people along the way. I don't know if it's going to work. I do know that, so far as my constituents are concerned, everybody is praying that we can forget about Reconstruction and the hurts of the war and get back to making a living for our families and living decently, having kids— just like my Jessica and your Geraldine. That's really what everybody wants, when you come right down to it."

" 'S'cuse me, gennlemen," Reuben Henry apologetically broke in, as he and his plump, gray-haired wife approached the table and set down plates of viands. "I took de liberty, suh," addressing Andy Haskins, "of fixin' you a plate of the specialties my wife 'n I cook for our best customers. Pork chops here, some of the beef stew, and a nice piece of liver with yams, and also hash-brown potatoes, jist in case you'd prefer those instead of the yams. Dey's some right nice fresh vegetables we wuz lucky to git, and I sho' does hope you like it, Senator Haskins."

"It looks and smells wonderful, Mr. Henry! Thank you very much, you and your nice wife, for being so kind to a stranger."

"Nossuh," Reuben Henry obstinately shook his head. "You ain't no stranger. Us black folks know exactly what you been doin', even when you wuz back in the House of Representatives here in town, to help us git a square deal. Besides, you bein' a fren' of Mr. Bouchard, you be doubly welcome. Now I'm gonna shut my big mouth, and let you'n Mr. Bouchard there enjoy your meal, suh."

Andy Haskins's fears concerning Rutherford B. Hayes were to be realized. For Hayes and Congress never did fulfill their part of the bargain of backing a Southern railroad, and the South was destined to wait many years before private initiative eventually accomplished the task. But on the other hand, the Southern politicians refused to vote for James Garfield to become Speaker of the House and they made no effort to strengthen the Republican Party in the South.

The Hayes era would be one of piety and peace: abundant platitudes but little performance. The high-sounding phrases of equality for all, however they might have been aimed at the situation of the freed blacks of the South, would really change nothing as regarded prejudice and oppression. And the Civil Rights Act itself would be declared unconstitutional only three years after Hayes was to leave office. The judge who was to write that decision would be none other than Joseph P. Bradley, whose vote on the electoral commission had made possible the infamous compromise that had put Rutherford B. Hayes into the presidency.

Midway through the last week of March, while Andy was attending the spring session of the Alabama Senate, he was brought word by a page that Jessica was delivering their second child. Exhaling a deep breath, Andy gestured his thanks with an abrupt wave of his hand and threaded his way between the seats to the exit. Once outside the capitol building, Andy saw that the sky was gray and the clouds darkening. The wind from the northwest seemed to blow them into a single, intensified mass. Glancing feverishly around, Andy spied an unoccupied carriage and made his way to it, stared down the surly, reluctant driver and gave his destination. "Don't be unhappy," he added crisply, "you'll get all you want and something extra besides if you get me home inside the hour."

Then, leaning back for the long ride, his eyes closed, he marveled at his good fortune. Once he was penniless and without hope for the future; now he was a productive member of his community, blessed with a loving wife and son, and soon—perhaps even at this very moment—another precious child.

When they arrived at Andy's house, the carriage driver opened the door for his passenger. The one-armed state senator nodded his thanks, thrust a greenback into the driver's hand, and then made his way into the one-story frame house. Entering the bedroom, he found the midwife, Mrs. Emily Norton, massaging and soothing Jessica, who groaned and trembled and kept her eyes closed as, her fists clenched, she prayed silently for deliverance of the child both she and Andy yearned for.

It was nearly midnight before Jessica finally gave birth to her child, a little girl, and Andy Haskins put his hand over his mouth to stifle his sobs of relief and gratitude that Jessica had been spared after her protracted ordeal. He moved beside her, his face haggard and lined, as he clasped her hand in his and stared lovingly at her. An hour later, blinking her eyes, still dazed and almost somnolent, Jessica looked at him and murmured, "Has it started yet, dear Andy?"

"It's over, sweetheart. I love you, Jessica. You don't know how happy I am that I can look at you and know that it's over and you're both safe. I love you very much, I'll love you till I die and beyond that, if the Lord lets me," he brokenly murmured.

Wanly, she put out her soft hand toward his, and he took it, brought it to his lips, and fervently kissed it. "My sweet Jessica, my dear one," he hoarsely murmured.

"Was it a boy for you, honey?" Not yet fully conscious, she spoke with a voice that was weak and distant.

"No, Jessica, a girl, and that's exactly what I wanted."

"I'm glad. I like girls, Andy," she quavered.

39

"Have you decided on a name for her, honey'" He anxiously bent to her, whispering as he held her soft hand in his.

"If you don't mind, Andy, I—I'd like to call her Ardith. She was my favorite of all my aunts, and she and Daddy were the only family I really knew."

"Of course. That's exactly what we'll call her. Now you just close your eyes and rest, Jessica darling. I'll take care of things. I'm here and I love you; don't ever forget it," Andy whispered. At that moment, he noticed Mrs. Norton hesitating in the doorway.

"I'll need a few more minutes alone with her," she said.

Reluctantly, Andy let go of his wife's hand, "I'll be just outside in the parlor, honey," he said, and retreated from the room.

No sooner was the senator seated in his favorite armchair than exhaustion claimed him. After dozing for some minutes, he shook himself awake and, with an effort, rose from the chair. Having no idea how long he had slept, he was alarmed that Jessica might have wondered at his absence. Entering the bedchamber, he was relieved to see that Mrs. Norton was still there, straightening the bedclothes. Bending to his wife, he kissed her forehead and whispered, "I love you, Jessica. You've made a new man of me, and I want us to have a lot of time together. I want to pretend that we've met for the first time and we're just courting and sparking. Please rest and get well, so we can have this together, my honey girl."

Jessica smiled, uttered a long sigh, and squeezed his hand. Then her long curly lashes fluttered as she closed her eyes and fell asleep. Andy eyed the midwife and breathed, "I'm thanking God that you were here to take care of my wife, and to give us a fine new daughter. God bless you. I don't know what I would have done if Jessica hadn't pulled through."

"Now, Senator Haskins, no need to fret at all. She's a fine, strong girl, she'll give you lots more kids, you wait and see. And, if you'll excuse my boldness, I couldn't help listening to what you were saying—you're a wonderful man, and she's mighty lucky to have a husband like you. I'll be going now. And God bless you and her and the baby."

Andy Haskins was very close to tears, as he quickly

40

pressed some greenbacks into the midwife's hand and then escorted her to the door and saw to it that one of his workers drove her back to her house in the new buggy he had recently bought in Montgomery.

He went back into the other room where Horatio was sleeping, and he knelt down and bowed his head and silently thanked God for the abundant blessings that had been vouchsafed him. And he prayed for a prolonged life for his benefactor, Luke Bouchard, without whose help back in those turbulent days just following Appomattox all of this could not have been possible.

Two days after the birth of Ardith Haskins, Luke Bouchard received a discreet message from Lopasuta to the effect that the will that the Comanche lawyer was to have drawn up for his adoptive father was now ready. Lopasuta had been delayed somewhat in the preparation of the will, for he had only recently received from Jason Barntry the information he needed concerning Luke's most recent stock acquisitions and also his trust funds; but at last the document was ready for Luke to read and sign.

Though Luke had experienced no recurrence of the fainting spells of December and January, he had not forgotten their ominous significance, and he was eager to conclude the matter of the will as quickly as possible. On his next regular visit to Montgomery, two mornings later, he went to Lopasuta's office and the document was signed in the presence of two witnesses from a neighboring shop.

That same week, Luke received a letter from his friend Edmond Philippet in Tuscaloosa. Philippet was on the county board of commissioners, having been a nonsecessionist and a landholder who, like old Lucien Bouchard and Luke, had managed to free his slaves and to take little part on either side in the Civil War. For this he had been vilified by his fellow townsmen. His wife had died of pneumonia four years ago, having been ill for several years prior to that—some malicious neighbors said that she had wasted away because she did not hold her husband's humanitarian views. Nonetheless, Philippet was now thoroughly vindicated, one of the most respected men in Tuscaloosa, and he gave a great deal of money to charity. He had, in fact, helped subsidize the private sanatorium into which he had placed the deranged former Confederate

41

captain, William Darden, after the latter's attempt to kill both Andy Haskins and Luke Bouchard.

Luke had just finished breakfast with Laure and his children when the letter was delivered to him. As he opened it, he turned pale and, glancing at his golden-haired wife, asked her in an unsteady voice to excuse him for a few minutes. Respecting his feelings and aware that the news he had just received must be serious, she at once turned to the children and diverted their attention by asking them questions about their schoolwork. Lucien and Paul enthusiastically piped up, vying to be the first to answer, while Luke swiftly went to his study and closed the door.

There, he seated himself at his escritoire and, before rereading Philippet's letter, pondered William Darden's story. A captain in the Confederate Army, Darden had returned at the war's end to find his wife insane, his daughter raped and murdered, and his plantation destroyed—all at the hands of Yankee soldiers. A bigoted neighbor told him that blacks had raped and killed his daughter, and from that moment forth Darden had been possessed by an insane hatred for the black race. Homer Jenkinson and his cronies had played upon this hatred four years ago, so rousing Darden to homicidal fury that the poor ex-Confederate captain had taken his Whitworth and twice tried to kill Luke and Andy—just because they had blacks working with them on their farms. Luke had ultimately found refuge for the poor man in Philippet's asylum, providing extra money so that the former captain would be well cared for.

Bringing himself out of his reverie, Luke perused Philippet's letter again, uttering a soft groan of heartfelt anguish as he did so:

Dear Luke:

I must sorrowfully report to you that William Darden died by his own hand several days ago. It was not discovered until the following morning. He had made a noose from a torn bedsheet, stood upon the table, fastened one end of this noose to an ornamental bracket, and then leaped to his death.

This suicide has deeply moved me because, when Mr. Darden entered the sanatorium, I personally interviewed him. I felt such compassion for this unfortunate, tortured man, whose misfortunes were exploited by those damnable carpetbaggers whom you described when you wrote seeking a place for him.

In all that occurred in his life, Darden felt an ineradicable guilt, as if it were he, and not those unprincipled scoundrels, who was responsible for all the misfortunes that befell him. I enclose a note that he wrote to the head of the sanatorium, Dr. Brandon Cullers. Dr. Cullers gave it to me and thought that perhaps you would want to see it.

God alone knows how many such tragedies have occurred as a result of that dreadful internecine war, which set brother against brother. Now, looking back, we may wonder why it happened, and what the real motivation was. Was it brought about solely by the pious Northern abolitionists who condemned the South for moral depravity—or was it caused by something still more sinister? Neither you nor I can judge. We can only stand by and bewail the tortures and the agonies of the innocent, like poor William Darden.

One day, if you ever come to Tuscaloosa, I would consider it my privilege to have you and your lovely wife, Laure, as my guests in my spacious house. It is empty now except for several very old and loyal retainers. I am left with memories. You, deservedly, have your family and your friends and those who know how much good you have done and how hard you have tried to combat the injustices of this world. Sometimes I think that you and I are like Don Quixote, as your wonderful grandfather was, valiantly testing our lances against the windmills, the malefactors. Granted that we cannot topple them into the dust; at least, may God be praised, the effort that we put forth in fighting evil rewards us inwardly and acts as an inspiration for the rest of our lives.

> Your devoted friend, I remain always,
> Edmond Philippet

Luke put Edmond Philippet's letter down on the escritoire and then slowly unfolded the single sheet of foolscap that his friend had enclosed, the last communication of William Darden. Tears ran down his cheeks as he read the short, poignant message:

To those whom this may concern:
People have been kinder to me than I deserve. But

there is no purpose to going on living, eating, sleeping, without any future or hope. What I have done I am deeply sorry for, and I beg the forgiveness of Haskins and Bouchard, at whom I fired shots from my rifle. I know now they had no part in what happened to me, and that is why I feel all the more guilty.

I can no longer go on living with the memories of how my wife and my poor girl Alice suffered—those two who were all that I lived for and gave meaning to my life—

There is nothing left, except nights when I cannot sleep and I am haunted by all that happened. God forgive what I am going to do, but at least I hurt no one except myself, and I take myself out of a world where my presence is surely needless.

William Darden

Luke Bouchard bowed his head, crumpled William Darden's pathetic letter, and pressed his hand against his heart. "What torture life must have been for him after losing his family in that dreadful war," he said aloud. "The poor soul, may he be granted peace. And may all of us who have sinned knowingly against our fellow man, or who have been sinned against by those who care nothing for life and decency, be given mercy in Thy wisdom."

He felt a trembling fit seize him, and he sobbed aloud and prayed not only to God, but also to the spirit of old Lucien Bouchard and his Dimarte. And then it passed as suddenly as it had come upon him, and he murmured, "When it be Thy will, into Thy hands I will commend my spirit."

# *Four*

Dr. Ben Wilson felt specially blessed in this spring of 1877. His practice in Wichita was thriving, and there were no more catcalls as he and his beloved Elone walked through the dusty streets of the town. Once spurned and derided as a "squaw man" for his marriage to the lovely, dusky-skinned Elone, the Quaker doctor was now loved and respected in his new home. The birth of their fourth child, Dorothy, left him in wondrous gratitude at the joys of his late second marriage.

Meanwhile, Thomas, now nearly twelve, and Sybella, now eight, went to school in Wichita and had made friends easily. These children from his first marriage were closely bound to their half brothers and sisters.

On a chilly spring evening, not long after Elone had regained her strength following Dorothy's birth, Dr. Wilson and his wife were entertaining at dinner their friends Dallas Masterson and his recent bride, Flora. Some years back, after Ben had removed a bullet from Masterson's chest, thereby saving his life, the latter had become a staunch advocate—and defender—of the mixed couple. Also present at dinner was Dallas and Ben's mutual friend, Dave Haggerson, a teacher who had tried his hand at farming for a while, until his wife died a few years back and he had returned to the schoolroom.

Ben felt very close to Dave, having himself known the grief of losing a wife—his gentle Fleurette. The Quaker doctor also took special pleasure in his friendship with the newlywed Mastersons. On the surface, he had little in common with Dallas, a professional gambler who had left the hard life of a trail boss to become a faro dealer at the local casino. And yet, looking deeper, there were undeniable similarities. For both men, unexpected happiness had come through late marriages to much younger women, both outcasts from their own societies: Elone, a refugee from her own Sioux tribe, had found shelter in the Creek village of Emataba, where Ben, as resident shaman, was devoting himself to the medical needs of the Indians. Flora, too, had been a victim. Escaping from her squalid home in St. Louis, the pretty twenty-year-old runaway had fallen in love with the gruff but good-hearted gambler. For both couples, the unlikely love matches had been no less than mutual salvation.

Now the two lucky couples and Dave Haggerson were assembled at the Wilson's dinner table, enjoying the sense of well-being that comes with friendly conversation and a homecooked meal.

Dave was in a jovial mood, and so he asked Ben playfully, "Well, now that your practice is thriving here in Wichita and you've seven young-uns clamoring for attention, I imagine you're ready to sit back for a time and enjoy being a family man. Lord knows, you deserve it, after all your good works."

"To tell the truth," replied Ben, smiling at first, then growing serious, "I've been feeling a bit restless lately. One day—and it will be soon, God willing—I mean to start a hospital here for the needy. Poor people shouldn't have to worry about paying doctor bills with money they just don't have. The sick should get medical treatment, plain and simple. Actually, I've already been working on this with Pastor Hartmann for some time, trying to raise the necessary funds. Most of our contributors can afford to give only a little, so we must be patient. Pastor Hartmann has agreed to donate a goodly sum out of his own pocket."

Dallas Masterson now shook his head and smiled admiringly. "I guess I should have known that Ben Wilson would be the last man on earth to sit back and take life easy." He reached for his wife's hand and, holding it in his own, said shyly, "We want you to know that we count it a . . . a whopping privilege to be your friends."

An altruist by nature, Ben had been feeling the need for another project, especially since he was reassured that the Creek village of Emataba was in the able hands of

Douglas Larrimer, whose timely arrival as Indian agent for the village had made possible his own departure. Unlike the evil and dishonest agent who had preceded him, Matthias Stillman, Larrimer fought for good-quality food and clothing and saw to their equitable distribution. Naturally his efforts were resented by many in Washington who, like General Philip Sheridan, believed that the "only good Indian is a dead Indian." Although they wrangled with Larrimer, in the end he was given considerable leeway in dealing with the reservation Indians and in looking after their health and well-being.

In a recent letter, Larrimer had written that Sipanata had been elected *mico* in Emataba's place, and the gentle Quaker doctor remembered this sturdy brave with great affection. For it had been Sipanata who had taught him the Creek language, though at first he had resented this white doctor who had come to live with his abandoned people, not understanding Dr. Wilson's true motives. And it had been Sipanata who had first revealed to Ben that Elone loved him and had urged him to acknowledge that love—a love that had ripened and given the Quaker doctor a joy he thought he would never know again after true, gentle Fleurette had been taken from him by diphtheria.

"I've also brought a few soldiers to the reservation," Larrimer had written.

These men either grew up with the Indians, or else actually have Indian blood in them, and therefore they don't resent the Creeks. Two of the men, in fact, actually volunteered to stay on by themselves for three months to go on with their work—something I knew you'd like to hear. It's heartening to know there are still decent men in this world who don't look down on others because of the color of their skins or because they happen to be on land that somebody else wants.

Yes, there were men of good will everywhere, and though at times corruption and scandal and sectional hatred made one forget this, Dr. Ben Wilson was sure that eventually such men would prevail. Yet he knew sadly that in spite of all Douglas Larrimer had done for the Creeks, they really could look forward to very little, and they would ultimately be forgotten. When they died out, there would be few who would remember that once they had come from the rich lands of Alabama and Georgia, where they ruled the Southeast.

Since the first week of last September, Arabella Hunter, now a widow, had been living with her daughter, Melinda, and her son-in-law, Lawrence. She had brought with her to the Davis household her precociously intelligent and poised daughter, Joy, who had been born to her at the advanced age of forty-five, the happy result of a quarrel between James and herself that had ended in an unexpectedly passionate reconciliation. Instead of having only her own memories to support her through late middle age, Arabella, now past fifty, had a remarkably lively and sensitive seven-year-old daughter as a loving companion.

For the first few weeks after James's death from the dreaded scourge of yellow fever, Arabella had felt herself irrevocably lost, isolated, and abandoned. Then she had courageously faced the inescapable reality of her situation. One night, while Melinda and Lawrence were out to the theater and she herself was acting as babysitter to their sons, Gary and James, and their little daughter, Denise, she had stared into the mirror and taken an objective account of herself. She was fifty-three, and there would be no more suitors, no more excitement, no more titillating adventures in the game of love. To offset this, she realized, there was the consoling fact that James had left her well provided for, in financial terms. And yet she had to admit to herself now that material comfort mattered little to her. All her life, she had never placed much value on financial wealth; things would not change now, even though James had done very handsomely by her, with a special trust fund for his last-born child, their love child, Joy.

Now, at this start of the first week of April, with Joy fast asleep, Arabella sat before her mirror, pensively combing her long hair, once black, now nearly gray. She smiled at her reflection in the mirror. "I'm very glad that James and I understood each other thoroughly before he died," she said, half aloud. "And best of all, dear James, you went to your grave knowing that your daughter Melinda and her husband had settled the breach between them and now are as much in love as ever. Yes, James, you always were the calm, reserved, and analytical member of our marriage. But I knew how deeply you were worried when

48

you learned that your son-in-law was seeing that woman, Marianne Valois. I'm pleased, too, that our daughter and her husband came together. Any day now, Melinda will bear her fourth child to Lawrence. I'm very grateful, and I'm at peace. Except that I'm beginning to think that Joy and I have worn out our welcome."

Abruptly she rose, blew out the candle, and lay down on her bed. A hundred different thoughts were running through her mind. She knew that Joy was self-disciplined, incredibly mature for her seven years, and that she need not go searching to see whether the girl had taken her bath and put herself to bed in the adjoining room. With a smile on her lips, Arabella fell asleep. And in her dreams, she was once more transported back to those heavenly days on Windhaven Plantation, when as a teenage girl she was first conscious of her own vivid beauty and of the attentive interest shown her by many men.

She had told Melinda and Lawrence when she had first come to live with them she would care for five-year-old Gary and three-year-old James and the two-year-old girl, Denise. Melinda had made only token protest, for actually she was eager to make certain that Lawrence would never stray again, as he had done with Marianne Valois. And so the two of them, as if they had just begun their courting, often went out to dinner and to the theater and symphony or to enjoy an operetta, leaving Arabella home with their three children and with Joy.

Joy had become a kind of little mother to her older sister's children. Arabella had watched delightedly as Joy had taken charge with an earnestness and interest far beyond her years. The serious-faced little girl was constantly devising new games to amuse her niece and nephews, and even little Denise, who had just begun to put words together with an adorable lisp, obeyed her and followed her suggestions.

On the second Thursday in April, Lawrence drove Melinda in his carriage to the hospital, where she delivered their fourth child, a daughter. Arabella stayed home to look after the other children, though Joy reassured her, "Mama, I can take care of them all right, I know I can. You really ought to go with Melinda, Mama."

"Sweetheart, she'll be fine; the nurses and the doctor

49

will take care of her. And besides, if I went and left you all alone, and if anything happened, I would never forgive myself," Arabella encouragingly assured her precocious daughter.

Joy sighed and nodded. "All right, Mama, but honest, I can take care of them. And they don't cry or make a fuss or anything when we play our games together."

"You blessed little angel—the luckiest thing I ever did in my life was to make James so angry with me that—" Arabella had gossipingly begun, only to catch herself, to clap a hand over her mouth, and then turn a vivid crimson. For she remembered only too well how her groundless suspicion that James was having an affair with an attractive young widow had forced him to remind her of her own flirtation with Durwood McCambridge and to spank her over his knee with a hairbrush. Anger was soon followed by an amorous act that gave her this enchanting, grave, poised daughter who would delight her in her old age.

When Melinda had come back from the hospital, Arabella was given a further proof of her older daughter's love and gratitude. "Mama," Melinda had exclaimed as she hugged the little black-haired baby to her bosom, "Lawrence and I are going to name her Arabella after you. She's got your black hair, Mama, see?"

"Bless you, Melinda dearest," Arabella had huskily whispered, tears blinding her for a moment.

On this Saturday night in the last week of April, as Arabella sat in front of her mirror, brushing out her long hair, she smiled philosophically at her image in the glass: "Bella, you've got to face it, you're a grandmother four times over now. But you've been very lucky with such a wonderful husband, and now this treasure of a little girl who's fast growing up—it's almost magical to think how smart she is at seven years old—"

There was a soft knock at the door, and Arabella called, "Come in!" Joy entered, in her muslin nightgown and robe and slippers. Her face was downcast and her eyes were red and swollen from crying. "Joy, sweetheart, what's the matter?" Arabella gasped, as she rose from her chair and hurried toward her daughter, then knelt down and took Joy into her arms and kissed her wet cheek.

"Couldn't we go back home?" Joy sniffled.

"Home?" her mother echoed, eyes widening questioningly.

"Oh, yes, Mama!" Joy blinked her eyes and put her arms around Arabella's neck. "They really don't need us any more, Mama. You know that?"

"No, honey, tell me," Arabella urged, intently searching her daughter's charmingly serious face for a clue as to Joy's inexplicable unhappiness.

"Well, Mama, I heard Melinda say to Mr. Davis—"

"He's your brother-in-law, sweetheart. I think it's all right for you to call him Lawrence," Arabella teased her, trying to adopt a bantering tone that would ease Joy's as yet unexplained distress.

"Yes, Mama. Well, anyhow, I heard Melinda say that she hoped everything would be as wonderful as it used to be. What does that mean, Mama? Doesn't it mean that they don't want us here anymore?"

"It means, dearest, that your big sister is falling in love all over again with your brother-in-law, even if they have four children. And that's very nice. Some day, when you're a little older, you'll understand it's nothing to do with you or me. But now it's time for your bed, Joy honey."

"I know, Mama, I was just going. But I was just wondering, couldn't we go back to our old house, our *real* house? Just the two of us?"

"We'll see," Arabella promised. Then, rising, she took Joy by the hand and led her to the adjoining little room that had been converted into a bedroom and playroom for her young daughter.

As she went back to her own bedroom, she snuffed out the candle and lay thinking, her head pillowed on her arms for a long moment before sleep claimed her. Her work was done here. And the most rewarding, wonderful thing of all was that Joy wanted to be just with her. She knew very well that Joy loved the children and would love the little baby, too. But just the same, it gave her a feeling of being needed, and Arabella fell asleep with a rapt smile on her lips.

"Melinda, darling, I think it's high time for Joy and me to go back home," Arabella said as she and her daughter were sipping coffee, having finished their breakfast in the kitchen. Lawrence had gone off to his work, and Joy was looking after her niece and nephews, while Melinda held little Arabella and was nursing her, her left arm encircling the cooing infant.

"But, Mama, Lawrence and I are ever so happy to have you with us, you know that. I hope you don't think we're chasing you away," Melinda protested. Then she looked down at the black-haired little baby and giggled, "She's so sweet, and she's so strong. I'm glad I've named her after you, Mama."

"You're happy again, darling. That's as it should be. Your father died happy, too, knowing that you and Lawrence had gotten back together again. And now that the baby is here I know in my heart that there'll never be another separation for you. That's exactly why I think it's time for me to leave."

"Well, Mama, if you've made up your mind—but I certainly hoped you haven't thought for a minute that either Lawrence or I want you to," Melinda anxiously protested.

"Of course not, honey. And Joy just loves your children. Just the same, she herself asked if we couldn't go back. You know"—Arabella gave her oldest daughter a radiant smile—"Joy is the most darling girl. I hope my namesake turns out to be just as sweet and smart—but then I'm sure she will." Then, in a serious tone, "We'll go back next week, if it's all right with you."

"Yes, of course, Mama, if you truly want to—but you know you'll always be welcome here."

Arabella firmly shook her head. "I like to hear you say that, sweetheart. And of course I'll come over to dinner every so often and I'll bring Joy. But it's time that the two of us had more time together. Joy no longer has a father, so I have to devote all the attention and love I can to her to make her feel wanted and needed."

"I love you so, Mama," Melinda sighed.

And so Arabella Hunter and her daughter Joy returned to the house that had been shared for so many happy years with James Hunter. The day after they moved back, Arabella received a letter from her son, Andrew. He was now twenty-three and living on a ranch near Austin with his young wife, Della.

As she opened the letter, Joy entered the living room, having just come home from school all by herself, much to her mother's pride. "How was school today, darling?" Arabella smilingly inquired.

"Just fine, Mama. The teacher was telling us about the Civil War, how things are changing and are going to be nice now that we have a brand-new President."

"I hope Mr. Ellison is right in his prediction, Joy. Well now, here's a letter from Andrew. Guess what?"

"What is it, Mama?" Joy came up to seat herself on the couch beside her mother, to put her arms around Arabella's neck, and tender her a warm, prolonged kiss on the cheek.

"He and his sweet wife, Della, are inviting us to come stay with them on their ranch near Austin."

"Oh, please no, Mama! I just want us to stay here and be together. I love you so, Mama, and even though I love my brother too, I'd much rather just be your little girl and have you tell me stories and ask me about school and things like that," Joy anxiously volunteered.

Arabella put down the letter and turned to take Joy into her arms and to kiss her. "God bless you, honey, you couldn't make me happier than when you say a thing like that. No, we shan't be visiting anywhere else for any length of time, not ever again. I promise that. But I'll tell you what we're going to do tonight. We're going to dinner in the nicest restaurant in Galveston, and then I'm going to take my sweet girl to the symphony. They're playing some Mendelssohn and Schubert, it's lovely music, and you'll like it very much."

"Oh, that sounds like a lot of fun, Mama. Now we're together again, and I'm your girl again, aren't I?"

Arabella nodded and, momentarily closing her eyes, breathed a silent prayer of thanksgiving for the serenity and joy that were accorded to her in these gentle twilight years of her life.

On Windhaven Range, Catayuna, who had once been Catayuna Arvilas, wife of the *jefe* of Maxtime, and then the squaw of the Comanche chief Sangrodo, felt out of place and useless. Now thirty-eight, in the full maturity of her ripe beauty, her black hair touched with a thin streak of gray down the center from the top of her scalp to the back of her proud, erect head, she observed the placid, serene life of her hosts, their workers, and their families. After Sangrodo's death from the bite of a scorpion last year, she had accepted the invitation of Lucien Edmond and Maxine Bouchard to take her children and to come live with them. This she had done, bringing her daughters, Miguerda, now six, and Consuela, not yet five, and her year-old son, Nahubiyaa. Lucien Edmond's vaqueros had built a little house for her, not far from the Belcher house, in the shade of some spreading oaks. One of the vaqueros had even helped her plant a little garden.

She thought now of the life she had known, two separate and distinct lives, really. First, she had been the envied and pampered wife of the head of a Mexican village—a man, she reflected, whom she had respected more than loved yet who was always considerate of her. She wondered, in retrospect, how it was that they had had no children; she had married him when she was twenty, and they had spent six years together without issue. Then Sangrodo had taken her from her Mexican husband. He had at first enslaved her to punish Manuel Arvilas for his cruelty toward peaceful Indians; and then, struck by her courage, he had made her his squaw and elevated her to the rank of "beloved woman." They had had five children in all; a sixth child had been lost before birth when the *bandido* Carlos Macaras had struck her in the belly with the butt of his rifle. Despite her agony, she had managed to kill the outlaw with her scalping knife.

She had borne a son, little Inokanti (He Who Is Loved) nearly eight years ago, but he had died of fever before he had lived to see five summers. Then, three years ago, after giving Sangrodo his two daughters, she had borne another daughter, this one dead at birth. That was why she took such concern with little Nahubiyaa: not only was he their only living son, but he was also the last living child whom the noble-hearted Comanche chief had given her. And he must live so that he would grow to manhood and be told of the heroism and goodness of his father, who had sought no fight with the white-eyes, who had in his own primitive yet honest way rendered justice for justice, and who had led his people to the little Mexican village where they had begun a life of peace, farming, and the protection of their families who would motivate them to keep the peace and live out their lives in contentment.

54

Perhaps it was the atmosphere of happiness and family devotion at Windhaven Range that touched her, and made her miss the strong, often brooding, yet always considerate Sangrodo. Here in this friendly, bucolic setting, she missed him more deeply than she knew.

And yet, the hospitality of Lucien Edmond and Maxine made her feel under an obligation that irked her, for in marriage to Sangrodo and in sharing his rugged life and its dangers, she had gained not only pride, but also a fierce spirit of independence.

And that was why this late April evening, after dinner, she approached Maxine, who had seated herself at the spinet, and murmured, "Dear Señora Bouchard, I love to hear you play and I pray you continue. But when you've finished, I would like very much to speak privately with you."

"But of course, Catayuna!" Maxine turned to send her a warm smile. She had grown to admire Catayuna as much as if she had been a sister: she had heard from Lucien Edmond the many stories of Catayuna's exploits of heroism and her unselfishness. And, having herself once been kidnapped by a renegade Indian who had wished to violate her and make her his slave, until Lucien Edmond had saved her, she could comprehend the tremendous adjustment that Catayuna had had to make in exchanging the pampered life of enviable respectability in a Mexican village for the stark primitivism of a Comanche stronghold.

After she had played a Haydn sonata and some Chopin nocturnes, Maxine rose and accepted compliments from her delighted listeners—Mara and Ramón Hernandez, Joe and Margaret Duvray, Eddie Gentry and María Elena, Henry and Maybelle Belcher, Lucas and Felicidad Forsden, and Pablo Casares and his Kate.

When they left, she turned to Catayuna, took the latter's hand in a warm grip and murmured, "Something's troubling you, Catayuna. I've seen it all these weeks. Is there something Lucien Edmond and I do that makes you uncomfortable?"

"Oh, *Dios*, no, Señora Bouchard!" Catayuna exclaimed, vigorously shaking her head. "It's only that I want to be of some service, of some use here. Otherwise, I could never stay on indefinitely. Your vaqueros were so kind in building me my little house, and I love all of you here, and I see what a peaceful life you have. Yet I'm doing nothing—"

"But you're bringing up your children, dear Catayuna. And I, a mother like you, surely know how important a task that is!" Maxine smilingly retorted.

"I know, I know, yet a thought has come to me—there are so many children here, and it's such a good thing to see. Might we not have a school? I think, since we are so close to the Mexican border, it would be very good if the white children knew how to speak Spanish. And, by the same token, the Mexican children should surely learn to master the English language, for they will need to use it most of their lives when they go beyond this ranch. Since I am fluent in both, I was thinking that I could easily be their teacher."

"You're quite right. That's a wonderful idea. I'm going to talk to Lucien Edmond about it. And all of us will sit down and discuss this tomorrow, Catayuna, I promise you, because we want you here as long as you want to stay with us." Impulsively, Maxine Bouchard hugged Catayuna, and the latter felt her eyes moisten with tears as she returned that compassionate embrace.

# Five

The next day Lucien Edmond's handsome Mexican brother-in-law, Ramón Hernandez, bade farewell to his beautiful wife, Mara, and to their children. He was about to set off on a long and hazardous cattle drive to Dodge City, the new boom market town, with twenty of Windhaven Range's best vaqueros to protect the herd. As he emerged from their house and walked to the black gelding that Pablo Casares had saddled for him, he turned back to his wife and softly said, "Now I have two Maras to love, and each has beautiful dark eyes and black hair, and each has a part of *mi corazón*."

"Come back to me safely, my dearest one," Mara called back, and blew him a kiss. Ramón pretended to catch and press it against his lips, and to send one back in turn. Then he swung into his saddle, took the reins, clacked his heels against the gelding's belly, and rode off toward the waiting herd, giving a last shout and wave as he went.

During these past few months, Ramón, Joe Duvray, and Lucien Edmond—all of whom had prospered through the careful regulation and interbreeding of their herds— had continued their policy of supplying such relatively nearby army forts as Camps Inge, Sumner, and Grant. Lucien Edmond held fast to the belief that well within the next decade the railroad companies would be certain to extend feeder lines down to Texas. With rail transportation available, the drives with all their dangers—stampedes, storms, bushwhackers, and rustlers—would forever be a thing of the past. As it was, Lucien Edmond had, four years ago, more or less permanently decided against further drives to Kansas, because the prices at market were just too low and because the risks were too great. Accordingly, he would not have planned to undertake a drive this year, except for the fact that in February, a courier from Joseph McCoy had arrived to tell the larger Texas breeders that this year they could count on better money for their herds in Dodge City.

Lucien Edmond had mulled over this news and then said to Ramón, "We've an overabundance of yearlings right now. They're prime stock and should certainly bring a good price. I'm not happy about a three-month trip across the rivers and into Indian Territory, knowing what we've all experienced in the past. Yet I think it would be sound business to send perhaps two thousand head. You, Ramón, my friend, will head the drive, and you'll be on your own. I'm going to need Eddie Gentry and Nacio Lorcas to help me with driving smaller herds to the army forts, and I'll want Simata to be our scout. Joe Duvray will look after things on both his property and ours, and Lucas will assist him. But I'm sure you can manage by yourself, Ramón—you'll have twenty of our best vaqueros to help you, all of them well armed with Spencer rifles and carbines, just in case there's trouble."

Ramón had eagerly agreed to this. Though attached to his family more than ever and happy in his life as Lucien Edmond's brother-in-law—and now a full-fledged partner as well—he was still young enough at thirty-seven to miss the challenge and beauty of wilderness life. For the next twelve weeks, he would be dependent on his loyal, durable horse and the companionship of the vaqueros; his pleasures would consist of simple but satisfying meals under the stars, and all the small talk and the camaraderie that came at night, when the cattle had been bedded down and when men felt free to share what was in their hearts and minds.

Now, as he rode alongside his men on this hot, dusty spring morning, Ramón was content. He let his mind wander, thinking over his life, reviewing its many blessings. The best part, of course was that his Mara, at the age of forty, had just given him their loveliest child of all. As he thought of this, Ramón touched the scar on his face—a constant reminder of the moment of passion that had marked the beginning of their love. Even with five children, Mara seemed today as young as ever, and as lively as that first, passionate day so long ago, when she had struck him with a quirt in childish anger and then had fallen headlong in love with him. . . . There would be no more children, though, Ramon told himself, for now that they had their family, he wanted to enjoy his remaining years with Mara as sweethearts, while the two of them watched the children grow up.

He was glad, too, for the adventure of the long journey ahead—though he was of an age when he was content to have its dangers and uncertainties at a minimum. Over the past few weeks, he had had numerous earnest discussions with Lucien Edmond, planning the route. The last of these had occured the day before yesterday, when Luke's blond son had invited Ramón into his study after dinner and offered him a cigar and a snifter of brandy.

"I'm glad that all seems to be in readiness for the drive," Lucien Edmond had declared affably. "I'll not keep you long this evening, because I know you'll want to get your sleep, in preparation for what's ahead. But I did want you to see these new maps, which I received by courier from San Antonio this morning." Lucien Edmond gestured to his favorite chair. "Come, sit over here and make yourself comfortable. Your horse is going to be the best seat you'll have for quite some time, so you'd better relax while you can!"

Ramón quickly took a seat, and the two men then proceeded to pore over the maps that Lucien Edmond spread out in Ramón's lap. They were silent as they studied the charts, Lucien Edmond looking over Ramón's shoulder, until at length Ramón ventured, "From these maps, I can see that you've been right to suggest that now the best route to Dodge City lies to the west of the trail we've followed to Kansas in years past. In a way, I'm sorry: I could follow the old route blindfolded!"

"Well, yes," Lucien Edmond replied. "But the man that Joseph McCoy sent down here had a good deal to say on the subject, and I think we'd best pay him mind."

As they continued to peruse the maps, Ramón paused to ask, "Did the courier have anything to say about the Indian situation this year?"

"I suppose most people would say that the news is good on that score," Lucien Edmond replied, settling back in his

59

chair. "But it makes me sad—and it makes me angry. You're unlikely to run into hostile Indians this year because most of them are gone. The soldiers are driving them out of their hunting grounds here and up to the north and northwest. To my way of thinking, the policy is no better than cold-blooded murder."

"It's a horrible injustice," Ramón agreed.

"I don't like to say anything against the dead," Lucien Edmond continued, warming to his subject, "but General Custer made the situation a lot worse. If he hadn't insisted on fighting at Little Big Horn, there never would have been a massacre, and maybe public opinion wouldn't have mobilized so strongly against the Indians." Lucien Edmond shook his head in exasperation, reluctantly shifting his attention to more practical matters.

"Now, Ramón," he began, "I've every confidence that you're going to make it to Dodge City—with or without hostile Indians. And naturally I want you to get a good price for the cattle there. But there's a good deal more resting on your trip than money. The cattle business is a complicated one, and it's changing every day. See if you can find out whether the railroads seem likely to extend their lines within the next few years. Look around. See whether our herd is competitive with the other cattle being traded. Talk to people, and above all listen. See if you can get wind of any new attitudes the Kansas homesteaders and nesters may have regarding the cattlemen. A lot depends on your report—perhaps the very future of Windhaven Range."

"I'll do my best," Ramón said earnestly, as he rose to take his leave. He was deeply gratified that his brother-in-law had entrusted to him the command of the drive. It would be an opportunity as well to show his gratitude to *el Señor Dios* for the happy life that he had been given, and it was with a high sense of satisfaction that he went to his bed, to rest for the morrow's work and for the long trek ahead.

A recent letter from Laure may well have been responsible for Lucien Edmond's concern with the future. She had written her stepson in confidence, late in January, mentioning her concern with Luke's health and alluding to his fainting spells. And she had concluded her letter by

60

saying that she had had a dreadful premonition that she prayed would never come true: that Luke's days were already numbered, but not through any fainting spell or seizure of the heart. She could not explain this, for she had never before been superstitious; yet the fear remained. She felt it her duty to tell Lucien Edmond, and clearly took some consolation in doing so. "Perhaps," she wrote, "when one sets down one's fears on paper, in the clear light of day, they seem so laughable that they no longer trouble the mind. At least, that's what I hope for, my dear Lucien Edmond. My warmest good wishes to you and Maxine and your children. Your father is very proud of you and of all those on Windhaven Range, even to the humblest vaquero. God bless all of you and keep you."

Toward evening, after Ramón Hernandez had departed for Dodge City, there was a momentary wind squall, and the sky turned an ominous black. A sudden fierce crash of thunder heralded a violent but brief thunderstorm: for ten minutes, the sky was ablaze with jagged bolts of lightning. Then, as suddenly as it had come, the storm vanished.

Lucas, one of Lucien Edmond's most loyal workers, mounted his gelding and rode out toward the western section of Windhaven Range, where there were many heifers and yearlings likely to be frightened by such a storm. Lucas, now thirty-seven, was taking an increasingly important part in the running of the ranch, and just last month, his lovely Felicidad, now twenty-six, had borne him a daughter whom he had christened Felicity. The name—as he had explained to his wife—was the English translation of Felicidad.

Felicidad Ramirez had come to Windhaven Range after Lucas had found her weeping in Nuevo Laredo, an orphan faced with the necessity of yielding to the importunities of the keeper of a *posada*, or having to earn her living as a *puta* to keep from starving. The young vaquero had fallen head over heels in love with her, and they had married. They had named their first child James, which was the translation of Djamba, the Mandingo name of Lucas's heroic father. James was sturdy, intelligent, and a delight to his parents, but for Lucas he was more than that: he was the reincarnated spirit of that brave and loyal black who had once been king of the Mandingos and then a slave to Henry Bouchard. Lucas had already taught little Jamie that here in these young United States, it did not matter what a man's antecedents were, so long as he himself had integrity, decency, honor, and a willingness to work to earn his bread.

Lucas had neglected to take along his Spencer carbine this evening; instead he wore a hunting knife strapped to his belt as he rode along to hear the lowing cattle and to listen for sounds of panic or stampede. There would be no real danger, he had reasoned: even if there were a minor stampede among the cattle, they would eventually find their way back to the fertile grazing land. If at worst a hundred head or more had galloped on to the north or west, it would be an easy matter for half a dozen vaqueros to round them up in the morning. Now that Lucien Edmond had made contracts with the army forts to supply them with cattle every three months, the daily routine at Windhaven Range was much more leisurely than at the outset, when he had striven to make his mark as a Texas cattleman and ensure the prosperity of his father's new venture.

After watching Lucas ride out of sight, Felicidad left her little daughter in a crib, instructing Jamie to look after her, as well as his little sister, Celia, now just five, and went to the well to draw some water. Unlike Lucas, she was careful to take with her a Spencer carbine. She had never forgotten how Coraje, her pet *aplomado* falcon, had saved the life of her tiny son by darting down and killing a snake that menaced him. Since then, she had always carried a weapon when she went for water.

At the well, Felicidad met Catayuna, who carried little Nahubiyaa in her arms. Catayuna had round her waist a handworked leather belt with a sheath for a knife, which her husband Sangrodo had presented to her a month before his death. Sangrodo himself had made the belt, a kind of wampum with beads and little stones that told a picture story of her courage. The knife in the sheath was a replica of the scalping knife she had used to kill the evil Carlos Macaras when he attacked the Comanche stronghold. Although Catayuna had lost Sangrodo's unborn son in the struggle, her bravery won his heart and she wore the wampum daily, as a constant reminder of his devotion.

The two women greeted each other in Spanish, and Felicidad marveled at the sturdiness of little Nahubiyaa. In return, Catayuna smilingly responded, "And your Felicity, she is as fine a child. Who knows if *el Señor Dios* will not one day bring the two together? When I see how Ramón Hernandez has given joy to his Mara, and Eddie Gentry to his María Elena, and Pablo Casares to his Kate, I am greatly at peace. Here it does not matter if the skins of the parents of a boy or of a girl differ; when people are good and honorable, it matters only that they are together and find love— But what's that noise?"

Both women had turned, drawn by the distant sounds of choking cries mingled with growls and snarls.

"It's Lucas—he rode out to look after the herd! Oh, Catayuna, we must go help him! But what can it be?"

"It sounds like some wild beast—hurry, there is no time to look for horses, we must run! It will not harm Nahubiyaa—from birth, the papooses of the Comanche are taught to endure hardships!" Catayuna gasped, as she began to run, holding the little boy in both arms to cradle him against the jostling of her swift-footed gait.

Near the little village of Miero, there was a forest where a wolf pack had spent the night after a successful hunt. At dawn, the grizzled old leader of the pack, an enormous gray wolf, had been challenged by a younger rival. They had fought nearly to the death, and the grizzled wolf had been driven off, bleeding and crippled. The young wolf, to show his contempt for the ousted leader, spared the latter's life, and the other wolves who had accepted his new leadership banded as a pack to drive off their former chief.

The gray wolf had loped along, hobbling at times because of the crippling wound in his left haunch. He had taken little food, and the hot sun made him irritable. He managed to kill only two field mice in three days, and he was starving. He sensed that there were no other wolves around for miles, and so he did not bother to roll his scent or to care whether his droppings would be observed by others who might be hiding in the mesquite bushes that marked his path. He had crossed the border of the Rio Grande early last night, and had taken refuge during the ferocious thunderstorm in a little ravine protected by stunted trees that grew over it.

When he emerged from his hiding place, he heard the lowing of cattle, and he made his way stealthily toward an

63

isolated group of three young cows and two newly born calves. His jaws salivated, and he had to master the savage urge to spring and kill at once. Old as he was, experience had taught him that where there were many cattle, there were also two-legged beasts with sticks that blazed fire and could kill—he had seen those fire-sticks, though he himself had escaped unharmed. No, this must be done very carefully. A calf would be tasty eating and easiest of all to kill. There were no bulls around to gore him. His tired, reddened eyes brightened at the prospect of a feast.

But just as he was about to lope forward and attack the nearest calf, it saw him and began to bleat for its mother.

The cows, seeing his bared jaws and bloodshot eyes, bolted in every direction, forgetting their calves. It was at this moment that Lucas rode up on his gelding. He put a hand to the saddle sheath, then swore under his breath to find it empty. Dismounting, he drew his knife and came courageously forward toward the little calf. With a raging snarl, the shaggy wolf sprang at him.

Lucas lunged to the left, throwing up his left arm to fend off those gleaming fangs and, at the same time, drawing his knife, thrust upwards. But the thick mane of the renegade wolf prevented the sharp knife tip from inflicting more than a minor wound, and its jaws closed on Lucas's left wrist.

The wolf's weight and forward lunge felled Djamba's son to the ground and caused him to groan with agony while he repeatedly stabbed upward. The wolf's snarls and growls were hideous. Twisting and writhing, the heavy, shaggy body of the brute evaded the sporadic thrusts of its two-legged assailant. Now, drawing its fangs back from Lucas's bleeding wrist, the wolf lunged at his throat. Once again, Lucas thrust up his bleeding wrist to fend off that fatal attack at the jugular, and again stabbed, his blade drawing blood from the wolf's shoulder.

The savage snarls and the groans and the yells had frightened the part of the herd that still lingered at this western section of Windhaven Range. The steers and the young bulls and the cows snorted and bellowed and galloped northward. Three little calves, bleating wildly, awkwardly got to their feet and stumbled off, leaving Lucas and the wolf alone in this primal battle.

Catayuna and Felicidad, breathless, ran toward the

scene of this duel to the death, guided by the crescendo of sounds. Suddenly there was a whir of wings and a shrill cry, and Felicidad looked up and uttered a startled gasp. "It's Coraje! He'll help us—oh, Catayuna, *Dios mío*—oh quickly, we must help Lucas!"

By this time, darkness had fallen, and the only light in the sky was from the moon hanging just above the horizon, but it was often obscured by fleeting clouds. The two women cautiously halted and saw the wolf and Lucas twisting and writhing and turning, as Lucas tried valiantly to fend off those cruel jaws. The wolf's muzzle was smeared with Lucas's blood, and the brave man was wearying, devoting all his strength to evading the one fatal bite to the throat that would end his life. His knife stabs became weaker and more erratic, though four or five bloody patches on the wolf's shaggy gray pelt testified to the extent of his defense.

The two of them rolled over and over, the wolf's snarls hideous and raucous with the savage lust to kill.

Felicidad hoisted the carbine to her shoulder and squinted down the sight. She could hear, but she could not accurately see, and she was afraid.

The wolf was distracted by these intruders, and Lucas freed himself momentarily, rolling over and over, but the wolf hurtled toward him, its jaws sinking into his shoulder. Lucas uttered a cry of agony.

At the same moment, Coraje, soaring aloft, darted down, and thrust his sharp beak against the left ear of the shaggy gray wolf.

With a frenzied snarl, the renegade wolf twisted its head and snapped at the intrepid, aging falcon. Felicidad pulled the trigger, and the wolf jerked and lunged to one side, only wounded in the shoulder. It righted itself, hobbling on its one bad leg, its bloodshot eyes fixed on this new danger.

As the enraged animal lumbered toward her, Felicidad uttered a terrified gasp, swiftly raised the carbine to her shoulder, and pulled the trigger. But the mechanism had jammed, and she cried out, "Oh, *Dios, ayúdame!*" The falcon had soared high again, and now plummeted down and dug his sharp beak into the wolf's left side. With an angry growl, the shaggy beast turned and snapped at Coraje,

65

while Felicidad frantically tried to clear the jammed trigger. And once again Coraje soared into the air.

Snarling in pain, the wolf turned back to Felicidad, ignoring Lucas, who tried to stagger to all fours, dazed by the agony of that savage shoulder bite. As Felicidad backed away—her eyes widening at the hideous sight of the wounded wolf hobbling slowly forward, its bloodied fangs bared—Catayuna, with a prayer, drew the knife from her belt. Then, laying her son down on the ground, she balanced the knife between right thumb and forefinger and, with all her strength, sent it flying forward.

The sharp hunting knife bit into the wolf's left side. Confused with pain, the beast halted, then tilted its head toward the sky, emitting a mournful howl. Coraje swooped down again and dug his beak into the wolf's throat, but this time, slowed by age and the furious exertion of his defense of his loved ones, he did not lift himself in time. As his wings wildly fluttered, the wolf's jaws closed on one of them, and the falcon screeched his final agony. At the same moment, Lucas, having at last got to all fours, grimacing from the pain of his wounds, crawled behind the wolf and, lifting his knife, jabbed twice with all his strength, imbedding the sharp knife blade in the wolf's neck. It sprawled lifeless, and Lucas, with a dull groan, bowed his head and fainted.

Felicidad, bitterly weeping, hurried to her husband and, exerting all her strength, rolled him over onto his back. "Oh, Catayuna! His poor hand, and his shoulder—he's bleeding badly—"

"*Momentito*—I'll make a bandage for his wounds. Somehow, we must carry him back to the hacienda," Catayuna exclaimed. Glancing back at her little son who lay cooing and clapping his hands where she had left him, she reached down to tear a strip of her petticoat to use as a tourniquet for Lucas's profusely bleeding wrist. Then, tearing another strip, she bound it round his shoulder, under his armpit, knotting it as tightly as she could till she panted with exertion.

Felicidad, still weeping, cupped her husband's face and bent to kiss him. "Lucas, *querido*, speak to me, it's Felicidad—you're safe now, the wolf is dead—" she sobbed.

And then, lifting her tear-stained face, she uttered an anguished cry: "Coraje—look, Catayuna, he's lying there—what's happened to him—my brave, heroic *halcón*, he doesn't move—I'm so afraid—he saved Lucas, you know he did!"

"*Sí*, Felicidad—but your husband will be well, he is alive. That is what counts. The *halcón* was old, and he died protecting those whom he loved. Be content with it, *querida*," Catayuna murmured.

Felicidad crawled toward the falcon. She put her palm to his heart, and then she bowed her head and wept. Coraje had given the last measure of his devotion to save Lucas, the *esposo* of the woman who had helped him recover from his broken wing and fed him and tamed him. A debt had been paid in full.

Both women turned now as they heard the drumming of hooves coming toward them. Then a young vaquero, tall and black-haired with an enormous *mostacho*, sprang down from his mustang and headed toward them. "The *patrón* told me to come this way to see if the storm had made the herd stampede. *Dios mío*, it's Señor Lucas!"

"Please help us," Felicidad sobbed as she rose and tottered wanly. "Take him back on your horse to the hacienda. He is very badly hurt—it was a wolf."

Catayuna had hurried back to her little son and lifted him, kissing him feverishly. "Blessed be *el Señor Dios* to have kept you well and safe, my little one," she murmured.

The young vaquero came toward Lucas and gently lifted him and with the help of Felicidad, placed him astride and behind the vaquero, who grasped both Lucas's arms in his and began the short ride back to the hacienda. The two women followed, eyeing each other with respect and with tears. Each knew that the other had helped save Lucas's life, and Catayuna felt at last that she was needed and wanted here on Windhaven Range. As they made their way back to the hacienda, she said to Felicidad, "Coraje's heart must have stopped in his attack to turn the wolf's jaws away from Lucas. You named him truly— Coraje, courage."

## *Six*

Maybelle Belcher had discovered that at fifty-seven, life could be quite as absorbing as it had been in her thirties and forties. If anything, it had improved: her marriage eleven years ago to Henry Belcher, five years her junior, had completely obliterated the loneliness and self-doubt that her unfortunate first marriage to Mark Bouchard, almost forty years ago, had brought upon her.

After Mark had callously abandoned her, with a curt note saying that he had no use for marital ties, Maybelle had thrown herself into the creek near the red-brick chateau. Djamba, her mother's loyal Mandingo slave, had saved her, at the cost of the child she had been carrying. Later, when the chateau had been burned, she had known crushing desolation once again; though she did not again attempt to take her life, she could not help feeling that there was no reason to go on living.

The move to Windhaven Range had done much to lighten the darkness in Maybelle's life; so, too, had the happy marriage of her daughter, Laurette, to Charles Douglas. But the greatest happiness of her life had begun when Henry Belcher had stopped briefly at Windhaven Range with his two children, Timmy and Connie. At Lucien Edmond's invitation, Henry had prolonged his stay, and Maybelle's life had suddenly brightened. She had been touched by the mature ex-Confederate's respectful admiration of her and his flowery praise of her cooking; and when he had proposed marriage, she had eagerly accepted. Now white-haired and plump, with robust health and a sunny disposition, Maybelle Belcher in no way resented the passage of the years.

In this spring of 1877, she found herself placed in a position of great responsibility—one that clearly showed how close she had become to her husband's children. For without her really knowing quite how, it had fallen to her to guide Timmy and Connie through their very first romances—for they were both in love.

It was hardly a question of puppy love. Though he was still freckle-faced and towheaded, wiry Timmy Belcher was almost twenty-four, and blue-eyed Connie—sandy-haired, and willowy—was already twenty-one.

By now Connie was a valued helpmate in the Bouchard kitchen, relieving her stepmother when the work became too arduous, as, for example, when the Bouchards gave large dinner parties, or invited the couriers who rode in to stay the night and enjoy the Texas hospitality of a home-cooked meal.

Ramón Hernandez had taken the gangling young Timmy under his wing, allowing him now to rope and brand the cattle. While preparing for the cattle drive to Dodge City last week, Ramón had put Timmy to work ensuring that each of the two thousand animals selected was of prime quality and properly branded. The Windhaven Range brand was already well known to eastern and midwestern cattle buyers, and Lucien Edmond took pride in knowing that his beef, which eventually graced family tables in New York, Cincinnati, St. Louis, Detroit, and Milwaukee, was the very best that money could buy.

As for Henry Belcher himself, he was quite content at the prospect that his only son would become a rancher, or even a farmer. Before enlisting in the Confederate Army during the Civil War, he had been a farmer near Sedalia—a farm he had found destroyed upon his return. The death of his first wife had determined him to head west in search of new, fertile land where he could bring up his children, teaching them the homely virtues of caring for the soil and getting a good living from it by hard, honest work. His modest aspirations had been satisfied at Windhaven Range, leaving only his desire to see his children settled.

He remarked to Maybelle one day, "Honey, I'd like to see my kids married to decent, God-fearing mates who'll give them the happiness they deserve. I don't figure that either Timmy or Connie will ever be rich—Lord knows I've never been and I don't expect to ever be. But I'm mighty grateful for my life here with you and the kids, Maybelle honey, and I wouldn't trade it for even a fancy palace and gold-plated service to eat off."

Now it appeared that Henry's fondest wish was about to become a reality. Timmy Belcher had fallen in love with Conchita Valdegroso, a shy, lovely Mexican girl of eighteen who, like Felicidad, had been brought from Nuevo Laredo some six months ago by one of the Windhaven Range vaqueros. The vaquero, Esteban Bernadon, had been visiting his parents; they had told him that one of their neighbors was a certain Juan Valdegroso, Conchita's middle-aged uncle. The girl's own parents had died when she was eleven, and her uncle and his wife, Marta, had taken her into their house and brought her up.

Last year, Marta Valdegroso had died, and Juan had begun pressuring his niece to take Marta's place in his bed. After all, he had argued, she was beholden to him for all the money he had spent on her upbringing. Horrified at this lubricious proposal, Conchita had run away and found work in a small *posada* on the other side of town. It was there that Esteban Bernadon had found her, after having heard her story from his parents. He had brought her back with him to Windhaven Range, assuring her that the generous *patrón*, the Señor Bouchard, would assuredly find her a position in the kitchen to cook meals for the ranch hands.

Esteban and some of his friends among the *trabajadores* had built a comfortable little cottage for the lovely runaway, and she had soon regained her self-esteem and overcome a good deal of her shyness, thanks to the cordial welcome that Maxine Bouchard and Felicidad, as well as Maybelle, had shown her. As for the vaqueros, having tasted her cooking and observing how conscientious she was in her work, they showed her the utmost respect and courtesy.

From the beginning, Timmy Belcher was smitten by the black-haired beauty. At first he brought her flowers; then once, after he had accompanied his father on a trip to San Antonio to buy supplies, he spent ten dollars on a lovely garnet bracelet, which he blushingly presented to Con-

70

chita. Delighted by the gift—the very first she had received from a man—and finding Timmy not only handsome but attentive, she impulsively kissed him.

Timmy was overwhelmed. It was his very first kiss from a pretty girl, and it confirmed his determination to marry her. Since her parents were dead and she was completely estranged from her lecherous uncle, Timmy went to Esteban and manfully explained his honorable desire to court and win Conchita as his wife, and the young vaquero clapped him on the back and bade him good fortune. "She is a fine *muchacha*, Señor Timmy," Esteban smilingly declared, "and I can see that she has already chosen you as her *novio*. I tell you, *hombre*, she is shy and sweet; that is the kind that makes a man the very best wife. Do not hurry, and she will be yours one day soon. I wish you good luck!"

And so, sometimes on a Saturday evening, after shaving and washing and donning a pair of clean breeches, Timmy would go walking with Conchita along the little creek. He was careful not to overwhelm her by too ardent a declaration of love. Though he longed to embrace her to his heart's content, he exercised commendable restraint and contented himself with an occasional kiss. But Conchita's increasingly ardent responses told him that she would not say no when he asked her the all-important question.

As it happened, the previous night, which marked the third day after Ramón Hernandez had departed for Dodge City, Maybelle chanced to take a bucket out to the well, located not far from the creek. She was taken aback to see her stepson and Conchita locked in a passionate embrace, and to hear the girl's sighs of pleasure and her tremulous words of avowal: "Oh, *mi corazón—te quiero mucho—sí, es verdad*—oh, Timmy, *te quiero!*"

Maybelle had the presence of mind to call out to warn the lovers of her approach. Timmy whirled round with a sheepish, guilty look on his freckled face while Conchita uttered a startled little cry and then hid her blushing face in her hands.

"It—it's a bit late, Timmy—and you know, sometimes there are snakes near the creek. Maybe you'd best say good night to Conchita," Maybelle hesitantly proffered.

"I—I must have lost track of the time," Timmy hoarsely stammered, and then turned to Conchita and said,

71

"I'll walk you back to your cottage so you'll be safe, sweetheart."

"And then," Maybelle softly rejoined, "I think you and I should have a little talk back at the house, Timmy."

She watched as the tall young man took Conchita's arm and slowly led her back toward the cottage. She uttered a sigh and shook her head. Young love, first love, was bittersweet—how well she knew; when she had met the dashing, mercurial, handsome Mark Bouchard, he had virtually swept her off her feet and imperiously told her that she was to be his girl and no one else's. Her mind drifted back to the disastrous outcome of that wooing. Having eventually found happiness and fulfillment, she naturally wanted the same for Timmy—only now she feared that he was about to make the wrong choice.

Filling her bucket at the well, Maybelle walked pensively back to the house. When Timmy returned, she said gently to him, "I know you like that girl very much, Timmy, and I made out just enough Spanish—though I didn't mean to eavesdrop on you two—to figure out that you want to marry her. Am I right?"

"Yes, you are, Mother." Maybelle was touched by the young man's spontaneous use of that endearing term, which indeed both children had granted her almost as soon as she had married their father. "Of course I'm serious about her—it couldn't be any other way with a girl like that."

"I know, Timmy. You've grown up to be a fine young man, just like your father. But what I'm thinking is—well, she's a Mexican girl. And—well, to be honest with you, Timmy, I hoped you'd be attracted to one of our own kind."

"I can't help it, Mother. She's sweet and nice and good, and she's a lady. You can see that all the men treat her with respect. I know all about her past and that she hasn't got a *centavo* to her name, but none of that's important to me. I can work hard here on this range and earn enough for both of us. I'll even build a house for her with my own hands, if I have to."

Maybelle put her arm around Timmy's shoulders. "I like the way you talk about her. I'm glad you respect her. Only I do wish you'd think a little before plunging into something like this. If you marry a girl, it ought to be for life. I've never told you very much about myself, Timmy, but now is as good a time as any.

"You see, I lived in Alabama with a sister who married Luke Bouchard. Long before we came out here and I married your father, I'd married a man who was Luke Bouchard's half brother. He said he loved me and I believed him. Only, well, after I'd had my daughter, Laurette, who as you know is in Chicago and married to Charles Douglas, Mark up and left me to make his own fortune in New Orleans. So what I'm trying to say—and I know I'm clumsy in saying it, Timmy dear—is that you have to be very sure. After all, she's the first girl you've really ever known."

"Well, Mother," Timmy assayed with a halfhearted chuckle, "I don't travel much, so I can't very well meet other girls. But she's right for me, I know she is."

"All right, son. Suppose you go get your sleep. You'll have a hard day working the horses tomorrow, and you need your rest. I'll see you at breakfast."

Timmy nodded, and started toward his room, then hurried back and gave Maybelle a resounding kiss on the cheek.

Maybelle sighed. Her confession had left her pensive at remembering her first love, who turned out to be such a scoundrel. Not that she thought that Conchita Valdegroso wasn't a decent girl, but she was a Mexican and she really had no background at all. How could one tell whether she would be the proper wife for Timmy?

With another sigh, she entered the bedroom, where she found Henry still up. Seating herself on the edge of the bed and putting out her hand to him, she smiled wistfully and said, "Henry, I guess your boy's got it bad for that Mexican girl, Conchita. I just saw them, and they were really spooning to beat the band. Oh, nothing wrong, mind you—your son's not like that, and she certainly is a proper girl—but what I mean to say is, he said he wants to marry her and she evidently feels the same way."

"And what's so awful about that. Maybelle honey?" Henry kindly inquired, realizing that Maybelle was upset. "So she's Mexican. Aren't you forgetting that Ramón Hernandez is Mexican, too, and he's made Mara Bouchard a marvelous husband."

"That's different—" Maybelle began.

"Not a bit, honey," Henry emphatically interrupted, as he shook his head. "And look at Eddie Gentry, married to María Elena, who just gave him that fine strapping boy they call Douglas after Charles. And then there's Pablo, and his Kate. Mexican and white, white and Mexican, and they're all happy. Remember, here at Windhaven Range there isn't any hostility—the prejudice we had back South before the war is fading everywhere, thank the good Lord. No, Maybelle, for my part, he's got my blessing. And I've a little money put aside—if he wants to buy a piece of land and build a house on it for his girl, I'll help him with it. He's a fine boy and always has been. He used to insist on helping me on the farm in Sedalia when he was only a tadpole."

"I know, he's a hard worker, and he does you credit, Henry, you and your dear wife Millie, may she rest in peace."

"Look, Maybelle," Henry said huskily, as he turned to her and drew her down beside him. "I never thought I'd find anyone worthwhile after Millie. Usually, when a man has one happy marriage, he figures that's his quota for a lifetime. And then I met you here. I sure didn't make a mistake with you, and I don't think Timmy's going to make one either, so now don't you worry any more. We'll both talk it over with Conchita and Timmy and see when they want to get hitched. We'll give them a big celebration dinner, and you can cook some of Timmy's favorites."

"Oh, Henry, you make everything so nice and easy. And I'm so glad you stopped by Windhaven Range when you did," Maybelle happily sighed as she gave him a tender kiss.

It was just as well for Maybelle's now-restored peace of mind that she didn't yet know about Connie's growing attachment to a new vaquero, a mysterious older man who had recently arrived at Windhaven Range. For undoubtedly Maybelle would have been doubly anxious to prevent the willowy blonde, so naive and warmhearted, from repeating her own mistakes.

Last December, a lean, dark-haired man in his mid-thirties had ridden a lathered, exhausted gray mustang toward the corral of Windhaven Range and dismounted, tottering with fatigue. For a long moment he pressed his forehead against the mustang's side, clinging to it for support.

Eddie Gentry had been first to see the rider, and he had hurried up to him and sympathetically declared, "Whatever you're running from, stranger, there's nobody in sight who's after you. You surely look tuckered out. Come along into our bunkhouse and you can lie down for a spell and rest. There's food and good, strong coffee when you've a need for it."

The man had uttered a long, weary sigh and then straightened, turning to face Eddie. In a hoarse, raspy voice he had ejaculated, "That's damn decent of you, *hombre*. I think I'll take you up on that. If it's not asking too much, would you look after my horse? He's come with me a long way, and he's just about on his last legs."

"Sure. You go on in and stretch out, and I'll take care of your mustang," Eddie had smilingly proffered.

The man had staggered toward the bunkhouse, thrown open the door, and, oblivious to the other curious occupants, flung himself down on an empty bunk. Pillowing his face on his arms, he had fallen dead asleep, not awakening until nearly nine that evening. Eddie had looked in on him several times and finally, seeing the man come drowsily back to consciousness, seated himself on a nearby bunk and grinned. "You certainly needed that sleep. Your horse is fine, mister."

"I'm obliged. My name's Walter Catlin. I've come a long way, from back east, if you want to know. Originally I'm from Virginia—but I left after the war."

"My God," Eddie gasped, his eyes widening, "not on that same horse, I hope?"

"Hell no, cowboy," the stranger laughed hollowly, as he wanly sat up and then cupped his stubbly face in his hands and took several deep breaths. "No, I've used up a lot of horseflesh. I'm right glad I happened by here—it's a great spread. How's chances for a job? I'm not bad with horses—even if I did ride that mustang of mine just about down to the fetlocks."

"We can talk about that in the morning. Right now, you better have some food. I'll get you some from the kitchen. It's just about time we went to bed—most of us for the first time," Eddie chuckled.

"Yeah, I was bone-tired, and I've been driving for

weeks now. I could use a cup of coffee and maybe some hardtack or whatever else you've got. Don't put your María to any trouble."

"Oh, so you know that María's what we call the chuck-wagon cook on our drives! I guess you've spent some time around cattle." Eddie grinned again. "My name's Eddie Gentry, by the way. Glad to know you, Mr. Catlin."

"Hell, sonny, that mister makes me feel like an old man, and I don't guess that I'm more than about ten years older than you are. I only look old because of all the riding I've been doing for the last year or so. Anyhow, I'd be mighty grateful for something to eat, like I said. And maybe in the morning you could steer me to the right man to ask for a job. I'm pretty good with horses, and, yeah, I know cattle, too."

"You can talk to Lucien Edmond Bouchard, who owns Windhaven Range, Mr. Catlin. And we can use some good vaqueros."

"You're a real friend. You're sure you don't mind bringing me a bite and that hot java you just mentioned?"

"Sure. Be right back with it."

Eddie Gentry went to the hacienda and beguiled one of the kitchen maids to heat up a pot of coffee and a bowl of the mutton stew that had been served at supper that evening. He brought the viands and coffee back to the taciturn stranger, who grunted his thanks, before ravenously devouring the stew and gulping down the coffee in a way that made Eddie shake his head in compassion.

The next day, Eddie introduced Walter Catlin to Lucien Edmond Bouchard. "He's looking for a job as a wrangler, Mr. Bouchard," the lanky Texan explained. "We could use somebody in the remuda, so I thought I'd ask you to talk with him, and see what you think."

Lucien Edmond affably nodded and escorted the tall, wiry stranger into his study. After half an hour, he declared, "Catlin, you've been straightforward with me, and I'll be the same with you. As long as you're not an outlaw and won't bring trouble down on us here at Windhaven Range, I'll certainly give you a chance, since we can always use a good man. There's a place in the bunkhouse for your gear and your bedroll. I'll introduce you to my brother-in-law, Ramón Hernandez, and he'll see just how good you are with horses. If you shape up, you can stay on here as long as you've a mind to."

"Thanks, Mr. Bouchard. You won't regret it. And I guarantee you, I'm not an outlaw."

"I'll take your word on that. From what Eddie tells me, you've ridden a long way to get here, and if your reasons are legitimate, I'll give you every chance to prove your worth to us."

"That's all I ask, Mr. Bouchard, and I'm grateful to you."

The two men shook hands, and Catlin went out in the afternoon to work in the corral with several ornery mustangs. As the other vaqueros observed, he went about his tasks in a careful and knowledgeable way, and before the sun set, he had broken in two of the horses.

About two weeks later, Walter Catlin volunteered to bring some water for his mates in the bunkhouse and walked toward the well with a wooden bucket. As it chanced, Connie Belcher also went to fetch water, for the evening meal. As they both approached the well, Connie blushed and lowered her eyes beneath Catlin's forthright gaze. Then Catlin spoke up. "Let me fill that for you, missy."

"Why, th-thank—thank you very much." Connie was flustered.

"I just signed on here for a spell, missy. My name's Walter Catlin."

"Glad to know you, Mr. Catlin. I'm Connie Belcher."

Catlin dipped Connie's bucket into the well and then straightened and pleasantly remarked, "I'll carry it back to wherever you're going, Miss Connie."

"That's very nice of you, Mr. Catlin. It's a heavy bucket, and I don't mind if you do," she blurted, and then blushed at her own audacity. "Are you from Texas?" she inquired.

His face was somber as he shook his head. "Not really. From Virginia at the start. I thought I'd come out west and see what was happening after the war."

"Oh, I see." Connie didn't, but tried to make casual conversation. She noticed that his bright gray-blue eyes stayed fixed on her. "I—I hope you'll like it here," she stammered.

"I'm sure I will, Miss Connie—is it all right if I call you that?"

"Oh, yes! Anyhow, that's my name—" She uttered a little giggle, and then inwardly berated herself for being too friendly, remembering how her father had always cautioned her not to be too frank and open with strangers. Yet there was something about this man, something she couldn't define, that held her attention. He looked sad, almost grim; not old, but as if he'd spent a lot of time worrying. She couldn't explain why, but she felt a sudden sympathy for him.

"Thanks, Miss Connie. Is this the house where you live?"

"Yes, it is, Mr. Catlin, with my brother, Timmy, and my father and my m-mother, you see," she awkwardly stammered.

Walter Catlin went up the steps of the porch and opened the door, then set the bucket down on the puncheon floor. "Glad to have been of service. Good evening, Miss Connie."

And that was how it had begun. Feeling guilty, and yet with an inexplicably growing excitement, Connie had volunteered several times to go out to the well to fill the water bucket; yet it had taken ten days before she met Walter Catlin again. This time he complimented her in a way that made her blush hotly and tremble with a feeling she had never known before. He said very simply, "You know, Miss Connie, you remind me of someone who was awfully lovely and meant a lot to me. I hope I don't offend you by speaking out so frankly, but I just had to."

"I—I'm not offended at all, Mr. Catlin. It's very nice of you to say a thing like that to me. Well now, I—I have to go in. G-good night."

Through the next two months, their paths had crossed again, not always by accident. Connie found herself offering to run errands that would take her past the corral where the vaqueros often worked, and timing her visits to the ranch house to coincide with mealtimes when the cowboys would be lingering over their coffee. She felt herself drawn toward this strange, reserved man who seemed somehow to understand what she was feeling: and in his presence she felt an unfamiliar yearning for some adventure that would make her life meaningful. He was un-

78

failingly courteous, always tipping his Stetson to her. Never once was he too forward or impertinent. But when she tried to question him, even obliquely, he always managed to avoid telling her why he had come to Windhaven Range. She sensed that he was well educated, far better than she was, and she did not know why he was content with a wrangler's job.

And then in April, she met him one afternoon about ten days before Ramón Hernandez began the drive to Dodge City. His face was set in a hard line, and he appeared not to see her as she came hesitantly down from the porch of the Belcher house, heading toward the kitchen of the ranch house where Maybelle had suggested that she might be needed. The chuck-wagon cook was busy preparing for the drive and might not have time to do his work for the regular vaqueros who would stay behind.

As she saw him, she brightened and impulsively asked, "How are you, Mr. Catlin?"

"Fine, Miss Connie, and you?"

"Oh, j-just fine, th-thank you."

She saw that he had holstered a pair of six-shooters around his waist, and that he was wearing new boots. Suddenly he looked menacing and she was worried for him; why, she could not explain.

"Well, I—I've got to go to the kitchen—" she began to explain.

"Wait a bit, Miss Connie. I—I've asked Mr. Bouchard to let me ride to Dodge City with the herd he's taking to market. I figure I'll be away about three months or so—at least, that's what the other hands tell me. I—I hope I don't offend you, but if I come back, I'd like to talk to you—about something personal."

Without knowing why, her cheeks flamed and she lowered her eyes. There was a sudden pounding of her heart, and she twisted her hands behind her back and stared at the ground. Finally, in a faint, faltering tone, she admitted, "I—I hope you do come back safe and sound, M-Mr. Catlin. I—I'd like to talk to you a lot—oh my gosh, I—I don't want you to think I'm that sort of—"

"No, Miss Connie, I don't. Now don't worry or fret any," he interrupted and gave her a gentle smile. Then, his face somber and taut, he added, "I've got some business to settle. When it's over, and if I do get back, I'd like to spend time with you, sort of private-like. Would that be all right?"

"Oh yes!" she impulsively gasped, and then put her hand to her mouth, turning away, aghast at her own daring.

"God bless you, Miss Connie. Wish me luck now. Maybe I'll bring you something back from Dodge City."

As he turned in his tracks and marched off toward the ranch house, she raised her eyes and looked at him, and felt herself trembling again, shaken by a feeling she could not identify. It was as well she did not tell either her father or Mother Maybelle, but she knew that she was going to pray when she went to bed tonight that he would come back safe and sound.

## Seven

Alice Steinfeldt was tearfully ecstatic this last week of April. She had just borne her loving husband, Max, their second son, whom Max named Philip after his father. Their first son, John, was now already three; thus they had two perfect little boys, despite the dire predictions of Alice's doctors, who once had assured the lovely auburn-haired young woman that she would never be able to bear a child.

Alice sighed happily and remembered the odd turn of events that had led her to such contentment, and how the most wretched period of her life five years ago had turned out to be the most fortuitous. She smiled to think that the man who had brought her such misery five years ago was, in a way, responsible for her radiant happiness today. For it was the unscrupulous dealings of her former employer, Arnold Shottlander, with that lecherous banker Calvin Jemmers—so determined to make Alice (then a lonely widow) his mistress—that had unwittingly given her this wonderful life. The two crooks had been determined to dupe Charles Douglas into purchasing land for a new department store in Houston, in what was a shady deal, to say the least. Alice had been equally determined that the kindly Charles would not become a victim of their machinations, and he had rewarded her probity with a good job when he opened his new store in Galveston. It was there that she had met the gentle, older contractor Max Steinfeldt, whose constant devotion and tender affection for her had fulfilled her every dream of wifehood.

Then, a year ago, Charles Douglas had finally opened a

store in Houston, urging Max to become the manager of the new branch. Alice was delighted: although she and Max knew that Max had had no experience in merchandising, they also agreed that work in the store would be a good deal less physically strenuous for the aging German than his contracting work. Because he was a dedicated, conscientious man as well as well educated, it did not take him long to develop the requisite skills, and now, only twelve months later, the Houston store was already a great success.

The day after Alice had given birth to Philip, Max Steinfeldt received a letter from Charles Douglas's Chicago lawyer. Hurrying into the hospital room that he had filled with an array of floral bouquets, he exuberantly declared, "Sweetheart, here is news that will really perk you up!" Alice was feeding her baby son, and a prim, disapproving-looking nurse beside her turned and gasped, "Mr. Steinfeldt, please don't raise your voice like that! We've some quite sick patients along this floor, you know."

"I beg your pardon, Miss Stanford," Max chuckled in his bluff, candid manner, "but this news was just too good to keep inside of me. Would you mind very much if I had a few minutes alone with my wife?"

"Very well, Mr. Steinfeldt. I suppose there'd really be no harm in it. But please don't tire her, and remember that she's nursing."

Max rolled his eyes ceilingward and held his tongue until the tall, homely, middle-aged nurse went out of the room. Then he turned to Alice with such a woebegone look that she could not help laughing as she beckoned to him to come sit beside her.

At once his face grew almost reverent, as he stared at the tiny infant. "Thank you, dear God," he said half aloud, "not only for two sons, but for the most wonderful wife and mother on earth."

"My gracious, Max Steinfeldt, whatever has got into you?" Alice exclaimed, blushing very becomingly.

By way of reply, Max kissed her soundly, saying, "I've got some news for you, sweetheart, as I was saying." Waving the letter from Charles's lawyer, he smiled. "There are many legal phrases, but the gist of it is, I'm to keep on managing the store here in Houston, and I'm to be a sort of superintendent of the original one in Galveston, too.

And Charles wants to make me a full partner with him, which means I'll receive a percentage of the gross volume of business from each store."

"Why, that is wonderful news, Max darling!" Alice breathed.

"Not only that, I will be in charge of selecting the personnel for both stores. And Charles himself added a postscript after the lawyer had signed the letter saying he was hoping I would also take over all the merchandising for both stores. Now isn't that something? I hope I can handle it all—this business is still new to me, you know. For so long I was just a plain, ordinary contractor who got things built—and I am getting on in years, after all."

"You're not a plain, ordinary anything, Max Steinfeldt, and you know it!" Alice hotly declared. "You're still a young man, and you've got brains and gumption and lots more imagination than you give yourself credit for. You're just trying to get me to flatter you out of your britches!" she boldly announced; then, realizing that she had voiced a highly risque innuendo, she blushed in embarrassment and preoccupied herself with their son.

Max guffawed heartily and exclaimed, shaking his head, "That was very naughty of you, darling! Besides, the doctor says it will be some time before—"

"Now you stop that, Max! I declare, you're just impossible sometimes!" Alice said in mock exasperation, trying to hide her smile. In a softer, more intimate voice, she went on, "Anyway, I will help you. As a woman, I know exactly what other women shoppers want in stores like Charles's. I can help you choose merchandise and maybe even make suggestions for adding new lines. And now that Charles has his warehouse along the bayou, we can order merchandise in before the summer quarantine season and have it on hand for the fall showing. You and I will be partners, too."

"Alice, dearest, I know you'll be invaluable to me. I only hope I can be as good a manager and superintendent as Charles deserves."

"You'll do just fine. The Houston store is already a great success. Besides, do you think Charles would have offered you this partnership unless he was convinced how good you are? Now give me a kiss, and then you'd better leave before Nurse Stanford throws us both out," she laughed.

Max pulled away from the tender embrace as he heard the brisk steps of the approaching nurse.

"Oh, oh, just what I was afraid of, here comes Miss Stanford to chase you out," Alice whispered as the prim woman briskly entered and glared at them.

"I really must insist that you let your wife and child rest, Mr. Steinfeldt!" she snapped.

"I was just going. Thank you, Miss Stanford. You be sure to give them the best of care; they are the world to me." He closed the door with a conspiratorial wink at his smiling wife, leaving the nurse sniffing her disdain, momentarily at a loss for words.

On the very day that Max Steinfeldt was visiting his wife and their new son in the Houston hospital, Laure Bouchard was on her way into Montgomery to see Dr. Kennery, being driven by Dan Munroe, as Luke had gone to visit Andy Haskins at Andy's house while the state senate was in adjournment for a brief period.

Laure, in her eighth month of pregnancy, was confident that she was in good health, having been given a brief, superficial examination by Dr. Kennery when he came for dinner at the red-brick chateau following Luke's own visit to him in Montgomery. She was going to see him again for a more thorough examination in his office, but she had another reason for wanting to see the young doctor, as well.

Abel Kennery courteously ushered her into the examining room and introduced Laure to his new nurse, Muriel Donahue. After the examination, while Laure was getting dressed, Miss Donahue excused herself and went out to the front office. Dr. Kennery announced, "I believe the child will be born toward the end of May, in about a month, Mrs. Bouchard. I don't foresee any complications, so if you like, when you think you're near term, have one of your workers drive in to bring me back to you. I'll have Miss Donahue with me to assist—although I would prefer your having your baby in the hospital, as more and more doctors are recommending nowadays."

"I appreciate your concern, Dr. Kennery, but I'd much prefer to give birth to my child at home. I know Luke would like that—and his grandfather's spirit would thoroughly approve, I'm sure." Laure gave him her most enchanting smile, then inquired, "Your nurse seems very capable and charming: is she from these parts?"

"She's from Pittsburgh. I learned of her from an elderly patient of mine, her aunt. Miss Donahue was a nurse at Pittsburgh General Hospital—well, it's a sad tale, really. She was engaged to a young doctor, and while he was out riding one day, his horse threw him and he was killed—a month before the wedding date. Her aunt felt that a change of scene would help her get over her tragedy, and she inquired if I couldn't use a good nurse. Thanks to your and Mr. Bouchard's ready acceptance of me, I've quickly found myself with quite a number of patients, so I was more than willing to hire her."

Laure sighed, then realizing that Dr. Kennery was looking at her questioningly, she explained, "A good friend of ours, also a doctor—Ben Wilson—worked for a time at Pittsburgh General. He was married to Luke's half sister, Fleurette, before she succumbed to diptheria. Your story about Miss Donahue brings back memories. . . ."

"I understand," he said gently. "Well, now," his tone lightening, "if there's nothing more—"

"Well, actually, Dr. Kennery, I wanted to see you for another reason today—something unconnected with my pregnancy."

"I see. By all means, tell me about it. I hope it's nothing troublesome—in my view, a woman with a child on the way should have a clear, happy mind at all times. No brooding, certainly no domestic spats—"

"Oh, Luke and I almost never quarrel, Dr. Kennery, that I can guarantee you." Laure gave him one of her famous roguish smiles, which made her look as beautiful and as young as that day when Luke Bouchard had first met her at the Union House. Then again her face was grave: "No, Doctor, what really concerns me is Luke himself, the state of his health. You know, he's had a few little attacks that were very disturbing. I'm thinking especially of one time in December—we were at his grandfather's grave—when I felt sure he was having a heart attack."

"I see," Dr. Kennery pursed his lips, remembering that Luke had sworn him to secrecy about the most recent attack. "How can I help, then?"

"Why, I was thinking that you might suggest to Luke that he slow down and accept the fact that he's over sixty. He really drives himself. Oh, he doesn't have any worries on his mind, but the long day he puts in, surveying the fields, and making sure that all the tenants are comfortable and working over the ledgers with Marius—the physical exertion is just too much. I think you know by now what sort of schedule he keeps."

"Yes, I do. Now mind you, I believe that, when a man ages and thinks of retiring and devoting himself simply to leisure and pleasure, he's more likely to die quickly than if he occupies his mind and body with work. But I see your point. At this stage of life, he should only work in moderation. Very well, I'll be sure to recommend that he not drive himself at the same pace as he did in his youth."

"Thank you ever so much, Dr. Kennery, I appreciate it. By the way, perhaps you could come to dinner again—and why not bring Miss Donahue? We'd like to welcome her to Montgomery."

Dr. Kennery grinned boyishly and seemed to lose his composure for a moment, leading Laure to believe that perhaps the young doctor harbored more than strictly professional feelings for his nurse. But the doctor quickly recovered himself and smiled graciously.

"That's very kind of you, Mrs. Bouchard. I'm sure Miss Donahue would be delighted. I know that she's going to miss all her friends back in Pittsburgh, and living here knowing only her aunt makes it a little trying for her. Besides, it may help take her mind off the sudden loss of her fiancé. You and Mr. Bouchard would be very good for her, and so would all the rest of the people who live out your way."

"Oh, I do hope so, Dr. Kennery. Now, when do you think you might wish to bring her?"

"Perhaps next Friday, if that's convenient?"

"It certainly will be. Be sure to tell her that she'll be warmly welcomed and we hope she'll like us. And thank you again, Dr. Kennery, for offering to speak with Luke. I love him dearly, and want him to live a good while yet."

"You two are remarkable people, Mrs. Bouchard. It does my heart good to see how you rejoice in your marriage. I think it's a wonderful thing that the two of you should be so much in love after all these years."

"That's very kind of you to say, Dr. Kennery," she smiled. "Well, then, we'll expect you and Miss Donahue next Friday—about six o'clock?"

"That will be fine, and thanks again."

The following Friday a hired carriage bearing Dr. Abel Kennery and his eastern-born nurse drew up in front of the Bouchard's red-brick chateau a few minutes after six o'clock. Luke welcomed them both, nervously glancing at the handsome doctor and putting a finger to his lips, silently reminding Dr. Kennery to reveal nothing of his condition to his golden-haired wife. Dr. Kennery understood, just as he had Laure's secret visit to him out of her deep concern for her aging husband.

Genially, Dr. Kennery suggested to Laure, "Mrs. Bouchard, I'm sure Miss Donahue would welcome the chance to see your lovely home. There's nothing like it back east, you know."

Realizing that Dr. Kennery was seeking the opportunity to speak with Luke privately regarding the discussion she and the young doctor had had in his office, Laure smilingly agreed.

Luke, ever proud of his beautiful home and its heritage, concurred. "That's an excellent idea, Laure darling. Take this charming young woman on a tour of our chateau. Tell her all of its history—and don't leave out Grandfather."

"You need have no fear of that!" Laure bantered, as she tapped him lightly on the cheek. "I know the story by heart now. Don't look so unhappy, Luke dear, I didn't mean to belittle or to joke. You know very well how much respect I've always had for Lucien Bouchard. After all, without him, there wouldn't have been you." And then, taking the arm of the attractive nurse, Laure swept her off down the corridor saying, "Come along, Miss Donahue. I'll give you the guided tour and I'll try to make the platitudes as brief and few as possible."

Luke Bouchard stared at Dr. Abel Kennery and sighed, then asked, "Tell me, doctor, in all candor, has my wife said anything to you?"

"Nothing, really, Mr. Bouchard. Please believe that we're not dealing behind your back, either of us. But after you told me about your fainting spells, I've been giving a good deal of thought to it, and all I'm going to say to you

87

is, please, for your own sake, and for your lovely wife's, take things moderately. You don't have to prove anything anymore. You're an honored and respected man here in Montgomery and you've accomplished wonders. It would not be an exaggeration to say that you're almost a legend, as your grandfather was. Don't jeopardize your health by taking undue chances. You don't have to ride a horse from sunup to sundown anymore, any more than you have to take a hoe and go out with the workers in the fields. They understand this, and you've already proved yourself to them a thousand times over. Please take my advice—and that's all I'm going to say on the subject tonight, for this is a social occasion. For the rest, I want to give myself up to the enjoyment of this beautiful home of yours, and to the fabulous dinner I understand I'm about to enjoy."

So the evening passed lightly and pleasantly, with much bantering conversation. After dinner, Laure, wanting to talk to Dr. Kennery alone, airily declared, "Luke, I'm going to be very selfish and ask Dr. Kennery to examine me. I'm close to term, and I might as well take advantage of his presence and avoid a bumpy drive to Montgomery. Would you mind waiting, dear, while Dr. Kennery, Miss Donahue, and I retire for a few minutes?"

Luke chuckled and flushed, then nodded, giving Laure a loving glance. Laure turned and touched his shoulder reassuringly, and then left the dining room.

Dr. Kennery and Miss Donahue, taking their cue from her, excused themselves and followed Laure to one of the guest rooms. There, Dr. Kennery, with the nurse's assistance, quickly examined Luke's golden-haired wife. After he finished, he suggested that Miss Donahue rejoin Luke in the parlor. Then he turned to Laure and said, "As I said, Mrs. Bouchard, I think you can expect the child to be born by the end of May, and I quite honestly don't expect you will have any difficulties."

Laure touched his wrist and smiled. "I know everything will go smoothly—I've perfect confidence in you, Dr. Kennery." Then she added, "By some chance, were you able to speak to my husband?"

"Yes, indeed—just as we discussed. If he listens to my advice, I'm sure he'll have many good years ahead of him."

"That's what I pray for, Dr. Kennery. God bless you for what you've told me and for your presence here tonight." Then, with a teasing look, Laure added, "You know, Doctor, Miss Donahue is a very lovely woman. I shouldn't be at all surprised if before the year is over, you tell me that you're interested in taking her into your practice more as a wife than as a nurse."

"Good gracious, Mrs. Bouchard," he chuckled uneasily, and then blushed as any schoolboy might. "Yes," he ruefully admitted, "she is very attractive. But needless to say, I don't intend to pursue that tack until there's some indication on her part that she's interested. She's still grieving for her fiancé. As of now, ours is a strictly professional relationship."

"Well, I must admit, Dr. Kennery, it would please me a great deal if something nice and romantic happened." Laure enchantingly smiled, then added, "Thank you so much for coming tonight. You've put my mind at rest."

Laure and Dr. Kennery then rejoined Luke and Miss Donahue, and after a few minutes' further conversation, the doctor pulled out his watch, looked at it, and decided it was time to depart. Luke accompanied the visitors down the steps of the chateau, as Laure waved good-bye, and then handed them up into the carriage that Dan Munroe had brought around for them.

On the drive back to Montgomery, both the doctor and his nurse were silent for nearly half an hour; then Dr. Kennery turned to the attractive young woman and said, "You know, I respect the Bouchards more than I can tell you. They're amazing people. I don't know what you feel about the South so far, but these people are a far cry from the stereotyped Southern plantation owner who brandishes a blacksnake whip on his slaves and dreams only of cotton, eternally cotton."

"I've already discovered that, Dr. Kennery," she said quietly.

"You know, I'm wondering just how much Mrs. Bouchard told you about the family history; for example, about their old grandfather who founded Windhaven Plantation back at the time of the French Revolution."

"She did talk a bit about that, but it seemed to me that she was almost apologetic, as if she didn't want to burden me with it. But I think I understand a good deal of the tradition and the pride that she'd naturally have—and truly, Dr. Kennery, what old Lucien Bouchard did was extraordinary. And I think Luke Bouchard's accomplishments are equally true to form."

"Indeed, if he hadn't been so modest and self-effacing, he could have gone far in politics, I'm sure. He might even have been a United States senator, or at least state governor. He's a man whose humanity and decency transcend sectional politics and prejudices. I'm very proud to count both him and his wife as friends."

"I think I'm going to like it here very much, Dr. Kennery. And if you won't think me too presumptuous, I'll say that I'm sure I'm going to enjoy working with a man like you. You're very enlightened and very wise."

Remembering the sly hint that Laure had introduced into their private conversation, Dr. Abel Kennery could not help flushing hotly. Drawing a deep breath, he abruptly changed the subject to discuss the patient suffering from asthma who was coming to them the next morning.

# *Eight*

On April 26, Daniel Fornage died in his sleep, and his death left Lowndesboro without a mayor. Mitzi Sattersfield, though only about a week from her delivery of their fourth child, remembered what her husband had told her of his conversation with Luke and Andy last January concerning the mayoral post. That evening, as they were sitting down to supper, she gave him a kiss on the top of his head and airily declared, "Dalbert, now's your chance to be the new mayor of this nice, thriving little town."

"Mitzi, you worry me sometimes," her husband exclaimed in irritation. "I've told you a hundred times that we ought to hire a woman to do the cooking and to give you a hand around the house, what with you so far pregnant."

"Dalbert, sometimes you exasperate me, the way you so quickly manage to change the subject!" Mitzi firmly countered, as she ladled out a generous helping of beef stew and then served herself before sitting down beside him at the kitchen table. "You know perfectly well there isn't anybody else in this town who'd be capable of taking that job. You're smart, and you've brought lots of customers into the stores; we're doing very well, with money in the bank, and soon we're going to have an addition to the family. So I don't know why you give me all these arguments."

"Because—oh, well, by the time I started explaining to you why I don't want to be a mayor, you'd have a hundred arguments for convincing me to run for office. Mmm, this stew is wonderful, Mitzi!"

"I'm glad you like it, darling." She sent him an adoring look. "I haven't told you lately, Dalbert, but I don't think any woman in the world could be as happy as I am with you. I'm proud to be married to you, and I only wish you'd begin to understand your own worth—"

"Oh, you conniving little minx you, I get your drift," he chuckled. Laying down his spoon, be got up from his chair, moved over to her, put his arm around her shoulders, and kissed her very sweetly and tenderly on the eyelids, then the tip of her nose, and finally her mouth. Mitzi sighed raptly and returned the kiss with ardor, then primly remonstrated, "There's time enough for that after the dishes are washed and the children put to bed, Dalbert. Now you sit down and finish your stew before it gets cold, do you hear me?"

He tilted back his head and burst into hearty laughter. This irrepressible, petite, delicious young wife of his had made a new man of him, and he felt as young as she was. For a few moments they ate in silence, and then he gave her a curious, sideways look. "Do you really think I should run, Mitzi?"

Mitzi Sattersfield looked exactly like the proverbial cat that had swallowed a canary as she nodded. "I do indeed. And do you know, it could be the start of a wonderful career in politics for you. I mean, honey, look at what Andy Haskins has done. He didn't know anything about politics, any more than you do. And yet he's now state senator, and he's getting a lot of favorable mention in the papers all over the state—even outside of it. They're even talking about running him for governor one of these days."

"Now, Mitzi, let's be sensible, that couldn't ever happen to an old duffer like me."

"Dalbert, I love you, I adore you, but when you talk like that I could—I could just dump this plate of stew over your head! Don't you know that nobody ever got anywhere by putting himself down? There'll be lots of others who'll try to do that for you, honey. Besides, you're a wonderful, decent man, and you're honest to a fault, so you'd be sure to make a wonderful mayor. Now, does that answer your question?"

"All right, then. If it'll make you happy—and you'll

stop nagging me every night and spoiling my digestion—I guess I'll file when they announce a special election."

"I love you so, Dalbert!" Mitzi breathed, giving him another soulful look.

After petitioning the state legislature, on May first the citizens of Lowndesboro were granted the right to hold a special election to replace the late mayor, Daniel Fornage. The date set for this was the twenty-eighth of May.

On the second of May, at dawn, Mitzi Sattersfield gave birth to her fourth child, another son, whom she insisted on naming Dalbert junior, since the baby had his father's hair and eyes. The labor had lasted only four hours, and Johanna, the midwife, exclaimed that she had never seen an easier, less painful birth.

Within two days, Mitzi was already pleading to be allowed to get up and resume caring for her beloved husband—an idea that left the gallant Southerner aghast. But when Dr. Abel Kennery rode from Montgomery to the Lowndesboro house and examined Mitzi, he pronounced her incredibly strong and recommended that surely she might be allowed to be up and about in just a few days, and even to resume light household tasks.

Standing with her husband at their son's crib a week after the baby's birth, Mitzi anxiously demanded, "Dalbert, honey, did you file your bid to run as mayor in poor old Mr. Fornage's place, I hope?"

He admitted that he had done so, adding somewhat sheepishly, "I know it was your dearest wish, honey, and I did it to please you. But I still don't think I'm qualified, and I know absolutely nothing about politics."

"Dalbert Sattersfield, you are the most exasperating man I ever met, and the dearest!" she softly giggled, as she reached up to him, entwining both arms around his neck and drawing him down to give him an ardent kiss. The baby cooed, as if in pleasure at the sight of this exchange, and Dalbert, touched by his son's response, had to blink rapidly to clear his eyes of the tears that had gathered.

"You know perfectly well," Mitzi whispered, "that you're the only possible candidate—I'm awfully glad you filed all by yourself, honey."

"There's only one other candidate running against me," Dalbert replied, "a freed black, name of Rafe Thomasson, who owns a little farm about twenty-five miles downriver. He's very well thought of, and he sells a little cotton and some fruit and vegetables down at Mobile."

"Pshaw, Dalbert, I don't care how nice he is, or how hardworking, you're the man that people know and respect. So the election's going to be a week from now, is that right?"

"Yes, my darling. But I'm not planning to do any campaigning. I'll just stand on my merits and leave the decision to the will of the majority."

"I'm sure you know what's best, Dalbert. Now you go back to your store, because Johanna and I can handle everything around here. She's the best midwife in these parts, and I'm glad you found her for me."

"There isn't anything I wouldn't do for you, Mitzi."

"I know that, darling. I'm the luckiest girl in the world. We've got four wonderful sons, and they'll all get married and have children, and when we get old and white-haired they'll run the stores, and they'll make us very proud."

"That's a long way off—for *you*, at least," he murmured, as he took her hand and kissed it.

"You hush up. Don't you start talking about how old you are, Dalbert Sattersfield. No girl could ask for a sweeter, more considerate lover and husband—you're everything I ever wanted. And I'm going to be very proud to be the wife of the new mayor of Lowndesboro," Mitzi triumphantly concluded.

Rafe Thomasson had had his black attorney file an injunction at the state capital to defer the election till the tenth of June, on the grounds that the original date had not given him sufficient time to campaign and garner suitable opposition to his opponent, Dalbert Sattersfield. An elderly judge granted the injunction and announced that the mayoral election would be held on the June date.

While Dalbert was away in Montgomery, filing additional obligatory credentials—including a copy of his Oath of Amnesty, a declaration of his present and past material holdings, and proof of his residency in the town of Lowndesboro—Buford Phelps paid a courtesy call on Mitzi and her new son. Mitzi had always liked Buford and his wife, Dulcie, and had been delighted when Dalbert had promoted him from clerk to manager of the Lowndesboro store after Dalbert had decided to open a second store ten miles downriver and was concentrating all of his own efforts on the new branch.

Mitzi had another reason for being pleased to see Buford aside from his kindly solicitude, and she eagerly explained, "Buford, you can do me a mighty big favor, if you will."

"Of course, if I can, Mrs. Sattersfield. You just name it," he amicably grinned.

"I've written a letter to Governor Houston. Are you by any chance going into Montgomery in the next day or so?"

"Matter of fact, I am, Mrs. Sattersfield. I'll be there tomorrow morning. I've got to buy some dry goods and darning yarn and needles—our store is running mighty low."

"That's just wonderful! I'd be ever so obliged if you'd take this—maybe you could take it right to the governor's secretary, Buford?"

"It'll be my pleasure, Mrs. Sattersfield."

"Thanks an awful lot. After this election is over, you and Dulcie and the children will have to come over for dinner—a celebration dinner, I hope. You will remember that, won't you?"

"My, oh my, Mrs. Sattersfield, I surely won't forget, you can depend on it." Buford Phelps grinned from ear to ear. "My mouth waters just thinking about that Creole gumbo you make, just like it's done in New Orleans."

"Well, I came from there, Buford," she reminded him, "but it's mighty nice of you to say so. You just tell me when you and Dulcie and the family can be our guests and gumbo's what I'll serve. And thanks so much again for taking the letter for me."

After Buford had tipped his hat and left, mounting his dappled mare, Mitzi giggled to herself. "Just wait till Dalbert hears what I've done!"

Just three days later, a letter bearing the official seal of Governor Houston was brought by a special courier on horseback to the Lowndesboro store. As it chanced, Dalbert and Buford were discussing the need to take inventory to be prepared for summer business, when the courier entered and exclaimed, "I've a letter from Governor Houston for Mrs. Dalbert Sattersfield. I was directed here. Can you see that she gets it?"

"I rather think so, young man," the one-armed storekeeper smilingly drawled, "considering that I'm her husband. I'll just take it."

"Thank you, Mr. Sattersfield. If you'll sign this receipt, I can go back to the governor and tell him that I've done as he requested."

Dalbert nodded, scribbled his name on a paper that the young courier presented, then wonderingly stared at the letter. "Now what in heaven's name can Governor Houston be doing writing to my wife?" he rhetorically asked.

"Why don't you open it, Mr. Sattersfield," Buford smilingly prompted.

"Buford, I'm not in the habit of reading Mitzi's mail. I'll bring it home tonight—and then I'll find out what it is. I'll admit, though," Dalbert chuckled, "I'm most curious. How is it that the governor happens to know my wife? Oh well, let's get back to work."

When he came back that evening, he found Mitzi preparing supper while keeping an eye on little Dalbert junior, gurgling and cooing in his cradle a few feet away.

"Mitzi, darling, I hate to see you working so hard," Sattersfield solicitiously remarked.

"Dalbert, honey, I'm not made of Dresden china. Besides, Dr. Kennery was here again today, and he said I'm doing just fine."

"All right, then, but I'm concerned about you. And by the way," his brows knitted as he grew stern and serious, "I have a letter from Governor Houston himself addressed to you. It came to the store—"

"Oh, my goodness!" Mitzi gasped, turning a vivid crimson and occupying herself more industriously than was necessary with the pots simmering on the stove.

"Exactly. Do I have your permission to open it, or would you rather open it yourself—and read it to me?"

"D-Dalbert, you—you don't think that I'm carrying on—" Mitzi stammered, very ill at ease.

"I hardly think that you'd be carrying on with Governor Houston, my dear. But I am most curious about his sending a special envoy with a letter, instead of entrusting it to the mails."

"I—I suppose you'd better read it, th-then," Mitzi's

voice faltered, and she didn't look at him, as she continued with the supper preparations.

He stared intently at her, uttered a faint sigh as if to say, "What in the world can a man do with a woman like this?" and then opened the official-looking envelope.

"Well now, let's see . . ." Dalbert opened the letter and started to read it aloud: " 'My dear Mrs. Sattersfield: I should be delighted to accept your kind invitation to appear at the campaign meeting to marshal support for your husband in the upcoming mayoral election in Lowndesboro. I have made inquiries, and on the strength of excellent reports from trustworthy individuals, I can say that your husband's reputation for honest business dealings—as well as his record of service to the Confederacy during the last war—recommend him most highly for public office. And may I add that your candor and devotion to him, in extending to me this invitation, speak volumes about you both.' Well, that's a pretty compliment, my dear. But he goes on: 'If you will let me know exactly what day you wish me to appear to endorse Mr. Sattersfield's candidacy, I shall see to it that my schedule is adjusted accordingly.' The letter is signed, 'Cordially yours, George Smith Houston, Governor of Alabama; given by my hand, this day from the Executive Mansion, Montgomery.' "

"Why, Dalbert, that's just wonderful!" Mitzi turned to face him, her eyes sparkling, her cheeks still very red. He did not answer at once, and she quailed before his unrelenting and unwavering gaze. "But, h-honey, I—I was just thinking of you—" she faltered.

"Good heavens, Mitzi Sattersfield! I ought to spank you, that's what. The effrontery of writing a letter to the governor of this state asking him to endorse me, when all I'm doing is running for mayor of a little town, just one of hundreds like it in this sovereign state. Really, Mitzi, I can't think what got into you!"

Mitzi took a deep breath, put her hands behind her back, and twisted her fingers together, much like a young girl who has been threatened by a stern parent and seeks to justify her behavior. "Go ahead and do it, spank me if you think you can. But the fact is, I'm not at all sorry I wrote the governor, and I never will be, so there!"

"Now, Mitzi . . ." he gasped, his eyebrows widely arched.

"Dalbert, you're the most deserving man around here, and I want to be sure that you win the election. I did it for your sake, because I admire and respect and I love you. Now, if you still want to raise your hand against me, go right ahead." There were tears in her eyes when she finished, but she faced him bravely all the same. He uttered a groan, clapped a hand to his forehead, and then burst out laughing and shook his head. "Mitzi, I don't know what I'm going to do with you."

"Don't you, really, honey?" she faintly put in, her eyes wide and appealing and moist with tears.

He looked down at the cradle where his infant son lay, and then at her again. Then tears came to his own eyes, as he went to her and hugged her and murmured, "Damn it all, sweetheart, I just can't believe that you'd care as much as this for an old codger like me. I know you did it out of impulse, and it was a wonderful thought. You're the most loyal wife any man could ever hope for, and I thank God for you every day of my life."

"Oh, D-Dalbert, Dalbert, I—I just love you so much—and I'm so worried that I'll do the wrong thing and that you'll be mad at me," she tearfully confessed, as she buried her face in his chest and clung to him.

Dalbert kissed her hair and stroked her shoulders. His face was beaming now. If he had ever had the slightest doubt that she might once have been in love with Luke Bouchard—and he could not have blamed her for that, in all fairness, since she had known Luke long before she had ever met him—he was now serenely assured that now there was no other man in her life.

"Mitzi, don't cry. I never want to make you cry, honey," he said, his voice hoarse and choked. He tilted up her chin and kissed her, and the two of them clung to each other with tears freely running down both their faces.

# Nine

The next day, Mitzi approached Burt Coleman and shyly asked if he would mind driving her to Windhaven to pay a visit to Laure, and then waiting to give her a ride home again.

The hardworking Southerner readily agreed. He felt close to the Sattersfields, for his wife, Marietta, also was about to have a baby. It would be Marietta and Burt's second child; their first, Matt, named for his friend who had been brutally murdered by the Ku Klux Klan, had been born early last year. He hoped this child would be a daughter, who would surely be as lovely as his wife. He smiled to himself as the buggy gently rolled along.

Arriving at the red-brick chateau, Mitzi carefully descended from the buggy and, holding her infant son, Dalbert junior, strolled toward the imposing edifice that had been restored, just as Luke had dreamed it would be, to the untarnished splendor of those days when old Lucien Bouchard had seen his dream come true and had built a replica of his Normandy birthplace near the banks of the gently flowing Alabama River.

Clementine opened the door to Mitzi's eager knock, and smilingly welcomed in Dalbert Sattersfield's petite wife. "Miz Laure's in her bedroom. She's not far from her time, and she was telling me early this morning she'd hoped you'd come visit her, 'cause she's pinin' on seein' your newest—my Lord, isn't he the cutest li'l feller ever!" She leaned forward to kiss the baby's head, and then volunteered, "I'll take you right there, Miz Mitzi, honey."

The knock at Laure's bedroom produced an enthusiastic

99

"Come in!" and Clementine opened the door and then withdrew.

"Thanks, Clemmie." Mitzi gave her a smiling nod. Then, entering the bedroom, she hurried to Laure, who reclined in bed with two pillows behind her. *"Madame, que je suis heureuse de te voir!"* she exclaimed.

"You little minx, that goes double for me. Come here and give me a big hug, and let me look at Dalbert junior!" Laure exclaimed.

Mitzi seated herself on the edge of the bed and tendered her infant son to Laure, as she reached over to hug her former employer, giving her a resounding kiss on the cheek.

"He's just beautiful, Mitzi. I'm so happy for you and Dalbert. But that look on your face tells me you've been up to something!" Laure teasingly declared.

Blushing as Laure laughed at her, Mitzi related the story of how she had written Governor Houston to urge his participation in her husband's campaign for the mayoralty of Lowndesboro.

At the conclusion, Laure tilted back her head and laughed heartily: "You're just impossible, *ma petite*! I wonder that Dalbert didn't turn you over his lap and give you a sound spanking!"

"He threatened to do it, and I dared him," Mitzi giggled. Then, her face serious, she leaned forward and murmured, "But I wouldn't have cared. I just want him to be recognized. He's done so much for the town, and everybody likes him, you know that yourself."

"Of course, I do, you silly girl! Now listen, I'm going to tell Luke, and I'm sure he'll make arrangements for our popular senator, Andy Haskins, to put in a few good words for your dear husband."

"Would you? Oh, that's just wonderful of you, Madame Laure!"

"I asked you to stop calling me that ages ago," Laure countered with a shrug. "We're a long way from New Orleans, Mitzi. And I don't have the slightest inclination to ever go back there."

"Do you know," Mitzi confided, "I don't think either of us ever dreamed we'd come up here and be so happy."

"I know. God has been very good to both of us, *ma*

*chérie,*" Laure mused. "Now come, you must give me the latest gossip from town."

Half an hour later, the two women parted with promises to meet again soon after Laure had had her baby. Happily, Mitzi went back to the buggy, and Burt Coleman drove her back quickly to the house she and Dalbert occupied in Lowndesboro, then he drove on back to the Williamson acreage that he supervised.

At dinner that evening, Laure informed her husband of Mitzi's audacious strategem in enlisting Governor Houston's support. Luke laughed heartily and shook his head. "Dalbert really has his hands full with that Mitzi, but I know he couldn't be happier. She's quite a girl!"

"I know, sweetheart," Laure teased him. "If you'll remember, when you were on your way from New Orleans to Texas with Lucien Edmond to start Windhaven Range, Mitzi had her cap set for you. I suppose by now it's safe to admit that at one time I was just a little jealous of that saucy little creature. I thought you might succumb to her."

"As if I could look at any other woman except you in those days—and now, too, my dearest Laure," Luke tenderly murmured, as he took his wife in his arms and kissed her cheek.

The next day, after having divulged to Laure his intentions of meeting with Andy Haskins and doing some business as well, Luke rode into Montgomery on his gelding. It was as if he had never had the warnings of his fainting spells: on this particular morning he felt as young and vigorous as he had twenty years ago. Tethering his horse to a hitching post outside the state capitol, he waited until the senators adjourned for lunch and, seeing Andy emerge with two of his colleagues, hailed him.

They went to lunch in a pleasant restaurant patronized by the legislators, across the street from the capitol building. Once they had given their order, Luke leaned forward to inform the one-armed Tennessean of Governor Houston's response to Mitzi's impulsive letter. "Andy, I think this would be an ideal time for you to take a strong stand, calling for state unity. What I mean is, you ought to come to that rally and speak along with the governor. To my

101

mind, it's a way of declaring an end to party rivalry since we'll have both Democrats and Republicans there who believe in decency and justice and fair play. It's a wonderful opportunity to put political differences aside, if only for the time being."

"I think that's a great idea, Luke," Andy energetically nodded. "And, as far as backing Dalbert is concerned, it would be my pleasure."

"I understand there's a freed black by the name of Rafe Thomasson opposing him. He's had no experience either, so I'm not worried about his candidacy at all. Of course, if anyone overheard me say that, they'd think that I was against Thomasson because of his color—and you know that isn't so. It's just that Dalbert is already known, and that gives him the popular mandate needed to do a good job. It'll give him stature, and of course it'll make Mitzi very happy, as you may well guess."

"I agree one hundred percent," Andy enthusiastically assented. "You know, I've met Governor Houston a couple of times, and I think very highly of him. He won't have anything to do with the Ku Klux Klan, and he'll work with both parties to do all he can for Alabama. You know, of course, the Alabama and Chattanooga Railroad issue is just about resolved. Naturally, there's a lot of grumbling about it, but Governor Houston has laid down the law, and it'll have to be accepted. I, for one, am grateful that we're through worrying about carpetbaggers who want to swindle honest citizens with fraudulent schemes in connection with that railroad line."

"I know. My blood still boils when I think of Judge Siloway and Homer Jenkinson—and that other unsavory character, Milo Brutus Henson."

"I remember them, too—with good reason," Andy grimly agreed. "But I think we've drawn the arrows in their quiver, rendering them all pretty harmless. Besides, Jenkinson died some time back, and I really don't know what happened to the judge. Henson's still around, of course, but I haven't heard a peep out of him lately."

"Good. Well now, I know you'll be wanting to get back to the Senate chambers, and I'd best be off myself. Among other things, I'm investigating two new shipping lines to take our crops from Windhaven to the markets in Mobile. Both companies seem sound, but I'd like to meet the owners and see which one can offer the most advantageous schedule. I'll be lucky to make it back to the plantation by midnight! Now, don't you forget to bring Jessica and the children over for dinner soon, preferably before the baby arrives."

"I'll talk to Jessica and see when it's convenient. You know, Luke, I'm eager to sit down with you and talk some more about the issues that are coming up in the Senate these days," Andy Haskins earnestly avowed.

"It will be my pleasure," Luke replied, "Just name the day."

Sometime past midnight, Laure was taken with protracted labor pains. She was terrified that something was wrong: the baby was not due for at least two more weeks! Turning to awaken Luke to see if he could summon Dr. Kennery, she discovered to her horror that he had not yet returned from Montgomery.

The pain intensified. Fighting to master the sense of panic welling up within her, her fear exacerbated by Luke's absence, Laure struggled to sit up in bed. In her confusion, she recalled vaguely that Luke had said he would not be back until late, possibly after midnight. This recollection was swept from her mind as yet another pain assailed her, causing her to cry out in agony. She knew she needed to have help; yet even if there were someone to go for the doctor, he would in all likelihood arrive too late. Struggling to her feet, she made her way uneasily across the room to the doorway into the hall.

At Luke and Laure's invitation, the Thorntons—Marius, Clementine, and the children—had taken up permanent quarters on the second floor of the red-brick chateau, and Clementine had in recent weeks proved herself indispensable in assisting Laure with the care of the children—for their regular nurse, Clarabelle Hendry, had been called away to Mobile to attend a sick cousin. Thinking now of Clementine, Laure stepped from her bedroom into the hall and passed down the long corridor, gritting her teeth against the sharp pains and leaning against the wall for support, until she reached the stairs leading to the floor above, where the Thorntons' rooms were situated. Bowing her head over the balustrade, clutching it with both hands, she imploringly called out, "Clemmie—Clemmie—h-help me! Please help me!"

As it happened, Clementine was in her room, but had not yet fallen asleep, for she was nursing her newborn son, her seventh child. She heard Laure's cry—a faint, distant sound—and, placing her infant in his crib, she went to the door and opened it. A second cry—this one louder—came from below. Clementine at once donned a robe and, giving a glance over to where her husband, Marius, was sleeping soundly—for he was just recovering from a fever—she hurried down the hall to the stairs.

By now, Laure's birth spasms were even sharper. Clementine guided her back to the bedroom and helped her get into bed. Working Laure's nightgown off her perspiring, shuddering body, Clementine murmured soothingly, "There, there, Miz Laure. You gonna be all right. I'll just get some water and towels and be back in a jiffy. You just hang on, Miz Laure!"

Later, Laure would not recall how much time passed, as she underwent agonies such as she had not endured with the births of her other children; yet it was in fact only a short while before she vaguely heard the first cries of life. Tears streaming down her face from both exhaustion and relief, she beseechingly inquired, "Oh, Clemmie! Is the b-baby all right? Is it—is it normal?"

"Why, Miz Laure, he's not only all right—he's just beautiful! A fine, healthy son. No need to fret, child. He'll be as fine and strong and handsome as his daddy."

"Oh, Clemmie—bless you Clemmie," Laure murmured as she began to sink into an exhausted sleep after her ordeal. "I want—" she whispered faintly, "I want to name him John, Clemmie. T-tell Luke it's for Jean, old Lucien's brother. I want Luke to know that his child, the child of our love, will become a good man—even with that name. Perhaps he will bring honor to the name, redeeming it from the dishonor brought to it by old Lucien's elder brother, all those years ago. Tell Luke—please tell him—C-Clemmie—" and her eyes finally closed, and she mercifully slept.

Ten days after the birth of baby John, Lopasuta Bouchard and his Geraldine, radiant with her advanced pregnancy, joined Luke and Laure for an informal dinner.

At Luke's request, Marius and Clemmie were also present, since Luke intended to confer with both the young Comanche lawyer and his foreman on the disposition of business affairs at Windhaven Plantation.

Luke had been concerned that a social evening would put too much of a strain on Laure so soon after her confinement, but Dr. Kennery had said that she might resume light activities, in moderation, for she had quite recovered from the rigors of John's premature birth, and an evening of pleasant diversion could only have a salutary effect. "Besides," Laure had added, "the Thorntons live here now, and Lopasuta and Geraldine aren't company at all—they're part of the family." And so the evening had been arranged.

At the conclusion of a leisurely and excellent dinner prepared by Annabel Leary, who continued to perform Hannah's culinary duties because of the latter's age and infirmity, Luke raised his glass of vintage red Bordeaux and proposed a toast: "Just as our bountiful crops are nurtured by the fertile and yielding land, so will the joyous and loving atmosphere of Windhaven Plantation nurture the lives of those who come after us. To the children, who will shape the future destiny of Windhaven, I propose this heartfelt toast!"

Geraldine, Laure, and Clementine exchanged knowing glances, for each understood that Luke's words were meant for the three of them.

They all raised their glasses and drank to the toast. And then Luke added, "I think of my grandfather tonight with affection—and humility. For I have tried in my own way to create a commune in which people of all colors can work together in perfect harmony and justify that word of the Bible that holds that all men are brothers under the sun—as did Lucien Bouchard."

With pride shining in his eyes, Luke addressed his beloved adopted son in a voice trembling with emotion. "I look at you, Lopasuta, and see that you, too, strive as both my grandfather and I have done, to make others understand and accept these tenets. I lift my glass in salutation to you, my son, for your courage in speaking out against injustices against those who are oppressed. You have restored pride and honor to the People, the Wanderers, the Comanche. May you and dear Geraldine have long, happy years and delight in the family that God in his wisdom and mercy will surely grant you. May there be no shadows of hostility and prejudice to darken your horizons."

Lopasuta reached for his wife's hand and gazed deeply into her eyes, which were glazed with tears. Then they all raised their glasses again and drank to Lopasuta and Geraldine and their kinship with the Bouchard family, as well as to the enduring bounty of Windhaven Plantation.

# Ten

Luke had casually mentioned during the dinner with Lopasuta and Geraldine that he was greatly concerned about Hannah's increasing infirmities, and although Annabel had substituted admirably in the kitchen on special occasions, she could hardly be expected to be solely responsible for preparing daily meals for all the residents of the chateau. Lopasuta had volunteered, "I might be able to find you somebody in Montgomery. There are many young women looking for work, but not very many jobs to be had. I'll look into it."

The following Monday, when the Montgomery County court had adjourned for lunch, Lopasuta went—as he so often did—to Reuben Henry's little restaurant. The dining room was nearly full this noon, but Reuben Henry genially came forward and whispered, "If you don't mind being near the kitchen, Mr. Bouchard suh, I can put you at a nice, cozy little table where you'll have some privacy. 'Sides which, you have first chance at the nice hot specials my wife's fixin' up right now."

Lopasuta chuckled and nodded, seated himself, looked back into the kitchen, and waved a greeting to the industrious black woman, who beamed and nodded her pleasure at seeing him. Because of increasing patronage, Reuben Henry had hired a young mulatto waitress about a month ago. (He counted Lopasuta mainly responsible for the increasing business, since the Comanche lawyer had recommended the restaurant highly to his colleagues in the courtroom, as well as his friends and acquaintances.) The new waitress, Emily Colton, was slovenly in her dress—

107

her white smock was often dirty and wrinkled—and she had a disconcerting habit of looking elsewhere when a customer was giving her his order and often had to ask him to repeat it. But Reuben Henry, being a mild-mannered and tolerant man, had put up with her thus far, knowing that the girl had endured hard times and might well, if she lost this job, turn to prostitution.

She ambled over to Lopasuta now and, with an audible sniff to indicate her disdain of him—because of his coppery skin, no doubt—drawled, "What you want, mistah?"

"Unless my sense of smell deceives me, you've got lamb stew today. I'd like a nice, big plate of it, miss, and whatever fresh vegetables are on the menu. And a cup of coffee, if you please."

"I'll go see," she arrogantly retorted, and shuffled off into the kitchen.

Lopasuta turned back and considered the other patrons. At a table next to his along the window that looked out on the side street, he recognized Carleton Ivers, a tall, bony-faced man in his early sixties, with sparse white hair, a small, lecherously ripe mouth and dark, greedy eyes. He was the president of the Montgomery Central Bank and Trust Company, which was housed in a one-story brick building two blocks west of the Montgomery County Courthouse. Seated across from Ivers was an attractive young octoroon woman of about twenty-five, who demurely lowered her eyes and adopted an attitude of humble deference.

Lopasuta had heard a good deal about Carleton Ivers from one of his colleagues, little of it flattering. Ivers was reputed to be a shrewd speculator in stocks and bonds and mortgages, and he owned considerable property in and around Lowndesboro. He had come to Montgomery about five years before the Civil War, purportedly from Boston, where he had been an investment broker for a well-known firm. With his capital, he had acquired a partnership in the Montgomery Central, and after its founder and chief owner had died, he had been elected president. Although reputed to be scrupulously honest in his business dealings, rumor had it that Ivers had coerced a succession of young mistresses to submit to his lechery. When he was tired of them, they were invariably cast off and forced out of town, several of them going to the houses of ill repute on New Orleans's Rampart Street.

Sitting with his back to Lopasuta, Ivers glowered when the insolent waitress, who had stopped briefly at Lopasuta's table to inform him that his order would be out shortly, had then gone toward the front of the restaurant. "Hey, gal, don't you have eyes?" he shouted after her. "Can't you see we've been waiting a lot longer than the fellow behind me?" Ivers irritatedly snapped.

"Now wait a minute, mistah, jist hold your horses," the waitress sullenly replied, "I have to take care of Mr. Stanley up front there. He came just ahead o' you."

"Damn it, girl, I don't like your tone! Where do you get off talking to a white man that way? I'm president of Montgomery Central, I'll have you know!"

"I don' care if you is President o' dese here United States, mistah. You jist waits your turn, git me?"

"You high-yellow bitch, you! I'll have your job for this!" Ivers snarled. Then, turning to the attractive octoroon seated opposite him, he growled at her in his most imperious manner, "Amelia, you go back to the kitchen and get me the two thickest pork chops you can find there, hear me, girl? And some sweet yams and hominy grits—and be quick about it!"

"Yes, Mr. Ivers," the young woman meekly replied, as she rose from her chair.

"Show some life, Amelia! Don't forget I gave your dad a decent job at the bank—then the ingrate left town with a bundle of my money. You're beholden to me, so hop to it! Damn niggers. You're all alike," he muttered.

Lopasuta could hardly believe his ears. He carefully turned his head to observe the banker, who contemptuously snorted and looked away. Meanwhile, the mulatto waitress came back from the front of the restaurant, pointedly ignoring Ivers as she passed him on her way to the kitchen.

The octoroon came back from the kitchen with the plate of hominy grits and a dish of sweet yams, which she set down before the banker. "Where the hell are the pork chops, Amelia? I told you to bring them, didn't I?"

"I know, Mr. Ivers, but they have to be cooked first—"

"So now you're getting uppity, just like that yellow bitch, are you?" Ivers reached out and viciously slapped

109

her across the cheek, the imprint of his fingers leaving a bright red mark on her pale skin. She uttered a stifled gasp of pain. Tears filled her eyes as she straightened, fought for self-control, and then stammered, "Y-you've no cause to hit me—specially not here—please!"

"Oh, don't I? You listen to me, Amelia McAdams. What you need is a good whipping, the kind we used to give niggers in the good old days before that bastard Lincoln set you all free with his damned Emancipation Proclamation. And when I get you home, 'Melia girl, I think that's exactly what you're going to get, to teach you your place. Don't think I haven't noticed that you've been forgetting to be nice to me for keeping a roof over your head and food in your belly, after what your thieving father did. I declare, he might have been of white stock, but he's just as trashy as that yellow bitch—or you."

"Oh, please, Mr. Ivers—don't raise your voice like that—everybody's listening and looking at us—" Amelia McAdams entreated in a low, tearful voice.

"I don't give a damn who's listening or looking. Now just you get back to that kitchen and bring those pork chops. Otherwise, when I get you home, I'll tan your hide till the blood runs down to your heels, you hear me, girl?"

Lopasuta could bear no more. Abruptly rising from the table, he turned and stepped beside the irate banker. "You really shouldn't pursue that subject of cowhiding this young woman any more, Mr. Ivers," he interposed in a cool voice.

Slowly, Carleton Ivers turned to stare up at him. "And who the hell are you? Wait a minute, I know you, I've read about you—you're Lopasuta Bouchard, that goddamned Injun-nigger lawyer Luke Bouchard adopted!"

"I'd lower my voice, if I were you, Mr. Ivers. And I'd be very careful about insulting someone who's done nothing to offend you, in a public place. I am a lawyer—which should tell you that I know the laws of slander. I also know the laws of civil rights. You made it impossible not to overhear your threats to this young woman. The days of slavery ended with that very proclamation that you so profanely discredited. Miss McAdams, there's no need for you to remain with this man and take that kind of abuse. If you care to, I'm prepared to introduce you to someone who is looking for a cook. It would be an excellent situation in a respectable household, where you'd be treated kindly and as an equal."

"Please, you're going to get me into terrible trouble," Amelia McAdams whispered, biting her lips and glancing frantically at the banker, who sat with his mouth agape at what Lopasuta had just said to him.

A slow, angry flush spread from the back of Ivers's neck to his cheeks, giving his sallow complexion an unhealthy, feverish look. His mouth twisted with hatred, he furiously rasped at the young Comanche, "Stay out of this! Since you're prying into business that isn't any of yours, I'll tell you about this bitch. Her dad's white, and he shacked up with a quadroon and had Amelia here as his git. I gave him a chance to work in my bank, and what does he do but up and take French leave with about five thousand dollars. So Amelia's working it off, she's my housekeeper. That's not slavery, so you mind your own business, or you'll be sorry!" Ivers pushed back his chair and stood up, glowering at Lopasuta.

"Miss McAdams, he can't compel you to pay off your father's debt; nor are you responsible for his actions, legal or illegal. So I'm suggesting that if you're interested, you come along with me now, and let me take you to a household where you'll be gainfully employed, treated with respect, and not subject to any kind of abuse."

"Are you—are you *sure* that would be—that would be lawful?" Amelia quavered, her tear-filled gray-blue eyes widening with wonder.

"I'm quite certain, Miss McAdams. He can't do a thing to prevent your leaving him here and now, if you so choose."

"I'm warning you, Bouchard, stop meddling in my business!" Ivers growled threateningly. "Girl, don't you heed him none, hear me? I tell you what, you just go get me my pork chops and be quick about it, and I won't cowhide you this time."

"No, sir, Mr. Ivers. I have been your slave ever since you forced me into your bed because of what my father did, even though I was a decent girl and didn't want to." Amelia stood up, her shoulders straight, declaring her right to leave. Turning to Lopasuta, she stammered, "I—I will go with you, mister. Just please don't trick me or anything like that."

111

"I'm not tricking you, Miss McAdams. I'd never do a thing like that. And I'll take you at once to the household I mentioned. Or would you prefer to go pack your things?"

"*No!* I don't ever want to go back to Mr. Ivers's house, not ever again!"

"Fine. Oh, miss," as Lopasuta perceived the mulatto waitress coming out of the kitchen with his plate of lamb stew and vegetables, "I can't wait for lunch after all. Perhaps Mr. Ivers here would care to enjoy my meal. And here, allow me to pay you for it." He took out his wallet and put down a greenback. "The rest is for you. Come along, Miss McAdams."

"Now wait a minute—you just wait a minute, Bouchard—" Ivers spluttered, his face so livid that it looked as if he might have a stroke at any instant. "I warned you before and—"

"You don't have to repeat it. And I wouldn't advise you to try anything like forcing Miss McAdams back into your house. The *Advertiser* would be very glad to print a story about slavery after Lincoln, especially if I were to tell the editor all that you've said to this young woman in my hearing. This way, Miss McAdams." Lopasuta took an arm of the trembling octoroon and led her out of the restaurant. As the waitress put down the Comanche lawyer's order on Iver's table, the banker turned and, with a violent curse, swept the dishes to the floor with a great crash as he hammered on the table. "That conniving Injun-nigger son of a bitch," he snarled, "he hasn't heard the last of this! That about settles his hash here in Montgomery!"

Once outside the restaurant, Lopasuta Bouchard hailed a carriage and, taking Amelia McAdams by the arm, soothingly murmured, "You don't have to be afraid of him anymore, Miss McAdams. Trust me. I'm going to take you directly to Windhaven Plantation. It's where my adoptive father, Mr. Luke Bouchard, lives. Only the other night he was telling me that he needed a new cook because poor old Hannah is ailing and doesn't have enough help. You'll be just fine there."

"I—don't know what to say—I can't thank you enough—"

"You don't have to, Miss McAdams. All right, now, driver, we want to go to the red-brick building down near Lowndesboro. And don't shake your head like that, I've got money enough to pay you for your time and effort." With this, Lopasuta extracted his wallet and held up a five-dollar banknote. The surly, squat black driver's face at once brightened, and he nodded, suddenly effusive. "Git right in, suh, you 'n yoah lady. Ah'll be glad to drive you dere!"

A little more than an hour later, the horse and buggy halted in front of the red-brick chateau. Lopasuta handed the driver the promised banknote, then gallantly helped Amelia McAdams step down from the buggy and led her to the door. Reaching out, he banged the knocker three times. Clementine hurried to open the door and, recognizing Lopasuta, smilingly invited, "Come right in, Mr. Lopasuta, suh. Mr. Luke is in his study."

"Thank you very much. Come on in, Amelia. Clemmie, this is Amelia McAdams. She's here to look into the possibility of helping out in the kitchen."

"Hannah sure could use some help, Mr. Lopasuta. Come with me and I'll tell Mr. Luke you're here."

Amelia McAdams held back a moment, her eyes wide with apprehension. "Look, Miss McAdams," Lopasuta urged in his most sympathetic tone, "from what you've already told me on our way here, you could bring suit against Mr. Ivers for enforced bondage, harassment of your person, and a good many other charges that I could make stick in court. Don't worry, he's not about to try to get you back, and he couldn't if he did try. I'm a good enough lawyer to tell you that, in all honesty. Now stop your fretting and come meet my adoptive father. As I told you, he's a warm, understanding man. If Mr. Bouchard can accommodate you—and I feel sure he can—you'll be safe here, you can start your life anew, and there won't be anything to remind you of the past."

"I—I don't know how to thank you enough."

"It's all right. I've met men like Carleton Ivers many times, even when I lived in the stronghold with my *jefe*, Sangrodo. They're bullies, all of them, and once you meet them face to face and show them that they're not quite so strong as they think, they become the cowards they really are. Here we are now."

Luke, who had been writing a letter to Lucien Edmond, put down his quill and rose, graciously inclining his head toward his two visitors. "Lopasuta! And who's this charming young lady you have with you?"

"This is Amelia McAdams, Luke. You remember that night you were telling us that poor old Hannah won't be able to do much more cooking for you? Well, Miss McAdams is in need of a position."

Turning to Amelia, Luke made her a graceful bow. "It's certainly very gracious of you to come see an old man—"

Though she flushed slightly at this gracious courtesy, Amelia boldly declared, "Your adopted son has told me what a kind man you are, and you're certainly not old, at least not to me, Mr. Bouchard. I—he told me that there might be a job for me here working in the kitchen. I'm a very good cook. I—I've had to cook for Mr. Ivers for quite a few years now."

"Carleton Ivers, the head of the Montgomery Central Bank?" Luke curiously demanded.

"Yes, sir."

Choosing his words carefully so as to avoid embarrassing Amelia, Lopasuta briefly described what had happened at Reuben Henry's restaurant. "To make a long story short," he concluded, "Amelia's father used to work for Mr. Ivers and apparently ran off with some money. Since that time, he has forced Miss McAdams to work as his housekeeper, and he has taken advantage of her in other ways as well—"

"I understand," Luke rejoined, with a wave of the hand. "It sounds like a nasty situation, obviously brought about by the selfishness of a contemptible man." He turned then to the attractive octoroon, who had lowered her eyes and clasped her hands behind her back. "Miss McAdams, you're more than welcome here. And there definitely will be a job for you. If you can cook, believe me, we can use you. Now, let me just call my wife, Laure. I'm sure she'll want to take you out to the kitchen and show you what's involved."

"G-God bless you, Mr. Bouchard," Amelia McAdams faintly stammered, and tried to hide her tears.

Carleton Ivers had stalked out of the restaurant in high dudgeon, his face still livid with anger, his lips twisted in fury, and his eyes blazing. He had brushed aside Reuben Henry's attempts to soothe him, pushing the middle-aged black aside and slamming the door of the restaurant. Several blocks east of the restaurant, he halted before an office window on which the sign, "Milo Brutus Henson, Surveyor" was painted in black lettering. He opened the door and brusquely entered.

Milo Brutus Henson was in the back, reading a document that he had dictated the previous day. It had to do with the disposition of a parcel of land not far from the Bouchard property. As he saw Carleton Ivers enter and stride toward him, the surveyor put down the document and stood up, managing a friendly grin by way of greeting. "Mr. Ivers, sir, you're a sight for sore eyes! I haven't seen you in weeks."

"Well, Milo, you're seeing me now. I'm just about ready to explode, too, I can tell you."

"Judging from the color of your face, Mr. Ivers, I'd wager you've just had a spat with someone you'd just as soon see either shipped back to Liberia, or taken out of town and hanged and buried in an unmarked grave," Henson remarked.

"You couldn't have put it better, Milo. And you're right. It's that meddling Injun bastard, Lopasuta Bouchard."

"Well now, come sit down, have a cigar, and let me pour you some fine old Kentucky whiskey."

"I don't mind if I do. I had to go without lunch because that damned Injun-nigger lawyer stuck his nose in where it didn't belong," Ivers angrily avowed, as he flung himself down on a seat facing the surveyor.

"Here's your cigar, and here's a good, stiff drink. I trust you don't mind if I join you." After pouring a quantity of dark amber liquid into two glasses, he settled back in his chair. "Now then, Mr. Ivers, supposing you tell me what happened."

By the time Ivers had finished telling the story, he was nearly purple with rage. "I'd like to fix that smartass lawyer good and proper!" he concluded.

"So you, too, finally have your craw full of Lopasuta Bouchard," Henson sneered. "You're late to the game. There's a couple of us here in Montgomery and a couple down near the Gulf who'd like to get rid of that bastard once and for all."

"All right then, you know where I stand—and don't forget you're in my debt. Not so long ago, I advanced you a couple of thousand dollars out of my bank so that you could get yourself a nice chunk of land and sell it on a speculative basis to suckers who thought maybe the Alabama and Chattanooga Railroad would come to life again."

"I remember that, no need of your reminding me," Henson gruffly declared.

"Just wanted to make sure," Ivers angrily snapped. "I'm not asking for you to pay that back, but if you'll help me get that damned interfering lawyer out of town once and for all, I might even make it worth your while beyond canceling the loan. I happen to know that you've got the chance of a snowball in hell to recoup on that investment for the Alabama and Chattanooga, no matter what our dear new President Hayes is promising."

"I suspect you're right," Henson grudgingly admitted. "Now look, you and I, we've made money in the past; you at the bank, and me doing surveying work with bills that were put through your bank and paid, and hardly a mite of real sweat-working-up work done for it. I won't blab on you, you don't blab on me, Mr. Ivers. And I'll let you in on a little secret. Fact is, for some time, a few of us have been thinking about settling this Lopasuta's hash for good."

"I'm all for that!" Ivers grumbled. "But if you've other fellows in on this scheme, why haven't you done something before this?"

"Patience, Mr. Ivers, patience. You, as a banker, should know that virtue above all others," the surveyor taunted him. "Those of us in on this little deal have bigger fish to fry than just Mr. Lopasuta Bouchard."

"What are you getting at, Milo?"

"All right, I'll put it to you so even a first-grader would understand. Lopasuta Bouchard took over when old Jedidiah Danforth kicked the bucket, including all the Bouchard legal affairs."

"You're not telling me anything new, Milo."

"Just wait a bit, I'm coming to the good part. I've got a friend, female gender—no need to mention names now—

116

but she struck up a friendship with this nice young nurse who came to work with Dr. Abel Kennery. And it seems that Mr. Luke Bouchard, who adopted this damned Injun and had old Danforth school him in the law, hasn't been feeling up to snuff lately. He might just kick the bucket any day—you never know. Now if that were to happen and Mr. Lopasuta Bouchard were to disappear, that big chunk of rich land they call Windhaven Plantation might just be foundering. Nobody to run the legal affairs, and the purty widow so beside herself with grief that she wouldn't have a nose for business. Are you beginning to get the picture?"

"Yes, I think I am," Ivers slowly said, then grinned evilly. "And your friends are going to hover around like vultures and maybe make a grab for that acreage."

"Stranger things than that have been known to happen when folks die. Mr. Ivers, I'm going to level with you. After all, you have put some good hard cash my way when I needed it. I've got a good friend, known him for some years, who moved to New Orleans when the Union took over. He's making it big in the Queen City now, has his own mortgage company and a few fancy houses on the side, catering to wealthy Creoles and rich visitors who come to have some fun and throw away their greenbacks."

"Very interesting," Ivers muttered, eyeing the surveyor with ill-concealed anticipation.

"This friend of mine has got connections so that things happen the way all of us want. And we're thinking that if we get Mr. Lopasuta Bouchard out of Montgomery, there are plenty of lawyers in this town who would give a loud cheer. Who knows? Some of them might even go so far as to pay us our costs in getting rid of him."

At this, Ivers burst into a malicious chuckle, which was shared by Henson. Then the banker drawled, "I'm all for it. And I'll just say this, Milo, if you've got a scheme that will really work and pay that bastard back for taking my octoroon bitch away from me, I'll even stand a good share of the expense myself."

# Eleven

Lopasuta Bouchard had asked Dr. Abel Kennery to visit Geraldine, since his wife believed that she was close to term with their first child. The day after the Comanche lawyer brought Amelia McAdams to Windhaven Plantation, Dr. Kennery concluded his afternoon appointments and then rode his bay gelding over to Lopasuta's house to give the prospective mother a thorough examination.

"You're doing just fine, Mrs. Bouchard," he reassured Geraldine. "From the look of things, I'd say you could expect your baby around the second or third week of June, or thereabouts." Then he gave her a boyish grin, which made him look even younger and completely won her confidence. "Of course, I *was* a bit off in my judgment of Laure Bouchard's due time—I have to admit that their little son sort of snuck up on me—but, judging from your estimate of when the baby was conceived, I'd say that my prediction is reasonably accurate. That doesn't mean that it couldn't be born a few days later or even earlier—errors can occur, as in the case of little John Bouchard. So don't be upset by a slight miscalculation."

"I won't be, Dr. Kennery. And it was awfully nice of you to come to see me."

"It was your husband's doing. He's a most concerned and devoted man, and a very intelligent and gifted one. And I'd say that he's exceptionally fortunate in having so fine a wife."

"Now you're making me blush, an old married woman several weeks away from her first-born," Geraldine giggled, and then held out her hand to the handsome doctor. "Do you think I should call a midwife in to stay by me for the next few weeks?"

"That would be a wise precaution. I've had time, now that I've been here a while, to talk to some of the midwives here in Montgomery. I can recommend the same woman who took care of Mrs. Haskins. She did a commendable job, and she believes in modern hygiene. You see, we learned back east that the mortality among infants comes mainly from lack of cleanliness—yes, even in hospitals. But this woman is very experienced and very knowledgeable. If you'd like, I'll have her stop by in a day or two."

"Thank you, Dr. Kennery. I'd be much obliged to you. I think Lopasuta, with his Comanche background, would think more of me if I had my baby—our baby—" she prettily corrected herself with another blush, "born here in our house."

"Though there's much to be said for a good, modern hospital, you'll get no real argument from me if you prefer to have the baby at home, Mrs. Bouchard," he reassured her. "I'll have Mrs. Norton come to see you tomorrow."

He took his leave and rode slowly back toward his house on the outskirts of Montgomery. He had acquired the home from old Dr. Medbury, who, at the time of selling his practice to Dr. Kennery, had offered him his own house at a reasonable price. Spacious enough for a whole family, it was solid, cheerful, and sturdily built. Moreover, it had a stable for Dr. Kennery's bay, and even a tiny attic with eaves and gables. This last feature delighted and made him quite nostalgic about the old houses in Boston and Salem where he had grown up. He found himself thinking, as he rode back to this old, comfortable house, that now that he had a practice and some property in the South, he might as well marry and settle down for good. The image of his lovely nurse sprang to mind along with Laure Bouchard's teasing comments, and he smiled wryly to himself.

Mrs. Emily Norton called on Geraldine Bouchard late the very next afternoon, and the two women got along famously. Geraldine insisted that the midwife remain long enough for Lopasuta to meet her. When Lopasuta came home and was introduced to Mrs. Norton, he enthusiasti-

119

cally agreed with his wife that she would be the ideal choice to look after Geraldine until their child was born. Financial arrangements were swiftly and compatibly agreed upon, and Emily Norton took her leave, assuring Lopasuta with a smile, "It's going to be a pleasure to work for you. She's such a sweet, lively, spirited girl, and I've heard a great deal about you, just from reading the papers. I almost hate to charge such a fine couple."

After seeing the midwife to the door, Lopasuta turned to Geraldine, took her gently into his arms and kissed her, and said, "You see, honey, we're making headway. There's a woman who's lived here all her life, and yet she feels as if we belong and are good people. I told you that one day this stupid prejudice would vanish. All you have to do in life, as my mother and my *jefe* Sangrodo constantly taught me, is to return good, even for evil—eventually, the Great Spirit will balance the scales in your favor. And I believe that sincerely with all my heart and soul."


Entering his office the next afternoon, Lopasuta found a letter addressed to him, postmarked New Orleans. He frowned as he opened it, thinking that it might be a communication from Jason Barntry of the Brunton & Barntry Bank. For the past eight weeks, he realized, he had received no statement of profits and losses on Bouchard investments, and he was reminded that he had meant to get off a letter to the bank on the subject.

But when he opened it, he discovered that the letter was not from Barntry, but rather from someone whose name was totally unknown to him. He read it with absorbing interest:

Dear Mr. Bouchard:
   You have been recommended to me by some of my friends in Montgomery as the most able attorney in that city. Therefore, I am taking the liberty of writing to you to acquaint you with a legal problem which perhaps you might be interested in solving for me—at a sizable retainer.
   I should tell you that I am a cotton factor, who is being sued for damages by a disgruntled plantation owner in Louisiana and Alabama. His claim, based on a misunderstanding that occurred nearly a decade ago,

120

pertains to contracts drawn up in Alabama as well as Louisiana. And because my adversary is attempting to win damages in both states, I believe that you might legitimately advise me in the matter, even though I realize that you may not have been admitted to the bar in the state of Louisiana.

Since I have no attorney handling my affairs at present—for reasons I shall acquaint you with, if you will be good enough to spare me some time—I should like at least to meet you and discuss the facts of this case, as I believe them to be. It would not take you more than a day to meet with me and to hear my story. I should be willing to pay you a retainer of five hundred dollars, in addition to your traveling expenses.

If you agree to these terms, kindly send a telegram to me at your earliest convenience, stating your expected time of arrival in New Orleans. As the matter in question is of the utmost urgency, I must request that you schedule your visit within the next ten days. Of course if—after hearing the details of the case—you decide you can advise me in the matter, and also represent me in the case to go before the Alabama court, then we can discuss any additional financial arrangements you may require.

> Yours respectfully,
> William Brickley

Lopasuta Bouchard sat staring at this letter for nearly a quarter of an hour, his forehead wrinkled, deep in thought. His immediate reaction was to accept this offer. Now that he was married, now that his first child was about to be born, the urge to be totally independent, free from any material aid from his revered adoptive father, made Brickley's offer overwhelmingly tempting. At the same time, he did not want to leave Montgomery during the next few weeks, when it was certain that Geraldine would give birth; indeed, he feared his departure would be tantamount to negligence.

He decided finally to share this letter with Geraldine, to learn her reaction. He had full confidence in Mrs. Emily Norton's expertise, and yet he wanted Geraldine to know he stood beside her in her time of trial. To be sure, the fee cited was more than what he could earn in at least six months; many of his clients were former Southern slaves who paid him either a few paltry dollars, or else gave him produce, chickens—even, on one occasion, a suckling pig—in place of a legal fee. Then, too, there were things he wanted to buy for Geraldine, frivolous gifts to express his adoration and his gratitude.

So, that evening, when he returned home to find that the midwife was already occupying the small room that was designated for their child when it was born, he exhaled a sigh of relief. He did not want to upset Geraldine at so critical a time, but the reassuring presence of the friendly midwife eased the stress and tension that Brickley's letter had evoked.

To his delight, Mrs. Norton had prepared supper, and as she served the meal, she carried on a friendly, rambling conversation that made Geraldine and Lopasuta feel as if they had known her for a very long time. Although most of his life had been spent as a stoic Comanche youth, Lopasuta secretly savored the luxury of being waited on. And Geraldine, her eyes moist with affection for him, reached out to squeeze his hand when Mrs. Norton served the entree and sweetly commented that it delighted her to see two young people so very much in love.

While Mrs. Norton was washing the dishes in the kitchen, Lopasuta broached the subject of the unexpected letter. Looking ardently at his smiling wife, he began, "Geraldine, I've had an offer today which could earn me more money than I'd make in six months here in Montgomery. And because you're going to have our baby, because I want you to have everything you need and more— presents and flowers and jewelry—I want to ask your opinion."

"You're very sweet, my darling. Tell me about this offer, then." She put out both her hands and squeezed his.

Lopasuta felt a tug at his heart, as he returned her affectionate look. "I got a letter at my office today from a man in New Orleans," he explained. "He's having some trouble with a plantation owner who used to be a friend some years back. There was some sort of misunderstanding—exactly what, I don't know yet—and now the plantation owner is suing the writer of this letter. He's offered me five hundred dollars and expenses to come down to New Orleans to talk this over. He says that, even if I can't practice law there—and I can't, of course—I can be of help to him. You know very well how I feel—I hate to leave you, but this man is offering so much money that it would make our lives a lot easier."

"Honey, if you feel you should go, by all means, don't hesitate. Besides, you've been working so hard lately that you deserve a little rest. Going to New Orleans would be a kind of vacation, wouldn't it?"

"I suppose so—but I only wish the offer had come at a better time—"

"Shhh, not another word. Mrs. Norton and I will do just fine."

"You're sure now? You see, there's another reason for me to go to New Orleans. I'd been hoping by now to have another letter from Jason Barntry—whose bank has always handled Luke Bouchard's investments. As Luke's lawyer, I'm supposed to receive regular reports on his holdings. If I go down to see this Brickley fellow, I could also pay a visit to Jason Barntry and get Luke all the facts he needs to manage the estate."

"Then I'd say you should definitely go, sweetheart, and if you leave right away, you may very well get back before our baby is born."

"You're sure it will be all right, my darling?" Lopasuta softly asked, and again he clasped her hands warmly in his own as he gazed tenderly at her.

"My gracious, I'm not the only woman who's ever had a baby! Besides," she laughed, "you really couldn't do a thing to help—and I still say that you'll probably be back before it even happens, so there's no reason for you to worry about it. The only thing I ask is that you send me word—a telegram—to let me know what you are doing and how long you'll be gone."

"You have my solemn promise on that, my love. Oh, Geraldine, I can't tell you how much I love you—"

"Now you hush, or you'll start me crying, and that won't be good for our child at all," Geraldine giggled, but there was a hint of moisture in her eyes, as she squeezed his hands back to tell him that she was wholeheartedly behind his decision.

The next day, after taking leave of Geraldine and again receiving her assurance that she would feel perfectly secure with Mrs. Norton in his absence (and then taking the midwife aside and urging her to call for Dr. Kennery if

123

any unforeseen complications should arise), Lopasuta sent a telegram to Mr. Brickley, informing him of his scheduled arrival in New Orleans, and then boarded the *Belle of the River*, a new, lavishly appointed steamboat that made the trip between Montgomery and Mobile twice a week.

Soon after boarding, Lopasuta encountered the captain, a loquacious, bearded man in his fifties who offered to give the young lawyer a tour of the vessel. As they made their rounds, Lopasuta saw that the ship had been designed to provide every comfort for river travel. In the luxurious men's bar—where a French Creole bartender served up anything from Maryland whiskey to mint juleps and *sangria*—the captain proudly pointed out the tables, which were round, with smooth stone tops, hand-wrought by a gifted New Orleans artisan, and covered by the finest thick velvet. The waitresses were dressed like French can-can girls, with sheer black net hose, calf-high laced black leather boots with narrow high heels, and a body corset from upper thighs to bosom, deeply cut to reveal the enticing cleft of powdered, satiny breasts. Their only other garments were arm-length red calfskin gloves, and the vivid exposure of bare shoulders and upper back was, as the captain roguishly explained, much to Lopasuta's amusement, a source of great profit for the *Belle of the River*. "It motivates ardent gentlemen to buy more than their normal share of drinks," the captain explained, "if only to have these flirtatious young beauties near them." In almost the same breath, he primly added, "You understand, sir, we permit no licentiousness aboard. Doubtless, if some of our charming girls wish to arrange meetings with patrons who have captured their fancy, that is entirely up to them—but I assure you, to the best of my knowledge, it is done for love."

Lopasuta went directly to his cabin after exchanging a few more pleasantries with the talkative captain, stretched himself out on the comfortable bunk bed, and drowsed until it was time for supper. The meal was served in a dining room even more elegant than the bar; here there were black waiters in resplendent uniforms, even wigs, suggesting a European court motif, and the viands served were exquisitely prepared.

After an early stroll around the deck, enjoying the

gentle cool breezes and the picturesque panorama along the shores touched by the silver rays of the full moon, Lopasuta went to bed and slept until late the next morning.

About an hour after supper the second day of the voyage, the *Belle of the River* docked at the wharf in Mobile, and Lopasuta Bouchard, carrying his single valise, disembarked, to stay the night at a comfortable little inn. Following breakfast the next morning, he boarded the packet for New Orleans.

Arriving in the Queen City about eight-thirty that evening, Lopasuta hired a carriage to take him to the same hotel where he and Geraldine had spent their honeymoon. He planned to see Jason Barntry first the next morning to ask for the summary of the Bouchard accounts, and then to visit his potential new client, William Brickley.

After an early breakfast of *café au lait* and *croissants*, the tall Comanche lawyer strolled from his hotel to the imposing building of the Brunton & Barntry Bank. Jason Barntry, white-haired and frail but still spruce, recognized him immediately and left his office to come forward to greet him. "What a pleasant surprise, Mr. Bouchard! You know, I owe you an apology—and I'm going to forestall your censure of me right off. When you sent me a copy of Luke Bouchard's will, you reminded me that I owed you another report on the Bouchard holdings. It was finished late last night, and only my desire to add a few last-minute listings held me back from dispatching it at once to Windhaven Plantation."

"That's quite all right, Mr. Barntry," Lopasuta pleasantly replied, as he shook hands with the elderly manager and accompanied the latter back to his office. "I was going to write you about it, but as it chanced, I had a letter from a Mr. William Brickley asking me to see him about a legal problem—apparently he feels I can be of help."

"Brickley?" Jason frowned, then nodded, as if to himself. "Oh, yes, now I remember. It's well known that he's a wealthy man, with a good many investments. He owns several houses of pleasure—but that shouldn't necessarily count against him—and I've heard that he represents several large cotton plantations in the matter of expediting sales and finding new markets for their crops. He also has other landholdings. Brickley now has an account with us—I can't say anything more specific, you understand, but you can safely infer that he's one of our larger depositors."

"Do you know anything about him personally?" Lopasuta asked.

"Very little, I'm afraid," Jason ruefully smiled. "At least, there's nothing bad to say: he's never figured in any kind of scandal that has reached the pages of our daily journal. I suppose you might say that this alone indicates him to be a man of at least some business acumen and propriety. But I'm afraid that's all I can tell you about him."

"I'm grateful for that, Mr. Barntry. Well now, I'm going to see him. Perhaps afterwards, if you are not too busy, I might have the pleasure of taking you to lunch or dinner at Antoine's?"

"Oh, dear. I would like nothing better, but unfortunately quite a few of my best investors have requested meetings with me during the coming week; I imagine they want to get their financial affairs in order before going upriver for the summer. In short, with great reluctance, I must refuse your gracious offer."

"Another time, then. If I decide to take on Mr. Brickley's case, I may well be returning to New Orleans before long. In any event, it's been a pleasure seeing you again, Mr. Barntry."

"And you, Mr. Bouchard," Jason Barntry graciously countered.

The two men shook hands warmly and Lopasuta, inclining his head respectfully to the older man, took his leave.

The day was pleasant, not yet oppressively humid, so Lopasuta Bouchard decided to walk from the bank to the Rampart Street address indicated in William Brickley's letter.

He came at last to a four-story building with cast-iron window grilles. The galleries curved at the corners of the building, and the colors of the exterior were the warm, gentle red of brick, black of iron, cream-white of fine woodwork, and soft green of the shutters. The front balconies extended over the entire width of the building, which was set back twenty feet from the sidewalk and enclosed by a wrought-iron fence.

126

As his eyes scanned the building, Lopasuta saw the name of the establishment delicately inscribed in the iron-work of a narrow gate that indicated the entrance. To his amusement, the sign read, "La Musée des Délices"—The Museum of Delights. Evidently his new client's headquarters were located in one of New Orleans's most elegant bordellos. He drew down the latch, opened the gate, and approached the teakwood door, to which was fastened a knocker of gleaming polished brass in the form of a naked nymph who beckoned with one hand while with the other she modestly covered her loins.

Halting a moment, he chuckled to himself, then lifted the knocker and rapped loudly three times. After a moment, the door was opened by a liveried manservant in red waistcoat adorned with gold braid, black breeches, and boots, a uniform that somewhat resembled that of the Queen City Zouaves at the outset of the Civil War. The man himself was bald except for a semicircle of graying hair; he had a full mouth and closely set dark-brown eyes.

"It is early for the entertainment of this house, m'sieu," the servant informed Lopasuta in a gently apologetic tone, almost effeminate in pitch.

"I have an appointment with Mr. William Brickley. My name is Lopasuta Bouchard. I should be grateful if you would announce me," the young lawyer affably explained.

"Oh yes, he is expecting you, Mr. Bouchard, sir. If you will come this way, you can be at your ease in one of our antechambers, while I fetch Mr. Brickley. This way, if you please, sir."

With impeccable, if somewhat obsequious manners, the liveried servant escorted Lopasuta down a red velvet-carpeted hallway and, opening the third door to the right, ushered him in with a florid bow. "I shall order some refreshments for you, Mr. Bouchard."

"I've breakfasted, thank you."

"A drink, then? Mr. Brickley is particularly proud of the libations here, sir. May I suggest a light rum, with cinnamon and cream—you'll find it unusual, and quite refreshing on a hot morning like this."

"As you like," Lopasuta said with an acquiescent nod.

"I'll bring it presently, Mr. Bouchard, just as soon as I've informed Mr. Brickley of your arrival." The servant executed his deferential bow again, and left the antechamber, closing the door behind him. Lopasuta looked around, finding himself in a luxurious room furnished with chaise longue, several settees, wicker-backed chairs with upholstered footstools, as well as a magnificent cherrywood sideboard on which reposed several decanters of wines and stronger spirits. The shutters were drawn to prevent the bright morning sun from filtering inside, so that the room had a warm, shadowy patina of opulence. Lopasuta seated himself on one of the settees and waited.

A moment later, there was a discreet knock at the door, and then a pause before the same servant entered with an exquisite silver tray on which was posed a handmade Venetian goblet partially filled with an amber liquid on top of which was a rich surface of thick clotted cream flecked with brown specks of cinnamon. "Here you are, Mr. Bouchard. You'll find it most palatable, I'm sure. Mr. Brickley wishes me to tell you that he'll be down to see you in about ten minutes, if that's satisfactory."

"Of course. And please thank him for his hospitality."

"Thank you, sir." The man again bowed and left the room, closing the door behind him.

Lopasuta lifted the goblet, admiring its expert craftsmanship. He took a tentative sip, found the drink pleasant indeed and, feeling somewhat thirsty because of the closeness of the room, drank about half of its contents before setting the goblet down on the silver tray.

How pleasant it was to relax here, he thought, to see a kind of microcosm of the gentle past when, for the affluent, life was placid and luxurious, when social unrest and poverty did not intrude upon their sybaritic lives. With bitter humor he imagined what Sangrodo would have thought of this sinful luxury, so in contrast to the primitive life of his stronghold, where strength and cunning were the Comanche's only tools in the daily struggle for survival.

He took another sip, set the goblet back down on the tray, and leaned back against the thickly upholstered settee, closing his eyes to await the arrival of William Brickley. He thought of Geraldine with a vague anxiety for her well-being, for the safe and untroubled delivery of their first child. And he smiled, thinking how much he loved her and how courageous she was.

He felt drowsy, and he reached up to loosen the cravat he had grown accustomed to wearing in the Montgomery courtrooms. He had often whimsically remarked to Geraldine that of the few Comanches who had ever worn white-eyes clothings, he was assuredly the most bedecked like a popinjay. He could almost see her smile and hear her saucy laughter.

He drew a long breath, and then his head began to nod. He tried to blink his eyes, but suddenly his eyelids seemed held down by weights. With one hand, he reached for his loosened cravat and tugged it off. It dropped unnoticed to the floor as he began to unbutton his shirt. The room seemed oppressively hot; he would give a great deal to be back in the stronghold, his skin naked to the gentle winds from the Rio Grande. The room was closing in around him; he tried to open his eyes again and could not. All at once he slumped to one side on the settee and lay sprawled there.

A few minutes later the door slowly opened, and the liveried servant tiptoed toward the unconscious lawyer. Staring down at him, he chuckled softly, then he hurried out of the room.

Shortly thereafter, two burly stevedores entered the room and roughly lifted Lopasuta's unconscious body between them, lugging him out of the house. In the courtyard a carriage was waiting with a black coachman.

"You know where we're going, Rastus," the older of the two stevedores barked at the coachman.

"Sho' 'nuff, I knows," the coachman bobbed his head. With a crack of his whip over the two horses, he started the carriage down a cobbled alley into the street and headed for the waterfront.

## Twelve

There was a roaring in his ears, and he felt as if he were disembodied, floating in space, listlessly without direction or purpose. He tried to open his eyes, but could not. Then, as consciousness gradually returned to him, Lopasuta Bouchard moved a hand to touch his throbbing forehead. It seemed to him that his skull was entirely permeated with pain, and when at last his groping fingers brushed his forehead, he felt the damp of his own sweat.

Now that he was becoming conscious of his surroundings, and could separate himself from the terrifying floating sensation, he groped with his other hand. He felt the hard outlines of a bunk, narrow and constricted, not much more than a hard wooden board, which horizontally supported his body. He lay at full length—no, his right leg had slipped off and the heel of his shoe bore down upon the floor. He made an effort to sit up, but he could not. He could feel the sweat redoubled on his forehead, and sticking in his armpits. He now became aware of his parched and aching throat. He wanted water; he felt feverish from the lack of it. His very clothes suddenly became oppressive.

As consciousness returned, his weakened body suddenly discerned that he was rocking, moving sideways—sometimes jerkily, sometimes regularly—from one side to the other. He could not explain it. Again he tried to sit up and again he failed.

Like a man who has been dazed by shell shock, Lopasuta experimentally made out the outline of his own face with his left palm. It was instinctive, this gesture, to reassure himself that he still lived, that he was still whole and intact. Against the sensations that assailed him, he needed this desperately. He was not dead, and yet he was still unable to open his eyes to find out where he was, or what had happened to him, and why.

He lay there a few moments, trying to summon back his strength, and then gingerly tried to slide his left leg down to the floor. At last, he managed it, but the effort cost him a ferocious throbbing in his head, and he groaned aloud and this time clapped both hands to his forehead.

Now that both his shod feet were on the floor, the sensation of rocking and rolling became more insistent than ever. As he lay there, both hands now clasped against his forehead in a futile effort to relieve the savage pain, he tried to remember what had last happened to him, where he had been. And then it came back to him. He had taken the packet from Mobile to New Orleans, seen Jason Barntry at the bank, and then walked to the address on Rampart Street that William Brickley had given him in the letter sent to Montgomery.

He remembered now the obsequious, liveried servant who had tendered him a goblet of—what had it been? Oh yes, now he could remember: a most unusual drink, comprised of rum, cinnamon and clotted cream. And after that—nothing.

He uttered a hoarse cry at the realization that he had been drugged. There could be no other explanation. Was he still in the salon where the manservant had left him? No, that would not explain the movement against his heels.

His hands dropped from his clammy forehead and he pressed them down against the hard surface of the bunk on which he lay. Agonizingly slowly, Lopasuta Bouchard hoisted himself to a sitting position, and he felt as if his skull would split apart at any instant from the pain. There were flashes of light and then darkness behind his eyeballs, and once again he clapped both hands to his head, trying to ease the sharp, piercing edge of his agony. He tried to blink his eyes and this time he succeeded. It was dark, yet there was a vague glimmer of light, a kind of grudgingly faint glow. He compelled his eyelids to open, and he saw that the room in which he found himself was narrow and confined. And then as he took in his surroundings, he felt himself slung forward by a sudden lurching movement.

At last, he dropped his hands into his lap, straightening slightly, and even that cost him another savage spasm of blinding pain. Tilting back his head and groaning, blinking his eyelids repeatedly, Lopasuta at last managed to clear the swirling black mists that had blinded him, and saw the dull, hazy outlines of an incredibly small room. He faced a narrow door, of thick, solid, dark wood. There was a little tabouret to the right of him, about four feet away. On it was a tray and an earthernware bowl that contained some greasy liquid. The ceiling was low—indeed he doubted he could even stand up fully—and he had a feeling of being in a narrow prison cell.

Very carefully, he turned his head to the left, and discovered the source of the vague filtering pale light: a round glass with a shining brass circle framing it. He shifted his legs up and then, kneeling up on the bunk, forced himself to stare through the glass. He uttered a startled ejaculation of complete incredulity and horror—for what he saw were the billowing waves of a vast expanse of water. And the water was near this round glass; even as he stared, a whitecap hurtled against the glass and spattered it violently.

Now he could comprehend the curious rocking movement under him; he was on a ship. But *why*, in the name of the Great Spirit?

The drink—drugged—yes, to be sure. At Brickley's orders? But why? What possible motive could this unknown client have had to drug him and put him aboard this ship bound for an unknown destination? It was beyond his powers of reason and logic.

He put his left palm down on the edge of the bunk, feeling a meager, thin blanket of wool. Then slowly he placed the other palm at his right side, gripping the wood for support. Lopasuta drew a long, shuddering breath and forced himself to rise. As he did so, his head bumped against the low ceiling, and he uttered a cry of pain: all at once, the piercing, flashing pangs of agony renewed and deepened.

He bent his head, hunching his shoulders, learning the cruel dimensions of his prison. He staggered as the floor beneath him rocked and heaved, but he managed to lurch toward the door. Huddling against it, his body weak, his head throbbing, he beat upon the door with his fists. "Let me out! Let me out—does anyone hear me—let me out!"

A moment later, he heard the click of a bolt being drawn, and even as he recoiled, the door was forcibly shoved back, nearly pinning him against the side wall of the cabin. A squat, stocky man with a grizzled, spare beard, bleak, closely set blue eyes, and jutting jaw, confronted him. "What the devil do you want, bucko?"

"I want to know where I am—what's happened—I want—I want to see your captain—" Lopasuta hoarsely whispered.

"Stow it, my fine bucko," the man sniggered. He wore a seaman's uniform with a round matelot cap. "Cap'n Jenkins ain't seein' no one now, not hardly. We got a sou'wester tryin' to rip away our topgallants. Reckon, though, we'll see a lot worse, when we get around the Horn."

"The H-Horn?" Lopasuta uncomprehendingly echoed.

"Stow me if yer not a landlubber for fair, bucko," the seaman brutally laughed. "Cape Horn, 'round the tip of South America. We're bound for 'Frisco—might have to hold up in Rio a spell until winter down there breaks up and until it's fit fer navigation."

"But, my God, I—I have to get back—my wife's going to have a baby—I've got no reason to go to San Francisco!" Lopasuta desperately tried to explain, pressing his hands against the wall, as the ship gave another violent lurch. "I beg of you, in the name of decency, take me to the captain. There's been some kind of mistake—"

"No mistake, bucko. Orders. You're down here, and you'll stay till we reach 'Frisco."

"By whose orders—at least tell me that!" Lopasuta pleaded.

"Can't say. Cap'n says we got strict orders to keep you safe 'n sound, mister, till we reach 'Frisco. So you'll be obligin' me, if you'll be a good bucko and go lie down till this storm's over. Later, I'll bring you some stew and hardtack."

"No—I demand to see your captain—let me go—" He struggled forward, and the seaman, with a muttered oath, drew a belaying pin from behind his back and savagely

133

struck the tall Comanche on the side of his head. Lopasuta Bouchard dropped like a log.

"Some folks jist don't understand plain English, I reckon," the seaman grumbled, as he stopped and dragged Lopasuta's inert body back to the bunk and, grunting with the effort, lifted the young lawyer back onto it. Going out of the cabin, he bolted the door behind him.

# Thirteen

It was the afternoon of June 9, 1877, an afternoon with a cloudless blue sky almost too dazzling for the eye to endure. There was little breeze, and the humidity from the nearby river was fortunately less oppressive than usual during the beginning of an Alabama summer.

Today the rally for Dalbert Sattersfield was being held, a day before the scheduled election for mayor of Lowndesboro to replace the late Daniel Fornage. Sattersfield's opponent had conducted his own rally two days before, with only about eighty persons attending. But for the citizens of this pleasant little town, the rally this afternoon was no ordinary event, since the governor himself was slated to speak on behalf of the one-armed storekeeper.

There had been a second letter from Governor Houston, this directed to Sattersfield himself, and not to the irrepressible Mitzi. In this letter, Governor Houston had declared that he was eager to come to Lowndesboro, as the Democratic leader of the state, to make this public attempt to ally the Republican faction with the Democrats. As he wrote, "Now that the Civil War has been over for more than a decade, and the evils of Reconstruction at last begin to recede from the tortured South, my own personal feeling is that all the sons of Alabama must be reconciled with one another, if the state is to grow and there is to be equal opportunity for every citizen, whether high- or low-born."

Luke Bouchard's and Andy Haskins's workers had spent two days erecting a sturdy speakers' platform with a side

135

flight of wooden steps, and had decorated it with bunting and pennants. Behind the platform, from a temporary flagpole, the flag of the United States hung limp in the still air. On a lower pole to one side was the state flag of Alabama. The men had also constructed a speaker's lectern, and brought a mahogany table down from the red-brick chateau in a long travoislike cart drawn by two horses. Straight-backed wooden chairs with upholstered seats had also been transported. The table was placed on the right side of the platform, near the American flag, with the chairs aligned behind it.

Although the rally was not scheduled to begin until two o'clock, already at least sixty farmers, workers, and elderly residents of the little town had gathered, gossiping, exchanging speculations not only on this election, but also on the future course of the nation under its newly elected (dubiously elected, in the opinion of many) President, Rutherford B. Hayes.

On a fringe of the crowd and to the left, there was a wooden stand where free refreshments were being served. Luke Bouchard had suggested that those who attended the rally would be hungry and thirsty and that such hospitality would be sure to make a good impression on the prospective voters the following morning.

Accordingly, for the past several days, Amelia McAdams, happy in her new status as cook to Windhaven Plantation (for Hannah had by now gratefully retired, leaving Amelia in charge) had prepared fried chicken with the most delicate batter, yams, hominy grits, and sandwiches of chicken and pork and beef; there were also jugs of cider, lemonade, and cold tea. All of this would be dispensed with the compliments of Dalbert Sattersfield.

The governor and his personal aide had spent the night in Montgomery's best hotel. Early this morning, the aide had gone out to the chateau to confer with Luke, Andy, and Dalbert on the procedure for that afternoon. Luke would begin with just a very few opening remarks, their sole purpose being to introduce Governor Houston, who would then present his address. The aide had showed the three men an advance handwritten copy of the speech that would be made; it contained a flattering reference to Dalbert Sattersfield's contribution to Lowndesboro and to the country in general, dwelt on his exemplary and courageous

136

record as a war veteran, and his integrity as a family man. Dalbert flushed hotly when he read this passage, and Andy Haskins clapped him on the back and chuckled, "You're blushing like a schoolboy, Dalbert. Which only goes to show how downright decent you are. An experienced politician would just smirk like a cat that had lapped up some cream and think it was his due. You're going to win hands down, by what we could call a landslide."

"I quite agree," Luke smilingly assented. "Now, Andy, after the governor delivers his address, you'll be next to speak. And then I'll get up again and introduce the man of the hour, Lowndesboro's next mayor, the Honorable Dalbert Sattersfield."

"Oh, my," the one-armed storekeeper sighed, "I never thought I'd come to see this day. And I know whom I've got to thank for it—that rather impertinent little wife of mine."

"Now, now, Dalbert," Luke banteringly countered, "you know very well you're delighted that Mitzi took her courage in her hands and wrote to the governor. And I'm sure Mr. Talbot here"—Luke turned now to the governor's aide—"will confirm that Governor Houston is very happy to be here."

"He is indeed, Mr. Bouchard," the aide cordially replied, "and I myself am completely satisfied with all the arrangements that you and Mr. Sattersfield have made for this afternoon's rally."

"Thank you. Now then, Mr. Talbot, will you convey the thanks of all of us to the governor and tell him that his speech is magnificent. It will certainly make friends for the Democrats here, and maybe even convince some of the die-hard Republicans that there are Democrats who don't believe in unleashing the Ku Klux Klan on them simply because they differ politically."

"I certainly shall, Mr. Bouchard. I know the governor will be pleased to hear your assessment—he's hoping to accomplish some kind of reconciliation. Well then, gentlemen, I'll bid you farewell until we meet again this afternoon."

The sun had become more intense now, at a quarter of two this summery June afternoon. The crowd, which had grown to over one hundred fifty people, among whom

137

were a scattering of black freedmen, was in a pleasant mood. The refreshments and the drinks had been well received, and there had been loud voices of praise for Dalbert Sattersfield's generosity. Luke overheard some of their comments and leaned over to Andy, seated next to him, to whisper, "It's a very good sign. They're not restless. And your idea, Andy, of having these three old Confederate musicians play the North's 'Battle Hymn of the Republic' as well as 'Dixie' and then to wind up with 'The Star-Spangled Banner' was a stroke of pure genius. It'll get them in a good, mellow listening mood."

"Thanks very much, Luke," Andy drawled with a modest grin. "I'll tell you something—I think this little mayoral rally is going to be so special that I wouldn't be surprised if the *Advertiser* has a reporter down here to witness it. I like this business of Governor Houston's speaking of healing those old wounds and offering peace to everybody—no matter which party they belong to—in the state."

"I'll agree with you there, Andy," Luke responded, "and I'll tell you something: even though I'm a Republican by choice and temperament—and that goes back to the days of old Abe Lincoln—I can still recognize a good man regardless of what party he's affiliated with."

"Amen to that," Andy soberly replied. Then he stiffened and whispered, "Here comes the governor now. We'd best be all ready for him. He's a fine figure of a man—I'll surely give him that."

As Governor Houston and his aide ascended the steps to the platform, the three musicians—seated just below the platform—played the "March of the Priests" from Mendelssohn's *Athalie*, which happened to be the governor's favorite musical composition. The state's chief executive smiled down at the musicians and saluted them in tribute. Before seating himself at the speakers' table, the governor walked over to shake hands with Luke, Andy, and Dalbert, who now stood erectly at attention.

The smattering of applause while the speakers took their seats was followed by a pleasant buzz of conversation as the audience waited for the opening of the formalities. The speaker's lectern had been placed in the very center of the platform, and Luke now rose to his feet and moved toward it. Resting his hands on the lectern and clearing his

138

throat, he declared in a firm voice, "On behalf of our good friend Dalbert Sattersfield, candidate for the office of mayor of Lowndesboro, I wish to welcome all of you. We'll try not to speechify too long"—at this there was a ripple of laughter from the audience—"but if you'll remember only one thing when we're finished—that Dalbert Sattersfield has been an industrious, honest, hard-working family man who can't be corrupted—you'll have found out just what we hoped you would."

Again there was a smattering of applause, and a few sporadic shouts of "Hear, hear."

"We are privileged this afternoon, my friends," Luke continued after a brief pause, "to present to you the man most qualified to replace the late Daniel Fornage as your mayor." He gestured in Dalbert's direction, then continued, "We are also greatly pleased to have our very own state senator, Andy Haskins, with us to tender his support. And we are indeed honored to have with us our illustrious governor, who has graciously consented to say a few words to you this afternoon. Therefore, without further ado, my friends, it is my great and distinct pleasure to introduce you to our distinguished keynote speaker, the chief executive of our fair state of Alabama, a man known and respected by all, Governor George Smith Houston!"

The applause broke out in full, and with a gracious smile, Luke inclined his head toward the governor as the latter rose from his chair and approached the lectern. As he did so, Luke happened to scan the cheering crowd, and he noticed that a heavy-set black man with sparse white hair, wearing a frayed waistcoat and dun-colored breeches, was edging his way through the crowd of spectators. Seating himself, Luke attentively waited for the governor's address.

Clearing his throat, the mild-mannered but sturdily built leader of the state of Alabama took hold of the edges of the lectern, both his hands resting lightly on the polished wooden surface, and smiled as his glance swept over the assembled listeners. "Thank you, Mr. Bouchard. It is an honor for me to be introduced by a man of your distinguished service to our sovereign state, and it is a pleasure to be reunited with our distinguished state senator, Andy Haskins."

Again he cleared his throat and looked slowly around

139

the attentive audience. "I am here to meet all of you, my constituents, whom I have the honor and privilege to represent in my efforts to restore our state after the painful trials of Reconstruction. I am here to visit this prospering community, which, small though it may yet be, is vital to the well-being of the entire state. Because of this, it is imperative that its affairs be handled by competent, dedicated men. Ladies and gentlemen, this is a task that calls for complete elimination of partisan politics, which have plagued us since our Northern domination immediately following Appomattox." With a quick grin lighting up his face, the governor continued, "I realize it is somewhat uncommon for a Democrat like myself to speak at a Republican rally, and what is more, endorse a Republican candidate—" Good-natured shouts of approval from the crowd now interrupted the governor's words. "However," he continued, "that is an easy and pleasant undertaking when the candidate in question is an honorable man. Which brings me to the principle reason for today's gathering, and one to which I am most happy to lend both my presence and my official support—the candidacy of Dalbert Sattersfield for mayor of Lowndesboro."

The applause from the audience rose and swelled, and the one-armed storekeeper, flushing self-consciously, felt obliged to incline his head and to lift his right hand slightly by way of thanking his supporters.

The governor leaned slightly forward as he went on: "Dalbert Sattersfield is a sterling example of the dedicated Southerner who is wise enough to see that a party label need not make his thinking inflexible. His candidacy lends credit to the Republican party, but if he were a Democrat, he would do equal credit and honor to my party.

"Dalbert Sattersfield is a former Confederate officer who gave an arm on the battlefield fighting for his beloved homeland, yet he bears no rancor for the victors. He has shown himself to be courageous and purposeful in beginning a new life despite his handicap—one which I need not remind you has done nothing to hinder the effect that Senator Andy Haskins has made in the state capital, a man who shares a similar burden. My friends, I firmly believe in putting party politics aside to think only of the well-being of the people of Alabama. Vote only for good men of sound and proper judgment—for men like Dalbert Sattersfield. I believe that he is eminently qualified to be your mayor, and I endorse his candidacy to the very fullest."

The cheering, whistling crowd went wild. Luke smiled as he looked out over the audience and now noticed that the heavily built black man had moved forward to the front of the audience. The man's brooding face looked hostile and his brown eyes were fixed on Governor Houston with an unwavering stare. As Luke gave Andy Haskins to his left a swift, uneasy glance, a slight movement from the man caught his eye. With infinitesimal slowness, the man's right hand edged toward the pocket of his breeches. Luke Bouchard was seized with a sudden irrational terror, a nameless dread, a premonition that compelled him to tense himself on the edge of his chair with such strain that he could feel the muscles of his legs quiver violently.

Suddenly the cheers of the crowd were split by a hoarse, hysterical shout. "Goddamn Democrat! You sent the Kluxers out on us niggers and dey done killed mah wife!"

Luke saw the man draw his hand out of his pocket and instinctively, heedless of any danger to himself, he leaped down from the platform and flung himself at the man.

"For God's sake, look out, Luke! He's got a derringer!" Andy Haskins cried as he sprang to his feet, seeing the little gun, its mother-of-pearl handle gleaming under the warm rays of the June sun.

Luke seized the man's wrist with his hand in a frantic effort to twist the weapon away before it could be fired.

"Let me go!" the black man hoarsely cried. "I got no grudge 'gainst you, mistah! I'm gonna kill dis here gobbenor for lettin' the Klan go raidin' before the last election! You look out now! I'm gonna kill him, so help me—"

The two men violently struggled. Luke managed to grasp at the wavering derringer and turn its sinister muzzle away from Governor Houston when suddenly there was a sharp report.

With a look of incredulity on his face, Luke staggered backwards and stared down at his ruffled shirt front, stained by a spreading circle of blood.

With cries of outrage, two men nearest the assailant wrestled the gun out of his hands. One of them put his

141

hands around the black man's neck and was trying to strangle the deranged attacker.

"No, don't hurt him—don't you see—it'll start up the old hatred between—white and black—someone help that man—" Luke Bouchard managed to gasp. Then his legs buckled and he sank down to his knees, his head bowed, shuddering violently as a black wave blotted out the sun and everything around him.

# *Fourteen*

As Luke Bouchard sank down from his knees and crumbled, horrified cries from the crowd rose like a veritable Tower of Babel. Governor Houston, his face pale and his eyes wide with alarm, beckoned to his aide and hoarsely ordered, "Get my carriage ready! Mr. Bouchard must be taken to the hospital in Montgomery immediately! He must receive proper medical attention! Hurry, man! My God, that bullet was meant for me! We must help him all we can!"

But it was Andy Haskins, managing with supreme effort to regain some composure, who took complete charge. Shouting to a farmer he knew who was standing near the platform, Andy commanded, "Jerrold Evans! You've come with your horse and buggy—that's just what we need to lay Mr. Bouchard in to take him to the hospital.

"Dalbert," he shouted to his friend, "get some bolts of cloth out of your store and lay them on the floor of the buggy! We've got to make Luke as comfortable as possible!"

Dalbert Sattersfield jumped down from the speaker's platform, elbowed his way through the crowd, and ran up the street to his store to grab whatever he could find that would ease Luke's journey. Rushing back to the buggy, he carefully spread out layers of cloth, and as Luke's inert body was carried onto the buggy, Dalbert ripped off his own coat and gently pillowed Luke's head onto it.

Andy Haskins leaped back onto the speaker's platform and shouted over the buzz of the crowd, "Who's got a fast horse here?"

A young man shot up his hand and came forward. "I've got a real fast mare, Senator—bred her myself, and I know she's strong—"

"Good!" Andy yelled. "Do you know where Dr. Kennery's office is in Montgomery, son?"

The youth solemnly nodded as he looked up at Andy. "Yes sir, I do."

"All right, then," Andy replied. "I want you to ride to him as fast as your horse will go and tell him to be waiting for Mr. Bouchard at the hospital. Mr. Bouchard's life may very well depend on the doctor's being there in time."

The young man ran for his horse, untethered it, and in a few seconds galloped out of sight, heading upriver.

Leaping back down from the platform, Andy ran over to the buggy. "Dalbert, I want you to ride with Jerrold. Get to Montgomery as fast as you can, but not so fast that Luke will be jarred and jolted."

"I understand, Andy," Dalbert solemnly avowed.

Andy climbed into the buggy to give his beloved friend one last look before he was driven off. Bending over Luke, Andy sucked in his breath and shook his head in dispair. Luke's waistcoat as well as his shirt were now drenched with blood. Sobbing aloud, Andy gently opened the buttons and assayed the wound. The round-nosed slug from the derringer, fired at such close range, seemed to have pierced the left side of Luke Bouchard's chest some two inches away from his heart. To staunch the flow of blood, Andy ripped off his own cambric shirt and tore away a jagged strip, pressing it against the wound. Tears ran unashamedly down his cheeks as he watched the blood ooze through the bandage.

Andy clutched Luke's left hand in his own and brought it tearfully to his cheek before gently placing it back. With a last, mournful sigh, Andy leaped out of the buggy and explained to Dalbert, "I'm going to ride to Windhaven and tell Mrs. Bouchard what has happened. She's got to know, and it'll help Luke if she's there at the hospital. We'll meet you there as soon as we can. Ride safely, now."

"You can depend on me, Andy," Dalbert hoarsely whispered.

The buggy took off, and Andy spared it one last, lingering look before he ran to his horse. Wheeling the horse's head around, Andy urged the protesting gelding on at a

144

gallop, leaving the governor and the rest of the assembled crowd in a stunned silence.

A quarter of an hour later, Andy rode up to the front of the red-brick chateau. The gelding reared and pawed the air, snorting in protest against the ruthless way it had been ridden. Running up the steps, Andy banged once loudly on the brass knocker, then impatiently flung open the door, not waiting to stand on ceremony.

Clementine was just coming into the hallway, responding to the clanger, and uttered an alarmed cry at the sight of Andy's haggard face. "Oh, my God, Mr. Andy! What—what's happened?"

"It's Mr. Luke," Andy sadly told her. "He's been shot—hurt bad. Is Mrs. Bouchard here?"

"Oh, Mr. Andy!" Clementine wailed, her kindly face wreathed in sudden tears, "I—I'll go fetch her. She's in her room—"

"No, no, Clemmie—I'd best be the one to tell her. But I want you to run out to the stable and have a carriage made ready. Mr. Luke's been taken to the hospital in Montgomery where Dr. Kennery'll be waiting for him, and I'll take Mrs. Bouchard to him. Clemmie," he softly continued, "Mrs. Bouchard will need us to help her. You take care of the children while we're gone."

"Don't you worry none, Mr. Andy," Clemmie sobbed. "I'll see that they're all right. You just take care of Miz Laure." Turning on her heels, she swept out of the house and headed toward the stable.

Andy sighed, then turned and walked down the long hallway toward Laure's room. Pausing before her door, he gritted his teeth and sighed again. He mustn't alarm his beloved benefactor's wife any more than she had to be. Still, she must be told—Resolutely, he knocked on Laure's door, and, bidden to enter, turned the knob and stepped across the threshold.

Andy's look of utter despair immediately told Luke's beautiful wife that something terrible had happened. Rising from her chair, she came toward him.

"Andy! You're white as a sheet! What's happened?"

"Mrs. Bouchard—Laure—I wish I could prepare you for what I have to say. There's been—there was a man at the rally, he had a gun—and Luke, he was—he was shot," Andy finally managed to whisper.

"Oh, God! What—how did it happen—who could have wanted to shoot Luke?" Laure gasped, as she put both her hands to her head, her face stricken and blank.

"It—it was a mistake." Andy forced the words out of his throat. "The bullet was meant for Governor Houston. Some crazy old black man hollered that the Democrats had used the Klan to kill his wife. He drew a pistol and your husband jumped down from the platform and tried to pull the derringer away—and it went off."

"Oh, my God!" Laure moaned. "He mustn't die! Oh please God, don't let him die!" She sank down to her knees and put a hand over her mouth to hold back her choking sobs.

Andy kneeled down and gently lifted her onto the bed.

"Dalbert Sattersfield's taking him to the hospital in Montgomery right now. We've sent a fast rider on ahead to summon Dr. Kennery, so he can be at the hospital when Luke gets there."

"I w-want to be with him, Andy," Laure cried.

"Of course. That's why I'm here," he replied gently. "I've already instructed Clemmie to get your carriage ready. We'll get to the hospital just as fast as we can."

Laure shook herself together, and, grabbing her wrap off the coat peg, she ran out of the room and down the hallway, with Andy in tow.

As they descended the front steps, the carriage drew up. Clementine, out of breath, came rushing up at the same time. "Miz Laure," she panted, "I don't want you to worry none, you hear? I'll look after Lucien, Paul, Celestine, and Clarissa. An' I'll take care of baby John like he was my own, Miz Laure. You can depend on me."

"Oh, Clemmie!" Laure cried. "What would I ever do without you? Bless you—and pray for Mr. Luke, Clemmie. Pray for him!"

The two women hugged one another tightly. Having such a short time before faced the miracle of John's birth together, the bond between them was closer than ever.

Andy gently urged Laure into the carriage, then, climbing up beside her, he seized the reins and they sped off toward Montgomery at a fast trot.

They rode in silence for a long while, the carriage bouncing and jostling its passengers occasionally as the steady clip-clop of the horses' hooves sounded against the

146

hardened surface of the road. Finally, Laure turned to Andy, and biting her lower lip to keep her tears in check, she bravely asked, "Do you think he will live?"

"I think there's a chance—if they can get that bullet out. He lost an awful lot of blood, but I think if he'll fight, he'll win."

She silently nodded, and once more fell into a silent reverie. *I'm coming, my darling,* she said to herself. *I'm coming. Hold on, my darling, my sweet love. Please hold on. You must live for me, for our children. It mustn't end like this, not over such a senseless, terrible thing. But, oh, my love, I'm so proud of you! You'll never know how very proud I am of you and your courage!* Her eyes widened, and she could no longer control the tears that streamed unchecked down her ashen cheeks.

Andy Haskins, driving the two mares with his single arm, quickened their pace, expertly guiding them over the familiar road. Looking around her, Laure knew that old Lucien Bouchard had walked this very same trail to the village of Econchate. How strangely comforting it was that this recollection should come to her now, as if to distract her tormented mind from its agonized worry. Remembering the legend of her husband's indomitable grandfather, she raised her eyes and mouthed a silent prayer to the benign ghosts of the Creeks and especially to Lucien's beloved woman, the beautiful Dimarte, that her spirit might watch over Luke and see him through this terrible danger.

It was almost seven o'clock when Luke Bouchard's tall form, draped in a white cotton sheet, was wheeled back into the private room where Laure was waiting, pacing the floor back and forth, her hands twisted and clenched into tight fists of tortured anxiety. Andy Haskins, his face drawn and haggard, had remained beside her these last few hours while they waited for the news of the operation. He had done his best to soothe her, but as the clock ticked off its remorseless seconds, his own secret concern deepened.

As the door opened and two attendants carefully lifted the still unconscious white-bearded man into the bed, Dr. Kennery appeared. Laure hurried to him, tears blurring her widened eyes: "Tell me, Dr. Kennery—for God's sake, tell me!" she cried.

"Mrs. Bouchard, the bullet is of small bore, but it lies so dangerously near the heart that, after probing, I dared not risk removing it. I fear if I try, there would most likely be a powerful and massive hemorrhage. It's true the outward bleeding was stopped, but there has been internal hemorrhaging, the most damaging of all. I wish to God our medical science were wiser than it is—"

"Does that mean—" Laure began, but could not finish. She bowed her head and put her hand over her eyes as she fought to hold back the choking sobs that assailed her.

"I've managed to suture the passage of the bullet." Dr. Kennery tried to force an optimistic note into his voice. "There have been instances, as I know from my own medical training and from cases illustrated in the Civil War, where men have lived with bullets still in their bodies—"

But he could not finish. He made a hopeless gesture and bowed his head. "I've done everything I can, believe me, everything. He's strong, he has a will to live, and the rest is up to God, Mrs. Bouchard. I'll leave now to allow you to be with him. Try not to excite him if he regains consciousness. I'll be back in half an hour."

Laure Bouchard turned to Andy Haskins and, bursting into hysterical sobs, flung her arms around his neck and buried her tear-stained face against his chest. "Oh, my God, Andy, what am I going to do if he dies? He's been my life—he's so strong, so brave, I just can't conceive of living without him. Oh, I love him so much. I wish to God I'd told him many more times what's in my heart for him—how much he's done for all of us, his kindness and goodness. Oh, Andy, I must pray for him!"

"We'll pray together, Laure. I think the Lord will give him every chance because he's needed so much, by everyone." Andy's voice was low and unsteady.

Laure made a valiant effort to dry her tears, and then knelt beside the bed, clasping her hands in prayer. Andy emulated her, staring at the drawn features of the still unconscious man who had lived all his life by the precepts of his beloved grandfather. Finally, after some minutes, Andy rose to his feet and withdrew, sensing that Laure needed to be alone with her husband.

About a quarter of an hour later, Luke Bouchard's eyes opened, and he slowly turned his head and saw her. "L-

Laure—be-beloved—" he managed in a whisper that barely reached Laure's ears.

"Oh, my dear one! Luke! You've come back to me. Oh, thank God!" Laure tearfully exclaimed as she rose to her feet and stood beside the bed, both her hands reaching for one of his. Bringing it to her lips, she covered it with kisses, smiling at him through her tears as he stared almost uncomprehendingly at her.

"I'm here, I'm with you, Luke," she softly reassured him.

"Lopa—Lopa—Lopasuta—is he here? Has—has he come back?" With an effort, Luke managed to murmur the words, and Laure had to stoop to hear them.

"Not yet, my love. He'll probably send a telegram soon—he's been busy with his new client, I'm sure. And when he does come back, I'll certainly give him a piece of my mind! The very idea, leaving Geraldine when she's about to have a baby and with just the midwife to help her—"

Abruptly Laure stopped herself, for she recalled Luke's own absence when John had been born—how unimportant that seemed now, and how glad she was that she had never spoken to Luke of this, nor uttered so much as one word of reproach or regret at his absence when she needed him. Nor would she ever reproach Lopasuta, either; life was too short and too precious.

Sitting on the edge of his bed and leaning toward Luke, still holding his limp hand in both of hers and bearing it to her lips, Laure stared at him, willing—with all her strength, her energy, and her love—his life, his recovery from the savage pellet that Dr. Kennery had not been able to extract.

"That's my g-girl," she heard Luke murmur, and for an instant there was a flicker of merriment in his eyes as he looked directly at her. A faint smile creased his lips, but he breathed with a visible effort. There was an ominous feeling in her heart as she watched him fight for breath. With all her strength, she fought to keep from breaking down and giving way to the emotions welling up inside of her. Instead, she smilingly whispered, "You must rest now, my dear one. I'll stay here with you. And when you've recovered, we'll go back home and you'll relax. There won't be any more riding for you for a good while, and no

149

more working out in the fields with a hoe. The very idea! Trying to prove that you can keep up with the young workers!"

"There you go—scolding me—now I know you love me—"

"Yes, Luke. I've always loved you. Even that stolen time we had when I was engaged to John—yes, I loved you then."

"I—I know that. God—God—God bless you for giving me your strong young life, for the ch-children—" He tried to lift his head, but with an alarmed gasp, Laure gently eased him back onto the pillow.

"The doctor says you must rest, my darling. No, you needn't thank me—I'm the one who should thank you for the wonderful times we've had together—for our love— yes, for the children I so happily bore you, my own true dearest love, my Luke."

His eyelids closed for a moment, and then they opened wide. His voice was coherent and his gaze was steady as he said in a faint voice that she had to bend to hear, "I know I'm going to die. No, don't say anything. I—I know it, and I'm not afraid. You—you've given me such happiness as I never dreamed of, my—my dearest. Laure, tell—tell the children how much I love them. And tell Lucien Edmond—tell him also how very proud I am of him and wh-what he has done at Windhaven Range—he and Mara, too—"

"My darling," Laure whispered, "you'll live to tell them yourself—you'll see." Now it was all she could do to keep from breaking down and sobbing in her grief. Her hands clutched his, loath to relinquish it, as if by holding his hand she could draw him away from the invisible shadows that were encroaching, soon to take him from her forever.

"You're kind, you're gentle, my l-love. No, I go to join G-Grandfather. Don't speak now—I'm very weak and I must finish what I want to say. I—I provided for you well, at least I've done that—"

"Oh, L-Luke, please—don't say that—" Now she was weeping bitterly.

"Hush, L-Laure. I've done well and I'm grateful—not because I wished for material th-things, but so that you and the children will have a happy l-life. I ask you— carry—carry on the work of Windhaven so—the ideas

150

Grandfather believed in as I believed in them, will n-never d-die."

"I promise you, I swear it, my dearest one, my Luke." Her voice was almost inaudible as the tears flowed down her cheeks. She bent to kiss him on the lips, and at that moment she heard a faint, long-drawn sigh. His eyes closed and he lay still.

Holding his hands in both of hers, she stared at him through her tear-blinded eyes. She memorized his face, the strong, peaceful face that was so dear to her. "You must know that you were never a sobersides, my Luke, my sweet one," she whispered. "You made me feel that I was a woman again, and in your arms I knew what love meant. I knew how you both desired and worshiped me as no woman should ever be worshiped—and yet, I bless you for it and thank dear God for that love. My own true husband, my sweetheart, my lover, I'll keep my promise— your spirit will always be on that tall bluff with Grandfather and his Dimarte, overlooking Windhaven. And all of you will watch over us in the years ahead. I must now say good-bye to you, but you will be in my heart and in my soul every waking and sleeping moment. Your spirit and mine will still commune as we've always done. It is only by believing in that, my own true Luke, that I can bear this grief."

She leaned forward to kiss his eyelids and then, for the last time, his mouth. Gently she released his hand, and drew the sheet over his bearded face. She sat there unconscious of the passage of time, until at last with a tremendous effort, she rose and walked slowly toward the door.

Andy Haskins was outside, pacing back and forth, his face twisted with concern. He saw her emerge and he started toward her. "How is he, Laure?"

"He's with his grandfather and Dimarte now, Andy. He had no pain. We are still one and always shall be. His death does not change this. His spirit will live."

"He was a great man, Laure. He was a great man every day of his life. All I have now, I owe to him." He stopped, his voice choked with emotion. Then he whispered, "I'll go see the doctor and make arrangements, Laure, and then I'll drive you home."

"If it's not asking too much, dear Andy, would you drive me over to Geraldine's house? I—I don't want to be alone right now. And you know, we haven't had a word from Lopasuta since he left—perhaps Geraldine has heard from him by now. That would be some comfort—just to know that he's coming home. I—" Suddenly she was exhausted, drained by the events of this tragic day. "I'm so weak and tired now—but I can't let myself go. I have to be strong for his sake and for our children. If we don't hear from Lopasuta soon, I'm going to have to go to the bank in New Orleans, Andy, to make sure that the affairs of both Windhaven Plantation and Windhaven Range are safe and sound."

"I understand, Laure. If there's anything I can do, just name it."

"You're so good, Andy. Luke was lucky in having a friend like you, just as I am."

"I've done nothing, Laure, when it comes right down to it, not compared to his giving me this new life with my Jessica; and now representing the people of this state—I swear to you I'm going to do everything I can to be a good senator, because he'd want me to. I want to dedicate my work to him, Laure."

Laure at last gave way to her pent-up emotions. Putting her arms around Andy Haskins's neck, she clung to him and wept unabashedly as he held her, stroked her hair, and awkwardly murmured such soothing words as he felt might ease her grief.

After a moment, he said, "I'll go see Dr. Kennery first, Laure, and then I'll drive you over to Geraldine's. I'll wait for you, too, so I can take you home."

"Thank you, Andy. I'll try not to be too long, and then I'll let you go home to your Jessica and your new baby. They both need you, Andy. People do need each other so—and it's so easy to become complacent. . . ."

# Fifteen

"I can't believe it—it's like some dreadful nightmare—why would anyone want to kill Luke?" Geraldine sobbed. Heavy with child, at most a week away from its birth, she struggled to get up, while Emily Norton, the solicitous midwife, hurried forward with a mild rebuke. But it was Laure Bouchard who came to her and, her hands firmly on Geraldine's shoulders, shook her head and insisted, "You're not to get up, dear Geraldine. But please—tell me and help to ease my grief: have you heard from Lopasuta? It was one of the last things Luke asked."

"No, no, I haven't, Laure—and he promised he'd send word. I'm beginning to be really worried. He's always been so reliable—I—I just know something awful must have happened!" Geraldine started to cry and covered her face with her hands while Mrs. Norton made token efforts to soothe her.

"Don't hover about her so!" Laure said, more sharply than was necessary. Then, softening those words with a faint smile, she added, "She'll be all right—but a glass of cold water would be good for her, if you'd bring it, please."

"Certainly, ma'am. I'll be right back. Now then, Mrs. Bouchard, you just stay there, and don't try to get up. Your baby is going to be born any time now. You just mind what I say and you won't have any trouble," the midwife solicitously ordered, as she hurried off to the kitchen.

Laure seated herself on the edge of the sofa facing the attractive young woman. "You say that Lopasuta got a let-

153

ter from a man in New Orleans offering him a case and that he went down there?"

"Yes, that's right. He didn't want to go, he was so worried about the baby and me—he's such a wonderful man, I'm so lucky, I think I'd just die if anything happened to him!" Geraldine sobbed.

"Now, now, Geraldine, honey, try to stay calm. I plan to go to New Orleans myself now since I'll have to go to the bank to see about our affairs. Lopasuta handles them as the Bouchard lawyer, so obviously something else has to be done during his absence. But what I'm getting at is I can visit that man who you say sent the letter to Lopasuta. Maybe he'll know something."

"That's a wonderful idea! Oh, would you, please, dear Laure?" Geraldine anxiously begged.

"Here's your water, Mrs. Bouchard. Now you drink it down nice and slow and easy," the midwife cautioned with a beaming smile as she watched Geraldine docilely obey.

"You're very nice to Geraldine," Laure told the kindly woman. "I'm very grateful." Once the midwife had left the living room, Laure turned back to Geraldine. "Do you remember who this client is? You know, when you first told us Lopasuta was going to New Orleans, you didn't tell either Luke or me his name."

"That's right, I didn't. It's William Brickley. I know, because Lopasuta said when he got to New Orleans one of the first things he was going to do was go to the bank and ask Jason Barntry about this man."

"I see. Well, it should be fairly easy to find him. Now, are you feeling all right? Is there anything I can get you?"

"Oh, Laure," Geraldine looked down again, "it just tortures me to have you so kind and sweet to me when all the time you're thinking about—about—"

"About Luke," Laure finished for her. "Luke would want me to go on living—especially for the children—and I pray I can continue Windhaven Plantation just the way it is. I'm going to do my best. But—oh God, Geraldine—I just don't know if I'll be able to. Luke was so strong, and though Marius Thornton is a very good man, and he's worth his weight in gold, he takes orders better than he can give them."

"I know. He's too gentle—"

"Yes—he's not really a doer the way Luke was. Well,

154

I'm hoping that perhaps Jason can help me find a good reliable man who can be a kind of overseer and know enough about business at the same time to make things run. Then I can devote more of my time to my children, just as Luke would want me to, and as I want to myself."

"I'm so afraid, Laure—" Geraldine's composure broke again.

"I know, my dear—and I'm concerned, too. It certainly isn't like Lopasuta not to keep his promise to send you some word."

"That's exactly the way I feel, Laure. We've always been so close; we've never had any secrets from each other—"

"I'm sure there must be a reason. When I go down to New Orleans, I'll do everything I can to try to find out what has happened. Clementine will take care of the children while I'm gone—she's such a treasure," she added with a pathetic sigh.

"I do hope you'll have good news for me, Laure—I feel just awful, sitting here, so big and ungainly and helpless. And to hear about Luke! It's so wrong, so unjust, so unfair!"

"Sometimes life is like that, Geraldine. But then, I have the children, and I have the knowledge of Luke's love, and it will always be with me as a kind of blessing. You know, the way his grandfather used to stand in the fields and look up at that tall red bluff where his Dimarte was buried, and commune with her spirit. It will be like that for Luke and me, I know, till the end of my days." Her eyes were distant and her voice otherworldly as she spoke, and then, with a little sigh, she turned back to smile at Geraldine, bending to kiss the distraught young woman on the forehead. "I'll leave you now, dear. Andy Haskins— such a self-sacrificing, wonderful man—has driven me here from Windhaven, and he's waiting outside to drive me home. And I'm sure by now that his Jessica is just about frantic wondering what happened to him. Unless someone rode by and told her, she doesn't know what— what happened this afternoon."

"I—I'll say prayers for Luke, Laure. And please, say a prayer for my Lopasuta when you say yours tonight," Geraldine Bouchard tearfully whispered.

\* \* \*

At twilight on June 11, Laure stood at the top of the towering red bluff, with Andy and Jessica Haskins, Marius and Clementine Thornton, Dan and Katie Munroe, and others from Windhaven Plantation in attendance.

Burt Coleman was the only loyal friend missing. Though he had expressed a fervent wish to pay his last respects to the man who had given Andy Haskins his chance and thus had made it possible in turn for Andy to give Burt an opportunity and a new life, his lovely Marietta had experienced the onset of labor pains just three hours before the funeral, and she was having a difficult birth.

Dan Munroe had dug the grave beside that of old Lucien, and Andy Haskins spoke a benediction as the simple pinewood coffin, lifted by three of the workers, was lowered into the waiting grave. Laure knelt, and murmured words that no one around her could hear, her last farewell to Luke Bouchard. Then, plunging her soft hands into the upturned soil and filling them, she let the earth fall upon the coffin in a symbolic leavetaking.

Later that evening, a sobbing Clementine answered a knock at the door. A courier from Governor Houston handed her a sealed envelope, directing that it be given to Laure Bouchard.

Tears formed anew in the eyes of Luke's grieving widow as she read:

My dear Mrs. Bouchard:

Words cannot express the sorrow that I felt upon learning of your husband's passing; indeed, I am painfully aware that no words from me could possibly soften the suffering of so tragic a loss. Let me simply extend to you and your family, on behalf of all of the people of Alabama, the most heartfelt sympathies. In addition, I wish to express to you my humble gratitude, in acknowledgement of the fact that your dear husband gave up his life in order to protect me. There is no greater sacrifice that a man can offer his fellow man.

I have this day drawn up and signed an official proclamation, summarizing your husband's achievements and attesting to his courage and his record of service as a private citizen to the people of Alabama. It will be my distinct honor and privilege to present this document to you, in an official ceremony, at some future date that would be convenient for you. For Luke Bouchard surely blessed this land with his presence, as he served it in his passing, and he will never be forgotten, so long as loyalty, freedom, and honor are held in high esteem.

Yours faithfully,
George Smith Houston
Governor of Alabama

Two days later, Laure Bouchard, wearing somber widow's weeds, a long-skirted black silk dress and heavy veil, closeted herself with Clementine Thornton and explained the purpose of her journey later that day to New Orleans. "Clemmie, because you're so dear to the children and they accept you as part of the family—you know, I'm very grateful, especially now that I'm alone—" She broke off, then continued, "If I were to stay here and grieve for my husband, I'd likely break down and be good for nothing, and frighten the children, besides. With Lopasuta gone, and no word from him, there's no one else but me who can take charge of what's happening here on Windhaven Plantation."

"I understand, Miz Laure," Clementine responded somberly.

"I realize that this is a terrible imposition—since you have your own dear baby to care for now as well as your other children—but I have no one else to turn to. What I'm asking, Clemmie, could you find a nurse for little John, or even nurse her yourself, if need be, just for a few days—a week, at most? And could you please look after the other children and make them see that I had to go away for a very good reason? Lucien will surely understand—he already has his father's keen mind."

"Miz L-Laure—" Clementine had begun to weep softly. "I swear before God I won't let you down. I'll nurse the baby myself, just like my own, and I'll look after the other children—try to make them understand—"

"Thank you, my dear Clemmie."

And then, just before she left on her journey, Laure called in Marius. "I have to say something to you, Marius, and please don't be offended," she began at once. "You're still foreman here, of course. You will be till either you decide to go elsewhere, or old age keeps you from working for us."

"Miz Laure—I'd work here for the rest of my life if I

157

was just a hired hand working for room and board, as long as you'd have me," Marius protested. "I'm sure you know how Mr. Luke saved my life in New Orleans when there was a mob of Creoles fixing to kill me. And then how he got my Clemmie away from a miserly old woman who had her indentured and who was making her life hell. I swear to God, and I mean it, I wish I had taken that bullet instead of Mr. Luke."

Laure Bouchard had to turn away and blink her eyes very quickly at this poignant expression of loyalty. She knew now, even as she had known when she had married Luke Bouchard, how his decency and kindness left its mark on all those with whom he had come into contact. Finally, when she could speak again, she turned back to Marius and said, "I'm very grateful to hear you say that, Marius. God bless you and keep you and Clemmie and your children safe and sound forever. But—you know that Lopasuta hasn't been heard from since he went off to New Orleans, and there's no one else to look after our affairs, so I'm going to New Orleans to see what I can do. I've been so upset and confused since Luke left us—I don't know exactly what's going to happen, in the direction and guidance of Windhaven Plantation. I may want to hire someone who'll be able to oversee things as Luke used to do—somebody who knows the markets in Mobile and New Orleans, and maybe even up in St. Louis and farther north. Not that you aren't the best foreman we ever had, Marius—"

"You don't have to apologize to me, Miz Laure, ma'am." Marius shook his head, his eyes wet with unshed tears. "And I know you're not putting me down when you say that. I learned a lot from Mr. Luke—I don't rightly know what I'll do without him. I taught myself a lot along the way, too, but I always felt better when Mr. Luke was taking charge of things—a man I could lean on. I tell you this, anyone you want to bring back, if you feel he'll be able to step into Mr. Luke's shoes, why then I'll take orders from him, just as if they came right from you and Mr. Luke. Not that anyone could fill Mr. Luke's shoes, if you understand what I mean—"

She pressed her hand to his, unable to speak, and then suddenly impulsively kissed him on the cheek and whispered, "God bless you so very much, dear Marius. No one will ever be able to take Luke's place, not really, but you and I will both feel better if there's someone here who begins to have his knowledge of how things should go."

Having said good-bye to her children, telling young Lucien, her eldest, to look after his brother and sisters, she ascended the gangplank of the *Belle of the River*, prepared to substitute for her dead husband as the head of Windhaven Plantation. What she would do, she vowed to herself, would be to make wise decisions that would help her keep her promise to Luke on his deathbed: with the help of a man like old Jason Barntry, she would try to allocate some of the profits of Windhaven Plantation into sound investments so that her children and Luke's might grow to maturity and not have the harrowing fear of poverty. Beyond that, she would work to insure the growth and the strength of this commune so that all workers on it, whether white or black, would have a livelihood, happiness, and the enjoyment of their families. For this was the credo of the Bouchards, and she clung to it now because it was a reminder of Luke's integrity and courage and his abiding love.

As she was shown to her private cabin by the deferential captain of the steamboat, Laure reflected on the irony of fate. It was barely a month after the birth of the infant John, the last child she and her beloved Luke had conceived in their desire for each other, their trust and their felicity. And John had been named in a blithe defiance of the history of the Bouchards: John was the English translation of Jean, the name of the older brother of the very first Lucien. He had been as different from Old Lucien as evil from good, as night from day. But this son of hers and Luke's would transcend his namesake, she vowed, and being the very last of their children, would have the very best of them both.

Once she had settled in her cabin, she leaned back against the pillows and mused that if fate had been kinder, she would be even now holding little John in her arms. Suddenly a tremulous sob rose up in her throat, and she began to weep bitterly, venting all of her grief in a torrent of tears. When she finally dried her eyes, Laure Bouchard murmured a prayer directed to the man she had most loved in all her life, and to his grandfather and his beloved woman, Dimarte: "Help me now to be strong, to think

159

and act like a man in your stead, my beloved Luke. And you who are Luke's grandfather and you, his blessed woman, look down kindly upon me who loved him so and respects you both and treasures your immortal love. Help me to achieve my vows. Amen."

The bald little telegrapher at the Montgomery railroad station glanced at the crabbed handwriting on the telegraph form that Milo Brutus Henson had just handed him, and scratched his neck as he read it. "This don't make sense, mister," he finally decided. "You sure you want it like this?"

"Exactly that way! My friend in New Orleans will know what it means."

The telegrapher regarded the short, dapper man with his elegantly waxed mustache and thoughtfully scratched again. "Well now, it reminds me of the codes that I saw used back when we were fighting those damn Yankees."

"Never you mind," the surveyor irritatedly retorted. "How much do I owe you?"

With an eloquent shrug, the man counted the letters and then decided, "That will be six-fifty, mister."

The telegraph was to William Brickley at the Rampart Street address and the code was eminently simple. When Brickley decoded it, it would read:

> Luke Bouchard died two days ago from a bullet meant for Governor Houston. His doctor's nurse told my girl that Mrs. Bouchard is heading to New Orleans. Since she has an affiliation with the bank where you do business, arrange to meet her and convince her that you should handle her affairs. If you can bring it off, we'll have not only the lawyer out of the way, but also Windhaven Plantation under our thumb. Profits galore!
>
> Henson

Two days after Laure's departure for the Queen City, where she would try to pick up the threads of her life, Geraldine Bouchard was delivered of a sturdy son. She named him Dennis after her favorite uncle, who had dangled her on his knee when she had been a little girl.

In her loneliness since Lopasuta's unexplained disappearance, Geraldine had confided in the friendly midwife,

160

who was indignant when she learned how Geraldine's parents still refused to recognize this marriage.

Shortly after Dr. Abel Kennery arrived at the Bouchard house to examine mother and child and to assert that both were doing extremely well, Emily Norton told Geraldine and the doctor that she was going out for a while to see a dear old friend, but that she would be back before midnight.

Mrs. Norton walked two blocks away from the house, and then hailed a passing carriage whose black driver was mournfully returning to the stable after having, as he dolefully told her, "Made only sixty cents all day long, would you believe it, ma'am! Seems like no matter how hard a man works dese days, he can't hardly make out. Don't seem rightly fair."

The midwife commiserated with him, and promised him a tip if he would take her to the address that she gave him, wait for her, and bring her back.

Fifteen minutes later, the horse and buggy came to a halt in front of the house owned by Geraldine's parents. The midwife descended, hurried to the door, and loudly rapped the knocker till at last George Murcur himself slowly opened the door and irately demanded to know why she was making so much noise.

"You don't know me, Mr. Murcur, but I know all about you," Emily Norton declared sharply. "Your daughter, Geraldine, just had a baby boy, I'll have you know. I delivered it for her, that's what, and Dr. Kennery says she and the boy are just fine. I thought you'd like to know. She said she was going to name it after Dennis, her favorite uncle."

George Murcur's harsh features softened and he bit his lip. In a low voice, he murmured, "That was my dead brother." His wife, hearing the conversation, hurried into the hall demanding, "What is it, George? Who is this person?"

"It—she's from Geraldine—our daughter just had a boy and she's named it after my brother Dennis."

"Oh, George, that poor girl—"

"And that's not all, Mr. and Mrs. Murcur." The midwife drew herself up to her full height. "Her husband went down to New Orleans to see a man about a law case, and he hasn't been heard from since. That poor girl is all

161

alone. I asked the doctor to stay until I could get back to her. You're her father and mother, and I know it's none of my business, but I just had to speak my mind. And then, as if poor Geraldine doesn't have enough to worry her, the other day Mrs. Bouchard came by from the big red house downriver, to tell her that Mr. Luke, Lopasuta's adoptive father, died of a wound he received trying to take a gun away from some crazy man who wanted to kill Governor Houston."

"Oh, George, our poor baby," Angela Murcur began to cry. "We have to go to her—we've been wrong—it's been hard on us, too, but now—"

"I hired me a carriage to bring me here, Mrs. Murcur," the midwife spoke up. "I think there's enough room for all of us if you want to ride back and see your daughter."

"Oh, do let's, please, George, right now," Angela sobbed.

George turned to look at the midwife, and he was fighting hard to control his tears. "If you'll just give us a minute, my wife and I will get our coats and we'll go back with you right away."

When Dr. Kennery opened the front door of Lopasuta's house in answer to Emily Norton's energetic knock, he saw the middle-aged, gray-haired hotelkeeper and his weeping wife standing hesitantly behind the midwife. It was Angela Murcur who spoke up first. "Doctor, could we—do you think it would be all right if we see our little girl, Geraldine?"

"I think it would do her all the good in the world," he declared. "By all means, go right into the bedroom. She and the child are doing splendidly. You've got a healthy grandson, with a good pair of lungs, I can tell you that. Well now," he turned to Mrs. Norton, "I don't think you'll need me any more this evening, so I'll be on my way." He affably nodded to the Murcurs and left.

"You've got company, honey," the midwife triumphantly announced as she walked smilingly into the bedroom where Geraldine lay propped up against the pillows, nursing her baby.

"V-visitors?" Geraldine wonderingly echoed. And then with a cry of surprise and joy, her eyes brimming with tears, she saw her father and mother enter the room. "Oh,

162

Mama, Papa—it's so good to see you—I've missed you so—please say you don't hate me any more—"

Angela knelt down beside her daughter's bed and hugged her, exclaiming as the tears rolled down her cheeks, "It's the other way around, precious! You have every right to hate us both for the shabby way we treated you and your husband. If you can find it in your heart to forgive us, we'd like to take care of you until he comes back."

George, on the other side of the bed, peered down at the suckling infant. "You named him Dennis, I'm told—your uncle would have liked that very much. Thank you, Geraldine. God bless you, and forgive a pair of old fools, please!"

# Sixteen

Burt Coleman, now thirty-five, tall, ingratiatingly pleasant of manner, with black hair and candid gray eyes, seemed to have aged by at least a decade.

An Alabama farmboy whose family had virtually abandoned him when they had left the state in search of a better future, Burt had been very grateful when Andy Haskins had hired him to work his acreage. Later, Burt had been ecstatic at being named foreman, and when he had fallen in love with and married his charming Marietta he had believed that his life had reached its zenith of happiness. Both of them had been enchanted with Matt, their firstborn son, and eagerly awaited their second child.

Then, on the very night of Luke Bouchard's funeral, his darling Marietta was taken from him, dying in childbirth while bearing their son Clarence. Burt had been crushed. He couldn't understand why his sweet wife, who had seemed so strong and vital, had died. Brought up from boyhood as a Methodist, he had not practiced his religion in recent years; nevertheless, he remained a devout believer. On the night of Marietta's death, he had knelt down in their little cottage and prayed, weeping unashamedly, asking God what evil he himself had done and why his Marietta had to be the one to be punished.

But mostly he had been utterly bewildered. With an almost naive trust, he had looked forward to a long life of domestic happiness: sharing the evening meals after hard work in the fields; watching Marietta raise their sons and taking joy in Matt's and Clarence's first steps and first words; savoring the keen delight he felt at the gift of

Marietta's love. He had always looked on his dear wife with a kind of awe—that a woman so lovely and generous should fall in love with him, a simple man. It had struck him as almost miraculous—and now it was so suddenly over.

He had been especially at a loss about caring for his infant son. Fortunately, as soon as Andy Haskins had heard of Marietta's death, he took it upon himself to ask the midwife who had attended her to find a wet nurse for Clarence. The midwife declared that she knew the perfect girl, a Cecilia Vanders, and Andy had promptly arranged to interview the girl.

The kindly midwife, herself a widow, had taken Cecilia into her home after the girl's adoptive parents had disowned her upon discovering that she was with child. From the time she came to live with them at the age of five, Cecilia had been treated cruelly by her parents, almost as a slave rather than a daughter. Finally, after almost fifteen years of intense loneliness and insecurity, she had fallen in love with a smooth-talking scoundrel who had callously abandoned her when he found out she was pregnant; her parents, meanwhile, had thrown her out of the house.

Cecilia, now twenty, was a tall, homely girl, shy and ingenuous. She had given birth to a little girl about a month before, and had been tearfully grateful when Andy Haskins had interviewed her—with Jessica sympathetically sitting in—and offered her this post.

Andy was deeply concerned about his foreman's overwhelming grief. Rather than talk about his loss, Burt Coleman—morose and taciturn—insisted on going about his tasks in the fields with a dogged stoicism. His coworkers, understanding his reticence, took pains not to mention anything about Marietta's death.

One June evening, while supping with Jessica, Andy revealed his distress. "Jessica, Burt's a wonderful man, and he's been through hell. I don't know how to manage it, but we've got to get him thinking about the rest of his life—he's only thirty-five, and I don't want him to get sour just because he's been dealt a bad hand."

"I know, honey." Jessica reached out to pat Andy's cheek and to give him a tender kiss. "Of course, it's far too soon to be thinking about a thing like this, but with those little babies of his, he'll feel bogged down if he doesn't have a woman to look after them and share his life. I'd like to see him get married again. It's not as if he's going to forget Marietta, not ever; she was his first love."

"Honey, when you say things like that, and show how much compassion and understanding you have, I feel like the luckiest man in the world," Andy said tenderly. "But right now, I guess he feels that his whole world has gone topsy-turvy and he doesn't know what to make of it."

"Maybe some additional responsibilities would take his mind off his troubles," Jessica suggested.

"Maybe so," Andy mused. "You know, Mrs. Bouchard has gone down to New Orleans to take care of the estate and to find out what happened to Lopasuta, if she can. His disappearance worries me a lot, too, much more than I've let on so far. There's something very funny going on, and I don't know what it is. I only hope to God she finds him and that he's all right. Anyhow, to get back to Burt, it might not be a bad idea for him to go have a chat with Marius Thornton up at Windhaven Plantation, and see what they're going to have by way of crops by early fall. Marius, I think, could use the help along about now, and it would be good for Burt, too—it'll take his mind off things."

"That's a wonderful idea, Andy. I feel so sorry for him. He's such a good, decent man."

"I know," Andy morosely agreed. "Why is it that the good always seem to die young? And there was something else that Shakespeare said—what was it now—"

"I know," Jessica offered with a sigh. " 'The evil that men do lives after them, the good is oft interred with their bones.' Isn't that it?"

"That's it, Jessica honey. And that's just what I was thinking. Oh, well, we'd better turn in. And tomorrow I'll have a chat with Burt."

The next day, Burt Coleman mounted his roan gelding and rode along the river trail to the red-brick chateau. Dismounting, he took his horse to the stable and then walked out to the fields in search of Marius Thornton.

The affable black warmly greeted him and, tactful almost to a fault, led him down the neatly sectioned rows to show him the progress of the varied crops that Luke

Bouchard had ordered for this year. Burt watched attentively, praising Marius's decision to devote a limited number of acres to cotton, planting it only after three or four years to give the fertile land a rest from this nutrition-draining crop, which had ruined so much soil and land prior to the Civil War because greedy plantation owners hadn't rotated it with other crops. "You see here, Burt," Marius enthusiastically explained, "here we're using one acre for snap beans, and another for yams, and two more for melons and berries. Mr. Luke always knew we could sell these in Montgomery and Lowndesboro, and a good bit down to Mobile, even. Cotton is perking up a bit, pricewise, but Mr. Luke was always leery of it—and I don't blame him any."

"You're doing a great job, Marius. In a smaller way, for Senator Haskins, I'm seeing that his land isn't ruined by just one or two crops. But then," Burt philosophically smiled, "he's at a stage now in life where he doesn't have to worry about what the land brings for him—it's what's in his head that counts. I wouldn't be surprised if one day he got to be governor."

"And he could do it, too, Burt," Marius enthusiastically nodded. "Now, we've got some prime suckling pigs that are just about ready for old Dalbert's store as well as for Mr. Graves's butcher shop in Montgomery. And we've even got some cattle out at the eastern boundary—you see out there? It's good grass, rich and thick, and the critters thrive on it. We can always sell a side of beef without any trouble, and once in a while the army post down near Mobile wants about ten or twenty head. I'll be sending them down in August, I reckon—leastwise, that's what Mr. Luke asked me to do, before he died."

"I've never seen such good rich land—even better than Mr. Haskins's spread," Burt confessed.

"It's got a history to it, Burt, maybe that's why. Maybe because old Mr. Luke's grandfather knew what to do with it and respected it. And that's what I was trained to do, respect the land."

"I feel the same way as you, Marius."

"It's getting hot out now, and it's nigh onto lunchtime. Why don't you come in and let our new cook fix you up something nice? I know you—" Marius stopped short, stopping himself just in time, as he was about to touch on an agonizing topic.

Burt eyed him, bit his lip, and then declared, "I'll admit I've got an appetite. And I could stand a good meal. I've been going around the last few days on just nerves and nothing else, Marius. Thanks a lot."

As he said these words, his eyes suddenly watered, and he turned away and pretended to cough to hide his emotion, remembering how lovely Marietta had teasingly asked him at the very outset of their brief marriage what foods he liked best and then gone out of her way to cook him special treats.

Marius pretended not to notice his friend's nostalgic recollections as he jauntily explained, "Our brand-new cook is a looker. Name of Amelia McAdams. Her previous employer treated her just terrible, but that's all over now, and she's happy as a lark. You know, she cooks as good as my own Clemmie, and I can't give any woman any higher praise than that. But come on, you'll see for yourself!"

Burt Coleman listlessly agreed and followed Marius to the back of the red-brick chateau and into the kitchen, where Amelia McAdams was busy cooking chicken and sweet yams. Her face was flushed from the heat of the stove, and she was obviously too busy to do more than give Marius a smiling nod of greeting.

"Miss Amelia," Marius respectfully spoke up, "would it be all right if the two of us had some lunch in the kitchen, that is, if it wouldn't be too much trouble?"

"Why no, it'd be fine. You and your friend just sit down at the table. These things are nearly done, so I'll serve you before I get lunch for the others. Your wife wants something light for the children, seeing as how the weather is so warm."

"That'll be just fine—mmm, that chicken and those yams smell scrumptious!" Marius beamed as he gestured to Burt to sit down with him. "By the way, Miss Amelia, this is Burt Coleman."

"I'm very pleased to know you, Mr. Coleman." Amelia turned and gave the tall Southerner a warm smile. She had already been told of Burt's tragic loss, although she had not as yet met him, working as he did on Andy Haskins's land.

"Likewise, Miss Amelia." Burt managed a genuine smile.

A few minutes later, the attractive octoroon served both men baked chicken and sweet yams and poured lemonade into tall glasses, before setting a loaf of home-baked bread on the table along with a crock of butter and a jar of jam. Amelia herself had made the jam, and Marius was loud in his praises, making the young woman blush as she laid out a tray of food for the four older Bouchard children and some of the chicken and yams for Clementine.

"Let me carry that tray for you, Miss Amelia," Burt volunteered, springing to his feet.

"I can manage. Thank you, Mr. Coleman."

"It's pretty heavy, and anyhow, it's my way of saying thank you for that tasty lunch, Miss Amelia. I'd appreciate it a heap if you'd let me," he offered.

Amelia blushed and lowered her eyes and then handed him the tray. As they walked down the hallway and up the stairs to the children's playroom, she said in a low sweet voice, "I'm so awfully sorry about your wife, Mr. Coleman."

He turned to stare at her a moment, and then tears welled into his eyes as he said hoarsely, "I guess time will just have to make me forget the hurt of it."

"I guess that's right. I—I know there's nothing I can really do to help—especially being a perfect stranger and all—but, but I want you to know that—that I've been through painful times, too, and I think I can understand a little of what you're feeling."

Burt was startled at this sensitive comment from a comparative stranger and gave her a sharp, almost suspicious look. But when their eyes met, he saw there was a warm sympathy in hers, and he felt his tears start in earnest. He had to content himself with a nod, and by then they had reached the playroom.

As they returned to the kitchen, Burt found himself looking at the attractive young octoroon, and despite the surging, grieving remembrance, he found himself saying to her, "You're a kind person, Miss Amelia. Thank you for saying what you did."

"I—I hope I didn't offend you, Mr. Coleman—"

"You didn't. I'm grateful to you for it. Well, I'd best be

getting back. I work for Senator Haskins, you know. Maybe I'll see you again."

"That—that would be very nice, Mr. Coleman," Amelia stammered.

## Seventeen

After arriving back at the red-brick chateau, following her husband's tragic and heroic death, Laure Bouchard's first impulse had been to send word to his older children, Lucien Edmond and Mara on Windhaven Range. However, during the preparations for the funeral, she could not bring herself to make the journey back to Montgomery to dispatch a message by telegraph, nor did she even, in her grief, take time to ask one of the workers from the plantation to go in her stead and send the message for her. Moreover, she was not certain whether the telegram should be sent to Corpus Christi or to San Antonio. In either case, it would then have to be carried overland by courier to the ranch, or perhaps—in the case of a message sent to San Antonio—be held for Lucien Edmond at his bank. There was, in short, no easy, quick, and reliable way to get word to her stepchildren—and they certainly could not possibly get to Windhaven Plantation in time for the funeral, no matter how quickly word was sent.

She decided that since she was very eager to get to New Orleans to consult with Jason Barntry, she would send Lucien Edmond a telegram from there, which would reach him just as quickly as a wire from Mobile or Montgomery. She would welcome his help in arranging Luke's affairs, but even without him she felt secure in the knowledge that she could rely on the business acumen of Jason Barntry in helping her find a competent overseer for Windhaven Plantation, as well as directing her to make such other investments as might be wise to strengthen her husband's estate.

171

Following her trip down to Mobile on the *Belle of the River,* Laure stayed overnight in a comfortable inn and boarded the packet rather late the next morning for the journey to New Orleans. Once the packet had docked along the huge wharf of the Queen City, she was able, thanks to the solicitous captain's help, to obtain a carriage that drove her to the small but elegant hotel she favored on St. Louis Avenue. It was rarely crowded, the clientele was usually of the best quality, and it was quiet—the ideal retreat for her stay.

As Laure began to think of the tremendous new responsibilities that Luke's untimely death had suddenly thrust upon her, she found herself reacting with exhaustion— more from nerves than real physical fatigue—and she decided to nap in her room. Upon awakening, she had the bellboy bring up a tray of food so that she would not have to dress and go out. It was a leisurely beginning, and it helped settle her nerves and crystalize her thoughts on what must be done to safeguard the plantation.

On the morning of the third day since she had left Lowndesboro, she awoke refreshed after a welcome, dreamless sleep, had breakfast sent up to her room, and then went down to the street to summon a *fiacre* to drive her to the Brunton & Barntry Bank.

New Orleans was already humid, a harbinger of the mercilessly torrid summer to come. By now, even though it was still only early in June, many wealthy Creoles would be making plans to travel upriver to their summer retreats, taking their leave of all business and practical matters to relax with their wives or mistresses. They would be escaping more than merely the heat: being located on the coast, this city, like Galveston, was vulnerable to the annual scourge of yellow fever.

As Laure entered the bank, a tall, attractive blond woman rose from a desk and cordially greeted her: "Good morning, ma'am, may I help you?"

"I am here to see Mr. Barntry. My name is Mrs. Laure Bouchard."

"Please have a seat, Mrs. Bouchard, and I will tell him directly that you're waiting to see him." The attractive woman gestured to a semicircular padded-leather bench to one side of the bank's entrance. Laure thanked her and seated herself.

172

"What is it, Judith?" Jason Barntry looked up from a sheaf of papers, frowning at the interruption. He was examining the estimated prices given by the New Orleans Stock Exchange for the cotton harvest this summer and fall: the price had risen a few cents since last year, but it was still far from the profitable high level that had been reached nearly a generation before the Civil War. There was too much competition abroad, in the West Indies, even Cuba. Since the English mills could afford to pick and choose, they considered the cost of transportation to England a vital factor in determining where and how much they bought of the South's most famous crop.

"There's a Mrs. Laure Bouchard to see you, Mr. Barntry," the young woman quietly informed him.

"My gracious! Show her in right away! And would you mind bringing some black coffee for both of us and some of the cornbread that Lois Marder was kind enough to bake and bring us this morning?"

"Right away, sir."

"Thank you, Judith."

As Judith Branshaw escorted Laure into Jason Barntry's office, the frail, white-haired bank manager rose from his desk and came forward to meet her, his kindly face furrowed in compassion. "My dear, dear Mrs. Bouchard," he began, taking both her hands in his, "I read of your terrible loss yesterday and I am still suffering from the shock of it. Words can never express my heartfelt sympathy. But how did it happen? The account in the *Times-Picayune* gave only the barest details. Please sit down and tell me everything!"

Laure Bouchard proceeded to give Jason Barntry a full account of Luke's tragic death, ending by saying, "So you see, Jason, it's important that I settle Luke's affairs—look into his financial holdings and the like."

"My God, how terrible for you—and for the children! Luke gone—as noble, as fine a man as his wonderful grandfather!" Jason sighed and shook his head. "But why isn't Lopasuta handling all of this for you?"

"I'm sure he will, Jason, but for the time being, at least, I'm looking after our affairs because Lopasuta hasn't been heard from since he came to New Orleans a couple of weeks ago. Geraldine and I are terribly worried. Have you seen him?"

"Good heavens, yes, of course I have—some time ago now. He came here to tell me that he had had a letter from a William Brickley, and he also asked about the monthly report on Windhaven. Then he told me he was going to visit Mr. Brickley. You say he hasn't been heard from? But I can't believe it!"

"Do you know this Mr. Brickley, Jason?" Laure earnestly demanded.

"Why, yes. He's quite a successful businessman in New Orleans, with many holdings. And he is one of the bank's larger depositors."

"I'd like very much to visit him, if you'd give me the address. Lopasuta didn't leave the letter with his wife, Geraldine, so that all she knows is Brickley's name, but not where his office is."

"I'll get that for you, of course. Oh, here comes the coffee now, and there's some fresh cornbread, too."

"I—I'll just take some black coffee. Thank you. I've tried to rest and numb my mind to everything that's happened, but I'm still overwhelmed by everything, as you can imagine."

"Yes, of course I can," Jason sympathetically agreed.

Judith Branshaw entered, set down the tray, poured out two brimming cups, and then, with a pleasant nod, she left the office and closed the door behind her.

"That's a very charming young woman, Jason. I don't recall seeing her when I was last here—but of course that was many years ago."

"Her name is Judith Branshaw. Four years ago she was coerced into helping some carpetbaggers with a black-mailing scheme, but Andy Haskins—whom they were trying to discredit—and your husband both felt that she should be given a new chance—especially after what had happened to her to bring her to Montgomery in the first place."

"And what was that, Jason?"

"She was raised on a farm near Tensaw, Mrs. Bouchard, and after her parents' death she stayed on to work it with the help of their loyal workers, four freed blacks. In her loneliness she fell in love with a handsome, deceiving, scoundrel who arranged for the Ku Klux Klan to—well, I shan't go into details, Mrs. Bouchard; let's say that they abused her in every way possible, giving her

174

fickle lover an excuse to renounce her. Soon after that, she went to Montgomery. With her self-esteem in tatters, she was easy prey for the carpetbaggers who used her as a pawn in their game."

"Oh, yes, now I remember! Good lord, you mean *that* was the girl whom they put on Andy's lap and had a picture taken to suggest that he was unfaithful to Jessica?" Laure demanded.

"The very same. She's started a new life here. She works hard at her job, and she has made friends for the bank. Yes, Mrs. Bouchard, her story is another of the many examples of your husband's great compassion and humanitarianism. He will never be forgotten, I assure you."

Laure sipped her coffee and her eyes momentarily closed to acknowledge this tribute to the man she had so fervently loved. Then at last she said, "I'd really like to have the benefit of your advice, Jason, in helping me select a manager for Windhaven Plantation. I've already spoken to Marius Thornton about this—he's the foreman right now, and a good one, too, but because of the growth and variety of the operations at Windhaven Plantation, I feel that it would be wise to have someone supervise him, someone more sophisticated, and aware of all of the various markets, not only up where we are but also in Mobile and New Orleans, and possibly up North eventually. Perhaps you can advise me as to where to find such a man."

"I'll do what I can, I promise you."

"While I'm in New Orleans I'd also like to investigate the possibility of an investment that may bring us a better return than what we have—perhaps a gambling casino."

"That's an unusual choice for you, Mrs. Bouchard."

"Not really, when you consider that Luke met me at the Union House just after the war, when it was made into a bordello to hide the fact that it was a bank still loyal to good, honest Southerners. Understand me, I don't propose to have fancy girls in such a place; just gambling, good wines and spirits, and attractive employees who will lend an air of elegance to the establishment. My husband often predicted that the Queen City would develop rapidly in the years to come with increasing flows of tourists, businessmen, speculators, and the like. So I should think that one might expect a quick return from such an investment."

"That's true enough, Mrs. Bouchard. But we'll talk again about this at a later date, I'm sure. Have you found comfortable quarters?"

"Oh, yes, I'm at the New Frontier Hotel on St. Louis."

"Ah, yes, a very civilized, quiet establishment. It embodies the very best of what New Orleans has to offer."

"Yes, I'll admit to you, I've been just a tiny bit homesick for New Orleans"—her face was shadowed—"though I never dreamed I'd come back here under the circumstances that forced me to make this trip."

"Nor I, certainly, God knows!" the old bank manager sympathetically responded. "Well then, since you wish to visit Mr. Brickley, I'll have Miss Branshaw write down his address for you. From what I understand, he makes his office in one of the several houses of pleasure that he owns on Rampart Street."

"Thank you very much. But before I visit him, I want to send Lucien Edmond and Mara a telegram. It's unlikely that news has reached them about Luke's death. Then, too, as Luke's oldest son, Lucien Edmond must have something to say about the decisions that are before me now."

Laure rose, and Jason rose with her and escorted her to the front door of the bank. "There's a telegraph office a block north of here, Mrs. Bouchard," the banker said, "I'll hail a carriage—"

"No, no, I'll walk. It's such a lovely day. I'll return later this afternoon, once I've seen Mr. Brickley. Until then, Jason. Good morning to you." Laure Bouchard extended her hand and Jason Barntry brought it to his lips in tribute, bowing low. Laure blushed, and there were tears in her eyes as she turned to walk down the street.

Entering the telegraph office, she sent off a brief message:

Dear Lucien Edmond:
    With great sorrow I must inform you that your dear father has been taken from us. He was brought down by a bullet meant for Governor Houston. We buried him beside Grandfather and Dimarte. Please accept my heartfelt sympathies and convey them to Mara as well. You are both in my thoughts and prayers.
    I am in New Orleans now and wonder if you can come to help me decide the future of Windhaven Plan-

tation. You can reach me in care of Brunton & Barntry Bank or the New Frontier Hotel. All my love to you and Mara, Maxine, Ramón, and the children.

Laure Bouchard

The telegrapher informed Laure that her message would be wired to San Antonio, where a mounted rider would take it on to Carrizo Springs in about four days. Laure nodded, frowning at the delay, but understanding there was nothing that could be done about it. She told herself that she would doubtless be staying in New Orleans for at least a week, in any case, and by then surely Lucien Edmond would reply with a message of his own.

She had no way of knowing that Luke's oldest son had left the Range ten days before, heading for the army fort near Santa Fe, to fill a contract for a thousand head of prime beef.

Leaving the telegrapher's office, Laure hailed a genial black driver of a *fiacre* and directed him to the Rampart Street address of William Brickley. She told herself that if she learned anything about Lopasuta, she would immediately return to the telegrapher's office and send back word to Geraldine.

## Eighteen

William Brickley rose from his upholstered chair in the luxurious private office of La Musée des Délices and came forward to greet Laure Bouchard with a deferential gravity. Observing her costume of mourning, he gave her a courtly inclination of his head and suavely said, "This is an unexpected honor you do me, Mrs. Bouchard. I perceive from your attire that you have had a grievous loss—permit me to offer my deepest condolences."

"Thank you, Mr. Brickley. It was my husband, Luke Bouchard."

"Forgive me—I was unpardonably *gauche*, Mrs. Bouchard. Yes, I read about his heroic death in the *Times-Picayune*. Please, Mrs. Bouchard, sit down here, you'll find this chair most comfortable. May I have my majordomo bring you some light refreshment? A glass of white wine, perhaps, or some tea, or our favorite Creole *café au lait*?" Gallantly, he gestured toward a sumptuous armchair with lace antimacassars at the top of the back and along the arms.

"No, thank you, Mr. Brickley. I appreciate your sentiments. You didn't, by any chance, know my husband?" Laure asked, as she seated herself.

William Brickley, wearing a white linen frock coat, flowery cravat, and neatly creased fawn-colored trousers, seated himself on the edge of a small settee opposite Laure Bouchard and shook his head. "Regretfully, only by reputation. As it happens, I do a good deal of my banking business at the Brunton & Barntry Bank, and Mr. Barntry has, on occasion, mentioned your husband. You see, Mrs.

178

Bouchard, I have many holdings and investments in and around New Orleans, and I was asking Mr. Barntry if he might suggest the names of some other depositors who might be interested in a kind of investment partnership in some of my enterprises. That was how your husband's name came up."

"Oh, yes, I see." Laure bit her lip nervously, looking down at the floor, and then leaned forward toward her suave host. "It's possible, now that I must of necessity look after the affairs of my late husband and the estate, that I may have a bit of business to discuss with you in the near future. However, my reason for coming here this morning—and I do hope that I have not disturbed you by coming without any appointment this early in the day—"

"Please, dear lady." The forty-eight-year-old entrepreneur held up his elegantly manicured hand, revealing the cuff of a fine monogrammed silk shirt with gold cuff links. "It is I, rather, who must apologize to you again for bringing up what I know is a distressingly painful subject. I am entirely at your disposal, Mrs. Bouchard."

"You're most kind, Mr. Brickley. Well then—you may or may not know that Lopasuta Bouchard, the Montgomery attorney, is my late husband's adopted son. I visited his wife, Geraldine, and learned from her that you had sent him a letter requesting aid with a legal problem, I believe—"

"That's quite correct, Mrs. Bouchard."

"Well you see, Mr. Brickley, the puzzling thing is that it has been a couple of weeks at least since your appointment, and yet there has been no word from him. When I left Montgomery some few days ago, Geraldine was beside herself with worry. And since she was about to give birth to their first child, you can understand her anxiety—it was quite out of character for him not to communicate in some way. That was why I came here this morning, Mr. Brickley, to ask if you can give me any explanation as to what might have happened to him. Did you retain his services? Is he still in New Orleans?"

William Brickley rose, clasped his hands behind his back, and frowned thoughtfully. "I am completely at a loss. I am deeply sorry that I am not able to give you much information, but I will tell you exactly what happened. When I explained the details of the suits with

which I am threatened, Mr. Bouchard felt I had best seek
legal counsel here. The plaintiff in these matters—a liti-
gious man, to say the least—is suing me about a number
of contracts, some signed here in Louisiana, some in Alabama. I had hoped Mr. Bouchard might feel able to advise
me and represent me in the matters coming under Alabama jurisdiction, but he seemed to feel strongly that the
Lousiana suits, being the first filed, would have to be
settled first, and that it would not be ethical for him to
comment on them. I confess the legal reasoning seems
fairly arbitrary to me, but the gist of it is that my primary
defending attorney must be admitted to the Louisiana
bar."

"I see," Laure faltered, "but did he say if he was going
back to Montgomery, or, indeed, do you remember anything he might have said to indicate what he would do,
since he had no further business here?"

"Let me try to remember—" Brickley closed his eyes
and passed his elegantly manicured hand over his high-
arching forehead. "I do know that he mentioned having
stopped in earlier at the bank—"

"Yes, Jason Barntry told me this morning that he had
seen Lopasuta briefly, but not after that meeting."

"I see. Now let me think again, Mrs. Bouchard. I saw to
it that he was recompensed for his transportation and expenses, and I said that I was very sorry he could not help
me, for I had read in the *Advertiser*, which is regularly
sent to me, the many stories of his courtroom victories. He
is a most able lawyer and a very personable young man—
he does the name of Bouchard great credit, may I add."

"Yes, yes," Laure blurted out, "but can't you tell me
anything else he might have said that would give a clue as
to what he intended to do after he left your office, Mr.
Brickley?"

"I do wish I could help you. For the life of me, considering his poised and well-organized demeanor and his
great caution regarding his own ethical position vis-à-vis
my case, I should have said that it was very much out of
character for him to be unaccountably missing, as you
now tell me he is. Unless, perish the thought, he might
have met with foul play. Wait a bit—is it possible that he
might have gone elsewhere to appraise the condition
of other Bouchard holdings?"

"My late husband's oldest son runs a large cattle ranch in Texas. Why, I suppose he might have gone there—though he certainly didn't mention anything to Geraldine. I certainly hope that is the explanation—though I cannot imagine why he didn't send word to his wife, as he promised he would do."

"That, I fear, is beyond my poor powers of divination, dear Mrs. Bouchard. I wish I could be of greater service to you in this matter—I feel my assistance has been so dreadfully inadequate in view of your great loss and now this assuredly disturbing situation." He faced her and gave her a rueful little smile as, in his suavest tone, he added, "If there's anything I can do to help you in your search, you have only to ask me. I have business contacts that extend even into Texas, as it happens. If you wish, I could send a telegram to one of my associates and ask him to look for Mr. Bouchard."

"No, thank you very much, Mr. Brickley, but I've already sent a telegram informing Lucien Edmond of his father's death, you see. Perhaps when he replies to me, he may give me the news that Lopasuta actually did go to visit him in Texas."

"I surely hope so, for your sake, Mrs. Bouchard! Are you quite certain you won't take some small refreshment?"

"No, thank you, Mr. Brickley. You've been very kind, and I appreciate it." Laure rose with a weary sigh.

"Allow me to escort you to the street and to call a carriage for you, dear lady," he proffered.

"Thank you again. I'm sorry to have disturbed you."

"I only wish I might be so delightfully disturbed each day of my life, Mrs. Bouchard." With this, William Brickley reached for Laure's black-gloved hand and brought it to his lips. She regarded him, her cheeks coloring, and her eyes momentarily moist. Luke had courted her in this very city and Brickley's gallantry recalled that of her beloved husband. Now the exquisite courtesy of this undeniably attractive, mature man with his Vandyke beard and imposing sideburns, at home in a milieu of elegance and luxury, had a forceful impression even through her grief and growing anxiety over the disappearance of her adopted son. And in a low, unsteady voice she murmured, "I thank you for your concern and your hospitality, Mr. Brickley. And yes, I should be grateful if you would call me a carriage. I think I'll go back to the bank and talk with Jason Barntry again."

"Perhaps, Mrs. Bouchard, if you plan to extend your stay in our beautiful city, you would grant me the esteemed privilege and honor of dining or lunching with me some day at your convenience. I believe you mentioned that you might wish to discuss some business with me. Perhaps in that way we could kill two birds with the proverbial stone, if you are so minded?"

"Perhaps, Mr. Brickley. I will certainly communicate with you, if I find, upon advice from Mr. Barntry, that an investment would be judicious. You know, since Lopasuta is also the family lawyer, it is up to me alone to try to conduct the affairs of the estate in a way that will safeguard it for all the Bouchards. I must be very cautious and examine every possibility very carefully."

"I admire your honesty and your refreshing candor, Mrs. Bouchard. Rest assured that, if the fortuitous occasion of our discussing business should arise, I would open my ledgers to you and otherwise fully disclose the details of my business affairs. And I'm sure that Mr. Barntry will confirm that my deposits are quite substantial at his excellent bank."

"Thank you again for all your kindness."

"Here comes your carriage—let me help you inside. A very good day to you, Mrs. Bouchard."

## Nineteen

When Jason Barntry had escorted Laure Bouchard to the door of the Brunton & Barntry bank, Judith Branshaw had watched her from her desk. She shook her head, thinking to herself what a pity it was that such a young and attractive woman as Mrs. Bouchard should be widowed. Mr. Barntry—such a dear man—how kindly and courtly he was in the way he treated her! He obviously cared a great deal about her. But then, that was his way—he cared about everyone. He was a fine old gentleman, and if he was a bit absent-minded at times, well, at his age he was entitled to be.

Picking up a sheaf of papers from her desk, Judith sighed, recalling the conversation that she had had with her employer the day before. She had gone to his office with the morning's mail, as usual, and as usual he had greeted her with that gentle, preoccupied smile of his. But then he had put down his pen and, clearing his throat awkwardly, as if seeking a way to begin, had surprised her with these words:

"By the by, Judith, I want to tell you how happy we are with you here. I know I've said this before, but it bears repeating: you have a secure future with us. We like your intelligence, your loyalty, and the helpfulness you show our customers—who are the very life blood of the bank, after all."

Judith had been quick to reply. "I'm very grateful, Mr. Barntry, for the chance you've given me. I think you can guess just how much."

Recalling this exchange, Judith set aside her papers and

183

reached into her reticule for a lace-trimmed handkerchief with which she surreptitiously dabbed her tearful dark-blue eyes. Jason Barntry's words had touched her to the core; they had also revived memories that were bitter and tortured.

She remembered how, four years ago, she had been betrayed by the treacherous David Fales. If only she had been more cynical, more sophisticated, she would have realized that his professed love for her was merely lust.

She would gladly see him roast in hell for the savage treatment he had arranged for her at the hands of his partners in crime, the Klansmen, believing that if she were sullied she would have had no choice but to submit to his demands that she warm his bed without the benefit of marriage. She had proved him wrong—but only barely. For having believed herself ruined for the rest of her life, and without a penny to her name, she had gone to Montgomery to ply that most ancient of trades.

Oh, she had been so bitter then, wanting to avenge herself on fine Southern gentlemen like Fales. She would always feel guilty over having been so easily convinced to become part of that horrible blackmail scheme involving Representative Haskins. Thank God it hadn't succeeded, and that he was able to continue in politics, doing so much good for people.

She was still almost overwhelmed at the kindness he and poor Mr. Bouchard had shown her, helping her get this wonderful job. She thanked God for the opportunity to lead a decent life in decent surroundings, where no one—except dear old Mr. Barntry—knew of the degradation to which David Fales had so cruelly subjected her. Indeed, her fear that her past might be disclosed to others in her adopted home had been so great that when she first came to New Orleans, it had been under an assumed name. But Mr. Barntry—bless him—had convinced her that such a device was unnecessary and that she needn't feel apprehensive. This had set her mind greatly at ease, for she was fundamentally an honest person to whom duplicity was unnatural.

Judith's striking beauty—her tall, slender frame, her luminous eyes, pert nose, and sweet full mouth—had attracted many handsome admirers during these past four years, and her comfortable and well-paying job at the bank had brought to her invitations from many respectable gentlemen. Yet she had refused all such overtures, even invitations to dinner or the theater, turning them aside with a gracious smile and a soft word to ease the bluntness of her refusal.

This purposeful aloofness was not entirely due to her determination to avoid further heartbreak and betrayal. Whenever she undressed before the full-length mirror in the bedroom of her small but comfortable apartment she saw the ineradicable scars of that vicious flogging years before. Even today, she could not help weeping and then loathing herself at the sight of them. She regarded them not only as physical scars, but also—far more devastatingly—as signs of moral downfall. She judged herself, with an almost punitive self-destructiveness, as being unworthy of a man of honor. She had never forgotten David Fales's insolent reference to her as "damaged goods" after the attack. And that was why she had steadfastly refused to accept even the most harmless social invitation from a man—yes, even when Jason Barntry had himself remarked that this or that customer of the bank was a person of innate good character and decency—and unmarried. Instead, she contented herself with many a long evening spent in conversation with the lonely, gossipy widow, Mrs. Dorcas Fulton, who ran her boarding house.

She had cut her long, honey-colored hair when she had first come to New Orleans and wore it in a modest, piled upsweep that made her look at least five years older than her twenty-five years. This, too, was her unconscious way of announcing that she was *hors de concours* to the opposite sex.

Yet she was happy in her work, at first out of sheer gratitude for this second chance, and then because Jason Barntry was a thoughtful, considerate man: appreciative of her energetic application to her job. She had been delighted when the simple tasks he had first assigned her had led to constantly increasing responsibilities. Her success had been rewarded by a sizable raise in salary at the end of each year of her employment, which enabled her to buy books and lithographs for her apartment. At times, he sent her on errands across the city to interview the officers of other financial institutions, as well as those of the Stock Exchange and some of the bond and mortgage houses. She had taken pains with her reports, and he had often complimented her on the depth and scope of her coverage and their consequent value to him in the bank. Gradually, Judith Branshaw had begun to regain her self-esteem.

But recently, she had chanced to meet an unusual man, a customer of the bank and a friend of Barntry's, and for the first time since her ill-fated infatuation with David Fales, she had felt a twinge of emotion, a buried need for love and trust. Yet even now, that brooding sense of moral inferiority held her back from candidly admitting to herself that for the first time since leaving Tensaw, she had come to care for someone. It was just last month that Bernard Marquard had entered the bank. He was as tall as David Fales, but stockier, with a pleasant face, a crisp little beard flecked with gray, and curly, short-cropped hair. He had been a captain in the Confederate Army and had lost his sight at Gettysburg. Jason Barntry had casually remarked to Judith that besides being an excellent customer of the bank, Marquard was a personal friend. The latter had been loyal to the Confederacy, but had been enough of a realist to understand that the South would inevitably lose the war because of the North's sheer strength and superiority in arms. Just before the attack on Fort Sumter, Bernard Marquard had converted most of the profits from his Virginia plantation into gold and deposited it into an English bank, not unlike what old Lucien Bouchard had done so many years before.

Jason had told Judith something else that had evoked a sympathy for this self-reliant man: before the war had ended, and immediately upon learning that her husband had been blinded for the rest of his life, Marquard's shallow, flirtatious wife, Elinor, had run away with a Union officer. Unselfishly, her blind husband had permitted her to obtain a divorce so that she could marry her lover; he had then moved to New Orleans two years after Appomattox, transferring most of his funds to the Brunton & Barntry Bank.

Although he was financially well-off because of his shrewd conversion of land into gold, he had determined to keep himself busy. He had become a patron of the opera and of the symphony, and helped young people who had skills in various arts and crafts to develop their abilities, and he had opened a shop that sold their handcrafted articles.

After the war, Bernard's orderly had stayed on as his companion to help him adjust to the total blindness that had rendered this robust man so helpless. Jesse Jacklin was a Tennesseean, now forty-nine years old, wiry and jovial of nature. Before he had been assigned to Bernard as an orderly, he had been a male nurse working in military hospitals on the battlefields, and had learned how to care for those who had suffered wounds and disability.

At the outset of Bernard's blindness, the former Confederate captain had depended on Jesse almost as a child would depend upon his father. But Jesse, because of his optimistic nature, had been a stalwart inspiration for his employer. He had constantly urged the blind officer to be grateful for the gift of life and its potential, despite the handicap of blindness. In fact, he had almost indignantly attacked Bernard's initial reactions of self-pity to his misfortune and then, shortly after that, to his wife's treachery. He had bought an English retriever in Virginia and trained it to be Bernard Marquard's constant companion so that the older man would have some mobility. Just a year ago, Jesse married an attractive forty-year-old widow who owned a house a block away from the two-story house that Bernard had purchased when he had come to New Orleans. The two men still remained close friends, but the difference was that Bernard Marquard, who had developed a stubborn independence with the help of Jesse Jacklin's constant and at times almost dictatorial exhortations, was no longer dependent on his former orderly.

Judith Branshaw remembered their first meeting. Bernard Marquard had come into the Brunton & Barntry Bank, with the retriever on a short leash. He had stumbled over the smooth floor immediately after crossing the threshold of the entrance, and Judith had risen from her desk and instinctively gone to help him. Brusquely he said, "Thank you, I can fend for myself, if you don't mind." She had blushed furiously, taken aback by his crochety irritation, and then he had said, "Is Mr. Barntry in this morning?"

And when she had answered in the affirmative, he had remarked, "I know the way. I'll find it. Thank you. I know my way about here."

She had watched him walk with confident steps toward the back of the bank and on to Jason Barntry's office, and seen Mr. Barntry come out and greet the blind gray-haired man before stooping down to pet the English retriever. And a flicker of admiration and respect for Bernard Marquard's independence had been her first real sentiment toward a person of the opposite sex since her terrible ordeal.

After Marquard had left the bank, she had taken the mail to Jason Barntry and he then told her the story of the blind man's past. That night, alone in her rooms, Judith Branshaw inexplicably burst into tears and then angrily rebuked herself for such a maudlin sentiment. After all, why should it matter to her that this man had been blinded and then betrayed by his wife?

But ten days later, Bernard Marquard came into the bank again. It was a rainy morning, and just as he entered, a slightly tipsy Creole dandy in a ruffled shirt and florid cravat lurched against the blind man and knocked him down. The English retriever growled his protest, and Judith sprang to her feet, came forward, and indignantly declared, "M'sieu Florieux, you should really be more careful—knocking down a blind man. You should be ashamed of yourself! Just go out of the bank quietly, if you can!" Then, stooping, she stammered, her face crimson at her own audacity, "This time, Mr. Marquard, I must insist you let me help you. That was very rude of M'sieu Florieux, and he didn't even have the courtesy to apologize!"

"That's very kind of you, M-Miss—?" Bernard turned his sightless eyes toward the attractive young woman.

"My name is Judith Branshaw, Mr. Marquard. Let me help you, please."

"Well, I can't refuse such charming aid, I'm sure. Thank you very much."

He grasped her hand and she drew him to his feet and steadied him. And then, unexpectedly, he put out his hand and slowly stroked her face, making her blush violently. She understood that it was his way of "seeing" her, although at first she flinched from a man's touch. And then he said, "You're very lovely, Miss Branshaw. Thank you again for being so kind."

She watched him head toward Jason Barntry's office,

and she felt herself trembling. There was a swell of deepest respect and admiration in her for his gentleness, which was at odds with a fierce self-reliance that he had originally shown her.

She returned to her desk and occupied herself with the paperwork that had been assigned to her, and when she saw Bernard Marquard leaving Jason Barntry's office, the English retriever faithfully at his side and glancing up at him to make sure that his master was following with an unbroken gait, she rose and said, "May I open the door for you, Mr. Marquard?"

"Thank you again, Miss Branshaw. I hope you'll pardon my having touched you—it's the way I've learned to see——"

"I—I understand, Mr. Marquard. There's no need for you to apologize."

"It's a curious thing," Marquard continued, "but my fingers have learned to understand more about people than ever my eyes did. Not facts and events, of course, but something far more important."

Judith found his words both compelling and calming, and she experienced an unfamiliar sense of good will—almost of trust. Before she realized what she was saying, Judith heard herself counter lightly, "Does that mean you've found out something about me?"

"Ah, Miss Branshaw, I'm afraid the brevity of our acquaintance does not permit me to say, but you should know that when I mentioned your loveliness a few minutes ago, I was not referring to physical beauty alone. I would, however, very much like to have the opportunity to get better acquainted. Would you think me importunate if I asked you for the privilege of dining with you some evening?"

To her own surprise, Judith found her voice unsteady as she almost eagerly responded, "That—that would be very nice, Mr. Marquard. I should like that very much indeed."

Three days later, when he came back to the bank on business, he invited her out to dinner that very evening, and Judith Branshaw accepted. He took her to the little restaurant on Eglantine Street, owned by old Felix Brissart. Felix Brissart had, eleven years ago, married young Aurelia Dubois, who had once been forced out of economic need to work in the Union House where Laure Prindeville had been hostess. It had been Laure, in fact, who brought them together by finding Aurelia a respectable singing job in Brissart's restaurant. Brissart, now in his mid-sixties, basked in his marital happiness; Aurelia had given him two sons and a daughter, and on occasion she still came to the restaurant to play her mandolin and sing the old songs of the Auvergne, a special treat for the regular customers who greatly appreciated her lovely voice and delicate accompaniment.

As it chanced, on the very evening that Bernard Marquard took Judith Branshaw to dinner there, the mature, still serenely beautiful Aurelia Brissart was singing some old pastoral love songs, and although she did not understand French well enough to comprehend all the words, Judith felt her eyes mist with tears at the poignant loveliness of the melodies.

For the first time since that terrible afternoon when she had been met by the four hooded assailants instead of by her trusted lover, Judith felt herself able to respond without wary suspicion to a man, and she realized that she could communicate with Bernard Marquard and empathize with him. To begin with, her respect and admiration for him in doggedly surmounting his handicap became the first bridge of trust between the two, and as he talked, simply but eloquently, about his previous life with his wife, and his own interest in the arts—especially music—not trying to impress her with his sophistication or with the adventures he had had during the war, she warmed to him. And yet, precisely because she had placed a blindly protective veneer around herself, she could not believe that one day there might be more than warm communication between them. Even now, even after four long years of adapting to the new life in New Orleans and exclusively dedicating herself to her job, she felt herself to be flawed.

As they listened to Aurelia's exquisite singing of those haunting melodies that suggested the bucolic joys of a simple life, the elemental emotions of love and despair and hope, she saw that tears had come to the blind man's eyes and she caught her breath to see him so moved. She had to control her instinctive impulse to reach across the table and touch his hand, as if to say, "I want to share this with you; I, too, know what it is to be lonely and rejected and

190

betrayed." But she dared not, for it would have stripped her of her protective cocoon, once again rendering her soul naked, and emotionally vulnerable to a man.

She looked down at Rory, the English retriever, who lay, his head on his paws, steadily regarding his blind master from a dark corner near their table. Felix Brissart had encouraged his blind guest to bring his dog and not to worry about complaints from other customers. And, indeed, there had been none in the many visits that Bernard Marquard had paid to this charming little restaurant.

At this moment, the proprietor of the restaurant now came over to chat with Bernard Marquard and gallantly, as befitted a Frenchman, complimented Judith Branshaw and solicitously inquired if she had enjoyed the cuisine. She stammered a few words of enthusiastic praise, blushing as he bowed and said to her blind companion, "Mam'selle is a most discerning and charming young woman. You are very fortunate, M'sieu Marquard. I hope to see you both here again."

When he had gone back to the kitchen, Bernard turned toward Judith and, with a soft little laugh, said, "You've made quite an impression on old Felix, Miss Branshaw. And what he just said gives me courage to ask if, whenever it is convenient, you might consider repeating this very delightful evening. I shall be frank with you, Miss Branshaw, I haven't felt so at ease and so comfortable with a woman in many years."

She caught her breath at this, and once again, to her annoyance, found her eyes misting with tears. Not wanting to betray her emotion, she forced her voice to be banteringly casual. "Why, you're very flattering, Mr. Marquard. It's been pleasant for me, too. Yes, I'd very much enjoy dining with you again."

"Good! An after-dinner cordial perhaps, Miss Branshaw?"

"No, thank you, I'm really—my gracious, I haven't dined like this, well, really ever before. The food was just wonderful—thank you so much for taking me."

"Thank *you*, Miss Branshaw. Come, I'll see you home in a carriage, if I may."

"I—I'd much rather be sure that you got home safely, Mr. Marquard—" she blurted, and then put a hand over

191

her mouth and turned crimson, realizing too late that the remark had been tactless.

But he did not take offense. With a faint smile, he countered, "Never you mind about me. After I've dropped you off in the carriage, I'll have the driver take Rory and myself home."

"Oh, yes—I—please forgive me—I shouldn't have said that—" she tried to apologize.

"You're a very warmhearted young woman, Miss Branshaw. Please don't think you've offended me in the least. In fact, I find that your concern for me is somewhat touching, and much too flattering for an old fellow like myself. Well then, I can tell from the silence outside that the light evening rain has stopped. There should be no trouble finding a carriage."

# Twenty

Laure Bouchard, waiting for an answer to the telegram she had sent to Windhaven Range, spent the day after her visit to Jason Barntry and William Brickley in sightseeing, like any first-time visitor to the Queen City. After breakfasting at her leisure in a little sidewalk cafe on melon, *café au lait,* and freshly baked *croissants,* with honey and thick, sweet butter, she hailed a *fiacre* and had herself driven around this quaint city, whose architecture—in the beautifully elaborate homes of the wealthy and also the churches—showed traces of Spanish as well as French influence.

At the end of the day, she went to the theater, after dining at the very same restaurant on Eglantine Street where, some days before, Judith Branshaw and the blind Bernard Marquard had had their first social meeting. Lovely Aurelia Brissart immediately recognized the golden-haired hostess of the Union House who had been instrumental in sending her to her future husband's restaurant. There was a joyful reunion, and Brissart, surreptitiously mopping his eyes of the tears that clouded them, loudly called for the very finest champagne, and poured the sparkling effervescent liquid into his finest goblets. This nostalgic meeting made Laure weep in memory of what she had been and then become: a widow who would always cherish the man with whom she had shared her life and whose constancy and idealism had earned her deepest respect.

All evening, Laure found herself musing about the past, remembering the chaos that had reigned during her days at the Union House when the Queen City was in the grip of Yankee occupation: the hated soldiers in blue, the insolent officers who treated all young women—even the most gently born—as if they worked in a Rampart Street brothel. How much more civilized and thriving the city was today: it had come to life again, like a phoenix rising from the ashes of defeat, with many new businesses and buildings; and even with the oppressive summer heat beginning, Laure had noticed a steady influx of visitors from distant parts.

Everywhere there was optimism, part of it, to be sure, derived from the change in the federal administration. Even the most fanatical Southerners were hopeful that with the election of Rutherford B. Hayes and the appointment of an incorruptible cabinet, people might once again plan confidently for the future, and look forward to prosperity as a reward for their hard work. It seemed that the terrible, towering wall that had made New Orleans a kind of ghetto of defeat had at long last been razed to the ground, and not a single sign remained that it had ever existed. Laure Bouchard found the rebirth of the Queen City enormously heartening. Although nothing could take away the grief she felt at losing Luke, somehow the vitality of the city was a good omen, a harbinger of better things to come.

That next noon, when she inquired at the desk for any messages, the pleasant, soft-spoken clerk regretfully informed her that none had come for her. Laure frowned, perplexed, and then told herself that Lucien Edmond's silence was understandable after all. If he was occupied with a cattle drive, as was fairly likely, it was quite possible that her message had arrived after his departure. Having thus logically explained her stepson's failure to reply, she had a *fiacre* take her to the bank, where the graciously attentive Judith Branshaw made her presence known at once to old Jason Barntry.

"Forgive me, Mrs. Bouchard, for not having stopped at your hotel to inquire if I could in any way make your stay more pleasant," he apologized.

"That's quite all right, Jason. You have more pressing matters to attend to, I'm sure. The reason I've come here today is to ask you to think very seriously about the idea you'll recall I mentioned—opening a gambling casino of the very highest calibre catering only to trustworthy customers and not the riffraff that one might find in one of the houses along lower Rampart Street."

"Yes, Mrs. Bouchard, since you first mentioned it, I've given considerable thought to the project. You know, of course, that William Brickley owns quite a few of the most elegant, shall we say, pleasure houses in all New Orleans. I should think that he would be able to give you more practical advice on the possibility of opening such a casino than I myself. As you know, I've always frowned on gambling and licentious entertainments, and I could not, in all sincerity, endorse investing any large sums into an establishment catering to an activity that we at the bank only accept as a necessary evil."

"You put it very quaintly and primly, Jason, but I understand your meaning," Laure laughed wholeheartedly, reaching out her hand to squeeze one of his. "You haven't forgotten the Union House, I hope," she said mischievously, referring to the establishment where she had worked as hostess during the war, "a brothel that fronted for this very bank."

With some embarrassment, the elderly banker replied, "Why, that was entirely different, Mrs. Bouchard, a question of the bank's survival. And we have survived very nicely indeed, through several wars and industrial panics, I might add, so that now I pride myself in saying that there is probably no sounder, more solvent bank in all of New Orleans."

"The credit for which, in the main, must surely go to you, Jason."

"No, Mrs. Bouchard, I have only been a kind of steward. The real work was done by your first husband, John Brunton, and before him, by our founder, Antoine Rigalle, who as you know did so much for old Lucien Bouchard years ago."

"Dear Jason, the Bouchard family has been very lucky in having such good friends and loyal helpers as you, who cared about their responsibilities above and beyond the call of duty."

"Please, Mrs. Bouchard, you give me too much credit.'

"Not at all, Jason. I know that you wanted to resign your post after your wife's death. It was at the urging of our adopted son, Lopasuta, when he was here on his honeymoon with Geraldine, that you agreed to stay on and

I'm very grateful that you did." Then, reverting to the subject that had moved her to visit the banker that afternoon, Laure leaned forward and soberly demanded, "What do you really think of my idea of opening a first-class gambling casino where there will be no women for sale, but that will cater to the well-to-do and give them the antique flavor of old New Orleans in its heyday?"

"My personal views are probably much too old-fashioned, but as a businessman and as your appointed officer in this bank, Mrs. Bouchard, I'd be inclined to agree that the idea is sound, financially. Providing, of course, that you don't invest too much capital and leave yourself thin here at the bank."

"That's where you'll help me, Jason. But please continue; I'm interested in your views."

"As I've said, William Brickley is probably the best man in New Orleans at the moment to give you the practical whys and wherefores on such a project. And so far as I've been able to determine, there's really no negative information about his integrity or personal reputation. He's a shrewd businessman, and his steady profits—at least judging by the deposits he's made here over the last six months—indicate that he steers clear of risky investments. I think you should certainly talk to him and then, if he, can offer you any concrete suggestions, let me know so that I can make further investigations. I feel a great responsibility for your affairs now, following your dear husband's death, as if I were a minister or a doctor sworn by the sacred honor of his profession to do everything that he can to help. Although I may sound a bit dramatic, I want to be this kind of advisor to you, Mrs. Bouchard. And, at the same time, I'm trying to think of what your husband himself might do if he had broached just such an investment to me."

"Jason, you're absolutely unique," Laure softly murmured. She then added, "Quite apart from this business venture, as I've already mentioned, I've been thinking about finding an overseer, a capable manager with a sound, varied background. I know you won't believe I'm saying this out of snobbery or because Marius has black blood in his veins, Jason—"

"Of course not. I know you better than that, Mrs. Bouchard," Jason Barntry smiled indulgently. "And it's an excellent idea. I know from the reports that Luke occasionally sent me about your various endeavors at Windhaven Plantation that the scope was broadening; it had already occurred to me that you might shortly need a man with the qualifications you mentioned. I'll keep my eyes open. But it's possible that this William Brickley, with so many irons in the fire as he has now, might be able to recommend someone who has worked on the land and also done business with the counting houses of New Orleans, Mobile, and even St. Louis."

"Very well, I'll go see him again. However, he might not be at the Rampart Street office I visited the other day."

"That's easily determined—why don't you let me send a messenger to ask for an appointment for you, Mrs. Bouchard?" the bank manager suggested.

"Would you, Jason? That's so good of you!"

"Not at all, it's my pleasure. I'll ask Miss Branshaw to go and she'll be back directly. If he's there now, and can see you, would you wish to leave at once?"

"Yes, I would, Jason. You're sure I'm not taking that nice young woman away from her duties here?"

"Not at all. I'll go fetch her directly. Just be at your ease till I come back, Mrs. Bouchard."

A few minutes later, he returned to tell Laure that Judith Branshaw was already on her way to the ornate house of pleasure, where Brickley maintained his office most of the time. Laure smiled and nodded her thanks, then remarked, "I've been wondering, Jason, now that Luke is dead, whether there might be any question about my owning stock in this bank."

"No, Mrs. Bouchard, on that point I can completely reassure you. Your late husband had Lopasuta Bouchard draw up a very binding and comprehensive article of title which clearly states that as the widow of John Brunton, you are entitled to retain the majority of voting stock. It's true that the laws today are quite exclusionary, giving women few rights regarding business ownership or personal property, but Mr. Bouchard made excellent provisions to protect you."

"That I didn't know—Luke never told me," she murmured, and uttered a faint sigh, for a moment overcome with emotion. More than she had dreamed, Luke had thoughtfully anticipated the problems that might arise if he should die and had protected her. Thus his love reached beyond the grave, and the knowledge of it humbled her and yet made her at the same time wonderfully proud.

Jason Barntry was silent a moment, observing that she was meditating on the past, and then when she regarded him again, proferred, "I don't want to overburden you with further legal matters, but there are a few other things I should mention, especially in view of Lopasuta's apparent continued absence. Ordinarily, of course, I would be discussing this with him, but since it seems to have fallen to you to manage your late husband's entire estate, at least temporarily, I can reassure you that things are very heartening. Fortunately, there is a will, properly signed by Luke, of which Lopasuta sent me a copy on your husband's instructions. So far as I can tell, it provides for everything. If you like, in Lopasuta's absence, I'd be glad to see that a Montgomery attorney undertakes to put it through probate for you; that's just a formality, but it should be completed as soon as possible, and I feel certain that your stepson would not object to our doing so on his behalf."

"I'd like that very much, Jason, thank you." Laure replied.

"Very well then, consider it done—and I assure you that you need think no more about the matter. The will is very tightly drawn up, and there will be no difficulty with it. Now, quite apart from that, you ought to know that things are very encouraging. Your husband left separate trusts for you and for each of the children in such a way that, regardless of his other holdings, even if there should be shortages or even bankruptcy, the monies could never be touched or attached, by law. In addition, there is a fund specifically designated for the maintenance of Windhaven Plantation. And the profits there are excellent: as of the end of last month, the plantation had earned a total gross profit of well over a hundred thousand dollars, and that is after deducting what is due to the original tenant owners."

"That's very good, indeed. It also reminds me that I've been wanting to discuss Luke's arrangement with the tenants. It was so clever of John Brunton to have a factor buy up all the original acreage of Luke's grandfather's grant from the Creeks—which he purchased officially before the Civil War—for black tenants. The provision, as Luke always told me, was that they would later sell back the land to him, yet retain an agreed-upon profit."

"That is precisely what was done, Mrs. Bouchard. As your husband set it up, they receive a percentage of the overall profits."

"Since that was what Luke always wanted, I want it to continue."

"And so it will. What a pity that we can't find Lopasuta Bouchard to draw up some additional documents solidifying the entire estate," Jason regretfully declared. Then, with a philosophical shrug, he added, "At any rate, I see no present obstacle or challenge to continuing the affairs of Windhaven Plantation. Considering that four years ago the entire nation sustained a grievous economic panic from which many firms had not yet recovered, it's a testimony to Luke's foresight that the estate is in better financial shape than at least half of the larger farms and plantations that have been restored since the easing of Reconstruction restraints. All in all, Mrs. Bouchard, I'd say that you are completely free to invest as you see fit—always with caution, needless to say—and you'll still be assured that you and your children are well provided for."

Judith Branshaw arrived at William Brickley's office and asked the driver of the calash to wait, since she intended to return to the bank. She eyed the imposing facade of the Musée des Délices and made a grimace of distaste as she took hold of the knocker and rapped it three times.

The same liveried manservant who had admitted Lopasuta Bouchard and brought him the invidious drink warily opened the door and eyed the tall blond young woman with a kind of cynical appraisal. "Yes, miss?"

"I'm from the Brunton & Barntry Bank. Mrs. Bouchard, who is there now, sent me to ask whether Mr. William Brickley would be able to see her. She has a matter of business to discuss with him."

"If you will wait in the salon to your right, miss, I'll go ask him. A moment, if you please."

With an almost contemptuous flourish of his hand, he indicated the salon, the very room in which Lopasuta had waited for his interview with his potential new "client." Judith stared after the man and again grimaced, then seated herself on a settee and patiently waited.

About five minutes later, the dapper William Brickley, his black hair touched with gray at the temples, wearing a white linen frock coat and matching trousers, his right hand grasping a sword cane with ivory pommel and a Cuban panatella cigar, entered the salon. "My majordomo tells me that you come as a messenger from Mrs. Bouchard, mam'selle?"

"That is correct, Mr. Brickley."

"I am delighted." His sensual lips curved in a slow, appraising smile, as his dark-blue eyes detailed her. "I have seen you working where I bank, have I not, Mam'selle—Mam'selle—?"

"Branshaw. Judith Branshaw."

Brickley's face was impassive, as he gave her a slight inclination of his head and murmured, "Enchanted to make your acquaintance, Miss Branshaw. You're certainly a very lovely courier. Well now, you may tell Madame Bouchard that I shall be at her disposal. I am free now, and will be for at least another hour or two."

"Thank you, Mr. Brickley, I'll give her your message."

"Thank *you*, Mam'selle Branshaw. By the by, are you from Alabama? I ask because I have some holdings in that state and, unless I'm mistaken, your voice has the accent of a native Alabaman."

Judith flushed hotly under his scrutiny and, lowering her eyes, hesitantly replied, "Why, yes, I—I used to live in Tensaw. But I've been in New Orleans four years now."

"I see. Well now, I haven't lost touch with that lovely state, it appears, since I detected a native daughter in you, Miss Branshaw. Please tell Mrs. Bouchard that I'm looking forward to seeing her again."

"Th-thank you, Mr. Brickley," Judith said as she rose. Brickley watched her walk back down the hallway to the door, which the manservant opened for her with an obsequious bow. After she had gone, the majordomo turned to his master and broadly winked, remarking, "She could bring a fine price, Mr. Brickley, in one of your houses of pleasure."

"I'm sure she could, Roland." A cruel little smile curved William Brickley's sensual mouth. "Unless memory fails me—and my recall of names hasn't let me down yet—she more or less pursued that ancient profession back in Montgomery, thanks to the rather barbaric but certainly effective behavior of a man I happen to know. Well now, Roland, let us prepare for Mrs. Bouchard's visit. Have some refreshments prepared by Pierre. And pacify him— our dear chef is a damnably irritable person so early in the day when it comes to special requests. Tell him that this is for a very beautiful and desirable woman and that, if the repast he prepares induces her to linger here and do some business with me, he may expect a particularly delectable bonus for his extra labors."

"I will tell him, of course, Mr. Brickley," the liveried majordomo smiled with a salacious wink.

"Roland, you're really worth your keep these days. You're a rogue at heart, and the smartest thing I ever did when I opened this house was to engage you in the dual role of majordomo and personal valet. You are also quite an expert procurer, though I trust"—Brickley's eyes were now heavily lidded in warning—"that you'll never see fit to try to exercise your talents on your own in competition with me. It would not at all be profitable for you, rest assured of that, Roland.'"

"Of course not, Mr. Brickley! I wouldn't think of it, sir. I—I'll go tell Pierre to prepare something very special for the lady."

As the majordomo went down the hallway toward the kitchen, William Brickley chuckled softly to himself. "So that is the young lady whom that idiotic David Fales was hot for. Most interesting. Considering what's just happened to him, I wonder what he would think if he were to meet her now, working for the very bank that has all the Bouchard money. The possibilities are extremely interesting. I shall have to give some thought to them." Then, with a malicious chuckle, he went back to his office. There was a letter he had to send off to Milo Brutus Henson, and he would have just enough time to finish it and have Roland take it to the post office for him before Laure Bouchard would be calling upon him.

Judith Branshaw was puzzled as she rode back in the calash to the bank. How curious that William Brickley had asked her if she had come from Alabama. As far as she

201

knew, there was nothing about her diction or her voice that could reveal her native region—well, perhaps it really meant nothing. But there was something about the handsome, obviously rich Mr. Brickley that made her wonder just what sort of man he really was.

She bade the calash driver wait once more, telling him that she would shortly have another lady to drive back to the Rampart Street address. She hurried into the bank and went directly to Jason Barntry's office, where she told Laure Bouchard that a carriage was waiting to take her to see William Brickley. Laure graciously thanked her, and then went out to the calash.

Jason Barntry smiled at the young woman and then said, "You were very thoughtful, and Mrs. Bouchard appreciates it."

"She's a very fine lady, Mr. Barntry."

"That she is. One of the finest it's ever been my pleasure to meet. I just hope—" He checked himself, for he still had some misgivings about Laure's idea of investing in a gambling casino. And yet, on the face of it, there was really no harm, and it would certainly make money for her. Still and all . . . He looked up and dismissed Judith with a kindly smile. "If you've some time today, you might begin to send out the announcements of our new private stock issue, Judith. The notices should go out before the first of next month."

"I'll get to it right away, Mr. Barntry, if you've no other errands for me."

"Oh, no, you've been most helpful, my dear. And by the way," Jason said with a paternal smile, "Mr. Marquard was in the other day and complimented you. He thinks you're a very fine person."

Judith bit her lip and blushed, stammered something unintelligible, and excused herself to go back to her work.

As Laure Bouchard descended from the calash in front of the ornate facade of the Musée des Délices, sudden sounds of screams and shouts were heard. The calash driver, with a violent, hoarse oath, cracked his whip to urge his mournful-looking, aging mare into a gallop, and the clattering vehicle veered to the other side of the street. Startled, Laure stood in her tracks, looking after him to learn the reason for this sudden commotion. And then, a hand to her mouth, she uttered a horrified cry.

Loping toward her was a mangy black mongrel. Its eyes were glazed and hideously dilated, and its yellowish teeth were bared in a grotesque grimace. As it came, it uttered whining, strident yowls, and there was froth around the edges of its mouth.

"Oh, God—oh, my God—" Laure ejaculated, petrified with terror.

"Mad dog, mad dog! Get out of the way!" the shouts came from storekeepers and passersby, who had hurried to keep out of the mongrel's path.

At this moment, William Brickley, having heard the noises, came out of the house. Quickly reacting, he drew out the gleaming blade of his sword cane and, advancing ahead of Laure, stood his ground, as the black, slavering mongrel sprang. Dexterously, with a single thrust, he impaled the maddened animal through the heart and, in almost the same movement of his arm, shoved it out onto the street, where it lay twitching a moment and then was still.

Then he turned to Laure who, tottering, was about to faint. "It's all right now, Mrs. Bouchard—it won't hurt you—thank God I heard and came in time—you had a narrow escape. Here, lean on me, you'll be all right now!" he soothingly assured her.

## Twenty-One

His arms protectively around her shoulders, Brickley
helped Laure back into the house and imperiously ordered,
"Roland, bring Mrs. Bouchard a snifter of cognac." The
liveried majordomo, his eyes wide with alarm, hurried off
to bring back the restorative drink.

"Here we are now, Mrs. Bouchard," Brickley murmured
as he eased Laure onto the settee. "That was a very close
call. I'm certainly glad I happened to have my sword cane
with me—it's a kind of battlefield souvenir, you might
say," the handsome entrepreneur amicably explained. "A
friend of mine, who was at Antietam, found it after the
Yankees had retreated, belted around a Union captain
he'd picked off with his rifle. He was so struck with it, he
brought it back and later gave it to me as a token of
friendship." Then, raising his voice that had taken on a
gently soothing tone for Laure's benefit, he exclaimed,
"Bring the cognac right here, Roland. That's fine. And
now, if you please, see that we're not disturbed. If there
are any callers here on business, give them my apologies
and tell them to make an appointment with you, and I'll
do my best to keep it."

"Very good, Mr. Brickley."

As the door closed behind the majordomo, William
Brickley solicitously murmured, "Take a sip of this, Mrs.
Bouchard. You'll feel a good deal better. Nothing to fear
now. I'm so dreadfully sorry that your visit to me had to
be marred by this violent and ugly incident."

"I—I do feel better now, thank you. You're most courteous." Laure exhaled a long breath, accepted the exquis-

itely wrought snifter and put it to her lips. She gasped upon tasting the fiercely potent cognac, but feeling much revived, did her best to suppress a soft little laugh, reacting to the contrast between the hideous, slavering mongrel with its jaws bared as it came for her and this quiet, ornately furnished salon in which she felt completely at peace.

"Take another sip," Brickley urged, as he moved to a tabouret and sat facing her in an attitude of respectful concern.

Laure did so, and then set the snifter down on the edge of the tabouret. "It'll make me tipsy, thank you. That's quite wonderful cognac, Mr. Brickley. And I'm deeply indebted to you for rescuing me. Well now, I came here to discuss business with you—"

"Then business it shall be, my dear lady. But you're sure you're feeling up to it? I'd never take advantage of a beautiful woman."

His suave, honeyed voice had a curious effect on Laure Bouchard. She stared at him, almost as if seeing him for the first time, and then, it suddenly, shockingly dawned on her that so soon after Luke's death, she found herself singularly fascinated, almost hypnotized by this tall, elegantly dressed, impeccably mannered man.

Overwhelmed by a tumult of emotion, Laure struggled to understand what was happening to her, and why. Suddenly she realized that Mr. Brickley's rescue, by some uncanny coincidence, was a virtual reenactment of the event that had decided her to marry Luke Bouchard just eleven years ago.

*Oh, God, it's impossible, and yet it's happening, I'm actually moved by this stranger's presence. I feel so empty, so lost without my dear Luke. . . . After Lucy's death, when he came to propose marriage, telling me that he knew the child I had borne to John Brunton was really his, I refused him still. Then I played the game of masked courtesan, daring him to make love to me because the chance might never again recur . . . until that day he won my heart by saving that little boy from the mad dog—killing the dog with his sword cane, just as William Brickley used his sword cane to save my life. What can it mean? Can it be a sign?*

*Oh, no! I'm distraught over Luke's death, over all my*

*responsibilities to the estate. Yet why do I feel so helpless before this man, so compelled to listen to his every word? I certainly don't want even to think of another man, not now. Luke was all the man I ever dreamed of. And yet I'm sitting here, my pulse racing, and I'm looking at William Brickley as if I were a young girl again—I can't let it happen—I mustn't!*

"Are you sure you're feeling better, Mrs. Bouchard?" William Brickley gently pursued. "It was a terrible scare, and I thank the Lord I was expecting you and went out to the street when I heard the outcry. I'd never have forgiven myself if that dog had reached you before I could turn it aside."

"Yes, I—I'm much better now." Laure closed her eyes and leaned back, drawing another deep breath to try to steady herself. But her mind was still dominated by the incredible coincidence, and by the unsettling emotions it aroused.

"Well then, Mrs. Bouchard, if you're quite feeling yourself again, I'm at your disposal."

"Thank you, Mr. Brickley." With this, Laure came directly to the point of her visit, outlining to the suave entrepreneur the proposal she had discussed with Jason Barntry. "I came from New Orleans and lived here for quite a number of years," she concluded, "so I'm familiar with the recreational tastes of the inhabitants here."

"An excellent idea, Mrs. Bouchard! A gambling casino for wealthy citizens, as well as visitors to our fair city who are in search of excitement and who have a good deal of money to back their play, is that it?"

Laure's voice was cool and composed now, for she had largely succeeded in thrusting from her mind her singular reaction to Brickley's valiant rescue. As she concentrated on the business at hand, however, she remained vaguely aware of the peril she had escaped, and the disturbing emotions that had followed.

"I'm convinced," she said, "that there is a good deal of money to be had here from those people who have become bored with the pleasures New Orleans has available at this time."

"Your reasoning is very sound, Mrs. Bouchard. Let me congratulate you. Well now, as it happens, I have been thinking about just such a venture myself. You probably know that I own several houses of pleasure, not only here on Rampart Street, but also a particularly fine one on Esplanade Avenue in the very heart of the wealthiest Creole section of this city. It has superb architecture and all the refinements of good taste and tradition that have made New Orleans so famous in this nation. While I have some ladies of pleasure there at the moment, they could easily be transferred to some of my other houses should you decide that the building would be suitable for your casino. Now, might I know what figure you had in mind by way of investment? Did you want to own such a casino by yourself, or had you considered a partnership?"

"I see no reason why a sound partnership would not be acceptable," Laure warily averred.

"Excellent. What would you say to an investment of—let us be modest to begin with, and because you are in mourning, rest assured that I have no intention of driving you to a hard and fast bargain—about fifty thousand dollars? The expenditure of such a sum would give you an equal partnership with me in the Esplanade Avenue property when it reopens as a casino."

"I would want to inspect the building first, of course.".

"By all means, dear lady! I would expect you to. Whenever you're ready, I'll send Roland with you as a guide. He's quite familiar with all of my affairs and holdings, and he's a most intelligent man—honest, too, a rarity in our age, I'm sure you'll agree."

"Honesty is very important to me, Mr. Brickley. My husband lived by it, as did his grandfather. And, first as his wife and now as his widow, I have always respected his credo."

"In a partnership, Mrs. Bouchard, both partners stand to gain an equal share of the profits—but I must remind you that each is responsible for one half of the losses."

"That's standard procedure, I'm sure. I do wish," Laure faltered a little, as she said these words, "that our lawyer could be here to work with me. We've already discussed Lopasuta's unexplained and prolonged absence, and I'm distressed to say that I've received no new information about him."

"Since you first saw me, dear Mrs. Bouchard," Brickley's voice was unctuous, "I've asked some of the managers of my houses of pleasure, as well as those accountable to me in my other business affairs, if they have seen a man answering to Mr. Bouchard's description. I regret to inform you that, to this moment, I've had no word whatsoever."

"I see." Laure closed her eyes and steadied herself again, then reached for the snifter and fortified herself with a last sip of the powerful cognac. "In that case, perhaps Jason Barntry can find a lawyer whose services would be acceptable both to you and to me, to draw up the necessary documents."

"I'm sure we'll have no difficulty in agreeing to such an arrangement, Mrs. Bouchard."

"You're certainly direct and honest, Mr. Brickley. I've been honest with you, and that's the only basis on which I'd consider striking an agreement with you. I also wish to discuss another matter, about which Mr. Barntry felt it might be worthwhile to speak with you, as well."

"You have only to name it, dear lady. To the best of my humble abilities, I'll certainly try to help you."

"Thank you. Well, what I'm thinking is that I'd like to find a very capable overseer for Windhaven Plantation." Describing her needs, Laure then added, "He must also possess the ability to get along with all of our workers and especially my present foreman, Marius Thornton. This foreman, I may add, Mr. Brickley, has been extremely loyal to my late husband and myself, and I wouldn't want him to imagine that my appointment of a more experienced overseer in any way diminishes his position. As you can see, it's a rather delicate situation."

"Your sentiments do you great credit, Mrs. Bouchard. I, too, have always been very fond of loyalty. Yes, I think I could be of some service to you on that score, as well. It happens that one of my associates is an Englishman who ran his father's estate—quite a sizable one, I'm given to understand—which made a very commendable profit. He's come to this country because he likes the American spirit and wants to be part of it."

"That sounds like a good recommendation, Mr. Brickley. I should like to meet him, if it's possible."

"But of course! After all, if you and I are going to be partners, we will each be somewhat dependent on the other's financial well-being; therefore, it will be to my advantage, as well as to yours, to assist you—altogether impartially, of course—with your holdings. I expect you, in turn, to investigate my ways of working, so that each of us has enough information to speak frankly. I tell you, I have no use for deviousness or hypocrisy when I'm engaged in business."

"I share your sentiments exactly, Mr. Brickley. Well, this Englishman may be the very man to take charge at Windhaven Plantation and relieve Marius of a good many of the more onerous responsibilities."

"Does he by any chance have black blood in his veins, Mrs. Bouchard?" Brickley discreetly inquired.

"Yes, he does. During the race riots in New Orleans just after the Civil War, my husband saved him from death at the hands of an angry, irrational mob, who were displeased that a black man was in their midst. By way of gratitude, Marius Thornton has plunged himself into his duties with an energy and a purposefulness that have often made me feel very humble and very grateful for such loyalty."

"The man I have in mind, Mrs. Bouchard, is the very soul of tact. That's a trait you can generally associate with the English. I expect he'll be visiting here in the next day or two, and as soon as I see him, I'll send word to you at the bank—unless you prefer that I contact you at your hotel—so that you may arrange to meet him and decide for yourself if he is your man."

Laure rose, her color brightening and at last in full control of her nerves. "You may leave word for me with Mr. Barntry, thank you, Mr. Brickley. And now I'll be getting back to the bank. You've been most kind and helpful. I shall think over your suggestions, and you may expect to hear from me within the very near future."

"It will be my pleasure and my obligation to serve you and yours, when you're ready, Mrs. Bouchard." Smoothly rising, William Brickley brought one of Laure's slim hands to his lips, kissing it debonairly. "I'll begin the remodeling of my house on Esplanade Avenue at once, Mrs. Bouchard. And, as soon as we've both agreed on an attorney, we can have him draw up the documents of our partnership in the casino."

"I'm deeply indebted to you, Mr. Brickley. Not only for saving my life, but also for your suggestions on behalf of the Bouchard estate. Thank you again."

He helped her rise, again brought her hand to his lips,

209

and escorted her to the door. "I believe that in order for you to accomplish all that you wish here, Mrs. Bouchard, you may have to consider remaining in New Orleans for a period of time. I know the weather is dreadfully oppressive, but I'm sure Mr. Barntry could arrange for you to stay at a pleasant little inn or hotel far enough upriver to escape the appalling humidity here in town."

"I—I daresay I can work that out if it becomes necessary. Thank you for the suggestion, Mr. Brickley. Goodbye for now."

He gave her a smiling bow as she left, and stood there waiting until the calash bearing her had disappeared from view. Then, with a malicious little chuckle, he murmured to himself, "I ought to burn a candle to the patron saint of mad dogs. If I had staged this meeting, the results couldn't have been better than what happened completely by accident. Yes, it *is* very lucky that I had my sword cane and came out to investigate—for all of a sudden this beautiful widow seems to look at me through new eyes. It's going to be childishly easy to take Windhaven Plantation away from her." He smoothed his impeccable hair with his hand and mused aloud, "I could do a good deal worse than to marry a widow like that—once I get hold of all of her property, of course."

Back at her hotel, Laure Bouchard refreshed herself with a cold bath; then she changed into a wrapper, sent for tea and a salad and toast, as well as the current copy of the *Times-Picayune*, and reflected on what had taken place this singular morning.

More detached now that she was away from the persuasive and magnetic aura of William Brickley and the almost decadent luxury of his sumptuous house of pleasure, she tried to analyze her reactions and reassemble her thoughts. It was vital for the future of Windhaven Plantation, for her children, to make no mistakes simply out of emotional impulsiveness.

It was only a coincidence—it could have been nothing else. And yet, how was it that he had killed that hideous mongrel with a sword cane, instead of a derringer, a weapon that would surely be in more common use? If it was only a coincidence, why did she find herself thinking back to that day when Luke Bouchard had shown her that he had physical courage, in addition to the intellect for which she had always admired him. She wondered again if it was the working of fate.

There was no real link between this tall, self-assured, almost glibly sophisticated man and herself, as there had been with Luke. She was sure that she would never remarry even though she was still a comparatively young woman. She knew that her life must be devoted entirely to the upbringing of her children and to the judicious stewardship of Luke's estate, so that the Bouchard tradition of loyalty and love and integrity could continue without impediment or lapse.

She picked up the paper, looking for some distraction from the troubling events of the day. There was talk of a strike by anthracite workers in Pennsylvania, as well as by those who mined bituminous coal. Widespread railroad strikes throughout the nation were also threatened. Federal troops might be called in, and that would doubtless mean bloodshed.

Laure dropped the paper to the floor in some dismay. Somehow all the unrest reported in the news—in addition to the strikes, there was a new campaign against the peaceful Nez Percé Indians in Idaho—made her feel even more keenly the burden of responsibility that Luke's death had placed on her shoulders. If only Lopasuta Bouchard were here to help her with the decisions she must now make, Laure thought to herself. Young though he was, he had such a level-headed understanding, not only of law, but also of financial matters. He could surely help advise her on the gambling casino project that on the surface seemed sensible and lucrative.

She shook her head sadly. How she wished she had come to New Orleans more frequently during her idyllic marriage to Luke and consulted with dear old Jason Barntry and perhaps some of his business associates. By now she would have gained a broader understanding of the economic tides of this developing city and would be better able to predict whether a particular new business— her casino—would be likely to prosper.

She also wished that Lucien Edmond would reply to her telegram. He must be on the trail—if only he'd return quickly and respond to her message! Laure sighed wearily and then, exhausted by the morning's near-misfortune and her own jumbled feelings about this prospective new partner of hers, sought solace in a nap.

Lopasuta Bouchard groggily stumbled to his feet off the hard bunk and shivered. Groping his way toward the narrow door of the tiny cabin, it seemed to him that he had been imprisoned for a lifetime. Three times a day, the New England seaman Noah had unbolted the door and brought him in food and drink, balancing the tray in one hand and a belaying pin in the other. Behind him, guarding the door, stood a younger, stockier seaman who glared in at Lopasuta as if daring him to escape.

With his fists, the tall Comanche hammered upon the door, agonized by the infinitely long days and nights, not yet knowing why he had been imprisoned. Then at last, he heard the rattling of the bolt as it was drawn back, and he moved aside instinctively, clenching his fists, ready to try anything to gain his freedom. His only thought was that of his lovely Geraldine, who had by now given birth to their child. What must she think of him, not having heard a word in all these long weeks, perhaps even months—for at times his nightmarish dreams had made him feel as if he had been separated from her for countless years.

"Get back there, mister!" Noah warned, as he entered with a tray on which were placed a mug of chicory, a plate of beans and salt pork and a piece of hardtack. "There ye be."

"For God's sake, man, tell me this—where are we—we seem to have stopped?"

"We'll be low at Rio, mister. There's bad weather off the Horn—it's nigh unto winter at the other end of the world." Noah permitted himself a mocking little cackle, as he moved back warily, raising the belaying pin to warn the prisoner against the folly of a sudden move. "We'll take on water 'n grub—some tasty fruit to cut the scurvy, ye know. But our cargo won't spoil—it's good Missouri wheat, and machine parts and stuff like that bound for 'Frisco."

"San Francisco? Oh, God—that will take months to reach by ship! Please, N-Noah, if you're a Christian, think of this—I've left a wife and by now a child behind me, and she doesn't know where I am and she thinks I've deserted her—" Lopasuta's voice was hoarse with agony.

"I'm sorry for you, mister, that I be, rightly. But I've orders, and the cap'n would have me catted raw, if I so much as let you talk about slipping off the ship. Now you just eat your grub and stay where you are. You won't be hurt, I'll tell you that much—and that's all I'll tell you. See you at suppertime, then, mister." Noah swiftly withdrew, slamming the door behind him, and a moment later Lopasuta heard the inexorable thrust of the bolt. He walked glumly over to the porthole and stared bleakly out. The water was glassy and calm and beyond it was the sky. There was nothing else to see.

Making his way to the little stool on which Noah had placed the tray, he took the mug in his shaking hands and gulped it down. Then he grimaced. It was violently bitter, but at least it was warm. Sitting on the edge of his bunk, he bowed his head and prayed to the Great Spirit: "Manitou, You who give the gift of life and the blessing of peaceful death, hear me now—let my wife know that I am not dead, that I long for her and the child. Let her know that I have not deserted her."

## Twenty-Two

Two days later, Laure Bouchard and William Brickley met in Jason Barntry's office. With the elderly bank manager was a bespectacled, meek-looking lawyer, Hollis Minton, whom Barntry had used for various legal transactions and recommended highly. Minton was thoughtful and soft-spoken; he knew his profession and was reliable. Laure told herself that, if Brickley had brought along his own lawyer, she might have had some reason to suspect that he was attempting to fleece her; the fact that he himself had proposed that they both use the bank's lawyer to draw up the articles of partnership registered greatly in his favor.

Brickley was accompanied by a tall, towheaded man with elegantly waxed mustache and neatly cropped beard, nattily dressed in a white linen suit and sporting a particularly ornate cravat held in place with an amethyst stickpin. He had large blue eyes, set well apart, prominent cheekbones, a high-arching forehead, and a firm jaw line. Judging from his face, he appeared to be about forty-five, but the vigor of his physique suggested that he might be perhaps five or even ten years younger. His manners and diction were impeccable. William Brickley introduced him as Danvers Willoughby and added *sotto voce* to Laure while Jason Barntry and Hollis Minton conferred by themselves for a moment, "After we've drawn up the articles of partnership, Mrs. Bouchard, I'd like to invite you to luncheon to chat with Mr. Willoughby about the possibility of his acting as overseer for Windhaven Plantation."

Again Laure was favorably impressed by Brickley's thoughtfulness. However, she demurred at the notion of

Willoughby's being present while the document of partnership was being prepared and so she responded in a soft voice, "I think that's a fine idea, Mr. Brickley. But—well, is there any reason why he has to be present at this meeting regarding the casino?"

"Why, no, not at all. Danvers, why don't you go take a walk around Honorée Street and look at the sights of our beautiful Queen City for about half an hour? Then we'll be ready for you."

"Quite, old chap." Willoughby made a gracious inclination of his head toward Laure and then added, "I look forward to the opportunity of proving my qualifications to you, Mrs. Bouchard. And may I say that I should certainly be privileged to work in any capacity for so gracious and lovely a woman."

Laure could not help smiling for a moment and, quite unconsciously, flushing at this flattery from a man who, even at first impression, was undeniably magnetic and handsome. But then, just as quickly, she dismissed him from her mind, with an imperceptible, angry shake of the head—*Good Lord, what's happening to me? I'm acting like a schoolgirl just because a handsome stranger pays me a compliment that, back at the Union House, I'd have laughed aloud at. And it's the same thing with Mr. Brickley—am I so lost, then, because dear Luke is gone forever, that I am susceptible to just any attractive man who approaches me? I mustn't let it happen, I just mustn't!*

Half an hour later, Laure Bouchard and William Brickley had agreed on the terms of their partnership: the four-story mansion on Esplanade Avenue was to be renovated and opened within two weeks as a gambling casino. Laure, with a contribution of fifty thousand dollars, was to have a half-ownership, Brickley the other half. The profits would be divided equally, as would the losses. At Hollis Minton's cautious suggestion—which Brickley himself approved with a hearty, "Of course, man, that's only common sense!"—there was to be an accounting, rendered monthly, of the gross intake and outlay of the casino, so that both partners could judge month-to-month the current financial status.

"And now, dear lady," Brickley smilingly remarked, "to you I leave the choice of naming our new joint venture. It was formerly known as 'Joies Inouïes,' untold joys. That

215

of course referred to the extraordinary pleasures that could be obtained by the fortunate visitor within its portals. But now that we shall allow only games of chance, the establishment obviously requires a new name, one that will induce our clients to play roulette, faro, *vingt-et-un*, baccarat, and the other games by which men hope to become rich overnight. The fantasy of instant wealth is an illusion, but it has survived for a good many centuries because, every now and then, as any gambler will tell you, the house sometimes loses."

"I should hope, Mr. Brickley," Laure engagingly retorted, "that *our* house of chance will be the most honest in New Orleans, and since I lived here before I married Luke Bouchard, I know at least by reputation most of the gambling houses and the mathematical odds they offer. If the wheel and the deck are honest, a visitor to a gambling house has the same chance as the house to win. What makes the profit for the house, of course, is the often desperate play of a loser who thinks that by doubling or even tripling his bet, he can recoup his losses, or a man who plays with his own system—I have the feeling that most gambling houses welcome such an optimist."

"I defer to your wisdom, as to your beauty, Mrs. Bouchard," Brickley chuckled as he gave her a gallant little nod of his head. "Let us hope that we attract many of these optimists and leave our profits to the very same mathematical odds that indeed do rule such games of chance."

"And I've already thought of the name of our house— 'La Maison de Bonne Chance'—The House of Good Luck," Laure merrily proffered.

"Excellent! The play on words underscores my tribute to your wisdom, Mrs. Bouchard." William Brickley again gave her a deferential nod. "We'll get along famously, I'm sure!" Turning to Jason Barntry and Hollis Minton, he remarked, "If you gentlemen are satisfied with the rough outline of our agreement as you heard it, might we not have it drawn up and proceed to the formalities of signatures and the deposit of Mrs. Bouchard's purchase of the half-interest?"

"You're satisfied, Mrs. Bouchard?" Jason Barntry warily eyed the golden-haired widow.

"I am, Mr. Barntry, And you, Mr. Minton, does it sound properly legal to you?"

"I confess I find no flaw in it, Mrs. Bouchard. Mr. Brickley is certainly forthright, and the monthly accounting would seem to protect both of you against any defalcations," the bespectacled attorney pedantically answered.

"Then let's draw it up. As to the money, Mr. Brickley, should it be placed in a joint account and the name of the account be that of our new venture?" Laure Bouchard turned to her new partner.

"So long as it is a joint account, Mrs. Bouchard, from which each of us is able to withdraw or deposit as the need arises, I see no reason why it cannot be arranged that way. Of course, you understand that the renovation of the mansion on Esplanade will require an immediate outlay, quite a considerable sum. The present decor would never do for the elegant gambling casino I propose to create for us, my dear lady."

"Would you then prefer that I turn the entire fifty thousand dollars over to you?"

"If you have no objections. We can deposit it into my business account here, so that this bank will still maintain it. Mr. Barntry, whom I commend as your personal advisor—and he is certainly a good and honest one—can transfer it into the joint account just as soon as it is open. I would ask only that I be allowed to retain in my own account a token payment from you to me, as I am the owner of the casino building. Mr. Barntry will see to it, and he will also make certain that our business henceforth is being conducted with integrity and on the highest ethical plane."

An hour later, William Brickley and Danvers Willoughby escorted Laure Bouchard to a pleasant restaurant just off Royal Street, where, according to her new partner, the gumbo was the most savory in all of New Orleans. After ordering for all three of them, Brickley promptly began, "Danvers has been a friend of mine for some years. As you can tell by his accent, he's an Englishman of the landed class. He had charge of his father's estate—a very successful farm with varied crops and livestock. That was why, Mrs. Bouchard, when you mentioned to me that you were looking for an overseer, I thought immediately of

Danvers. Now, I wish you two to become better acquainted, but without doubt, Mrs. Bouchard, you yourself must be perfectly satisfied with his ability before you engage him. That goes without saying."

"You've been most helpful, Mr. Brickley, and I appreciate your having gone out of your way to suggest Mr. Willoughby to me." Laure gave him a grateful smile. Then, turning to the tall, towheaded Englishman, she suggested, "Tell me something about yourself, and especially as it concerns your father's estate. Of course, you must understand that farming in Alabama differs a good deal from what is practiced in England."

"I'm sure that's true, dear lady." The Englishman lifted a glass of Madeira and suavely toasted her before continuing. "But there are also many degrees of similarity. My father's estate was in Devonshire, one of the most beautiful and fertile regions of all of dear Albion. We had several thousand acres, and of course we had many tenant farmers. My duties were to oversee them, to collect their rents, and to work with them when their tithes were delayed because of either their own personal misfortunes or—in some instances, to be sure—their sheer stupidity in not making the most of the resources of the land and its proper cultivation."

"I see," Laure politely ventured, waiting for him to go on.

"Mr. Brickley tells me, Mrs. Bouchard, that you have a very varied agricultural program on this magnificent plantation of yours."

"That's quite true," Laure proudly told him. Explaining the concepts that her beloved husband had believed in, and how Luke's love and understanding of the land had restored Windhaven Plantation to its former glory, the golden-haired young woman concluded, "And so you see, Mr. Willoughby, Marius Thornton has himself said to me that he would much prefer to be in a more subordinate position, and not have to bear the entire burden of every decision that will, of course, have to be made—and made carefully if we are to continue as my late husband wished. I have therefore decided that an overseer is of the utmost necessity. Incidentally, I have brought with me a copy of Mr. Thornton's report for the month of April. I believe that you will find it most enlightening. You'll notice, for

218

instance, that only a few acres are given over to cotton this year—my husband always believed in giving the land a chance to rest and be strengthened—"

"A very wise precept, which does both you and your late husband great credit, dear lady," Willoughby ingratiatingly broke in. "I should like very much to see this report you mentioned. Thank you—" He quickly perused the sheets, took a sip of his Madeira, and then sagely nodded. "This quite abundant variety of your plantation, Mrs. Bouchard, is very similar to my father's Devonshire estate. We too produced milk and cream, butter and cheese, and there were hogs and horses as well as cattle. And on some of the acreage, we even had sheep—the rolling meadows of Devonshire offer such rich grazing that sheep and cattle alike may find ample nourishment there. This is unlike some parts of your West, as Mr. Brickley himself has pointed out to me, where there are ranchers who become quite violent when they speak of sheep invading the cattle-grazing land, and vice versa, isn't that so?"

"I'm afraid it is, Mr. Willoughby." Laure laughed softly. "May I ask how many years you ran your father's estate?"

"About five. With my father's death, I felt a great loss and a desire—since I was unwed and had no attachments of a romantic kind—to seek my fortune in this brave new world of yours. You see, my older brother returned from the army at about that time, to claim the farm as his inheritance. I'm not sorry, mind you: it's certainly more exciting in America, although at the same time more hazardous. I came to New Orleans because there is a gentility here, a culture and a tradition which reminded me of my own native shores."

Laure Bouchard found Danvers Willoughby's flowery speech amusing, but also fascinating. He spoke with conviction and appeared to know a good deal about the planting and harvesting of crops; he also seemed capable of communicating with the tenantfarmers and of aiding them in achieving the full potential of the land that had been allotted to them. At the end of the meal, she turned to William Brickley and said, "I'm convinced enough to offer Mr. Willoughby a trial as overseer of Windhaven Plantation."

"I am greatly honored, Mrs. Bouchard, and I promise you that I shall justify your trust in me," the Englishman spoke up. Then, startling Laure with his effusiveness, he took her black-gloved hand and bore it to his lips and kissed it respectfully.

The golden-haired widow flushed hotly, and after a wide-eyed look at Willoughby, turned back to her new partner. "Perhaps it would be wise business practice to have Mr. Minton draw up a contract—shall we say for a trial of six months, with my option to renew if Mr. Willoughby's services prove adequate?"

"I think that would be quite satisfactory, wouldn't you say, Danvers?"

"Quite, old chap! In six months I should certainly be able to show Mrs. Bouchard some concrete achievements."

"Then we may as well discuss terms, Mr. Willoughby." Laure turned back to the Englishman. "Salary, for example. Would one hundred dollars a month and expenses be satisfactory? To be sure, you would have your living quarters and your meals and such incidentals—including your own horse, that goes without saying—as perquisites of the situation, as you call it in England."

"That's exactly true, dear lady. Why, that sounds most generous. I accept, and I'm eager to begin to prove myself to you."

"Then we can go back to the bank. I happen to know that Mr. Barntry was taking Mr. Minton to lunch and they were planning to confer on some banking matters upon their return," Laure smilingly suggested. "That way we can draw up the contract then and there."

The contract with Danvers Willoughby was drawn up by Hollis Minton according to the terms that Laure Bouchard had proposed, and witnessed by Jason Barntry. Then at Laure's dictation, the bespectacled lawyer wrote a letter of authorization that Willoughby was to present to Marius Thornton. "You must understand, Mr. Willoughby," she concluded, "that the two of you should work together very closely. Naturally, because of the years of loyal and hard work that he has devoted to Windhaven Plantation, I know that Marius will be anxious to cooperate with you to the fullest extent. He'll be able to quickly acquaint you with the details of how Windhaven operates so that you can begin to find new markets for our products, and perhaps devise other ways to increase profits as well, with the least possible delay."

"Of course, I shall work hand in hand with your Mr. Thornton," Willoughby beamed. "And I assure you that I am the very soul of tact—in no way will I lord it over him because you have appointed me your overseer. I realize that I am on probation, as it were, dear Mrs. Bouchard. Deeds, not words, shall henceforth be my way of justifying your trust in me. Well then, I shall plan to take the ferry to Mobile tomorrow, and then the very next steamboat up to Lowndesboro."

"You can disembark at our own wharf, from which we receive goods and ship them as well, Mr. Willoughby," Laure smilingly informed him. "Every captain on the Alabama River knows Windhaven Plantation, rest assured. Well now, I feel we have accomplished a good deal. I shall stay on here for a few weeks to see how the casino goes, and I hope to return home by the middle or at most the end of July."

"By the time you return, I grant you that you'll be able to see some pleasing results, Mrs. Bouchard," the Englishman assured her.

"Thank you, Mr. Willoughby. I have every confidence in you. By the way, I shall go to the telegraph office and send Marius Thornton a message that I have engaged you, so that he can prepare for your arrival. Well then," Laure turned to offer Danvers Willoughby her hand, which he again kissed, somewhat to her discomfort, and then shook hands with William Brickley, "it has been a most eventful day. I have a happy feeling about our association, Mr. Brickley, and about you too, Mr. Willoughby. And now, if you'll excuse me, I think I shall go back to my hotel."

That evening, Danvers Willoughby was admitted by the majordomo Roland to William Brickley's elegantly furnished office. The Englishman grinned wolfishly as he observed that a willowy, black-haired *soubrette* was engaged in giving the entrepreneur a haircut. He hesitated a moment on the threshold, but Brickley, leaning back in a huge overstuffed armchair, a linen cloth tucked into his loosened shirt collar, beckoned him forward. "This is Nellie, Danvers. She's one of my newest protégées at the Musée des Délices. And she has some excellent domestic talents besides those which, in only six months, have already made her one of my most desired girls. Wouldn't you say, Nellie, that your gentleman callers pay more for you per visit than just about any other girl in the house?"

"Just about, Mr. Brickley. 'Course, there's Daisy, she's only there a month and Madam Rose keeps selling her cherry—whereas I lost mine months ago."

"Quite true, my dear. As a matter of fact, it was I who initiated you into the tender pleasures of Cythera, wasn't it?" Brickley looked up and chucked the tall brunette under the chin. "Keep on with your work, my dear. Well, now, Danvers, you handled yourself superbly. And you leave for Windhaven Plantation tomorrow?"

"I do indeed. Now exactly what instructions do you have for me? We've only talked in general about this situation, and you haven't yet come to the point. What exactly do you expect of me for the fee you promised?"

"Let's level with each other, Danvers. Nobody knows that you are a remittance man and on your uppers—isn't that your quaint English phrase? Oh yes, you did run your father's estate in Devonshire for five years, but you neglected to tell Mrs. Bouchard that you ran it into the ground. Or that your mother, after your father's death, disowned you and told you that she would send a monthly check to any post office in the United States that you selected, with the proviso that you never darken her door again."

"I say, old man, that's ancient history—" Danvers Willoughby's face had darkened with a suffusion of blood, and his eyes narrowed angrily.

"Don't play the haughty toff with me, your lordship," the entrepreneur scoffed. "You came to me because those maternal checks were beginning to dwindle. It appears that you did such a good job of ruining the estate that your mother was forced to sell it to some commoner for a pittance. Oh no, you need me, and you're going to do what I tell you to do."

"Get to the point, Brickley."

"I will. Hold it, Nellie dear." William Brickley sat up and leaned forward, his eyes narrowed and his right forefinger, gleaming with a massive ruby ring, pointed at the Englishman's chest. "If you and I work this carefully, Danvers, we can ruin this haughty bitch, Laure Bouchard. We can run the estate into the ground, for starters. At the same time I'll see to it that the new casino venture, which I told you about, will flourish—for a while. Then, suddenly, there'll be huge losses that will wipe out her contribution and a good deal more. So much more, I hope, that she'll be forced to sell the plantation just to get out of debt. We can acquire it then for a pittance, through a third party of course, so that no one's the wiser. So, you see, it's all set. You'll have orders from me as to what to do. The plantation itself can meet with a few unfortunate accidents whereby crops don't get harvested or, if harvested, don't get to market."

"I understand you perfectly."

"All right, then. To seal our bargain, we'll have a drink together. Nellie, my love, go fetch that bottle of tawny port on the sideboard and pour out a glass for yourself too, love."

The girl obeyed, approaching Willoughby with an appraising, lewdly inviting look as she handed him his glass. He clinked his glass with hers and eyed Brickley with a speculative smile.

The latter chuckled. "All right, we'll drink, and then to seal the bargain, after Nellie has given me my haircut, you may take her upstairs to the room with mirrors, where she'll exhaust you. That will be your first dividend as my secret partner."

# Twenty-Three

Marius Thornton was waiting at the Windhaven dock to greet Laure Bouchard's appointed overseer as the spanking-new *Alabaman* sounded its shrill steam whistle at the bend before the towering red bluff, heralding its arrival.

When he had received Laure's telegram, Marius had confided to his faithful Clementine, "Honey, don't look so sad for me. It's all right. Miz Laure's not putting me down, not one little bit, don't you never for a minute think it. I know I had experience looking after this place, learning as I did from Mr. Luke, but I don't think I could manage it all by myself. I'd like to have someone to talk over things, like I used to with Mr. Luke. Besides, I'd rather be working right here on the land instead of going off to town, and the Lord knows where else, to hobnob with storekeepers and shippers. It'll be all right, you wait and see. Miz Laure wouldn't have picked this Danvers Willoughby 'less'n he knew what she wanted done."

"Just the same," the attractive mulatto woman loyally remonstrated, "stands to reason you've worked here so long, you're bound to know more about what this land can do than this fancy new overseer, like she calls him. Oh, all right, Marius honey, don't look at me like that, you know I'll mind my manners and be real sweet to him."

"Not too sweet, Clemmie," Marius smilingly teased, and his wife giggled as she hugged and kissed him.

The stevedores laid down the gangplank and Danvers Willoughby walked slowly down. Scanning the magnificent red-brick chateau with its twin towers that was set back imposingly from the river bank, he whistled soundlessly to himself. "That's quite an estate! Brickley knew what he was talking about, all right. Well now, let's make our presence known, old chap, shall we?" He had dressed himself resplendently, despite the torrid weather: a fawn-colored frock coat with matching trousers, elegantly créased; gleaming polished leather shoes, the finest he could purchase in old Armand Durois's little shop off Chartres Street; and a cane with a shining brass knob. Also, he had set atop his head at a rakish angle a broad-brimmed summer hat of the latest continental style.

When Marius Thornton saw him coming down the gangplank carrying a broad valise, the former's first impression was that Danvers Willoughby resembled a greedy carpetbagger setting foot on the soil of the conquered South for the very first time. But he brushed this thought aside and swiftly flashed a cordially welcoming smile, as he advanced and said, "You're Mr. Willoughby, I take it?"

"Quite right, my good man. And, speaking of taking, would you mind awfully carrying my valise? It's a bit heavy."

"I'll be glad to. I'm Marius Thornton. Glad to know you, Mr. Willoughby, and welcome to Windhaven Plantation. You come right this way. I'll get you fixed with a nice cool pitcher of lemonade and some biscuits 'n honey and there's a melon just picked this morning out of our fields—sweet and meaty."

"That's very nice. I think I shall enjoy it here." He turned with an affected wave of the hand to the grizzled old captain, with whom he had shared a festive supper last night and divided a bottle of excellent red Bordeaux. The captain, as it chanced, was a fellow countryman, and the evening had been spent more delightfully in exchanging reminiscences about the English countryside, the congenial barmaids in the little country pubs, and the superior merits of fish and chips and kidney pie against the overpowering gumbos and spicy Creole dishes of New Orleans.

With a satisfied chuckle, he turned back to Marius Thornton. "Lead the way, my good man. What quarters have you reserved for me? I may say I'm extremely particular about my lodgings."

Marius's eyes widened, but otherwise he gave no sign of the mild impatience he was beginning to feel with his new superior. "We've a cottage at the back of the fields, Mr. Willoughby," he ventured with an amiable grin meant to propitiate the standoffish newcomer. "It's been cleaned spic 'n' span, and there's a good bed in it and a table and—"

"A cottage in the fields? Well, really, my good man!" Willoughby drawled. Halting in his tracks, he delved his hand into the inner pocket of his frock coat and produced Laure's letter, which he proceeded to unfold and hold up for Marius to see. "I suggest, my good fellow, you acquaint yourself with my letter of authorization here. It will show you that Mrs. Bouchard has placed me in command. And a leader does not relegate himself to a humble cottage in the fields. I'll have you know, Marius, that back in Devonshire our estate possessed an acreage far vaster than this small tract of land—yes, and some fifty or sixty tenants with their families. So you see, I am accustomed to having only the very best. No, Marius, you will lodge me in that elegant chateau. It has a French style to it, I perceive."

Marius doggedly acquiesced in a resigned tone, "That's right, Mr. Willoughby, old Mr. Lucien Bouchard—he was the first here just about a hundred years ago—he had his son Henry build it for him. It was just like the place he was born in, back in France."

"At least, he acknowledged the value of tradition. I'm happy to see that. Well then, you'll find me a comfortable set of rooms in that chateau, Marius. And you may serve me the collation you were kind enough to mention earlier. I shall take my ease till this dreadfully oppressive sun goes down and there's some cool air for a tour around the fields."

"All right, Mr. Willoughby. I guess I can put you up in one of the guest rooms."

Danvers Willoughby coldly eyed Marius, arching his bushy eyebrows as he indicated his disdain. "Not just any room, if you please. I want the very best. The kind that would be offered to an important guest. As you see by this letter which I've just shown you, I shall be in charge of Windhaven Plantation from this moment forth. You will have the goodness not to forget it."

Marius colored hotly under this insolent rebuke, but again he showed masterful self-control by merely nodding and rejoining, "I'll make sure that you're satisfied with the arrangements, Mr. Willoughby. Now if you'll come this way, we can get out of the hot sun all the faster."

"Quite, old chap," Willoughby crisply agreed. Marius had taken his bulky valise and the supercilious remittance man sighed with relief. He glanced around at the river and then up toward the red bluff, and made a distasteful grimace. If it weren't for the profits involved and the bonus Brickley had promised him, he would never have left the delights of the Queen City for this primitive, uncivilized spot. There would, he hoped, be distractions. . . .

"We'll go in by the kitchen," Marius said. "And in case you're wondering if the vittles will suit your fancy, after coming up from New Orleans, I'm here to tell you that we've got ourselves a brand-new cook, Amelia McAdams, and she's as good as any of those fancy cooks down there, I'm sure. But you'll find out for yourself this evening, when it's time for supper. Come along, then, we'll go to the kitchen first."

Willoughby brightened when Marius led him into the kitchen and he saw the attractive young octoroon. He paid her a florid compliment, winked at her as he was leaving, and then, when he was walking down the hallway with Marius, slyly hazarded, "Er, old chap, I was wondering—is it possible that one might have a wench at one's disposal here?"

"I don't rightly take your meaning, Mr. Willoughby," Marius replied guardedly.

"Oh, come now, Marius, we're men among men," Willoughby snickered nastily. "From what I've heard, on these Southern plantations an overseer always had the pick of the wenches."

Marius drew himself up with injured dignity. "Mr. Willoughby, that was before Mr. Lincoln set the slaves free all over the country. You won't find any *wenches* here, now that I take your meaning. That Miss McAdams is a fine, upstanding young woman, if you mean her. Matter of fact, it was Mr. Lopasuta Bouchard himself—a mighty fine lawyer in Montgomery—who brought her to us. He overheard her being abused by her former employer, a bank president in Montgomery, he was. Well, Mr. Lopasuta wouldn't stand for it, and he helped her get a job as cook here. So I don't think you'd better treat her—or any of the other women here who are married to the

227

men who work in the fields—as wenches. No sir! If that's what you've set your fancy on, I don't doubt you could find some if you went looking in Montgomery—but you'd have to pay them and that wouldn't be right for a gentleman of quality like yourself, sir."

It was an unusually long speech for Marius Thornton, but he felt honor-bound to stand up for his late employer's ethical code, even if it meant appearing to rebel against Laure's letter. Marius thought to himself that maybe Mr. Danvers Willoughby knew a lot about farming, and then again maybe he didn't. "I'm going to find out tomorrow," he said to himself, "that's for sure."

Willoughby stood frowning at Marius, not quite certain whether the latter's reply was meant to be sarcastic or simply factually edifying. Then with a shrug he grumbled, "Well, I'm tired from my journey, so do let's get to my quarters. And then," he added, "you might ask Miss McAdams to bring up that pitcher of lemonade."

"I'll tell her that's what you asked for, Mr. Willoughby. Up these stairs now, and to your right. It's the biggest, most comfortable guest room we have here."

Marius Thornton opened the door to the room and the Englishman stood on the threshold, appraising his new quarters. "Not too bad, old chap," he allowed. "I daresay I can get used to it."

He sat down and tested the huge, four-postered bed. Then he put his hat in the closet and eased out of his frock coat, taking off his cravat with a sigh of relief. He tugged off his shoes and lay at full length, pillowing his head in his arms. When Marius returned to tell him that Amelia McAdams was preparing a tray for him, Willoughby coyly suggested, "I expect you want to take me on a tour around the fields, but really, that can wait until tomorrow, can't it? And preferably late afternoon, when that damnably hot sun goes down. Perspiration simply ruins my cravat and underlinen."

Marius didn't know whether to laugh or cry. Could this be the man to whom the entire economic future of Windhaven Plantation was entrusted? For an instant, Marius couldn't help staring at Willoughby, his brow deeply furrowed in thought.

The tension of the moment was broken by the entrance of Amelia with a pitcher of lemonade and a plate of bis-

228

cuits and honey, which she placed on the nightstand beside the bed. Purposely, Marius remained there, to prevent any embarrassment for the attractive octoroon while Amelia deftly poured out a brimming glass. "Here you are, sir, and I hope you enjoy it," she said pleasantly. "If there's anything else you need from the kitchen, you can just tell Mr. Thornton. It's nice to be knowing you, Mr. Willoughby." She left the room with great dignity. Marius was hard put to conceal the flicker of a smile, for Danvers Willoughby had been very deftly outwitted.

The new overseer of Windhaven Plantation had slept until nearly noon the next day before going down to the kitchen to commandeer breakfast. On the way down the stairs, he encountered Clarabelle Hendry, the children's nurse, who a few days earlier had returned from Mobile, after caring for her sick cousin.

Shortly after she had arrived in New Orleans, Laure Bouchard realized that her stay in the Queen City would last longer than she had at first anticipated. She therefore had telegramed Clarabelle Hendry to ask if the latter could possibly cut short her sojourn in Mobile and return to Windhaven Plantation to take over the care of the Bouchard children. Clarabelle had immediately wired Laure at the bank that she would be pleased to do so, and that she would secure the services of a wet nurse, as Laure had further requested. Clarabelle's arrival at Windhaven had come as a considerable relief to Clementine, for whom the demands of caring for twelve children, including the nursing of two infants, had begun to be quite burdensome.

Finding Mrs. Hendry a personable and attractive woman, Danvers Willoughby now essayed his usual florid charm. "Good morning, dear lady. Let me introduce myself. I am Danvers Willoughby, just appointed by Mrs. Bouchard to be the overseer—as I believe the term is in these parts—of this expansive estate. I do hope that I shall see more of you."

"My name is Clarabelle Hendry; I'm the children's nurse, Mr. Willoughby. Pleased to meet you. Now, if you'll excuse me, I must go down and prepare lunch for them."

"Oh? May I be of service? Perhaps I could order the food you wish and bring it up to you—"

"Thank you, no, Mr. Willoughby. I'm quite capable, and besides, it's my job." With a pleasant smile, she dismissed him and went on ahead of him downstairs into the kitchen. Willoughby plucked at the tips of his neatly waxed moustache with irritation, aware that he had been rebuffed again. Then, with a philosophical shrug, he sauntered down the stairs and went into the kitchen.

Amelia McAdams and the nurse were chatting cordially. Amelia eyed him and proffered a cool, "Good day to you, Mr. Willoughby. If it is breakfast you're after, I'll be happy to serve it to you in the dining room. But it *is* a bit late, and I was just preparing lunch for the children— so, if you'll bear with me and be patient, I'll see that you don't go hungry."

This was his second dismissal of the morning, at the hands of mere servants, and Willoughby glowered at the two women for a moment, then stomped off to the dining room, where he sat in solitary state. Then, again comforted by his own egotism, he craftily smiled and murmured to himself, "Never mind, old chap, I'll have occasion to be alone with that tasty kitchen wench before I'm finished here. And she'll come around, once I devote my full attention to her. Ah, well, Danvers boy, you must needs be patient. But what a dreary place this is to have to wait for Brickley's orders, when I could be having myself a fine fling back in New Orleans with a gay widow I've had my eye on for some little time."

A quarter of an hour later, Amelia entered and silently placed a tray before him. There were fried eggs, crispy fried potatoes without a speck of grease, some biscuits and honey, a melon, and strong coffee. Willoughby reached for her wrist and, fixing her with his most ingratiating smile, propitiatingly murmured, "That's a lovely breakfast, my dear. I'm grateful to you. Don't take offense, Miss McAdams, but you see, I'm new to these parts and it's a bachelor I am."

"I am sure, Mr. Willoughby," Amelia frigidly replied as she extricated her wrist from his grasp and moved away, "that you will find someone worthy of you. As you know, I'm only a lowly cook."

There was nothing in her words at which he could take

palpable offense, yet when she had left, he ground his teeth and muttered a savage imprecation: "The hoity-toity bitch! Oh, she's a clever one—but I'll have her drawers down before I go back to New Orleans, or my name isn't Danvers Willoughby." This vow seemed to hearten him, and he fell to his breakfast with a ravenous appetite. At least, he ruefully mused, the wench was an admirable cook.

It was four in the afternoon when he deigned to accompany Marius Thornton out into the fields. The congenial foreman, learning that Willoughby could ride a horse well, had a gelding saddled for him, and the two men rode out in leisurely fashion to look over the acreage of Windhaven Plantation. At the end of the tour, Marius turned to Willoughby and respectfully inquired, "Do you have any orders for me, Mr. Willoughby?"

"I was thinking, Marius, that you might plant some rice."

"*Rice*, Mr. Willoughby?" the foreman echoed in surprise. "But this soil is red clay; it's rich enough in minerals and the like for what we're growing here, but it doesn't have the dampness. I'd say that rice would be at its best down New Orleans way, where there's plenty of marsh land and swamp and all the water one could wish for."

"All the same, you might try planting a few acres over by the river. There's some low-lying land there, and you can get your workers to connect it to the river with irrigation ditches."

"With all due respect, Mr. Willoughby," Marius rejoined, with just a hint of sarcasm, "I don't think it will work. The soil's not right, and I'm not sure that land by the river is low enough to flood properly. Besides which, digging ditches is going to take the men away from their other crops, which need work right now—"

"You are under my orders, let me remind you," Willoughby contemptuously broke in. "I want you to instruct your hands to start digging those ditches and planting rice within the next week or two. I'm sure you'll be able to find a way to produce a profitable crop."

"We'd have to send down to New Orleans for the plants, Mr. Willoughby. And we'd have to determine whether we should grow long grain or short grain—"

"The devil take you, Marius! You'll plant both kinds, and that's a direct order from your overseer! Do you wish

231

me to tell Mrs. Bouchard that you have been making trouble for your new supervisor? Don't forget, you're not only my subordinate, but you're a man of color."

With this remark, Marius's patience was all but exhausted. It was all he could do to keep from clenching his fists and driving them into Willoughby's smugly smiling mouth. With a visible effort, he mastered his fury at Willoughby's insulting tone and blandly retorted, "Very well, since that's your order, I'll do my best to follow it. And now, Mr. Willoughby, have you seen enough of Windhaven Plantation, or shall we continue?"

"Good heavens, man, I'm exhausted. You seem to be doing well enough, but I'd like to postpone further observations. Perhaps tomorrow at about the same time, when the sun is low, I'll take another look at what you have here. Meanwhile, I'd like nothing better than a bath and a nap before supper."

Marius Thornton had invited Dan Munroe, Hughie Mendicott, and the other tenants of the plantation to supper that evening, so that the new overseer might meet them and exchange views. Danvers Willoughby spent most of the evening with self-serving and grandiose anecdotes of his own experiences in Devonshire, but when Dan or Hughie tried to pin him down on actual farming methods, he turned extremely evasive. At the conclusion of supper, when Marius had a chance to take the tenants aside, to a man they declared that the new overseer was personable and likable, but, as Dan phrased it, "I wonder if he ever had a hoe or a spade in his hands, for all he talks about running an English farm."

After lunch the next day, Marius felt he ought to sit down with his new superior and go over the records of the year thus far, as they pertained to the various crops. Willoughby scanned the records with an occasional exclamation to indicate his interest, but again he seemed to have little to contribute. He did tell Marius that he proposed within the next few weeks to go down to Mobile and talk to some of the larger store owners with a view toward inducing them to buy some of Windhaven's produce. This, at least, was a positive step forward; but Marius still had grave doubts.

Once again, he led Willoughby around, this time giving

232

him a more careful and lengthier tour of the acreage, wanting to give the Englishman every advantage in which to take charge of the decision-making. At the conclusion of the inspection tour, Willoughby turned to Marius and drawled, "You know, old chap, I'm wondering why you don't try oats, barley, and a good bit of wheat. It did wonders for my land back in Devonshire. As you've praised the fertility of this soil so much, I'd say it should do well with more acreage planted with grains."

"Well, Mr. Luke gave that a lot of thought at one time, but then decided against crops like that," Marius explained. "According to him, Alabama has never really been a wheat state, because the midwestern and eastern markets buy mainly from Illinois, Iowa, Missouri, and Kansas, which are closer to them and better connected by railroad."

"Oh yes, I see. Well, Marius, I will say that your work around here so far seems good—not that it couldn't be better, mind you. And you must give me a little time to acclimate myself, so that I have the feeling of the land. Devonshire isn't Alabama, after all."

"It certainly isn't, Mr. Willoughby." Again Marius couldn't quite eliminate a gentle sarcasm from his tone. The Englishman gave him a sharp look, then decided to ignore it.

After supper, Marius told his wife, Clementine, that he was going to ride over to Andy Haskins's place and have a little chat. "I'm not going behind anybody's back, honey," he explained, "but I don't cotton to this new overseer, and I can't help it. He gives a man the idea that he's the big know-it-all, but when you try to pin him down to cases, it sounds to me as if he's bitten off more than he can chew. I can't for the life of me think where Miz Laure ever got the notion to put him in charge of this whole place. It just doesn't make sense, honey."

"Now, Marius, don't you go getting all upset," Clementine soothingly advised her sturdy husband. "He has that letter from Miz Laure, and you know you have to do what he says. When she gets back, there's time enough to have it out with her, and then maybe she can tell you what she saw in this Mr. Willoughby."

"I guess I'll have to settle for that. You always know how to cheer me up, honey. But I'm still going to ride over to see Mr. Andy right now. Maybe he can straighten me out. I just don't feel right about this strange fellow."

"You do what you think best, Marius honey," Clementine murmured. "Don't you worry none, Miz Laure will straighten things out when she gets back. Don't forget, she's been so crazy in love with poor Mr. Luke, all of a sudden she's found herself having to decide everything without a man to stand beside her. I don't know who she met down in New Orleans, but it's a cinch she was really hurting. Maybe that's why she picked the man she did. You just go on doing your job the way you always do, Marius honey, you'll see, things will work out all right."

Marius went to the stable, saddled his black gelding, and rode downriver to Andy Haskins's farm. As he rode in, he caught a glimpse of Andy's horse through the open barn door, and he uttered a sigh of relief: if Andy hadn't been home, he would have been vexed at himself for disturbing Jessica, especially now that she had a new baby to look after. Dismounting and tethering the gelding to the hitching post, he hurried up to the front door and anxiously knocked on it. A moment later, Jessica opened the door to him and at once welcomed him with an engaging smile saying, "Why, Marius, what are you doing here so late at night? I hope nothing's wrong?"

"No, Miz Jessica, not really. I sure hope I'm not disturbing you folks—"

"Not at all, Marius. Andy came home late from the senate, and he's just resting a spell till I have supper ready for him—some nice pork chops, yams, snap beans, and a big piece of apricot pie and coffee."

"Man oh man," Marius smiled, "if that doesn't give him back his strength after a hard day in the Senate, I sure miss my guess, Miz Jessica, ma'am!"

Jessica put out a hand and patted Marius on the shoulder. Then her face was shadowed with remembrance. "Have you heard from Mrs. Bouchard yet, or Lopasuta?"

"Miz Laure sent us a telegram, all right, but with nary a word about her adopted son. I reckon that's why she's still down in New Orleans—trying to find out what happened to him. I'll also bet she's trying to get Mr. Lucien Edmond to come up from Texas and talk with her about what's just happened."

"Well, you come sit down now, Marius. I'll heat you up

234

some nice, strong coffee. I'm sure Andy will be up and about pretty soon and eager to talk to you."

"Thank you very much, Miz Jessica," Marius gratefully agreed.

He seated himself on a low chair and, twisting his hat between his hands, waited for Andy to waken.

About half an hour later, the one-armed senator sauntered into the kitchen, yawning and rubbing his knuckles against his eyes. "Jessica, I'm awfully sorry I fell asleep. I didn't intend—why, Marius, you rascal, what are you doing here?"

"I had to come over and tell you what's been happening lately, Mr. Andy."

"Sure, Marius. Tell you what, Jessica'll put another plate on the table—now don't you shake your head, Marius, we can get a lot more done talking over good food—and that way, I'll have plenty of time to listen to what you've got to say."

Marius grudgingly agreed, insisting that he had eaten only shortly before and he wasn't in the least hungry and didn't want to put Mrs. Haskins to any extra trouble. But, half an hour later, over savory pork chops, he was expansive on the subject of the new overseer. "You know, Mr. Andy, I'm real worried about Miz Laure. I've seen the letter that this Mr. Willoughby takes out of his pocket at the drop of a hat, to prove that he's who he says he is and that he's got authority from Miz Laure to do what he's done. Only, just between you and me, he hasn't done a thing, and he really doesn't know as much as he thinks he does."

"I'm listening, Marius. Mmm, Jessica honey, you outdid yourself for fair with this supper." Andy looked over to his lovely wife and paid tribute to her culinary skill, for which she rewarded him with a dazzling smile. Then, turning to stare intently at Marius, he went on, "Now you just get it off your chest, Marius, and tell me what's been bothering you."

Marius uttered a long, weary sigh and shook his head. "Well, Mr. Andy, he comes here off the steamboat and starts lording it all over everybody. First thing he does, he asks me if we've got any wenches to service him. Mind you now, it's as if he never heard of old Abe Lincoln."

"I catch your drift, Marius. Go ahead," Andy encouraged. Jessica, who was cleaning the dishes, turned halfway toward the table to listen.

"Do you remember that sweet gal Mr. Lopasuta brought to Windhaven to work in the kitchen after he found out how the man she was working for was treating her like a slave?" Marius asked, and, at Andy's encouraging nod, he continued, "I'll be doggoned, Mr. Andy, if he doesn't start making a play for her. But she put him in his place, all right. And then, after I've taken him out to the fields he starts talking about growing rice."

"Rice?" Andy gasped, then shook his head. "This is Alabama, not Louisiana."

"That's what I told him, Mr. Andy. So he wants me to cut irrigation troughs out to the river, start planting rice, and he figures the Alabama will give him all the water he needs."

"And you say he's got this letter in Mrs. Bouchard's handwriting?"

"That's the gospel truth, Mr. Andy," Marius proclaimed, wanting desperately to have a more educated opinion than his own. "He talks a lot of stuff about running his father's big farm in England, Mr. Andy. But he sure doesn't like to be out in the fields—he's mad the sun's so warm—and he spends an awful lot of time sleeping in his room. Now I ask you, Mr. Andy, why would Miz Laure hire a fellow like that to run the whole works?"

"I think I have an explanation, Marius." Andy shook his head in commiseration. "What I should have done, if only the legislature hadn't been in session these past weeks, was to have gone with Mrs. Bouchard and done my best to fend off all those fellows with greedy eyes and empty wallets who'd be looking for a helpless, rich young widow like her. I think that's what happened, Marius. I don't know what this new overseer of yours has in mind, but I'll come over and talk to him one day soon, I promise."

"Would you really, Mr. Andy? I'd be real beholden to you if you did." Again Marius sighed and shook his head. "That's a big weight off my mind, I can tell you that."

"To tell you the truth, I'm getting pretty worried," Andy frowned. "I don't know what's happened to Lopasuta, and I can't understand why Mrs. Bouchard has to hang around New Orleans when it's so humid and sticky you can't even breathe. But she must have a reason—maybe she went off to Texas to look up Lucien Edmond."

"That's what I've been telling myself. Only it's been an awfully long time. I wish she'd come back."

"I know, but you have to be gentle with her, Marius," Andy softly said. "What happened to Mr. Luke was sheer hell for her, there are no two ways about it. Her mind's preoccupied, and we have to be careful not to judge her harshly. You and I will just have to keep our eyes open and our ears, too, and find out what this Danvers Willoughby fellow is up to. But right now, all you can do is go along with him, because if Mrs. Bouchard put him in charge and sent along a letter to prove it, you just have to swallow your pride and give him enough rope to hang himself by. At least, that's what I would do if I were in your shoes, Marius."

# *Twenty-Four*

Maxine Bouchard had left Laure's telegram unopened for a week, and then, perhaps out of some fearful premonition, or simply because she knew that her husband would not return until nearly the end of July, she decided to open it.

Horrified at the news of her father-in-law's tragic death, she at once shared the sorrowful news with Mara, who tearfully agreed that they should dispatch a vaquero to San Antonio with an answer to be wired back to Laure in care of the bank in New Orleans:

> Dearest Laure:
> Our deepest condolences on your irreparable loss—which is ours as well. Lucien Edmond is driving a herd to Santa Fe, then stopping at other army forts on his way back. Expect him back by middle of July or early August at latest. Can we do anything to help?
>
> Maxine Bouchard
> Mara Hernandez

When Laure received this telegram, she turned to Jason Barntry and, with a helpless shrug, declared, "Jason, Lucien Edmond may not be here for more than a month, so I can only hope that the decisions I've made so far have been the right ones for Windhaven Plantation."

"Now, now, Mrs. Bouchard," the white-haired bank manager tried his best to reassure her, "Mr. Minton and I have investigated this casino investment of yours as carefully as we could, and we think it will be a profitable investment. And so far as the contract you've given this

238

Mr. Danvers Willoughby, you were wise to insert an escape clause that allows you to discharge him after six months, if his work is found to be unsatisfactory. I should say, Mrs. Bouchard, that you've been most prudent. And you can rest assured that all of us here are going to look after your interests." Then, after she had nodded and leaned back with another weary sigh, he asked, "How long do you expect to stay here in New Orleans?"

"For about two weeks after the opening of the casino, Jason. I want to make sure that Mr. Brickley has thoroughly remodeled the house on Esplanade, as promised, and that he is attracting the kind of clientele who will appreciate a luxurious setting and be willing to spend their money regularly in honest games of chance. Once I'm satisfied, I must get back to my children. And of course I'm anxious to see how well Mr. Willoughby and Marius Thornton are getting along."

"Of course. Well then, if Lucien Edmond Bouchard should contact me after you've gone back to Alabama, I'll instruct him to take the fastest transportation to confer with you there. It will be my own personal project, I promise you that, Mrs. Bouchard."

"Jason, I'm deeply grateful to you. I've always admired your loyalty and your purposeful hard work for the benefit of the Bouchard name and interests; Luke did, too, but now, as never before, I appreciate all that you've done and are doing for my children and me. God bless you, Jason."

"It's my duty. You've made me your financial manager, a great responsibility indeed, and I must justify it, Mrs. Bouchard," he replied simply, but his voice quavered because of the deep emotion he sought to minimize.

Laure sent Clarabelle Hendry another telegram from New Orleans, thanking her for her early return and asking her indulgence in looking after the children at least another three weeks. She also asked the nurse to bring Marius and Clementine up to date on the most recent developments. Meanwhile, the golden-haired widow was growing more and more alarmed at the lack of news from Lopasuta; as soon as she had received Maxine and Mara's reply to her original message to Lucien Edmond, she sent off another, inquiring of them whether Lopasuta had visited Windhaven Range. The negative reply made her more and more uneasy, and she asked Jason Barntry's advice on the feasibility of employing a private detective to try to track her adopted son's movements after his interviews with Jason Barntry and then William Brickley.

Cautiously, wanting to protect Laure from a fruitless expense and fearing that no real facts could be learned, Jason tried to dissuade her from such a move. Nonetheless, on the day before the Fourth of July and ten days before the casino was officially to open, Laure Bouchard conferred with a former Pinkerton detective who had formed his own private agency, commissioning him to do all he could to track Lopasuta Bouchard. A week later, the man ruefully reported that, although he had sent several of his associates out to question those who might possibly have seen the tall Comanche, there was absolutely nothing to report. William Brickley had seen one of the operatives and repeated the very story he had told Laure.

More and more distressed, Laure had decided to call off the search, but had purposely sent a consoling wire to Geraldine, which avoided any direct declaration of Lopasuta's whereabouts and said only that the search was continuing and that Geraldine was not to worry: thus far, there had been absolutely no indication of any foul play. For the operatives had visited the city morgue and the various police stations throughout New Orleans, armed with a detailed physical description of Luke's adopted son, and they had further asked questions of individuals known to them on the New Orleans docks. No one had seen him. He seemed to have disappeared without a trace just after his meeting with William Brickley.

The casino was opened on Friday night of the second week of July. When Laure Bouchard entered the imposing four-story house on Esplanade, she saw that William Brickley had indeed kept his part of the bargain, in offering the citizens of the Queen City a glittering and beautifully ornamental gambling palace. On each of the floors, there were rooms devoted to the most popular games of chance: *vingt-et-un*, poker, roulette, baccarat, dice, and faro. There were salons on each floor as well, where refreshments were served without charge: the finest French champagne, wines, and brandies, and buffets for patrons visiting the establishment during the luncheon and dinner hours.

William Brickley had cleverly chosen a number of women from his other houses of ill-repute to act—for the time being—as hostesses and waitresses. They had been very carefully instructed to avoid soliciting casino patrons; and if any of the customers were to recognize them from previous patronage of the bordellos and question them, they were to reply that they were beginning a new life.

He had costumed the women in superb lace-trimmed gowns, and an expert hairdresser had devoted hours to their pompadours and chignons as well as to their makeup of rice powder and lip rouge to make them look both glamorous and deliciously young without any suggestion that they might be of easy virtue.

Brickley had also recruited some of the city's best gamblers, paying them an enviably high percentage of the house's take, to run the games of chance. He had chosen a stunning auburn-haired widow in her mid-thirties to preside over the faro room, and from the very first night on, hers was the table most patronized by the avid Creoles who looked upon gambling with the same obsessive reverence that they accorded horse racing, masked balls, and the festival of Mardi Gras.

The hallways were carpeted with green velvet, and the playing rooms themselves alternated between red and green velvet carpeting. Throughout the salons, there were statuettes, lithographs, and oil paintings: the total impression was one of sybaritic luxury and elegance.

Laure was gallantly escorted by the suave entrepreneur, and, from the throngs of patrons and onlookers, she judged that the casino had been enthusiastically welcomed by the citizenry of the Queen City. Indeed, at the end of the first week, the gross profits of the house amounted to nearly eighty thousand dollars—and Laure reported this to Jason Barntry, declaring, "I think I've found a good investment on my own, and I believe that my beloved Luke would have been proud of me."

Feeling that Jason might be suffering from the loneliness of a widower, Laure invited him to have supper with her the following evening, Saturday, at the Maison de Bonne Chance, to see for himself how crowded the casino was with affluent, well-groomed patrons.

Evidently, William Brickley had publicized the new casino skillfully, for there had been an article in the *Times-*

*Picayune* that very morning, lauding this luxurious and elegant addition to New Orleans's splendid array of houses of entertainment. "This new casino," the article glowingly avowed, "has brought together *tout le beau monde*, the very elite of our illustrious citizenry. The furnishings are tasteful, the food and spirits lavish, and the many games of chance, operated by honest and expert dealers, are attracting all who pray for Lady Luck to smile upon them—several proved exceptionally fortunate at roulette and faro on the gala opening evening."

Saturday afternoon, Clarabelle Hendry had sent Laure a telegram that conveyed the love of the Bouchard children and reassured Laure that they were healthy and happy, but missed her. In addition, she remarked that the wet nurse she had found was a kindly woman who took great care and trouble with the baby. This news heartened the golden-haired widow, and eased her mind about having stayed away from Windhaven Plantation so long. Now she felt she had accomplished all that she could here in the Queen City, and she planned to return after the second week of the new casino's operation.

When Laure and Jason visited the casino that evening, William Brickley, debonair and handsomely dressed in black frock coat with buff-colored trousers, a blazing ruby stickpin in his flowery cravat, came forward to kiss Laure's hand and to escort her to the second floor of the gambling house. Jason Barntry exclaimed over the sumptuous furnishings, particularly the thick velvet carpeting of the winding stairway that he ascended. Once in the salon, Brickley imperiously snapped his fingers and two young male attendants, dressed in livery like all the employees of the casino, hurried forward to prepare a comfortable table with luxurious stuffed chairs for the honored guests. One of them brought a bottle of champagne and Brickley himself poured out a glass for Laure, then one for the bank manager, and finally one for himself. Lifting the glass, he proposed, "To our prosperous partnership, Mrs. Bouchard. Our association has been a lucky one from the very start!"

Bemused, the elderly bank manager turned in his chair to watch the patrons assaying their luck at the various games of chance. There was a moderate hum of conversation followed by an electrifying silence at this or that table as the ball slid along the roulette wheel, coming to rest at

242

last on a number that drew either groans or joyous exclamations from the avid gamblers.

Laure turned to William Brickley and smilingly remarked, "It's a great success, Mr. Brickley! I congratulate you. If this throng is any indication, I'm sure this casino will be popular with the people of New Orleans for a long time to come."

"To be sure, dear lady," he suavely replied, "you must remember that Fridays and Saturdays—particularly Saturdays—will mark the high point of the week. During the Lenten season, of course, Fridays will not show the patronage that you see before you now, but at other times of the year, the two weekend evenings should be equally busy—and this is only one floor of our casino. Yes, I'm quite gratified that the citizens have taken La Maison de⁻ Bonne Chance to their hearts. Perhaps you'd like to try your own luck at *vingt-et-un*?"

"Why, I think I'd like that," Laure laughed, her eyes bright with anticipated pleasure. "Jason, will you play with me, or do you prefer to watch?"

White-haired Jason Barntry uttered a dry chuckle and shook his head. "As a banker, Mrs. Bouchard, it's against my nature to gamble. But I'll be delighted to attend you and to bring your whatever luck I may."

"Thank you, dear Jason." Laure put out her hand and squeezed his. "Spoken exactly like a banker," she gently teased. Turning to look up at Brickley, she smilingly added, "I must thank you also for the delicious supper."

"My pleasure, dear lady. I've engaged one of the best chefs in all New Orleans. And I've made it a point to let every patron know that food and drink are provided gratis, even if he spends no more than a single dollar at any of our tables. It's a policy that, as you can see for yourself, has already aided in bringing good will for our venture. Well now, come along, I'll find you a dealer who's free at the moment—there's one right now, Henri Gistain. Do you see him? The handsome, black-haired young man wearing a ruffled silk shirt, whose classically mournful face might have come out of the Renaissance. It so happens that he comes from one of the most distinguished families in New Orleans but, alas, his parents disowned him because of his mania for gambling. I chanced to meet him one evening in a noisy saloon, and determined to train him to become one of our best dealers. He had been on the other side of the table, the losing side, so much of his life, that he welcomed the change."

He offered Laure Bouchard his arm and, approaching the table, presented her to Henri Gistain. "Henri, this is Madame Laure Bouchard, the coowner of our casino. She has expressed a wish to play *vingt-et-un* with you. Mind you, she is to be treated exactly like any other customer: an honest deal, an honest cut, and may the cards fall as they will. *Entendu?*"

"*Mais bien sûr*, M'sieu Brickley." The elegantly mournful young Creole had risen, and he now turned to Laure Bouchard and made a low bow. "*Je suis enchanté de faire votre connaissance*, Madame Bouchard. If you will be seated, we shall begin. Would you like me to explain to you the rules of the game?"

"That won't be necessary, M'sieu Gistain. You see, I came from New Orleans—and my father at times frequented a gambling house." Turning to smile at Jason Barntry, who stood at the side of the table, she whimsically added, "He was a banker, too, you know. Fortunately, he wisely allowed himself only a very small stake for his gambling, and as soon as he had lost it, he always left the casino."

"Ah, madame," Henri Gistain laughed softly, "your father was indeed a very wise man. But of course for the sake of M'sieu Brickley and yourself, I do hope that the customers we attract here will not be deterred by an occasional loss."

William Brickley cut in, "I shall leave you now, my friends, to court Dame Fortune. Your very devoted servant, Madame Bouchard. And a good evening to you, Mr. Barntry. You honor us with your presence here." With a courtly bow, Brickley walked to another table to greet a wealthy patron who was accompanied by his young quadroon mistress.

"Well, then, M'sieu Gistain," Laure brightly began, "what are the stakes?"

"They are completely at your discretion, Madame Bouchard."

Laure played five dollars on each card and won the first hand. She lost the second hand but won again on the third and fourth. "I'm quite satisfied," she laughingly announced. "My thanks, M'sieu Gistain, for a very pleasant half-hour. And here is a *pourboire*." With this, she handed him a five-dollar counter. He gallantly rose, drew out her chair for her, and then kissed her hand. "I hope, Madame Bouchard, to have the great honor of playing with you again. And meanwhile, I shall try very hard to make *beaucoup d'argent* for you and Mr. Brickley."

"I couldn't ask for more than that, *merci bien!*" Laure smiled.

The second week the operation grossed nearly one hundred ten thousand dollars—even better than the first. Laure Bouchard, satisfied that she had not made an error in judgment, booked passage the next morning on the steamboat that would take her back to Windhaven Plantation, after first urging Jason Barntry to tell Lucien Edmond, if he should come to New Orleans, to visit the casino himself. The morning before her departure, she sent off another telegram to Windhaven Range, informing Lucien Edmond that she was returning home and that she hoped he could spare time from his family and the management of the ranch to visit her and to see his father's grave.

## Twenty-Five

Toward mid-July, Ramón Hernandez and his vaqueros departed from the westerly route they were following with the herd on the cattle drive to Dodge City, and stopped at the Creek reservation, where they were welcomed by the new *mico*, Sipanata, to whom they gave a gift of twenty steers. After a night of feasting and rest, during which Sipanata urged Ramón to convey his greetings to Lucien Edmond, the vaqueros returned to the herd and continued northwest, following closely the route that Joseph McCoy's courier had recommended to Lucien Edmond and Ramón.

As they neared their destination, Ramón reflected with satisfaction that there had been few incidents to mar the welcome monotony of the three-month drive to this bustling new cattle market. The rivers that they had had to ford—the Colorado, the Red, the Canadian, and a number of smaller streams—had been at surprisingly low water and thus easy to cross, and there had been only one or two instances when the cattle had spooked—once during a dust storm in northern Texas and once during a thunderstorm. But the expert vaqueros, most of whom had accompanied Lucien Edmond and Ramón on previous drives, had rounded up the strays with very little trouble.

Now, only about eight days out of Dodge City, the drive again swung northwestward toward the Cimarron River, near the border between Kansas and Indian Territory, and there they encountered a sudden brief sandstorm, which forced them to make camp for the night just south of the river. The stream itself was nearly at its lowest as Ramón sought a good place to cross. He found it about two miles to the northeast, and he ordered the crossing for just about dawn the following morning, wanting to strike on for Dodge City, still some sixty-five miles away.

Mounted on his black gelding, Ramón supervised the fording as the vaqueros drove the lowing herd, impatient for water, toward the shallow fork of the river. It took about three and a half hours to see all the cattle safely across, and Ramón had been pleased to see that, as a trail worker, the taciturn new cowhand Walter Catlin was about as good as any he had.

The midmorning sun had begun to beat down on them when suddenly there was a sound of gunfire and distant shouting. Ramón's eyes narrowed and he reached for his Spencer carbine, thrust into the saddle sheath, as he spurred his eager mount across the shallowest part of the Cimarron to ride to the front of the herd.

Suddenly his horse stumbled in a gopher hole, and as the gelding went down, Ramón leaped clear. The animal lay sprawled, whinnying in agony from a broken fetlock. With a sympathetic oath, Ramón pulled his carbine free and ended the gelding's suffering with a well-aimed bullet.

He could see in the distance that several of his vaqueros had turned southeastward and were riding at a gallop, crouching low in their saddles and firing their rifles and carbines. Loping forward, holding his carbine at the ready, Ramón raced toward the scene.

Reaching a small wooded knoll, he found that six of his vaqueros had encircled a panting, bearded man in his mid-twenties. The man's black hair was disheveled, his shirt was ripped, and his breeches were tattered. One of the vaqueros dismounted, a hand pressed to his bleeding left shoulder, and gave an order. Two others seized the young man and quickly marched him toward a tall cottonwood tree, while a third, making a noose out of his lariat, hurled it over a high, sturdy branch some seven feet above the prisoner's head. Two other vaqueros then seized the noose and fitted it around the man's neck.

"Hold off now," Ramón cried; and when his voice did not reach the cluster of vaqueros circling like vindictive birds of prey around their captive, he lifted his carbine in the air and fired a round. The reverberating shots made them turn.

"¡*Momentito, hombres!*" Ramón exclaimed, cupping his left hand to his mouth to make the sound of his voice carry.

At last he reached the scene and turned to the vaquero whose hand was still pressed to his bleeding shoulder. "*Qué pasa*, Narciso?"

The vaquero, Narciso Duarte, a stocky Mexican in his early thirties, turned and angrily declared, "*Patrón*, this *gringo* was cutting out one of our strays and driving it east. We called him to stop, but he had a good start, and when I fired my *pistola* over his head to halt him, he turned and drew his own *pistola* and wounded me and Felipe Sanchez. He's a rustler, *patrón*! And out here, there's no need for a trial! We hang the *gringo*."

"Not so fast, Narciso!" Ramón sharply rebuked the glowering vaquero. "At least not until I talk to this *hombre*."

He walked forward, scowling at the trembling young man who, his hands already bound behind his back, the noose tight around his neck, glanced fearfully at the squat vaquero who was about to hoist the end of the lariat and send him to his maker.

"Slack that rope, Juan!" Ramón crisply ordered. "That's better. Now then, *hombre*, you'd better talk and tell me the truth, or my vaqueros will hang you for certain."

"I—my wife is starving—my kid too—you had all these steers, you wouldn't miss one—" the young man hoarsely stammered, with a pleading look at his captors, staring fixedly at the stocky vaquero who held the noose, which was already tightly compressing his thin neck. For an instant, his eyes flickered upwards to the branch of the cottonwood tree, then back to Ramón's questioning, weatherbeaten face.

"Starving? You wife and *niño*? Where do you come from, *hombre*? What's your name?"

"My name, it's—it's Robert Markey. I—I've got a little farm east of here—it's just about worthless, can't raise wheat, or rye or barley—came out here two years ago from Indiana with my wife, Marcy—and last month we had a—we had a kid—we don't have any food—the neighbors think we don't belong—you had so many steers—"

"I see. But why, in God's name, did you try to shoot my vaqueros? You wounded two of them, you know," Ramón indignantly averred.

"I—I was just scared—they took after me—I didn't think they'd see me cut out just that one steer—they shot at me, so I shot back without thinking—I didn't mean to hurt anybody—oh please, I don't know what Marcy and my little girl will do if you hang me—" The young bearded man bowed his head and burst into choking sobs.

Ramón shrugged. "Let him go, vaqueros. Yes, that's what I said! And let him take the steer along. You, Rodrigo, get him a sack of beans and one of flour and a little coffee. We've supplies to spare and we're not far from Dodge. Don't look at me like that! Do what I tell you to! *¡Adelante!*"

With a glowering sneer, the man who had been holding the noose tight around the captive's neck loosened it, then moved away. The young farmer crumpled now on his knees, bowed his head and covered his face in his hands, and began to sob wholeheartedly.

"It's all right, *hombre*. You're safe now. Take what my men give you, and take the animal, too. I wish you better luck." Ramón came forward, bent and clapped the sobbing young man on the back. Then, turning to Narciso, he demanded, "What did you do with his horse?"

"It was shot, *mi jefe*," the vaquero grudgingly replied. "By all the devils in hell, are we to let a *gringo* steal from the herd and go free? It was not done this way in the days of *mi padre*."

"But you were not starving, Narciso. When you were hungry, your mother or your sister gave you a taco or an enchilada, and you knew there was more where those came from. This young man is not a *ladrón*—he did it for the sake of his wife and *niña*. Now, you will get a good horse from the remuda and bring it to him."

"This is the way you reward thieves, Señor Ramón?" the astonished vaquero gasped.

"There is a difference between thieving and having to eat or die. And this man did not think of himself, but of his wife and child. So long as I am boss of this drive, Narciso, you will take orders from me. Go get him that horse and make sure it has a saddle. And don't look so angry, by all the saints in heaven!"

In a few minutes, the vaquero, his face dark with anger, led a yearling mare out of the remuda. "Take it and get out of our sight, *hombre*," he growled at the incredulous captive.

The latter did not wait for a second invitation: he swung himself into the saddle, and one of the other vaqueros grudgingly handed him the end of the lariat with which he had roped the steer. He looked questioningly back at Ramón, who nodded with a grin and a wink, saying, "*¡Vaya con Dios, amigo!*"

For a moment he sat silently, not believing his good fortune. Then he said, in a voice that threatened to break at any instant, "God bless you, Mister—Mister—?"

"You're talking to Ramón Hernandez from Windhaven Range, the Bouchard spread near Carrizo Springs."

"I'll make it up to all of you," the young man brokenly faltered, "I don't know how, but I swear to God I will. And now I want to get back to Marcy. We'll both thank God for you for the rest of our lives."

The other vaqueros who had ridden up, wondering about the lengthy delay at the front, silently crowded around and watched, their mouths agape, as the whispered news of how Ramón had pardoned a rustler reached them. They watched him ride off on his new horse, to which had been attached saddle bags filled with the beans and flour and coffee Ramón had ordered for the farmer. As he disappeared in the distance, they turned to stare at Ramón Hernandez who, finding amazed gazes fixed on him, swore violently: "That'll be enough of this daydreaming! How in ten thousand hells are we to get to Dodge City if you stand there and look at me? You've seen me before, and you'll see a great deal more of me than you'll care to! Now, to horse! *¡Adelante!*"

Then, to the stout, black-bearded vaquero who had been put in charge of the remuda, he barked, "Cut me a gelding out of your remuda, Diego, saddle it, and bring it here. My gelding broke his leg in a gopher hole just across the river, and I very nearly didn't get here in time to stop a lynching!"

"*Sí, patrón.*" The vaquero touched his forehead and hurried off to execute the order.

Sheepishly, the men who had tried to hang the young man began to move about, not wanting to look again at Ramón Hernandez in his tautly drawn mood. Then his face softened and, just as Diego brought up the horse, he casually remarked, "In this herd we're bringing to Dodge, *amigos*, there are two hundred head from my own grazing land. I shall pay for the steer I gave that *pobrecito* out of my profits when I sell them in Dodge and I'll pay back Señor Lucien Edmond for the supplies I gave that poor fool to take back to his wife and child." There was a murmur of approbation from the men, who still did not turn around to look at him, fearing the lash of his biting sarcasm.

He swung into the saddle and took the reins in his left hand, adjusted his sombrero against the heat of the Kansas sun, and then, leaning toward the little group, added, "And you, Narciso, Sanchez, who took those bullets from our poor young thief, patch yourselves up—they're only scratches. There'll be a twenty-dollar gold piece for both of you as a bonus for taking the risk of being shot on the trail with me, as soon as I'm paid off in Dodge."

"*¡Gran vaquero!*" the group lustily cheered, waving their sombreros at Ramón. He flushed, wheeled the gelding, and rode back toward the river.

On the outskirts of Dodge City, a gray-haired, heavy-set rancher, wearing a broad white Stetson and with a pair of ivory-handled six-shooters holstered round his waist, rode out toward the south, followed by his trail boss and half a dozen top hands. Reining in his white palomino stallion, he greeted Ramón: "Mighty fine-looking critters you're bringing to Dodge, *amigo.*"

"Thank you, señor," Ramón Hernandez replied. "Just under two thousand head this time. My partners and I weren't too sure of market conditions in Dodge."

"They're probably right to be wary. My name's Carl Hartmeyer, from the Panhandle. I brought in ten thousand just last week, and we stayed over to let the boys have a little fun. But to be sure, Dodge isn't what it used to be."

"I'd be grateful, Señor Hartmeyer, if you'd give me some pointers. My name's Ramón Hernandez, from Windhaven Range—that's near Carrizo Springs."

"Yep, heard about your good spread. You and your

partners are trying Brahmas, I hear. They can stand the heat better. But to get back to your wanting to know about Dodge, Hernandez—you know, these damn railroad strikes aren't going to help much, so a lot of the herds are being sold to Injun reservations, because that means they won't have to be shipped too far. And they've got most of the northern Injuns out on reservations now, except for the last batch with Crazy Horse and Sitting Bull up Yellowstone way. A lot of the boys are driving trail as far as Wyoming."

"I see. What is the market paying now, Señor Hartmeyer?" Ramón asked.

"Hell, you'd be lucky to get fourteen or fifteen dollars a head. Even though you've got prime beef, there's too much of it around. And then, to make matters worse, you've got farmers yelping about damage to their haystacks and crops, holding up the trail bosses by making them pay fines. Still more herds are being held up with this damn notion that all Texas cattle carry fever ticks."

"That's an old story, Señor Hartmeyer," Ramón knowingly grinned.

"Damn it all, you're right, Hernandez, but even though the Supreme Court said that the Missouri quarantine law against Texas cattle was unconstitutional, they're still mighty concerned about ticks around here. What I heard, a couple of weeks ago, just before my boys and I got in, was that old Dick King drove thirty thousand head from his coastal ranges and divvied them up into a dozen herds, each with a crew of fifteen top hands being paid good money for their work—like, for instance, the trail boss drew down a hundred bucks a month, and the cook got thirty. Anyhow, King went on north beyond Dodge, and he tried to stay away from the heavily settled farming areas. But it seems that some of the northern stock got sick and they say that even stray milk cows that happened across King's trail came down with fever and died. So, of course, the farmers shot off letters to the governor, and they're still circulating petitions to get wider quarantine areas all the way from the Red River to Montana."

"That's not good news at all."

"No, it's not. If we ever get this damn railroad strike settled, maybe there'll be feeder lines down into your neighborhood and mine, Hernandez, and then we won't

252

have to waste good meat pounds driving our critters eight hundred miles or more all the way from Texas. Well, my boys are getting restless. I wish you good luck in Dodge— but you better look for another market next year, that's my tip to you."

"I'm greatly obliged, Señor Hartmeyer. May you and your men have a safe journey back home!"

"*Gracias*, Hernandez. All right, boys, let's hit the trail back!"

Ramón was quietly reflective as he rode ahead of the herd and his vaqueros into Dodge City. He saw rows of sun-dried wooden shacks, false-front wooden buildings that boasted saloons, gambling dens, and theaters like the Long Branch, the Alamo, the Comique, and even a Dodge Opera House. For those cowboys who had ever spent time back East, there was a restaurant named Delmonico's in imitation of New York City's most luxurious dining establishment.

The herds could water in the nearby Arkansas River, and in the railroad yards there were huge bone ricks that had once held as many as a hundred thousand buffalo skins at a time, baled and piled high, waiting for empty freight cars. But now the buffalos were gone, and Dodge's hope was the beef bonanza and the railroad. Only, as Hartmeyer had just told Ramón, there was a strike on, and it was hurting. Probably there wouldn't be too many buyers on hand, not if the cattle couldn't be shipped on to either Chicago or St. Louis, the two cities vying for leadership as the meat market's main clearinghouse.

Ramón and his riders circled the town to the north, driving the lowing herd toward the cattle pens. He noticed, with some chagrin, that most of the pens were filled, and that there were no railroad cars along the tracks. What Hartmeyer had told him now seemed to have a doubly ominous ring to it. What if he had come all this way in all these long, dreary weeks, with two thousand prime head, only to find no buyers?

Three men were standing near one of the empty cattle pens, one of them with a huge paunch and a dirty gray Stetson pulled down to one side over his double-chinned, flaccid face. He was consulting a gold-plated watch with an ornamental fob, making certain that his two cronies noticed the expensive timepiece with due respect. Advancing a step or two forward, he lifted his pudgy right hand and called out to Ramón, "That's a fine herd you've got there, stranger! I might give you an offer, if we can agree on a sensible price." Then, turning to his two friends, he barked, "Open up those pens and herd those critters in. I think maybe this greaser will come to terms, all right. He's seen how crowded we are with cattle that aren't going anywhere."

Ramón's lips thinned and his eyes narrowed at this palpable insult. But, remembering that he was Lucien Edmond's partner and Joe Duvray's as well, and that the vaqueros had ridden in their saddles loyally behind him for three months on a dusty trail, he quelled his resentment and dismounted. He stood aside while the two men, in chaps and jackets, waved their Stetsons and hurrahed the steers into the pens, his own vaqueros flanking them from the side and the rear, so that none would escape. At last, the gates were closed and the job done, and Ramón exhaled a secret sigh of relief that yet another drive had been accomplished with no fatalities or serious injuries to his men.

"My name's Jeb Cornish," the fat man perfunctorily introduced himself. "I'm a federal buyer, 'n Injun agent, and I must say, I like your herd. How'd you like to sell them right now so's you and your men can enjoy Dodge hospitality?"

"That depends on what you offer for them, Señor Cornish," Ramón guardedly countered.

"Well now, you see, we'll use this herd of yours for the Injuns up north and hold about four hundred head for the army fort that's keepin' tabs on those murderin' redskins," Cornish chuckled. "That's good prime stock there, so I'm not about to haggle. Give you thirteen-fifty a head."

"I was looking for fifteen," Ramón proposed.

"Nope. If that's the way you're figgerin', you kin jist let yer herd set there till the railroad strike's over. Land o' Goshen, haven't you heard jist about every line in the country's shut down because the railroad men want a hefty pay raise? Well, that's the truth of it, so you better take my offer because you won't find any better. There's nobody here right now from Chicago or St. Louis, if that's what you're countin' on."

Ramón scowled, in a quandary. He wanted a better price, but knowing that much of the beef would go to feed

Indians, at least it was a sure bet that Lucien Edmond would approve of the sale on moral grounds; and the rest would go to soldiers, which was, in effect, exactly what was already being done down in Texas with the rest of the herd. All in all, he thought, the offer could have been much worse. He made a quick decision: "All right, then, but I want cash."

"Nope, can't give you all that cash. I got government vouchers; they're jist as good. Now, we got a new President, like I'm sure you heard, and he's standin' behind the vouchers. I'll show you my credentials, 'case you're thinkin' I'm not what I say I am."

"Just the same," Ramón interjected, "you see I've got twenty men with me, and they expect to have a little fun before we ride back to Texas—and I've got to pay them off. So I've got to have some cash—as much as you can manage." Several of his vaqueros had come up behind him and were listening intently to the conversation. From the looks on their faces, Ramón could tell that there would be trouble if some hard cash wasn't forthcoming.

"Tell you what," Jeb Cornish decided, first glancing at his two helpers and apparently reading from their faces what his decision should be, "what would you say to twenty thousand in vouchers and the rest"—he did some quick mental calculations—"nearly seven thousand in hard cash of the realm?"

"I'd take it!" Ramón promptly answered.

"Good! I like a man who makes up his mind fast. S'pose you come over to my office near that old caboose, and you write me a bill of sale and I'll pay you. Fair enough?"

Ramón amiably nodded, and gestured to Narciso to accompany him. As they entered the ramshackle office, Cornish squinted at the vaquero and grumbled, "First time I ever done bought a herd from greasers. Hope you've got some papers on you to prove you didn't rustle that herd."

Ramón Hernandez clenched his fist and fought the impulse to smash the fat, smirking face of the agent. "I happen to be the brother-in-law and partner of Lucien Edmond Bouchard of Windhaven Range, Señor Cornish," he replied in a cold, incisive voice. "I've credentials enough to satisfy even your Congress, if need be."

"All right, all right, no need to get techy. I jist said

255

'greaser' in fun, mister. Everybody does around here," Cornish sought to propitiate the handsome Mexican.

"That may be, but I'd appreciate it if you wouldn't use the word again in front of either me or my men," was Ramón's answer.

"All right, no offense meant, mister. Okay, we said twenty thousand in vouchers, the rest in cash. Now let's see those papers you got to prove the herd is yours," Jeb Cornish demanded.

Ramón produced a letter that Lucien Edmond Bouchard had signed appointing him as trail boss with two thousand head of cattle bound for Dodge City—a precaution that Ramón himself had suggested to avoid just such a problem as this. Convinced now of Ramón's legitimacy, the fat Indian agent became affable and even comparatively gracious. "There you are, Mr. Hernandez," and he turned over the vouchers and the cash. "Tell you what, this is a good piece of business for you 'n' me alike—suppose I stand you treat at the Long Branch. Better still, if you're in the mood for the purtiest dance-hall girls west of the Mississippi, I'll take you over to the Comique."

"First off, if you don't mind, Señor Cornish," Ramón countered, "I'd like to get my men settled. Are the hotels crowded?"

"Not so much now. You see, when this railroad strike started, the buyers didn't come around, some of the trail bosses decided to leave their cattle here in the pens and go riding off to Ellsworth or maybe even farther north, to see if they couldn't swing a deal. But a lot of their hands are still holed up at the hotels. You might try the Dodge House, 'n' there's two boardin'houses down off Front Street. First corner north of the big saloon with the painted doll sign at the front—you'll find it right enough. Nice respectable widows run the houses, and they don't charge too much. They set out a mighty good breakfast 'n supper too."

"Thanks for the information, Señor Cornish. First I'll see to my men getting settled and then I'll be glad to join you at the Comique to seal our bargain. Only I'll stand the treat."

"Now, Mr. Hernandez, you're talking like a reg'lar white man—oops, sorry. That jist slipped out. I didn't mean to—all right, all right, don't look at me like that. I

256

apologize. Anyhow, what I'm gettin' at is, I like a man who does business the way you do, Mr. Hernandez. Let's let bygones be bygones."

With this, the Indian agent put out his sweaty, plump hand, and Ramón, after a moment's hesitation, shook it. "No hard feelings," he repeated. "It'll be sunset in a couple of hours. Why don't I meet you over there then."

"Suits me fine, Mr. Hernandez. A pleasure to do business with you. And when you go back to Texas, you can jist tell your friends 'n' neighbors that old Jeb Cornish gives a square deal on cattle every time, 'specially when they're prime stock like yours."

# Twenty-Six

Ramón and his vaqueros rode to the boardinghouses, where, by dint of assigning two and three men to a room, he was able to find lodgings for all of his hands.

This done, Narciso called the vaqueros to the room that he and Ramón shared, and Ramón paid them off one by one. Bonuses were included in the pay handed to those who had shown extra diligence, with special bonuses to Narciso and Felipe, as promised, for being shot, and to the two men who had ridden drag at the end of the herd, "eating dust" all the way to Dodge City.

"I wouldn't spend all that in the saloons, *amigos*," he told them as they stood there, grinning, counting their money. "From all I've heard, this is an open town. The marshal's a fellow named Larry Degler, and Charlie Bassett is the sheriff of Ford County. I heard someone say this afternoon that a couple of brothers, Ed and Bat Masterson, are their new assistants, and they're supposed to be pretty good with their guns. Still and all, about the only law I can figure they're enforcing here is the one against riding your horse into stores, dance halls, or saloons."

This gained a hearty laugh from the vaqueros, then Ramón continued in a more serious vein: "There are plenty of *putas* who will want to separate you from your *dinero*. My advice to you is to go in groups of threes and fours, so you don't get fleeced—and keep your weapons loaded and handy. There's lots of shooting in this town. I've seen their Boot Hill on that big rocky height northeast of Dodge—and I've been told that every morning there's a man killed for breakfast. Go and amuse yourselves—but be careful!"

Walter Catlin filed by last, feeling that as he had been the last to be hired, he should be the last one paid. "Don't spend it all here in Dodge," Ramón cheerfully cautioned him, as Walter Catlin's lean, tight features brightened when Ramón handed him his wages for the three-month drive—thirty-five dollars for each month plus a bonus of thirty dollars. Seeing his look of puzzlement over this unexpected windfall, Ramón seriously declared, "You're a good man, Walter; you did quite a job rounding up some of those balky young heifers, and you're also a very good hand with horses. When we get back, if you're still interested, I'm going to talk to Señor Bouchard and see if we can't give you a job with more responsibility—and more *dinero*."

"Thanks, Mr. Hernandez," Walter sincerely responded. "I'm very grateful. And I'm glad you let me come along to Dodge. You don't have to worry—I'm not going to spend my hard-earned money in a dance hall or saloon. I don't drink hard liquor very often. Only now and then, when I need it to forget—well, something that's been on my mind a long time. Thanks again." He touched the brim of his Stetson and walked out of the room.

Turning to Narciso, Ramón shook his head. "He's one of the best cowhands I've ever seen, a real vaquero—but about all I know about him is that he came from Virginia. He's been ridin' all this time with something bottled up inside him, and I hope he gets it out—whatever it is."

"If I may say something, *señor patrón*," Narciso cheerfully put in, "I know that he has been seeing a good deal of Señorita Connie—and I think she likes him *mucho*."

"That is very good news, *amigo*," Ramón declared. "I would like to see him come back with us—and maybe her presence will be an incentive. She's a fine young lady. Somewhere, I get the idea that he comes from a much better background than just an ordinary trail hand. Well, perhaps we'll find out someday."

Ramón yawned and stretched as he told Narciso, "I don't think we'll stay here more than a night or two—just enough time for the men to get the liquor out of their systems and to have their fill of the *putas* who are no doubt ready and eager to entertain them. By the way, Narciso,

259

since we'll be traveling light and fast going back, I'd like to stop off briefly in Wichita and say *buenos días* to the *médico*, Ben Wilson."

"But of course, *patrón*," Narciso nodded with a smile. "I, too, like that man very much. *Patrón*," Narciso continued, somewhat sheepishly, "I wish to go with you, as does Felipe Sanchez, when you meet Señor Cornish at the Comique. I think—if you'll forgive my boldness for speaking what I have no right to say to you—but I feel that the señor paid you much too little for your fine *ganado*."

"Perhaps, Narciso, but I couldn't afford to gamble. You see, I might have gotten as little as ten dollars a head if I had turned him down. Now that I've seen Dodge City, I'm going to tell Señor Lucien Edmond that we had better go on trying to sell most of our cattle to the army posts and wait until those railroad feeder lines come into Texas, so we don't have any more long drives like this one, only to have them end up not worth the effort. You've seen yourself how the farmers are trying to stop Texas cattle again, just as they did right after the Civil War.

"But," he wearily declared, "let's stretch out now and get a bit of rest before we go in search of Señor Cornish."

Narciso readily agreed, and only moments after the two men sank down on the hard bed that they shared, they were fast asleep.

It wa sabout an hour before sundown when Ramón Hernandez, Narciso Duarte, and Felipe Sanchez left their boardinghouse and walked down Front Street—Dodge's main thoroughfare—heading for the Comique. Though it was still early, the raucous sounds of a Dodge City night were already beginning to be heard all around them. They reached the Alhambra, a restaurant and saloon owned in part by Dodge City's mayor, James "Dog" Kelley (so named because at one time he cared for General Custer's hounds, and to this day maintained a large pack of dogs). As they were passing this establishment, its doors were flung open, and two burly men emerged, holding a drunken cowboy by the scruff of the neck and the seat of his pants. They flung their victim ignominiously out into the dusty street, and one of the men, having taken the cowboy's revolver and emptied the chambers, tossed the unloaded gun toward the half-conscious figure now sprawled in the dust. "Don't try coming back in here again, Jimson, if you know what's good for you," the man growled and then, clapping his partner on the back, went back into the saloon.

"What are you thinking, *patrón*?" Narcisco spoke up, seeing the frown on his boss's face.

"I am thinking, *amigo*, that my vaqueros had better heed my warnings about Dodge's night life—I don't want to be missing any men before we ride out tomorrow."

Turning off Front Street, Ramón and his two companions crossed the railroad tracks and walked south until they reached Maple Street; then they turned again and walked along Maple until they reached the Comique, where, with Ramón in the lead, they pushed through the swinging doors and entered the noisy saloon.

At one end of the dance hall was a raised stage, for the Comique prided itself on being a theater as well as a drinking and gambling hall. At the other end, numerous gaming tables were in operation, cowboys crowded around them. To the right, along the wall, was a long, wide, polished walnut bar, behind which a huge mirror ran the entire length. Centered above the mirror was an oil painting in a gilt frame depicting a voluptuous Rubenesque blonde lying naked on a chaise longue, one of her knees coyly raised; she was sending a provocative smile to all who beheld her.

There were three bartenders working, serving schooners of beer, shotglasses of whiskey, and here and there an occasional tequila to Mexican vaqueros. For the motto in Dodge City was, "Get the money fast and get them out so there's more room at the bar for the next customer."

As Ramón entered, his Spencer carbine lowered toward the floor, the nearest bartender, a bald-headed, middle-aged man who looked as if he had once been a pugilist, to judge from his broken nose, called out, "Better leave the carbine with me, mister. Handguns are okay, but shotguns and carbines and rifles are checked in here. Pick it up when you leave. No offense, mister."

"And none taken," Ramón amiably replied. As he spoke, the fat Indian agent detached himself from two of his cronies at the bar and came forward, beaming with obsequious cordiality. "I'm glad you came, Mr. Hernandez.

261

You and your friends are welcome. Let's go find a table—it's too noisy and crowded here at the bar."

With this, he turned to the bartender and, with a grandiose wave of his arm, commanded, "Three bottles of your best whiskey for my friends, and put it on my tab."

"Right you are, Mr. Cornish." The middle bartender, who sported a walrus mustache and spoke with a Cockney accent, reached down to produce three bottles that he placed on a tray with flyspecked, dusty glasses.

"Señor Cornish!" Ramón laughingly protested. "Just one of those will be quite enough for my friends and myself. That whiskey looks as if it was just made—it's a little too raw for comfort and we won't be in town long enough to nurse the three-day hangovers it would give us."

"See 'ere, me good man!" The bartender drew himself up to his full height, with an injured look on his face. "That's good Maryland rye—and it's over a year old."

"All the same, just one bottle, if you please." Ramón's smile took the edge off his refusal.

"Well, we can always get more, if we want it, can't we gentlemen?" Jeb Cornish guffawed. He handed two of the bottles back to the bartender, then carried the four glasses and the bottle to a table near the rear of the large dance hall. At the back was a narrow stairway carpeted in green baize, which curved to the right and showed a kind of mezzanine with four closed doors along the landing.

As Cornish seated himself and uncorked the bottle, proceeding to fill the four glasses with generous portions, the farthest door at the top left of the landing opened, and a stunningly handsome young woman emerged. Her gleaming, coppery-red hair was set in an imposing pompadour to make her look older than her twenty-one years. She wore a spangled blue dress with flounces at the sleeves and the shoulders, its décolletage suggestively dipping to show most of the wide valley between her opulent breasts. The black net of her stockings made a disturbing contrast to her high-button shoes, and the gown was slashed at the left side so that, as she slowly descended the stairs, one could see the contours of her beautifully rounded thigh and long, sleek calf.

From the opened door on the landing a man now strode forward, black-haired, with bushy eyebrows and short, pointed beard, wearing a rust-colored frock coat and

262

trousers. "Get to work, Doris! I want to see some action out of you tonight You aren't worth your keep, girl!" he called out in a loud, domineering voice.

"I—I'm going, Mr.—Mr. Thompson!" The redhead turned to look up at him, her face congealed with fear.

"See that you do, then, or I'll have to give you another taste of the quirt," he drawled, and then, with a mocking little laugh. he descended the stairs to the ground floor, turned right, and disappeared through a door behind one of the gaming tables.

Ramón considered the young woman, as she came slowly down the stairs, her head bowed, and Jeb Cornish leaned forward and muttered, "That's Doris Taylor. She's only been here about a month, and she's having hard times. It would be a nice thing if you bought her a drink, Mr. Hernandez."

"I can do that much, I suppose," the handsome Mexican shrugged, but before he could beckon to her, a cowboy seated near the stairway had roughly grabbed her wrist, drawing her to his table where he was drinking with a companion.

"Later will be soon enough," Cornish chuckled. "Anyhow, I must be forgettin' my manners," he continued. "We still haven't drunk to that mighty fine deal we made, *amigos*. To cattle trading, the best dang business there ever was," he exclaimed, downing his drink. The three men followed suit, as was customary, but Ramón couldn't help noticing that Cornish had served himself barely half the liquor he had given the others.

Again Cornish filled their glasses, and although Ramón held up a hand in protest, it was to little avail. Knowing it was his turn to propose a toast, Ramón courteously said, "To you, Señor Cornish, with all our thanks for providing ready cash to pay off the Windhaven vaqueros." Everyone drank again, except Ramón, who managed surreptitiously to spill out most of the liquor from his glass. He couldn't fathom the reason, but fearing that Cornish was trying to get them drunk, and hoping to prevent more toasts, Ramón took the opportunity to hail Doris Taylor, the red-haired young woman who at that moment was sauntering down the room toward them.

To Ramón's relief, as the young woman came forward, Cornish excused himself. "Well, I think I'll leave you to enjoy your night in Dodge," he chuckled as he got up from his chair. "Anyhow, I want to get back to my office. And thanks again for the quick deal we made, Mr. Hernandez."

"It's been a pleasure doing business with you," Ramón politely retorted.

Doris now reached their table, and Ramón could see that she was an attractive woman. Her cheekbones were high-set, her nose was small and delicate, and her skin had the pale, milky tint of the true redhead, with just a touch of rosiness. Yet it was clear that she was upset: her hazel eyes were blurred with tears, and she was obviously forcing a smile to her tremulous, softly curved lips. "Welcome to Dodge, gentlemen," she said in a husky voice.

"May I buy you a drink, señorita?" Ramón rose from his chair and made a sweeping gesture with his right hand toward the seat that Jeb Cornish had just quitted.

"Thank you very much. I can see that you're a real gentleman." She uttered a cynical little laugh. "I think, in the month I've been here, you're the first one of that kind I've met. At least, nobody's ever bothered before to get up from the table when I came to cadge drinks."

"You mustn't downgrade yourself, señorita. I am Ramón Hernandez and these are my friends, Felipe and Narciso." Ramón introduced his two friends.

"Happy to know you. You're Mexican, then?" Doris queried, as Ramón beckoned to the bartender to bring another glass. The Cockney ambled over, set down a glass with a clatter, and gloweringly demanded, "How about another bottle, mister?"

"In time. Thanks for the glass, señor," Ramón pleasantly dismissed him. Then he poured from the bottle into the glass until Doris lifted her hand and said, "Whoa, Mr. Hernandez, that's plenty!" He watched as she put it to her lips, shuddering as she swallowed, then set the glass down and suddenly burst into tears, bowing her head onto her crossed arms. Her shoulders convulsively heaved, and the two vaqueros seated at the table glanced at each other, not knowing what to make of this behavior.

"Come now, señorita, don't cry—it can't be as bad as that," Ramón soothingly offered.

"I—I'm sorry—what—what must you think of me—but—but, I just can't help it—" the redhead sobbed, as she

264

slowly lifted her tearstained face, her eyes poignantly wide and fixed on Ramón's handsome face.

"Tell me what is troubling you, señorita," he urged.

"I—did you hear that man upstairs who ordered me down here—did you?" she chokingly asked. Seeing him nod, she glanced fearfully back at the stairway, then turning to him again and leaning forward, she went on in a low, agitated voice: "That's my b-boss, Frank Thompson. He owns this place. I have to work to—to pay off debts—you see, Mr. Hernandez—I—I married a salesman back east, and we came out here about six months ago—and my husband—my husband was shot playing cards here—because—because—oh, it's just too awful—" Again, she burst into tears.

Ramón shifted uneasily in his chair, glancing at Felipe and Narciso, then bent to her and murmured, "Don't be afraid, we'll see that no harm comes to you, señorita."

"You're so kind—I haven't dared tell anyone—but you're new to Dodge—and Frank Thompson is a mean, cruel man. He—he's whipped me already with that awful quirt of his—"

She straightened, drew a deep, shuddering breath, took another glance at the stairway, and then quickly dragged down the edge of her gown as she twisted to show him the faint welts of a recent whipping that marred the dimpled round of her shoulder and upper back. Then, pulling her gown back into place, she stammered, "You see, my husband—my husband called the dealer a cheat—and so he shot him and killed him—but then Frank Thompson told me that I—I had to pay off my husband's debt—he apparently took to drinking and womanizing, and gambling in a big way, and he'd run up a big tab of several thousand dollars. I didn't know what to do—and there wasn't any other work to be had in Dodge—so I—I came to work here about a month ago. Oh, Mr. Hernandez, I'd do anything if you'd help me get away—please, won't you try to help me?"

"I—I'll do what I can, of course," Ramón dubiously replied, "but I don't exactly see how—"

"Oh, please!" Doris leaned forward again and, in a confidential, tremulous whisper, breathed, "I have to—I have to report for work every night except Sunday, whether I want to or not—and he—he wants me to go upstairs to

265

my room with the—with the cowhands—and I just can't bring myself to—that's why he whipped me—"

"*Pobrecita*," Felipe sympathetically murmured, shaking his head and looking to Narciso for his reaction.

"That is surely wrong," Ramón declared, looking toward the stairs and scowling. "But I can't very well take you away without being forced into a showdown with guns with this Señor Thompson."

"Mr. Hernandez—if you'd come upstairs with me, if maybe you'd give me just enough money to get out of town—or if—if you're going to leave Dodge right away, you could let me ride with you to some town where I could hide out until I could figure out what to do, I'd—I'd be ever so grateful to you—I'd say prayers for you every night, Mr. Hernandez, believe me. I'm so afraid of Frank Thompson—but I just can't—I'd rather die than let any stranger—you know what I mean—" Again she began to weep, stifling her sobs and covering her face with her hands as she bowed her head.

"Very well, señora. I'll come to your room with you," Ramón murmured in a low voice.

Doris breathed a shuddering sigh of relief and added in a confidential whisper, "I'll pay you back for your kindness by helping you in turn."

Ramón looked at her quizzically, wondering what she meant by this remark.

As she saw the look on his face, the redhead dried her eyes and in a husky whisper said, "You're such a gentleman, Mr. Hernandez. So kind and good. Listen carefully to me—don't think it peculiar when I go to the bar and order a bottle of whiskey to take upstairs. Wait a few minutes before you come up—and have your friends make a very obvious exit from this horrible place. Around the corner of this building is a stairway leading up to the second floor. Tell your friends to climb it very quietly and come back into the building through the fire door up there. You all saw the room that I came out of before?" When Ramón assured her that they had, she continued, "Well, there's a closet at the end of the hallway just outside my door. Have your friends wait for you in there."

When Ramón professed some bewilderment at this plan, she pleaded with him not to question her, telling him that as soon as he came to her room, she would make everything clear. "Only, please—" she begged, "don't say anything to your friends while you're down here that anybody might overhear."

With that, she rose and sauntered over to the bar, where with a lewd wink, she told the bartender to give her a bottle to take upstairs—for her and the handsome stranger. Then, with a last long look at Ramón, she quickly ascended the staircase and disappeared into her room.

Felipe and Narciso immediately leaned forward and the former, in an excited whisper, demanded of Ramón, "*Patrón*, are you going to help that poor *muchachita*? She is *muy linda*, that one. Narciso and I saw the marks that man put on her. Me, I would never use a quirt—not even on a balky mule!"

"I'll try to help her, *amigos*," Ramón said in a low voice as he described the plan that Doris had explained to him. "We'll finish our whiskey together, and then I will go upstairs while you two make your way around the side." Downing his drink in a final gulp, Ramón looked carefully at his friends. "*¡Adelante, amigos!*"

Doris Taylor was sitting expectantly on the edge of the sagging bed in the small, cramped room when the knock sounded at her door. Rising, she crossed to the door, opened it, and saw Ramón standing before her. From behind him came the bawdy gales of laughter and raucous shouts of the men in the saloon below, as well as the muffled sounds of the tinny piano. Swiftly she reached for Ramón's arm and drew him toward her. "Come in quickly," she urged.

"That I will do, señora," Ramón replied.

Doris had exchanged her dance-hall gown for a pink wrapper with a green cloth belt. The belt was loosely fastened and revealed that she wore camisole, corset, and knickers underneath, as well as the black-net hose she had worn with her gown. She wore no shoes. The cloying fragrance of her perfume, together with the alluring sight of her scantily clad body had a potent effect on Ramón, who found himself attracted in spite of himself to this beautiful young redhead.

She moved toward him now, her eyes red and swollen, and then suddenly she threw her arms around him.

"Mr. Hernandez, I'm so glad you came. I—I was afraid that you'd changed your mind. You *will* help me, won't you?"

"I said I would, Señora Taylor."

"Please—please call me Doris, and—and I'd like to call you Ramón—may I?"

"Of course. Now, as I am a man of my word, and I said I would help you, tell me what you know." He took a step backward, extricating himself from her trembling grasp.

"It is as I told you. I had to—to pay off my hsuband's debt. Well, Mr. Thompson has a partner in this place, Jeb Cornish—"

Ramón swore at this revelation. "Go on," he said tensely.

"Anyway, Mr. Thompson and Mr. Cornish told me that if—if I wanted to pay off my debt in full immediately, and not have to—to take just anybody—dirty and cruel and treating a decent woman like—like a—"

*"Puta,"* Ramón finished for her.

"I knew you would understand," she sighed. "They told me to bring you upstairs and get you drunk—so they could steal back the money and the vouchers that Jeb Cornish had paid you for your cattle. They—they told me that if I wasn't willing to do it, they'd have one of the other girls work their dirty little scheme. And, oh, Ramón, after you showed me so quickly what a kind man you are, I just had to help you back."

Again her arms went around him, and she started to cry. Ramón reassuringly stroked her shoulder, murmuring, *"Pobrecita,* it's all right—please, don't cry."

"Ramón," Doris breathed heavily, "I—I like you very much. Pl-please don't think unkindly of me, but—oh, Ramón, you are so good and so kind—please hold me and—make me feel wanted a little—I haven't—I haven't had any love since my—my husband died—please, Ramón dear. We have a little while before—before Thompson and Cornish are planning to—expect to find you dead drunk. Couldn't you pretend—just for a little while—"

Her arms tightened around him and Ramón flushed with embarrassment to feel the thrust of her breasts against his chest. Clumsily, his hands on her shoulders, he tried gently to ease himself from her clinging embrace.

Then her lips sought his, and her soft pink tongue insinuated itself between his lips as she uttered a little moan of pleasure.

"You take my breath away, *querida*," he confessed, as she at last ended the kiss. "But I'm a married man, you see—I've a wife and *niños* back in Texas."

"It doesn't matter—she will never know. I'll be ever so good to you, and we can have this moment together for ourselves and remember it always, dear Ramón," she whispered, her eyes starry and her lips moist and quivering. "I'm so very grateful to you for helping me get away from that awful man—I want to show you how much."

"Ah, señora, love should never be given in mere gratitude," Ramón gently replied, as he looked into her eyes moist with tears. "You must save that special love for a time when it has a deeper, more eternal meaning. You will see, *querida*—as soon as you leave here and are able to start a new life for yourself, you will find someone who is worthy of your beauty and your devotion." Giving her a tender kiss on her tearstained cheek, he suddenly drew back and, taking her by the hand, led her over to the small bed and bade her to sit down. He then grabbed the chair that stood in front of her dressing table and pulled it over to face her.

Sitting himself down, Ramón smilingly mused, "Since we no doubt have a bit of time to kill before your Señor Thompson will assume I am drunk enough to be easily robbed, why don't you tell me all that you know about this town—and Jeb Cornish's influence here?"

In anxious tones, Doris proceeded to tell Ramón all that she knew about the cattle buyer, embellishing her tale with many facts about her own life in Dodge.

After about thirty minutes, when Doris had nearly finished, Ramón suddenly interrupted her by putting a finger to his lips, signaling to her to be silent. He had caught the faintest audible sound outside her door. Quickly pushing the chair out of the way, he stepped to the door and flung it open, moving behind it as he did so. With a loud curse, Frank Thompson came hurtling into the tiny room.

Realizing that he had been tricked at his own game, Thompson sprang at Doris, who sat quaking in terror. "I'll get you for this, you bitch!" Thompson spat, raising the back of his hand to her face.

269

"I wouldn't do that if I were you," Ramón angrily suggested.

"You stay out of this, greaser. She's my property until she works off her debt to me."

"She's nobody's property—and especially not yours," the handsome Mexican retorted.

Thompson whirled to face Ramón, drawing his pistol. "If you don't want to be gunned down, greaser, you'd better get the hell out of my saloon and out of my sight."

Wordlessly, Ramón put his fingers between his lips and emitted a shrill whistle. At this prearranged signal, Felipe and Narciso rushed into the room, their six-shooters drawn.

Thompson stepped back, his finger tightening on the trigger. There was an explosion and Ramón ducked as the bullet nearly grazed his shoulder. Almost simultaneously, the guns of the two vaqueros went off, and Thompson dropped his pistol, stumbling to one side before sprawling flat on his face, where he lay completely still.

Doris sobbed, almost swooning in her relief. Then she ran to Ramón, tearfully asking, "Are you all right? Oh, I don't know what I'd have done if you'd been hurt!"

"Not even a scratch, señora," Ramón assured her. "My vaqueros are excellent shots. But as for you, I would advise you to leave as soon as you can. You have shown courage in telling about your employers' little scheme, and you deserve a chance to start life over. I will give you some money to go back home with. Where *is* your home, señora?"

"Back—back in Chicago. My mother's still there, but my dad died a long time ago."

"You should go back to Chicago. You will be able to find a good job there, I'm sure—a woman of your character," he told her with a soft smile.

The look of a cornered animal came into her eyes and she stammered, "But—but what—what will Jeb Cornish do to me when he finds out that I double-crossed him and his partner?"

"Do not fear, señora. You will take the first train out of Dodge City tomorrow morning—and while you are doing so, I will let it be known around town that I am wise to Señor Cornish and his tricks—and if he wants to keep his fine-paying government job, he had better think twice before trying anything more."

Rising up onto her tiptoes, Doris planted a firm kiss on Ramón's blushing cheek. "Thank you, dear Ramón. I think your wife is the luckiest woman in the whole world."

Ramón awkwardly thrust a fifty-dollar bill into her hands, his head bowed so that he couldn't see the looks on his friends' faces. Then he turned to the door and barked, "¡*Vamanos, amigos!* Let's get some sleep, and then we'll head back to Windhaven Range by tomorrow afternoon. I do not think Señor Lucien Edmond will ever want to ship cattle here again."

As they started to file out the door, there was the sharp report of a weapon fired just outside on the street, followed by several more shots and the tinkling of glass, in rapid succession. Instinctively all the men in the room ducked, and Ramón pulled Doris down, out of the path of any stray bullets that might shatter the window. Then Felipe, during a brief pause in the firing, crawled over to the window and cautiously peered out.

"*Patrón, patrón,*" he called out hoarsely, "it is Señor Catlin—he is being shot at!"

With that, there was the sound of more breaking glass, and then the gunfire resumed.

# Twenty-Seven

After quitting Ramón Hernandez's room earlier that afternoon, Walter Catlin had wandered through the streets of Dodge City before returning wearily to her own boardinghouse. His room was on the second floor of the ramshackle wooden frame building, and when he had first taken a look at the room, he had decided that at least it had the advantage of being in the front of the building, so that its window commanded a view of the street—not that there was anything much to look at in this godforsaken town.

After carefully stashing his pay, Walter Catlin stretched himself out on his bunk, intending to get a few minutes' rest; but he promptly fell asleep, and when he awoke, it was late afternoon. Rubbing his eyes and rising from the narrow cot, he took a last look around at the meager little room and headed out into the streets of Dodge.

He walked south from the boardinghouse, across Front street, across the railroad tracks, and into the south side of town. As he paced a steady cadence along the dusty street, the spurs on his low-heeled boots jingled in time to his steps. He hadn't shaved in five days, and the dust of the trail clung to the growth of beard on his chin and jaws, his chaps and jacket, and stuck to the creases in his forehead and his hollow cheeks. His normally bright gray-blue eyes were narrowed and cold, and they fixed each passerby with more than a mere casual glance. From time to time, he patted the double-action colt T.44-40 that was holstered in a well-oiled leather belt slung around the hips of his dark blue tweed breeches. Once or twice he reached for it with his right hand, as if reassuring himself that the smooth, polished walnut grip was easy to draw.

Except for the stares he directed at passersby, he was detached from the scene around him; he saw but did not register the groups of cowboys who tethered their horses to hitching posts in front of the saloons, then drew their revolvers to fire into the air, whooping and cussing, letting off steam, venting the fear and tension that had built up by the end of their cattle drives. He merely strode on, in resolute silence.

The sun was just starting to set, but the hard drinking that went on in Dodge was already under way. The sharp clinking of glasses and loud talk emanating from behind the many swinging doors of the saloons came only as vague sounds to Walter Catlin's ears.

Turning and walking west, he saw ahead of him the sign proclaiming "The Comique," and he watched as a group of five cowboys staggered out of the dance hall, laughing uproariously and shooting their revolvers into the air.

Suddenly he caught his breath. A tall, thin man with a wide-brimmed black Stetson astride a black mare rode toward the dance hall. He watched as the man dismounted and tethered his horse to the hitching post, wiping the dust off his gleaming black boots. His full, sensual lips held a contemptuous smile as he regarded this group of cowhands, a look that declared that he thought these drunken trail hands would be easy marks—for his black frock coat and breeches, along with his Stetson banded in gold braid with five silver dollars glued upright around its crown, proclaimed the man to be a professional gambler, or a "tinhorn," as the cowhands called his type—particularly when they lost their trail wages to him.

Walter Catlin began to tremble as he stepped off the sidewalk and into the dusty street. "Ed Brainard!" he called to the man in a hoarse, hollow voice.

The man turned away from the cowhands and moved into the street facing Catlin, his hands on his hips and his handlebar mustache twitching in expectation. He slowly unbuttoned his frock coat, and Walter could see that his pair of holstered six-shooters were adorned with mother-of-pearl grips that gleamed in the rays of the setting sun.

For a long moment the two men just stared at each

other. Finally, the gambler called, "Who might you be, stranger?"

"You spent a little time in Virginia during the war, if I'm not mistaken," Walter harshly declared.

"I think you've had one too many, stranger. Besides, I've got to go to work—I can't make a living if I stand out here and chew my cud with you. If you've money to play with, come in and try your luck." The tall, black-hatted man started to turn back to the swinging doors of the dance hall.

"Twelve years is a long time, Brainard, but I'd never forget your face. I've tracked you from Virginia to Missouri, down to New Orleans and Laredo. I don't suppose you remember a sweet young girl by the name of Sarah Catlin?"

"So!" Brainard whirled around. "It's you! Walter Catlin, in the flesh, come for me after all these years!" Brainard walked out into the street. Facing Walter Catlin, he was now completely oblivious to the noise emanating from the dance hall to his right. "Why don't you go home, Catlin? No sense a poor yellow-bellied sap like you gettin' hurt, now, is there? Hell, Catlin, all I did was keep your woman happy—which is more than you could do. You might say you made me do it, Catlin," he mocked, and turned his back on his enemy.

Walter Catlin rose to the bait and took several steps toward the retreating gambler. "I ought to kill you," he cried out in an angry voice.

"Aha, so now you're threatenin' me," Brainard sneered over his shoulder. "Well, Catlin, I'm goin' to teach you your final lesson about how to be a *real* man!" The gambler whirled, crouching, both hands plunging to his holsters.

Walter Catlin flung himself down flat on the dusty street, his right hand drawing out his Colt at the same time. Already, Brainard's guns were blazing, and bullets kicked up spurts of dust near the prostrate cowboy. Catlin's Colt barked twice, but both shots missed their target: one of them whizzed past Brainard's head and imbedded itself in the end of the hitching post in front of the dance hall, the second went wildly off to his right and shattered the glass of the Comique's window, bringing a chorus of angry shouts from inside. Immediately Brainard turned and dashed for the cover of a watering trough in front of the dance hall. He threw himself lengthwise on his belly at the end of the trough, peering around it to get a bead on Catlin.

As Brainard ran for his cover, the cowboy got off another shot at his retreating figure and then scrambled to his feet and ran back to the general store across the alley from the Comique. Seizing a broad wooden bench from the porch, he hastily toppled it lengthwise as a rough barricade against Brainard's bullets, two of which now whined past his ears. He got off another shot from behind the bench, aiming just at the point where Brainard's head was disappearing behind the watering trough; the bullet went off the mark into the trough, leaving a hole from which water began to flow out in a fine, steady stream.

The bench, though thick and sturdy, afforded Catlin too little cover, so the cowboy leaped up during a pause in Brainard's fire and made for the general store. He moved in a half-crouch, throwing himself through the door, knocking over a sugar barrel, and then ran over to a side window inside and to the left of the door, to give himself a clear view of Brainard's prone figure by the trough. He smashed the pane of glass with a violent blow from his revolver, then pulled the trigger. The hammer clicked against empty chambers and he swore, turned back around, hunkered down, and reloaded.

From up the street came Brainard's harsh voice. "You goddamned coward! Come out and face me like a man!" With this Brainard recklessly stood up from behind the water trough, seeking to dash across the alley to take closer aim at his adversary holed up in the general store.

The element of surprise was on Walter Catlin's side this time. Taking careful aim through the broken window, he loosed two more shots. One of the bullets found its mark. The gambler uttered a piercing cry, fell backwards, and lay still.

Slowly, Walter walked out of the store toward the fallen man, and then he stopped. Brainard was dead. As he holstered his pistol, Walter noticed that men were pouring out of the dance hall. Soon they were clustered around him, and there was a buzz of conversation.

Just then, Ramón Hernandez, Narciso Duarte, and Felipe Sanchez came out through the swinging doors and rushed up to their friend. "Walter, *amigo*," Ramón asked, "are you all right? Who *was* this man? What's the meaning of this?"

Before Walter could respond to Ramón's questions, a tall, burly man with a star on his chest strode toward them from a building just up the street. "What happened here, mister?" he demanded of Walter. "Who started it?"

"He did, sheriff," Walter spoke up, "but I won't say I wasn't glad to finish it. It was a fair fight—some of those men over by the dance hall will vouch for that."

The sheriff turned to the group. "You gents see this action?"

The several men who had been outside the saloon when the shooting started now spoke up. "Brainard pulled his gun first."

"That cowpoke was acting in self-defense."

"Brainard always was trigger-happy."

The sheriff listened to the comments, then turned to Catlin. "Guess you're in the clear—you got enough witnesses here sayin' Brainard went for his guns first. What might your name be?"

"Walter Catlin. I rode in today with Mr. Hernandez here, bringing in a herd from the Bouchard spread at Windhaven Range, back Texas way."

"All right. You can go, I guess. But I hope you and your outfit will be out of town before you kill any more gamblers—you'd be takin' all our fun away," the sheriff dryly chuckled. "Besides, there's plenty of gunslingers around who might take it into their heads to challenge you—and I don't want no more killings."

"I've no reason to kill anybody else, Sheriff. I'll say good night to you and go back to my boardinghouse now."

The sheriff nodded and then called to one of the men in the crowd whom he recognized: "Jake, the city'll pay your fee for burying this galoot in Boot Hill. Give him a marker, though. He played a pretty damn good game of poker, I'll grant him that."

"I think I could use a drink, Mr. Hernandez," Walter Catlin declared as he stood watching the body of Ed Brainard being borne up the street.

"All right, *amigo*," Ramón responded, "and I want to know all about what's been going on."

With this, Narciso and Felipe, sensing that their boss wanted to talk with Walter privately, took their leave and walked off in the direction of their boardinghouse, knowing that sooner or later they would hear the whole story.

Ramón clapped Walter on the back and said, "Let's go find another place. I think this dance hall isn't the place for you to be right now—whether the men inside think you're a hero or a villain, either way there'd be too much staring and whispering for my comfort."

Walter Catlin readily acquiesced, and the two of them wandered up the street, then turned into a small, reasonably quiet saloon.

Ramón ordered a bottle of whiskey and two glasses and took them over to a small table in an empty corner of the establishment. Pouring out a generous portion of whiskey for Catlin and a smaller amount for himself, he waited for his friend to begin his story.

With an anguished sigh, Walter said, by way of a preamble, "I sort of involved you in my life, Mr. Hernandez, you and Mr. Bouchard both, and I owe you an explanation. If you decide that I've been fairly paid for fair work and want to be done with the sight of me, I'll understand and I won't have any hard feelings."

Ramón took a sip of the whiskey before replying, "Look, Walter, I've known from the day I met you that something has been troubling you deep inside. But I also know, *amigo*, that you are a good worker, a good horseman, you handle yourself well, you keep your mouth shut, and you do the jobs asked of you. I couldn't want more from any vaquero. So don't worry about getting fired. Just tell me what's on your mind."

"I—I really appreciate that, Mr. Hernandez. Because now that I've finally finished something that had to be finished for a long time, I'd like to think that I can go back to Windhaven Range. Sorry," Walter ruefully smiled, "I guess I'm digressing a bit. It's just that—well, it's kind of hard for me to tell this. . . .

"I come from a town in Virginia—a small place that keeps to itself and doesn't cotton to outsiders. Well, my father moved us there from the North when I was a small boy—he owned the general store—and we were never really accepted, if you know what I mean."

"I know only too well, Walter," Ramón replied sardonically. "I'm Mexican and an awful lot of people don't like us 'greasers'—I've already been called that here in Dodge City."

"Well, me, I judge a man by what he is and does, not by the color of his skin, his religion, or anything else that some people consider different."

"Then you're wiser than most men, Walter."

"I don't know about that," the trail hand confessed, uttering a short, humorless laugh. "I sure didn't judge one man very wisely . . . but I'm getting ahead of my story. Anyway, after my father died and I inherited the store and our house in town, I thought I had the world by the tail. Here I was, barely twenty years old, and I already had a prosperous business all my own. Then I met a girl. She was eighteen—and as sweet and gentle as you could ever wish. Actually, I had known her as a sort of acquaintance way back in school, but suddenly there she was, all grown up and as pretty as a picture. Well, we got married and I felt then that there was nothing better in life than this. The war had just started, but I hadn't thought of joining up—Sarah and I were hoping to start a family and I was even thinking of getting some more education, maybe even going into teaching. I sort of thought that I'd like to help young kids who weren't sure where they were going."

Ramón watched him intently as the cowhand bit his lips and looked down at his hands, splaying his long fingers and knotting them into fists. "Go on, Walter."

After a moment, Walter Catlin resumed. "A year went by and Sarah still wasn't with child. Then I guess you'd say something just happened. Neither of us wanted it to, or even expected it to, but it happened all the same. A stranger came into town, a man of about thirty or so. He was a drifter, though he didn't seem to want for money. He came into the store one afternoon—I remember Sarah looking up with surprise from behind the counter, because we seldom got strangers passing through our town—and started talking real friendly like. Said his name was Ed Brainard. . . ."

"I think I'm beginning to see the picture, *amigo*," Ramón interjected.

"Yeah. Well, he seemed like a nice enough fellow at the time—if a bit slick. Anyhow, he seemed to take a shine to

278

us and started coming into the store just to pass the time of day, and before long, he was coming to dinner a couple of nights a week.

"Later I heard that he'd owned a gambling house up North and was a real wizard with a pack of cards—but at the time I didn't question his past. We enjoyed his company—I suppose we were even a bit flattered that he liked us—because we didn't have many friends in town. It wasn't till later that I realized he wasn't interested in my friendship at all—he was just after Sarah.

"Well, right about then I began to get restless. I loved Sarah—God, how I loved her—but I was beginning to feel that maybe I should enlist after all. I sure didn't want to have to kill anyone, but—hell, I don't know. Maybe it was all those years of being snubbed, of being an outsider, thinking I was a Southerner after all and I should defend my homeland. . . . Anyhow, I joined the Virginia Volunteers. Sarah didn't want me to go, of course, but I guess I felt it was my duty."

"I understand, Walter," Ramón told him. "A lot of men went to war for the same reason. You certainly don't have to defend yourself."

"Thanks, Mr. Hernandez—"

"Please, call me Ramón."

"Okay. Well, I went off to war, under Stonewall Jackson—but then we lost him, and the South began to lose. I'd been away from home maybe four months when a letter from Sarah arrived— Oh, God!" He nearly wept at the anguish he had locked up inside him. Struggling to get hold of himself, he finally blurted out, "In the letter she said she was going to have a baby—but she wasn't sure if it was mine. She told me that after I'd left she was so terribly lonesome. Ed Brainard had swept her off her feet, telling her they would start a new life together in some exciting city, not the little backwater town in Virginia that she had known all her life—and she sort of lost her head. She told me she was sorry now that she had been unfaithful, but since she had betrayed me, she was sure I wouldn't want her—or the baby—any more. So she was going to go off with Brainard.

"I damn near went crazy when I read that. It just tore up my guts. Hell, I loved her—of course I was hurt and, I'll admit it, damned angry that she'd been with another man—but I loved her more than anything in the world. I wouldn't have cared whose baby it was. I know I could've loved it, regardless.

"The worst of it was that I couldn't even get word to her. We were surrounded by Union troops and there was no chance that a courier could get through. Then I was wounded in the battle and cashiered out of the army. But by the time I got home, all I found was an empty house and a three-line note tacked to the mantel. I can remember it word for word, to this day: 'I love you, Walter,' it said, 'but I don't deserve you. I spoiled everything we had together and now it's too late for happiness. I know you can never forgive me.'"

"*¡Diablo, hombre!*" Ramón groaned.

"I damn near fell apart after reading that note. I felt so helpless. All I wanted to do was find her and bring her home, but I'd no idea where she'd gone. Then I thought of Mrs. Bundy, our next-door neighbor. She was an elderly spinster who'd always taken a motherly interest in Sarah. I ran over to her house, but the moment I set eyes on her, I knew the news was bad. . . . Ramón," he interrupted himself, "I think I need another drink, if you don't mind."

"Certainly, *compadre*." Ramón solicitously poured another generous libation into the cowboy's glass. Walter quickly took two gulps of the drink, then resumed his narrative.

"After Mrs. Bundy took me into her parlor, she told me that the two of them had left town very suddenly about six weeks before. It seems that Brainard had been running a crooked card game and had to skip town before the law got onto him. I don't know if it was because his lucky streak seemed to have run out on him or what, but Mrs. Bundy got a letter from Sarah from Baltimore saying that Brainard had turned mean and he—he had beaten her so bad that the baby had come too soon and was born dead.

"'Mr. Catlin,' she told me—as if I had needed any urging—'go find her and take her away from that awful man before something even more terrible happens to her. I hate to say anything against a Christian soul, but that man is no good.'"

"How horrible for you!" Ramón sympathetically averred. "What happened then?"

"I made my way immediately to Baltimore—Lee had

surrendered at Appomattox by this time so people could travel freely between North and South—but I was too late. They'd already moved on to Columbus, Ohio. By the time I got there, my darling Sarah was dead." Walter's voice was choked with grief. He surreptitiously wiped his eyes with his sleeve and blew his nose hard on his handkerchief.

"Take your time, Walter," Ramón murmured. "I know how hard this must be for you."

"They—they told me she had been beaten, but they weren't sure if internal injuries had been the cause of death or not; they said it may have been a fever that took her. I know better, Ramón. She did die of internal injuries, sure as I'm sitting here, because I think that poor little girl died of a broken heart! And that bastard Brainard murdered her as surely as if he had plunged a knife into her breast.

"He had lit out fast, leaving her to be buried in a pauper's grave. I didn't have much money, but the sisters in the hospital where she had died took pity on me—you see, Sarah and I were Catholics. Anyhow, I promised I would send them the money if they would see to it that she got a proper funeral and they trusted me, God bless them. I took off after Brainard's trail, tracking him back down to Virginia, then over to Missouri, on up to the Badlands of Dakota, then back down again to New Orleans. I've tracked that man for twelve years and I'd fairly much given up hope of ever finding him. Then I got wind that he had gone to Laredo after another crooked card game again forced him to flee the law; I guess he figured he'd be safe in a border town. So I went down there after him. But then apparently he heard about the fact that Dodge City was a boom town, filled with cattle drivers with a lot of hard cash to spend and willing to lose it—not to mention that nobody here really gives a damn whether the law's looking for you or not. When I left Laredo, I chanced to stop off at a ranch not far from the Bouchard spread to water my horse, and they told me that you were probably planning a drive up here. You know the rest."

"I would have done the same thing in your place, Walter, I know I would have," Ramón said fiercely between his teeth. "You have done nothing to punish yourself for, amigo. And I hope you'll be riding with us when we head

281

back to Carrizo Springs tomorrow—now that you're free and you've buried your ghosts." Ramón stood up and held out his hand to the emotionally spent cowboy. "Come, my friend, it's late and we've got a long journey ahead of us. Let us walk back to your lodgings. I think you have earned a good night's rest."

Catlin rose and clasped Ramón's hand in his. "Thank you, Ramón. Thank you for everything."

They walked out of the nearly empty barroom onto the dusty street, side by side, in complete silence, each lost in his own thoughts.

Walter Catlin slowly climbed the stairs to his room, walking as if his feet were made of lead. Sitting down heavily on the bed, the springs creaking alarmingly, he began to weep, tears cutting crooked paths through the dusty grime of his stubbly cheeks. He rose and walked over to the window, looking up at the half-moon rising in a cloudless sky. "It's over, Sarah," he whispered. "I've paid him back for you, honey. Now I can begin my life all over again, God willing."

# Twenty-Eight

Ten days after their first social engagement, Judith Branshaw had readily accepted another dinner invitation from Bernard Marquard. Looking forward to their second meeting, she felt an eagerness she hadn't known since the days in Tensaw, when she had still believed that dapper, suave David Fales had truly been in love with her and intended to marry her. She had, to her own surprise, eagerly told her landlady, Mrs. Dorcas Fulton, all about the blind man with whom she had gone to dinner and whom she was planning to see again.

"He's probably twice my age, but it doesn't seem to matter, Mrs. Fulton," she had told the lonely, gossipy widow. "When he was wounded in the war and lost his sight, his wife fell in love with someone else—and he was generous enough to let her divorce him, so that she could go away with her lover. He's so good and kind and gentle. Surely there can't be many men like that."

"You're right, Judith. And age really doesn't matter. You know, it's none of my business, but you and I have a lot in common because we're both lonely, and we've both been disappointed in love. But you're young, Judith, and you've got your whole life ahead of you. I'm glad to see you coming out of your shell and taking interest in another man."

"Oh, not that way, Mrs. Fulton," Judith had protested, with a furious blush. "It's just that—well, after what happened to me in Alabama, I haven't wanted to go with any man. But Mr. Marquard isn't like most men. He's so courteous, and sometimes you hardly realize he's blind. And he's thoughtful and—"

"You see, Judith," Mrs. Fulton had knowingly smiled, "you think you shouldn't fall in love with him, but the fact is, I believe you are, even if you won't admit it."

The second evening together had delighted Judith as much as their first. This time, Bernard had taken her to Antoine's, where he had ordered a gourmet dinner and a fine white Bordeaux to accompany the fresh crayfish and the superbly baked chicken.

Because she had become so interested in him, Judith had asked him questions about his shop and the work he did, and he had warmed to this and told her many amusing anecdotes that further revealed his sensitivity and compassion. She found, too, that they had music in common: Bernard, though blind, played the spinet, practicing at least an hour each day. He had taken lessons as a boy and had never lost his love for the instrument. She found herself exclaiming that she would like very much to hear him play, and he had promised that she would.

By mid-July, they had gone to dinner some eight times, the last time at his own house. Marquard's loyal friend and former orderly, Jesse Jacklin, had been there to lend an occasional hand and Judith had marveled how easily the blind man was able to prepare food in his own spacious kitchen, with only a little assistance from his friend. Jesse acted as a kind of waiter, and Bernard, having introduced him to the lovely blond young woman, told her how, after losing his wife and his sight, his friend had taught him to avoid self-pity and make the most of his advantages and abilities to start a new life.

After Jesse did the dishes, he excused himself to Judith and Bernard Marquard, and then went back to his own house. Rory, the English retriever, lay contentedly before the fireplace, his head on his paws, while the blind man sat on a settee with Judith at a modest distance away from him.

"You promised me that you'd play some music for me, Mr. Marquard," Judith Branshaw softly said, as she turned to look at the spinet in the corner."

"I shall gladly keep my promise, if you really want to hear me play."

284

"I wouldn't have asked if I didn't," Judith replied.

"Very well, then. I'll play you some Haydn and Mozart—they were always my favorites. And their music is especially suited to the spinet, which doesn't quite have the percussive quality of a modern piano, Judith—you don't mind my calling you Judith, do you?"

"Why no—I—I prefer it, Mr. Marquard."

He laughed softly. "Then it's only fair that you should call me Bernard. I know I'm much older than you are, my dear—old enough to be your father. I'm fifty-two."

"That doesn't matter to me. I—I like you very much. No man has ever been so kind and thoughtful to me."

"You know, Judith dear—yes, I find myself saying that easily—you've come to mean a great deal to me," he gently went on. "I feel there's a good deal about you you've never told me. I'm not one to pry, but somewhere, somehow, a man has hurt you. I've sensed this from the very first time we spoke in the bank. No, you don't have to tell me. I don't want to open old wounds that have healed. But, for whatever reason, I'm deeply grateful that you've allowed me to know you, to have your friendship. I treasure it, Judith."

Unexpectedly, she felt tears well into her eyes, and quickly dabbing at them with her handkerchief, she struggled to reply in an even voice. "What a lovely thing to say to me, Bernard—but you mustn't flatter me so; it might go to my head."

"No, Judith, you're too wise and sensible for that. But I'll tell you this very frankly, you've aroused feelings in me I thought I'd never have again, after Elinor left me. The fact is, I've fallen in love with you. And mind you, there's no obligation whatsoever on your part. I shouldn't be at all hurt, if you laughed at me and told me that you couldn't dream of caring for an old man."

She could not help bursting into tears, for his candor and gentleness had entirely disarmed her, melting at last the icy barrier that she had erected between her innermost need for love and her terror of being hurt, as she had been hurt by David Fales's betrayal.

"Judith, my dear," his voice had a tremor of alarm in it, "I didn't mean to make you cry. Please forgive me—"

"Oh no, it's not that at all—oh, Bernard, I—I care for

you, too. Please—won't you—won't you play the spinet for me now—I—I think some music is just what I need," she quavered, as again she dabbed at her tear-filled eyes.

Bernard then went unerringly to the spinet, reached down to find the stool, and seated himself.

He began to play a sonata of Haydn, and then one of the earlier sonatas of Mozart. The limpidly clear, joyous music was exactly the counterbalance needed to halt Judith's tears. Yet, at the same time as she listened and watched him play with such artistry, she felt herself more deeply moved than she had ever been before.

When he had finished, he turned his sightless eyes toward her and jauntily asked, "Are you still there, my dear? Or did you run away?"

"Oh, Bernard! You silly man," she said warmly. She rose and walked toward the spinet, put her hand on his cheek, and then bent down to kiss his forehead. He reached for her, his hands gently touching her neck, then her cheeks, and suddenly she felt his lips on hers.

A shuddering warmth surged through her entire body. Though she had been violated by the four hooded men whom David Fales had hired to ruin her, she was a virgin insofar as genuine love was concerned.

"Judith—sweet, lovely Judith—forgive me—I—I've wanted to do that for a long time," Bernard confessed.

"And I—I've wanted you to do it, too, Bernard."

He rose from the stool and took her in his arms. Judith closed her eyes and clung to him, as their lips met again. Her bosom rose and fell, and the warm surging of desire thrilled her loins. The tenderness of his hand, the exquisite sweetness of his kisses convinced her more than his words ever could that he desired her, and not in mere lust. And, moved by the music, by her admiration for this resourceful and courageous man, Judith felt herself almost giddy with rapture in his embrace.

"I love you, Judith. I think I started falling in love the very first time we met, when you tried to help me at the bank—though I was rather churlish then, I'll admit."

"Oh no—I—I was thoughtless—I shouldn't have reminded you that you were blind—but you see so much better than most men who have their vision, Bernard. And you're not old, you mustn't ever think that—you're good

286

and kind—oh yes, Bernard, I do want you, as much as you want me," she avowed in a tremulous, low whisper.

She had not dreamed it could be like this. He had undressed her almost reverently, kissing her, praising her beauty, and the delicate caress of his fingers had made her overwhelmingly desirous to withhold nothing from this gentle, lonely man.

Their lovemaking had been beautifully spontaneous, and she was completely unaware that he was blind, or that he was more than twice her age. He had treated her like the shyest of virgins, almost apologetically and yet with a thrilling gentleness that wakened her deepest sensitivies. He had wooed her, not possessed her, with his lips and fingers and his soft words of ecstatic praise and almost humble gratitude for the beauty of her nakedness. She had cried out with rapture at the culmination of their love, and she had felt herself fulfilled as a woman was meant to be, in total love, in sharing, in unselfish giving. After their mutual consummation, her face had been wet with tears and she had nearly swooned in ecstasy to know that she could achieve such total unity and joy in the arms of a man. She gloried in knowing that she had given him equal joy, though he had not demanded it, and that was the most beautiful joy of all for her.

He lay beside her, his fingers caressing her gently, insistently, until she felt once more the sweet pulsations of desire. Then she caught her breath as she felt him again touch her hips and buttocks, but this time allowing his fingers to linger on the still-discernible welts of that vicious flogging four years ago.

"Judith, my dear one, my sweet one, how did this happen? These are dreadful scars, and you've had them a long time, haven't you?" he gently inquired.

As she turned away from him, bursting into agonized tears, he awkwardly pleaded, "Forgive me, forgive me, my sweet darling, I shouldn't have asked—forgive me, it's not my business—it's only—I love all of you, and these are not flaws, but I thought—"

"No, B-Bernard—you've every right to know. And I—I want to tell you now. You've told me everything about yourself, but you really know very little about me. Bernard, of course you realize I'm not a virgin—"

"It was never my concern, my darling. You were to me tonight. When we come together, each of us is virgin to the other. There are no remembrances of the past in love, only the delight of now and the future."

"Oh, Bernard, I've never known anyone like you before! I wish to God—I wish I'd known you instead of D-David Fales!" She blurted out and then began to sob again.

He stroked her hair, kissed the back of her neck, and murmured, "Please, my darling, I didn't mean to make you unhappy. Please don't cry like that."

"I—I'm crying because I'm so happy, because you've given me such joy, dear Bernard."

"Would you think me a fool, an old silly fool, if I asked you to marry me, dear Judith, my love, my sweet Judith?"

"Oh Bernard—I—I couldn't—I'm not worthy of that—"

"Hush, Judith. Never accuse yourself of that. It's not true. I'm the one who isn't worthy of you—old as I am and blind. It's true that I have money, but you deserve a strong, young man—"

"Oh, no—that's so absurd, if you only knew, Bernard—listen—yes, now I want to tell you. After I do, you won't want to marry me, but I'm glad that we had tonight together because I wanted you so—I needed you as much as you needed me, Bernard."

"Thank you, my darling."

She turned onto her back, an arm under her head, looking up at the ceiling as if it would reflect back the memories of that evening near old Fort Mims, when she had ridden out to meet her fickle, treacherous lover.

"Bernard, I was born on a farm near Tensaw in Alabama. I'm twenty-five now, and I was an only child. After my parents died, four wonderful, loyal blacks who, though they'd been freed and could have found jobs elsewhere, stayed with me and looked after me, helping to run the farm."

"Please, Judith, you needn't tell me anything you don't wish to. All I know is that I love you and I want to marry you," he murmured, as his hand reached for her neck and stroked it gently and then tenderly gripped her bare, soft shoulder.

"I want to tell you everything. It's important that you know everything about me, Bernard—especially now. No,

288

don't try to kiss me, darling—I—I want to tell it now just as I remember it."

"Yes, my dear one. But no matter what you say, it won't change my feelings for you," he reassured her.

There were tears in her eyes as she forced herself, in a cool, impersonal voice, to tell him the events of that unforgettable evening. But when she told him of her hideous violation at the hands of four men, she sobbed bitterly, crying, "I was a virgin till then, but they used me, do you understand?"

"It does not change things, Judith, not for me, not ever for me, my dearest," he murmured back.

She told him about David Fales's part in the scheme. Bernard groaned in anguish and burst out, "That vicious bastard—now I understand a great deal about you, my darling, and it makes me want you all the more. You have such courage, you've overcome your sufferings, you've started a new life here in New Orleans—Mr. Barntry says many complimentary things about you, and they're all true, Judith. I want you to marry me, now more than ever."

"But you can't, Bernard! That isn't all! Hush. Please don't touch me again or try to kiss me, or I'll—I won't be able to tell you—and I have to tell you. When I told David Fales what I thought of him, he laughed and said that I should go to Montgomery because carpetbaggers could use my services. I felt horribly crushed at the time, thinking I was ruined forever. I did go to Montgomery, where I even—s-sold myself a few times. Then I let these carpetbaggers convince me to help them blackmail a fine politician, Representative Haskins. Luckily the scheme didn't work. He was a kind, good man—he only has one arm, you know—and he and his friend, Luke Bouchard, took pity on me. Without them, I'd never have found my job, working for Mr. Barntry. I've made a new start, but you know now, dear Bernard, that I'll never be worthy to be your wife. I've been a whore and—"

"Hush, darling. You were never that. I love you, Judith. I want you to be my wife. I respect and love and desire you—I would be honored and made happier than I ever thought possible if you'd agree to marry me, Judith."

She turned to him, and his arms enfolded her as their

lips met. She began to weep again, but this time, it was from wonder and joy at a love so tender and compassionate. It transcended all she had ever believed love could be, even before she had met David Fales.

# Twenty-Nine

A week after Bernard Marquard asked Judith Branshaw to marry him, William Brickley, at his ease in his office in the Musée des Délices, was indulging himself in a sensual pedicure. Wearing only a red silk dressing gown, he smoked a fine Havana panatella as he lazily looked down at the attractive dark-brown-haired young woman who was bathing his feet in a silver bowl, rubbing a tiny fine-bristled brush against his toenails and between his toes, then laving his feet with a mixture of perfumed rosewater and scented bath oil. She was a newcomer to one of his elegant bordellos on Rampart Street, just eighteen this very day. She wore only a black silk shift that descended to her dimpled knees, the black provocatively setting off the smooth milky pallor of her skin, and as she leaned over his feet, it revealed the lush cantaloupelike globes of her narrowly spaced young breasts with their small, dark aureoles and dainty pink nipples.

"You have a gentle touch, Claudine," he praised her in a soft, husky voice, feeling himself throb with desire for her. He had not yet enjoyed her, but when the madam of the house had reported that she had started to work there, he had instructed the woman to be extremely selective with Claudine's clients: she was to sleep only with older men who would not be exceptionally virile, and she was not to be delivered to any sadistic client, no matter what price he offered.

"*Merci, mon maître,*" she murmured, without looking up at him, as her slim, long fingers continued to knead his instep and arch and heel and then massage each toe with a delicate slowness that excited him.

"Tell me again why you came to seek employment from Madame Morel," he encouraged her.

"But it is in my dossier, *mon maître*."

"I have asked you a question, Claudine, and for not answering you have earned yourself a little punishment. Now tell me!" His voice hoarsened in lascivious anticipation.

She blushed exquisitely, all the way down to her suddenly swelling bosom as she stammered her reply, "My—my father left my mother for another woman six months ago, *mon maître*," she said dutifully, still without looking up at him as she continued her diligent labor. "My mother, in turn, took a lover and one day he tried to force me and my mother came home unexpectedly and saw it. She told me I was a little *putaine* and that she would send me to a convent school where they would whip me every day to teach me to be a good girl. So—I had a friend in school, Cecile, who knew Madame Morel—and I went to see her. That is how I came to be here, *mon maître*."

"And before that, you had never had a man? Is that correct, *ma petite*?" Now his voice was caressingly gentle, and he leaned forward to stroke her hair, which was combed into a thick sheaf, gathered with a barrette, and descended below her shoulder blades.

"*Oui, mon maître.*"

"But I wager that you had *amour* with this Cecile, did you not, *ma petite*?"

Again she blushed, and in a faint voice responded, "*C'est vrai, mon maître.*"

"Excellent. Now you may leave off what you are doing and put your hands on me. But first, let me tell you exactly what you must do." With this, Brickley leaned down and whispered in her ear such explicit and lascivious instructions that once more she blushed. "*Eh bien, ma petite,*" he concluded, "*tu peux commencer.*"

Obediently, Claudine sidled forward on her knees, her hands spreading apart the folds of his robe before beginning to caress his body, touching him delicately but with increasing boldness. Brickley leaned back, closing his eyes and surrendering himself to this potent stimulation.

There was a sudden knock at the door and, irritably, Brickley called out, "Who is it?"

"It's Roland, sir. There's a David Fales to see you," came the answer.

"Very well, show him in." With a sadistic chuckle, Brickley leaned forward and opened a drawer of his desk, drawing out a slim, flexible riding crop. "Claudine, you are to withdraw for a few minutes, but you must return— to get your punishment," he smiled perversely.

With a stifled sob, the attractive girl withdrew to a room off Brickley's sitting room, closing the door behind her just as David Fales entered.

"Well now, Fales, what brings you here? I'm busy at the moment, so don't bother to make yourself comfortable. Just tell me what you have in mind."

"I thought, Mr. Brickley, I could be of some use to you working that casino deal against Mrs. Bouchard."

"You could, Fales, except for the fact that I don't trust you. You see, I've found out that your wife, Henrietta, killed herself last month because of your many infidelities, to say nothing of your gambling and your physical abuse of her."

"That's not fair—"

"Allow me to be the judge of that," Brickley harshly interrupted. "You cast aside that Judith Branshaw to get Henrietta and her plantation. Well, she brought you the plantation as her dowry, and now that she's dead, you own it. The only trouble with that is you've practically ruined it because of your mismanagement. I understand you want to borrow money to salvage what you can."

"That's why I want to work for you and earn enough to bail myself out, Mr. Brickley. Yes, I do gamble, and I'm not lucky, but the way I understand it, you want a shill—"

"I do—not just one, but several. But I want men who aren't in financial difficulties. If someone comes in here and breaks the bank and it leaks out that he's in a desperate situation, even Mrs. Bouchard would catch on. And I happen to know that she has some capable friends who would be certain to look into it. No, Fales, my little scheme wouldn't work if I used you."

"For God's sake, Mr. Brickley, you've just got to help me!"

"I don't have to do anything, Fales," Brickley spat. "But I'll tell you what—why don't you try the Brunton &

Barntry Bank for a loan? Ah, yes, that's one of life's more delicious little ironies—"

"What are you talking about, Mr. Brickley?" Fales demanded.

"Well, Fales, that delectable young blonde you so shamelessly used has been busy coming up in the world while you've been busy going down—"

"Do you mean Judith Branshaw?" Fales angrily interrupted.

"The one and the same," Brickley snidely retorted. "She's now a valued and respected employee of old Barntry's—and who knows, perhaps she's willing to let bygones be bygones to help out an old, ah, friend. . . . But enough of this, Fales." Brickley's tone became curt. "I'm extremely busy and I wish you to leave."

David Fales, his face at once both flushed and haggard, swore under his breath, then turned on his heel and left the room, slamming the door behind him.

William Brickley chuckled maliciously and then pushed back his chair from his desk, calling out to Claudine as he fingered the riding crop. "Come in at once, *ma petite*, and let us return to more important matters. You know, I really should give you a little punishment for being such a saucy little *fille*; but, on second thought, I may be persuaded to commute your sentence, if you are very, very good to me."

David Fales went directly from the Rampart Street bordello to his shabby boardinghouse. Changing into his best suit, he left the house and walked up to a barbershop, to have a careful trim and shave. The unexpected bit of news that Brickley had imparted seemed like a lifeline to a drowning man. "Fales, my boy," he muttered to himself, "your goose may not be cooked yet. Not while dear Judith is still on the fire." He laughed aloud at this mixed-up analogy, oblivious to the curious stares of passersby.

When he entered the bank to seek an interview with Jason Barntry and to apply for a loan, he was somewhat disappointed to learn that Judith was out to lunch. Nevertheless, he was determined to make a good impression on the elderly bank manager. He had brought with him the deed to the plantation, which Henrietta Aylmers had given him at the time of their marriage, and several other documents and letters attesting to the financial worth of the estate.

Jason studied the credentials carefully and then earnestly replied, "Well, Mr. Fales, you understand that I'll have to investigate the current status of your holdings, but if everything is as it appears to be, I'm confident that you should have no trouble securing a loan of five thousand dollars."

"Thank you, Mr. Barntry. I'm delighted to hear that. When do you think you might give me the final word?"

"I'll telegraph our appraiser in Mobile at once, Mr. Fales. I shouldn't imagine it would take him more than a week or ten days at most to ascertain that the title is clear and there are no outstanding debts or delinquent taxes. Why don't you stop back toward the end of next week, Mr. Fales? We should have the answer for you by then."

"Thank you, Mr. Barntry," Fales said as he rose to leave. Hesitating a moment, he then declared, "By the by, Mr. Barntry—I believe a good friend of mine, Judith Branshaw, is employed by your bank."

"She is to be sure, Mr. Fales. We think very highly of her. I must say, young man, that your being a friend of Miss Branshaw's is recommendation in itself."

"Yes," Fales replied unctuously, "she's a wonderful young woman. Well, then—thank you for your time and kindness, Mr. Barntry, and I'll see you next week. Good afternoon, sir."

As Judith left the bank at the conclusion of work that afternoon and directed her footsteps toward the boarding-house, her face was radiant with expectation. Bernard Marquard had again invited her to dinner this evening at the Brissart restaurant, and she wanted to look her very loveliest, for it had been at this restaurant that they had had their first rendezvous. Her landlady would, she knew, ask many prying questions about tonight; one of them, to be sure, would be concerning the date of the proposed marriage.

"Good evening, Judith," a soft voice came behind her. "I must say, you look lovelier now than you did four years ago."

With a startled gasp, she whirled. David Fales wore a top hat, which he promptly doffed, making her an ironic little bow. "Indeed you do, Judith," he went on. "Now you're quite a woman, a very beautiful one."

"How—what are you doing here? How did you know where to find me?" Her voice was strained and trembling, and her widened eyes fixed him as if he were a ghost whose reappearance she simply could not credence.

"I have some business here, my dear. And some of it is with you."

"With me? I have nothing to do with you, David Fales—and I don't think I need tell you the reasons why. And now, if you'll excuse me, I'm on my way home to dress for dinner. I have an engagement for which I don't care to be late—certainly not on your account."

"My, you certainly have regained your self-esteem. But I wonder, my dear, what your employer would think, if he knew that you were, shall we use the antiquated but very apt phrase, a fallen woman?"

Her cheeks flamed with anger and humiliation. "And who, need I ask, was responsible for that? Besides, Mr. Barntry knows all about my background. Luke Bouchard and Mr. Haskins arranged with Mr. Barntry to have me work there."

"But I'm quite sure that none of them ever knew that you'd gone to bed with the niggers on your farm, honey."

"How dare you! I want you to know something, David Fales. I'm engaged to a decent man who knows about my past and who doesn't hold it against me."

"How nice of you, my dear!" he smirked. "Have you told him about the niggers, too? Or doesn't he mind?"

With a shuddering cry, she slapped his face. Fales caught her wrist and twisted it, till she winced with pain. "Be careful, my dear, you don't want to cause a scene. See? People are looking at us already. Now listen to me. I've applied for a loan at your bank. I don't like the word blackmail—let's just say, I, ah, won't use my knowledge about you to your disadvantage, if you agree to put in a favorable word about me with your employer, Mr. Barntry. Tell him what a respectable gentleman I am, trustworthy and deserving of a loan. If you do that, I'll use the money to set you up real fine—Henrietta is dead, you see, and I own the plantation, so I'm fancy free at the moment. You could live very well as my mistress—"

"I'd rather die than give myself to you, you—you filthy, contemptible swine!"

"Careful, my dear. If you continue to treat me so scandalously, I'll have no recourse but to tell your boss, Mr. Barntry, that you're very rude to customers. Besides, I have quite a few connections in this town," he added, lying blatantly, "and many of them happen to do business with your bank. I doubt that many of them would feel quite the same amount of trust if they were to know that their hard-earned savings were in the hands of a whore. The same might be true of your upstanding fiancé, my dear. Would he think so highly of you if suddenly all of his friends were to desert him when they learned of your—your reputation? And of course, I have proof of your indiscretions, because I was a friend of some of the men you went to bed with. So, Judith, you'd best reconsider."

"I'd die first! Get away from me—I never want to see you again!" Trembling with rage, Judith Branshaw quickened her pace as she walked toward the boardinghouse. David Fales looked after her, then uttered a sardonic little laugh. "We'll just see, Judith dear, we'll just see whether you do or not."

Despite the upsetting encounter, it was another wonderful evening for Judith. Lovely Aurelia Brissart sang songs to a hushed and appreciative audience of diners in the little restaurant on Eglantine Street. Bernard Marquard reached for Judith's hand and pressed it to his lips. "You've made me a very happy man, my darling. I want us to get married the third week of October, if that's all right with you. My birthday is on the twenty-first, you see, and it will give me a glorious double celebration."

"Bernard, oh, yes, I want to marry you more than anything! But—but I have to tell you something. You remember that night—you know—when we first—when I knew I really loved you—how I told you what had happened to me in Tensaw?"

"I've already forgotten. For me, it never happened. Or, if it did, my dearest one, it led you to me, for which I'll always thank God."

Tears came to her eyes, and she leaned forward and quickly kissed his cheek, then blushed as old Felix Brissart, who had seen her tender gesture, nodded and blew her a kiss to show her that he wholeheartedly approved. "You're very good to me, you're wonderful, Bernard. No, but this is important. This afternoon, as I left the bank to go home, David Fales came up to me. He—he tried to blackmail me. He said that if I didn't agree to become his mistress now, he'd injure Mr. Barntry's bank by telling our customers that Mr. Barntry has a deceitful whore in his employ. And he also threatened to harm you, my darling, through the same insidious means. Oh, Bernard," she sobbed, "what can I do? The two most decent, kind men I've ever known will be disgraced if I don't leave their lives immediately!"

"Judith, my dear, please calm yourself and listen carefully to me. You needn't fear that man any longer. He's just playing on your feelings, hoping that you'll do exactly what you're talking about doing. My darling, I have known men of his type, and believe me, if Fales were challenged to make a move, he would slink away with his tail between his legs like a whipped dog. Judith, think with your head for a moment, not with your heart. You must realize that you have lived in New Orleans for four years now, and you have proved to everybody who has ever met you that you are an honest, forthright woman. No one would ever take the word of a scoundrel like Fales over the actions that have proved your merit over and over again."

"Oh, but Bernard, I—I—"

"Enough, my dear. You were young and vulnerable when you knew Fales, and you have accepted a terrible burden of guilt for what you did. But it is high time that you stopped living in fear and stopped punishing yourself for what you see as your sins. You're decent and honorable. I love you, and I will till I die. And now, are we going to be married the third week of October?"

"Oh, Bernard, yes, oh yes, my sweetheart, my love! Even sooner, if you wish it!" she softly sobbed.

Ten days after David Fales's application for a loan on his plantation, he entered the Brunton & Barntry Bank, once again dressed in his very best, neatly shaved and carrying a silver-knobbed cane, which he had purchased in an antique shop, just before coming to the bank, as a kind of good luck charm.

Judith Branshaw was at her desk, occupied with her work. Fales again doffed his top hat and moved over toward the counter, then with a sibilant hiss to attract her attention, winked at her and whispered, "I trust you've spoken to your employer. Remember what I told you, my dear. I'll meet you after banking hours, and we'll have dinner together—to celebrate my getting this loan."

She gave him an icy stare, and then went back to her work without a word. Tightening his lips, he shot her a furious look and then muttered, "Well, we'll just see. Just wait till I get my loan. If you're still of the same insulting opinion, I might just have something more to tell Jason Barntry, that sanctimonious old fool!"

Straightening, he walked toward Jason Barntry's office. The elderly bank manager, looking up from the financial report in the *Times-Picayune* that he had been reading, recognized him and rose to meet him. "Good afternoon, Mr. Fales," he said rather brusquely. "Just this morning I received the information I had requested concerning your application."

David Fales made himself at home in the seat across from Jason Barntry's desk, crossing his legs, nattily smoothing his trouser leg so that it would retain its sharp crease. "And I trust that everything is satisfactory." He gave the white-haired man an affected smile.

"I'm afraid not, Mr. Fales. My sources in Mobile tell me that there are a number of questionable points. For one thing—it appears that the taxes on your plantation haven't been paid in nearly two years, and that you yourself are almost totally without assets—in a word, bankrupt. The two letters of credit that you showed me when you first came in here to make application for the loan, Mr. Fales, are regrettably outdated and no longer pertain. I'm afraid that you are a very bad credit risk, and I suspect that every other bank in New Orleans will say the same thing. Of course, you are at liberty to try elsewhere."

"Why, you insufferable prig, you! I'll have you know that the land itself is worth a good deal of money——"

"There's no need to raise your voice or to insult me, Mr. Fales," Jason quietly interposed. "It's true that the land is good, but the plantation is run down and further-more, it's very likely that it may be put up for public auction because of the delinquent taxes. I'm afraid I can't help you, Mr. Fales. I'm sorry."

"You'll be sorrier still! The idea, rejecting a Southern gentleman with my breeding and background, when you have the effrontery to engage in a position of trust a shameless harlot like that Judith Branshaw!" Fales raged.

"I must ask you, sir, to leave this bank. Your remark about Miss Branshaw is scurrilous and ill-founded. She is certainly not a harlot, and I am proud to number her among our employees. And that is all I have to say on the subject, or for that matter, on any subject to you, Mr. Fales. Good day!"

David Fales turned, livid with anger. He stalked out of Jason Barntry's office and then stopped to confront Judith Branshaw at her desk. "So, you told tales out of school to your fine Mr. Barntry, did you, you dirty little bitch! I suppose you're sleeping with *him*, too—"

Judith's eyes were wide with alarm, but they weren't looking at Fales. Bernard Marquard had just entered the bank, stopping dead in his tracks when he heard Fales's outburst. "No, Bernard! Please don't—oh, God, no—" Judith cried as Bernard, locating Fales by the sound of his voice, clenched his fist and drove it against Fales's chin, felling him.

The silver-knobbed cane clattered on the floor as Fales, with a savage oath, drew a knife from his inside coat pocket. "I'll fix you for that, you bastard!" he snarled.

"Bernard—my God, Fales has a knife—look out—he's going to stab you!" Judith cried, beside herself with terror, as she rose from her desk.

But with uncanny accuracy, judging by the sound of his adversary's voice and movements, Bernard thrust out his right hand and caught Fales's wrist, then twisted it till, with a cry of pain, the latter dropped the knife to the floor. In almost the same movement, the blind man groped for and clutched Fales's collar and dragged him to his feet, once again drawing back his right fist and smashing it with full force against the Southerner's mouth. Fales crumpled with a heavy thud and lay unconscious.

Judith, weeping hysterically, ran to her fiancé, flung her arms around him, and sobbed, "Oh, darling, darling, thank God you weren't hurt—I was so afraid he'd kill you— you've knocked him out—you took the knife away! You're blind and yet you disarmed him and knocked him out! You're an amazing man, Bernard, and I love you so much I could die!"

The other employees hurried up, ready to intervene if need be. Jason Barntry strode forward and beckoned to one of the young clerks. "Andrew, go get a policeman. Tell him there's been a disturbance here and that I want a man ejected and jailed, if he doesn't go quietly by himself. You, Nelson," designating another young clerk, "get some brandy in a glass so I can revive this scoundrel."

When the young clerk brought the brandy, Jason stooped and, putting his arms under David Fales's shoulders, partly lifted him up while, at his gesture, the clerk put the glass to the Southerner's lips. Fales, blinking his eyes and groaning, swallowed a sip of the brandy, then coughed and choked.

"Now then, sir, I've sent for a policeman. If you're well enough to leave, I suggest you do so—and if you ever come into this bank again, I'll swear out a warrant for your arrest on the grounds of assault and disturbing the peace. Do I make myself clear?" Jason Barntry severely demanded.

David Fales stumbled to his feet, retrieved his silver-knobbed cane, just as the policeman arrived with the other young clerk. "I'm going, I'm going! To hell with your bank and all of you!" he snarled. Then, fixing Judith with a last, malevolent glare, he walked unsteadily out of the bank.


That night, David Fales, having pawned the silver-knobbed cane, went to the Maison de Bonne Chance, where he ordered supper and wine. He had in his wallet not quite two hundred dollars, all the money that was left to him after squandering his dead wife's legacy. He seated himself at one of the faro tables and won the first few rounds, but then his luck decisively turned sour. Within an hour, he had lost every penny. By that time, too, he was drunk, having consumed a full bottle of wine and then some brandy.

As he staggered out of the elegant mansion, he was jostled by a streetwalker who giggled, linked her arm through his, and insinuated, "Well now, dearie, somebody ought to take you home and put you to bed. I'll do that and give you pleasure—for just five dollars. Whaddya say, dearie?"

"Let go of me, you dirty bitch—I don't go with whores—get away from me, I said! Oh, you won't, eh? That'll teach you—and that, too!" Fales, drunk and enraged, slapped her face and then, as she staggered back, clenched his fist and drove it against her cheek, knocking her onto the sidewalk.

"Hey! Nobody treats my girls that way." In his stupor, Fales heard a rough, raspy voice behind him. As he turned to confront this intruder, he felt a sudden, sharp, blinding pain in his back as a knife was driven in up to the hilt. The pimp helped the prostitute to her feet and both hurried down the darkened street into an alley, where they disappeared.

David Fales lay gasping, choking in his own blood. He had just enough time to gasp out, "Someone—help me—" before he was silenced forever.

# Thirty

Lucien Edmond, along with Eddie Gentry, Nacio Lorcas, Simata, and several other riders, returned to Windhaven Range during the fourth week of July.

As tall as his great-grandfather, old Lucien Bouchard, had been, Lucien Edmond did not show his thirty-nine years. His high forehead, deeply cleft chin, and large, alert eyes were very much like his father, Luke's, but there was hardly a gray hair on his head, and his lean muscular body, inured to outdoor life from the many cattle drives he had undertaken in the dozen years since he and Luke had founded Windhaven Range, made him seem ageless and indomitable.

Luke's oldest son was quite satisfied with the drive, having sold the bulk of the herd to the army fort at Santa Fe and the remaining cattle to the smaller forts on the return home. In addition, he had procured regular contracts with the two army posts that had hitherto done no business with Windhaven Range, and this surely augured well for the future. He looked forward to sharing this good news with his partner Joe Duvray, and also with his faithful friend Lucas—who, he hoped, had by now completely recovered from the wounds he had received earlier in the year.

Maxine, hearing Lucien Edmond ride toward the ranch, ran out to meet him, holding the telegram that Laure had sent to him from New Orleans.

"Oh, my God, Maxine, I feel so helpless. To think—to think that he should die like that—" Lucien Edmond groaned, after he had embraced her and tenderly wiped

303

away her tears. "I couldn't possibly have been there for his funeral, and by now, I'm sure that Laure has gone back to Windhaven Plantation. Maxine, I know this will be a disappointment to you, but I'm sure you understand that I have to go to her to give what help I can in arranging Father's affairs. I'll stop first at New Orleans, of course, on my way to Windhaven Plantation, to call on Jason Barntry and find out what she's already done and how the estate stands. He's such a capable, loyal man that I know I shouldn't be worried—but I am. More than anything, I want Laure and the children to be protected."

"I understand, my darling. Of course, you must go. But spend a few days here and rest first—it must have been terribly hard on you riding all the way into New Mexico and circling back to those other forts," Maxine solicitously told him. She then added somewhat shyly, "Besides, I have another reason for wanting you with me right now. You see, my dearest, I've just learned that I'm carrying another child."

"Oh, Maxine," Lucien Edmond softly breathed, "how happy this makes me! What wonderful news! Somehow knowing that another Bouchard is coming into this world eases Father's passing. . . . My darling, you know I want to stay here with you, but I won't be able to live with myself if I don't get started first thing tomorrow morning."

Mara, also having heard Lucien Edmond ride in, now came up and tenderly embraced her brother. "Oh, Lucien Edmond," she cried, "has Maxine told you the terrible news?"

"Yes, Mara, she has. Let us go to the chapel and pray for Father." Turning to his wife, he asked, "Will you come with us, my dearest?"

And so, their arms linked, their heads bowed, each remembering Luke as he had been and what he had meant to all of them, Mara, Maxine, and Lucien Edmond went to the little chapel that Friar Bartoloméo Alicante had dedicated, and there they knelt in prayer for the soul of Luke Bouchard.

The next morning, Maxine handed Lucien Edmond a wire from Ramón Hernandez that had been awaiting his return, but that his thoughtful wife had withheld the night before, knowing he would be distraught from the news of his father's death. The telegram advised him that the railroad strike had depressed the Dodge City market, but his brother-in-law had been successful in disposing of the herd to an Indian agent at a price that, although somewhat low, was still sufficient to ensure a decent profit for the operation. As Lucien Edmond packed provisions for the ride to Corpus Christi—the first leg of his journey to New Orleans—he ruminated on this news that confirmed his previous hunch: the boom towns were dying out and he had been wise, indeed, to concentrate on selling to the army forts.

Then, putting all thoughts of the ranch's business aside, Lucien Edmond again took leave of his wife and promised that he would send her a telegram from New Orleans as soon as he reached there safely and another when he had rejoined his stepmother at Windhaven Plantation. Their parting was tearful and long, until at last Lucien Edmond reluctantly disengaged himself from Maxine's embrace, mounted his gelding, and, turning to blow her a kiss, rode off toward the east.

When he reached Corpus Christi, driving the gelding harder than was his wont and cutting a half a day off the usual time of such a journey, Lucien Edmond was elated to find that the steamboat for New Orleans was waiting at the dock. He had just time to leave the gelding with a hosteler and to pay him for looking after the animal until his return, telling the man it might be a month or even more, and adding a bonus for the hosteler's trouble.

The journey to New Orleans was uneventful and marred by no delay, and arriving at the dock he was able to hire a *fiacre* that took him immediately to the Brunton & Barntry Bank.

After half an hour's time with Jason Barntry, he had learned all he wanted to know about his stepmother's activities in the Queen City after his father's death, including the fact that thus far, the casino appeared to be a profitable venture. Telling Lucien Edmond about Danvers Willoughby, the white-haired bank manager ventured, "He appears to be a rather glib man, although Mrs. Bouchard's partner, William Brickley, vouches for him. He's had farming experience in England, managing his father's estate—but to be sure, European farming methods and those employed in the South are vastly different." The old man permitted himself a nostalgic smile. "I can remember that your great-grandfather used to hold forth on that subject—but don't let me get started on that. No, I think your first duty would be to see if this new overseer is really carrying out his responsibilities. Your stepmother is an extremely able, fine woman, but it's very possible for a quick-talking, amoral man to pull the wool over her eyes, particularly in view of her bereavement. It's a lamentable fact, Lucien Edmond, that widows are marked down as easy prey by confidence men. I have made some personal checks of Brickley's business acumen and character, and so far, I must say that I find nothing really against him. But I must admit, a man who runs houses of ill repute, regardless of how much profit he derives therefrom, is not in my books the most savory of characters. But then, Lucien Edmond, I'm old and inclined to be quite conventional and circumspect—my work in this bank has taught me that."

"Don't apologize, Jason," Lucien Edmond smilingly reassured him. "And after all, don't forget that Marius Thornton is still on hand at Windhaven Plantation to help my stepmother. He'd be the first to know if this new overseer wasn't up to snuff. Well then," as he abruptly rose and extended his hand, which Jason Barntry warmly shook, "I'd best see if I can make connections immediately to Mobile and then on to Lowndesboro. Is there any message I can take my stepmother, Jason?"

"You might give her a copy of this report from the casino. I'm sure it will hearten her. On your way back, perhaps you would care to meet this Brickley."

"I would, indeed. Meanwhile, Jason, take care of yourself. On behalf of all of us, let me thank you very sincerely and appreciatively for the loyalty and devotion you've shown in managing the Bouchard affairs. If it weren't that San Antonio is ever so much closer to the ranch, I'd be tempted to shift all of my holdings from that bank to yours."

"Thank you, Lucien Edmond, that's very good of you to say. But I think you made a wise decision, and the San Antonio bank is one of the most solvent in the Southwest. Still and all, if one day you feel that you have some extra capital, I might suggest that you try to invest it with us here. There's a good deal of building going on now, and business continues to improve steadily—as do the crowds of visitors who come and spend their money. That, indeed, was one of the very points your stepmother made in supporting her decision to form a partnership for this casino."

"Thank you again, Jason, I'll be in touch with you, as soon as I get to Windhaven Plantation." Once again, Lucien Edmond shook hands, and then hurried out of the bank, hailing a *fiacre* to take him back to the dock where he could make connections on to Mobile, and thence up the Alabama River to Lowndesboro.

The steamboat dropped anchor at the Windhaven dock just beyond the little town of which Dalbert Sattersfield was now mayor. Lucien Edmond raised his eyes to look up at the towering red bluff where his father had been buried to share the eternal sleep with great-hearted Lucien Bouchard and his Dimarte, unable to hold back his tears. He went down the gangplank to be welcomed by Marius Thornton, who greeted him with almost a pathetic eagerness and explained, "Mr. Lucien Edmond! I'm so glad you're here! Soon as Miz Laure got your telegram that you were coming, she told me to start figuring steamboat schedules and to make it my business to be here at the dock to welcome you back home. She's with the children just now, and she'll be mighty happy to see you."

"You're looking very fit, Marius. And I take it you're working off all of Clemmie's good cooking, now that you're in the middle of your harvesting season," Lucien Edmond laughed, as he strode forward toward the red-brick chateau.

"That's right, Mr. Lucien Edmond," Marius grinned. "All of us are busy now, and the crops are doing pretty well—those that were planted already, that is."

Lucien Edmond caught the note of caution in the foreman's voice and stopped to look steadily at him: "Marius, that didn't sound like you just then. I have the feeling that you're not too happy about the new overseer, Danvers Willoughby. Jason Barntry at the New Orleans bank told me that my stepmother had hired him over you."

"Now you just hold on there a minute, Mr. Lucien Edmond, I'm not badmouthing anybody because, if I was to say I didn't like him, then I'd be saying that Miz Laure was wrong, and she's the finest lady I ever met— 'cepting, of course, my sweet Clemmie."

"That's better," Lucien Edmond grinned, and gave Marius a good-natured light jab to the shoulder. "But seriously, does this man know his business?"

"Well, he had charge of a big estate back in England— or so he said—and he's gone to Montgomery and to Mobile a couple of times already and got some orders for business we didn't have before," Marius grudgingly admitted. "But—hell, Mr. Lucien Edmond, he's made us put in rice."

"Rice?" Lucien Edmond echoed, with an incredulous stare at the handsome black foreman. "Whatever for? That land isn't made for rice."

"That's what I think, Mr. Lucien Edmond, but he had different ideas. We put a paddy at the southwest section, spending three days digging water trenches over to the river. Yes, sir, that's a fact."

"And is the rice thriving?"

"No, sir, it is not—he says that maybe next year it'll be all right. But here I am holding you up when you ought to be seeing Miz Laure! She won't take kindly to my keeping you out here talking my fool head off," he laughed.

Laure had seen the two men from the window of the children's playroom, and she ran down to open the huge door to the entrance of the chateau, her face aglow with joy.

Lucien Edmond hugged and kissed her, and smilingly exclaimed, "Laure, it's so good to see you! You don't know how sorry I am that I couldn't be here for Father's funeral, but I want to see his grave as soon as I can."

"We'll go there together right now, dear Lucien Edmond," Laure said, as they walked to the main guest room. "Your father thought so much of you—just before he died, he asked me to tell you how proud of you and Mara he was, and how much he loved you both. That was his way, unselfish to the very last—and the way he gave up his life to save Governor Houston was so typical of him. I was blessed to have been his wife and the mother of his children, Lucien Edmond." She turned away for a moment to hide the tears.

As soon as Lucien Edmond had put his traveling bag away, he and Laure walked across the fields to take the gently sloping path up the bluff to the gravesites. He knelt before the fresh mound and bent down to kiss the ground and to say a prayer as Laure, kneeling beside him, repeated her own.

It was nearly twilight when they rose and descended the hill, walking slowly. Behind them came the faint hoot of an owl. Lucien Edmond turned back, his eyes widening. "You know, it's almost as if his spirit were telling us that he's at peace," he murmured, as he put his arm around Laure's shoulders. "I remember how he used to tell me that my great-grandfather, heartsick after Dimarte's death, was consoled by the sound of an owl, knowing that she was with him in spirit."

"Yes, I believe that, Lucien Edmond, and I think just now it *was* Luke communing with us. He and his grandfather are immortal for what they did, and what they lived for will always be with us—in our minds and hearts and souls. It makes all of us want to live up to the heritage that they left behind."

"That's my feeling, too, Laure," Lucien Edmond murmured, as they went back to the chateau.

"I know it would be a great imposition, and I don't want to keep you from Maxine and your children"—Laure anxiously turned to him—"but I'd like it very much if you could stay here for a few weeks, Lucien Edmond."

"Maxine will understand, and everything's gone very well at the ranch this summer. I want to stay on here and give you what help I can. Jason Barntry tells me that you've invested in a casino."

"Yes," Laure confessed, "I guess it was a bit impulsive of me."

"I trust that you've confidence in the partner of this venture?" Lucien Edmond carefully inquired.

"Oh, yes. Jason himself said that Mr. Brickley has an excellent business reputation."

"Well then, it will be an interesting diversion from the usual way of making money off the land by hard work," Lucien Edmond said. "Perhaps there's a little of the gambler in all of us. And now, I'd like to see the children."

Lucien Edmond found the presence of Laure's children at dinner that evening enormously cheering, for his visit to

309

his father's grave had deeply sobered him and made him reflect on the past that they had shared. In Texas, engrossed as he had been in developing the ranch and in working with Ramón, Joe Duvray, and the loyal vaqueros who were like family members, he had kept up the bond between Luke and himself through letters. Now that Luke was dead, his visit to Windhaven Plantation communicated to him a sense of irreparable loss, but it also convinced him that Luke would live on in his children. Already Lucien, now eleven, was articulate and serious, as well as tall for his age: the questions he asked Lucien Edmond about the latter's ranch showed a precocious perception. Paul, Celestine, and Clarissa were more effervescent and gregarious than their older brother, but they all showed the breeding and courtesy that Luke had tried to impart to his children. It was a courtesy born not out of fear, but rather of respect and love—and that, Lucien Edmond thought to himself, was the key to the Bouchards' success since those first days when old Lucien had come from Yves-sur-lac to begin his new life in Econchate.

Marius and Clemmie Thornton and Danvers Willoughby were dinner guests that evening. Lucien Edmond took an immediate dislike to the new overseer. The Englishman was too inclined to florid speech and boasting promises of the profits he would bring to Windhaven Plantation to suit Lucien Edmond's more practical turn of mind. And when he asked Willoughby why the latter believed that rice would be a profitable crop on land that was not really suited to it, Willoughby glossed over the heart of the question, loading his reply with glowing phrases. Lucien Edmond could not help being reminded of the quotation, "Full of sound and fury, signifying nothing," but he decided to reserve his judgment till after he had seen more of the man at his work.

Proposing the toast of the evening, Lucien Edmond averred, "To my stepmother, Laure Bouchard, and to you her children, my admired and loved brothers and sisters—long happy years and the knowledge that, though I live in Texas now, I shall always be here for you whenever you need or want me."

# Thirty-One

He had lost track of time, for the days followed the nights
with only a faint brightness filtering through the narrow
porthole of his tiny cabin to mark their passage. Cell was
a more accurate word, he morosely reflected, for there was
hardly any room to move about. This was maddening for
the young, vigorous Comanche lawyer, and he forced himself, as soon as he had eaten what he presumed was breakfast, to make a deliberate tour around the narrow confines
of this prison, counting off paces aloud to hear a human
voice—if only his own. And the sound of his own voice
was indeed some small relief from the maddening hours of
despondent loneliness.

Thus far, through all this incalculable period of time, he
had seen only the squat man with his grizzled spade
beard—who, he learned, was named Ebenezer—and Noah,
who usually, though not always, brought his meals. At
times, when they brought food, or water for bathing, he
tried to plead with them, repeating his poignant need to
communicate with his by now frightened, distraught wife;
he urged them, in the name of humanity, to let her at
least know—her and the child who had surely been born
by now—that he was safe and alive, if nothing more.

But they were laconic and curt with him, and regardless
of whether he wheedled ingratiatingly or was righteously
indignant, they would do nothing for him nor tell him why
he was imprisoned on a ship sailing around the Horn.

For quite some days now, the ship had been stationary,
anchored, Noah had mockingly told him, off Rio de
Janeiro. With a flickering surge of cunning and hope, he

311

imagined himself crouching just beyond the reach of the cabin door, and when it was opened at mealtime, he could take the seaman bringing his food by surprise, and, with luck, make his way to the deck. There he would hurl himself overboard and swim ashore.

That evening, when Noah, lanky and possessed of an even longer beard than Ebenezer, came to bring Lopasuta his supper, he meekly thanked the seaman and, as Noah was about to leave, asked casually, "How much longer do we hold over in Rio for fair weather?"

Before he could catch himself, Noah snapped back, "Two more days, matey—" and then, his eyes narrowing and his lips curling in a mocking little sneer, he countered, "It's no skin off your arse, my bucko—you're here till the end of the voyage, so don't get your hopes up. We'll be putting out to sea again before you know it, and Ebenezer and I aren't about to let you out on deck even to stretch your legs. If you need exercise, try walking around in the cabin where you belong, and that's an end o' it!" With this, he shot the bolt of the door home, but Lopasuta had his answer. He had two days before the ship set sail for its voyage round the tip of South America and on to San Francisco. He had no idea how long the journey would take, but he knew that he must act quickly and desperately, if he were to prevent its taking place with him aboard. And he wept that night, when he thought of his sweet Geraldine waiting there with their baby—waiting for the word that never came, perhaps by now thinking that he had deserted her. *Help me, Great Manitou*, he prayed, as he stared up at the low ceiling of the dingy, almost airless cabin.

He ate his meager supper, but this time with ravenous energy, for he had determined to break out of his prison the next morning. For the first time since he had been drugged and carried aboard the four-master, Lopasuta Bouchard had regained full possession of his faculties: he imagined himself once again back with his Comanche brothers, honing all his faculties and senses for the attempt to regain his freedom. Indeed, he could hardly wait for the dawn of the new day, and after he had eaten and drunk the bitter, chicory-loaded mug of hot liquid that passed for coffee, he began to pace his quarters with deliberate calculation. Six good paces forward, six to the left, then six back, and finally six to his left again, making the square.

His sinews and muscles quivered with a keenness that reminded him of the old days when he had been young and eager to bring honor to the People, as the Comanche called themselves, with a fervent pride earned by centuries of valor against the marauding Spaniards and other would-be conquerors. All the proud blood of his father's ancestors, together with the wise, knowing dignity that his Mexican mother had imparted to him almost from birth, surged through him, strengthening his resolve to get back to Geraldine and his child.

A pulse throbbed in his temples, and he finally stretched himself out on the hard bunk, pillowing his head in his hands, staring up at the low ceiling and thinking how he would achieve this feat. Only his escape could prove he was the rightful heir to his father's pure Comanche blood; only this—far from the Montgomery courtrooms where he had first announced his adaptability to the white-eyes world—could show that the Comanche blood of his birth was still powerful. As his eyes began to droop with fatigue, he pledged himself again to the Manitou, the all-knowing Creator, the Great Spirit who judged each brave by his courage and craftiness in battle when the stakes were nothing less than survival to live and be free, as the Comanche was meant to be, from the earliest dawn of time.

He came to keen wakefulness in the early dawn, and sprang out of bed, lithe and eager. Making his way toward the porthole, he stared out and saw glassy, calm water. In the distance, it seemed to him that he could make out the shape of a huge mountain, and the unchanging scene sufficed to tell him that the ship was still at anchor.

He waited. He did not know what time it was, except that it was past dawn. The rays of the sun touched the still water and made it glisten with an unearthly mixture of blue and green and startling white. For an instant, he felt fearful of this unknown setting, where he was ignorant of weather and signs and the feel of the air. But he knew that it was now or never again that he must try to escape.

He felt his heart pounding rapidly as he crouched to one side of the door, his clenched fists his only weapon. The seaman would carry the heavy belaying pin that could punish and maim, but now he did not fear it. If it were meant to be, he would somehow get back to Montgomery, to Geraldine, to their son—ot must be a son—and then he would learn who had done this to him.

Straining with all his senses, he thought he heard the faint sound of approaching footsteps, and he tensed himself in readiness. Then, as the steps sounded more clearly, he told himself that his instincts were still as sharp as they had been back in the stronghold with Sangrodo. The footsteps neared, halted, and then there was the snicking of the bolt, as one of the two seamen—Ebenezer this time, surely—shot it back and opened the door to his prison.

The seaman entered warily, the belaying pin in his right hand. Silently, Lopasuta sprang at the man and knocked him back into the narrow corridor, spilling the tray with a clatter. Running blindly to his left, he suddenly came to a narrow stairway, but as he pulled himself up, he found himself weaker from his long incarceration than he had thought. Beyond the calm harbor waters, the shoreline beckoned and his breath exhaled in a gasp as he crouched, gathering all his strength to hurl himself overboard.

Just as he straightened, ready to leap, there was a sudden blackness as he was dealt a vicious blow from behind. Lopasuta Bouchard sprawled forward on the deck; blackness engulfed him, and he knew nothing and heard nothing and saw nothing. . . .

He wakened in pain, his temples throbbing, and his hand groped for his head and tried to soothe away the agonized pounding. Then, as his consciousness more fully returned, he could feel the gentle rocking—and he knew with dismal anguish that the ship had drawn anchor and was continuing its journey . . . its journey around the Horn to San Francisco.

Tentatively, he tried to sit up, and groaned aloud, as fiery waves of torment leaped through his skull, and with both hands he gently rubbed his forehead to try to ease the pain. He was breathing heavily. The air in the little cabin had become stifling. He felt suffocated, as if he could scarcely move.

Only vaguely did he perceive the sound of the bolt being drawn back, and then in the doorway there appeared a man whom Lopasuta had not seen before, with both

314

Ebenezer and Noah behind him. The trio grinned mockingly at him, each gripping a belaying pin and whispering to each other.

"I'm the first mate of this ship, mister, and I'm here to tell you that was a fool stunt you tried to pull," jeered the stranger. He was a man in his thirties who sported a mustache that was slightly redder than his light brown hair. "You didn't have a Chinaman's chance in hell to get free. But I admire your courage, so I'll do you one favor—and it's the last you'll get on this ship, till we hit San Francisco—and give you a piece of advice."

Lopasuta, groaning, finally managed to sit up. Bowing his head, his hands still pressed against his throbbing forehead, he waited with a dull, resigned torment for words that somehow he knew would only plunge him into the pitfall of total despair.

They were long in coming, for the first mate sardonically grinned and exchanged a whispered conversation with the two seamen. And then at last, he declared, "Real foolish, mister. You didn't change a thing, except get yourself another bump on your noggin. So I'm warning you, you'd better not try it again, because Cap'n Jenkins says next time you do, we'll see that you get a taste of the cat."

"But where—please, in the name of—" Lopasuta hoarsely stammered, as he forced himself to raise his head and look at the sneering face of the first mate.

"Shut your uppity mouth and listen to me. I don't chew my cabbage twice, mister. We've been in Rio taking on cargo and letting the weather get a little better before we reach the Horn. We're going to make it, but it's going to be a little rough. It won't do you any good to tell Noah or Ebenezer that you're not exactly comfy in your first-class cabin, ha, ha!" At this, the two seamen echoed the first mate's laughter and exchanged a knowing wink. "But we'll make 'Frisco, you can depend on it. And when we do, you're bound for Hong Kong."

"Hong Kong?" Lopasuta sprang to his feet, only to bump his head against the low ceiling before dropping to his bunk with a cry of pain. "But why? Why am I being taken there?"

"That's Cap'n Jenkins's business, not mine. I'm just telling you what's going to happen. And if you're thinking of jumping ship in 'Frisco, mister, you'll get worse than I just gave you. They'll clap you in irons, and they'll gag you, too, and they'll put you in the hold. And if you die, it'll be your own fault, 'cause you were warned. So I'm doing you a favor, mister, telling you what the score is. Just make up your mind you're going to Hong Kong, and that'll do it. All right, men, back on deck!"

Lopasuta staggered to his feet and tried to put out a restraining hand, but the first mate brutally knocked it away with his fist. Then, with a raucous burst of laughter, he left the cabin and shot home the bolt.

Lopasuta began to weep. He was lost—irretrievably lost. He might never get back to Geraldine and their child. Bowing his head to his hands, he wept unashamedly. No Comanche would have wept, it was true. But he was a man shanghaied from his wife and child, unable to fathom the reason why any man, however cruel, would wish to inflict such inhuman punishment.

With a hopeless anguish, he thought over the words that the first mate had so contemptuously flung at him. The long, terrible journey around the Horn, where the winter weather of the Southern Hemisphere might buffet the four-master and send him lurching from side to side, bruised and shaken, unable to see how the ship was taking the waves and the winds of that terrible cold and isolated region. How long—if ever—would it take him to return to Montgomery from Hong Kong far across the Pacific? The prospect was annihilating to his spirit, to his will. He had tried his best, and he had failed. Now, in the darkness of his cabin, as the ship began to pitch gently from side to side with the soft breezes off the Rio harbor, Lopasuta Bouchard could only pray to the Great Spirit. Pray and wait, and hope that somehow those he loved the most in this world would not be lost to him forever.

Ramón Hernandez and his vaqueros rode back to Windhaven Range, after stopping for half a day in Wichita while Lucien Edmond's brother-in-law visited with Ben and Elone Wilson, giving the Quaker doctor and his loyal Indian wife presents that Lucien Edmond had commissioned Ramón to purchase for them and to give with his and Maxine's warmest greetings.

They took the old familiar route home from Wichita and came within sight of the ranch house near the end of

August. Ramón smiled as he thought back to the teething ring he had purchased in Wichita for little Dorothy, the last child born to the Wilsons. It reminded him of the daughter he had named after his beautiful, black-haired wife, Mara, the woman who had given him new life and joy beyond his wildest hopes after he had been shot down by the treacherous supposed *Juarista* leader, when he had refused to take part in the massacre of a peaceful little Mexican town. He was eager to see Mara and her namesake. He thanked *el Señor Dios* that this drive to Dodge City had been comparatively easy. The treacherous game that Jeb Cornish had tried to play on him, to regain the money from the herd, was now a thing of the past. He felt that one day, Cornish was certain to make a mistake that would be so glaring that he would be brought to justice by the federal government itself. Meanwhile, the government vouchers and the cash that he had given Ramón were bona fide. As far as Ramón was concerned, it was the end of a chapter, and with Lucien Edmond Bouchard concentrating on supplying army forts in the southwestern area, they might never have to consider an arduous, eight-hundred-mile drive to a Kansas market again.

He sat back in his saddle and enjoyed the warm thoughts of reunion with Mara and his children. At the sound of hoofbeats, he turned his head and saw Walter Catlin riding hard, crouched over the head of his gelding, and he smiled again. Catlin was certainly eager to get back to Windhaven Range; the reckoning in Dodge City had changed him from the loner, the inscrutable, mysterious stranger who had come in search of a job and revealed nothing of himself, his hopes or his dreams. Now, unless Ramón was greatly mistaken, those dreams could be realized. And there was a warm, good feeling that he had, in a small way, helped make another man's happiness possible.

This feeling was abruptly tempered when, following his arrival back at Windhaven Range, Ramón was reunited with his family, only to learn from a tearful Mara that her father had been killed and her brother, Lucien Edmond, had gone to Windhaven Plantation to meet with Laure. Ramón was profoundly saddened by this; he still recalled how kind Luke had been to him when Ramón had ridden to the ranch, many years ago, to warn the Bouchards of an attack by the man who called himself *jefe*, the so-called patriotic Juarista who had murdered and raped and stolen to aggrandize his own fortunes.

Leaving Mara with the promise that he would speedily return, Ramón went across to the hacienda to report to Maxine and Joe Duvray the results of the cattle drive and the sale of steers in Dodge City. Eddie Gentry, Simata, and Nacio Lorcas joined them, both to welcome Ramón home and to share with him their own good tidings of the sales of beef to the army forts. But further discussions of business were deferred until another day; for the moment, Ramón needed to be alone, to absorb the overwhelming news of Luke's death.

Leaving the hacienda, Ramón directed his steps to the chapel, where he knelt to offer a prayer to *el Señor Dios* for the soul of Luke Bouchard, as well as his own prayer of thanksgiving for the safe return of him and his men from the long trail drive. Then, crossing himself, he rose and left the chapel, and made his way to the little house where his beloved Mara awaited him. And as she clung to him fervently, while darkness descended slowly on the prairie, he felt lucky and grateful to be alive.

Walter Catlin had put his saddlebag and blanket in the bunkhouse, washed, and gone to supper with the other vaqueros. The other men noticed that he was friendlier now, and they welcomed him as one of them. The news had spread from those vaqueros who had ridden with Ramón to Dodge City that this taciturn man had had a showdown with a gunman and had come out alive. From now on, Walter Catlin's life would be eased, and he could begin to plan again for the future.

After supper, Walter took a walk down by the creek. He lingered there, awkwardly, looking this way and that, biting his lips like a schoolboy waiting to confer with his teacher. He frequently turned to look over at the Belcher house, hoping that eventually Connie Belcher would come out to the well to fill a bucket with water.

Henry Belcher had seen Ramon and the vaqueros riding back to the hacienda, and at supper he had mentioned this to Maybelle, surreptitiously eyeing lovely young Connie as he did so. "They all seem to have come back in good shape, Maybelle honey," he jauntily declared, as he helped

318

himself to more pork chops. "I declare, Maybelle, nobody anywhere else in this country can make pork chops taste the way you do."

"Now, Henry, you're just spoofing me," Maybelle happily declared, and unconsciously smoothed her hair. When she caught her husband's gaze, she lowered her eyes and blushed like a schoolgirl.

"Yessirree," Henry went on, "every man jack of them got back. I guess Ramón did a good piece of business up in Dodge City—and nobody got hurt, that's the best part of it." His smile faded as he continued, "Sure seems a shame, though, that after that long, hard drive Ramón'll have no chance to relax a bit, now that Lucien Edmond's had to go off to Alabama."

"I know what you mean, Henry," Maybelle commiserated, "but it can't be helped. Ramón has plenty of men here to assist him in running the ranch, and poor Laure needs Lucien Edmond right now more than any of us do."

"That's for sure, honey." There was a moment's silence, and Henry looked at Connie, who was busy eating her dinner with more concentration than the task required. "You know, I think we ought to have another bucket of water before we go to bed tonight. I'd like to shave some 'cause I'm getting to look as grizzled as an old bear."

"You look fine to me," Maybelle innocently rejoined.

"All the same, woman, if you've no objection, I'm going to shave. Connie, would you mind very much?"

"No, Pa, I'd be glad to." Connie slipped out of her chair and hurried to the kitchen to fetch the bucket, then went out the back door. She walked quickly toward the well and then halted, as she saw the shadowy figure over by the creek. She began to tremble, and her eyes were wide and eager, as she called out, "Who's there?"

"It's me, Miss Connie, Walter Catlin. Just got back today from Dodge, you know."

"Why, yes, I—I heard Pa tell. Was it bad, all that time driving those cattle, Mr. Catlin?"

"It was easy, Miss Connie." He approached her, smiling, and yet he felt awkward as he stood before her. "I want to say something to you, Miss Connie, and I hope you don't think I'm too fresh."

"Why, Mr. Catlin, you've always been a perfect gentleman. What did you wish to say to me?" Connie suddenly dropped her bucket, and then gasped with exasperation at her own clumsiness, and stooped to pick it up. But already Walter had come forward and retrieved it, lifted it up, and gently suggested, "Why don't I fill it for you, Miss Connie, then I can walk you back safely to your house? It's getting dark now, and I want to be sure there aren't any snakes or anything dangerous around."

"That—that's very nice of you, Mr. Catlin," Connie quavered. She lowered her eyes, and a furious blush suffused her cheeks.

There was a long pause as Walter Catlin walked over to the well, lowered the well bucket, drew it up again, and poured the water into Connie's bucket. "There now, it's nice and full. Nice evening, not too warm."

"Yes—yes, Mr. Catlin, it's very nice out here." From afar came the twitter of night birds and the gentle, reiterated chirping of crickets.

"It sure is." There was an uncomfortable silence, as Walter bit his lips again and shifted the bucket to his left hand. Connie walked back very slowly, once glancing back over her shoulder to make sure that he was following, and then, when their eyes met, quickly turning away with her cheeks flaming scarlet in confusion.

"I said—that is, I want to tell you something, Miss Connie. Could you wait a few minutes before you go back to your house? I know it's late, but I just have to say this. I've had it inside me ever since I left for Dodge City, but I couldn't do anything about it then. Now maybe I can. And, if I'm wrong, then I'm going to apologize right now in advance, before I even say it."

"Why, Mr. Catlin, whatever are you trying to say to me? You don't have to apologize for anything. I—" She could go no further, and her voice trailed off into the silence as her blushes deepened.

Nevertheless, she halted, turned slightly away from him, waiting, another fit of trembling seizing her as she sensed that somehow this moment was very important to both of them.

"I know I'm lots older than you, Miss Connie. I'd say close to fifteen years. And—well, I want you to know something about me, about my past. I came from Virginia, where I had a little store. And I was married—"

"Oh?" her voice was faint, almost disappointed.

"Wait—please wait just a second. I've only just started, and it's sort of hard for me. You'll just have to bear with me, Miss Connie. And if you don't want to listen any more when I finish, I'll understand."

"All—all right," she timidly acquiesced.

"Th-thank you, Miss Connie. Well now, as—as I was starting to say, I was married awful young, and we didn't have children yet when after a while I went off to the war. My wife wrote to say that she was with child, and nothing could have made me happier—except it wasn't that simple."

In low, halting tones, Walter Catlin recounted the heart-rending story of his young wife's untimely death soon after that of her first-born child, and of the vicious gambler who had callously left her to a pauper's grave.

"Well, maybe I went a little crazy after that," he groaned, then coughed to hide his emotion as he turned away to compose himself. "I swore I'd find him, and after twelve long years of tracking that man, I finally did."

Connie still hadn't moved, but stood turned slightly away from him, her head bowed, her fists clenched, her heart beating very rapidly. "Was it in Dodge City, Mr. Catlin?"

"Yes, Miss Connie, it was. He was working in a saloon in Dodge. I saw him and called out his name. He drew leather on me, and there was a battle, and I—I killed him. I had to, to save my own life. Miss Connie, I know it was wrong to take his life, just like the Bible says a man shouldn't, but I couldn't stand what he'd done to my wife and child."

"I—I think I understand, Mr. Catlin." Her voice was hardly audible in the darkness.

Walter set down the bucket and came forward to her, took her by the shoulders and made her face him. "Look, Miss Connie, I know this sounds crazy. But I just have to finish it. You remember when I came here, I looked at you a lot—"

"I—I know, Mr. Catlin. But—but I didn't mind, h-honest—" she faltered, averting her eyes from him.

"You know why, Miss Connie? The first time I laid eyes on you, I almost couldn't believe what I was seeing. You reminded me of my wife—she was young and sweet just like you—and I never knew just why it was she went away with Ed Brainard. But she did, and he ruined her, and he made her die, and my kid, too. But now it's over."

"You say—you say I look like your wife, Mr. Catlin?"

"Yes, a lot like her. But I see you're also quite different. Like I said, it's all over now, Miss Connie. Look, I—I like you a whole lot. And it's not because you look like my wife. It was sort of funny coming here and seeing you the first time and being reminded. But now I see you for yourself—a sweet, nice, decent girl, and I want awfully to get to know you."

She was crying a little now, and she turned to him and put her arms around his neck and buried her face against his chest. "Oh, honey, don't cry, please don't cry like that," he said hoarsely, stroking her hair.

"I—I missed you an awful lot, Mister—Walter—I did, for a fact. And I'm glad you came back. I feel just awful about what happened to you, and I think you're an awfully nice man and a good one—and yes, I—I really want to get to know you, too. But I hope you don't think that I look like your wife *too* much, because I want you to want *me*, Connie Belcher."

"Oh, my sweetheart, my darling Connie, you don't remind me of her at all now, I promise—you're just you." Walter could not hold back the tears as he kissed her almost reverently on the cheek. Shyly, with a soft little nervous giggle, Connie turned her head and kissed him on the mouth, then tightened her arms around him. And when the long, tender kiss was over, she murmured, "I was sort of dreaming that you'd do that one day, Walter."

"Oh, Connie honey, I can't think of anything I'd rather do just this minute. But somebody in your house sent you out to fill this bucket, and is probably wondering just where it is, long about now," he laughed. "And I'm sure glad you came, because I don't know what I'd have done if you hadn't come out tonight. I was just praying you would, Connie."

They walked back to the little house, each holding the bucket, exchanging long, happy looks.

## Thirty-Two

During the last part of August, Danvers Willoughby made an extended trip to Mobile and New Orleans, ostensibly to talk to large greengrocers and factors of commodity warehouses to open new markets for the bounteous crops of Windhaven Plantation. He returned during the first week in September and asked for a conference with Laure Bouchard and Marius Thornton.

Lucien Edmond had spent that morning out in the fields surveying them and talking with some of the workers, and when he came back to the house, Clemetine told him that the new overseer was in old Lucien's study with his stepmother. He went directly to the door and knocked. Laure called out, "Come in!" and, seeing Lucien Edmond, smilingly invited, "I'd like it very much if you'd join us, Lucien Edmond. You'd be interested in knowing what Mr. Willoughby has done to sell our crops and produce and even some of our livestock down in Mobile. Why, he's even had a few orders from New Orleans."

"I have indeed." Danvers Willoughby puffed himself up with pride and glanced around the table, giving Marius a particularly triumphant look. "I'm doing just as conscientious a job as I know how, and I'm here to report my accomplishments on behalf of this beautiful plantation, Mr. Bouchard."

"If that's the case, Mr. Willoughby, I'll be the first to praise you," Lucien Edmond coolly replied, as he seated himself and, sitting back in an attitude of attentive expectation, waited for the Englishman to continue his report.

Willoughby produced an imposing sheaf of papers and,

shoving them out into the center of the large cherrywood table, cleared his throat and drew out two of the sheets. "These, Mrs. Bouchard, Mr. Bouchard, are annual contracts from two New Orleans commissaries—one is the Villeneuve Hotel just off St. Louis Avenue, and the other is from one of the largest greengrocers in the Queen City. Melons, yams, and snap beans for the greengrocer, and for the hotel, chickens and hogs and more melons."

"That's very good, Mr. Willoughby," Laure smilingly nodded, then inquired, "Don't you agree, Lucien Edmond?"

"Yes, it appears to be a nice piece of business." Lucien Edmond had picked up the two papers and was examining them. "They seem to be genuine."

The Englishman's face congealed, as again he drew himself up. "Genuine, Mr. Bouchard? Good gracious, I've known Mr. Catesby of the Villeneuve for several years, and I'd swear to his signature in a court of law. As to John Benedict, everyone in New Orleans knows that he's the largest greengrocer in the French Quarter."

Seeing that Lucien Edmond was still studying the papers and had remained silent, he felt it necessary to add, "I may say, sir, that I obtained these two contracts not only through my own efforts, but through the good graces of Mr. William Brickley, who, as you may know, is the coowner of the Maison de Bonne Chance and thus has the honor to be associated with Mrs. Bouchard."

Lucien Edmond looked up and then tossed the contracts back onto the table. "I see," he tersely admitted. "Well then, you appear to have done excellent work for Windhaven Plantation. I must say, however, that I do not approve of your experiment with rice. From what little I know of the crop—and I had occasion to see a few rice paddies in lower Louisiana years ago when my father and I passed through there on our way to Texas to start Windhaven Range—it seems to respond very poorly to this kind of clay soil. Indeed, I believe this ill-advised project should be abandoned. The troughs that were built to draw irrigation from the Alabama River, far from helping the rice grow—which it definitely has not done at all, from my view—may in fact be endangering some of the nearby crops that do not need so much constant water."

"Yes, perhaps I misjudged the quality of the land, Mr.

324

Bouchard," Willoughby glibly retorted, "but I made this experiment with the enthusiastic hope that I could justify my new post here by opening up new sources of revenue."

"That certainly is commendable, Lucien Edmond," Laure put in soothingly.

"Yes, the motive is commendable enough, but the execution was not. However, we'll let that pass. Marius, what do you think of this new business?" Lucien Edmond turned to the handsome black foreman.

"It looks very good, Mr. Lucien Edmond. And we've had fine weather all this summer, not too much rain, and even the little bit of cotton we put in is going to be prime."

"I've arranged for the sale of that, too, at Mobile, Mr. Bouchard," Willoughby self-importantly interrupted, as he cleared his throat to call further attention to himself. "I think Marius and the workers are about ready to gin the cotton and bale it, and I was talking to Elbert Simmons, the cotton factor down at Mobile, just before I came back here, and he thinks we can get about nineteen cents a pound. That's two cents more, he says, than he's been paying, but he knows the Windhaven crop from the past."

"I should think he would," Lucien Edmond dryly retorted. Then, shrugging, he added, "Well, Laure, if you're satisfied, I've no objections to the business that Mr. Willoughby has proposed to transact for us."

"It seems quite satisfactory to me, Lucien Edmond," she replied.

"Thank you both for your time and consideration, Mrs. Bouchard, Mr. Bouchard. You too, Marius." This last was by way of an afterthought and was accompanied by an almost contemptuous glance. "Well now, I'd best gather up these papers and get out to the fields to see how the workers are doing and to tell them to lay aside quantities of the merchandise we plan to ship on these contracts," Willoughby declared.

Laure Bouchard rose, as did Lucien Edmond, and left the study room. Marius Thornton remained behind with the Englishman, slightly frowning, as he watched the latter roll up the sheaf of papers and grasp them in his right hand like a club, a satisfied smirk on his face. "You think we have enough help on the land for all the harvesting and picking of these orders, Mr. Willoughby?" he ventured.

"Quite enough. Why add to our labor costs? Unfortunately, that Moses Turner is getting old and decrepit and can't do a proper day's work, but men like Hughie Mendicott and Dan Munroe can more than make up for that old fool's feeble efforts. Well, now, let's you and I have a bite of lunch, shall we? I want to say hello to that charming cook of ours," Willoughby grinned wolfishly.

"I might tell you something right now, though it's not really my place, Mr. Willoughby," Marius spoke up and the smile left the Englishman's face. "While you were away, Miss Amelia and Burt Coleman came to what you might call an understanding."

"I don't follow you, my good man," Willoughby haughtily averred.

"Well, maybe you know or maybe you don't that ever since poor Mr. Coleman lost his sweet wife, when their second baby was born, he's been moping and downright lonely. And it just so happened that he and Miss Amelia hit it off, and last week I overheard them sort of talking about maybe getting married someday. So I don't guess you'd better go traipsing around the kitchen with any sweet talk on her account."

"I'll thank you to keep your black nose out of my personal business," was Danvers Willoughby's savage retort, as he strode out of the study.

That Saturday night, Laure Bouchard had retired early, and Clarabelle Hendry had put the children to sleep with the promise to Lucien and Paul that they could go riding with their mother the next morning. Although it was midnight, Lucien Edmond was still awake. Earlier that day he had sent off a letter to Jason Barntry, saying that he was not entirely satisfied with the stewardship of Danvers Willoughby. After dinner, he retired to his room with a solitary glass of wine and a cigar and paced for what seemed like hours before flinging himself down, almost fully clothed, on the comfortable bed to lie there pondering the several mysterious aspects of this alteration in the management of Windhaven Plantation.

He still could not understand how a man who purported to know farming as well as Willoughby had done could insist, over the strong objections of Marius Thornton—and even Dan Munroe, who had once spent six months on a Louisiana rice plantation—on having the workers dig the long troughs to the Alabama River and devote two full acres to the planting of this grain. Why, it seemed almost perverse. And yet, after all that work, at the conference the other afternoon, Willoughby had as willingly shrugged the project off as he had formerly been passionately dedicated to its inception.

But why? And why also did Laure continue to treat Willoughby with such high esteem, when his behavior toward Marius Thornton—who had for so long been loyal and devoted to the Bouchards—was that of an exalted superior toward a lowly menial?

These were unanswered questions, serving only to intensify his growing doubts of the merits of this new overseer who was all talk and no performance. Was it possible that Laure had been hoodwinked by Willoughby's oily and ingratiating manner? Had his father's death so affected his stepmother that her judgment of character had lapsed? True, the contract that engaged the services of the new overseer surely could be reconsidered when the six months were up, but that would not be until the end of the year—and by then the damage might well be done.

Lucien Edmond made a mental note to return to New Orleans as soon as it was feasible to interview this William Brickley, Laure's partner, who had recommended the new overseer.

He wished fervently that he could convince Laure—and for that matter, Marius as well—that the genial black foreman was sufficiently educated and experienced to take on additional responsibilities, thereby eliminating the need for outside help. His own experience on Windhaven Range of giving self-taught men more important roles had certainly proven that a man like Marius was qualified to be overseer. Besides, the handsome black man had an unsurpassed understanding of what this land could produce and to what extent it could be taxed for greater production. And he was also competent to make reports and surveys and could even—assuming that several new workers could be added to the fields to relieve Marius of the monotonous burden of appraising each land section by himself—go after new markets, just as Danvers Willoughby had boasted he had done.

The names of those two New Orleans buyers whom the new overseer had so gloatingly described as his own discoveries were vaguely familiar and made Lucien Edmond struggle to recall where he had heard them before. The Villeneuve Hotel was, as he remembered it, an old, rather seedy building whose clientele had been dwindling the last several years. As far as he knew, there had been no changes made in that hotel's operation, decor, or services in over a decade. To be sure, he was relying on quick impressions from the infrequent trips he had made to the Queen City during the last ten years. Nonetheless, it would be interesting to learn why this, of all New Orleans's hotels, should have made a contract with Windhaven Plantation for such a quantity of fruits, meat and poultry. It suddenly occurred to him that almost any sales representative who made a long-term deal with an establishment like a hotel would be expected to yield a sizable kickback as a guarantee against the possibility that a competitor could offer better prices later on. What kind of deal had Danvers Willoughby made with the Villeneuve Hotel management?

He lay pondering these unanswered questions until at last sleep claimed him. Just before he dozed off, he thought briefly of Maxine and his children, but he did not regret having told her that he was prepared to spend as long a time with Laure Bouchard as was necessary to put his deceased father's affairs into lasting order. How those affairs would be affected by the curious failings, as he saw them, of the new overseer, he was not yet certain, but he had a kind of presentiment that his stepmother might well have chosen a more able man in Danvers Willoughby's place.

Soon after Lucien Edmond had fallen asleep, there sounded three strident cries from the screech owl perched in one of the tall trees surmounting old Lucien's grave on the distant red bluff. At that moment, as the full moon went behind a dark cloud, the dappled rays of silver that had tinged the fields vanished and shadows took their place.

More shadows came, moving upriver from the direction of Lowndesboro, along with the muffled sounds of horses' hooves. And as the moon peered reluctantly from behind the cloud, it shone down on twenty men clad in the white robes and hoods of the Ku Klux Klan—outlawed by federal statute, as well as by state law, yet here in force on Windhaven Plantation.

Two of them dismounted, holding improvised torches of fir branches coated at one end with pitch. They struck lucifers, flamed the torches, and then ran down the fields, one toward the cotton, another toward the vines laden with ripened melons. Even as they ran, four others behind them dismounted and followed suit, running with their lighted torches into other parts of the sprawling, fertile fields of Windhaven Plantation, till flames were leaping in eerie patterns throughout the acreage that once old Lucien Bouchard had won for his toil from the powerful Creeks of Econchate.

Old Moses Turner, whose arthritis had been plaguing him with the sudden dampness brought by the river breezes, could not sleep tonight. He sat up, rubbed his eyes, and then thought of taking a short walk outside his cottage, fearing his restlessness would wake his sleeping wife. As he stepped out the door of the cottage, he saw the blazing pyres of blackening vines and shriveling cornstalks and the white pods of cotton scorched and dropping to the baked earth. He uttered a cry of alarm: "Dey set fire here! Help! Dan, Hughie, come out quick, 'n bring yer guns! Dey's Klansmen all over de fields!"

With an oath, one of the riders reached inside his robe and drew out a six-shooter, leveled it at the old black, and pulled the trigger. Moses Turner uttered a strangled cry and fell over backwards, dying.

Lucien Edmond woke at the sound of that shot, and springing to the window, saw at once the many fires rising before his eyes, casting a ghastly glow upon the towering red bluff where his father and great-grandfather lay buried. Still wearing his shirt and breeches, he stumbled over to his boots and tugged them on. Hurrying to the closet, he retrieved the Spencer carbine that he had brought with him and hurried down the stairs toward the kitchen exit.

But by this time, Dan Munroe and Hughie Mendicott had wakened, seized their own carbines, and come out running, crouching low so as to furnish poor targets for the attackers. Kneeling down, Dan aimed his carbine at one of the nightriders and leveled off several shots, catching the man broadside. The white-robed Klansman was flung, as if by a giant hand, out of the saddle, and the gelding whinnied wildly as it galloped madly forward, dragging its dead rider beside it, one booted foot still caught in a stirrup.

Some of the other riders drew their guns and fired at the distant defender, whose carbine flare had brilliantly blazed like a pinpoint of light across the fields near the cottage of the workers. Dan swore under his breath as one of the bullets grazed his sleeve, but inflicted no wound; then he triggered off two more shots. Another Klansman, in the act of leveling his six-shooter, stumbled back and then fell on his side, rolling over, his dead eyes staring up at the full moon.

Hughie saw the other riders mount their horses and wheel them back downriver, and he fired off all the rounds in his carbine. Angry cries responded, as the bullets found their marks, but not fatally, in three of the Klansmen. And then there was the pounding of hooves receding in the distance.

The men lost no time in trying to prevent the fires from spreading over the land. They succeeded, ironically, largely because of the readily available water from the irrigation ditches dug for the ill-fated rice fields. However, a great deal of damage had already been done. After casting one last sorrowful glance over the charred remains of the night raid, Dan Munroe, Hughie Mendicott, Marius Thornton, Lucien Edmond, and the others stumbled exhausted and broken-hearted to their much-deserved rest. Silence returned to the night, and once more from the top of the bluff the screech owl hooted, this time a mournful, plaintive cry, before all again was still.

330

## Thirty-Three

Shortly before noon the next day, Laure and Lucien
Edmond Bouchard conducted a simple burial service for
Moses Turner, who, old and crippled by arthritis though
he had been, had proved himself to be one of Windhaven
Plantation's staunchest defenders. At the grave, which was
near the little cottage where Moses had lived with his
ailing wife, Mary, there was yet to be another tragedy: for
just as the coffin was lowered into the ground, Mary Turner uttered a sobbing cry and, collapsing, toppled forward
onto the edge of the newly dug grave. Dan Munroe and
his wife, Katie, hurried to try to revive her, but they found
that she was dead.

Pale and shaken, Laure turned to her tall stepson. "How
could all this have happened, Lucien Edmond? I thought
the Ku Klux Klan was finished, having been outlawed
throughout the South. There was almost no sign of them
during the last election—why in the name of a just and
merciful God did they strike here? What was their purpose, their motive?"

Gravely, Lucien Edmond shook his head. "Laure, ever
since the attack last night, I've been thinking. One thing
I'm going to do is see if any other farm or settlement was
attacked. They left two of their dead here, but Dan and
Hughie and Marius have assured me that they don't recognize either of the nightriders." . .

"What a tragedy—and what a bad omen for the future
without my brave Luke to stand by me," Laure murmured. Then, turning to Dan, she said in a choked voice,
"It's too much for me—poor Mary—and yet perhaps it's

331

better. She'd been so sick the last few years, and to die with her husband is in a way a beautiful ending, for they were so devoted to each other and so good and kind to everyone else. Can you—would you do what has to be done, please, Dan?"

"It goes without saying, Mrs. Bouchard," Dan Munroe respectfully murmured.

Lucien Edmond put his arm around his stepmother's shoulders and walked slowly with her back to the red-brick chateau. "There's so much I don't understand around here," he said at last when they had gone inside and Laure had seated herself in the comfortable armchair at the end of the study room, closing her eyes and putting her hand over them, as she tried to regain her composure. "For one thing, isn't it customary to post a night guard around the fields, particularly when they're being harvested? Why didn't Willoughby see to that?"

"But we haven't had any trouble all this year, Lucien Edmond," Laure wanly protested. "And with Luke gone, what enemies could we have? You remember the two Cournier brothers, Henri and Armand—they both hated Luke because he bore the Bouchard name and because old Lucien's brother Jean had crippled their grandfather in a duel—and yet, they are both gone. And Luke's only other enemy was Hugh Entrevois, the illegitimate son of Mark Bouchard, Luke's half brother. He brought the Klan upon our fields once, but he's dead, too. There's no one I can think of who would have hated either my husband or me or indeed the Bouchard name itself enough to make them want to burn and pillage—and even murder—as they did last night."

"I know—I have been thinking along the same lines. And yet there is something very singular about this—I can't yet put all the pieces together, but I have a few suspicions."

'What are you driving at, Lucien Edmond?"

"Just this, Laure. Why has Lopasuta disappeared? How is it that the last person to see him in New Orleans is this partner of yours in the casino venture, William Brickley? And it is also a coincidence that it was through Brickley's recommendation that you hired this pompous ass, Danvers Willoughby—"

332

"Now, Lucien Edmond, you're being too harsh," Laure broke in with a worried look.

"Forgive me, Laure. I didn't mean to distress you, not after the terrible aftermath of last night's raid. But, these odd connections keep coming back into my mind. And Willoughby's experiment with the rice field borders on the ridiculous. I only wish you'd overridden him. I understand that Marius did approach you once and rather hesitantly suggested that Willoughby's idea about planting rice wasn't really an outstanding one."

"Well, yes, it's true he did, Lucien Edmond, but Mr. Willoughby, just as he said the other day, was trying so hard to justify his position and authority here and wanted to try something new."

"Well, we'll let that pass for the moment. I still don't like the idea that the man didn't have the forethought to stand some kind of guard last night, just when we were about to harvest most of the cotton and the best of the melons and the yams and the corn—to say nothing of the fact that we lost quite a few head of livestock, cattle as well as pigs. That is going to diminish this year's profits from Windhaven Plantation by a good-sized amount, I'm afraid."

"I—I don't really care about the money, Lucien Edmond. I'm most concerned with preserving this place as old Lucien and your dear father wanted it, and to make sure that our children obtain their rightful heritage. Understand me, Lucien Edmond, I'm going to try to bring them up with the steadfast belief that they must expect nothing except what they can do themselves with God's help and their own diligence. What they inherit they will appreciate as a kind of unexpected dividend, and I hope they will be wise enough to save and put by for the proverbial rainy day. Luke was never much interested in material possessions for themselves nor in the accumulation of wealth; nor am I," she added with a bitter little laugh, "especially after what happened to my poor father and his bank. I was a very young girl then, and I thought that the world was mine and that my beauty was a weapon that would get me through the worst adversities. Well, it didn't. But I learned very early the meaning of survival and adaptability to circumstance. My children shall learn that, too."

She laughed again, this time apologetically. "I didn't mean to make a speech, dear Lucien Edmond. Bear with me. I'm afraid my nerves are terribly jangled from all that has happened. I'm so glad you're here to stand by me and to give me your shoulder to lean on when I need it."

"With your permission, Laure, I should like very much to go back to New Orleans in a few days. I want to do a little investigating of my own. I honestly think that the answers to what happened here and, more than that, perhaps even the disappearance of Lopasuta, will be found there."

"If you feel that's the right thing to do, Lucien Edmond, then certainly you should go. But I can tell you only that, thus far, according to reports that have been forwarded to me by Jason Barntry and by Mr. Brickley himself, my casino profits should certainly counterbalance the losses we suffered last night."

"If that's true, then I'm very glad for you. And I appreciate and understand your reason for deciding, even impulsively, to go into a speculative venture like that. I only would to God I'd known of Father's death sooner; then I could have gone to New Orleans with you and given you the benefit of my own suggestions. But what's done is done. What matters most now is to get to the root of this—this malignancy, because it may fester deeper, and involve a good deal more, than even you or I suspect."

"You sound so ominous and mysterious, Lucien Edmond." She stared at him, her eyes widening with a hundred doubts, then filling with tears. Immediately he regretted alarming her, and he rose and went to his stepmother, his hands on her shoulders, bending to kiss her forehead. "Laure, forget what I've said. Remember only that what I'm going to try to do is to make all that Father worked for come out right in the end, just the way you deserve to have it, you and the children. So, as I said, in a day or two I'm going back to New Orleans. But I'll keep in very close touch with you from there."

"Will you stay at that pleasant little hotel where I was, Lucien Edmond?"

Lucien Edmond shook his head with a faintly derisive smile on his lips, "No, I think I'll go to the Villeneuve Hotel. It's quiet and small and convenient enough to all the places I expect to visit. Now, I think you should rest. I'll go back out there and help Katie and Dan arrange for Mary's burial. God bless you, Laure."

"And you, Lucien Edmond. I can see in you the wonderful stability and decency and perserverance that I loved so in Luke himself."

"That is the nicest thing you could ever say about me. Thank you for it." Again he kissed her on the forehead, and then left the study.

# Thirty-Four

Lucien Edmond Bouchard arrived in New Orleans four days later, carrying only a small valise. At the dock, he hired a carriage to take him to the Villeneuve Hotel, striking up a casual conversation with the elderly, soft-spoken freed black who was driving the vehicle. "I haven't been to New Orleans very often," he began, "so I'd like your advice."

"Mighty glad to be what help I can." The driver turned back with a grin. "What was you wantin' to know, suh?"

"One of my friends suggested that I stay at the Villeneuve. Do you know anything about it?"

The driver made a grimace, then gave a deprecatory shrug. "Well, suh, to be real honest with you, it ain't de best we got in N'Awleans." His voice had the rich dialect of a Mississippi-born black. "Sort of run down, if you gits my meanin', suh. 'Course, mind you now, it's comfortable and all dat and it's clean, but it don't do much business. Mostly folks what comes here on business or fo' fun, dey stops at de Exchange or mebbe de Verandah. 'Course, dey costs a lot mo' den where you'se gwine, suh."

"Thank you, driver. What's your name?"

"It's Josiah Morris, suh."

"I'm pleased to make your acquaintance, Josiah. You're very helpful. My name is Lucien Edmond Bouchard, by the way. Well, as long as the Villeneuve is clean and convenient, it will do for my needs. Incidentally, do you happen to know who owns it?"

"Oh, sho' 'nuff, Mrt. Bouchard. Ah sho' 'nuff does. It's

Mr. Brickley—he owns dem fancy houses on Rampart Street. He a big, rich, important man here in N'Awleans."

"I see. Well then, if the hotel is under his management, I'm sure it will be comfortable enough for me. One more thing, Josiah—I'd like to meet this Mr. Brickley. Do you know where he has his office?"

"Most of de time, Mr. Bouchard, suh, you kin find him at de Rampart Street house he calls—my French ain't too good, Mr. Bouchard, but so far as I kin make out, it sounds something lak Musay Delicesses. I kin take you dere, if you wants."

"I tell you what, Josiah. I'd like to check into the hotel and leave my valise in my room. If you'll wait for me, you can then take me to this house."

"Dat would be mah pleasure, Mr. Bouchard. You'se a fine gentleman of quality. You'se friendly wid old Josiah. Not too many white folk still wants to be friends, you know. Well now, here we is, suh, de Villeneuve."

It was not, Lucien Edmond Bouchard admitted to himself, too prepossessing an edifice. Yet the driver had been correct in saying that it was clean and would most likely also be comfortable. As he entered the lobby, he saw a narrow stairway whose faded carpeting had seen better days, as indeed, had the lobby itself. There were some potted palm trees, a few tall straight-backed chairs upholstered in a worn red velvet at one end of the room, and at the other, a desk behind which was a compartment box for the room keys. It was presided over by a nearly bald man in his early fifties, whose mournful expression and black frock coat made him look rather more like an undertaker than a hotel manager.

Lucien Edmond pleasantly introduced himself and asked for a room, indicating that he might stay a week or more, depending upon the success of a business venture about which he had come. "Most happy to have you here with us, Mr. Bouchard. You may certainly stay indefinitely, as it fits your pleasure or your business. We are not crowded, as it chances, so you may have your choice of rooms. We have one suite that is unoccupied now—"

"No, I am a man of simple habits, coming from Texas and living on a ranch as I do," Lucien Edmond chuckled. "An ordinary room with bathing privileges will quite suffice."

"Very well, sir, in that case I will give you 203. It is accessible by that stairway and, if you have no objection to carrying your own valise, here is the key, sir. Welcome to the Villeneuve."

"Thank you." Lucien Edmond took the key and gave the mournful-looking man a smiling nod. "By the way, I should like to see Mr. Brickley. Do you think he would be in his office at this hour?"

"Very possibly, Mr. Bouchard. That would be at the Musée des Délices on Rampart Street. Any *fiacre* or carriage driver knows where it is. You have only to mention the name."

"Thank you again." Lucien Edmond ascended the steps, found his room, opened the door, and placed his valise on the bed. His quick glance confirmed his expectation that the furnishings of the rooms of the Velleneuve would be as dreary as those of the lobby. Then, locking the door and pocketing the key, he went back downstairs to the waiting driver. "Now you can drive me to the Musée des Délices on Rampart Street, Josiah," he told the man.

But then, just as the driver started up, Lucien Edmond had a sudden change of mind. He wanted first to see the casino that Laure Bouchard coowned with Brickley. So, leaning forward, he called out to the driver, "I've changed my mind, Josiah. Do you know where the Maison de Bonne Chance is?"

" 'Sho 'nuff does, Mr. Bouchard, suh. Take you dere in a jiffy."

"Good. Thank you, Josiah." Lucien Edmond settled back and contented himself with observing the streets and the shops of New Orleans. The weather was still warm and humid, but, since it was mid-September, the worst of it was over.

"Here we is, suh," Josiah gently drew in the reins, bringing the carriage to a gradual stop. "Hope I's been helpful to you, Mr. Bouchard, suh. A real pleasure fo' me to drive a fine gentleman like you."

Lucien Edmond got down from the *fiacre* and handed the driver a banknote. "Ain't got enough change for this, Mr. Bouchard, sorry—I ain't done well at all today drivin' folks."

"That's for you, and well worth it for your friendship

338

and your helpfulness in acquainting me with the city, Josiah," Lucien Edmond smiled.

"Ah thanks you wid all mah heart, Mr. Bouchard, suh. That's mighty kind of you, Mr. Bouchard."

"I hope I'll meet you again, Josiah. I'll look for you whenever I need a carriage. Thank *you* again, and good afternoon to you."

Lucien Edmond approached the door and struck on the knocker, to be promptly admitted by a charming, copper-haired young woman in her early twenties, dressed in flesh-colored tights, her hair carefully coiffed, her lace-trimmed gown cut simply and elegantly, yet showing off her slender waist and swelling bosom to great advantage. Lucien Edmond stared for an instant, impressed despite himself by the demure yet enticing charm of her costume, then smilingly inquired, "I'm a visitor to New Orleans, mam'selle, and I thought I might try some games of chance. I've been told about this house, and its name suggests that even I might have good luck."

"But of course, m'sieu. You will find on each floor tables of roulette, faro, poker, *vingt-et-un*, baccarat. There is always someone representing our house ready to play with you. If you give me your hat and cape, m'sieu, I will have them held for you until you are ready to leave—which I sincerely hope will not be for quite some time and also that you will be very lucky on your first visit."

"Thank you very much. And business is good here?" Lucien Edmond inquired.

"Very good, m'sieu. By the way, all guests of this house are provided with food and wines of their choice. I could arrange to have the attendant on duty at the floor where you prefer to stay bring you a collation and whatever beverage you prefer, m'sieu."

"That is indeed superb New Orleans hospitality," Lucien Edmond replied. Then, after inquiring as to her opinion on which floor was preferable at this hour, he added, "Very well, I shall go up to the next floor and try my hand at *vingt-et-un*. As for wine, a glass of dry white will do very nicely, and something light in the way of food. I haven't eaten lunch, but the weather is so humid here in New Orleans that my appetite isn't especially strong."

"Thank you, m'sieu. May I inquire as to your name, and would you mind signing our guest book? M'sieu

339

Brickley likes to keep a record of all of our guests so that he may call upon them on occasion for suggestions on how we can make this house more entertaining to them."

"You've been ideally trained, Mam'selle—Mam'selle—"

"I am Suzette Delcroix, m'sieu, at your service." She made him a charming little curtsy, inclining her head and bending one knee.

"And my name is Lucien Edmond Bouchard."

"Thank you, M'sieu Bouchard. Claire is the attendant on the next floor: simply tell her that you've already given me your order for food and wine, and she will serve it to you. By the way, you might want to know that M'sieu Brickley himself is here this very moment, playing at a side table for special stakes with one of his very old friends. If you have no objection, I shall let him know that you are a first-time visitor, and I am sure that he will want to welcome you himself, M'sieu Bouchard."

"I have no objection whatsoever, Mam'selle Suzette," Lucien Edmond Bouchard smiled and shrugged. He thought to himself: *Well now, how fortuitous! Since Brickley's here, it'll be interesting to see him in action.*

Aloud, he said, "Then I'll go up to the second floor and take my chances. I thank you again for your great courtesy, Mam'selle Suzette."

"It is my pleasure, m'sieu."

Lucien Edmond gallantly inclined his head toward the lovely *soubrette* and walked toward the velvet-carpeted stairway that wound upwards to the second floor of the casino. As he drew open the door, a dazzling honey-colored blonde, whose hourilike figure was not unlike that of Mitzi Sattersfield's (and quite as petite), came toward him with an enchanting smile. "Good afternoon, m'sieu. My name is Claire. May I conduct you to a table of your choice?" After being informed that Suzette had taken his order for refreshments, she added, "I will serve you shortly, m'sieu, once you are at your ease. Now, what is your gaming pleasure?"

"I should like to try *vingt-et-un*, Mam'selle Claire," Lucien Edmond declared.

There were few patrons in the elegantly furnished casino. The petite blond hostess led him toward a table in the corner at the right-hand side of the spacious room, where a tall, slim, rather effete-looking dealer not much more than thirty, with a stylishly trimmed goatee, cordially welcomed him and introduced himself as "Eugène D'Onorio, *à votre service, m'sieu.*"

"A pleasure to meet you, M'sieu D'Onorio. I am Lucien Edmond Bouchard. This is the first time I have come to your lovely casino, and I fancy that a few games of *vingt-et-un* will pleasurably while away the time this afternoon till my dinner engagement at Antoine's."

Lucien Edmond seated himself, and Claire swiftly took several banknotes and exchanged them for counters. Amiably, he put down two five-dollar chips as the dealer shuffled the cards and then began to deal.

Lucien Edmond won the first hand and called for a second round. Again he won, this time staking three five-dollar counters. At that moment, as he was leaning back and making pleasant conversation to the amiable dealer, honey-haired Claire approached with a tray on which was a beautifully worked Wedgwood platter holding savory meats and cheeses and a goblet of chilled white wine. Another attractive girl appeared, this one a willowy black-haired attendant, who set down a small tabouret at Lucien Edmond's left, on which to rest the tray.

Lucien Edmond lifted the glass of wine and smiled at each lovely hostess, then took a leisurely sip. "My compliments to your wine steward. The wine is deliciously dry, as it should be. And the collation you've just set before me seems equally tempting. And now, M'sieu D'Onorio, whenever you are ready, let us try a new game."

He watched as the dealer shuffled the cards, then leaning to the table, he placed two chips beside his place and waited to be dealt his first card. Nodding, he received a second and, deliberately pausing to take another sip of his wine, casually upturned his first card and said, *"J'ai gagné, M'sieu D'Onorio, n'est-ce pas?"*

"Indeed you have, my compliments, M'sieu Bouchard. Luck favors you this afternoon. *Encore, peut-être?*"

"I have no objections." Lucien Edmond now turned to the plate and forked a mouthful, washing it down with another sip of the chilled white wine.

"Well now, M'sieu Bouchard, you do us great honor by visiting us." A suave voice behind him made him twist his chair around and then rise to face his interlocutor.

"You have the advantage of me, m'sieu," Lucien Edmond chuckled.

"My name is William Brickley. I am the coowner of this casino. Your name was relayed to me while I was concluding my own little game with M'sieu LeVeau, who has tried for the last five years, but with unfortunately no success, to defeat me at baccarat. Let me welcome you to New Orleans and refill your glass." Brickley turned and autocratically snapped his fingers. Lovely, petite Claire hastened forward, nodded and vanished, to return a moment later with a fresh goblet filled with the pleasant white wine, and Lucien Edmond thanked him for his courtesy.

"My pleasure, M'sieu Bouchard," William Brickley drawled. "You are related, then, to my partner, Madame Laure Bouchard?"

"You might say so, Mr. Brickley. I am her stepson."

"I see. And are you in New Orleans on a visit or perhaps on business?"

"As you doubtless know, my stepmother recently lost her husband, and I have just come from visiting her and offering my condolences. I personally live in Texas."

"That was most thoughtful of you, M'sieu Bouchard."

"It turned out to be fortunate that I arrived at the plantation when I did. We had an incredible disaster—some men dressed in the costume of the outlawed Ku Klux Klan raided the plantation after midnight and set fire to the crops. We sustained quite a heavy loss—although it might have been far worse."

"How dreadful! Please convey to Madame Bouchard my sincerest regrets for the misfortunes she has suffered, coming as it does so soon upon the lamentable death of her husband."

"I shall do that. And thank you, Mr. Brickley, for being so concerned." Lucien Edmond turned and casually looked around the room. "I understand you do an excellent business."

"Yes. Naturally weekday afternoons are far from our busiest times. As I'm sure you must realize, m'sieu, there is tremendous competition among the, shall we say, 'polite' gambling houses such as this one for the dollars of our clients. Thus, I am letting it be known that at the Maison de Bonne Chance, the proverbial sky is the limit for our more affluent players.

342

"You see, M'sieu Bouchard," he added in a low, confidential tone, "that is what attracts the big money—and it also attracts those who play for less but who are intrigued by being at the heart of the action. Besides, if it were to be known that our casino has a low ceiling, we would lose prestige and overnight our customers would vanish—and to stay in this business, it is imperative that we have a continual flow of people willing to risk a loss. So you see, I am completely on top of the situation here, and I can say with total confidence that your stepmother has no reason to regret her investment."

"I'm glad to hear that. By the way, I believe I'm staying at a hotel you own, Mr. Brickley, the Villeneuve."

"It is not, I must tell you, one of the finest hotels. But it's pleasant and comfortable and moderately priced."

"I have found it so. And now, before the rest of this food gets cold, would you allow me to complete my belated luncheon?"

"Of a certainty, M'sieu Bouchard. I shall be in my office for a bit. Do stop by and say good-bye, when you've finished. Oh, by the way, are you returning to Alabama to confer with your stepmother?"

"No, Mr. Brickley. The work on my cattle ranch has been rather taxing, and I'm in need of a vacation. I think I shall stay in New Orleans and enjoy myself for a bit. Thank you again for your hospitality."

"My pleasure, sir." William Brickley made a stately bow, and then left the room.

Lucien Edmond tried two more games of *vingt-et-un* but lost each time. Nonetheless, he had made about forty dollars and had consumed an appetizing lunch and two glasses of excellent French white wine. He tossed a five-dollar chip to the dealer, thanked him, and rose and left the casino.

Once on the sidewalk, he hailed a *fiacre* and directed the driver to the Brunton & Barntry Bank. A few minutes later, Jason Barntry ceremoniously ushered Lucien Edmond into his office, where Lucien Edmond, after first obtaining the bank manager's permission, lit a cigar, leaned back, and regarded the aging man.

"Jason, I've just spent some time at Laure's new casino."

343

"I see, Mr. Bouchard. And how may I be of help to you?"

"I'm going to ask a special favor of you, Jason. I understand that William Brickley is a large depositor in this fine bank."

"That's true, Mr. Bouchard."

"Well then, without violating any confidences, could you possibly tell me the status of that account over the last two months? Before you answer me, I will tell you exactly why I ask that. A few nights ago, after midnight, some twenty men riding horses and disguised as Ku Klux Klan members rode in on Windhaven Plantation and torched the crops. There was utter devastation. Worse, poor old Moses Turner was shot down. For the life of me, Jason, I can't understand why we were attacked and no one else. What research I've been able to do thus far has led nowhere. I can't prove anything as yet, but I'm beginning to be suspicious of this Brickley fellow. Anything you can tell me about him as it affects his association with my stepmother would be deeply appreciated."

Jason Barntry rose from his desk and, turning his back on Luke's oldest son, clasped his hands behind his back and stood staring and silent for a moment. Then he turned and said in an uneasy tone, "You know of course that your stepmother came here and in this very office, with our attorney, Hollis Minton, signed articles of partnership on the casino venture. At the time, the agreement seemed reasonably equitable to me, although I harbored reservations based on my own personal disapproval of gambling as a pastime. But I realize now that the clause that makes Mrs. Bouchard responsible for half of the losses renders her vulnerable in the event of any chicanery or dishonesty. If that happens, she could very easily find herself in financial difficulties."

"That is precisely the kind of information I want from you. Now, I know you were uneasy from the start about choosing Danvers Willoughby as the new overseer at Windhaven Plantation."

"And I sincerely hope my fears have proven unwarranted," countered the elderly banker. "What do you think of the job he's doing?"

"I consider him an insufferable prig, a colossal egotist, and a man whom I suspect of playing both ends against the

344

middle. I can't prove it, mind you, but I don't like him. And just now, at the Maison de Bonne Chance, I had the unexpected pleasure of meeting William Brickley. He's a very glib man, quite prepossessing and undoubtedly clever. But it does not follow that he has been dishonest in his dealings with my stepmother."

"Are you, by any chance, suggesting that there is fraud or collusion involved here?" Jason Barntry looked alarmed.

"Not yet, Jason, but I do have some damaging evidence that I'll reveal to you in a bit. Meanwhile, just pretend that I've been talking to you off the record, as one might say. There are a few more questions I want to ask William Brickley. One of them concerns Lopasuta—you've still not heard from him, by any chance?"

As Jason dolefully shook his head, Lucien Edmond went on, "Again, I have no way of proving or disproving my suspicions, but I have a strong feeling that William Brickley knows more about Lopasuta Bouchard than he cares to tell. Of course, I didn't mention the subject this afternoon to Brickley—it's too soon to reveal my hand—however, one of the things that worries me greatly are two contracts that Willoughby made a great fuss over. He obtained them here in New Orleans—one from a greengrocer and one from the manager of the very hotel at which I am stopping, the Villeneuve. And today I learned that the Villeneuve is one of William Brickley's holdings. Now I'll admit that it's possible this coincidence is innocent, but I believe a more sinister interpretation is far more likely. That's why I'm asking you, not only as a faithful friend, but as an honest banker, to tell me anything that might be relevant about William Brickley's business with this bank as it might concern the Bouchards."

Jason frowned and looked down at the floor. Then, with a weary sigh, he stared directly at Lucien Edmond and said, "You put me in a difficult position, Mr. Bouchard. You know that my life depends upon my association with this bank—how your father, and then Lopasuta, inspired me to continue my work. I owe a great debt of gratitude to the Bouchard family—and yet—"

"All this I know, Jason." Lucien Edmond interrupted. "Come now, I know what you're about to say, that you're in the same position as a priest or a doctor or an attorney who may not vouchsafe confidential admissions."

"Exactly. But I will promise you this as a friend and as a counselor beholden to the Bouchards: As soon as you have more palpable evidence of unlawful collusion, I will examine Brickley's transactions to see if they support your claims. But until then I'm honor-bound to say no more about a client of this bank. Believe me, Mr. Bouchard, I'm deeply sorry."

"I quite understand, Jason, and I'm convinced that in a matter of weeks, Mr. Brickley will go too far." Lucien Edmond rose in preparation for his departure. "Until then I'm going to stay here in New Orleans and prepare for a showdown."

During the next week, Lucien Edmond Bouchard acted just as an ordinary tourist might on his first visit to the Queen City. But there was one stop he made, out of sentimental nostalgia, and it was to the shop of old Emile Dagronard, just past the Vieux Carre.

To his delight, he found the wagonmaker still alive and, incredibly, as voluble and fault-finding as he had been when Lucien Edmond's father, Luke, had visited his shop and commissioned special wagons to be built for the journey to that territory which would become Windhaven Range. That had been twelve years ago, and Dagronard had been sixty-four, with a long white goatee and thin, reedy voice. Now, at seventy-six, he seemed frailer than ever, but his eyes still blazed with anger when he upbraided a clumsy worker in the most fluent French *argot* Lucien Edmond had ever heard. He waited until the tirade was over, and then smilingly hazarded, "You are still the same as you were a dozen years ago, M'sieu Dagronard."

The wagonmaker whirled, his bushy eyebrows arching with suspicion. "And who in the name of seven thousand devils out of hell may you be, m'sieu?"

"I am the son of the man who commissioned some of the finest wagons you ever made about twelve years ago, M'sieu Dagronard. Is the name of Luke Bouchard familiar to you?"

"*Diable!*" the old man swore, hurrying up to Lucien Edmond and extending his hand. "Of course I remember, and they were the best, and I'll wager they're still usable, aren't they?"

"They are indeed. I have been in Texas running a ranch, M'sieu Dagronard, but," and here Lucien Edmond's face grew sober, "my father died just a few months ago, a hero's death saving the life of the governor of Alabama. I am here in New Orleans for a few weeks, and I wanted to come by and thank you for the sturdiness of those fine wagons."

"Do you hear that, you imbeciles?" Emile Dagronard wheeled and, arms akimbo, harangued his six surly young workers. "Here is a customer, if you please, who tells me twelve years later that my wagons are still the best he had ever had. And who built them? I, with the useless help of idiots like you. Let that be a lesson to you all. You may well be remembered because you worked for me, not because of your own paltry skills." Then, turning back to Lucien Edmond, he chuckled and said, "One must use the lash on these would-be hopefuls every now and again, but I'm very happy, I'll tell you this in all sincerity, that my wagons still work for you, M'sieu Bouchard." Then, with a sigh, "And what bad news you bring me, because I do remember your father very well. He was a fine man. You have my sincerest condolences, M'sieu Bouchard."

"Thank you, my friend. But may I say you're amazing, hardly a day older, M'sieu Dagronard," Lucien Edmond chuckled. "No, I need no more of your wagons, but it's good to see you again. I shall be here for some few weeks, until I learn what I've come to New Orleans to find out. Perhaps you'll do me the honor of dining with me some evening—why not this evening?"

And when Emile Dagronard agreed, Lucien Edmond smiled and said, "We shall share a bottle of wine tonight and drink to the many unanswerable mysteries of God's universe. But rest assured, what you did for my father and me will never be forgotten. You are a craftsman, and your work will endure."

347

# Thirty-Five

On his eighth day in New Orleans, Lucien Edmond Bouchard returned to the Brunton & Barntry Bank to confer again with Jason Barntry. "Do you know, Jason," Lucien Edmond fiercely declared, "sometimes one has a feeling that can't be justified by logic or facts; it's just a kind of inner awareness. All along, I've had just such feelings about my stepmother and this man William Brickley. But I feel as if I were suspended just out of reach of the truth, unable to seize it for myself."

Jason Barntry, shaking his head, murmured, "Looking back, I think I helped your stepmother to go into the casino venture; and while I was never entirely happy about the new overseer, I didn't actually discourage Mrs. Bouchard from engaging him. However, from all you've told me lately, I'm beginning to regret that I didn't actively dissuade her from either association."

"So am I, Jason. But let's keep our suspicions to ourselves, and I'll be in touch with you constantly to let you know what information I obtain. It's very curious, and I can hardly justify it, except perhaps by instinct, but I'm also concerned that Lopasuta's disappearance is connected with all this. My God, it's going on four months since he left Montgomery to come here! I somehow feel that his vanishing so mysteriously is tied up with the raid on our fields a few weeks ago, and my stepmother's sudden decision to plunge so much money into a gambling casino!" He rose and stretched. "Meanwhile, I'll go back to the Villeneuve and take a nap. If you hear anything before I do, please let me know."

Jason nodded and accompanied Lucien Edmond toward the entrance of the bank. Judith Branshaw, working at her desk, looked up and gave Lucien Edmond a pleasant greeting. "I hope that you're enjoying your stay in New Orleans, Mr. Bouchard."

Jason Barntry had introduced the two of them previously. Now the white-haired manager turned to him and smilingly remarked, "I'm not sure that we'll have Miss Branshaw with us much longer. She's going to be married very soon—isn't that right, my dear?"

Color flamed in Judith's lovely face, as she shyly nodded. "Yes, Mr. Barntry. Bernard Marquard and I plan to be married the third week of October. But I shan't leave the bank, not right away—that is, Mr. Barntry, if you'll still have me?"

"That goes without saying, Judith. You're going to make him a wonderful wife, and I've already noticed how happy he is, now that he has someone who really cares for him."

At this warm praise, Judith bit her lips and bowed her head, and her eyes filled with tears. Looking up, all she could do was send Barntry a look of intense gratitude.

Outside in the street, Lucien Edmond turned to the bank manager and said, "Do you know, I've just thought of something else that's extremely curious in this whole mixed-up affair. I've told you that the Villeneuve is owned by Brickley and that Danvers Willoughby showed me a contract from that very same hotel commissioning the purchase of various food items. Now, the singular thing about that—apart from its indicating possible collusion between the men—is that the hotel has absolutely no restaurant and serves no food on its premises. A contract for food supplies would hardly be legitimate under the circumstances."

"That puzzles me, too, Mr. Bouchard. What exactly do you think it means?"

"I'm not yet certain. But I'm going to stay in New Orleans until I've an answer to that and other parts of this mystifying riddle that it appears some very ingenious people have gone out of their way to concoct. Well, I'll be in touch with you when I've something to report. A very good day to you, Jason."

349

Lucien Edmond Bouchard spent the following week enjoying the sights of New Orleans, dining at attractive restaurants in the French Quarter, and even attending a performance of *Mignon* at the French Opera House, a four-storied, plastered brick structure of Italian design. The luxury and comfort of the building made quite an impression on him. From his seat in an upholstered armchair, he saw that above the first floor there rose four elegantly curved tiers of boxes and seats. The color scheme inside was white, red, and gold, and the two broad flights of stairs led to the foyer, which was hung with chandeliers and immense mirrors. The architect, Lucien Edmond learned, was James Gallier, Jr., the thirty-two-year-old son of the same man who had built the famous St. Charles Hotel, the City Hall, and the Pontalba Buildings.

He sent a telegram to Maxine, briefly recounting what he had learned thus far about the tribulations that had beset Windhaven Plantation. He avowed his intention to return home once he had straightened out Laure Bouchard's complicated affairs and, in a tender postscript, promised that he would bring her to New Orleans to enjoy opera and symphony concerts, as a kind of second honeymoon, when all this was over.

As he returned to his hotel from the telegraph office to change his clothes for a luncheon appointment with Jason Barntry, the officious manager of the Villeneuve called out, "Mr. Bouchard—there's a telegram here for you."

Lucien Edmond thanked the man, took the telegram, and went upstairs to his room. Only then did he open it, and he uttered an incredulous gasp at its contents:

Brickley telegraphed me today that three men broke the bank at the casino. Loss estimated at $400,000. My investment wiped out. Brickley demands I share losses with him. Please see him and wire me what you learn about this dreadful turn of events. My very best wishes and thanks for your help.

Laure Bouchard

Laure had been utterly horrified by the news that William Brickley had telegraphed to her. Within an hour after she had received Brickley's message, she had met Danvers Willoughby coming in from the fields with Marius Thornton and had asked in great agitation if she might have a word with him. Marius had rallied the other workers to do everything possible to salvage the crops that remained after the incendiary attack by the nightriders; nevertheless, at least half of the expected revenue from Windhaven Plantation had literally gone up in smoke.

"I'm at your service, dear lady." Willoughby made Laure a polite little bow as he followed her into the study.

"Mr. Willoughby, I've just received a wire from Mr. Brickley telling me that three men came into the casino to gamble and won over four hundred thousand dollars, and he expects me to make restitution for half the balance of the loss."

"That is indeed an unfortunate situation, Mrs. Bouchard, but as you know, I'm sure, a business partner would be liable for half the debts, as well as reaping half the profits."

She gave him a quick, suspicious glance, feeling his reply had been much too glib. Then, shaking her head and with a heavy sigh, she went on, "I have asked my stepson, Lucien Edmond Bouchard, who is in New Orleans, to investigate this matter for me."

"But debts in a gambling house, Mrs. Bouchard, are debts of honor and must be paid. There is no other alternative. Possibly your manager, Mr. Brickley, should have put a ceiling on the betting, and someday there may be laws regulating casinos on this very point—but, in the absence of those two contingencies, I'm afraid that you've no choice but to make good on the obligations of your establishment."

"But it's such a huge sum of money—more money than I have available; maybe even more than was in my husband's legacy. How in the world—" Laure stammered, her face bleak with the realization of this staggering loss.

"Well, if you were to draw upon your capital and then also sell this estate, I'm sure you could not only pay the debt, but have a considerable sum to put aside for yourself, so that you could retire as a *grande dame*, Mrs. Bouchard," the Englishman slyly suggested.

Laure indignantly drew herself up and shook her head, then replied in a firm voice, "That's unthinkable, Mr. Willoughby! Windhaven Plantation will never be sold! To sell it would be to destroy everything my husband and his grandfather worked for and dedicated their lives to."

"You may have little choice in the matter, Mrs. Bouchard." There was a malicious smile playing about Danvers Willoughby's mouth. "I am sure the creditors will press you and Mr. Brickley for immediate payment, or at least compel the two of you to make some acceptable arrangement for the payment of that debt."

"Mr. Willoughby," Laure said, trembling with indignation, "I do not care for your attitude in this matter. You were recommended by Mr. Brickley to help ensure the maintenance of this plantation, and I hired you on trust. But from the way you talk, I'm beginning to think that you would prefer to see me forced to sell my house to the first buyer. I declare, Mr. Willoughby, I've had nothing but trouble since you came here."

"Now then, Mrs. Bouchard, I can understand that you are distraught because of all that has happened. But what you have just said to me defiles my reputation and puts my honor at stake. You must really retract those words and apologize to me, or I fear that our relationship will become quite strained."

"I—perhaps I was hasty," Laure falteringly amended, and then burst into tears. The cumulative effect of Luke's tragic death, the attack by the nightriders, and now this financial catastrophe that had come upon her without warning, broke her gallant self-control. She bowed her head, covering her tear-stained face with her hands, and turned away from him, fighting to regain her composure. He stood watching her, a mocking little smile curving his sensual lips. Then, placatingly, he murmured, "Forgive me, Mrs. Bouchard. Perhaps I spoke too hastily in my own turn. I give you my word as a gentleman that all I have done here is to try to run the estate as well as I know how. You certainly do not believe that the nightriders were my fault?"

"No—no, of course not—please, Mr. Willoughby, I—I'm beside myself. We—we can resume this conversation some time later, if you don't mind. I—I'm going to the children now. If—if I've offended you, I—I apologize."

"There is no need, dear Mrs. Bouchard. I understand exactly how you feel," Willoughby ingratiatingly murmured, as he watched her turn and walk out of the study.

# Thirty-Six

As he read Laure's telegram over again, Lucien Edmond Bouchard had the eerie feeling that all the recent tragedies had been contrived and calculated. A furious anger began to smolder within him, and he fought against it, because his father had once told him, "Giving way to irrational anger clouds the mind and obscures the real reasons for that anger. Try to think of yourself in the third person, as if you were standing in the wings of a stage and watching what was happening, and see how it relates to you." And he knew it was sage advice.

Yes, it was true: he was even eager to attribute his father's death to the cunning and treachery of an outsider who had sought to bring the Bouchards to financial ruin. When Laure had told him how Luke had died, he had been crushed with a sense of utter futility. In turn, that had been tempered by his agonized admiration for his father, for the courage Luke had shown in being willing to risk his own life to save that of the governor of the state. And now that he tried to see clearly all the events that had been brought to his notice, he had to admit that, from what Laure had told him, there was absolutely no hint of a plot to kill his father. No, that had been merely a dreadful coincidence, a malignant accident. If destiny had decreed that Luke was to die, he would have died that day by some other means, if not from the bullet of his unwitting assassin.

Thus he put that thought aside as forcibly as he could, and thought deeply of all the rest of the singular events that had taken place following his father's death. But foremost, there was the recollection that Lopasuta had left for New Orleans for the very purpose of meeting William Brickley, and to this day had not been heard from. Could this be part of the master plan of the rogues who were trying to undermine Windhaven Plantation?

In his room, Lucien Edmond took pen and paper and began to set down all of the events that had begun with Lopasuta's disappearance: his stepmother's impulsive decision to invest in a gambling casino, which had led her to William Brickley; Brickley's recommendation of Danvers Willoughby as overseer of Windhaven Plantation; then the latter's contracts for the sale of crops to the New Orleans greengrocer, and, most puzzling of all, to the Villeneuve Hotel when the establishment had no restaurant or room service of any kind. Then there was the burning of the fields and the destruction of over half of the harvestable crops. And now, the sudden announcement from Brickley that the casino was in danger of bankruptcy because three men had broken the bank, rendering Laure liable for half the losses.

When he laid down his pen, Lucien Edmond picked up the paper and began to study it carefully. Finally, crumpling it into a ball and flinging it into the corner, he rose, his features hardened and cold, and made his way down to the lobby, where he asked the obsequious manager of the desk where William Brickley was most likely to be found this time of the day, and was told that it would be at the casino. Going out into the street, he hailed a *fiacre* and gave the driver the address. But then, countermanding the order, he directed the driver to the Brunton & Barntry Bank, adding that they would go next to the Maison de Bonne Chance. Arriving at the bank, he bade the driver to wait for him and hurried into Jason Barntry's office. The white-haired manager was dictating a letter to Judith Branshaw, and when Lucien Edmond entered, he started to rise to his feet, but Lucien Edmond shook his head and exclaimed, "Please don't get up, Jason! My apologies for disturbing you. There's just one question I have to ask you: can you check your records and see if William Brickley sent any money to Danvers Willoughly within the last month or so? It would be a draft that probably a bank in Montgomery would honor. I ask you because this is vitally important. I now have evidence—although it is circumstantial—that Brickley has been the evil genius behind Laure's present misfortune—and I even suspect him of being involved with Lopasuta's mysterious disappearance."

"Good God! In that case, Mr. Bouchard, I'll turn my back on the conventional rules of not revealing confidential matters relating to depositors and get the information for you. Judith, my dear, would you please be kind enough to check the account of William Brickley and see if there is a draft such as Mr. Bouchard has just mentioned? If there is, please bring it to me."

"Certainly, Mr. Barntry; right away." Judith excused herself with a lovely smile and hurried back to the window of the head cashier, quickly explained what she sought, and then waited there while the bearded, middle-aged Creole went down into the vault to examine the records.

He emerged about five minutes later with a draft dated August 2, 1877, and brought it directly to Judith. Thanking him, she hurried back into Jason Barntry's office and handed it to her superior.

"Your suspicions are quite right—though I'm not yet sure what you're getting at, Mr. Bouchard. Here is a draft for three thousand dollars to the order of Danvers Willoughby and signed by William Brickley. It was cashed"—the elderly man turned over the draft and squinted at it, —"by the State Bank & Trust of Montgomery."

"Thanks, Jason. This may well be the final piece of the puzzle. You see, I've come to the conclusion that Brickley saw a good thing in my stepmother's widowhood and inveigled her into making a substantial investment in his casino, planning to force her to sell Windhaven Plantation in order to raise capital to pay off a fraudulent gambling debt. I believe that he recommended Danvers Willoughby to be overseer for the sole purpose of hampering and obstructing the normal production of crops—and the usual profit therefrom—to further this end, although I must confess I cannot conceive of why this stranger would be so interested in the destruction of Windhaven Plantation and all that it stands for. Finally, as I told you before, I am quite sure that Brickley has the answers regarding Lopasuta's disappearance."

"But Mr. Bouchard," Jason put in, "surely the occurrence at the casino, while highly unusual, is by no means unheard of. It is my opinion that the situation may well have come about because of poor judgment on Mr. Brickley's part. Perhaps he found himself up against some very lucky players who had what I believe is called a winning streak. Then, too, there is the possibility that he was himself the victim of some unscrupulous professionals who were working a system calculated to break the bank; a casino manager is prey to all kinds of chicanery on the part of his employees. Really, Mr. Bouchard, I would caution you to tread cautiously, and not make charges like these publicly before you have ascertained all the facts."

"Thank you, Jason, for your advice," Lucien Edmond warmly told the frail old man. "I appreciate your discretion, and I promise you that I won't do anything foolish." With a final grin, he rose and held out his hand to Jason Barntry. "I'll be in touch with you as soon as I confront this ingenious schemer!"

"A pleasure to see you again, Mr. Bouchard. May I have Maude bring you a glass of champagne?" William Brickley smilingly rose from his desk, gesturing toward a tall, slim, dark-haired *soubrette* wearing the elegant livery of the gambling house, who was acting as hostess at the casino that day.

"I haven't come here to socialize with you, Brickley, and still less to drink your champagne. I'd appreciate it if you'd send the young lady away, because what I have to say to you is strictly private," Lucien Edmond coldly informed him.

"As you please." The entrepreneur shrugged and made a gesture of dismissal toward the young hostess, who promptly left the lavishly furnished office, closing the door behind her.

"Now then, sir, I'm at your disposal. Is something troubling you? You seem to be quite upset. Why, I can't imagine."

"Can't you, now?" Lucien Edmond angrily snapped. "Ever since she met you, my stepmother appears to have been involved in difficulties that I consider to be of your making."

"Sir," Brickley drew himself up and frowned, "that is an audacious and unfounded charge. I advise you to think better of slandering me—I have ample means to defend myself against nonsense of this kind."

"Hardly nonsense, Brickley, when you consider the rather strange sequence of events. After becoming involved with you in this gambling casino, Mrs. Bouchard hired Danvers Willoughby—at your recommendation—and then for no apparent reason, Windhaven Plantation was singled out to receive the ravages of so-called Klansmen; hard upon the heels of this destruction, you suddenly wired my stepmother to let her know that the bank of this casino was broken and plunged into an incredible debt—a debt that at this point could not be met without selling the plantation—"

"Now wait a minute, Mr. Bouchard—"

"No, Brickley, you wait till I finish!" Lucien Edmond stepped toward the entrepreneur, his eyes blazing with anger. "I know all about the phony contracts Willoughby obtained here in New Orleans. Did you think I wouldn't find out that the Villeneuve, which you own, does not even serve food to its customers? The Villeneuve contract alone is enough to convince me that you two are scheming together, to my stepmother's disadvantage, and I'm even prepared to charge you both with masterminding the attack upon Windhaven Plantation."

"And that's a damnable lie, Bouchard!" Brickley snarled, his face purpling with anger. "There is nothing like what you impute between me and my good friend, Danvers Willoughby."

"Nonetheless, I do make the charge. From the beginning, every move you've made has been calculated to bring financial ruin to my stepmother."

"You think so, do you? But you've really no proof," Brickley sneered. "Besides, you've nothing to say in the matter. Gambling debts have to be paid. If your stepmother has to sell the plantation, so be it. She came into our deal with her eyes open, you know. And kindly remember that I invested considerable money of my own to establish this venture—money which, I might add, I have now lost to three gamblers."

"And I shouldn't be surprised if these men who broke the bank at the casino were confederates of yours," Lucien Edmond vehemently declared.

"That's a damnable falsehood, sir. Although it really isn't any of your business, it just so happens that I discovered that those three gamblers were working with two of my dealers. Needless to say, when I discovered this, I dismissed those employees immediately. However, since I cannot prove the collusion, I have no alternative—nor does your stepmother—but to pay off the debt. The reputation of the casino is at stake here, sir, as well as my general business reputation in this city, and that of your stepmother as well. It must be known that we honor our obligations. Now, if you persist in this slander, I shall have no choice but to challenge you to a duel. I advise you very strongly, sir, to retract all of your statements."

"I shall retract nothing. You almost succeeded in duping even Jason Barntry, but just before I came here, I discovered that you had sent a draft for three thousand dollars to Danvers Willoughby. That, Brickley, could only have been payment for having those Klansmen, or whoever they might have been, set fire to Windhaven Plantation."

"I warn you, Bouchard, you're going too far!"

"I haven't really gone far enough," Lucien Edmond riposted.

"From what I understand, you spend most of your time in Texas, and it's clear you can't know too much about your stepmother. But you see, I've made inquiries. It appears that she once worked at the Union House, which, during the war, was a bordello for the servicing of Union officers. Surely, since your stepmother is a woman of the world, she certainly understands that in a gambling house, as in a brothel, one takes one's chances."

Lucien Edmond sucked in his breath, his cheeks crimson with fury. "How dare you make insinuations about Mrs. Bouchard? And who are you to challenge the morality of anyone? In my opinion, you're no better than a common thief, and not a very smart one at that. You have left a few traces behind you in your scheme, Brickley. And, when I get back to Windhaven Plantation, I think I'll be able to draw the truth from your glib confederate, Danvers Willoughby."

William Brickley bit his lips, momentarily flustered. Then, with a great show of indignation, he put his hand into his pocket of his fawn-colored breeches and drew out a glove. Advancing to face Lucien Edmond Bouchard, he angrily exclaimed, "You have impugned my honor, sir! *This* is my answer to you." Hardly had he finished that phrase before he drew back the glove and slashed it across

358

Lucien Edmond's cheek. "I challenge you to a duel. I warn you, Bouchard, I'm going to kill you for all the slurs, the unproved slurs, you've made here today!"

Much against his will, Jason Barntry agreed to be Lucien Edmond's second in his duel of honor with Brickley. The next morning, Brickley's own second called upon Lucien Edmond at the Villeneuve, to formalize the arrangements for the duel; he was a lean, sallow-faced Creole named Maurice Lazard, who was actually the manager of one of Brickley's bordellos and also the chief procurer of *filles de joie* for all of his pleasure houses.

Since Lucien Edmond had been challenged, he had the choice of weapons and dueling site, and he promptly chose pistols at twenty paces. He remembered his own father's duel with Armand Cournier on the Allard estate, celebrated for its towering line of oak trees whose outer branches touched the earth. Many of the duels on that property had been fought near a trio of the largest trees, which were called "The Three Sisters."

That had been nine years ago, Lucien Edmond recalled, in 1868. And when Armand Cournier, in his vindictive desire to kill Luke, had turned before the count of twenty, Luke's second, Arthur Traylor, then deputy chief of New Orleans police, had killed the Creole for having violated the dueling code. Luke himself had then been forced to shoot Cournier's second, who had been about to kill Traylor in retaliation.

And then, the following year, Cournier's brother, Henri, swearing to avenge Armand's death, had dueled Luke with rapiers, badly wounding him before Luke managed to kill him and thus avenge Laure's rape and the kidnapping of little Lucien, which Henri Cournier had so heinously arranged. And, in this recollection, Luke's oldest son saw a kind of strange coincidence of fate, for in a sense he was also about to avenge his stepmother's betrayal and violation—though this time it was not a physical act against her, but rather against the fertile land that his dead father had bequeathed to her.

"We must have a judge, M'sieu Lazard," he declared.

"My principal leaves the choice to you, so long as the man is honorable and known to both of us," was the sneering answer. "Also, since my principal was certain that you would choose dueling pistols, rather than the traditional rapier, he requests that your selection be of a weapon carrying several shots in its chambers, rather than the single-shot dueling pistol itself."

"I see," Lucien Edmond coolly retorted. "He is out for my blood. So be it. Ask him if he has heard of the new Colt that carries six cartridges."

"He has, and himself owns a pair."

"Very well, I choose those. Of course, the judge and my second as well as you yourself will examine these weapons before the duel takes place."

"That goes without saying, M'sieu Bouchard. Really, m'sieu, this entire conversation is odious to me, but I am honor-bound to observe the formalities. Do you have a judge in mind and a satisfactory time? My principal has affairs to handle and wishes this business to be over with as quickly as possible. Tomorrow morning would be his own preference, if you have no objection."

"I have no objections whatsoever. I, too, have business that concerns me, which M'sieu Brickley's interference has already annoyingly interrupted," was Lucien Edmond's sarcastic counter. "As to a judge, what would you say to M'sieu Felix Brissart, the restaurant owner? He is the very soul of honor. And as for the time, tomorrow—at dawn—would suit me."

"My principal knows M'sieu Brissart. I will accept for him in advance. Tomorrow at dawn, then? And where?"

"At The Three Sisters, where else?" Lucien Edmond disdainfully replied.

It was just past dawn and the mists rising off the ground gave promise that the dankness of this early hour would blossom into intolerable heat after the sun fully rose. The Spanish moss clinging to the gnarled old oaks was an eerie backdrop for the scene about to unfold. The setting seemed devoid of all life, except for the five men now advancing upon the scene.

One of the men, Felix Brissart, who had reluctantly consented to act as judge, wore a black top hat and black frock coat and trousers, as befitted his role. He stood off to one side, preparing for the grim task of officiating. The two seconds met beside their principals, and each asked the obligatory question as to whether the grievance might not be settled before the duel took place. Brickley shook his head, glowering at Lucien Edmond, who in turn answered no when the question was put to him. And then old Felix Brissart inspected the revolvers, double-action Colt .44s with six shots.

They were ready at last, and the two men, standing back to back, their guns in their right hands, awaited the count. Felix Brissart intoned it solemnly and slowly, and then, hesitating an extra second because of the momentous denouement he feared, he at last called out: "Twenty!"

Lucien Edmond Bouchard had whirled and crouched low, pulling the trigger as he faced his opponent. William Brickley, not expecting this maneuver, had fired at where Lucien Edmond's head would have been had he stood erect: the bullet whistled harmlessly past. But Lucien Edmond's bullet took the bearded entrepreneur in the left chest near the heart. There was a gasp of astonishment from the small entourage, as he dropped the revolver, staggered forward a step or two, then sank down on one knee and toppled onto his side.

"I declare that honor has been satisfied, m'sieus." Felix Brissart's voice broke with the strain of his emotion.

Lucien Edmond moved forward toward his fallen rival, his gun still leveled and ready if need be. "I think you are dying, Mr. Brickley," he said dispassionately. "And since confession is good for the soul, admit now that you plotted to make Mrs. Bouchard lose a fortune—so that you would thus gain control of Windhaven."

William Brickley slowly, painfully, turned his head to stare up at his tall opponent. He coughed, and drops of blood seeped from the corners of his mouth. His left hand scrabbled towards his fallen revolver, about two feet away. Hoarsely, almost incoherently, he gasped, "Yes, you b-bastard—and if you hadn't pried, it—it would have worked—"

"I thought as much. And it was you who must have done away with Lopasuta Bouchard, or, if you didn't murder him—and may God pity your soul if you did!—you arranged to imprison him somewhere where he can't be found. Confess it, Brickley, before you face God's judgment."

William Brickley's face was contorted with agony, and his eyes were already glazing. He coughed again, and a

361

spray of blood spurted from his mouth. He made a last desperate try to reach the butt of his revolver, but Lucien Edmond stepped forward and kicked it away. The entrepreneur's eyes stared up at Lucien Edmond, wide and agonized, and then faintly there came the hoarse, stammered words, "You—you'll never know—you can all go to—h-hell—and—"

A violent shudder seized him, as he sprawled onto his back and lay motionless.

Lucien Edmond Bouchard turned to Jason Barntry and Felix Brissart. "Gentlemen, my sincerest thanks for assisting me today. Jason, you heard him—at least the danger to my stepmother has passed. I intend to see that your attorney has the means by which to quash any claim to that fraudulent gambling debt that my stepmother is supposed to owe."

Before he left New Orleans, Lucien Edmond Bouchard conferred that afternoon with Hollis Minton, the bank's lawyer, and told him of William Brickley's confession. "Since my stepmother is the legal coowner of the Maison de Bonne Chance, and since her own attorney, Lopasuta Bouchard, is still missing, I authorize you, for her, to proceed. As soon as I see Mrs. Bouchard, I'll ask her to convey to you, in writing, formal power of attorney until such time as Lopasuta returns. Meanwhile, you may take my word of honor that she authorized me to act in her name."

"Of this I have no doubt whatsoever, Mr. Bouchard. Mr. Barntry has also informed me of the chicanery by which that nefarious man tried to fleece Mrs. Bouchard," the attorney agreed. "I plan to examine Mr. Brickley's books and question the employees at the casino. Very likely, it was just as you believed; he had paid confederates to pose as visitors and contrived with his dealers to let them win that staggering sum of money so that Mrs. Bouchard would be liable for half of the debts. Believe me, sir, if that is the case, the claim will not stand up in a court of law."

"Thank you, Mr. Minton. I will see to it, as soon as I turn to Windhaven Range, that you receive a separate retainer from me for your services on Mrs. Bouchard's behalf. If you are able to turn up the evidence we both are

362

certain can be found, once you complete your investigation at the casino, you may wire me at Windhaven Plantation, where I expect to remain for approximately one week. Then I shall be in transit back to Texas, and Jason will know how to reach me. Again, my appreciative thanks for all you've done. As for me, I leave for Windhaven Plantation tonight, to evict the new overseer before he can do any more damage, either to the land or to the name of Bouchard!"

# Thirty-Seven

Three mornings after the duel, having made excellent connections with the fastest steamboat on the Alabama River, Lucien Edmond disembarked at the dock of Windhaven Plantation and went directly to the red-brick chateau. He was admitted by Clementine Thornton, who exclaimed her delight at seeing Lucien Edmond again so soon. With a broad smile on her gentle face, she ushered him into the library at once, and then went to inform Laure that her stepson had returned from New Orleans. A few moments later, she entered, an anxious look on her lovely face. "What has happened, dear Lucien Edmond? You didn't send me a telegram, and I was so worried—"

"I apologize, Laure, but I've been rather strenuously occupied, straightening out your affairs with the bank, so that I might get back here quickly. Let me just say that in this case the old saw about no news being good news is certainly true; you have nothing more to fear from William Brickley."

Wasting few words, Lucien Edmond recounted the details of Brickley's vicious plot and explained how he had uncovered it. He alluded as briefly as possible to the duel, making light of it; nevertheless, Laure's face grew pale with fear upon learning that it had taken place.

"A duel? Oh, Lucien Edmond, you—you weren't hurt, were you?" she anxiously demanded.

"Thank God, no," he admitted with a wry smile. "My training fighting bandits in Texas served me in good stead. You might say that I fought Indian-style, and Mr. Brickley wasn't expecting it. So much for that—and now my only

364

great concern is finding Lopasuta. No, Laure"—he added quickly, seeing her gasp and step forward—"Brickley didn't tell me a thing, but left me with no doubt that he was responsible. With his dying breath, he cursed me and told me that I'd never find out what happened. All we can do is pray."

"I have done that already. Last night I walked up to Luke's grave and there I begged his forgiveness for having endangered all that he and his grandfather held so dear. Looking back, I can't understand how I could have been so gullible, Lucien Edmond."

"I can, Laure. You told me how Brickley had saved you from that mad dog; it was such an uncanny coincidence —so similar to what happened before, with Father—that you thought surely Brickley must be a trustworthy man. But I believe everything will run smoothly for you from now on—at least, it will as soon as I fire Brickley's collaborator, Danvers Willoughby. I'll stay on for a day or two to make sure that everything goes well from now on. And after I finish with Willoughby, I'd like your permission to have us both sit down with Marius Thornton and give him the position he justly deserves."

She made a helpless gesture. "I know now how wrong I was. By all means, I want to give him the job as overseer."

"Good! And now, if you'll excuse me, I'm going out to discharge that scoundrel so that Marius can take his place as quickly as possible," Lucien Edmond grinned.

"You won't find Mr. Willoughby in the fields, Lucien Edmond," Laure confided with a nervous little laugh. "He's sulking in his room, I'm afraid."

"No doubt that's the product of a guilty conscience. But, so much the better! I'll have him out of here all the sooner," was Lucien Edmond's comment, as, bowing in respect to his stepmother, he turned and went up the stairs in search of William Brickley's egocentric cohort.

The door to Danvers Willoughby's quarters was closed, and Lucien Edmond peremptorily knocked. After a moment, a rather petulant voice responded, "Oh, very well, you've awakened me, so you might as well come in."

Lucien Edmond turned the knob of the door and entered. He saw Willoughby lounging at his ease on the four-postered, canopied bed, and barked out, "Have the

365

decency to get to your feet when I talk to you! On your feet, man!"

"Very well, Mr. Bouchard, but I must say—"

"You will say what I expect you to, Willoughby, and what's more, you're going to reveal a few truths. Come on—get up, I said!"

"All right, all right. I don't understand why you're so dreadfully angry, Mr. Bouchard, I've done nothing—" Willoughby slipped his legs down to the floor and rose, tottering a moment, then yawned. "I really don't understand what has upset you so—"

"First off, your friend and employer William Brickley is dead," Lucien Edmond angrily interrupted, as he approached the Englishman.

"D-dead?" Willoughby gasped incredulously.

"Precisely. He died in the course of a duel to which he had the bad judgment to challenge me—but not before confessing the scurrilous scheme to defraud Mrs. Bouchard. Your part, aside from gross mismanagement, was, I'm quite certain, to arrange to have those night-riders descend upon us at midnight!"

"But I assure you—stop—what are you doing—ouch, you—you've fair broken my jaw—help!" for, as Willoughby had lifted his hand to protest, Lucien Edmond, unable to contain himself any longer, had stepped forward and sent his right fist smashing into the Englishman's jaw, toppling him to the floor.

"Get up and take your medicine! I'm going to thrash you until you admit everything that you've done here! Do you understand me? On your feet, I told you!"

"Please—I—I can't stand p-pain—Mr. Bouchard, I—I couldn't help myself—I was into Brickley for a great deal of money, you understand, and he told me I could get out of my debts and have sufficient monies left over to—perhaps to go back to England, if—if I'd play along with him."

As Lucien Edmond bent down to stare menacingly at the crestfallen and cowering dandy, Danvers Willoughby uttered a sob like a terrified child and covered his face with his hands to protect himself from any further blows. "I implore you! Don't hit me any more! Don't you see I'm down? I'm no match for you, sir!" he whimpered.

"You're a disgusting specimen! All right, then, admit

366

your part in this. Isn't it true that Brickley and you arranged that, at a proper time, you'd have men dressed as Klansmen attack us when we weren't prepared for it? Quickly, or I'll beat the truth out of you, so help me!"

"Yes—yes, I—I couldn't help myself, I told you—but I didn't think they'd kill anybody—honest to God, Mr. Bouchard, I swear I didn't! I told them—that is to say, I said—I said they were just to set a few fires and then leave. But they—they were too enthusiastic—"

"Indeed they were. The only thing that balanced the account of poor Moses Turner's death is that some of those cowardly, skulking rogues died along with him. But that doesn't excuse your part in this. What you did was criminal, but you're too pitiable to send to prison, Willoughby. Pack your things and be out of this house before half an hour is gone, or I'll kick you each foot of the way, until you're past the door. Get on with it!"

"I will—I'll do anything, if you only won't—if you only won't hit me again, Mr. B-Bouchard," Willoughby sniveled.

"You're a yellow coward, so I wouldn't get any satisfaction from thrashing you as you deserve. One last thing— what do you know about Lopasuta Bouchard?"

"I swear, as God is my witness, all Mr. Brickley told me was that he would take care of that interfering lawyer— those were his very words. He didn't tell me what he was going to do—"

"I believe that for once, you're telling the truth. All right, you've got your half hour, and you'd best not stay beyond it, unless you want to try my patience."

Turning on his heel, Lucien Edmond strode back to Laure. "I've got rid of your overseer, so nothing stands in the way of elevating Marius Thornton to the post, as we agreed. It may be true that he doesn't have the book learning of this cowardly fop I just discharged for you, but I think he can run the plantation very well, and you don't need to go looking for some stranger to do it for you. If you ever need me, Laure, I can always arrange to come back to Windhaven Plantation and spend some time with the workers—but my feeling is that Marius had handle it very nicely."

"Yes, I—I guess I was so overcome by your father's death, Lucien Edmond, that I wasn't thinking clearly. I

367

should have realized Marius could handle the work, and I should have tried harder to make him see that, too. I'm very grateful to you—I can't possibly express it in words."

He took her in his arms and kissed her forehead and gently said, "There's no need for thanks between us. I'm in your debt, not you in mine; you gave my father great happiness and joy—his letters told me of this. I respect and admire and love you, and I always shall."

She clung to him, weeping, but this time in relief, feeling a kind of benign solace after all her tribulations and despair.

Presently he said, "It goes without saying that you needn't worry any more about being in debt to Brickley or his estate for the money lost at your casino. Hollis Minton is investigating that, and he's going to wire me, but I'm very sure that you'll become the sole owner now that Brickley is dead, unless he's left some heirs I know nothing about. If you wish, I'll have Jason Barntry pick a good, loyal man who will manage your end of the casino in return for a small profit and a decent wage."

"Of course, Lucien Edmond, do whatever you think best."

"I'll try. Well then, I'll head back to Texas in a day or so and I'll stop in New Orleans to make certain that things are in proper order once again."

She took a handkerchief and dried her tears. And then, in a low, trembling voice, she said, "God bless you, Lucien Edmond. And I promise I'll rely on you again in the future, and not make the mistake of believing I can do everything Luke used to do, single-handedly. No one could do that."

"You mustn't deprecate yourself that way, Laure—you were blinded by grief, but you are a very intelligent, able woman. You'll manage just fine, I'm sure. And now I think it's time I began preparing for my journey back to Texas and to Maxine—you know, she's going to have another baby at the end of the year."

They clung together again, and Laure gave him an ineffable look of gratitude.

It was the last week of September 1877. Milo Brutus Henson had learned of the death of William Brickley, as well as that of David Fales, through articles in the New

Orleans *Times-Picayune*, to which he subscribed. He swore violently, and then brightened. There was still no word from Lopasuta Bouchard, so at least Brickley had succeeded in getting that accursed adopted son of Luke Bouchard out of Montgomery. If he hadn't, the surveyor reasoned, Lopasuta would have returned by now and it would have been mentioned in the Montgomery *Advertiser*. It was just as well. Indeed, it was not without feeling a certain relief that he learned of Brickley's death: that powerful, sinister man could no longer exert a hold upon him, nor could he or Fales blackmail him by disclosing the plot in which the two of them had participated. And of course, with Brickley dead and no letters of communication between them on record anywhere—they had always used their agreed-upon code in any communications in the past—there was no way that he, Milo Brutus Henson, would ever have to fear a future accounting with Lopasuta Bouchard, or the heirs of that nigger-loving scalawag, Luke Bouchard. And as for Carleton Ivers—well, he was sure he had nothing to fear from that quarter. After all, Ivers was too much the respected businessman here in Montgomery, and the last thing he would ever do would be to say or do anything that would damage his own reputation.

Milo Brutus Henson thought to himself that perhaps one day, since there was nothing really left in Montgomery for him to do and since the Alabama and Chattanooga Railroad was a dead issue, he might take his latest mistress and move out to California. There, he could live the life of a pasha, beholden to no one and accountable to no one, either. Nothing really mattered to him any more except enjoying the pleasures of the flesh for what years he had left. Besides, it would appear that under the righteous President Rutherford B. Hayes, the chances to turn a few dishonest dollars were being minimized. And, for the time being, anyway, his zest for risky undertakings had begun to wane. No, assuredly, it was better to make plans for the future in some other state besides impoverished Alabama.

# Thirty-Eight

As Lucien Edmond prepared for his homeward journey, he had no way of knowing that the Gulf coast of his adopted state was about to be buffeted by the forces of nature. During the last week of September, a powerful storm, originating in the West Indies, was reported from Miami. A telegrapher there, somewhat sheltered in his office from the violent winds that toppled towering palm trees and blew horse-drawn carriages along with them to crash in parks and into houses, frantically sent out his message in Morse code, until suddenly the wall of the building in which he was working started to give way and he was forced to flee.

His message was received by an amateur telegrapher in Atlanta and relayed to the Northern cities, as well as to Gulf seaports such as New Orleans and Mobile. But by then the storm—carrying winds of a hundred miles an hour—was destined to bypass those cities and concentrate its fury upon the Texas coast.

By four o'clock on the following afternoon, the skies were ominously dark and there was a terrible stillness around Galveston, which occupied about six square miles of an island off the coastline, extending twenty-seven miles east and west, and seven miles at its greatest width from north and south.

Nearing Galveston, after embarking from New Orleans, the steamboat *Clorinda Mae*, heavily laden with goods for Charles Douglas's stores in Galveston and Houston, tried to reach port. But by now, the winds had gathered momentum, and the *Clorinda Mae* was hurled upon a shoal about twenty-five miles from its destination, where it foundered. The stevedores put down a skiff and tried to get to safety, but the skimpy boat capsized before they could reach shore, and seven of the crew, including the young captain, were drowned. The *Clorinda Mae* itself sank with all its cargo aboard.

A shrewdly practical merchant, Charles Douglas had begun to cut costs and lower inventory after the 1873 panic so as not to incur great losses. The goods aboard the sunken steamboat were to have replenished both stores for the oncoming holiday season; by the caprice of nature, he had just lost ten thousand dollars in new merchandise, leaving him in financial straits until the following year.

Back in Chicago, where there was no news of the tropical hurricane, Charles and Laurette, together with the children and their nurse, gaily greeted Charles's partner, Lawrence Harding, and his reddish-blond-haired wife, Sylvia. This dinner was a very special occasion because Sylvia, now nearing forty, had just given birth to her first son—after two daughters—whom she and Lawrence had christened Alfred, after her own beloved father, who had died in his sleep just six months ago. Before dinner, the two men had discussed the possibility of opening still another Texas store, perhaps this one in Dallas or Fort Worth, or even in the state capital of Austin. The Chicago venture was doing very well indeed, and Lawrence suggested, "Perhaps, Charles, it might be more sensible to think of another store in the Hyde Park area of Chicago, which is beginning to boom now as a residential area for the well-to-do."

"I'll certainly think about it. But one of these days, I'd like you to come down to Galveston and Houston with me and see how well we're doing there. Then you'd catch Texas fever for sure, as I did," Charles enthusiastically declared.

The winds had begun to sweep down upon Galveston Island. In their home, Arabella and Joy saw the sky darkening and then heard a strange moaning sound from the southeast. "Mama, it's so awfully dark—and what's that awful sound, Mama?" Joy put her arms around her mother's waist and anxiously looked up.

"It must be a storm of some kind, darling. Don't worry,

it'll blow over," Arabella hopefully answered. All the same, she turned her head in the direction of that ominous sound, which seemed to grow louder now. Suddenly there was a jagged flash of lightning in the sky, and the windows were illumined with a ghastly brightness.

"Oh Mama, I'm afraid! And—oh my—hear how hard the rain is falling against the windows!" Joy tearfully exclaimed, as she hugged her mother even more convulsively in her fright.

Alexander Gorth had decided to close his shop early. There had been almost no customers since one o'clock, and he hadn't liked the look of the sky. He locked the doors and hurried down the street toward the little house he had been able to buy a few months ago, thanks to his earnings in the store that Henry McNamara had sold to him for a virtual pittance. He chuckled to himself when he recalled how McNamara—so certain that the store would fail under Alexander's management—had made him a sporting offer: if the shop was still in business in six months, then Alexander could forget about making any further payments, and the store would be his. Well, he'd sure called McNamara's bluff, and he remembered how proud Katie had been when, exactly six months later, McNamara had been forced to send him back the paper the two of them had signed outlining the agreement.

Alexander and Katie had been married almost four years, and now that Katie was pregnant again, Alexander hoped their second child would be a boy. Their daughter, Jennifer, now nearly three and red-haired like her mother, was staying in Austin with Alexander's second cousin, Ethan.

Just last month, one of Ethan's twins had died of pneumonia after contracting a summer chill, and Ethan and his distraught wife, Jacqueline, had come to visit Alexander and Katie. In the course of their visit, Ethan had taken Alexander aside and asked if little Jennifer could come to stay with him and Jacqueline in Austin for a while. "It would ease my poor wife's grief," he had said, "to have another little one in the house—just for a bit—until she gets over this. You can't imagine how it's been for both of us, with Susan gone. Jacqueline needs someone else to look after, someone who depends on her and can take her out of herself."

Alexander had been understandably reluctant to agree to Ethan's request, because several years earlier, when Ethan and Jacqueline still lived in Galveston, they had haughtily refused to help Alexander following the death of his parents. Jacqueline had just had the twins at the time, and they said they didn't want another mouth to feed.

But Katie, compassionate Irish girl that she was, had urged her husband to let bygones be bygones, and Alexander had at last relented. And now, though he missed his saucy, red-haired daughter, Alexander was secretly pleased to be alone with his Katie in their little house, as they had been that wonderful day when they were married, and they had come back from the church and made love for the first time. . . .

He had never been so happy in his life. Katie was a treasure, and she had given him back all his confidence as a man. The acne that had plagued him in earlier years had vanished, along with his nervousness and insecurity. All of his fears had evaporated, and it was Katie's love that had accomplished the miracle. He often went down on his knees late at night after she had fallen asleep to thank God for the blessings vouchsafed him.

As he entered the house and moved toward the kitchen, where Katie was preparing lamb stew for dinner, his wife exclaimed, "You're home early, Alex dear."

"I know, honey. There's going to be an awful storm. Good gosh! You can hear that wind moaning way off there in the Gulf! It's coming closer all the time—and now just listen to that rain! If big waves start hitting along with that heavy rain—I don't even want to think about what might happen!"

"What can we do, Alex?" Katie dropped the ladle into the stew pot and anxiously turned to her husband.

"If a hurricane really hits here, Katie, the streets will be flooded, and I don't know how high the water will get. It could be enough to drown everybody. Listen, I've got an idea. There's a rowboat in front of the shed next door—"

"But it doesn't belong to us, honey," Katie protested.

"I know that, but Mr. Callison is off in California visiting his kinfolks, and he's not due back until November.

373

I'll just borrow it. If the water starts flooding up to here, Katie, a lot of people are going to be in danger. And I'm not going to let anything happen to you, especially now that you've got my son—"

"Oh, you're already sure it's going to be a boy, Alex, are you?" she giggled, and gave him a quick kiss that made him sigh with delight. Her face instantly sobering, she murmured tenderly, "The nicest thing that ever happened to me, my sweet Alex, was when you came running up to the bakery that day and asked me out to dinner. The other girls thought I was daft for going with you, but I'm so very glad I did. You're the sweetest man, the best husband, and the best lover any girl could ever want, and I want you to know that."

"Oh, Katie, Katie," Alexander's voice was tight with emotion, as he hugged her, "Yes, it's going to be a boy. And we'll name him after your father, Patrick."

Even as he spoke, another savage flash of lightning seared the leaden sky, followed by a furious crash of thunder. The rain intensified its force, slashing against the windows, and he heard the crackling of glass. "It's getting real bad, Katie, but all we can do is wait and see what happens. You know, I just happened to think about that Mrs. Hunter, just she and her little girl alone in that big, fine house. You remember—her husband was a partner in Charles Douglas's big store before he died."

"Yes, I remember. She's a grand lady. Wasn't there something in the paper a few weeks ago about her donating a sum of money to the opera?" Katie asked, wincing as another deafening clap of thunder resounded, seeming to shake the house itself. "Oh my goodness, Alex, now I will admit I'm getting a little scared. And that's not usual for me. This is a really special storm, this one is."

"You're right, honey. If that stew's ready we might just as well eat a little bit now. I figure we might not have time later on, and we'll need our strength if that storm really floods the city. We're only about two miles from the Gulf itself, you know, and Mrs. Hunter's place is about four blocks south of here, she'd get it first," Alexander declared.

"Do you think the hurricane could damage our store, Alex?" Katie nervously faltered.

He grinned with the confidence of youth as he put his arm around her shoulders. "Never you mind, honey. If it did, we'd just patch it up and carry on. And even if it was carried out to sea, what would it matter, really? We're young, and we have our whole lives ahead of us. I love you, and I'd lick my weight in wildcats for you and Jennifer—and our boy."

"I never saw such a man so sure that his unborn child was going to be a boy," Katie giggled, as she put her hands on her hips and made a face at him. Then, instantly serious, she hugged him and murmured, "I'll get our dinner right off. You know, I'm sort of glad we didn't have another child right away after I had Jennifer—although to tell you the truth, I wanted one. You were like a granny, saying we shouldn't have another until we had plenty of money in the bank."

"I know. And I'm not sorry. Like I said, we're still very young. We can have a flock of kids—that is, if you've a mind to."

Katie blushed and then turned back to the stew and began to ladle it out into the bowls she had set upon the kitchen table. "I hope Jennie'll be all right—do you think she'll be in this storm, Alex?" she asked.

Alexander smiled reassuringly at his wife. "I doubt it, honey. Austin's a long way from the coast, and most of these Gulf storms blow themselves out once they get over land. Don't fret, she'll be fine." Then, to lighten the mood, he demanded peremptorily, "Now then, Mrs. Gorth, how about some of that nice bread you baked last night? It's as good as what I used to get at Gottlieb's. In fact, I'll tell you a secret—I married you because I knew *you* were responsible for Gottlieb's delicious bread!" He grinned and kissed her again as they sat down to supper.

But even as they ate their supper, Alexander and Katie could hear a new sound, even more terrifying: the thunderous crash of waves to the south as the ferocious winds drove the water in Galveston Bay against the island.

"I—I can't eat any more, Alex," Katie quavered, suddenly afraid. "Do you really think we ought to leave the house?"

"If that sound's what I think it is, honey, we'd better go and see about that rowboat before we don't have any time

375

left to do it. This island is practically at sea level, and when the waves roll in, they won't take long to flood most of the island," Alexander gravely informed his frightened wife. "You'd better take along anything you really value, just in case."

"You—you mean the house might be completely flooded? All the way over the roof?" Katie incredulously gasped.

"It could happen. I wish they'd built a seawall or something—this little island is so vulnerable out here with nothing but the Gulf to the south of it and very little protection at the north end. Go ahead, what about that music box your mother gave you?"

"Oh, yes—I'd just die if I lost that—I'll hurry and get it, Alex. And my clothes—"

"Don't worry about those. I've got a feeling we might have to use all the space in the rowboat for saving people, if this really gets bad. And clothes get awfully heavy when they're wet. Now you go get the music box."

At this, Katie, though distraught, gave him a hearty kiss on the cheek, then ran off to her bedroom to get the music box.

The waves had already begun to roll into the south end of the city, flooding the basements of the elegant houses in that district. The occupants had fled, taking what possessions they could carry. Some of them frantically strove to lead rearing, terrified horses out of their stables to hitch them to buggies, but many of the horses bolted and ran blindly down the water-soaked streets. There was a wash of two feet of water now, and more was coming, as the crash of waves resounded again and again, the wind unrelenting in its fury.

In a nearby Catholic boarding school, four Sisters of Mercy did their best to soothe the terrified children in their dormitory. Finally, in despair, the Mother Superior decided that they should seek refuge in the cathedral, which was the highest point in the city of Galveston. She instructed the older children to run with her as fast as they could toward the cathedral; meanwhile, the other three sisters went in search of ropes and bound the smallest children to them, then led them in a procession through the wind and rain. They began to pray as another flash of lightning and clap of thunder resounded. And then suddenly a giant wave, cresting over the little group, inundated them, and they were lost from view. A block away, the Mother Superior, hearing their faint screams, crossed herself and tearfully prayed aloud as she urged the older children on.

Now it was a city of darkness, for the citizens had extinguished their kerosene lamps and their gas, terrified that there might be explosions or fires caused by the flooding. Arabella Hunter and Joy, petrified with fear, had hurried up to the second floor of their house and there knelt to say prayers that they could barely hear over the wailing of the winds and the creaking of timbers. A window in the western bedroom suddenly shattered, and the full fury of the wind entered, as if to ferret out the two helpless occupants. Arabella clutched her daughter to her and raised her tear-filled eyes heavenward, as she prayed for deliverance.

The relentless wind and the frightening waves driven before it from the Gulf were covering more and more of the island. Alexander and Katie Gorth had left their house and found the rowboat already floating in two feet of water that covered the area as far as the eye could see. He had just time enough to catch it by a rope dangling from its stern before it was driven away by the force of the wind. They clambered into it and took the oars, dipping them into the murky, brackish water. "I'm going to try to row over to Mrs. Hunter's house, Katie," he called to his trembling young wife, as another clap of thunder crashed over them. "It's likely to be a lot deeper over there, and they could be trapped in their house. Don't worry, honey, I've got strength enough to row, and nothing's going to happen, I just know it."

She nodded, her fists clenched, looking imploringly up at the dark sky. Now, at least, the thunderstorm had stopped, although the winds continued unabated and the flood waters still were rising. As she glanced down the street, she gasped at the sight of bleak, dark houses, which seemed to be more like mausoleums than dwellings, with not a light showing anywhere.

Alexander began to row with all his young strength, and

the water had already risen another two feet. As he passed Elston Street, Katie cried out, "Look, there's a poor old woman with her cat on that roof! Alex, you have to save her!"

He craned his neck to look and nodded, then bent to the oars and redoubled his efforts. It was a small, dingy cottage, and the sixty-year-old widow who owned it had lost her husband, a packet captain in his day, in just such a hurricane as this fifteen years before.

"Poor old soul—just look, Alex, she must have dragged that heavy ladder out and put it up against the wall and climbed up to the roof," Katie commiserated, as the rowboat neared the cottage.

Alexander did not have time to answer, straining at the oars as he did. Gratefully, he observed that the wind seemed to have died down, or it might well have buffeted the small, though sturdy, rowboat away from its goal. At last, he came up to where the ladder stood by the side of the cottage, and Katie beckoned to the frightened, white-haired woman. "Climb down and get in! Hurry!" she called.

Swiftly pulling one of the oars over to the side and holding it in the lock, Alexander extended his right arm and seized the old woman's hand, virtually dragging her into the rowboat. The cat, a large Maltese, uttered a terrified meow, as it leaped out of her grasp and perched on the side of the rowboat. Viewing the water lapping about, it turned and hid itself at the bottom of the boat as close to its elderly mistress as it could, howling in piteous fright.

"The wind's not so bad, I think we can make it down to Mrs. Hunter's place, Katie," Alexander shouted as he lifted the right-hand oar and dipped it back into the water, then began to pull with all his might.

As they neared the street on which the Hunters lived, Katie and Alexander could see the desolation wrought by the hurricane. At least six feet of water inundated the southernmost streets, and the starkly outlined upper expanses of the houses were visible, as if they were individual islands rising out of the yellowish, churning water. The winds had spewed up the sands from the bottom of the bay and spattered many of the houses with a grim, ochre patina.

378

"There's the Hunter house!" Alexander triumphantly cried, as he steered the rowboat toward it. "My God, the first floor's half submerged already! Look, Katie, there's an open window. I'll head for it!"

It was the window to the west that had been blown in, and he reached it and leaned to his left, shouting, "Mrs. Hunter, Mrs. Hunter, it's Alexander Gorth—you know, I've got that small shop. . . . If you're in there, you and your daughter, come on out this way, I've got a boat for you!"

"Mama, Mama, it's a man with a boat—oh, Mama, hurry, please, I don't want us to drown, please let's see where it is, Mama," Joy wept. Arabella Hunter staggered to her feet and, taking Joy by the hand, hurried toward the open window, trying to avoid the shards of glass.

"Thank God, oh, thank God," she sobbed. "Can you keep the boat steady there? I'll hand Joy down to you, and then I'll get in."

"Sure I can, Mrs. Hunter—I thought you and your daughter might be here—there now, Katie honey, can you just try to hold the oars a minute while I get the girl— there we are—I've got her!"

The rowboat had now swung away a little toward the west, and Alexander hastily took the oars again and turned the rowboat back up under the window as best he could. "Now you, Mrs. Hunter! It's a sturdy boat, thank heavens for that. Just clamber in any old which way— there now—all right now, we'll head for the cathedral!"

Arabella had unceremoniously flung herself out of the window, but she was safe, and Joy, weeping now in gratitude over their salvation, helped her mother regain an upright posture in the rowboat.

"The worst is over, sounds like." Alexander cocked his head toward the south and listened. "The wind is dying down. We'll make it fine. Once we get as far as the cathedral, there won't be any danger of drowning or anything. But your husband's store, Mrs. Hunter, and mine too, I'm afraid will probably have to have a big damaged-goods sale, once this mess is all cleared up."

"Don't you worry about that, Mr. Gorth." Arabella began to laugh through her tears, as she hugged Joy to her. "I suspect Charles Douglas, my husband's partner, will get down here once he hears about the hurricane, and he'll have things fixed up right enough."

"But he probably won't be able to get here for a few days, and, you know, I'm sure a lot of his merchandise could be salvaged if it's gotten to quickly enough. Tell you what I'll do," he offered. "Just as soon as I've cleaned up my own store a bit, I'll go over to Mr. Douglas's and help out. I've got pretty good judgment about what can be rescued from the trash bin," he chuckled, "and I'd be glad to help out. I'm sure Mr. Douglas's losses are going to be mighty big, so if I can reduce them even a little bit, it'll be of some comfort."

"You're a dear man, Mr. Gorth," Arabella declared, "and Mr. Douglas will help you, too—you wait and see! And I'm certainly going to tell him how you saved my little girl's life and mine. God bless you!" Then, turning to Katie, she asked, "You're Mrs. Gorth, I assume?"

"Oh, yes, Mrs. Hunter, I'm Katie, and I'm pleased to meet you, even under these dreadful circumstances!" Katie tried self-consciously to smooth her wet, rumpled skirt about her shivering legs. Old Mrs. Nealey sat huddled beside her, crooning to her cat. Still crouched against her leg, it continually hissed its distaste over the inclement weather and the inconvenience of having to quit the comfortable pillow beside its mistress's favorite armchair.

Alexander cheerfully called, "Look, I think the water's starting to go down. And I don't hear the crash of waves any more. Boy, we certainly were lucky! But I sure hope they build a seawall here that'll prevent this from happening again. I don't even want to think how many people might have drowned in this flood. And imagine the damage to all the houses, the businesses, and the schools and everything."

"Yes, Alex," Katie spoke up, forcing a wan smile to her pretty face. "I think it's right and proper we should row over to the cathedral. And when we get there, I'm going to say a prayer of thanks to Him for saving people from storms like this—and for saving me too, so I can give you the son you want, Alex honey!" Then, aware that she had touched upon a highly intimate subject, she turned a most becoming crimson. But Arabella, her own fears now overcome, uttered a joyous laugh and hugged the pretty Irish girl. "I promise you, Katie Gorth," she declared, "that I'll

380

have Charles Douglas set the boy up with a bassinet and all the clothes he'll need for the next few years, you just see if I don't. And if you'll let me, I'd be proud to be at his christening."

## Thirty-Nine

Friar Bartoloméo Alicante had felt the weight of his years as an increasingly onerous burden this spring. The brutal tarring and feathering he had endured at the hands of the comancheros four years ago when he had been living with a band of Penateka Comanches near Big Spring, had done no lasting damage. But at sixty-three years old, though his spirit remained strong, his health had begun to fail. After his abduction by the Comancheros, he had come to Sangrodo's stronghold and lived there, teaching Christianity to the peaceful braves, instructing the children of the Mexican mothers in their first catechism and communion. And though he was dearly loved by this now-peaceful tribe whose dead chief had once been one of the most feared warriors among the Wanderers, he was beginning to think that his days of usefulness were numbered.

That was why, in May of this year of 1877, having learned that there was a younger and more tolerant new bishop in Santa Fe, Friar Bartoloméo had written a letter detailing his missionary work among the Indians and his earlier experiences in Santa Fe, where his dedicated service had enraged the affluent and arrogant Spanish families who had demanded his removal. He had asked the new bishop to send a young priest to the stronghold of Sangrodo to replace him, that his own efforts might be continued. "It has been said, most reverend Bishop," he had written, "that the Comanche are the most feared *indios* in all of the Southwest. And so they were, because their lands were stolen from them, their buffalo herds slaughtered to drive them away, so that the railroads might extend the white man's settlements. And all this was done cruelly, so as to render the *indios* helpless. Yet these people of Sangrodo's, I swear to you by my hope of God's grace, have exchanged the lance and the arrow for the plow and the spade. They grow their own crops, they are at peace, they think of their families, and they are concerned with the education of their children who will one day replace them. Some, like a brave named Lopasuta—who was adopted by Luke Bouchard of Windhaven Plantation in Alabama and is now an attorney who champions the downtrodden—have brought honor and fame to this tribe. You, most reverend Bishop, a Franciscan, as I also am humbly proud to be, know the virtue of helping the indigent and the needy and renouncing selfish material gains. Just so, I implore you to send someone who is young in flesh and eager in spirit to spread the blessed teachings of our dear Lord. I am not strong enough to do this daily work, though my spirit remains unquenched in the service of Him who watches even the fall of a sparrow from the heavens."

By July, a letter had come from Santa Fe informing Friar Bartoloméo that a young priest, Friar Jorge Mendoza, a man in his mid-thirties, had asked for the assignment to the stronghold of Sangrodo and would arrive in early August.

Kitante, Sangrodo's son and now the chief of the tribe, had taken instructions from Friar Bartoloméo and had become a devout Catholic. His lovely young wife, Carmencita, had been overjoyed to be able to go to mass again and to receive communion from the aging friar. She had not forgotten the horror of the old days, when her bandit father had forced her to ride away with him—abandoning her dying mother. Nor had she forgotten how he had taken her to a neighboring village and there made her wait, while he forced a priest at gunpoint to marry him to a young wanton of the town. Carmencita had feared for her immortal soul because of this sacrilege, and when Kitante had rescued her from the bandits and the cruelty of her stepmother, she had thanked God for His mercy. It delighted her that her stalwart husband, who had saved her by dueling her father's most skillful lieutenant and winning her freedom, had taken the vows and now knelt beside her to receive Friar Bartoloméo's blessing. And to crown her happiness, she was pregnant again. This time, she hoped, it would be a daughter to be a companion to their little son.

The new priest came during the first week of September to the little Mexican village that had become the stronghold for Sangrodo's peaceful tribe, and was tearfully welcomed by his predecessor. Together, the two celebrated a mass for all the villagers, and Kitante and Carmencita knelt holding hands, as they joyously joined in the ritual of the mass.

"Where will you go, *mi padre*?" Carmencita inquired at the end of the service, after she and Kitante had enthusiastically welcomed the new priest.

"I had thought of going to Windhaven Range, my daughter," the portly old Franciscan replied. "I want to visit the chapel that I dedicated years ago for that good man, Lucien Edmond Bouchard. There are vaqueros there for whom I will say mass and listen to their confessions, and it will strengthen me, weak as I now feel myself to be. For the eternal word of Him who created us is forever a joy, and yet I, knowing my own sins as a young man, feel the weariness of age and infirmity. That is why it was time for me to leave, my daughter. Father Mendoza is a good, kind man, and I believe that he has the same sympathy I do for the *indios* whom so many *gringos* consider little more than savages."

"My *mujer linda* and I should like to go with you to Windhaven Range, *mi padre*," Kitante spoke up, his arm around Carmencita's shoulders. "She will not have her child until the beginning of next year, so why do we not all go together, and take two of my best warriors to accompany us, as escorts. It is not a long journey, and I long to see Catayuna, the beloved woman."

"I, too, my son. Yes," Friar Bartoloméo's face lighted up, "I shall never forget her courage and how she won great love and honor among strange and alien people, when she had believed her life was over. I know now that to judge an *indio* as a savage simply because he is an *indio* is intolerant and hateful. And these prejudices, my son, of intolerance and hatred, destroy the hope we have of an eternal brotherhood of mankind. Thank you for wanting to come with me, my son, and you, my daughter. I will bless you both before we undertake the journey.

The next morning, Kitante, Carmencita, Miraldo—a warrior of twenty-six and an expert with bow and lance—and Rimado, another brave, set out for Windhaven Range with the old friar. Rimado's young Mexican wife, who had recently borne their first daughter, had eagerly agreed to stay behind to care for Carmencita's little son during her absence.

On the second day of their journey, just before they reached the Rio Grande, Kitante drew on his mustang's reins to halt the spirited animal as he pointed eastward. "A wagon train, *mi linda*! I want to see what it is. One does not often see such wagons south of the Rio Grande."

"That is true," Carmencita agreed, her eyes wide with curiosity. "It cannot be *gringo* settlers, surely?"

"I am certain that it is not. But we shall not know until we ride up to them. *¡Adelante!*" He lifted his right hand as a signal to his braves to ride forward with him, telling Carmencita to remain beside the old priest, and the three Comanches galloped up toward the two bulky weapons, each drawn by two pairs of sturdy, brown workhorses. As Kitante neared the wagon, he uttered a surprised cry: "They are women, *monjas*!" Then, turning to Rimado, he said wonderingly, "Do you see how they are dressed in black? They are the holy ones, the *religiosas*, who teach the *niños* and who help the poor. Do not frighten them—do not show your guns and your bows as we ride up to them."

With this, the three Comanches rode slowly up to the wagons, and then Kitante moved ahead to the foremost wagon, driven by a tall, gaunt-faced, white-haired woman in the black robes of a nun.

"Do not be afraid, sister," Kitante said in Spanish, with a friendly smile. "My men and I saw your wagons and wondered how it was that you were traveling in this direction. One does not usually see wagons this side of the Rio Grande, unless they are being used to bring trade goods, either to Chihuahua or up to Santa Fe and Taos."

"You are an *indio*, are you not, my son?" The white-haired lady drew in the reins and made the horses come to a halt, as she smilingly turned to contemplate Kitante.

385

"And yet you speak excellent Spanish. Also, you are of our faith, for you called me 'sister,' did you not? I am Sister Martha."

"And I am Kitante, *jefe* of the Comanche. Our stronghold is in Mexico now because we did not want war with the white-eyes. We have with us a holy man, Friar Bartoloméo Alicante. He will be very happy to see you. But tell me, Sister Martha, where do you go?"

"Alas, it is a long story, Señor Kitante. These two wagons contain twenty-five nuns and I am their Mother Superior," the white-haired woman replied in fluent Spanish. "We are called the Sisters of the *Indios* because it is our wish to work with *indios* and *peones* who have taken the holy vows of our faith. It was my hope to set up a mission and to grow our own crops and even build our own simple quarters. You see, my son, the nuns with me are mostly daughters of farmers and landholders, and a great many of them came from the provinces of Durango and Chihuahua."

"And you, Sister Martha?" Kitante asked with interest.

"My story is a simple one, my son. I was born across the sea, in England, and when my mother died, I came to this country with my father, who was a teacher. We lived in Ohio; then my father died, some twenty years ago, and I was left alone. Shortly afterward, I met a Spaniard from Madrid who had emigrated to America. We fell in love, and I adopted his faith in Catholicism; then, after a year of marriage, my husband decided to go to Mexico City where I, of course, followed him."

Kitante listened raptly, for he admired this old, yet remarkably energetic woman who had had so adventurous a life. He nodded sympathetically. "And then, Sister Martha?"

"Then, after we had been married some three years, my husband became involved in a senseless duel, and I saw him die before my eyes. More alone than ever before, I joined the convent in Mexico City, took my final vows, and finally, two years ago, was appointed Mother Superior of a group. And these are the nuns I bring with me now, seeking to find some land where we may settle. For we are called by God to lead lives of service, not only to subsist in our own humble way, but to be with those who need our help."

"Let me bring Friar Bartoloméo Alicante to talk with you, Sister Martha," Kitante urged. Then, to his two braves, he ordered, "Remain here and guard them, while I bring the *padre*."

Galloping back to the friar, Kitante quickly explained the identity of the woman who was driving the foremost wagon, and Friar Bartoloméo's eyes shone with joy, as he exclaimed, "But this is a fateful omen indeed, my son! We go to the hacienda of a good, God-fearing man who treats his vaqueros as if they were his family, and I believe that he will be equally glad to receive these good sisters. Yes, my son, I will go talk with her at once!"

So saying, the aging friar gently urged his horse forward, until he rode up abreast of the driver's seat of the first wagon and, making the sign of the cross, introduced himself to the white-haired woman. "Sister Martha, I am Friar Bartoloméo Alicante. For some years now, I have lived with the Comanche, whose young chief you have just met. I feel the burden of my years upon me, and he and his young wife are taking me to a hacienda just across the Rio Grande, owned by a man who is also of our faith. It is my thought, Sister Martha, that this man will welcome you and perhaps help you find a place for your mission. And it is possible that you could have much to offer him—there are always the children of the vaqueros needing instruction, and there is a chapel that I myself dedicated some years ago. I believe you will be warmly welcomed."

"It is kind of you to tell me of this, Friar Bartoloméo. I must confess," the white-haired woman said with a soft little laugh, "that we have traveled many days and many miles in search of a place that would take us in. But the landholders, though they are Catholic, too, do not wish nuns near them—they fear we may corrupt their peons by teaching them the gentle love of human brotherhood. Those men would rather keep their workers in ignorance and serfdom."

"That is true, Sister Martha. But I tell you and I know from my own experiences that Señor Lucien Edmond Bouchard, who owns this hacienda of which I speak, is good at heart and humble in his thanks to our dear Lord for the blessings extended to him. He is beloved by all his

387

workers because of this. Will you not let me guide you to him?" The friar smiled appealingly.

"I am grateful to you, Friar Bartoloméo. We have had bad luck these last few months, even as Joseph and Mary did when they sought a resting place where Mary might bring forth the Holy Infant, and I will gladly go with you and speak with this man of good will. The Lord has shown us infinite mercy in directing us so that our paths have crossed."

With this, Sister Martha made the sign of the cross, and the women with her bowed their heads and murmured a rejoicing prayer.

Because of the dreadful reports of the hurricane, which had reached New Orleans, Lucien Edmond Bouchard had lain over in the Queen City for three days, until the storm had passed, then had proceeded without difficulty to take a boat to Corpus Christi. When he reached that city, he found that the storm had inflicted much damage—though in fact it was less than the damage that had been caused in Galveston. But when he at last rode his horse through the gate at Windhaven Range, Lucien Edmond was overjoyed to find that the ranch had been largely spared the fury of the storm, which had done little more than blow over some fencing and tear loose a couple of boards of the bunkhouse.

Two days after Lucien Edmond's homecoming, the procession consisting of Kitante and Carmencita, the two braves, and Friar Bartoloméo, riding beside the wagons carrying the nuns, came to the gates of the sprawling hacienda. Lucas, seeing them, ran to welcome the friar and then hurried to the door of the ranch house to summon Lucien Edmond.

Kitante helped the old priest down from his horse, as Lucien Edmond came forward, his face aglow with pleasure. "What a happy surprise, Friar Bartoloméo! It is so good to see you again after all this time!"

"My son, I thank you for your gracious welcome. I ask you, I intercede with you, indeed, to extend your warm hospitality to these holy sisters who have come all the way from Mexico City seeking a place in which to build a mission."

"Of course they are welcome. I will have Lucas call the vaqueros to unharness their horses and take them into the stable to water and feed them. And I will have our cook prepare a good dinner for the sisters."

"Thank you, my son. I wish you to meet Sister Martha, who is the head of the order they call the Sisters of the *Indios*. They have sworn to help the Indians and the peons even as I did when I was young and strong."

"You are strong in spirit, and that will never change, Friar Bartoloméo," Lucien Edmond smiled, as he took the friar's hand and reverently kissed it. "I ask your blessing, and I have much to tell you when we are alone." Then, turning to Lucas, he exclaimed, "Have the vaqueros take charge of the horses, and then see that the sisters are brought into the hacienda and given rooms and a chance to refresh themselves after their long journey!"

"Yes, Mr. Lucien Edmond, at once!"

Lucien Edmond had decided that dinner should be a kind of festival held outdoors, since, gratifyingly, the evening was pleasantly cool. The nuns were seated at one table, with Sister Martha at one end and Friar Bartoloméo at the other, while Lucien Edmond and Maxine, Joe and Margaret Duvray, Eddie and María Elena Gentry, Ramón and Mara Hernandez, and Lucas and Felicidad Forsden were seated at the second table—their children making up yet a third and fourth table. Lucien Edmond had requested that several of the vaqueros who played guitars, violins, and accordions should make the evening joyous with music and singing, as well, in which all the guests joined. Lucien Edmond bent to Maxine and whispered to her, "We are blessed in everything, my dear one. We have been spared the ravages of a terrible storm; we are going to have another child; the range is fruitful. Surely, the coming of these nuns and our beloved Friar Bartoloméo is a very good omen."

"Yes, dear Lucien Edmond, and it is also a kind of celebration for the way you saved your stepmother from the ruin that those evil schemers were trying to bring to Windhaven Plantation—just as your father would have done," Maxine murmured back. Lucien Edmond put his arm around Maxine's shoulders and kissed her tenderly on

389

the mouth, then turned back to gesture to the musicians to play one of the hymns used in the service of the mass. A hush fell upon the assemblage, as Friar Bartoloméo rose and intoned the words in a cracked but still pleasant bass voice.

There was applause from the vaqueros, and the old priest flushed with pride as he seated himself. Lucien Edmond Bouchard rose now, a glass of wine in his hand, to offer a toast: "Sisters, and you, Sister Martha as Mother Superior, I bid you all welcome to Windhaven Range. You have met our beloved Friar Bartoloméo, and although your acquaintance has been brief, I am sure that you know already the devotion and the love he bears in his heart for the poor and the needy. And now, I wish to introduce to you a woman whom I deeply respect and honor. She lives with us because her husband is dead and because she wishes to bring up their children here where we recognize God as our judge and counselor, and welcome all men of good will as our brothers, regardless of their faith or their color. Catayuna, rise and let all see you."

The beautiful, mature Mexican woman who had been Sangrodo's wife rose, her eyes downcast, her face flushed with self-conscious embarrassment at this public tribute. Lucien Edmond Bouchard went on: "She is Mexican-born and an aristocrat in her own right. She became the captive of a Comanche chief, yet because of her goodness and the strength of both her chastity and spiritual convictions, Sangrodo, the Comanche chief, became her husband and they brought forth children blessed and baptized. She is wise enough to be chief of the Comanches, but her stepson, Kitante, is now chief, and she has helped him become strong and good while teaching him to walk in the footsteps of his wise father. Now he is Catholic, too, as his wife and child are, as will be the child she now carries. I drink to Catayuna. May all our children grow up emulating her many virtues."

A hush had fallen over the assemblage. Catayuna continued to stand, her head bowed. Lucien Edmond went on, "There are fifty acres of land in the southeast part of Windhaven Range, Sister Martha. I would be honored if you would build your mission there. Our vaqueros will help your nuns build all the shelters they need, as well as a church. I would also like to see a schoolhouse constructed—it is Catayuna's deep and generous desire to see that our vaqueros' children learn English and also further their knowledge of their Spanish heritage. And now that you good sisters have blessed us with your presence, the knowledge of instruction you bring with you will make Catayuna's school in which to teach the children even more effective.

"Friar Bartoloméo, I ask you to stay with us and with these good sisters, to be our priest and our confessor. Years ago, you dedicated our chapel, a place for prayer and meditation used thankfully by our vaqueros. Now you have returned to us, and now you shall dedicate a large church that will accommodate many, and especially the children who are the coming generation and who will one day shape the future of our beloved country."

Friar Bartoloméo Alicante rose, tears streaming down his cheeks. Again silence fell as they eagerly awaited his words. For a long moment, he could not speak, and then finally raising his face to the cloudless sky, he murmured, "I am not worthy, oh, my dear God, for such joy and such blessing. But I swear to You that, by all I have lived for, I shall make my final stopping place a blessed mission where these good sisters will do deeds of love. I am proud and humbly privileged to do what little I can in this great work. And I ask You, *Señor Dios,* to grant Your blessing unto Lucien Edmond Bouchard and his wife and family and all those who work with him on this ranch. Truly am I grateful unto Thee, to have brought me here in my declining time upon this earth of Yours, oh, blessed Lord."

Catayuna now moved from her place at the head of the table toward the old priest and knelt at his feet. His face was transfigured with joy as he put his hand upon her head and blessed her.

Finally Kitante, with Carmencita timidly following a step behind him, came to Catayuna and bowed his head, his arms folded across his chest, and said to her in Spanish, "Truly, you are still our beloved woman. Our tribe will remember you long after the Great Spirit summons you. What has been said of you tonight is only a little of what I know and what my father knew before me, Catayuna. And in the name of him who was my father and the greatest *jefe* of the Comanche, know that I respect you and that I and my *mujer* will keep your name alive through all the days of our lives."

Late that night, as Lucien Edmond got into bed beside his beloved Maxine, he took her in his arms and kissed her and murmured, "I am glad that in the name of Sangrodo I can help Catayuna and our beloved Friar Bartoloméo and the good sisters he guided here. And I think that bringing them here will prove a greater blessing than we can imagine, Maxine. Catayuna will be fulfilled as she watches the children grow and come to adulthood."

"Yes, Lucien Edmond, I know she will. And Kitante loves her, as much as if she had been his own flesh-and-blood mother."

"That's true." He uttered a sigh and shook his head. "If only we could teach everyone that it is possible for those of different races and religions to live peacefully together, as we do here. When I was in New Orleans, I read an account of the war this country is waging against the gentle Nez Percé Indians in Idaho. I have heard of Chief Joseph and what an honorable man he is. But he and his men will inevitably be defeated by the soldiers who outnumber them. You see, Maxine, it is the old story, of land being taken from those who were here first, and the Indians being driven into lands where there will be no hunting, so that they will die."

"It's a terrible thing, my darling. I know your great-grandfather would be pained to see this persecution that is so unjust and so unnecessary continuing."

"Yes, Maxine, for as with the Creeks in his time, it is still happening, and we are powerless to prevent it. My father taught me how to live peacefully with the warlike Comanche, and tonight we saw the fruit of this gentle creed—the creed of sharing, instead of taking, the creed of seeking to understand, instead of condemning that which is different." They were silent a moment, and then Lucien Edmond kissed his wife and whispered, "We shall teach this to our children—just as the nuns will teach love, kindness, and the desire to understand one's neighbors to the children of the vaqueros. It is my prayer that, long after you and I have gone, our children and the others will continue our beliefs. Tonight, Maxine, I feel very close to my father. It's almost as if I were in Alabama, on top of that bluff, feeling his presence."

# Forty

Following his unsuccessful escape attempt in which, rather than gaining his freedom, he was dealt a vicious blow on his head by a belaying pin, Lopasuta Bouchard had lain in a torpor. He remained semiconscious in his cabin for nearly forty-eight hours—partly because of the blow's aftermath, but mostly from the despair of knowing that he was destined for Hong Kong. Ebenezer, out of a grudging compassion, at last brought the ship's doctor to see him. Lopasuta had taken some food and water and submitted passively to the doctor's ministrations; he had no further will to resist. Indeed, the hopelessness of his situation had begun to undermine his courageous spirit, just as the beatings that the seamen had administered during the voyage had begun to weaken his physical stamina.

From Rio, after taking on cargo, water, and more food supplies, the four-master made its way around the Horn. It was winter there, but the captain had ably calculated that by the time they reached the tip of the Southern Hemisphere, the violent storms would have abated, and passage—though rough and chancy—would be possible. Indeed, he had his own reasons for wanting to reach San Francisco by mid-September: a substantial bonus awaited him when he docked at the Embarcadero in the City by the Golden Gate. And besides, he had a pretty Eurasian girl waiting for him in a little apartment on Green Street, and he was anxious to see her and spend a month in her embrace before taking the four-master back with a cargo from the San Francisco docks once again around the Horn and thence to Boston. That voyage would be even longer than the one he had made with Lopasuta, and it was certain to be dreary and lonely.

By now, the young Comanche lawyer had virtually lost track of time. Days and nights merged into a monotonous, agonizing eternity. All he could tell, from the violent rocking of the four-master when it passed into the wind-swirled waters around the Horn, was that this journey had become an ordeal that taxed his powers of survival.

During three of the days around that stormy point near the southernmost part of the globe, Lopasuta was often flung from his hard bunk onto the floor of the cabin and, crouching on his knees, had to grip the edge of the bunk to steady himself before he dared rise. Seasickness also took its toll of him during these harrowing days, and he lay feebly on his bunk, filled with self-loathing at having vomited and been left without the strength to clean himself.

Once again, Ebenezer, this time with a Portuguese lascar and the ship's doctor, attended to Lopasuta, bathing him and giving him some plain broth, which Lopasuta managed to hold down, thereby regaining some vestige of his former strength.

When at last the four-master docked at the Embarcadero, there was a new ordeal in store for him. The door was flung open and the first mate stood glowering at him, a belaying pin gripped in his right hand. Behind the first mate were three seamen, whom Lopasuta did not recognize.

"Your Lordship's going to change ships, so don't give us any trouble," the first mate crookedly grinned, then made a gesture as he stepped away from the door of the cabin. The three seamen hurried in and, although Lopasuta feebly tried to defend himself, he was bound, gagged, and blindfolded. He heard the first mate say, "We'll keep him in the hold until nightfall, my buckos. Then we'll transfer him to the *Eldora*. He's a lucky man—not many passengers get accommodations like this all the way from New Orleans to Hong Kong and the best of care, even the ship's doctor to call on him!" Then he guffawed with brutal glee before the sound of a door being shut and bolted closed off the harsh laughter.

Lopasuta writhed in his bonds, trying to cry out, to call for help, but the gag stifled all but a feeble moaning sound. Abject in his despair, thinking of his wife, alone and abandoned with their first child, he wept—and then he lapsed into unconsciousness.

When he wakened, it was to find himself lying on the floor of a cabin, no longer gagged and blindfolded, his limbs free of restraining bonds. He felt the pitching and tossing of the hard wooden floor beneath him, and he uttered a tortured cry: "Oh, Manitou, You are deaf to my prayers! I am lost! How can I return to her who is my heart and my life? May I never see the child?"

And then gradually he fought off the debilitating trap of self-pity. It would be all too easy to acknowledge a total defeat, to resign himself to the daily horror of his imprisonment. . . . But no, he must be strong, he must resolve within his mind and his sinews to return somehow to Geraldine and their child in Montgomery. There was nothing else to live for. During the first weeks of the voyage, he had imagined that he could cope with the overwhelming odds against him by reverting to the primitive cunning that his Comanche father had possessed, in whose veins had flowed the blood of the People, undaunted, unchallenged, and undefeated. But he had tried this, and he had been clubbed into unconsciousness and treated like a mutinous animal. Now he must resign himself, use his intellect to adapt to the new life to which some unknown and malignant person had condemned him.

Hong Kong. From his Mexican mother's teachings, the name summoned up a vague recollection: a distant, Oriental port, a free port where the British dominated. Now it came back to him, from the early lessons of his mother. Well, she had known how to cope with both the intellect and the practical world, and she had given him a heritage that had made him worthy of the honored name he now bore as adopted son: Lopasuta Bouchard.

This being so, he would accept his fate, and somehow, using both his native gifts and all he had learned among the white-eyes, he would one day return to his wife and child.

He uttered a long, weary sigh, for it was difficult to cast aside the primal role of Comanche against the enemy. Instead, he would play the game of whoever had arranged to take him from his home and send him halfway around the

396

world. And one day, when he came back to Montgomery, he would learn who had done this, and then it would be his time for vengeance.

At last, he was able to summon up a wan smile before fatigue once more claimed him, and he again slept.

Charles Douglas had received a telegram from the Galveston wharfmaster that his cargo-laden steamboat had been dashed to pieces during the furious hurricane that had swirled up from the West Indies to smash the Gulf Coast and wreak great havoc on the vulnerable city. He went to Laurette at once and told her, "Honey, I've lost a lot of money, but the hurricane was an act of God. I'm not worried at all, and I don't want you to worry, either. What I've lost in Galveston is balanced by my profits here in Chicago, thanks to Lawrence Harding. I'll try to get back as soon as I can, but I have to go down there and see just how bad that hurricane was. From what I gather, it damaged the big store quite a bit, but I'm sure we can come out of it. You know, Laurette honey, I'll always be an incorrigible optimist."

She smiled and hugged him and murmured, "I wouldn't care if you didn't have a penny to your name, Charles Douglas. You've given me a wonderful life, and even the downs don't bother me at all. I know you love me, we've got our children, we're together, and that's all that counts."

He stepped back, his hands on her shoulders, and grinned at her. At forty, Laurette Douglas was still as saucy and provocative as she had been when he had first met her; and, in her eyes, he at forty-two was still the energetic, amiable, and boyishly enthusiastic lover who had brought himself from the clerkship of a Tuscaloosa store to the ownership of one of Chicago's largest department stores with two branches in Texas. "Laurette," he murmured huskily, as he leaned forward to kiss her cheek and then the tip of her nose and then her eyelids, "you and I have had lots of excitement in our lives, more than I ever thought possible. You'll always be my girl, and don't you ever forget it."

"Don't *you* ever forget it, Charles Douglas," Laurette teasingly murmured, as she drew him to her and kissed him hard on the mouth. "Now you just go down to Texas without me and try not to get into trouble with another woman. I saved you from the last one, that Pansy creature."

Laurette smiled to herself as she thought back to four years ago when a nefarious man, Henry McNamara, had tried—unsuccessfully, thanks to her intervention—to blackmail Charles. She recalled how McNamara had used his mistress to try to seduce Charles—wtih the intention of then denouncing him as a scoundrel. McNamara had decided on this scheme when the success of Charles's department store was forcing the unscrupulous McNamara's own store to founder. With a little giggle, she remarked to Charles, "Well, we're getting to be staid old married folks, and I don't think I want any more excitement, thank you very much. You must come back to me and tell me that everything's fine and that you still love me, and I'll settle for that and thank the good Lord for all our blessings."

Charles Douglas arrived in Galveston the second week in October. The steamboat captain had told him that the hurricane had wrought a good deal of destruction to the city, but fortunately only some fifty persons had been killed. The damage, however, had run into the millions, and soldiers had been sent from Austin to enact martial law, arresting looters and digging into the collapsed houses to find the dead.

The energetic Chicago merchant had initially planned to go directly to his department store, but he uncharacteristically procrastinated—sensing that the visit would not be a particularly pleasant one—and went first, instead, to the mayor's office. He had in any case intended to pay a visit there, for he was eager to talk with the leading city authorities, to get their official views on the situation in Galveston.

"It will take at least another month, Mr. Douglas," the mayor gravely told him, "before we will be functioning again. Our water supply was contaminated by salt during the hurricane, and the men of the sanitation department are working night and day to correct that. We've had one or two cases of yellow fever and another of typhoid, but they've been isolated. In general, I'd say, the devastation has been less than we might have expected. Unfortunately, the city cannot afford to give financial aid to its citizens.

But I've issued a proclamation that for the next twelve months the merchants and the citizens will have no increase in taxes, and if they plead hardship and can prove it, we'll cut their taxes by two thirds."

"I appreciate your frankness, Mayor. And I'm not looking for any assistance. You and your officials can't be penalized for the winds and the hurricane, and I'd be a selfish fool if I thought otherwise." He extended his hand, and the mayor shook it cordially.

Leaving the mayor's office, Charles walked slowly around the town, watching the soldiers who were clearing away the debris and digging away the mud left by the hurricane and the flood. The sun was shining, and Charles—somewhat to his surprise—found his sense of sadness at his losses somewhat alleviated. He felt a profound sympathy for the people of Galveston, many of whom had lost loved ones as well as property, and this put his own losses in perspective. And after a while, his own infallible optimism took over, and he came to the conviction that even after such a catastrophe as the hurricane, life could return to normal and be better than ever.

He went next to pay a call on Arabella Hunter, to learn how she was faring—for he had not seen her since the death of her husband. Turning in at the gate to her two-story frame house, he rapped twice with the knocker, and a moment later Arabella herself opened the door and uttered a startled cry: "Good heavens, why it's you, Charles Douglas! I didn't expect to see you in town. Just you come right on into the parlor."

"I had to come as soon as I got a telegram that there'd been a hurricane here, Arabella. Belatedly, let me offer my sincerest condolences over James—he was a good, honest man, and there aren't many like him anymore."

"He—he died happy, Charles. He was so pleased that in his last years you'd given him a chance to enjoy a totally new life. I, too, am grateful to you for that, Charles."

"Don't thank me. James was a fine man. You know, somehow I feel a lot older after walking around Galveston and seeing what the hurricane did. But in spite of everything, I'm determined to restore the department store, and I've more ideas in mind to recoup what losses I've had to endure."

"I admire your optimism, Charles."

"Without optimism, Arabella, a man can't reasonably plan ahead. And I allow for acts of God as much as I do acts of faulty judgment. We all make those, you know."

"That's true." Arabella uttered a nostalgic little laugh. "But I'd like to tell you about someone who certainly saved my life, and Joy's, too, during the hurricane—that young Alexander Gorth, who took over Henry McNamara's store. He worked very hard, and he's made his store a really fine place to shop in. He and his wife, Katie, are the nicest young couple I've met in a long time. Why, just imagine: there we all were, with the water rising all around us, and what did that kind, generous man worry about? Your store, Charles Douglas!" She laughed. "I'll tell you—it's hard to believe that he's your competition for all the concern he's shown. I wouldn't be surprised if, when you get to your store, you find him hard at work. You can't miss Alex—he's a tall, rather boyish-looking fellow, a bit on the thin side—with brown hair that looks like it will always resist what a comb might do for it."

Charles smiled at Arabella's rather fond description.

"I'm glad to hear you speak so kindly of him. I've had a few ideas about Mr. Gorth's store. James used to mention him from time to time, in his letters to me—said young Alex was a real comer, someone to keep an eye on. Yes, I'd like to see him, and also find out just how much damage the hurricane did to his place. Maybe we could pool our resources. I could think of a lot worse business associates. Well, is there anything I can do for you, Arabella? I wish now, come to think of it, I'd brought Laurette, sort of help you get straightened out—"

"Oh, thank you, Charles," Arabella smilingly shook her head, "but I'm just fine. I'll have this place cleaned up in no time. My Joy and I are getting things done wonderfully—she keeps me young, I can tell you that."

"I'm sure she does, judging by the way you look right now. Well then, I'll be going now, but I'll see you again before I go back to Chicago. God bless and keep you and your family."

As he turned to go, Charles shook his head with exasperation at himself. "I've had my mind so occupied worrying about the damage done by the hurricane and the loss of the steamer with all my goods on it, Arabella, that I almost forgot the other reason I came to see you. I wanted

400

to tell you that your husband invested capital with me to become a partner in my Texas store, so as long as the stores continue and we have a profit-and-loss statement, you, as his widow, will receive a share of the profits, based on not only the amount of his original investment, but also as a kind of payment for the help and inspiration he gave me."

"Why that's—that's awfully generous of you, Charles!" Arabella blinked away the sudden tears. "You know, I contribute to the symphony and the opera, and I take part in fund-raising affairs to benefit the city—in fact, right now, I'm trying to raise money for the poor and needy who were left homeless by this terrible hurricane. But I've been thinking that I'd really enjoy working a few hours every week in the store itself. You see, I know most of the society women of Galveston, and perhaps I could increase your profits by promoting certain items that women like to buy. In a way, too, Charles, that might help make up for the losses you've suffered."

"That's really a wonderful offer, Arabella. I want to think about it. Perhaps perfumes and jewelry, or evening dresses—things with a feminine flair—might be just the ticket. When I get back to Chicago, I'll write you in detail what I have in mind." He gave her a rueful smile. "I have to admit to you that I lost a good deal of money on that sunken steamer, but the way we're doing in Chicago and the gradual profit increase that the Houston store is showing leads me to believe that I'll be able to expand here, too, after this temporary interruption to my plans. Well, let me say how good it was seeing you again. I wish you and Joy health and happiness and a long life. Goodbye, Arabella."

Though the hour was late, Charles decided to go at last to the Douglas Department Store, for a thorough survey of the damage. As he made his way there, he saw a number of black laborers as well as state troopers still at work, clearing the mud from the streets. Other men were working feverishly to get the salt water out of the cistern that serviced Galveston. Still others were busy repairing and painting the elegant private houses that stood to the south of Galveston's business district.

When he entered the store, Charles uttered a groan as he beheld the counters, which were in a shambles, many of the goods having been swept away. The floor was still thick with the mud and debris brought in by the fierce winds and the surging water from the Gulf, but there were already men with shovels working throughout the first floor of the store. His dismay gave way to a grin when he saw a tall, lanky young man with a shock of dark-brown hair efficiently directing the workmen and taking charge of the cleaning-up operation.

From Arabella Hunter's description, he recognized Alexander Gorth, and he gingerly made his way along the muck-stained floor toward where the young man was standing. "Mr. Gorth, I believe?"

"That's my name, sir. Wait a minute—aren't you Charles Douglas? I remember seeing your picture in the newspaper when you first opened the store."

"Guilty as charged, Mr. Gorth." Charles offered his hand, and Alexander warmly shook it.

"I'm pleasantly surprised to find you taking charge of getting my store cleaned up, Mr. Gorth," he chuckled, "—though not unduly so, since Arabella Hunter suggested you might be here. But tell me, what about your own shop—were you able to clean it up? I've heard, by the way, that you've done pretty well for yourself, since a certain notorious character by the name of Henry McNamara sold you his store for practically nothing after running afoul of the code of ethics and beating a hasty retreat from Galveston."

"That's true, Mr. Douglas, I have been pretty lucky. As far as the destruction goes, my store is smaller than yours, and it received proportionately less damage. Most of it's all cleaned up by now—I did the job myself, because that way I knew things would get done when I wanted them to."

"That's an admirable precept for any merchant. You certainly seem to know what you're doing. Come outside, I'd like to talk to you for a minute, Mr. Gorth—and it will be less distressing than standing here amid this ruin."

"I'd be glad to, Mr. Douglas." The two men made their way out to the sidewalk, where Charles, grimacing with distaste, finally found a place to stand that was not so thickly covered in mud as the rest of the sidewalk. "This is better—I think. Mr. Gorth, you probably know that Henry McNamara tried to put me out of business using the old badger game which, thanks to my smart wife, Laurette, didn't come off at all. That was the main reason he left so abruptly. And from all I hear, you've turned that scavenger store—for that's what it was—into a profitable, going enterprise that does you a great deal of credit. The bank and the other merchants talk very highly of you."

"That—that's very flattering of you to say, Mr. Douglas, but I'll never be in your class."

"Nonsense!" Charles gave him a boyish grin and clapped him on the shoulder as he went on, "How would you feel about a junior partnership in this store? In view of the damage of the hurricane and the rebuilding that will be going on, there'll be lots of demand for my goods. I'm even thinking that I'll need another outlet to serve customers, so what would you think of selling me your store at wholesale cost for the undamaged inventory, plus a small profit—I'll be honest with you, I lost about ten thousand dollars' worth of merchandise on the steamer that was off Galveston when the hurricane broke—plus a good job here and, of course, as a junior partner, a specified share of the annual profits, to be paid twice a year?"

"Well, Mr. Douglas! That's mighty generous of you! And—let me think now—yes, I think I would like that. You know, I've always wanted to be my own boss, but at the same time I've admired you right from the start—ever since you first opened your store here in Galveston. There's a lot to be said for teaming up with a man like you—particularly after a natural disaster like this hurricane, which sort of makes a man want to hitch his wagon to a bigger star. Yes, I—I'd be honored and proud to accept an offer like that, Mr. Douglas, and I'm sure Katie would say it's a good thing, too—we've even discussed it from time to time."

"Good!" Charles replied, shaking Alexander's hand enthusiastically. "Now, Max Steinfeldt, my senior partner, is in charge of the Houston store, and he also has supervisory responsibility for the branch here in Galveston. He's the merchandising director for both branches, and he'd handle the merchandising for your store as well, once it becomes part of the Douglas chain."

"I understand, Mr. Douglas."

"Still and all—" Charles Douglas was thinking aloud as he glanced around to see how ably the workmen were carrying out their task, which almost reminded him of the labor of Hercules in having to clean out the Augean stables, and then turned back to Alexander Gorth. "Since I want to spend the next full year in Chicago with my family and perhaps open another store in the Hyde Park area of town, I'm thinking that in addition to your continuing to manage your own store, I could offer you the temporary managership of this store." He waved his hand at the building behind him. "Of course, you'd be under orders from Max Steinfeldt regarding the merchandising, but Max devotes most of his tremendous energies and capabilities to increasing the business of the Houston branch. There's quick full rail service now between the two cities, so that you two can confer within a matter of hours over essential points and decisions."

"This is really wonderful of you, Mr. Douglas!" Alexander breathed. He was thinking of the look on Katie's face when he came home tonight and told her the good news. "I'd like nothing better than to try to make good for you, Mr. Douglas. I've heard a lot about you, and you're the sort of partner I've always wanted to have."

"One thing's for sure, Alexander—let me call you that—I'll never browbeat you the way that scoundrel McNamara did. By the way, I wonder what happened to the man? Well, that's of no importance. I'll tell you what, Alexander, I'm going to make rail connections tomorrow to Houston, and see Max Steinfeldt and his sweet wife, Alice, and their kids. I'll tell him exactly what I've got in mind, and then he'll probably be coming down here in a day or so to talk with you again and see when you think you can reopen this place. You've really got those fellows working!" Charles admiringly declared, as he looked around again. "I think we're going to get along just fine together, Alexander."

## *Forty-One*

On October 21, 1877, in the Little Church of St. Mary, Judith Branshaw and Bernard Marquard stood together before the altar as the kindly old priest intoned the words that would bind them together for the rest of their lives. As best man, Jesse Jacklin, Bernard's former orderly, stood waiting with the ring, dressed in the traditional black frock coat and white cravat. His affable, attractive wife, Edith, wore the yellow organdy of a matron of honor.

It was also Bernard Marquard's fifty-third birthday, yet the rapturous look on his face belied his age, more than twice that of his young wife. He turned to her, his sightless eyes straining as if, by a supreme act of will, he might just once see the tall, honey-haired young woman who had consented to share his life and who had given him peace and joy at an age when he had thought that he would never know the priceless gift of love. And in this newly born delight, he rejoiced in the knowledge that Judith Branshaw had not judged him by material possessions or wealth, and that the difference in their ages had meant nothing except to lead him toward the most tender consideration in his wooing. Now, as the priest asked for the ring and his former orderly handed it to him, Bernard reached for Judith's hand and unerringly slipped it onto the proper finger, whispering, "Bless you, my darling, I never knew that such joy could be mine. I don't know how many years God will grant me, but I swear to you here and now I'll devote each day and each waking hour to you so that you'll never regret becoming my wife."

Tears welled in her eyes as she turned to him and whispered back, "No, no, my dearest, it's I who am grateful to you for having such faith in me and giving me back my self-respect and, most of all, the happiness to know that I'm a woman who can give you happiness in turn. I love you so, my husband."

The old priest smiled as he overheard this pledge: it was more devout, more meaningful than many a vow glibly taken. Here indeed, he told himself, was a couple who came to the altar with love and unselfishness. That was what St. Paul had taught. When the ceremony was completed, Bernard reached for his wife and kissed her on the mouth, trembling with an exalted ecstasy.

They turned, she taking his arm and gently guiding him down the narrow church aisle bordered on each side by pews where well-wishers had come to witness this joyous union.

Outside the church, a carriage waited to take them to the wharf, where they would embark upon the steamboat *Niagara* that would take them to New York for their honeymoon.

Edith and Jesse Jacklin followed, and the Tennesseean helped the couple into the carriage. "I'll look after Rory real good till you get back, Cap'n," he avowed. "Now you and Miss Judith have yourselves a wonderful time, and don't you worry about anything."

"God bless you, Jesse. You've been the best friend a man could ever ask for."

As the carriage pulled away, some of the wedding guests threw rice after it and called out happy encouragements to the newly married couple. Jesse Jacklin turned to his wife. "I swear, Edith, he's the finest man I ever met in all my life. I still can't get over what he just did for me, recommending me to Jason Barntry as manager of the casino that Mrs. Bouchard took over, after that no-good William Brickley tried to cheat her and—good riddance to him—got killed for his pains."

"And you'll be the most honest casino manager in all of the Queen City, Jesse honey," his wife smilingly assured him. "Only just don't let me catch you spending my household allowance at one of those tables, honest though they are."

"No chance of that, Edith. I'll just make sure that the customers get a fair shake. Well now, I'm going to take you to Antoine's for dinner to really celebrate this day and my fine new job!"

Just before midnight, on the very day that Judith Branshaw and Bernard Marquard were married, the *Eldora* dropped anchor in the harbor of Victoria, the main port city on the north side of the island of Hong Kong. The waters were sheltered there, and there were facilities for replenishing the ship's water supplies from the "fragrant stream," the narrow passage between the island and the mainland that the native fishermen called *Heang Keang,* thus giving the free port its name.

The island of Hong Kong was small—only eleven miles long, with an area of only twenty-nine square miles. Troubles in Canton over the opium trade had made the island the ideal base for British shipping, and a settlement had been established on its shores in 1837. Two years later, when the Chinese emperor had appointed a special commissioner to eliminate the opium trade, this commissioner surrounded the foreign factories in Canton with troops and insisted that all opium supplies be turned over to Chinese authorities for destruction. The Chinese commissioner also issued an edict requiring the masters of arriving ships to sign an oath that they would not trade in opium, on pain of death.

Protesting this edict, the British foreign secretary, Lord Palmerston, sent an expeditionary force in 1840 to enforce his demand for either a commercial treaty allowing open trade, or, failing that, the cession of a small island where British citizens might live without fear of oppression. A year later, a British naval squadron was landed on Hong Kong, and the island began its history as a British colony. Through the Treaty of Nanking, signed in 1842, Hong Kong was formally given over to the British, with five other Chinese ports also being opened to trade.

It was a strange new world to which Lopasuta was being delivered against his will, a lush world full of mysteries and contrasts. On the south side of Hong Kong Island lay the fishing village of Aberdeen, once a pirate stronghold, named after Lord Aberdeen, the British foreign secretary during the colony's early days. Here were moored hundreds of little sampans, gently rocking on the waves, a virtual city upon the sea, where families earned their livelihood by fishing, and were born, married and died. Beyond Aberdeen, to the east, were the bathing beaches of Repulse Bay and Shek-O, but these were deserted, for it was the time of the winter monsoon, a generally cool period, with winds from the northeast, and periods of heavy rainfall alternating with spells of drier weather.

Lopasuta had not attempted to escape again, once he had been locked in the even tinier cabin of the *Eldora*, bound for Hong Kong. The waters of the Pacific had been peaceful, and so the days and nights had passed with endless steady rocking to and fro, to which he had resigned himself. The only relief from the atrocious monotony of the voyage had been the sympathetic kindness of a Portuguese lascar who had told Lopasuta simply that his name was Rodrigues. A bearded, black-haired, darkskinned man in his late twenties, he had guarded Lopasuta's cabin during the day, while a stolid, taciturn Chinese from Macao, with huge biceps and glowering mien, looking the more formidable because his head had been shaved bald except for a traditional queue, guarded the cabin at night. Rodrigues spoke execrable English, but he had managed to give Lopasuta some moments of relief throughout this seemingly endless voyage by cheerfully remarking on the weather, or the excellent time the vessel was making as it crossed the Pacific. And, observing that Lopasuta ate ravenously, he contrived on many an occasion to bring a bowl of pork cooked with greens and rice, which helped the Comanche gradually to regain his vigor.

But as the *Eldora* dropped anchor, Lopasuta lay unconscious on his hard, narrow bunk. Two days before the vessel had tacked around the south shore of Hong Kong Island, the captain had ordered that a powerful dose of laudanum be put into the unwilling passenger's food, and the dose had very nearly been lethal. Now, as the bolt to the cabin door was slipped back and three sturdy lascars entered, Lopasuta still lay like one dead. The captain, a little man with an enormous beak of a nose, was behind them giving orders.

"You'll take him in a dinghy—and be careful no British policemen see you. Take him to one of the alleys beyond Government House and leave him there. My orders were to deliver him to Hong Kong, and that's just where he's

408

going. What happens to him after that's not my affair—that is if he's still alive. . . . Is he?"

"Yes, Captain," the man known to Lopasuta as Rodrigues grunted assent, as he bent over the unconscious Comanche, rolling back one of Lopasuta's eyelids, and then feeling for the throat pulse. "The laudanum, it works too well. Maybe too much was given him."

"Shut your mouth, Rodrigues! It's none of your business. Just get him into the dinghy and be off with you!"

The three lascars approached the bunk and trundled the unconscious Comanche off as if he had been a sack of potatoes, descended with him into the dinghy, and set out across the harbor of Victoria. One of the men, glancing down at their unconscious captive, shook his head and chuckled, "Someone does not like this man, paying much money to have him taken from the Estados Unidos to San Francisco and then here."

"That is his *ming yun*, his fate," the Chinese sailor philosophically retorted.

"He wears the clothes of a foreigner," Rodrigues gloomily spoke up. "If we leave him where the captain has told us, he will be robbed, perhaps beaten to death or have a knife in his ribs."

"But that is not our concern," the burly Chinese countered. "Each man has within himself the seeds of his own destruction—that is the word of our beloved Confucius. If this man is destined to perish, he will, and our help will not save him. If he is to live, that, too, is beyond our doing. We have our orders, we carry them out, and we are paid for it—and that is the end of it. Now, row and do not talk so much."

His two companions glumly nodded and bent to their oars. Lopasuta mumbled something incomprehensible in his torpor, his face contorted with desolation. The burly Chinese glanced down at him and shrugged. "He is troubled in his dreams. Perhaps the laudanum is not so satisfying as the pipe, and though that is forbidden, I know secret houses in Hong Kong where, for a price, a man can sleep and dream happily with the poppy."

His two companions said nothing as they dipped their oars into the water, eager to end their mission and return to the ship. They would not sail back to San Francisco for another week, but already they begrudged this night: they might have gone to some of the floating restaurants, or even to some of the larger junks where painted women were to be had for the night at the cost of a few Hong Kong dollars.

At last, the dinghy was moored near a slip used for one of the cargo ships, and the muscular Chinese lascar nimbly leaped onto the narrow dock and made the dinghy fast as his companions passed the rope to him. The two Portuguese lifted the unconscious body of the Comanche, grunting with the effort. "He's strong, this one, and the color of his skin is one I have not seen before," the man called Rodrigues vouchsafed.

"Again I'd say it is not your business," the Chinese angrily cut in. "Lift him to me—there. Now quickly, we go to the alley. Let us cover him first with a tarpaulin, so if the British patrol sees us, they will not know that we carry a man. Quickly now—we will have done our work and then we can go back and think of tomorrow and our pleasures."

Through the winding, tortuous streets of the oldest section of Victoria, creeping near the buildings so that they would not be seen, the three lascars carried the tarpaulin-covered body of Lopasuta Bouchard. They reached at last a squalid alley, black as night itself, and they laid him down none too gently. Whisking off the tarpaulin, they turned and hurried back to the dinghy.

A few drops of rain had begun to fall. Lopasuta's eyelids fluttered, but he didn't regain consciousness. He lay sprawled, wearing the filthy, tattered suit that had once been his best, the very suit in which he had come to visit William Brickley in New Orleans so long ago.

An occasional passerby, hurrying home, passed Lopasuta in the night. From a nearby restaurant at the very end of the alley, a young Cantonese opened the door and threw out a pail of slops; then, uttering an imprecation because he heard his master calling him, he went back into the restaurant.

The night engulfed Lopasuta Bouchard, sleeping his drugged sleep, having at last reached the destination to which the now-dead William Brickley had consigned him.

## Forty-Two

Marianne Valois sat before her gilt-framed mirror in the boudoir of her elegantly furnished San Francisco apartment above her bistro on lower Lombard Street, and contemplated her reflection. At thirty-four, she was still as enticing and desirable as she had been four years ago when Lawrence Davis had been her lover back in Galveston before she had broken off that liaison and sent him back to Arabella Hunter's lovely daughter, Melinda. As she put her slim fingers to the ringlets of her dark-brown hair, which she had had cut only the other day, her soft, Cupid's bow mouth curved in a reminiscent smile. How naive and ardent Lawrence had been—and how infatuated! Yet the wisest thing she had ever done had been to break off the affair; she knew that by doing so, she had saved Lawrence's marriage from breaking up—an event that would have left her with a burden of guilt that she had never had the least desire to assume.

Having read of the recent hurricane in Galveston, she had thanked her lucky stars for having moved to the city by the Golden Gate. For one thing, the oppressive summer humidity of the Gulf Coast had never been to her liking; here in San Francisco, regardless of the season, the cool winds and the fog blew in from the bay almost every evening and made the air invigorating. Hot weather created a kind of spiritual torpor; ever since she had come out here to live near her sister, Odalie, she had felt herself to be younger, more alert and vivacious, more eager for the unexpected promises of each new day.

From time to time, she had thought fondly of Lawrence

411

Davis. His almost boyish adoration of her had certainly been flattering—that had to be admitted. And if he had been single, she might just have been sentimental enough to have married him—but no, the prospect of living the rest of her life in Galveston, even with so devoted a lover as he, was not really to her taste. Yes, she had nothing to reproach herself for now, as she looked back over these four years.

Indeed, perhaps it had been her guardian angel who had directed her to San Francisco. If she hadn't broken the affair off when she did, she thought cynically to herself, all her good fortune would not have happened.

Her sister, Odalie, had married David Serat, the only son of wealthy parents, about fifteen years ago, and they had had four children. David Serat, now nearing fifty, was something of an esthete; he had opened a fashionable antique shop on Buchanan Street, just beyond Van Ness, and led the life of a dilettante. But his parents' wealth and his own social background had made him one of the city's elite. He had been visiting Chicago on a buying trip, having gone there to acquire some heirlooms and costly brick-a-brac for his shop, when he met Odalie and soon after took her back to San Francisco as his wife.

When David and Odalie had married, they had urged nineteen-year-old Marianne to come with them to San Francisco. She had almost accepted this evidently sincere invitation; the lovely, naive young woman was now virtually alone in the world—for her father, a widower who had brought his children over from Paris, had died three years earlier, leaving the sisters to fend for themselves in Chicago. But rather than go with Odalie and her new husband, Marianne had rallied her courage and boldly decided to strike out on her own. Having recently suffered the pains of an unhappy romance in Chicago, she had decided to leave the Windy City and go to St. Louis.

Not long after she had reached St. Louis, she secured a position as an apprentice milliner at a hat shop where, after a brief romance, she had fallen in love with the son of her employer. A rather diffident but thoroughly likable young man, he in turn fell in love with Marianne, idolizing her. He was in line to inherit the shop; indeed, his aging mother had made it plain that as soon as he married a nice girl—and Marianne qualified in every sense—then she would turn the shop over to them and retire.

For six months after their festive wedding, Marianne and her husband, Gaston Valois, were ecstatically happy. But late one night, there was a knock at their door. A policeman was standing there to tell Marianne that Gaston had been found in an alley, dead from stab wounds. It seemed he had been attacked while coming home late from work, and his attempt to struggle with his assailant had cost him his life.

Within a week, the grief-stricken young widow had packed her bags and left St. Louis forever. Armed with a recommendation from her mother-in-law, she had found employment in a millinery shop in New Orleans. After a few years she had put away enough of her earnings to enable her to have a business of her own and, hearing that Texas was booming, she left the Queen City for Galveston, where she opened her own shop. Her brief affair with Lawrence Davis had made her decide to rejoin her sister at last, in the City by the Golden Gate.

Marianne was happily reunited with Odalie, but barely six months after her arrival in San Francisco, the serenity and peace of her new life had been shattered by the revelation that her sister was dying of consumption. A week before her death, Odalie told Marianne, "*Ma soeur*, I know it will not be long. And I welcome the end because I am so weak and it has been such a terrible ordeal for *cher* David. He has been a good, kind husband, truly, and he will look after our children. I have already told him that he should remarry as quickly as he can. No, do not cry for me, Marianne—I have had a good life, and I regret nothing. But I can do something for you at last. I have put away four thousand dollars out of the generous gifts David has given me since I became his wife, and I have written a will that leaves it all to you. I want you to take it and open a bistro. Perhaps the kind we used to have in Paris when Maman and Papa were alive. Promise that you will do this for me. But do not have it on the Barbary Coast; it is too dangerous for a woman there."

Marianne well understood why her sister warned her about the Barbary Coast. Ever since the early days of San Francisco's rapid growth, during the Gold Rush, the Barbary Coast had been a district filled with rough drinking

413

establishments and houses of ill repute. The ineffectiveness of the police in those early days had twice spurred the citizens of San Francisco to organize committees of vigilance to stamp out crime. The committees had long since disbanded, and by now large areas of the city were safe; nevertheless, the Barbary Coast retained its unsavory reputation as a district to be shunned by the more genteel elements of the populace.

Knowing this, Marianne had no hesitation in keeping her vow to her sister. Four months after Odalie's death, she had opened Chez Marianne, a beautifully decorated restaurant in an old building that she had been able to buy for two thousand dollars—in a location that was, to be sure, not far from the Barbary Coast, but it was still clearly outside that evil district, so that it could attract the wealthier clientele who had no desire to venture into the worst parts of town after sundown. Marianne herself presided as manager, welcoming the patrons, and she had gained a reputation as a charming hostess who unerringly suggested just the proper dishes to please each client's palate.

Gradually, she had added entertainment to what she pleased to call a bistro, although in scope it was far more ambitious than its Parisian equivalent. She had prospered, and if she was thinking of Lawrence Davis at this moment, it was not with regret but relief that she had found Kevin Anderson, an unattached man who would never cause her to feel the guilt that her previous liaison with a married man had engendered.

Kevin Anderson was twenty-five, six feet two inches tall, with closely cropped, light brown hair, a frank, pleasant face and the innocent blue eyes of a baby. Indeed, his guilelessness had very nearly led him to be shanghaied last year in a Barbary Coast saloon. Quite by chance, since Marianne had known the owner, an outgoing, bawdy but genuinely honest henna-haired woman in her early forties known as the Duchess, she had been able to save Kevin from the not infrequent fate of strangers to the Barbary Coast who found themselves waking from a drugged drink aboard a four-master bound for the Dutch East Indies, Macao, or the Sandwich Islands.

Kevin Anderson had been born in Boston, and his father had been a shipbuilder who had gone bankrupt when three of his sailing vessels had been sunk or burned by pirates off the China coast, after which he had taken his own life. Kevin's mother had remarried a saloonkeeper who often got as drunk as his customers, becoming irascibly quarrelsome when he did so. Wearying of this life, Kevin left home forever at the age of eighteen and, after working at odd seamen's jobs for three years, finally decided to seek his fortune in San Francisco. There he had gone one evening to the saloon owned by the Duchess to keep an appointment with a first mate who had promised him a berth on a schooner bound for Cuba. Actually, the first mate was a procurer for a disreputable vessel that often carried contraband and was captained by a sadistic German who was wanted on suspicion of murdering two young homosexuals in whose company he was known to have been seen.

The Duchess was not adverse to hiring dance-hall girls who would later go upstairs to their cubicles to entertain customers for a price—a portion of which she herself retained as a commission for providing the young harlots with living quarters, food, and a bed for plying their trade—but she abominated the practice of duping an unwary young man and carting him off to work in virtual slavery on a ship. Consequently, when she had seen Kevin Anderson come into her saloon and go to the table where the first mate was seated, she suspected what was likely to happen and sent a messenger to Marianne Valois, who she knew was always on the lookout for good help. Marianne arrived with two of her sturdy bouncers. They sent the first mate packing without his prey, and Marianne suggested to Kevin that she might have a job for him that would keep him out of trouble and danger.

He had begun as a waiter and busboy, doing double duty when her bistro was crowded on a Friday or Saturday night. She found that he was conscientious and personable and that the customers liked him, and just four months ago she had made him assistant manager. On that night, after the last customer had left and the doors had been locked, she had taken him by the hand and led him upstairs to her bedchamber.

She was more than fond of him, because, as so often

happens with a mature woman, she discovered that she was his very first love and that he was incredibly sentimental and even worshipful, as if he could not believe his good fortune that so beautiful and desirable a woman would choose him as her lover. Now, as she smiled at herself in the mirror, she told herself that everything had turned out for the best and she even vaguely entertained the hope that Kevin Anderson would marry her.

She thought to herself now that it was as well that she had never become pregnant; and yet now, even though she was thirty-four, it was well within the realm of possibility that she could bear Kevin Anderson a child of love. She remembered Melinda Davis and her children. She had met James Hunter in Charles Douglas's department store in Galveston and saw how happy marriage had made him, and how he idolized his children. Perhaps she had become a little cynical over the years, but she still retained, thanks to her Gallic forebears, a yearning for romance and a totally successful marriage.

She took her time dressing, for business was slow this Wednesday evening. She made a mental note to stop in the kitchen and pacify the temperamental Belgian cook. He had threatened to quit half a dozen times since Marianne had hired him, but she had always managed to cajole him into staying, usually by dint of raising his wages. His tenure, she mused to herself, was not permanent, for with the money she had so thriftily set aside, she believed that it would one day be possible to open a really elegant restaurant that would cater to the affluent clientele of Nob Hill and Twin Peaks, and when that occurred she would seek a really first-class chef who would add tone to the establishment.

At last, having completed her dressing, and also her coiffure, which made her look appealingly young, Marianne Valois went downstairs to the kitchen. There she sympathetically listened to André Soultanbieff's customary complaints, mollified him by praising him to the skies, and hinted that there would be five dollars more in his wages at the end of the week. He kissed her hand, praising her in flowery terms, and even made her laugh aloud—not without a blush—by intimating that his real reason for remaining on the job was that he was madly in love with her.

416

This done, she went out to greet the dozen couples who were eating dinner or enjoying a light collation, and encountered Kevin Anderson, who was playing the role of headwaiter tonight. His quick and sincere smile at the sight of her sent a slow tingle of delightful anticipation through her body. She smiled back and, certain that no one else was watching, blew him a swift kiss.

The door opened and a bulky, gray-haired, lantern-jawed man, in a natty gray tweed suit and gleamingly polished shoes with spats, entered. When he saw her, his mouth opened and his brown eyes widened with recognition. At about the same moment, she recognized him as Henry McNamara, who had had a store in Galveston and who had been pointed out to her one day as an unscrupulous profiteer who took advantage of any colleague undergoing financial difficulties.

"By all that's holy, I don't believe the testimony of my own eyes!" Henry McNamara purred as he scanned her swiftly up and down with a speculative and lecherous look. "This is the first time I've come to this nice bistro of yours, and I might add that my timing couldn't be better. Let me see now, you had a hat shop back in Galveston, didn't you?"

"Yes, I did. And you're Henry McNamara. My name is Marianne Valois."

"That's it. I know I'd have remembered it in time! Dear lady, what a pleasure, and what a small world it is, after all!" Gallantly, he reached for her right hand and put it to his lips.

"May I order for you, Mr. McNamara?" she coolly asked.

"Hmm, let me see your bill of fare." He lifted the menu, hand-written on a half-sheet of paper, which Marianne nightly prepared for her dinner customers, studied it a moment, and then decided, "If your cook knows how to prepare a genuine chateaubriand, I'll take that without question. Also, since the evening is chilly, I'd like some French wine—red, of course, to complement the beef."

"I'll give your order to the kitchen, and since we're slow tonight, you shouldn't have to wait very long, Mr. McNamara."

"And you, dear lady, shouldn't have to wait at all, I'm

thinking." He grew more and more aggressive, eyeing her with a discernible leer.

She nodded, went back to the kitchen, placed the order, and then returned to his table. Kevin Anderson was eyeing her intently, and she found it amusing: it was so nice for a change to have a virile, pleasant, devoted young man so jealous that he couldn't bear to have an old fool like McNamara even look at her. Yes, that was very good indeed. So long as he felt that way, their liaison would endure.

To make conversation, she turned to McNamara and blithely asked, "Well now, as I recall, you sold your store to your clerk and left Galveston."

"That's true, *ma belle*." He chuckled, watched as one of the waiters brought to the table a bottle of Chateauneuf du Pape and proceeded to open it and pour it.

"I believe you left Galveston about the time I did, Marianne, back in '73. Well, I've been here ever since, and doing very well, I may tell you. But everything else dwarfs into insignificance now that I've seen you again. My dear, I don't know how I missed you when I was in Galveston."

"Come, come, Mr. McNamara. You're beginning to repeat yourself. What are you doing these days for a living?"

"Oh, I don't keep a store any more, nor shall I ever again. But I rather like San Francisco."

"I can take it or leave it," was her cool reply.

McNamara sipped his wine, then appraisingly declared, "Quite pleasant, and just hearty enough for a cool evening like tonight. Well, if you'd like to know what I've been doing, I volunteered my services to the city, because I've done some land surveying in my time. That doesn't bring me very much money, but it has a certain prestige to it, you understand, Marianne." He looked around warily, then leaned forward and murmured, "But the really exciting thing is that I'm onto a gold mine up near Grass Valley, in the Sierra Nevadas. I found a large hill, you could almost call it a mountain, which assays rather high in gold ore and dust. What I want to do is organize a company and issue stock in the mine, to defray the necessary expenses of hiring a crew to mine this gold."

"I see. But from what I know of history, the gold rush back in '49 pretty well cleared out the gold in the Sierras," Marianne observed.

418

"You're right again, dear lady. I assure you it was quite a lucky accident that I stumbled upon this rich vein of gold. Most of it is too deep for the old-time prospectors to have been able to reach it with the equipment they had back then. I've already filed a claim on the land, and I should have a clearance within the next fortnight." As the waiter brought his food and set it down before him, McNamara glanced at it and smacked his lips. "That looks mighty fine. Do you know, Marianne, you might turn a tidy profit if you went along with me in this stock deal of mine."

"I could always use more capital—who couldn't? I plan one day to open a really deluxe restaurant. We're getting in more and more ships from the East, and a lot of them are bringing single men and families with enough of a grubstake to get along very nicely here."

"As I remarked before, you're a very enterprising and hardworking young woman. But there's really no need for you to scrounge around looking for capital, when you could get your investment back in a few months from me. Why don't you think about it, Marianne?"

"Perhaps I shall. How much would I need to invest, Mr. McNamara?"

"I'd say between five and ten thousand dollars. For that, Marianne, I'd make you a full partner, enjoying half the profits."

"And you're certain that you found gold in this hill—or mountain, as you call it?"

"Beyond the shadow of any reasonable doubt. Believe me, dear lady."

"You know, Mr. McNamara," she eyed him with a mocking little smile, "I have the feeling that this isn't the first of your little speculations."

McNamara maintained his poise, retorting boastfully, "I can assure you that this one is on the up and up, my dear Marianne. And just to show you my good faith, I'll give you the opportunity to be a part of the business with a minimum of risk on your part. For just a thousand dollars' investment, I can make you quarter-partner—I can use the money for printing the stock, and promotion, and some of the expenses of excavation and my own personal costs."

"Well, I suppose I could spare a thousand dollars, Mr. McNamara. Of course, I wish I could see this mine of yours. Suppose you tell me where it is—I'm not adverse to a little rough travel—"

"Never you mind the exact location," he wagged a reproving finger at her with a crafty smile, "I've already staked my claim on the land, and I don't propose to have any outsider learning my secret. I confess to you I've had rather shoddy luck in the last year or two in this city, but this mine is going to make all the difference. Why, I shouldn't be surprised if even your thousand-dollar investment would bring you back ten times as much once we start the actual mining. I've already had an assayer look at the ore—and part of that thousand dollars will also enable me to pay him for another analysis as soon as we do more testing."

"All right, Mr. McNamara, I'll go along with you. As a former neighbor from Galveston and knowing you to be a shrewd operator, I'll see what happens."

"Splendid!" McNamara had begun to tackle his dinner and was wolfing it down, pausing now to gulp down half a glass of the good French wine. He belched, uttered a hearty sigh of pleasure, and then said, "Suppose I come in late next week and we'll work out the articles of partnership. And you'll have the thousand dollars for me?"

"Of course. Do you spend much time at the mine?" she innocently asked.

"I'll be going up the day after tomorrow. So, when I see you, I'm sure I'll have a really exciting report. Why, this assayer is one of the best in the business, Marianne."

"I'll look to see you next Friday, then. Enjoy your supper, Mr. McNamara. And the bottle of wine is complimentary."

"Why, thank you very much! You're as generous as you are beautiful, my dear lady!"

As she sat in her boudoir sipping a glass of white wine, Marianne summoned back her memories of him in Galveston. She remembered Henry McNamara much more than even he imagined. During her stay in Galveston, many of her millinery customers had bitterly commented on the outrageous prices that he charged for shoddy merchandise. And she had heard other stories of his philandering liaisons with women like Pansy Lowell. There was no

420

doubt about it, Henry McNamara was not the most trust-worthy of characters.

And that was why, when Kevin Anderson discreetly tapped at her door about an hour later, she urged him to enter and, even as he was beginning to kiss and caress her, murmured, "Kevin, my sweet, I want you to do me a big favor, something that means a lot to me."

"You know I'd do anything in the world for you, Marianne." He moved away from her, trembling, his face flushed, but the respect and adoration in his eyes heartened her: it was not the lustful look of a man who merely wanted her body.

"I'll make it up to you, dearest," she promised. "You saw that man who came in and had supper a little while ago, the one whose table I was sharing for a time?"

"Yes, Marianne, I did. I don't like him."

Marianne tilted back her head and laughed deliciously. "Kevin, you're dear, you're unique, and I do love you. I've made you jealous. But that wasn't why I did it, believe me. I'd never try to hold you with a cheap trick like that, not ever." The smile left her face as she moved back to him, and put her arms around his neck. "But listen: you know that I came here from Galveston. Well, I met that man there, and he hasn't always been honest in the past. Now he claims he has a gold mine near Grass Valley that's loaded with ore and he wants me to invest a thousand dollars—he'd rather have five, but we temporarily settled on one. I'm just not sure whether to believe him. But from what I gather, he's going to go up to the mine in two days, and then he's coming in here next week to tell me what a killing I can make if I go in with him."

"I understand, Marianne. What do you want me to do?"

"Well, it's just a gamble, but it might work. You know where Grass Valley is? Well, maybe you could disguise yourself as a miner and go up there. Once you're in town, ask around for the whereabouts of a man answering to McNamara's description, or somehow get on his trail and find his mine. The area's not so big that you won't be able to find out where he is—people around town are bound to talk. I doubt very much there's any gold left in those hills, but you never know, and if there really is gold there, one thing is sure: I want my share."

"I'll be happy to go—anything for you, Marianne."

421

"You're a perfect darling, Kevin. And now you may kiss me properly."

She closed her eyes and shivered as his strong arms enfolded her, and she knew that she had made no mistake in this new, faithful love.

# Forty-Three

Despite the lateness of the hour, Lu Choy had decided to visit her cousin Wong Lu, who worked in the little restaurant just off Dragon Lane, beyond Government House. He was, after all, her only kin. Born near Canton to impoverished peasant parents, Lu Choy had been abandoned by them at the age of thirteen, when her two older brothers, her mother, and her father had suddenly moved to Peking. But she understood their behavior—as a girl, she would only be another mouth to feed, and they would doubtless have sold her anyway to the madam of the lupanar in Hong Kong, or, worse yet, in Canton or Macao. In those circumstances, she could never hope to live to even the age of thirty. She was only a humble peasant girl without education, and though she was sturdy and healthy, the wealthy mandarins and their retinues who patronized such houses demanded girls of many accomplishments. Besides, her feet had never been bound, and even some of the older fishermen pointed to her sandals and mocked her with calls of, "Stupid girl—who would want you as even a slave, with your big feet and your coarse skin?"

At twenty-three, she had not taken a man, and what she knew of them from the illiterate fishermen whose sampans crowded all around hers as far as the eye could see, she felt no desire to do so. It would be in a sense exchanging one kind of hard, exhausting life for another that was as yet unknown, hence one that would offer the most terrors. At least on this sampan, when she drew up the small anchor and the wind carried her little boat out to a fine school of fish, she felt free. Then there was the excitement of going into Victoria and haggling with Ah Ling, the old shopkeeper who boasted that he offered only the freshest and finest fish taken from the waters of the China Sea. And if she was lucky, as sometimes happened, she would make as much as twelve or thirteen Hong Kong dollars, and could afford a pair of new sandals or a round hat with a peak to protect her from the blazing sun when she was out on the water dropping her net or, sometimes, special lines for the really big fish.

Wong Lu was not really good to her, but at least he and she shared the same blood, for he was the son of her father's brother. He was about ten years older than she. There were times when the fish had not come to her net or her lines. Hungry, she would go to the little restaurant and entreat him with all the humility and pathos she could summon. He would berate her, make embarrassing comments about her big ungainly feet, but in the end he would give her a packet of food to take back, sometimes rice cooked with tiny prawns and onions, or again a bowl of delicious mussel stew.

She tried not to visit him more than twice a month, but she knew that it pleased him to grumble and scold her. He could not entirely dislike her, Lu Choy reasoned, for in between the scoldings he had taken the time to teach her a few words of English that he had learned from serving English-speaking customers in the restaurant. Sometimes, too, although very rarely the last two years, there was a letter to him from her father that her cousin read to her, even though her father never mentioned her existence.

From those letters, she had learned that her brothers worked as bricklayers and that both had married and had children. Of course, they were older than she was, and it was only natural that her father should do all that he could for sons to carry on his line. She no longer counted, and she had resigned herself to that fact years ago. Besides, as Wong Lu was so fond of saying to her, "If you do not like your lot, you can always go to the *p'in min yuan*, the alms house." And, of course, that was true, but because she had survived so long by herself on the little sampan, she could look back at her cousin's severe face and sometimes, if he was not in too bad a mood, reply, "I am sure, honored cousin, that if one day I must go there, you at least will send me off with a ricksha and a strong coolie to draw it."

There were times when Lu Choy allowed herself to think of what could have been, if her parents had been well-to-do. Her feet would have been bound, and perhaps she might even have been offered as a second or third wife—or at least as a concubine—to a venerable old mandarin who would treat her gently as if she were a little child who should not know pain. There would be food with rice wine aplenty, fine clothes of silks and brocades, and jade and turquoise rings or bracelets that he would give her if she pleased him. Coming out of her daydreaming, she would see the water lapping against her boat and hear the conversations on the next sampan and smell the cooking fires and realize that nothing had changed, nor would it ever.

Yet in many ways it was a good life. Perhaps tonight Wong Lu might have a tasty bit of squid for her, because the restaurant where he worked offered that as a special delicacy. It was reserved for wealthy customers, to be sure, and she herself had never yet drawn one up in her nets. There were others, like Kim Goy, who owned the big junk with the orange sail down toward the end of the port, who could go farther out than she dared in her little rickety boat and pull in squid and the biggest prawns, and even once last spring, a giant octopus, which he had sold to Lum Kee, who ran the big fish market on Kowloon Road.

She made certain that the sampan was properly anchored and that her cooking fire was completely out. It would be a long walk around the side of the island into Victoria, but the night was pleasant and she had a sudden craving for prawns. Also, it pleased her to concoct a kind of fantasy about her monotonous life: tonight, for instance, she would pretend that she was going stealthily to meet a wealthy merchant, who decided that he needed a fourth wife. No—better yet, it would be a young artisan, or even a scholar who had never had a girl and therefore would not find her too ugly. And she would walk behind him with head bowed, rapt with attention, listening to his every word as he spoke of things that were far beyond the ability of her intellect to comprehend—yet they would delight her simply because she could hear the sound of his voice and know that he was speaking to her and for her.

It was midnight when she reached the restaurant. Observing that there was only one customer, who was finishing a bowl of rice and drinking his tea, she quickly entered. Wong Lu was preparing to clean up the restaurant and close it for the night. He was the chief cook and, sometimes, when he was in very good humor, he would intimate to her that the man who owned the restaurant was getting old and would one day sell it to him for not too many Hong Kong dollars. If that happened, and she maintained this not too frequent relationship with him, it was conceivable that he would be even more generous with scraps and tidbits.

She had taken with her a little wicker basket to carry the food that he would give her. She effaced herself against the front wall just inside the door, waiting for him to notice her. He did, and he made his awareness of her known by directing disparaging remarks to her, berating her for daring to visit him at such an unseemly hour and wondering if she had had the good sense to make certain that her sampan would not drift away from its moorings.

At last, the elderly customer finished his late meal and, nodding his head and folding his hands in his sleeves, went out of the restaurant. "Have the goodness at least to pull the curtain down, worthless cousin," Wong Lu reproached her, and Lu Choy hastened to obey.

"Well, I suppose you wish me to fill your basket. Food becomes dearer and dearer, and you know that. Still and all, I have done well for the owner, and tonight has not been too busy. Wait until I throw out this bucket of slops. Better yet, go out ahead of me to the back and open the door so that I do not have to set the heavy bucket down and then open the door and lift the bucket again. This much at least you could do to earn your dinner," he grumbled.

They were hard words, but she had heard them many times before and she was used to them. With the apologetic smile of a poor relation, huddling and stooping to make herself as small as she could—for Lu Choy was taller than the average Chinese woman, being about five feet six inches in height, rawboned but with a pleasingly winsome face, under black hair cut short almost like a boy's—she hurried ahead of him into the back of the restaurant, past the storeroom where the smoked meats and the fish were kept in a dark room to prevent spoilage, and opened the door that led into the dead-end alley. Wong Lu, still muttering to himself over the impositions that a hardworking man was obliged to endure at the end of a trying day, toted the bucket toward the threshold and, gripping it with both hands, prepared to fling its contents out into the alley.

"Look, Wong Lu, a man!" Lu Choy exclaimed. Lopasuta Bouchard lay sprawled on his side, his body huddled in a fetal position.

"A vagrant, a derelict, one who perhaps has smoked too many pipes of the poppy," was Wong Lu's contemptuous comment.

"Not so, honored cousin. You can see from his clothes that he is not Chinese, and by his face also. It is red, and I do not know what this means except that he is not from this part of the world. Perhaps the poor man is hurt. Perhaps he has been beaten."

"What concern is it of yours, Lu Choy?"

"If he is not given care, he may die."

"And you wish to take in this man? Truly, you have ideas beyond your station. Poor girl that you are, living on the sampan, how can you give comfort to this stranger?"

The young Chinese woman held her head high as she boldly retorted, "I know that I am lowly, that I am a woman, and that I come to you on my knees, most honorable cousin. But all this does not prevent my feeling sympathy for this stranger. I will take him to my sampan, I will find a coolie with a ricksha to carry him there, for he probably cannot walk."

"Oh, well, since you are so stubborn, I will yield to you. Take him, then. And give me the basket, and I will fill it. He will be hungry when he wakens," Wong Lu grumbled.

"I ask but one more favor, esteemed cousin. Help me carry him into the restaurant. It is not good for him to lie there out in the cold and the filth."

"Woman, I swear that you have the devil in you! Oh, very well—but it is late, and I must go home, so let us make an end of it quickly," Wong Lu irritatedly declared. Nonetheless, glancing curiously at her, he stooped down, and with Lu Choy helping, the two of them lifted Lopasuta's inert body into the back of the restaurant, then closed the door. Wong Lu bolted it and snapped, "Now go

427

find your ricksha and be quick! I will fill the basket, but do not take too long. I do not want this nobody in the restaurant through the night. If the owner were to come ahead of me tomorrow and find him, I should be discharged in disgrace, and it would be all your fault, worthless cousin!"

"I'll be quick; I'll find someone. There are always ricksha boys on Cormorant Lane," Lu Choy eagerly proffered. Swiftly opening the door, she disappeared into the night and hurried down the cobbled pavement till she came to a broader square. There was a post topped with an oil lamp sending a flickering, eerie glow down the narrow street. "Come, I have work for you, and I will give you three coppers," she called out to one of the two ricksha coolies she saw squatting beside their vehicles.

"Where do you go, woman?" one of them, a man with a short queue, grumbled.

"To Aberdeen, to my sampan. I have found a man who is very ill. I will make it four coppers, then."

"Make it five and I will come with you."

"Come, then, we waste time talking," Lu Choy imperiously commanded.

With an indifferent grunt of assent, the coolie grasped the poles of his ricksha and trotted docilely beside the intrepid young woman back to the restaurant. Wong Lu was scowling as he opened the front door, then pressed the basket into her hands. "Here, girl, this is all I can spare now. Be quick, you have cost me an hour of sleep at least. And do not come back again so soon. I've done more for you than I should."

"I am very grateful, honored cousin." Lu Choy humbly bowed her head. Placing the basket to one side on the ricksha seat, she beckoned to the coolie, who accompanied her to where Lopasuta Bouchard still lay in his drugged sleep. "I do not know what manner of man he is, girl," the coolie said, "though he seems young and strong, and I can carry him alone—I do not need your help." With a show of his muscles, he stooped down, lifted Lopasuta in his arms, and bore him out to the waiting ricksha with Lu Choy hurrying beside him.

"Careful, do not sit him down on that basket. It's food he will need to get back his strength," she insisted.

"Woman, you give orders like a princess. I have

changed my mind. The price is too little—but we will talk of it when I have brought this *wai kuo jen,* this foreigner, to your boat," the coolie complained.

Lu Choy trotted beside the coolie, glancing back at Lopasuta, whose head lolled forward. She spoke but a few words of English, and she did not know what tongue this foreigner spoke, but it was as if one of her venerable ancestors had put within reach the answer to her prayer: one day there would be a man who would not look upon her with scorn at her ugliness.

When the sturdy coolie again began to complain that the journey was far too long for the scant handful of coppers he would earn, Lu Choy berated him with withering scorn. "I have seen you before. You boast that you are as strong as any sumo wrestler, and now you weep like a woman. If you are so tired, I will pull the ricksha myself. Oh, very well, I will give you eight copper coins, but nothing more, be that understood!"

"You drive a hard bargain, woman, but so be it. Well, the worst of the journey is over; we have not far to go."

When they reached the shore of Aberdeen, the rickshaw bearer squinted at the vague outlines of the vertical masts that stretched out into the inky darkness. "I will not go there. I do not swim and I do not wish yet to join my ancestors, woman."

"You will leave this man for me to drag all the way along the walk? If I can do it, so can you! Let it be nine coppers then!" Lu Choy indignantly declared.

With a shrug, the coolie lifted Lopasuta Bouchard's limp body from the ricksha, while Lu Choy nimbly made her way along the wooden plankings that led from sampan to sampan in this city of boats. Scowling and muttering oaths that he had been bilked by a creature whose feet had not even been bound at birth, the coolie carried Lopasuta until they reached Lu Choy's sampan. She crawled aboard and put her basket near a little metal grill where there were coals and kindling wood. She would warm it for the handsome *wai kuo jen.* She wondered how far he had come, for she had never seen the likes of such a man—young and tall, with skin that was the color of a copper skillet, and a fine, sturdy body. How had he come here, and what tongue did he speak? She would learn this when the time came, if the gods so willed.

"Here is your money, ricksha man." Lu Choy cautiously took out a round leather purse, counted out the coins, and dropped them into the ricksha man's hand. He bit several of them, suspiciously glaring at her, then nodded. Soon he was lost in the darkness as he made his way back to the shore and his empty ricksha.

Lu Choy knelt over the unconscious Comanche, clucking her tongue in a cooing, sympathetic sound as she saw the new scars on his temples from the bruises inflicted by blows of the belaying pin and the dirt and the filth of the alley begriming his cheeks and chin. She began to tug off the black frock coat, using all her strength to lift him first so as to ease off the sleeves. It was fine material, this she recognized, and she had never seen its like before. She loosened the cravat, examined it, then shrugged and shook her head. Now, dipping a clean rag into the placid water, she began to clean his face. She was hungry, but that could wait until he had come out of his deep sleep. By putting her hand to his heart, she knew that he was not dying: the beat was strong and good. But he would need food and rest.

It would be possible to clean those clothes, beating them on the rocks, sponging them off with clear water, then brushing them carefully with hard bristles. She opened his shirt and was struck by the sturdiness of his body. She took another clean rag, dipped it in the water, and rubbed his chest and throat. And then suddenly she uttered a tiny cry: he had blinked his eyes and was staring at her, dully, without recognition, and his lips moved, as he tried to speak.

"Who—you—" he mumbled, and then closed his eyes again. Greatly encouraged, Lu Choy took a fresh cloth and, soaking it, pressed it gently against his eyes and forehead, knowing that the cool water would refresh him. As the drug slowly wore off, Lopasuta again opened his eyes and feebly tried to rise.

Lu Choy shook her head, and with one hand gently pressed him back. Now she saw him fixing her with an intent stare as lucidity returned to him.

"Hong Kong?" His voice was feeble and husky. But these words she understood and she smiled and nodded her head emphatically.

Gradually, feeling himself stronger, he again tried to sit

430

up, but Lu Choy shook her head, uttering birdlike little cries of mingled sympathy and warning, as she insistently held him down with the flat of her left hand. She continued to pat his face, delighted that his eyes now fixed on hers and seemed to be clear. He did not seem ill, and yet he was so weak for so large a man.

The moon shone full and bright after the rain had passed, and by the silvery light wafting down through the hundreds of wooden masts, Lopasuta saw Lu Choy's face as she bent over him, eyes wide and dark and yet comforting. Then he groaned aloud, realizing that his journey had come to its destined end, and that he was thousands of miles from Geraldine and their child.

"My God," he murmured to himself, "Manitou, help me now. How will I ever get back to her? Who is this girl, and why am I on a boat again? Where will they take me—"

"You *wai kuo jen*—foreigner—yes?" Lu Choy brightly asked, wracking her brain for those few words of English that her cousin had taught her. Mostly—since her days were spent with the boat people of Aberdeen or, when she visited Victoria, the Chinese shopkeepers and her haughty cousin—she had no need to use anything more than her native Cantonese dialect.

Lopasuta struggled to utter a few words. "I come—from the United States. In a ship," he told her, but she shook her head, shrugging to tell him that she could not comprehend his meaning. Then an idea seized her: reaching for the basket of food that Wong Lu had given her, she showed it to him, and with her right hand made a gesture of putting food into her mouth, then cocked her head and eyed him. *"Chi e te?"* she said, asking if he was hungry.

He stared at her, wanting desperately to understand what she was trying to say to him. Then he saw the prawns and the rice and he nodded. Lu Choy gave a happy little laugh. At last he understood her, this strong, tall foreigner.

"I will heat the food for you. We will eat it together. I, too, am hungry," she told him in Chinese. He watched her, blinking his eyes, straining to regain the full measure of his physical senses so that he could cope with this new situation. He watched her make a little fire in the shallow wide iron brazier; then, taking out a crude metal skillet, she put in the food and placed it over the fire. Taking another cloth, she held the handle, turning the skillet this way and that until the food was ready. Then she upturned the skillet's contents back into the basket, set it down between them and, nodding at him with a glowing smile, put her hand to the rice and a few prawns and conveyed them to her mouth, chewing them and nodding again. Then she gestured that he was to imitate her.

He was hungry, ravenously hungry, and the aroma of the prawns and the rice had become tantalizing. Warily he scooped up a handful and brought it to his mouth and began to chew. It was very good, and as he met her gaze, he nodded and said, "Thank you. It is good."

Lu Choy was enchanted with him. She let him eat nearly three quarters of the food, satisfied that his appetite showed he was recovering. There would be time for talk later. Then she would learn where he had come from, which must be very far away, indeed. When the basket was empty, she made the sign of sleeping, pressing both palms together and putting her hands to one side of her head as she closed her eyes.

Lopasuta nodded. The meal had been delicious. Now fatigue again claimed him. He hardly noticed as she quickly removed her jacket and folded it, making it into a pillow. Then, with both hands against his shoulders, she lifted him up until she could place the folded coat beneath his head.

He fell back into an untroubled, restful sleep. Lu Choy sat for a long while studying him, and then at last she lay herself down beside him, drawing her knees up to her belly and making herself small so that he could have most of the space at the bottom of the little sampan.

The water of the bay splashed softly and the hum of conversation died out at last as deep night overtook the boat people of Aberdeen.

# Forty-Four

On the day after Henry McNamara's visit to the bistro, Kevin Anderson took the morning train to Sacramento, where he transferred to another train into the Sierra country. In the town of Colfax, he disembarked and went to a livery stable, where he secured a sturdy mare and rode for another two hours before he reached the busy little community of Grass Valley, the center of a number of gold mines still active in the region. There, using a supply of greenbacks that Marianne had given him, Kevin secured lodging for himself for the night, as well as a stable where he could feed and bed down his horse.

He awoke the next morning and, after dressing, looked into the cracked, cloudy mirror over the bureau and grinned at his reflection. He had taken care to disguise himself as a miner, so as not to attract attention, and the night before last he had even, with Marianne's help, dyed his hair. Should he happen upon Henry McNamara—not entirely impossible in a town the size of Grass Valley—he would in all likelihood not be recognized, for McNamara had barely taken notice of him on his one visit to Marianne's bistro.

Shortly before eight o'clock, he left his boardinghouse and walked down the main street of Grass Valley. Having acclimated himself to the town by exploring its streets and even looking in on one or two saloons, Kevin directed his steps to the office of an assayer, for he was anxious to learn if there were any information he could glean as to the whereabouts of the wily McNamara. Entering the office, he approached the assayer, a genial, mustachioed man who nevertheless had a shrewd look in his eyes. He was seated behind a long, dusty table on which were a number

433

of rock samples—ore, Kevin assumed—and a set of scales.

"Good morning, sir," Kevin spoke up brightly. "I wonder if you could give me some information."

"I'll try, my friend, but you'll have to make it quick. I've got a load of ore to evaluate before the day's out."

"Well," Kevin went on, "I wonder if you've had any inquiries from a big man, name of McNamara, obviously an easterner, to judge from the way he usually dresses. He may have claimed to have found a new mine in the area."

"New mine? Not likely; in fact I'd say most all the veins of gold in these parts have been discovered and claimed by now. Mostly now it's the big companies that are working the mines on a regular basis—and there's no saying how long they'll continue to yield high-grade ore. But—wait a minute now, hold on a bit. I do recall a feller coming in here a couple of weeks ago—big feller, just as you say, with a bowler hat and a pompous way about him. He had a sample for me to test. It tested pretty good, too, and I was mighty curious about it. But he was damn sneaky and wouldn't say where it came from—just that it was from somewhere north of town."

"I see," Kevin replied slowly. "So you couldn't surmise anything from the ore?"

"Oh, I'm not saying that, young feller. I've been in this business a damn sight longer than you've got years, and I know these parts well. Sure as I'm sitting here, the ore that feller gave me came from Casper's Gulch, northwest of town—I could tell from the particular composition of that rock. There's a whole hillside of stone like it back there, and they'd have pulled the ore out of there years ago if it hadn't been easier and more profitable to mine the other side of the valley. But as I say, this ore tested pretty rich—maybe a bit too rich for that site—and I was a mite suspicious of this dude."

"I can understand *that*," Kevin cynically replied. "Now, I wonder if you could tell me how I might reach this Casper's Gulch."

"Sure thing, young feller. Just take the road heading north of town and go on up that way for about ten miles. Then turn left at the fork and keep on going about five more miles. It's up in that area. The rock you'll be looking for is spread over a four-square-mile area. Still and all, you won't have too far to look: there isn't much countryside up there that's at all accessible and worth looking into, for a mine."

"Thank you, sir. I'll bear that in mind," Kevin responded. "I'll head up that way and see what I can find."

Leaving the assayer's office, Kevin went immediately to a general store, where he replenished his supplies of food. He then proceeded to the stable, mounted his sturdy mare, and rode out of town. As he headed north on the road the assayer had described, he felt the reassuring bulge in his trouser pocket—a loaded Colt revolver he had brought with him from San Francisco, just in case there was trouble.

The landscape grew more desolate, the hills steeper, as Kevin approached the fork in the road where he remembered he was supposed to turn left. The sun was by now high in the sky, but there was very little traffic on the narrow road. The road became steeper and steeper still as Kevin rode along, and he surmised that this western fork led away from most of the big mines in the area, since the right fork had appeared to be wider and better traveled.

Finally, Kevin reached a small path that veered off to the left again, and reining in his horse to peer down at the ground, he could make out a number of footprints, of both men and horses, which appeared to him to be recent. He turned his horse into the path and slowly followed it as it wound upward toward the steep face of a rocky cliff now looming above him. Then, reaching a plateau, Kevin stopped and dismounted. He looked around and saw a yard-wide crevice through an outcropping of boulders. Leading the mare by the bridle, he wended his way through to the other side, and determining that it could not be seen back there by anyone coming along the path, he fettered the horse to a poplar and made his way back through the opening.

Proceeding on foot along the plateau, which was largely bare of trees, Kevin reached a point at the far end where a large opening could be seen, the entrance of a cave in the rocky side of the slope of the hill. At the mouth of this cave, Kevin could see more footprints of several different kinds, and again he discerned that they must have been made recently. The footprints disappeared into the cave, and so he took out a piece of tallow candle that he had brought along in the pocket of his jacket, lit it with a lucifer, and entered.

Once inside the cave, Kevin could see that it had been enlarged with tools, and timber beams had been applied to brace up the top and sides of this partial excavation. As far as he could tell, it was an authentic mine; nevertheless, he recalled to mind the words he had heard from a grizzled old prospector, with whom he had talked just before leaving San Francisco. The loquacious old-timer, Elmer Whittens, who could remember panning for gold in the days of John Sutter, had warned Kevin that a phony mine shaft looked like a genuine article, and if he was on the lookout for any flimflam, he'd have to catch the schemers in the act. With graphic gestures and loud sound effects, Whittens had described what Kevin might expect to see and hear.

Satisfied that he had found what could well be McNamara's gold mine, Kevin crawled out of the tunnel and walked back down the plateau until he found another smaller cavern facing the mine site, and from this vantage point he settled down to wait and watch. He had brought along plenty of food and water in his saddlebag to sustain him throughout the night if need be; indeed he would have been ready to endure a far longer vigil for Marianne's sake.

All through the long, hot afternoon, there was no sign of any visitor to this lonely stretch of hills. For a time, Kevin dozed and then, after sundown, made a hasty supper from some biscuits, smoked ham, and cheese, washing them down with a swig of water from a canteen. Then, as a precaution, he took out his revolver and made certain that it was loaded, in the event there was trouble.

It was nearly sundown when he heard the sound of horses approaching in the distance from the eastern side of the plateau. Soon after came the sound of men's voices, and Kevin stiffened and cautiously peered from out of the mouth of the little cave. The riders dismounted, and as Kevin strained his eyes in the darkness, he could vaguely make out the outlines of three men clambering up to the large cave that he had already inspected.

Two of them were carrying sacks, and one, whose size and girth led Kevin to believe that he was Henry McNamara himself, carried a shotgun.

436

Holding his breath, and sharpening all his senses, he tried to hear their voices. One of the trio said hoarsely: "We'll do just like you said, Mr. McNamara. Where do you want it salted?"

Then he heard McNamara's voice before it faded as the men entered the cavern, "Right by the end of the shaft, Mason. And don't overdo it."

His eyes widened, as he remembered what the old prospector had told him. After the feverish days of the California gold rush, there had been many ambitious and scheming men who had tried to stake a claim to worthless sites and then proceed to high-grade, or as the old man put it, "salt" the supposed mine by firing a shotgun charged with gold dust at the desired locations in the rock, or even by blasting the rocks with dynamite packed with gold dust. It would be easy to get a crooked assayer to pronounce that there was a rich vein of ore, the evidence of which would be visible in the salting. A number of such schemes had worked in the past, and their perpetrators had flimflammed many honest but greedy backers into putting up a large capital, ostensibly to pay for working the mine, but actually to line the pockets of the schemer, leaving the investors sadder, poorer, and wiser.

Moving back into the protective cover of the little cave, Kevin waited. A few minutes later, there was a muffled explosion; then, four or five minutes after that, a second, quickly followed by a third. He chuckled to himself, grateful to Elmer Whittens. He would tell Marianne that the old man should have a standing credit at the bistro for helping him to expose the scheme. Now he understood precisely what Henry McNamara was up to, and she would be very pleased with him for having found out. He closed his eyes and imagined her waiting for him, and he smiled in eager anticipation. He thought to himself that even if she had not given him the unexpected bounty of her love, he would still be indebted to her, for she had saved him from being shanghaied, from a life of enforced labor whose brutality was legend along the Barbary Coast.

The three men were now emerging from the larger cave about two hundred feet beyond him, and he again strained to hear what they were saying. The first voice he heard, hoarse and surly, now declared, "That should do it, Mr. Mac. Jake and me, we'll stand ready to swear you got a rich vein here. And you remember, Mr. Mac, I told you about that fellow Dan Weinbold who used to be an assayer up in the Dakotas. He's been down on his luck and he'd go along with you, if you handed him some good hard cash."

"I'll do just that, Pete, once I get that uppity Galveston bitch to go along as a partner with me," Kevin heard Henry McNamara avow, ending his words with a cynical laugh. Marianne's young lover ground his teeth and clenched his fist at the insult. He restrained his impulse to avenge her honor then and there, feeling certain that, once he told her what McNamara was up to, Marianne Valois would think of a way to pay him back.

"All right, our job's done. Let's get back to 'Frisco," McNamara ordered. "Tomorrow evening, I'll divvy the money I get out of her with you, and then start selling the stock. It'll be a killing for us all."

"Better make sure there won't be any slips, Mr. Mac," the man called Pete warned. "We don't want anybody to have any reason to suspect this mine's been tampered with. I don't exactly like the idea of getting in trouble with the police."

"Nobody's going to suspect anything, so stop worrying." It was McNamara again, in a swaggering, confident tone. "Don't forget what old P. T. Barnum said six years ago when he opened what he called the greatest show on earth—'There's a sucker born every minute.' The suckers who'll buy my stock have plenty of greed in their hearts, and they'll fall hook, line, and sinker for the mine. And once all the stock is sold, we'll beat it out of town. You know, I've always hankered after going to the South Seas and maybe having a harem of sweet island girls to look after my needs. Well now, that's enough talk. Let's get the horses."

Kevin Anderson waited until he heard the horses' hooves grow fainter and disappear in the distance, and then crawled out of the cave, stretched his limbs, and chuckled to himself. There was no hurry. He was relishing all he had heard. And Marianne would relish it even more.

Lopasuta Bouchard eased back into the world of consciousness after a dreamless sleep. He awoke to find him-

438

self inside the little cabinlike shelter of the sampan, wearing only his drawers and socks and shoes. He uttered a startled cry and tried to sit up, then sank back with a groan of pain: the heavy dose of laudanum had left him with an excruciating headache. He began to feel a throbbing discomfort, and groaned softly again. Suddenly he was conscious of the young woman kneeling beside him, her face solicitous, her eyes searching and questioning, as they peered down at him. "My—my clothes—" he weakly stammered.

Lu Choy swiftly turned her face to one side and permitted herself a titter of amusement, which she concealed with a hand over her mouth. While he had slept, she had carefully moved him, taking pains not to waken him, and worked off his shirt and trousers. Then, groping for some English words from her limited vocabulary that he might recognize, she averred, "Me wash. You dirty. Maybe take bath later. Feel better now?"

She had interspersed Chinese phrases with the English words and Lopasuta failed to comprehend her meaning completely. But at least he knew he was no longer a prisoner, though the dull ache in his skull served as a reminder of his ordeal. He realized he had slept through the night and it was now at least midday, from the way the bright rays filtered in through the open entrance behind him.

He finally managed to sit up, and Lu Choy gleefully clapped her hands and smiled, taking this as a good sign that the handsome stranger she had saved was out of danger.

He stared at her, and since she was smiling, he smiled back, although he was crushed with despair at the knowledge of where he was. He reflected on the irony of the fact that while at last he was no longer a prisoner held incommunicado, it would still be virtually impossible for him to tell Geraldine what had happened. A cable that could be sent across Asia and Europe to England and thence to America would cost dearly, and while he had been unconscious on the ship sailing from New Orleans, he had been robbed of everything he had—except for the clothes on his back. He realized bitterly that even sending a letter, which wouldn't reach his beloved wife for nearly a month, even by the fastest steamship, would necessitate having the money to buy paper, an envelope, and stamps.

He rallied, trying to shake himself out of his black mood. He was still alive, he was strong, and he could work. Yes, that was the answer. Somehow, he must get to the city and find some kind of work, with someone who spoke English. In that way, he could earn his passage back to Geraldine. And yet this girl, this utter stranger, had been so kind to him—more thoughtful and considerate than many of the citizens of the town where he and Geraldine had lived together—that he must take care not to offend her, not to be rude.

"The main city—Hong Kong—is it here?" he asked, repeating the words and pointing to the bottom of the sampan with his forefinger.

At first she appeared puzzled by his words, but then she smiled and laughed—an exquisite, tinkling sound—and shook her head. "This Aberdeen." Her pronunciation was quaint and charming to his ears. "Big city—Vic-to-ria—she other side. You want go? I take you when you feel good."

"I want to go now. My name—" remembering that her English was limited, he pointed to himself, "my name, Lopasuta Bouchard."

Conscientiously, she repeated the syllables of his name again and again with so delightful an accent that he could not help smiling. Then she nodded and beamed her understanding. "*Shih jan!* Me unnerstan'! Me"—imitating him by designating herself with her forefinger—"Lu Choy."

"Thank you, Lu Choy. You have been very good to me. I go now," he said slowly. Then he proceeded to drag on his trousers, arching and twisting himself because the roof of the enclosure was too low to allow him to stand, and Lu Choy again turned her face away from him and put her hand over her mouth to smother another delightful little giggle.

She had managed to brush away most of the filth and grime from his coat and trousers, and she had washed his shirt. Although the temperature outside was warm—and certainly warmer than it would have been in Alabama in this month of October—his clothes were still uncomfortably damp. But at least he was presentable, and now he was determined to find some kind of work. He remembered that Hong Kong, as a British Crown colony, would have many trading firms, banks, and both importing and exporting companies. It was a kind of melting pot for the Asians, the English, even the Dutch and Portuguese. Therefore, there would be many officials and workers who would be able to understand him, and undoubtedly some of them could guide him to find remunerative work that would earn him his passage home.

His head had stopped throbbing now, and, stooping, still weak but at least able to control his movements, Lopasuta ducked his head under the opening and straightened up to stare around him at the city of sampans. The sun was descending in the west, and he decided it was too late today to go look for work—but tomorrow, he assuredly would. Then the awareness of his being without money struck him: against his will he would have to accept the kindness and hospitality of this Chinese girl, because he had no way of paying for his own food and lodging. But he promised himself that he would make it up to her. Still, he was curious to know how this young woman had found him and why she had had him brought aboard her boat.

She had followed him out and stood beside him, looking quizzically up at him. When he turned to look back at her, her shyness moved him. A slow blush spread over her cheeks, and she looked quickly away.

Her shyness was so different from his wife's bold demeanor—but this fond remembrance soon turned to pain. It tortured him to think that perhaps Geraldine's mother and father might, even now, be condemning him, telling her, "You ought to have known what sort of man he was. He's decided to leave you, to desert you and go where you'll never find him again." He prayed that that would never happen, but he was not so sure. He recalled how they had disowned her for marrying him, and he remembered how it had hurt her, even though she had tried not to show it. And perhaps—the horrible thought crept into his already despairing mind—if she were to hear all those vilifications, she might begin to believe the worst of him.

Gloomily, Lopasuta turned to stare at the tall, vertical masts of the junks and the sampans, but the beauty of the sky and the placid water only added to his misery. He would much rather have seen the sluggish, sometimes muddy current of the Alabama River as it crept past Pintilalla Creek before quickening its pace toward Montgomery.

Lu Choy moved beside him, studying his strong, anguished face. Although she did not understand him or know yet whence he had come, she could sense the torment seething in him, and very hesitantly, shyly, she put her slim hand to his elbow, then hastily drew it back as he turned to stare at her.

He was touched, because it was as if the Manitou to whom he prayed had sent him a sign: a sign that his beloved Geraldine had thought of him, prayed for him, and that somehow her thought and prayer had been transmitted across the continent and an ocean to this poor lonely Chinese girl in her sampan. Now Lu Choy furtively glanced up at him, half-fearful that she had offended him. And even though his heart was sinking, desolate at the thought that another day in a long procession of days and nights had widened the gulf between him and his wife, Lopasuta reached out to touch her hand and to give her a bleak smile of gratitude.

## Forty-Five

Henry McNamara returned to the bistro on Friday evening at about six o'clock, grandiosely appropriated the best table for himself, and ordered an excellent meal accompanied by a bottle of French wine. He directed the waiter to let Marianne Valois know that he was there and that—at her convenience, to be sure—he would welcome the opportunity to chat with her.

The attractive Frenchwoman received this news with Kevin Anderson present in her room upstairs. Earlier, she had coached her lover on the role he should play in the event that the Galveston con man proved obstreperous or threatening, telling Kevin that she was deeply indebted to him for having gone to Grass Valley and lain in wait for McNamara and his two confederates, thus proving that the alleged gold mine had been salted. And now she planned to turn the tables on the crook and make sure his swindling days were at an end.

So, half an hour later, she went downstairs, crossed over to the elegant bar to confer with the bartender, and then sauntered casually over to McNamara's table. After wiping his mouth with his napkin and smothering a belch, he got to his feet and bowed to her with a great show of gallantry. He greeted her effusively. "What a joy to see you again, my dear Marianne!"

"Thank you, Mr. McNamara. I see that you are enjoying yourself. I trust you find my place to your satisfaction?"

"I do indeed, my dear lady! In fact, seeing how many

443

customers are here so early in the evening, I have been thinking that you must be doing extremely well."

"Reasonably so—enough to make an honest livelihood, Mr. McNamara," Marianne blandly retorted.

"Do sit down. I'd be honored if you would join me in a glass of wine," he urged, designating a chair to his left.

Marianne smiled and seated herself, and attentively regarded him. "I recall that you had a proposition for me the other evening, Mr. McNamara," she began.

"Indeed I do! And I've the very best of news for you, dear lady. Incidentally, I believe the patronage of your fine establishment here reinforces my belief that you could surely afford at least a thousand dollars to go into partnership with me. Remember, the more you invest, the more percentage of profit you can expect to get."

"I understand. But what about the gold mine? As I recall, you were going to go over there with an assayer to find out whether the prospects were as good as you thought."

"They're even better." He set down his fork and leaned forward and, with a dramatic pause, waited until she had absorbed his remark, then continued, "There's a very rich vein of gold, which we discovered just inside the shaft of the mine, Marianne. But I will need more capital to continue the excavation farther down—in order to mine the entire vein. Our current discovery is merely the tip of the iceberg, so to speak."

She gave him a sweet smile. "But exactly where is this fabulous mine of yours, Mr. McNamara?"

"Dear lady, you could search for days and days and never find it. But believe me, it's going to make you and me rich. How rich it will make *you* will depend on the size of your investment with me, and that's really why I'm here tonight. Not that this dinner isn't as fine a meal as I've ever had anywhere, you understand, but I know that you're a businesswoman—and an astute one, at that."

"You have sized me up correctly, Mr. McNamara. That is exactly what I am. And that is why I certainly wouldn't dream of giving you a thousand dollars—or even one penny to invest in your gold mine."

He goggled at her, his jaw dropping, and then, recovering himself, gasped, "Surely you must be joking! Why, Marianne, I thought we had a deal—an agreement—I have my assayer standing ready—everything is planned—"

"I have my own plans," she airily retorted, putting a hand to her head and smoothing her curls. "The police would like nothing better than to put you in jail for a long, long time. If the Vigilantes still dispensed justice in this town, you'd probably have a rope around your neck."

"My dear lady," he frowned, "what are you talking about? What has my gold mine got to do with the police—and why would they want to arrest me?"

"Exactly *because* of this gold mine of yours, Mr. McNamara. You thought that I was going to be taken in by your ingenious little swindle—but you are quite mistaken."

"For the life of me, dear lady, I don't know what you're talking about. Would you please elaborate?"

"With pleasure, Mr. McNamara. The police hate swindlers—especially those out to dupe innocent women—almost as much as they do murderers. And when I tell them just how you salted that mine of yours out in Grass Valley—"

"S-salted the mine? You're absolutely mad!" Henry McNamara's face turned ashen and he began to finger the collar of his shirt as if its tightness was an uncomfortable reminder of something else.

"You see, Mr. McNamara," she blithely continued, "my partner, Kevin Anderson, went out to Grass Valley last week and found this mine of yours. And he saw you and your two men go into the mine carrying sacks and a shotgun—and he clearly heard you discuss your plans. Shortly after, he heard several explosions from the shotguns. He tells me it's a very old trick, known to prospectors since the days of the Gold Rush."

"My God!" was all that McNamara could hoarsely ejaculate as he mopped his suddenly sweating forehead with a monogrammed linen handkerchief.

"I assure you, Mr. McNamara, Kevin Anderson would be very willing to testify against you if you decide to ask for a trial in front of a jury."

"I—I'm sure we can settle this amicably, dear Marianne." McNamara's voice was unsteady and his eyes began to shift about nervously.

"Incidentally," she coldly interjected, "I resent your using my first name so freely. To you, I am Madame Valois, and I would be thankful if you would remember that."

Again he mopped his brow, staring frantically at her. "Damn you, anyhow!" he finally muttered under his breath. "Look, Mrs. Valois, all right—since you're a woman of the world, I'll admit that I salted the mine. But the suckers to whom I would sell stock wouldn't ever know that—there's a killing to be had there. Now, if you'll just be sensible and go along with my proposal—why, I wouldn't even charge you! Listen, I've still got three thousand dollars, and I can prepare the stock certificates and pay off the assayer just as I planned, and we can be partners—a fifty-fifty split. What do you say, Mrs. Valois?"

"Mr. McNamara, you don't seem to have understood me at all. I have no intention of being a part of any dishonest plans—yours or anyone's. Furthermore, I have no intention of allowing you to swindle anybody else. This conversation is over, Mr. McNamara," she declared, as she began to rise from his table.

Henry McNamara started sweating profusely again. "Now—now just wait, Mrs. Valois. Please. I haven't harmed you at all, have I? It—it was a bad idea, I admit it. Please—please sit down."

Reluctantly, she seated herself. "Well, Mr. McNamara? Do you have something further to say that could possibly be of interest to me? You know perfectly well that when Kevin Anderson tells the authorities all that he has witnessed, it will clearly show that yours is a case of *être pris sur le vif*—in other words, you've been caught with your pants down."

"Mari—Mrs. Valois," McNamara stuttered, "I beg of you. Let's keep this a little secret between you and me. Here," he extracted his well-worn wallet, "here's twenty-two hundred dollars. Take it. I'll get out of town with the eight hundred I've got left. I've been thinking of going on to the Yukon. There's sure to be gold there—real gold—that hasn't been found yet. And I won't have to salt a mine once I stake a claim."

Marianne Valois seemed to reconsider, then she shrugged. "All right. I'm in a generous mood tonight—more than you planned to be with me. I'll take the money if you and your friends promise to leave town for good."

"We will, we will!" he avowed. "Just give me a day or

two to make my plans." Grudgingly he handed over the banknotes. "There you are; your 'conscience' money."

"A very small price for saving the freedom of such an imaginative businessman, Mr. McNamara," she mocked as she folded the bills and thrust them into the bodice of her dress. "I wish you good fortune in the Yukon. You can count yourself lucky that I'm not a swindler like you—or else I'd take your money and tell the police about you into the bargain."

His face was livid as he rose from the table, turned, and began to stride out of the bistro. But Marianne stopped him with a cool, "Haven't you forgotten to pay for your dinner, Mr. McNamara? I would say four dollars should about cover it."

He turned, and there was murder in his eyes as he walked slowly back, took out his wallet again, and, with an oath, slammed the bills down onto the table so hard that the empty dinner plate toppled to the floor. He stared at her as if to memorize her face, and then turned on his heel and went out into the night.

It was past midnight, long after Marianne Valois's restaurant had closed. The building was dark, but Marianne and Kevin were still very much awake. In her rooms, the shutters and curtains were drawn so that no light passed through. The glow from a kerosene lamp on the nightstand beside her canopied bed lit the attractive Frenchwoman as she stood in Kevin's embrace, huskily murmuring, "*Chéri*, you've helped me more than I ever dreamed any man would. But I've a premonition that my Galveston swindler will be back tonight. I'm sure he would like to kill me to keep me from talking—and I think those two friends who rode with him to this cave of yours in Grass Valley will come with him."

"I have a feeling in my belly about it too, Marianne," Kevin Anderson hoarsely murmured, as his hands slipped down her shoulders and caressed her smooth, supple back. "When I heard them talking the other night, I knew they were up to no good—they're the kind who won't even stop at murder. But they won't get away with it if they try. I've still got that gun I bought for the trip to Grass Valley, and I know how to use it. I'm going out to the alley right

447

now to watch for those scoundrels," he avowed, as he gently disengaged himself from her embrace.

"Darling, it's far too dangerous for you to face them alone," Marianne protested. "I wouldn't want to lose you—" She drew him close to her once again, murmuring, "You know, I've been thinking a good deal about us. Even though you're younger than I am, maybe that's one reason I love you. That's all I'm going to say right now," and she gave him a prolonged kiss on the mouth.

Tearing himself away with difficulty, Kevin said huskily, "I'm going out there now, honey. I couldn't live with myself if anything happened. I love you, Marianne."

Marianne softly replied, gently stroking his cheek, "Go if you must, but please be careful."

Kissing her playfully on the nose, Kevin rejoined, "Pretend that I'm just your bodyguard, precious. And try not to worry."

As Kevin moved toward the door, Marianne called out in warning, "Do remember to stay in the dark so they can't see you."

Kevin nodded, halted a moment as he stared ardently at her, and then left her room. He went downstairs to the back of the bistro, then into the deserted kitchen, thinking fondly of his mistress. Never before had he met a woman who had so many ways of enthralling him, and whose inexplicable instincts for anticipating his desires made her without doubt the most unusual woman he had ever known, one who surpassed his wildest fantasies. He could not believe that she had chosen him to love, and he swore to himself that he would be her defender, her champion. Through all his life he had been afraid of violence, but now, curiously enough, he was resolved to do what was necessary—even to kill—if it meant saving her and protecting her. As he waited in the kitchen just inside the back doorway, he drew the revolver he had bought and examined the chambers to make certain they were still loaded. He remembered also the scornful, denigrating way Henry McNamara and his two cohorts had talked about Marianne; his eyes narrowed, and his face tightened with anger at the thought.

Close to the Barbary Coast as Marianne's bistro was, the raucous night sounds drifted to Kevin's ears. Music blared from honky-tonk pianos, and drunken laughter and angry shouts wafted from the cheap saloons two muddy blocks away. Once there was the shattering of glass, followed by angry shouts and the sounds of a fight.

His heart beating quickly, Kevin put the gun back into the belted holster. Suddenly the husky voice of the bartender, Ed MacDonald, was speaking behind him. "Kevin boy, I'll lend you a hand. The boss just told me that we might have some trouble out here. I've got my own gun, so we'll be ready for anything that happens. Mrs. Valois gave me the whole story. Now don't get your back up— she likes you a lot, and she trusts you. Only she thinks that an ounce of prevention is worth a pound of cure, and that's why she wanted me to be on your team, if you take my meaning."

"I do, and I'm glad to have you help, Ed. Wait, what was that?"

Kevin pricked up his ears as he heard a muffled sound out in the alley. Putting his forefinger to his lips, he crept forward to the kitchen door that led to the alley, opened it a crack to peer out, then quickly closed it again. He nodded excitedly. "They're here! All three of 'em, Ed. From the looks of it, they're going to try to start a fire that will hit us from the rear, and then shoot us down like sitting ducks as we run for it. Way I figure it is, we'd better get them first."

"I'm with you on that, Kevin boy," the bartender whispered. "Pull that door open again and let's you and I take some pot shots and see if we can't put an end to their shenanigans."

Kevin nodded and drew out his revolver, gripping it tightly in his right hand with his forefinger on the trigger. With his left hand, he took hold of the knob of the door, and then, eyeing the bartender, nodded. When Ed nodded back, he pulled open the door and flattened himself on his belly, as he stared out into the alley.

Pete and Jake, the two men who had salted the mine for Henry McNamara, had lit their torches, made of branches dipped into tar. At the moment the door opened, they were advancing toward each side of the frame building, and the light from their torches lit them up brightly in the murky darkness of the cold San Francisco night.

"No, you don't, you bastard," Ed yelled, as he fired his revolver at Jake, who had moved over to the bartender's right and was in the act of placing the pinewood torch against the dry wooden shingles of the building. Jake uttered a yell as he dropped the torch and spun around, sinking down on his knees, both hands pressed over his bleeding left shoulder. Meanwhile, Kevin had followed Pete to his left, and, lifting his revolver, pulled the trigger. There was a frenzied scream of pain as the older man dropped his torch and clasped his right wrist, wailing, "You broke my wrist, goddamn you, you broke it! You broke it!"

"We'll kill you both, unless you get the hell out of here," the bartender bawled. Then, sighting Henry McNamara crouching against a wall at the entrance of the dirty alley, he aimed his revolver at the shadowy outline of the Galveston swindler's body and called, "And you, mister, you better turn tail and get the hell out of here unless you want to be shot along with your friends. I'll count three, and then I'll let you have it!"

"Don't shoot, for God's sake, I'm going, I'm going, don't shoot!" McNamara wailed and, turning tail, ran for his life, disappearing in the darkness.

Jake and Pete had lifted their hands in surrender, and now stood side by side as Kevin and the bartender emerged from their hiding place in the kitchen, their revolvers trained on the two rogues.

"Now, boys," Ed taunted them, "I'll give you a choice. Either you stay put and wait while my friend here goes for the police, or you get the hell out of here as fast as your legs can carry you—and then get out of San Francisco altogether. Savvy?"

"Don't shoot! That's fine with me! Yeah, we'll go," Jake gasped hoarsely. "We only did it for the money. Mr. McNamara had lots of it to spread around, and we've been broke ever since we got to this lousy town."

"I hear you. All right, drop your guns where I can see them and then get out of here. If I ever see you again, I swear I'll have a bullet for each of you, and I won't just wound you. I'll do you in for good," the bartender threatened.

"I gotcha, mister! We're going! You won't see us again. Hell, Mr. McNamara ran off like a yellow skunk and we won't even get our dough. All right, we're going. Don't shoot again, though," Pete whined.

The two men hobbled off down the alley and were soon lost from view. Kevin rose and stamped out the last embers on the smoldering torches, then he and Ed went back inside, and Kevin slid home the bolt on the kitchen door. "I couldn't have done it without your help, Ed. I owe you," he said.

"The hell with that—it was the best fun I've had in a long time. Besides, those bastards had it coming. Now I'll tidy up in here, and you go back up and tell Mrs. Valois she won't have anything to worry about—not from those three sons of bitches," the bartender vehemently declared.

Kevin Anderson exhaled a sigh of relief. He walked slowly toward the stairway and up to the landing, then down the carpeted passageway. Thrusting the revolver into his breeches pocket, he lifted his right hand and hesitantly knocked at Marianne's door. Marianne opened it, clad in her dressing gown, which, although belted, barely concealed her enticing contours.

"Marianne, it's all over now. Ed and I sent them packing. Mr. McNamara was there, just the way you figured he might be, with his two friends—the ones who salted the Grass Valley mine," Kevin exuberantly declared.

Marianne smiled gently. She came toward him, linking her soft arms around his neck, and on tiptoe pressed her mouth against his. In response to this delicious provocation, he trembled with delight.

After a long moment, she whispered, "I want you to manage my place; I want you to be the boss man, Kevin. And if you wish, I'd like to be your woman on a permanent basis."

"You—you mean you'd marry me, M-Marianne?" he stammered.

"I would, indeed, *mon cher*—if you'll have me."

"Will I ever!" Kevin Anderson joyously exclaimed, as he took her into his arms and kissed her with all his heart.

Henry McNamara left San Francisco the next afternoon, taking a steamboat up beyond the Canadian border. Out of the eight hundred dollars he had left, he bought supplies, a sled and four sturdy malamute dogs, blankets, and a thickly lined fur coat. Then he started out for the Yukon.

In the store where he bought his supplies, two heavyset,

bearded Canadians watched him and then told the store-keeper, "There's a tenderfoot out looking for gold, but he's much too late."

They emerged a little later, and drove their own dog teams down the trail that McNamara had taken toward the fabled Yukon.

They caught up with him a few hours after midnight as he lay sleeping exhaustedly in his thick sleeping bag, the dog team tethered to a stout fir tree. The two Canadians deftly took his revolver out of its holster, then unfastened his bags of food supplies and trundled them over to their own sled. Then, adding McNamara's dogs to their own team, they started for the northeast. When McNamara woke the next day, it was midmorning and bitterly cold.

He found himself lying in the snow in the middle of a little forest with nothing but his sleeping bag. He sprang to his feet, looking around for the men who had intercepted and robbed him. And then terror claimed him, for he realized he had neither provisions nor dog sled nor dogs, nor even a map to show him how to get back to the Canadian border.

By sunset, he had managed to follow his own tracks back only a few miles. The sky was a sullen solid gray, and the wind had begun to moan in the tops of the trees.

McNamara violently swore, cursing Marianne Valois for his misfortunes. Then, doggedly, hopelessly, he continued to trudge through the snow.

That night, a sudden blizzard swept through the Canadian province. Henry McNamara huddled in his sleeping bag, but it was not enough to protect him from the bitter cold. In the morning, his face was glazed with ice, his sightless eyes fixed on the sky.

## Forty-Six

Lopasuta Bouchard, feeling his strength returned, had determined to go into Victoria that morning to look for work so that he might earn money for his passage back home. Lu Choy prepared a nourishing breakfast of rice, fishcakes, and tea. As he ate this simple meal, he was struck by her concern for him and her unselfishness in sharing what little she had, and he thought of how frightened and lonely his own Geraldine must be after all this time, without a word from him. He was suddenly quite excited at the prospect of finally being able to cable her, just to let her know he was alive. He would follow the cable with a long letter in which he would explain that he was trying to find work so that he could earn his way back home to her and their child.

But he had not a penny in his pockets for a cable, nor even enough for paper or a stamp for a letter. All the more important, therefore, that he find work.

At the same time, he reasoned that whatever work he might find would be unlikely to bring him enough money to rent a room in the thriving city of Victoria. So, for a time, at any rate—even though he disliked the notion—he would have to remain on the sampan with this kind young woman who had found him and cared for him.

After their breakfast together, he managed to explain to her what he wanted. He repeated the word "Victoria" and then made his fingers move back and forth as if they were walking, and she nodded delightedly and in her soft, clear voice insisted, "You walk Vic-to-ria, long way. Lu Choy go, show you way."

453

It was good to stretch his legs and to move about again—actually for the first time since leaving New Orleans. How long ago was it now, he wondered. Lu Choy herself seemed delighted at his rapid convalescence. He observed that, as he walked along, she kept at least a foot or two behind him, as if in deference, and he realized that the traditional subservience of woman to man in the Orient prompted her behavior.

It was a long and wearying walk, but the sights were unforgettable. Even in his despair, he could not help being absorbed by the fascinating, colorful scenes: the dark green hills with their forests of pine, banyan, and camphorwood, the terraced rice paddies, the archaic waterwheels, and here and there an ornate temple. There were fishermen working their nets, and he could see farmers and their wives plowing their small fields, their crude wooden plows tethered to huge, docile water buffaloes. And dominating his view was the towering Victoria Peak that rose some eighteen hundred feet to provide a backdrop for all that unfolded before him.

In the distance, and yet clearly visible under the sunny sky, were other tiny islands where he imagined life was just as primitive as among the boat people of Aberdeen. It was truly a different world, and yet one to which he must necessarily adapt if he were ever to be reunited with his family.

He motioned now to Lu Choy that he wished her to walk by his side, and she obeyed, after an initial hesitation. And as they walked on, he tried to explain to her what he wished to do. She understood only a little of what he was telling her: that he had to find work so that he could earn money to pay for food and, in turn, to repay her for her kindness. The words she did understand she repeated in their Chinese equivalent, so that Lopasuta learned some basic Chinese vocabulary: the word for money was *chien pi;* that for work, *kung tso*. He marveled that this girl who lived by herself on a tiny fishing boat should even know some English, as he did not think that Oriental women were encouraged to have much formal education. From what old Jedidiah Danforth had once told him, girls in China and Japan were looked upon as useless mouths to feed and were very often sold into slavery, particularly by poor peasant families.

By the time they had reached the outskirts of the city, Lopasuta had managed to assure the friendly Chinese woman that he would come back to her on the sampan and that, if he could, he would bring some food. She bobbed her head with a little smile and tucked her hands inside of the sleeves of her coarse coolie coat, which she wore over trousers. This time she wore sandals, but at times, as he had already observed, she went barefoot, walking with great nimbleness and sureness. Suddenly, to his surprise, she bowed low to him, turned, and trotted back the way she had come. For a moment, he stared after her and then, with a desolate sigh, turned forward to seek what fortune he could in this new, strange world.

The streets of Victoria's oldest district were narrow and bustling. Lopasuta's senses were overwhelmed by the cries of vendors, the clattering of the rickshas, and, at times, the angry rivalry between ricksha men who vied for an impatient customer—who would then walk away and choose a third man who had peacefully stayed away from the discussion. He marveled, too, at the smells of cooking, of sandalwood, incense, and fish.

He had thought his best course would be to walk to the very heart of the city, for there he might find businesses where English was spoken. Yet now he found that it was like looking for the proverbial needle in the haystack, to expect to encounter some man who would have a job for him. All he could do was try.

As he moved along, he was jostled by lascars, coolies, ricksha men, old women going to market with baskets on their heads. He tried to efface himself alongside the wall of a shop or building, to avoid the crowds, and then found that he was beginning to tire—it had been a long walk around the island, and already it was noon.

When he came to an intersection, he turned. Here the street broadened, and there were more buildings along it. Ahead of him, he saw a stocky, nearly bald man with thick muttonchop whiskers and dressed in a white linen suit threading his way past the jostling throng. Even as he watched, he saw a coolie dart from across the street toward the man, plunge his bony right hand into his trouser pocket, and then, having drawn out the man's wallet, scurry away.

Instinctively, Lopasuta reacted. Calling out, "Stop,

thief!" in his loudest voice, he lunged at the coolie with
both arms, tackling him and flinging him down on the
cobbled street. The man ahead turned, clapped a hand to
his pocket, and discovered the loss, then began to run
toward Lopasuta. The passersby, chattering, curious, had
formed a kind of circle around the two. The stocky white-
suited man pushed his way through them and hoarsely demanded, "Ye've caught the beggar, and I'm beholden to
ye, whoever ye are! Let him up now—ye be twice his size.
And gi' me back me wallet, man!" From his thick brogue,
it was clear that he was Scottish.

Still gripping the coolie's arms, Lopasuta got to his
knees and, observing that the wallet lay on the cobble-
stones at the coolie's side, retrieved it and tendered it to the
Scotsman.

"Thank ye, friend. Let the poor beggar go."

"As you wish." Lopasuta rose to his feet and gestured to
the frightened Chinese, who needed no second encourage-
ment. Springing to his feet, he ran pell-mell down the
street and disappeared at the intersection.

"Well now, friend—as I said, I'm much indebted to ye.
Me name's David Brorty, and I've a trading office near
Government House." He stared at Lopasuta, then added,
"For sure, man, ye not be native to these parts, not with
that frock coat and trousers. And though ye speak the
King's English, ye not be white, surely?"

"No, Mr. Brorty. My name is Lopasuta Bouchard, and I
have Mexican and Comanche blood in me. I'm from
Montgomery, Alabama."

"Man, that's halfway around the world, that is! And why
would ye come here?"

"Not by my own choice, Mr. Brorty." Hope quickened
in Lopasuta's heart at the encouraging interest shown him
by the man whose accidental benefactor he had become.
"If you've time, I'll tell you my story—or better still, perhaps you'd have a job for me."

"Now that's odd indeed, Mr. Bouchard. Just t'other day,
I was telling meself it was high time I had someone to
help me with the books and such. But come along, and
we'll talk it over in me office. First off, though, what
would ye say to a bite of lunch? It's well past noon, and
I've been busy all morning with letters and the like and
hardly time to breathe. It was lucky I met ye, for in gen-

eral I do not come down this Street of Fragrant Flowers—it was only because there's the best tailor here in all of Hong Kong, and I'd just come from commissioning him to make me two pairs of trousers for me special girth." David Brorty patted his considerable paunch and chuckled in self-derision. "So we'll stop at a place where we can get some real Shanghai cooking, Mr. Bouchard. There's Shanghai crab and a fine stew they call Empress Chicken."

"That's very kind of you, and I'm grateful for your invitation—but I must tell you," Lopasuta embarrassedly stammered, "I—I have no money. What money I had was taken from me before they brought me here to Hong Kong and left me for dead in an alley."

"Man, even if ye be broke, that story sounds intriguing enough to be worth the price of a luncheon. Come along now; mind that broken cobblestone."

# Forty-Seven

At a pleasant little teahouse, David Brorty listened with mounting interest as Lopasuta explained how he had come to Hong Kong. When the Comanche lawyer had finished his story, the Scotsman chuckled, shook his head, and averred, "I'd say, man, that somewhere along the line ye'd made yourself a powerful enemy. For certain, he went to much trouble to get ye out of that town. And ye've no idea who it could be?"

"I have some suspicions, naturally, Mr. Brorty. I told you that this Mr. Brickley had sent for me on a retainer to give him legal advice about a problem he claimed to have had. I suspect it was at his instigation that I was drugged, and yet I had never met this man Brickley before in all my life, so I cannot imagine why he would have done this to me."

"Aye, lad, that ye cannot," the Scotsman agreed, thoughtfully pursing his lips and frowning in concentration. "But the man might well ha' been in cahoots with yer real enemy from Montgomery—had ye thought o' that?"

"Yes, Mr. Brorty, I have, but right now there is little I can do about it. Either way," Lopasuta ruefully went on, "I must find work so I can buy my passage back home. Somehow I must get a cable and a letter off to my poor wife—but I can't even afford a postage stamp."

"I see, I see. I'm truly sorry for ye, Mr. Bouchard. But, as I told ye, I think I might be able to use yer services. Of course, ye understand I couldn't pay much. I've only a small trading firm, and labor is very cheap here. But ye've the advantage of being educated and also a lawyer—so it's possible ye may be able to gi' me some good advice. I've a partner who was foisted on me when I took over this post some years ago, and he's rarely around. Frankly, I suspect he's up to no good. Now, if ye're willing, I'll take ye on—but again, man, I can't afford to pay ye too much."

"I understand, and I'm grateful to you for giving me a chance. I'll work hard, and I'll try to learn quickly," Lopasuta promised.

David Brorty nodded, then reached out to tap Lopasuta on the shoulder as if he were conferring an accolade. "I couldn't ask for more than that, lad. Now—let me fill ye in on the way business works here in Hong Kong. Basically, we import everything we need. Half our food comes from China, which also supplies some textiles, fabrics, and base metals. Japan supplies about a quarter of our needs. And yer own United States sends machinery, tobacco, raw cotton, fruits, and medicines."

"I had no idea the country was so dependent on imports," Lopasuta murmured.

"Yes, we are. But we turn that around to our advantage. Because Hong Kong is a free port, great profit comes from reexporting all those imports to other countries needing textile fabrics, diamonds, and medicines—especially to Japan and Singapore. Believe me, the profits can be very big indeed. And as I told ye, I'm but a small cog in the wheel of export firms—but there are many traders here who would love to see the end of David Brorty." He chuckled again, then apologized. "I didn't mean to talk yer head off. But now, as to yer own situation, Mr. Bouchard. Yes, I can use ye in my office, working with bills of lading and me accounts—and ye can write letters, I'll be bound?"

"Of course."

"Most of the traders with whom I deal speak English as well as ye and I, so that's no problem there. But mind ye, as far as salary goes, the best I can do is twenty-four Hong Kong dollars a week."

"How—how much would that be in American money, Mr. Brorty?" Lopasuta falteringly asked.

"Let me think a moment." The Scotsman closed his eyes, tapped his high-arching forehead, and then declared, "About four dollars, Mr. Bouchard."

"My God," the young Comanche blurted in disappoint-

459

ment. "At that rate it will take me forever to save up passage money!"

"Of course if ye prove of service to me, we can talk about an increase to yer wages, Mr. Bouchard," Brorty insinuated. Then, with a stern look, he went on, "And I'd need ye Saturdays as well. I've been so busy traveling and working on deals that I haven't finished all me paperwork, which is where ye can help me most. Well, what do ye say?"

Unhesitatingly, Lopasuta Bouchard smilingly nodded and extended his hand, which the Scotsman took. "There is only one thing, Mr. Brorty. I—I'd like to send a cable back to my wife immediately, as well as a letter, to let her know that I'm safe. Perhaps—if it's not asking too much, might I have an advance on my wages to pay for these?"

"Come in tomorrow morning as early as ye can, Mr. Bouchard. We'll talk about it then. I'll arrange to have them sent for ye—after I've seen the quality of yer work." Brorty chuckled and winked. "Ye can tell from me brogue I'm from the land o' William Wallace, and ye know that we Scots are as tightfisted when it comes to a penny as to a shilling. I will see ye tomorrow."

Lopasuta strode back to the little fishing village of Aberdeen, his face aglow with hope. On the way back, he had stopped at several little restaurants where he heard pidgin English being spoken, and he made signs to the shopkeepers to inquire the cost. Food was cheap indeed, yet four dollars in American money would scarcely leave him enough money after buying food to get him even a squalid little room at the farthermost end of the city—much less enable him to save any of his wages. No, he must continue to accept Lu Choy's gracious hospitality, but at least he could contribute some food for the both of them. As he walked back, drinking in the sights of the landscape and glancing back up at Victoria Peak, he thought excitedly to himself that tomorrow at last he would be able to send off a cable to Geraldine to assure her that he was alive and had not willfully abandoned her.

Lu Choy was back in her sampan when he arrived, already preparing the evening meal. She sprang up with a cry of joy, then folded her hands in her sleeves and bowed low to him. "You find work?" she asked, and he, pleased

460

that she had fully understood his quest, eagerly nodded and exclaimed, "Yes, Lu Choy, I have found work. Tomorrow I will go back, I will work, and I will buy food." She eyed him uncomprehendingly for a moment, but then he improvised the signs of eating, and she tittered delightfully and nodded to show that she understood.

The dark evening was pleasantly cool, and he stretched out on the deck of the sampan outside the small cabinlike enclosure, wanting to sleep as his forebears did, under the starlit sky. He fell asleep at once, and that was why he did not know that the Chinese woman crept out to him and, carefully lifting his head with one hand, slipped her own bolster under it to make him more comfortable for the night.

And so he woke at dawn that first Saturday in Hong Kong, cleaned himself as best he could, ruefully aware that he had only the clothes he wore. Preoccupied with the maddening thought of his poverty, he gobbled down some rice and tea, and bade Lu Choy a smiling farewell. He welcomed the long, arduous walk around the island to his work, for the exercise was restoring his vitality, if not his high spirits. He told himself that he must try to put out of his mind the torturing images of Geraldine and the child—was it a boy or a girl?—as well as the anguish she must be feeling. He was here by some will of Manitou, though he did not know the meaning of it, and so he must cope day by day with this new life until the meaning was made clear to him.

Lopasuta found the little frame building near Government House, trudged up the stairs, knocked at the door, and was told to come in. "Ye're late, man!" David Brorty scolded him, fuming with impatience. "For a moment there, I thought ye were just another drifter—Hong Kong is full o' them. But I'm glad that ye didn't disappoint me. And now, let me show ye my books and teach ye what I need ye to do for me."

The offices of the Brorty-Hamill Trading Company were not even so well furnished nor ample as Lopasuta's own law office back in Montgomery. In one room, there was a huge wooden chest which, upon being opened, revealed piles of invoices and bills of lading. There was a crude desk and high stool where, Brorty indicated, Lopasuta would do his work. And Brorty's own office, though it boasted a superb teakwood desk and hand-carved chair of the same gleaming, dark wood, was hardly more impressive. The Scotsman drew out a ledger book with entries in his own crabbed writing, and after half an hour of explanation, Lopasuta could see the scope of the Scotsman's diversified operations. Goods were received from Japan and elsewhere, just as he had outlined to Lopasuta; the raw materials were then let out to contractors for manufacture, and they in turn submitted a bill for their services. Finally, the goods were exported with invoices and bills of lading, and when the money was received in drafts upon a major Hong Kong bank, the credits were inscribed on the right-hand side of the ledger.

And so, weary with figures, but fiercely eager to master them, Lopasuta Bouchard sat down on the stool and began to work.

David Brorty kept him till nearly six that evening, and the only kindness he showed was taking the Comanche out to a cheap teahouse near the office for a hasty lunch.

At the end of the long day, Lopasuta timidly broached the subject that most concerned him. "Mr. Brorty, as I mentioned yesterday, I'd be very grateful to you if you would provide me with the means to write a letter to my wife—and to send a very brief cable, as well. You may deduct any costs from my wages next week."

"Oh, very well," Brorty testily retorted. "Sit down here and write yer letter and the cablegram. I'll dispatch them Monday before I come to work—and mind that ye're not late the way ye were this morning, man!"

Gratefully, humbly, Lopasuta nodded. Brorty grunted, opened the drawer of his desk and drew out paper and envelope, and handed it to the young Comanche. "Now be quick about it," Brorty demanded. "I've a pert Chinese lass waiting for me on Kowloon Road."

Lopasuta flushed at Brorty's brusque vulgarity as he hurried back to the stool and began to write. He penned first the brief cable message, in which he simply stated that he was safe, in Hong Kong, and that a letter would follow. Then, taking a second sheet, he wrote a letter, the words tumbling out as he gave expression to his mingled despair and hope, after all that had befallen him.

When he had finished, he folded both the cable and the

letter, sealed the envelope of the latter, and brought them into Brorty's office, saying, "I've finished them, Mr. Brorty. Thank you for sending them on for me."

"Aye, man. Cables aren't cheap, ye know. I'll advance ye the money, but I'll deduct it from yer wages a bit each week until it's paid back. Mind ye're here early Monday."

"I will be, Mr. Brorty, you have my word on it. And thank you again."

He went down the stairs and out into the street, where, exhaling a deep breath of joy, he began to hurry back to Aberdeen and Lu Choy on her sampan.

David Brorty regarded the cable and the letter that Lopasuta had entrusted to him. He opened the letter, and read both it and the cable, turning them over and over. "That lad is too valuable to me to let him go back too soon," he declared to himself. "Besides, with all the fair lasses here in Hong Kong, one day he'll thank me for this."

So saying, he carefully, methodically, tore both the cable and the precious letter into tiny fragments and discarded them.

In the month that followed, Lopasuta Bouchard plunged himself into the complex clerical work of David Brorty's trading firm. He worked six days a week like a virtual slave, for the paunchy Scotsman was constantly critical of him and his shortcomings. "Man, ye'll never make a bookkeeper," was his judgment at the end of that first week, when he paid Lopasuta his wages, less a part of the cost of the cablegram and postage to America (callously planning to deduct a portion of the charges each week for the messages he had never sent). But by the end of the second week, he grudgingly conceded, "I can see ye'll soon get the hang o' things."

Still, he was helpful to the young Comanche. He had advanced Lopasuta just enough money to enable him to acquire a cheap new suit of clothes, for as Brorty explained, it would not do for his clerk to appear less than respectable during office hours. The suit would be paid for out of additional weekly deductions from Lopasuta's salary. Brorty also continued to take his clerk to lunch at the cheapest teahouses two or three times a week. He was fond of the sound of his own voice, Lopasuta wryly concluded, but his anecdotes—about the chicanery and the politics and the colonization of Hong Kong, with its constantly increasing flux of Chinese from the mainland—absorbed Lopasuta as he strove to learn all he could about his unchosen home. And what steeled him against the reprimands, the sarcasm, and the niggardliness of his employer was the thought that his cable and letter were on their way to his beloved wife, and that finally she would know that he had not died, nor had he forsaken her.

One thing that made him curious was the continued absence of the partner named Hamill, whose name appeared on the door, the bills of lading, and the invoices of Brorty's exporting firm. He assumed that one day the man would come into the office and that he would then be introduced to him, but the weeks went by without any sign of this absentee partner, against whom Brorty continued to rail.

Most of what remained of Lopasuta's wages after Brorty's deductions was spent on food for himself and Lu Choy. At the end of the third week, wanting to please her and to show his thanks for her solicitude and kindness, he bought her a little pin in a Portuguese shop on the outskirts of Victoria, a butterfly worked in imitation lapis lazuli. It cost all of a dollar and a half of American money, but after buying the food, it completely depleted his wages for that week. That evening, when he laid down his purchases and then showed her the little gift, she uttered a joyous cry and, seizing his hand, kissed it. His face crimsoned as he tried awkwardly to dissuade her from such kowtowing; he felt that it was he who was beholden to her, for if Lu Choy had not shown concern and kindness that first night, he might well have died in that alleyway, and his beloved Geraldine would have been left a widow without ever knowing what had happened to him.

# Forty-Eight

Judith Branshaw Marquard was radiantly happy this late November day. Bernard had urged her to go on working at the bank as long as she wished, so she had felt herself both emancipated and yet deeply loved by a husband who was in no way possessive. Yet this afternoon, as Jason Barntry came by to thank her for having written up a report on one of their customers who sought a rather large loan, she smiled to herself in secret joy. She had missed her period, and she knew that she was with child, a child of love, by a man she loved totally, eagerly, and joyously. She could hardly wait to get home that evening to tell her blind husband that he would be a father. Perhaps it would make up to him for his unfaithful first wife. And for herself, she thanked God that the planned sadism of David Fales had not spoiled her; that her enforced whoring had not taken from her the blessed privilege of conceiving a child by an honorable man.

At the celebration of the Thanksgiving holiday two days ago, Lopasuta's wife, Geraldine, had sat at the table with her father and mother, and Geraldine had prayed that she would have news from her husband. George and Angela Murcur had tearfully consoled her, telling her that they felt that he was a good and decent man who assuredly had not abandoned her willfully.

This morning, Laure Bouchard had paid a visit to Geraldine at her parents' house, and the two women had clung together and wept. Laure had murmured, "One day he'll return to you and me, dearest Geraldine. I'm sure that he's still alive—I have a feeling in my heart. One day, though our patience costs us both so much, we'll learn that he's safe. But for now, Geraldine, you must live for your child because he would want it so. And I, as Dennis's godmother, also desire this."

Burt Coleman had, that same Thanksgiving Day, knelt in the chapel at Windhaven Plantation, tendering his own special prayer of thanks to God. For Burt, it seemed as if a new life had begun. The heavy burden of grief for his Marietta had at last begun to be eased, for Amelia, the beautiful young octoroon with whom he had struck up so warm and tender a friendship, had only last night agreed to marry him the following year.

Burt was now assistant to Marius Thornton, and the two men worked together, each dedicated and grateful, with no thought of differences of color or creed to come between them—only the communication between men of good will who love the earth and its bounty.

On this last Saturday in November, Lopasuta, exhausted by the merciless tasks imposed upon him by David Brorty, had collected his meager wages for the week and stopped at a shop to buy some smoked fish, a roasted chicken, a sack of rice, some melons, and bamboo shoots and Chinese pea pods. Like a beast of burden, he carried the heavy sack over one shoulder, bent over as he trudged back to Aberdeen.

The sky had darkened faster than was usual, and there was a stillness to the air that sent a curious premonition through him. On the American plains and in the Comanche stronghold, he had seen skies like this that portended a violent, furious thunderstorm, strong enough to shatter the tepees of his people.

It made him uneasy as he hurried back to Lu Choy. He had learned from David Brorty that the typhoons, which averaged some thirty a year, occurred most often from July through September—and yet the signs this evening were unmistakably those of a typhoon.

His sack was heavy, and he was glad that at least he was earning enough money to buy food, because Lu Choy's fishing the last two weeks had been very scant, and she had earned hardly enough for her own needs. After all she had done for him, he was pleased that if nothing more, he could help provide food.

In just one short month, Lopasuta had learned many Chinese words, and he found it easier now to converse with Lu Choy. He learned something about her background—how she had been shunted into this lonely life on the tiny sampan in Aberdeen harbor—and that despite her lack of schooling and orphanlike existence, she was good and kind of heart. Impoverished though she was, she had unhesitatingly saved his life and shared her paltry possessions. There were not many people back in Montgomery who would have done the same for him, he thought bitterly.

He went down the connecting walk from the dock out to their sampan and boarded it. He called out her name and saw her turn from the brazier where she was preparing their supper to smile at him and hurry out to him, her face aglow. When he lifted the sack from his shoulder and let it down to the floor of the sampan, she clapped her hands like a child and gleefully exclaimed, "Very good. We are almost out of food. You work so hard. You are very kind to Lu Choy."

"Because you have been kind to me," he sincerely countered. Then, looking up at the ominous, leaden sky, he pointed and said, "Maybe it will be a great *pai feng yu*, Lu Choy. It looks very bad."

She moved beside him, looking up at the sky, then nodded. "Not happen often this time of year," she murmured. "We are near the shore. Many boats around us. We should be safe. Come now, we have our meal."

She still spoke with a mixture of English and Chinese, but by now he could almost readily understand; what words he did not know, he could sense by reading her face, her expression, her gestures. Although Geraldine was so far away from him and so unattainable, he had nonetheless told himself that to fall in love with Lu Choy was wrong, and that it would not happen. And he had been glad that he had not been lustfully drawn to her, for that would have been a gross abuse of the kindness she had shown him.

They had scarcely finished eating when the wind began to howl, and the water lapped noisily at the sides of the little sampan. He stooped and went outside and, with a

467

gasp, saw that the tall masts of all the sampans and junks in the harbor were bobbing erratically, although it was so dark that one could barely make them out.

Lu Choy had already unfolded her sleeping mat, and Lopasuta went back inside to help clear the dishes and empty the brazier of its coals. He dumped them into the water because he knew that if there was fire aboard and the typhoon should strike, the danger to them would be even greater. She looked shyly at him, and gave him a long look and a tender smile as he returned to replace the brazier on its stand. The howling of the wind had increased, and she suddenly clung to him and began to sob. "Lu Choy afraid—hold me, Lu Choy afraid!"

He closed his eyes, and his arms enfolded her. Her young body was firm and tender, and he could feel her heart beating against his chest. There were tears on her cheeks and her lips were trembling, and the little sampan had begun to jerk from side to side as the wind increased from the typhoon sweeping over the island.

Lu Choy was whimpering like a frightened child, and as she clung to him, she emitted tiny, piteous sounds like an abandoned waif. Lopasuta trembled, and though his hands clasped her shoulders, smoothing and stroking her supple back, trying to comfort her, desire played no role in his movements. He saw Lu Choy as a companion, a kind of consolation for his agonized loneliness.

The sudden jostling of the boats on either side of them made him stagger, and Lu Choy clung the more tenaciously to him as she pressed her face against his shoulder, in tears. Her firm breasts were thrust against his thin cotton shirt, and he tried to disengage his hands from her so that she would not mistake his actions. And then suddenly, with a sobbing little cry, Lu Choy hugged him even more tightly and they sank down upon her sleeping mat, he atop her. Lopasuta closed his eyes and prayed to his Manitou that he might neither offend Lu Choy nor break his vows to Geraldine.

The water slapped loudly against the sides of their sampan, tilting and rocking it, and as their bodies automatically imitated the motion, Lopasuta had to fight the elemental urge to comfort Lu Choy—and seek his own consolation—in the primal act of love.

Each was silent and alone, he with his anguished

thoughts, she with her loneliness. He could feel her fingers entwined around his neck, her nails biting into his flesh, as her breath came more and more quickly. And, virile and young, he could no longer resist the hunger of his own body or of hers. The wind leaped high over Victoria Peak, as the typhoon finally spent itself far out to sea. But the waves continued to sway and roll the sampan, and Lopasuta Bouchard felt himself engulfed and welcomed by the yearning Chinese woman.

# Forty-Nine

On December 18, 1877, in the annual tradition of Windhaven Plantation, Laure Bouchard, dressed in mourning, stood beside the graves of Luke; his grandfather, old Lucien Bouchard; and the beloved woman, Dimarte. She was alone except for Geraldine Bouchard, whose eyes were swollen with weeping.

Laure turned to Geraldine and murmured, "I'm glad at least that your father and mother have made peace with you, dear Geraldine. And don't despair—Lopasuta isn't dead. He's somewhere in this world, I feel it deeply, and one day he'll come back to you. Here today on the anniversary of Lucien Bouchard's birth, you and I will pray for Lopasuta's return. We will ask the blessed spirits of our beloved forebears to watch over us—and him."

"I know he never left me of his own will, Laure," Geraldine tearfully whispered. "But I thank God that my father and mother no longer hate me and now accept our child, because I wouldn't have been able to endure this if my parents were still estranged. And I'll devote my life to bringing up my son as Lopasuta would have wished."

Laure turned, her face haggard and wet with tears, and touched Geraldine's head in a kind of benediction. "All of us must rebuild from the ashes of the past, dear Geraldine. I most of all, and literally from those ashes that by my own mistakes I brought upon me. But at least now I know that Marius and Burt Coleman will ensure that Windhaven Plantation will continue in the vision of old Lucien Bouchard and my beloved husband. And you and I will share in this glorious future, and I pledge to you here at

470

Luke's grave and those of his grandfather and Dimarte, that our lives shall be entwined in meaning and fulfillment. For this I pray, a week before the birth of the sweet Christ child."

On Windhaven Range, Lucien Edmond Bouchard and Maxine, three months away from bearing a child, entered the chapel and knelt to pray for his father's soul and for that of his great-grandfather. Friar Bartoloméo and the vaqueros had earlier celebrated a mass for the new church, at the southeastern part of Windhaven Range, which was almost completed. Catayuna and her child had also attended the service on this warm Texas morning, and afterwards she remarked to the mother superior, "I have never been more content, Sister Martha. We have begun our school—your nuns and I are sisters together. And I am blessed by the joy of working with these children who will one day shape the future of our country. I am as American as I am Mexican, and I feel the borderline that separates our two countries means little."

"Amen to that, my child," Sister Martha replied. "I will be forever grateful to Friar Bartoloméo for bringing us together."

On this same day, Connie Belcher and Walter Catlin, who had some time ago pledged their love to one another, decided at last that their wedding day would be the first Saturday in the new year.

"Connie darling," Walter avowed, "I've been saving my wages carefully for weeks and weeks, and by now I think I could get you just about anything you'd ever want or need. I like the life of a cowboy, but we could get some land and maybe start our own little farm, too. I could buy some of Mr. Bouchard's steers and maybe a few cows, with what I've got set aside. Oh, Connie, you've made me so happy—you've made me forget all the misery I felt, during all those years of wandering."

Connie fought to hold back her tears and put her arms around his neck as she buried her face against his chest. "Oh, Walter," she cried, "I love you so much—I never knew a girl could be so happy. I've been wanting for us to set the date, but I knew you were working and putting money by—that's just the kind of man I want, and I'm lucky to have you!" Then, with an enticing little smile, she declared, "You know, it's going to be hard to wait until we're married—I want to love you like the way the Bible says a man and woman should." Blushing at this bold suggestion, she quickly added, "But now let's go in and talk to Pa and Ma and tell them what we want to do. They've been expecting it for a while!"

Planting a firm kiss on Walter's smiling mouth, Connie took his hand and led him back to the little house she shared with her family.

In Wichita, two days after Christmas, Pastor Jacob Hartmann died of a heart attack, and Ben Wilson was unanimously elected to replace him in the Quaker church. The homely doctor from Pittsburgh had found a new, richly satisfying life with his Indian wife, Elone; he cherished Fleurette Bouchard in his memory, but never alluded to her in Elone's presence. He knew unerringly, with a great peace and joy, that the God in whom he believed had granted him, as to few men, a second life, a wife as dear and good and devoted as Fleurette had been.

It was a new year, the year of 1878. With President Hayes at the rudder of the American ship of state, two years past the centennial, the jarring hatreds of North for South seemed to have eased. The land was rich, and though the panic of 1873 still had its aftereffects, there were signs of a greater stability and financial security. Perhaps it was an illusion, yet people were hopeful and had begun to plan for the future once more, as in the old days before the Civil War.

On the tenth day of January of this new year, the Woman's Suffrage Amendment was introduced in its final form into Congress by Senator A. A. Sargent. Four days later, the Supreme Court ruled at last on the famous case of *Hall v. de Cuyr,* that a state law requiring a railroad to give equal accommodations to all passengers without respect to race or color was unconstitutional because of its bearing upon interstate travel. It was a sign that, despite the Fourteenth and Fifteenth Amendments, the freed black had not yet achieved the equality that the martyred Abraham Lincoln had championed in his immortal Emancipation Proclamation.

And in February, the Bland-Allison Act was passed over President Hayes's veto, authorizing the purchase of from two to four million dollars' worth of silver each month to be turned into dollars, thus restoring the silver dollar as legal tender. The act symbolized the will of the farmers and the homesteaders to have easier money, after the poverty that the panic of 1873 had engendered.

Lopasuta Bouchard continued to work six days each week for David Brorty. Out of his paltry wages, the Comanche had saved perhaps eight dollars of American money toward his return home to Montgomery. The rest of it was spent on Lu Choy's food and occasional clothing, for his one carnal act with her during the November typhoon had resulted in pregnancy, and the conscience-stricken Comanche sought to make what amends he could. He waited in eager hope for a letter from Geraldine, thinking that surely by now the letter he had written, which David Brorty had sent, had long since arrived, and Geraldine's joyous reply would be on the way.

Yet it did not come. With Lu Choy pregnant and knowing that the child was his, he anxiously petitioned the Scotsman for an increase in wages, only to be denied on the grounds that business had still not improved, and that all the collections still on the ledger had not yet come into the till. By way of compensation, the Scotsman continued to take his hardworking employee to lunch at least three times a week and made flamboyant promises about what he might expect in the future. "Do ye know, Mr. Bouchard," he said one day at the beginning of April, after they had finished lunch in a teahouse near the office, "yer work is mightily improved, I'll give ye that. If ye persevere in the same way, it may be by the year's end that I'll consider offering ye a junior partnership in the firm. The man Hamill is shirking his responsibilities."

Lopasuta sighed and nodded wearily. He had heard such promises before. What puzzled him was the continued absence of this unseen partner whom his employer continued to accuse as the one largely responsible for the firm's financial crisis. So far as the ledger was concerned, Lopasuta could find only gradually increasing profits. And his concern for the kindly young Chinese woman who

473

would bear his child, together with his increased worry over Geraldine's failure to respond to his letter, made him nervous and despondent. There were some nights when he hardly slept at all, and when he wakened before dawn to find Lu Choy huddling close to him, a smile on her pretty face, he bit his lips and prayed he would not hurt her, and that Geraldine would not blame him for what had taken place.

In April of this second year of President Hayes's administration, a deadly yellow fever epidemic swept through the Gulf states and Tennessee, striking New Orleans, Corpus Christi, and Galveston. Arabella Hunter and her daughter, Melinda, had met for lunch in a fashionable hotel restaurant in Galveston.

"Do you know what I've decided, Melinda honey?" Arabella stared intently at her older daughter. "I'm going to offer my services to a hospital."

"But Mama," Melinda protested, "that's terribly dangerous."

"Not really. You forget that I nursed your father during the worst time of his own fatal bout with the disease, and the doctor said that since I didn't become ill, I must have a natural immunity against the fever."

"Well, if you can do that, Mama, so can I," Melinda stoutly declared. "I don't want to see the epidemic spread so that my own children are threatened."

"I'd talk to Dr. Parmenter, then, if I were you, honey," her mother advised. "You may not have the immunity, and I don't want you to get the sickness."

"Then I'll go to him, Mama," Melinda enthusiastically avowed. "Because I want to work with you to help the sick and do what I can to make this city free from yellow jack."

The next day, with Dr. Parmenter's approval, Arabella became a volunteer nurse at the Galveston General Hospital. Melinda, following her valiant mother's example, went there the day after, but the gray-haired, soft-spoken physician shook his head and said, "You aren't immune, Mrs. Davis, and so the danger for you would be as great as for a patient. But if you really want to help, you can try to raise funds from your friends and neighbors to purchase sulphur and quinine, bandages, new clothes, and other commodities for the General Hospital."

Three weeks later, Arabella Hunter, wearing a bedraggled white nurse's uniform, exhaustedly slumped in a chair in Dr. Parmenter's office at the General Hospital. He reached out to touch her forehead and said, "One of these days you might be called the Florence Nightingale of Galveston, Mrs. Hunter. You're a very brave woman. And your wonderful daughter has helped raise something over five thousand dollars, which this hospital will gratefully use in fighting the scourge of yellow jack. Your late husband would be very proud of you both, Mrs. Hunter."

Arabella uttered a sob, then covered her face with her hands and wept silently. She wished that the spirit of James Hunter could have heard Dr. Parmenter's words. At last, she told herself, she had proved her usefulness as a public-minded citizen, casting aside forever the foibles of a pampered, beautiful young woman, and she knew James would have been vastly proud of her.

It was late August in Hong Kong; the weather was hot and humid, and Lu Choy was near her time. There was still no letter from Geraldine, and Lopasuta had managed to save barely thirty dollars of American money toward his passage home. Once again, just last week, he had almost begged David Brorty to raise his salary, but there had been the usual excuses. The young Comanche knew that he had no recourse against this, and by now, with Lu Choy about to give birth, he was bound irrevocably to her. He asked himself how he could ever explain this liaison to his beloved Geraldine—and there were nights when he rose from his sleeping mat and went out on deck on the sampan and, looking up at the starlit sky, prayed to Manitou to give him a sign that his sin was forgiven, and that Geraldine in her turn had not abandoned him.

Lu Choy had been feverish and weak during these last few days, and Lopasuta had been alarmed each time he returned from work late in the evening to find her on the sleeping mat, her face drawn with pain, pale and trembling. She had tried to make light of it, but he did not like the way she looked. And so tonight, after they had had a simple supper of sweet-and-sour ribs and rice and tea, he stroked her damp forehead and murmured, "I will clean up, Lu Choy. Then I want to go into the village and find someone to help you."

"No, I can do it alone, if you will but help me," she replied in the mixed Chinese and English that he had learned to understand.

"You must rest now, Lu Choy," he gently said. "Besides, I want to go for a walk. It is cooler now this evening, and I will sleep the better beside you after I've had my walk."

She gave a little sigh and lay back on the blanket. He stared at her, then stooping to kiss her forehead, he turned and went down the wooden walkway to the dock. One of the elders of the village stood there, greeting him. Lopasuta bowed to the old man and asked him, in halting Chinese, "Is there an *amah*, a nurse, who knows how to help a mother about to give birth?"

"Yes, foreigner; Mai Soo, who lives on the junk *Kowloon Lights* there to the north, is such a one," the elder replied.

Lopasuta thanked him, and then strode quickly along the shore till he came to the large junk and then carefully made his way along the narrow wooden walkway to the side of the vessel. A burly, pigtailed Chinese amicably hailed him: "Ho, foreign one, whom do you seek?"

"Mai Soo, the *amah*," Lopasuta replied. "I come from the sampan of Lu Choy, who is with child. I need the help of Mai Soo now, honored one," Lopasuta earnestly avowed.

"Oh, yes, Lu Choy is known to us. You are her man. It is known also that you are good to her, and for a foreigner, you respect our ways. I will bring Mai Soo to you now. Wait here."

A few minutes later, the owner of the junk returned with a frail, elderly Chinese woman, who bowed low before Lopasuta and, in a piping voice, declared, "I will help you, young master. Is she near her time?"

"I—I think so, Mai Soo. I am grateful to you," Lopasuta faltered.

The elderly woman whispered something to the captain of the junk, then nimbly clambered over the rail and followed the Comanche lawyer along the wooden walkway to

476

the sampan of the young Chinese woman. As they neared the little boat, the silence of the night was suddenly shattered by Lu Choy's shrill cries. "It is the child—it struggles to be born!" the *amah* exclaimed.

"Go to her, quickly, in the name of mercy," Lopasuta hoarsely exclaimed.

The elderly *amah* stared a moment at his contorted face, and then hurried aboard and into the cabin of the sampan. Lopasuta began to pace back and forth, staring at the sky and praying to Manitou to grant this kind Chinese girl a safe delivery and to pardon him who had been unfaithful to Geraldine.

He heard gasps and groans, and he dug his nails into his palms, closing his eyes and wincing at each sound of Lu Choy's pain. He damned himself for her suffering, and he mercilessly denounced himself as unworthy of the tribe of the Wanderers. Sangrodo would have driven him out of the tribe for this monstrous unfaithfulness to the woman who had borne him a child in the eyes of the white-eyes church.

And then there was silence, followed by the cry of a newly born child. A few minutes later the old *amah* came slowly to him and murmured, "Young master, she is dead—but your son lives, and he is strong. And he looks like a *wai kuo jen.*"

"Like a foreigner," Lopasuta murmured, bowing his head and fighting back the tears. "She died in giving me this child, and now I can never tell her how much she helped me, how I owed my life to her. Now it is over."

Stooping, he went back into the little cabin, where Lu Choy lay pale and still. He knelt down and kissed her forehead, then folded her arms across her bosom and gently closed her eyelids. For a long moment he prayed, as he would have done in the stronghold of Sangrodo, and then he went out to join the *amah*. "Can you find a woman for this son who can give him her milk, honorable old one?" he asked in his combination of English and Chinese.

"I know of such a girl; she is very young, and she had a child a week ago, but her baby died shortly after it was born. Her name is Mei Luong, and she lives in a sampan to the south against the wharf. I will go to her, young master, and because she has no one to care for her now, she will be glad if you will give her a few coppers."

"Tell her I will do more than that," Lopasuta Bouchard said in a voice that was choked with emotion. "Bring her back here and let her look after my son."

# Fifty

In this November of 1878, Lucien Edmond, Joe Duvray, and Ramón Hernandez looked back on a prosperous year at Windhaven Range. Thanks to their policy of selling their beef to army forts, they had this year avoided the hazards of the traditional long cattle drive to Kansas. They had also continued the crossbreeding of Brahmas and Herefords, to produce prime stock to be held for the next year when, as they hoped, railroad feeder lines would extend close enough to enable them to ship their cattle profitably to more distant markets. Their current profits had already been put to excellent use, for the building of the new church for Sister Martha and her nuns, on the southeast acreage that Lucien Edmond had provided. And beside the church was the one-story schoolhouse, as good as any rural schoolhouse in the East, where the children of the vaqueros—as well as of those of Lucas and Felicidad, Pablo Casares and his Kate, and Eddie Gentry and his María Elena—attended, with the radiant Catayuna presiding as one of the teachers.

Maxine and Lucien Edmond were delighted with the antics of their fast-growing last child, a daughter whom they had named Ruth. And Connie had just made Walter Catlin a proud and happy father with the son they had named Henry, after her adoring father. Timmy Belcher had, the previous summer, married the beautiful young Mexican woman Conchita Valdegroso, and Maybelle now scolded herself for ever believing that this devoted and intelligent woman was not good enough for her stepson. Timmy and his bride were happily ensconced in a small but ample house near that of his parents, a house that Timmy proudly and almost single-handedly had built himself.

In New Orleans, Judith Marquard had a few months earlier presented her blind husband, Bernard, with a little girl whom he had urged her to name after her dead mother, Nancy.

Meanwhile, under the management of Bernard's former orderly, Jesse Jacklin, the Maison de Bonne Chance continued to prosper, and the profits that were continually deposited in Laure Bouchard's account in the Brunton & Barntry Bank had made her financially independent in her own right, without any need to touch Luke's considerable legacy. Laure had instructed Hollis Minton, the bank attorney, to devise from her own share of the legacy separate trusts for each of her five children, to be recorded in each of their names with herself and the attorney as coadministrators.

The yellow fever epidemic had raged all through the year and caused hundreds of fatalities in the Gulf cities, as well as in the larger cities of Tennessee. Arabella Hunter spent two days a week as a nurse at the Galveston General Hospital and two days more in the Douglas Department Store. Since the terrible hurricane last year, Alexander Gorth had assiduously taken charge of not only his own branch store, but also of the main Galveston branch, renovating the store, changing the displays, and—under Max Steinfeldt's tutelage—initiating a series of attention-compelling advertisements in the local newspaper to draw customers. There, as in the Houston store, headed by the genial Max, with his adoring Alice herself spending a day or two behind the counter each week, the resurgence of good business had erased Charles Douglas's disastrous loss when the steamboat carrying merchandise slated for both stores had been wrecked by the savage winds of the hurricane.

For Windhaven Plantation, too, this second year of the Hayes administration had been a rewarding one. Thanks to the concerted labors of Marius Thornton and Burt Coleman, the crops had been bountiful, and sales of produce, livestock, dairy products, and chickens had not only wiped out the deficit caused by the incendiary attack engineered by William Brickley and Danvers Willoughby, but also had enabled Laure to announce a large wage increase to the faithful workers.

The statewide elections had just been held, and it was evident that the Democrats would gain control of both houses of Congress for the first time since 1868. Senator Morgan of Alabama had spoken of the "Solid South" to indicate the unified Democratic outlook in those states that had once seceded from the Union. Senator Andy Haskins, though an avowed and loyal Republican, had been assured by his campaign managers that he would retain his seat in the state senate in November, and the returns had proved them right. He and Jessica had celebrated the birth of another daughter in September whom he had insisted on naming Margaret, his own lovely wife's middle name. Dalbert Sattersfield was overwhelmingly reelected mayor of Lowndesboro, and he rejoiced also in the birth of a daughter this month, his fifth child, whom he and his irrepressible Mitzi decided to name Laure as a tribute to Laure Bouchard.

Lopasuta Bouchard had been profoundly affected by the death of Lu Choy in the months that had passed since that event, and he was deeply grateful for the help of the nurse, Mei Luong—for without her, he would have been completely at a loss to care for his infant son. He had been unable to resist calling the child Luke—though he knew that Geraldine might have given this very name to her first-born; if so, Lu Choy's child would, Lopasuta decided, be christened with another name. Until then, he would be—in his father's eyes—Luke, and Lopasuta only hoped that he could be as good a father to this boy as Luke had been to him.

Though bereaved, Lopasuta nonetheless had continued to work for David Brorty in order to earn his passage home, and he put in long hours writing letters to clients and customers and in general acting as operations manager of the trading firm. During this period, his employer had spent a good deal of time away from Hong Kong visiting his manufacturers, and just last week Lopasuta had received an unexpectedly flattering comment from young

Morrison Edgers, the chief clerk of the trading firm of Camp & Raleigh, one of the port's largest import-export firms.

But after praising Lopasuta, Edgers had said something that had made the young lawyer puzzled and concerned: "You know, Bouchard, your boss isn't very well thought of here in Hong Kong. It's mainly his own fault, of course. He used to have a partner, but he cheated him, and Hamill left for Macao about five years ago. By rights, Brorty ought to take Hamill's name off of his letterheads, invoices, and his door, because Hamill won't have a thing to do with him—even if Brorty tried to make restitution at this late date. I'm just tipping you off, Bouchard, because you're an honest fellow, and I like you. Just keep your eyes open. There may be some skullduggery going on."

One morning early in the fourth week of November, when Lopasuta went to his employer's office as usual, he found David Brorty sitting at his desk, staring depressedly down at a rumpled pile of invoices, lost in thought.

"Good morning, Mr. Brorty. You seem very worried today. Is there anything I can do?" he asked.

"Lad, I've a right to feel this way. My business is doing very badly—ye yerself have already called my attention to quite a few invoices that haven't been paid yet. But it's all because of that scoundrel, Hamill. I want ye to go through my books again and spend all day, if ye have to, to find out what's wrong. I seem to be losing money, and I can't figure out why."

"Of course I'll go over your ledger, Mr. Brorty. Why don't you go out for a walk now and just relax? But to be frank with you, Mr. Brorty, so far I haven't found that we're losing money, as you claim."

"But we are, Bouchard, we are! And don't get beyond yer station—remember, ye're still me clerk."

"I know," Lopasuta gloomily responded. "I thought by now my work would have impressed you enough to increase my salary. I have, as you certainly should know, worked very hard to collect many of the foreign invoices and have them credited to your account. That's why I find it hard to understand your saying that you're losing money."

"Damnation, ye've hounded me long enough, Bouchard! All right, lad—this Saturday I'll increase yer wages by two

American dollars. But mind ye, I'll expect more work out of ye, and it's the last raise I'll be able to give until ye find out why my profits are continuing to go down in spite of all the business I'm doing."

"Thank you, Mr. Brorty. I'll be able to put that raise away for my trip back home. By the way—I don't suppose you have a letter for me—"

"O' course I don't, ye idiot! If I had, I'd ha' given it to ye the moment ye came in the door," his employer snapped. "Now I'm going out and ha' a bite to eat—I was too upset to enjoy me breakfast earlier—then I may go to see my lass. Meanwhile, dig yer nose into those books of mine and find out what's happening."

With this he abruptly rose and left the office. Lopasuta shook his head, shrugged, then went into Brorty's office. He went to the desk and drew out the ledger, then, putting it onto the ink-stained, dog-eared blotter, he opened it and began to study it assiduously.

As Lopasuta stared wearily at the book, Morrison Edgers's remark came back to him, but he dismissed it as he pored over the ledger, intent on carrying out his employer's instructions. He studied the familiar figures for hours, checking and then cross-checking them against receipts and bills the firm had received, hoping to find some evidence that would satisfy Brorty. Alas, he could find nothing; all was in order, the figures were correct as he himself had recorded them. There was absolutely nothing to support Brorty's contention that the business was losing money.

Lopasuta leaned back and for a long while pondered what he should do next. Clearly he had no idea what his employer could be referring to, when he complained about the firm's poor showing. Could there be some expenditures, some costs of doing business, that Lopasuta had failed to take into account because Brorty had failed to report them? Fearful of his employer's wrath if he should fail to find these missing expenditures, the Comanche desperately opened several drawers in Brorty's desk, looking for bills, receipts—anything that could be added to his own books. He found nothing of this kind, but as he was searching, his hand fell upon a ledger, one smaller than his own. He pulled it out of the drawer, placed it on his desk, opened it, and began to read.

An hour later, Lopasuta put aside the ledger with a sigh and rubbed his eyes wearily. He had not found what he was looking for; instead, to his shock and chagrin, he had found something a great deal worse. Now he knew exactly what Edgers had meant, when he had spoken of skullduggery. For Lopasuta had found that Brorty's firm, far from being unprofitable, was doing much better than even his own figures suggested—because his employer was regularly charging outrageously high prices that he had never reported to Lopasuta. Not only that; he had a number of clients whose existence he had never even mentioned to his clerk—important clients in Japan, China, and the United States. He was cheating these customers as well, charging them thirty percent more than he should.

And yet, in spite of this inflated profit, David Brorty continued to plead that he could not afford to raise Lopasuta's wages. It was intolerable. He saw at last that he had been exploited and used.

Lopasuta nearly cried aloud in his anguish. The money that he rightfully should have been receiving all this time—more than a year—could have done so much to ease the hardship of the simple Lu Choy, the gentle woman who had died giving birth to his child. And he knew, after having read this secret ledger, that by now he would have saved enough money to have enabled him to buy passage on a ship that would take him back to Montgomery.

He rose abruptly from the desk, put away both ledgers, and then stalked out of the office, slamming the door so hard as he left that the glass shook in the frame.

He arrived at the office the next morning a full half hour before the Scotsman was due to appear, and when David Brorty ascended the steps and saw Lopasuta standing there with folded arms and grim expression, he uttered a nervous laugh. "What is the trouble, Mr. Bouchard? Dinna tell me that ye wish more money from me, because ye know my circumstances."

"I know them better than you think, Mr. Brorty. And since I have had no letter from my wife, I must go back and find her for myself, to learn whether she has abandoned me."

"Dinna be so hasty, lad. Here, I'll unlock the door. Now

then, come in and sit down in me office. Besides, ye dinna have enough money saved, ha' ye?"

- The falseness of his employer only served to make Lopasuta the more determined to put an immediate end to this long, dreary slavery. "I am no longer willing to hear excuses or apologies, Mr. Brorty. I have something to tell you. All these months you have claimed that your partner, Mr. Hamill, cheated you. Yet I was told by Morrison Edgers of the firm of Camp & Raleigh that your former partner is in Macao and has been there for some years. Also, I have found your own private ledger." He angrily flung open the desk drawer and extracted the secret ledger as he detailed what he had learned to the Scotsman. "You knew, of course, that I'd see at once how you were cheating, and so you hid your ledger in your bottom drawer—"

"Why now, that's a terrible thing to be accusing a man o' so early in the day." Brorty tried to bluster it out.

"I won't accept that, Mr. Brorty. I realize now how little you've paid me all these months for all the work I've done for you. Now I'm telling you this: you're going to give me enough money to buy passage home. And if your conscience doesn't tell you that you owe it to me, I'll accept it as a loan, and I'll repay you when I get back to Montgomery. But I want the money now; do you understand me?"

"I told ye not to be too hasty, lad. Besides," Brorty again uttered a nervous laugh and shrugged like a man of the world, "I'll wager ye that yer wife's long since left ye for someone else."

"Not if she received my cable and letter, Mr. Brorty. Wait now—you said you sent them on the Monday after you engaged me to work for you. Tell me, Brorty—were they sent? Did you see to it as I asked—no, begged you to?"

"Well now, man, to tell ye the truth—"

Lopasuta Bouchard uttered an agonized cry and seized the Scotsman by the shoulders, his fingers digging cruelly into the trader's flesh. "You never sent them—is that the truth? I'll kill you if you don't tell me! I will not tolerate a lie now, not when that poor Chinese girl who saved my life died because of me. And all the time—yes, I see it all now—all the time I've been waiting for my wife's reply,

485

she never even received word telling her that I lived and still loved her and would come back home to her. You did this because you did not want to lose me as your slave. Admit it, before I kill you!"

"All right, for God's sake, man, all right, I'll admit it—I was wrong, yes I was, but ye dinna know the trouble I've had all alone here with all me enemies—"

"And you have made one of me, David Brorty," Lopasuta uttered in a growling voice. "The only restitution you can make now is to give me money enough to go home. You know you have it, and you know that I worked hard and faithfully for you. You paid me barely enough to buy food and a little comfort for Lu Choy. But now I have her son, and I mean to take him back with me to my wife, and thus Lu Choy's memory will live. Even if my wife does not accept me after what I have done, I will pray that at least my son will have his chance at life." Lopasuta's grip tightened around Brorty's neck. "Speak quickly, or I'll lose patience with you and then I cannot say how I will repay you for all the evil you have done!"

"Dinna—dinna kill me—man, for God's sake no! I—I'll give ye money, I swear I will—I'll give it to ye right now, only let me be!" the Scotsman pleaded, his voice trembling and his face ashen and damp with sweat.

Lopasuta let him go, and the Scotsman scurried to the chest in which he kept the old bills of lading, opened the lid, and then touched a little spring at the base of the chest: a secret false-bottomed drawer sprang out, and Lopasuta saw bundles of greenbacks. Brorty retrieved one of them, rose, and feverishly counted out the bills. "Here are two thousand Hong Kong dollars. 'Twill buy ye passage all the way home, believe me."

"Thank you. And today, I shall write another cable to my wife—but this time I shall send it myself. I will say good-bye to you now, David Brorty."

"Well now, take yer money and good riddance to ye," Brorty sullenly declared. "Ye think ye're a smart feller, but I can do without ye, that I can. I've done for meself all me life, and I'll do so long after you've gone back to America."

"Then there's nothing more for either of us to say." Lopasuta turned to stare at the uneasy, stout little man. "In your way, you were kind to me, so I cannot find it in

486

my heart to hate you completely. But for what happened to Lu Choy, and for your base deception in not sending my messages, I ask your God to pardon you. Good-bye, David Brorty."

## Fifty-One

Lopasuta Bouchard's first act after leaving David Brorty
was to go to the trading office of Camp & Raleigh to
thank Morrison Edgers for having warned him about the
Scotsman's chicanery. "I must send word to my wife immediately," the Comanche lawyer earnestly declared. He
explained Brorty's deception to the kindly clerk, adding, "I
am beside myself! Surely after not hearing from me for
over a year, Geraldine must believe me dead—or even
worse, that I've abandoned her. I must send her a cable,
just to let her know that I am alive and will be coming
home soon—and I will then send a long letter detailing all
that has happened to me."

Edgers smiled gently at the distraught Lopasuta, assuring him, "Don't worry, my friend. I'll help you any way
that I can. Write out your wire and I'll have it sent for
you—fortunately, this firm is so large that we employ our
own telegrapher, though of course I have to ask that you
absorb the costs. And then, by all means take all the time
you wish to compose your letter to your wife. As it happens, our very fastest cargo vessel is sailing late this afternoon, bound for the States—stopping first at San
Francisco, where the letter can be sent on by rail. I'll personally take it to the sailing master for his safekeeping,
and guarantee you that it will reach your wife by the
middle of December—surely not more than a day or two
later in the event of inclement weather. And in the mean-
time, your wife will have received the cable telling her
that you are indeed alive and safe. Let's see—I should say

488

that it will reach her within forty-eight hours, at the latest."

"I shall be forever in your debt," Lopasuta solemnly replied.

"Nonsense, Bouchard. 'Tisn't anything you wouldn't have done for me, if our positions had been reversed. Now then," he took Lopasuta by the arm and led him into an unused office, "you sit yourself down here where you can be alone with your thoughts."

"Thank you, Mr. Edgers. There is so much I must say to my wife, so much I must explain. It must make up a bit for all these terrible months of silence from me. I can only pray that she hasn't given me up for dead——"

"If she loves you, she hasn't, my friend. And take all the time you need."

Lopasuta could not speak for the lump that had formed in his throat. But he sent Morrison Edgers a look of ineffable gratitude that conveyed his feelings more than words could have done. Then, turning to the spotlessly clean desk, he picked up the quill pen and began to write.

Emerging from the office nearly an hour later, Lopasuta entrusted his letter to Morrison Edgers and explained to his new friend that before writing the cable, he would like to have some information on sailing schedules for transpacific ships. "I would very much like to be able to tell Geraldine on what day I'll be leaving, so she will know when to expect me home. Unfortunately, much as I would like to be able to leave on the ship sailing this afternoon, it will take me a week or two to arrange for the necessary papers for my son and the nurse I have secured for him, for them to accompany me back to America."

Mr. Edgers went over to his schedule book and ran his finger down the columns of sailing dates. "Let's see, now—ah, yes. This one should be just about right. There's a fast steamer sailing directly to San Francisco—with only a brief stopover in the Sandwich Islands to take on supplies—and it will be putting out of Hong Kong on the seventh of next month. I can reserve space for you, if you like, through our regular agent. And I trust that this journey will be happily uneventful!" He smiled broadly, then added, "I would estimate that you will find yourself back in the arms of your dear wife—what with the rail trip to

Alabama—just about the first of January. Not a bad way to start off the new year, I should say."

Lopasuta smiled in gratitude and quickly wrote out a brief telegram—albeit not without a trace of fear that his darling wife would no longer want him in her arms. But he shook off this feeling and promptly booked a small stateroom for himself and an adjoining one for Mei Luong and the baby. Although this was a somewhat presumptuous action, he hoped that he would be able to persuade the young nurse to accompany him and his child back to Montgomery.

With a feeling of incredible lightheartedness, Lopasuta ran nearly all the way back to Aberdeen and leaped onto the sampan, startling Mei Luong, who had just finished nursing the infant. He managed to convey to the Chinese woman what he had planned, and she readily acceded to his wishes. Her own lack of prospects and the death of her baby determined her to accompany the young Comanche, for she was devoted both to this strange, coppery-skinned man and to his child. Her pidgin English was good enough for her to be able to share in his joy at finally being able to rejoin his white wife far across the ocean.

It was the last Thursday of November, and Laure Bouchard was planning a Thanksgiving dinner for all of her dearest friends. Although the celebration would be subdued because of Luke's untimely death and Lopasuta's continued mysterious absence, nonetheless it warmed the beautiful golden-haired widow that in her and Geraldine's time of need, there were so many good people there to support them.

And so, while not exactly happy, she was feeling reasonably content at the thought that she was once again opening the red-brick chateau and extending its hospitality to those people who mattered most in her life. She looked forward with eager anticipation to welcoming Geraldine and her parents, Andy and Jessica Haskins, Mitzi and Dalbert Sattersfield, Burt Coleman and his dear Amelia—and here she smiled somewhat ruefully to herself. Burt and Amelia had married the previous summer, and while she certainly was glad that they had found such happiness together, she had to admit that she did miss the lovely octoroon's cooking! Laughing aloud at this selfish thought, she continued to smile as she laid out the place cards for Dan Munroe and his wife, Marius and Clementine Thornton, and those for a new couple about to share the traditional Thanksgiving feast at Windhaven Plantation: Dr. Abel Kennery and his dear nurse, Muriel Donahue, had recently gotten married. A mischievous grin played around Laure's lovely mouth in anticipation of being able to tell the handsome doctor, "I told you so!"

She had invited dear Clarabelle Hendry to join in the festivities, but the governess had firmly declined, insisting that she would much prefer to take charge of all the children and occupy them so that the adults could dine at their leisure. Laure had laughingly hugged her, thanking her for her consideration, promising that she would make it up to the woman who had been so helpful to her during her time of bereavement and all else that had ensued.

And now, having put the finishing touches to her hair and adjusting the folds of her gown, Laure Bouchard swept down the hallway to answer the sound of the brass knocker on the front door, which heralded the arrival of her first guests. She had barely reached the knob when Geraldine Bouchard fairly flung herself into the room, her parents following her, with the baby.

Geraldine's face was streaked with tears, and if Laure had not at once perceived broad smiles on the faces of Geraldine's parents, Laure would have believed that her dear friend had at last received some dreadful news about her missing husband. As it was, Geraldine threw herself into Laure's arms, laughing and weeping at the same time, and finally managed to blurt out, "Oh, Laure—he's—he's safe. He—he's alive! I—I just received this telegram—" She reached into her reticule and, extracting the much-fondled cable, handed it to Luke's beautiful widow.

Laure managed to calm the excited young woman, inviting Geraldine and her parents to sit on the sofa while she read the brief—but so long awaited—message. "My darling," it read, "am safe in Hong Kong. Will depart December 7 to arrive around first of January. Hope you will forgive me. Letter to follow." Laure burst into her own happy tears and managed to enfold Geraldine, young Dennis, and her parents all at the same time in her trembling arms. Through her sobs she managed to ask of Lopasuta's wife, "What do you suppose he means by 'Hope you will forgive me'?"

"I don't know, Laure," Geraldine responded. "I'm sure he will tell me everything in his letter. All I care about is that he is alive, well, and coming home to me. Oh, Laure," she started to cry again, "this is the most wonderful Thanksgiving I've ever had in my whole life! I still can't quite believe it. I certainly have much to be thankful for on this day, and I thank God that my prayers have been answered." Holding her baby in her arms, she softly murmured to him, "Your daddy is coming home, my darling. Soon, I promise you. And he will love you as much as I do."

# Fifty-Two

On December 7, Lopasuta, his son, and Mei Luong boarded the *Southern Belle* for the voyage to America. As the ship slowly steamed out of Hong Kong harbor, they stood at the rail, watching Victoria Peak diminish to a tiny speck and then melt completely into the horizon. Lopasuta's happiness was tinged with the bittersweet memories of his time on this island, of the Chinese woman who had made his isolation bearable, and who had borne him this sturdy son. "Farewell, Lu Choy," he whispered into the wind. "The Great Spirit will surely reward you for all your kindness and goodness."

Once on the high seas, the *Southern Belle* made excellent time. The amiable, middle-aged captain of the vessel told Lopasuta that if the good weather that they had been enjoying continued to hold out, they should reach San Francisco by Christmas Day. By then, Lopasuta was certain, Geraldine would have received his letter and would at last understand what had befallen him. He prayed that she would forgive him his transgression against the sanctity of their union, yet he told himself that it would be within her right to declare their marriage at an end because of his liaison with Lu Choy. If that were to happen, he would humbly ask only that she bring up the child, who was without sin.

Before the *Southern Belle* reached the Sandwich Islands to take on water and supplies, the weather worsened. From the activity of the seamen, Lopasuta sensed that they were preparing for a storm. Meeting the captain near

493

the latter's quarterdeck, the young Comanche asked, "Could it be a typhoon so late in the year, Captain Jackson?"

"Aye, Mr. Bouchard, that's what it looks like. With luck, we'll be able to skirt the edge of it, and I've told my pilot to alter his course in order to do so." Seeing the anxious look on Lopasuta's face, the kindly, bearded captain smilingly added, "But we'll continue to make good time all the while, even if we have to go off course for a short while. Don't you worry, I'll have you safe and sound at the San Francisco docks within a day or two of the time I've slated for our arrival there."

All that afternoon, the ship pitched and tossed, and Lopasuta, accustomed though he was to the movement of a ship on water, was extremely queasy. Solicitously, he went to Mei Luong's cabin, to ascertain her condition and that of the baby, and the Chinese nurse wanly informed him that she had managed thus far to keep the infant from crying and being upset. She had held the baby close to her, rocking him in her arms and crooning to him, and he saw that beads of sweat were on her pretty face. Tenderly, he touched her head and murmured in Chinese, "You are kind and good, Mei Luong, and I pray that soon this storm will be over. But I must go on deck now, for it seems that you are stronger than I am." He gulped spasmodically and hurried up to the deck, for he suddenly felt horribly nauseated.

After the sickness had passed, he slowly turned his head and saw a well-dressed man in his early forties clutching the rail, evidently a fellow passenger in the same distress as himself. Suddenly, the ship violently lurched, and the man, who had been half-bent over the rail, nearly lost his balance. With a cry of alarm, Lopasuta rushed forward and seized him by the wrist, as his other hand gripped the rail with all his strength. Then, leaning back and pulling hard, he managed to drag the man back onto a secure footing on the deck.

"Th-thank God—you saved my life, friend," the man gasped, as he tottered a little, then gripped the rail with both hands and stared at Lopasuta's anxious face.

"We'd best go below decks to the salon," the Comanche proposed. "Perhaps some brandy or wine would settle your nerves."

"My stomach, you mean," the passenger wanly grinned. "Well, I'll chance it. I'd much rather try spirits than salt water, which I would have had more than my fill of if it hadn't been for your quick thinking. You look a little under the weather yourself. My name's Leland Kenniston, from New York."

"I'm glad to know you, Mr. Kenniston. My name is Lopasuta Bouchard, and I'm from Montgomery, Alabama. Be careful, now. Hold on to me and we'll make it." As he shook Kenniston's hand, Lopasuta observed that the man was nearly as tall as himself, with friendly blue eyes, a firm jaw, and a Roman nose. His black hair was cut in a curly fringe along the top of his high-arching forehead.

Lopasuta opened the door leading into the hallway, and the two men made their way to the main salon of the vessel. As they seated themselves at one of the empty tables, Lopasuta beckoned to a steward and ordered two snifters of brandy to be brought to the table.

"Thanks again, Mr. Bouchard, and here's to your health and good fortune." Leland Kenniston lifted his snifter, then took a sip, smacked his lips, and nodded. "I think this is exactly what the doctor ordered. Now tell me about yourself, Mr. Bouchard. What's a man from Alabama been doing in Hong Kong?"

Quickly, the Comanche lawyer narrated the events that had led him from his marriage and law practice in Montgomery, the death of Lu Choy, and his eventual departure. When he had finished, Leland Kenniston shook his head. "That's a yarn good enough to write a book about, Mr. Bouchard. You've really had more than your share of misfortune, none of it of your own making. Well now, maybe our meeting out on deck just now was more than chance. You see, I run an importing and exporting firm in New York, and my reason for visiting Hong Kong was to open a branch office there. Also, by the middle of next year it's my hope to open still another branch in New Orleans."

"I see," Lopasuta politely interposed.

"By the time the New Orleans branch gets going full steam, I'll be needing a good lawyer. I don't know too much about the fine points of the law—I'm no scholar or intellectual; no one in my family ever was. You see, Mr. Bouchard, I'm Irish by birth, and my father and mother had no formal book learning except what they could teach

each other. I once asked my dad why he picked the name of Leland, instead of Michael or John, and he just laughed and said he saw it in a book and liked the sound of it—he did a lot of reading on his own, you see. We were immigrants, coming out of County Mayo, and poor as church mice. When we came here, I was still very young. My dad and mother sacrificed and slaved to get me a little schooling so I could amount to something."

The man looked away, a thoughtful expression on his face, then lifted his glass to take a sip of brandy and went on. "Well now, Mr. Bouchard, what I like about you—aside from saving my life—is the way you adapted to hard knocks. You might say I'm a graduate of the same school myself. I had tough going until about two years ago, and then I started to get contracts and to deal with honest people who kept their word—and that's a hell of a sight better than any contract, let me tell you—and so now I'm doing very well indeed. My instincts are invariably sound, and right now they're telling me that you're one of the best lawyers this side of Killarney. Now, I don't suppose you'd be interested in a post in New Orleans?"

Lopasuta smiled at the ebullient Irishman's forthrightness. "I really don't know what to say," he declared. "To begin with, I'm only licensed to practice in Alabama—"

"I'm being selfish, Mr. Bouchard—let me call you Lopasuta, and you call me Leland. You see, my feeling is that a good man is hard to find, and once you've found him, you want to do everything you can to keep him. Of course, with my new branch, you'd have to be admitted to the Louisiana bar. But I'm sure with your experience you'd have no trouble passing that examination."

"Probably not," Lopasuta cautiously agreed. Then he brightened as a new idea came to him. "Perhaps I could be helpful to you in New Orleans right away, Leland, because I represent the Bouchards of Windhaven Plantation near Montgomery. And their bank is the Brunton & Barntry Bank in New Orleans, which for many years has handled the family's holdings. If you don't have a particular bank in mind to handle your finances in the Queen City, I couldn't recommend the Brunton & Barntry Bank more highly."

"Now that's worth remembering, Lopasuta. You see, you're already valuable to me. We'll talk this over in greater detail before we dock at San Francisco, I promise you. And I'll just say one thing more—I'll pay you what you're worth, and if you do well for me, you'll prosper. My word is my bond, and I've never broken it yet."

"I feel that you haven't, Leland." Lopasuta held out his hand and the two men smilingly shook hands.

It was December 18, 1878, the one hundred and six-teenth anniversary of the birth of Lucien Bouchard, the founder of Windhaven Plantation. The sun was shining brightly and the weather was pleasantly cool as Geraldine Bouchard, her little son, Dennis, in her arms, and Laure Bouchard made their way up the gradually ascending path to the summit of the tall red bluff that looked down upon the gently flowing Alabama River and the fertile fields of Windhaven Plantation.

Geraldine's face was radiant with joy, and tears shone in her eyes as the two women stood before the graves of Luke and Lucien Bouchard and Dimarte. "Dear Laure," Geraldine murmured, "I'm so grateful today of all days. Bless you for asking me to share this moment with you. And, Laure, I have at last received Lopasuta's letter, which came only this morning. This will make your com-munion with your loved ones even more joyous and hope-ful. And I think their spirits will share the news with us and rejoice in it."

Laure Bouchard, dressed in black for this solemn occa-sion, turned to the younger woman. "Oh, Geraldine, my dear! What wonderful news, indeed. I trust that nothing has happened in all these long months that will place any barriers between you and Lopasuta."

Geraldine burst into tears as she fumbled in her reticule for a letter that she had read and reread so many times that very morning that it was already rumpled and creased. Wordlessly, she handed it to Laure who, with a wondering look, opened it and read.

My adored wife Geraldine:
I ask your pardon and forgiveness for not having been able to tell you long before the cable—which I presume you have received—that I am still alive and still devoted to you and to our child, whom I am so anxious to see.

497

You know that I went to New Orleans to see a William Brickley. While waiting to see him, I was given a drugged drink, and when I wakened, I found myself aboard a ship bound around the Horn for San Francisco. I tried to escape when we put into Rio, but it was to no avail. When we reached San Francisco, I was bound and blindfolded, and put aboard another ship bound for Hong Kong.

Upon reaching Hong Kong, I was left for dead in an alley, and I cannot think what might have happened to me had I not been found by a kind Chinese girl who found me lying unconscious and took me aboard her sampan. She shared what little she had with me and helped me to survive the terrible months that followed.

As soon as I could, I found work, but with a miserly man who paid me such scant wages that I and the girl, Lu Choy, could barely subsist, much less earn my passage home. Worst of all, my darling, when I began work for this man, he promised me that he would send both a cable and a letter I had written to you explaining what had happened, and I found out—only this very day on which I send you my wire and this letter—that he had torn them up because he wished to continue to profit from my work and keep me practically as a slave to him.

But I have at last learned what has been done, and I have forced him to pay me enough to buy passage on the next ship leaving for San Francisco—and by the time you are reading this letter, I shall be on it, coming home to you.

But before you prepare to welcome me and to forgive my unintended neglect, I must confess to you that I have sinned against our marriage vows. Lu Choy, truly my only friend and companion in Hong Kong all these despairing months, became fond of me—although I resisted with all my strength because I wished to remain faithful to you. However, during a terrible typhoon, my darling Geraldine, I consoled her fears through an act of love. Later, she died giving birth to the fruit of that one, single union.

I swear to you in the name of the Manitou and by the God in whom you fervently believe that I never intended to betray our love. I can say only that it happened as an act between two frightened and lonely friends—though that does not excuse my lapse.

I am bringing my son back with me, Geraldine, together with his nurse, a young Chinese woman named Mei Luong. If you cannot find it in your heart to forgive my sin, my beloved wife, I ask only that you give this little boy a home. He has not sinned, or offended anyone; he would be blessed by the love and the tenderness and the care you could give him, and the wisdom of your keen mind and your honesty. He would grow up to be a better man than his father with such guidance, I know.

Please convey my sincerest good wishes to my adoptive father and mother, and I wish you and them a truly happy holiday. I regret that I will not be there in time to share a small part of it with you all. My love to their children, and above all, to our child, the child you gave me. I ask again that you let me see him or her, and if you decide you no longer wish to share my life, I will understand.

But believe this, that you are my life and my hope and my joy, and it was through your love and companionship that I fulfilled Sangrodo's hope that I would speak for my people, as for all those who are oppressed and cast down by the influential and the wealthy and the selfish.

God bless you, Geraldine, and our child. I cannot wait to see you—even though it may be for the last time.

Humbly,<br>Lopasuta

Laure Bouchard was weeping as she finished the letter and turned to Geraldine. She took the young woman's hands in hers and, her voice choked, asked, "And will you take him back, Geraldine?"

"Oh, yes, Laure, with all my heart and soul!"

They knelt down together beside the graves, and Laure prayed aloud for the souls of old Lucien and his beloved woman and for her martyred husband, Luke. And then, her face radiant through her tears, she said, "You have heard, Grandfather Lucien, and you, my dearly beloved and sorrowfully mourned husband, Luke, how our foster son has fared and how his wife and I long for his return. And we cannot blame him in our hearts, for the sin for which he unjustly condemns himself was the result of unhappy circumstance, my dear husband Luke, as was my own ill-fated partnership with a man who tried to destroy the Bouchard name and fortune—all that you, dear

Grandfather Lucien, lived and worked for and believed in with your very last breath of life."

Laure tenderly put her arm around Geraldine's quivering shoulders, as the younger woman bowed her head and sobbed softly. And then she said aloud, "Yes, Lucien, Luke—and you, beloved Dimarte, who forgave your Lucien his own self-ascribed sin in possessing Shehanoy, who was your friend—all of you know the good that Lopasuta had done here in his adopted home, by speaking with truth and conscience on the side of the oppressed and the needy. The good he has done obliterates this sin, to my mind, and to his sweet wife's as well, and equally I pray, in God's all-forgiving vision.

"And it is right that we should learn he is returning to us, after incredible hardships, having loyally upheld the honorable Bouchard name, as we are communing here on the birthday of Windhaven's founder. Oh, blessed spirits—Grandfather Lucien, who began the great and humane tradition in your day, and you, my beloved husband, who continued it until your own heroism took you from me—now, with Christmas but a week away, we have more reason than ever to thank Almighty God for His gracious bounty. And Geraldine and I pray that it will continue so, as long as there are Bouchards upon this mortal earth."

# The Windhaven Saga
## by Marie de Jourlet

**Over 4,000,000 copies in print!**

☐ **41-691-1 WINDHAVEN PLANTATION** $2.95
The epic novel of the Bouchard family, who dared to cross the boundaries of society and create a bold new heritage.

☐ **41-692-X STORM OVER WINDHAVEN** $2.95
Windhaven Plantation and the Bouchard dream are shaken to their very roots in this torrid story of men and women driven by ambition and damned by desire.

☐ **41-784-5 LEGACY OF WINDHAVEN** $3.50
After the Civil War the Bouchards move west to Texas — a rugged, untamed land where they must battle Indians, bandits and cattle rustlers to insure the legacy of Windhaven.

☐ **41-643-1 RETURN TO WINDHAVEN** $2.95
Amid the turbulent Reconstruction years, the determined Bouchards fight to hold on to Windhaven Range while struggling to regain an old but never forgotten plantation.

☐ **41-258-4 WINDHAVEN'S PERIL** $2.75
Luke Bouchard and his family launch a new life at Windhaven Plantation — but the past returns to haunt them.

☐ **41-690-3 TRIALS OF WINDHAVEN** $2.95
Luke and Laure Bouchard face their most bitter trial yet, as their joyful life at Windhaven Plantation is threatened by an unscrupulous carpetbagger.

☐ **40-723-8 DEFENDERS OF WINDHAVEN** $2.75
Out of the ashes of the Civil War, the south rebuilds. Laure and Luke Bouchard continue to uphold Windhaven Plantation as Frank's niece and her husband forge a new frontier in Texas.

☐ **41-748-9 WINDHAVEN'S CRISIS** $3.50
With the fires of civil war still smoldering, our nation prepares for its first Centennial — as the proud Bouchards struggle to preserve the legacy that is Windhaven.

**Buy them at your local bookstore or use this handy coupon**
Clip and mail this page with your order

**PINNACLE BOOKS, INC. — Reader Service Dept.**
**1430 Broadway, New York, NY 10018**

Please send me the book(s) I have checked above. I am enclosing $_____ (please add 75¢ to cover postage and handling). Send check or money order only — no cash or C.O.D.'s.

Mr./Mrs./Miss _____

Address _____

City _____ State/Zip _____

Please allow six weeks for delivery. Prices subject to change without notice.

# Patricia Matthews

## America's leading lady of historical romance.
## Over 20,000,000 copies in print!

☐ 41-203-7 **LOVE, FOREVER MORE** $2.75
The tumultuous story of spirited Serena Foster and her determination to survive the raw, untamed West.

☐ 41-513-3 **LOVE'S AVENGING HEART** $2.95
Life with her brutal stepfather in colonial Williamsburg was cruel, but Hannah McCambridge would survive—and learn to love with a consuming passion.

☐ 40-661-4 **LOVE'S BOLD JOURNEY** $2.95
Beautiful Rachel Bonner forged a new life for herself in the savage West—but can she surrender to the man who won her heart?

☐ 41-517-6 **LOVE'S DARING DREAM** $2.95
The turbulent story of indomitable Maggie Donnevan, who fled the poverty of Ireland to begin a new life in the American Northwest.

☐ 41-519-2 **LOVE'S GOLDEN DESTINY** $2.95
It was a lust for gold that brought Belinda Lee together with three men in the Klondike, only to be trapped by the wildest of passions.

☐ 41-518-4 **LOVE'S MAGIC MOMENT** $2.95
Evil and ecstasy are entwined in the steaming jungles of Mexico, where Meredith Longley searches for a lost city but finds greed, lust, and seduction.

☐ 41-516-8 **LOVE'S PAGAN HEART** $2.95
An exquisite Hawaiian princess is torn between love for her homeland and the only man who can tame her pagan heart.

☐ 41-064-6 **LOVE'S RAGING TIDE** $2.75
Melissa Huntoon seethed with humiliation as her ancestral plantation home was auctioned away—then learned to survive the lust and greed of a man's world.

☐ 40-660-6 **LOVE'S SWEET AGONY** $2.75
Amid the colorful world of thoroughbred farms that gave birth to the first Kentucky Derby, Rebecca Hawkins learns that horses are more easily handled than men.

☐ 41-514-1 **LOVE'S WILDEST PROMISE** $2.95
Abducted aboard a ship bound for the Colonies, innocent Sarah Moody faces a dark voyage of violence and unbridled lust.

---

**PINNACLE BOOKS, INC. — Reader Service Dept.**
**1430 Broadway, New York, NY 10018**

Please send me the book(s) I have checked above. I am enclosing $_____ (please add 75¢ to cover postage and handling). Send check or money order only—no cash or C.O.D.'s.

Mr./Mrs./Miss_____

Address_____

City_____ State/Zip_____

Please allow six weeks for delivery. Prices subject to change without notice.
Canadian orders must be paid with U.S. Bank check or U.S. Postal money order only.

# Paula Fairman

### Romantic intrigue at its finest—
### over 2,500,000 copies in print!

☐ **40-105-1 FORBIDDEN DESTINY** $1.95
A helpless stowaway aboard the whaling ship *Gray Ghost*, Kate McCrae was in no position to refuse the lecherous advances of Captain Steele.

☐ **40-569-3 THE FURY AND THE PASSION** $2.50
From the glitter of Denver society to the lawlessness of the wild West, Stacey Pendarrow stalks the trail of her elusive lover for one reason: to kill him.

☐ **41-783-7 JASMINE PASSION** $2.95
Raised in a temple and trained in the art of love, the beautiful Eurasian Le' Sing searches California's Barbary Coast for the father she has never met and for a man who can win her heart.

☐ **40-697-5 PORTS OF PASSION** $2.50
Abducted aboard the *Morning Star*, heiress Kristen Chalmers must come to terms not only with immediate danger, but the desperate awakening of her own carnal desires.

☐ **41-015-8 SOUTHERN ROSE** $2.75
Amidst the raging furor of the Civil War, the beautiful actress Jaylene Cooper is torn between her passion for a dashing Southern rebel and the devoted love of a handsome Yankee officer.

☐ **40-474-3 STORM OF DESIRE** $2.25
The only woman in a rough and brutal railroad camp in the wild Southwest, young Reesa Flowers becomes enmeshed in a web of greed, sabotage, and lust.

☐ **41-006-9 THE TENDER AND THE SAVAGE** $2.75
In the wild and ravaged plains of the Dakota Territory, beautiful young Crimson Royale is torn between her savage lust for a Sioux Indian and her tender desires for his worst enemy—a captain in Custer's Army.

**Buy them at your local bookstore or use this handy coupon**
Clip and mail this page with your order

---

Ⓞ **PINNACLE BOOKS, INC.—Reader Service Dept.**
**1430 Broadway, New York, NY 10018**

Please send me the book(s) I have checked above. I am enclosing $_____ (please add 75¢ to cover postage and handling). Send check or money order only—no cash or C.O.D.'s.

Mr./Mrs./Miss _____

Address _____

City _____ State/Zip _____

Please allow six weeks for delivery. Prices subject to change without notice.

# HELP YOURSELF TO THREE
# BESTSELLERS BY LEADING EXPERTS

☐ **41-777-2** *POSITIVELY PREGNANT*
**by Madeleine Kenefick**                          **$3.50**
A provocative, step-by-step guide through the nine months of pregnancy. "It is a pleasure to read this good advice to pregnant women in a day when there is such hysteria surrounding the medical profession and, particularly, pregnancy and obstetricians."—Frederick H. Berman, M.D.

☐ **41-193-6** *TEENAGE SEXUALITY*
**by Aaron Hass, Ph.D.**                            **$2.95**
Find out the shocking facts about today's youth in this candid glimpse into teenage sexuality. Based on questionnaires and interviews with over 600 adolescents, *Teenage Sexuality* is "...the first book in which teenagers talk about sexual feelings and activities"—*Los Angeles Times.*
"Like having access to hundreds of unlocked diaries"—*Chicago Booklist.*

☐ **41-137-5** *SEXUAL JOY IN MARRIAGE*
**by Dr. Michael Clarke and Dorothy Clarke**    **$7.95**
                                       **(large book format)**
Now, for the first time ever, a tasteful and authoritative guide to sexual communication that incorporates explicit photographs with do-it-yourself therapy, *plus* frank discussions and candid advice—written by a world-renowned sex therapist.

Canadian orders must be paid with U.S. Bank check
or U.S. Postal money order only.
**Buy them at your local bookstore or use this handy coupon**
Clip and mail this page with your order

⊙ **PINNACLE BOOKS, INC.—Reader Service Dept.**
1430 Broadway, New York, NY 10018

Please send me the book(s) I have checked above. I am enclosing $_____
(please add 75¢ to cover postage and handling). Send check or money order
only—no cash or C.O.D.'s.

Mr./Mrs./Miss _____

Address _____

City_____ State/Zip_____

Please allow six weeks for delivery. Prices subject to change without notice.